# Earth's End

PAUL CUDE

Cover design by GetCovers

ISBN: 978-1916352490

# GRAB A FREE 'WHITE DRAGON SAGA' STORY

**FREE STORY:** As new friends face ruthless enemies that have designs on not only their bodies, but their minds as well, will an ancient mantra come to their rescue? Treachery, intrigue and a bare faced lie lead to gruesome negotiations. Will a cold hearted, duplicitous, double-crossing dragon fire the opening salvo in a wicked and unwarranted war, or can virtue and the moral high ground turn things around at the very last moment?

A Selfless Sacrifice is available for free when you join Paul Cude's newsletter at www.paulcude.com.

# CONTENTS

# PROLOGUE
# HANGING IN THE BALANCE

They say ignorance is bliss. That's certainly true for the dragons and humans all toiling away, desperately trying to find survivors amongst the devastation both above and below ground which extends across the whole planet. Such widespread destruction was all caused by the war instigated by the demonic dark dragon leader Manson and his vile other half and would-be queen, Earth. Little did they all know that an SLBM (Submarine Launched Ballistic Missile), with around four minutes to go, was on a crash course for a specific point in northern France.

A nuclear explosion in Europe: catastrophic, I hear you say. And of course you'd be right. Unbelievably, that wasn't the worst of it. The nuclear tipped warhead was heading for a monorail borehole test site, designed by dragon society to provide an almost direct route from Europe to Australia, just about skirting the planet's core.

Still not so bad, huh? However, in addition to all that, a great deal of the valuable, volatile and magic-enhancing metal, laminium, lays deep within the opening part of the tunnel itself, meaning that a potentially planet-destroying reaction remained in the offing.

To emphasise the seriousness of the situation, Fate, Luck and Time had all, in absolute desperation, hunted down the one entity they'd never had cause to interact with before. They'd only been able to observe from a distance, someone they were forbidden to cooperate with under any circumstances by the causality of the universe. Yet one they hoped could turn the tide against the pervasive evil that had so far, against all odds, got its way. Seeking out the meadow they knew he loved to hang out in, they were shocked and appalled to instead arrive in a dystopian desert that looked not only unfamiliar, but reeked of despair and defeat. If adversity could be thwarted, is this what the future had in store?

*"I FEEL SO OLD!"* a frightened voice echoed out from behind a sandstone boulder being battered by the wind.

The three entities, aware that the sand in Future's hourglass continued to trickle at quite a pace, homed in on the haunting words, strolling purposefully around the gigantic rock.

*"I FEEL SO OLD!"*

There, cowering on the ground, an emaciated old man lay curled up, his frail and feeble limbs shivering profusely, ragged white beard bobbing in time with the uncontrollable movements of his head. A more desperate and sad sight it was hard to think of.

*"Uhhh... this isn't what I was expecting,"* whispered Time to the other two.

*"It can't be him. It just can't be,"* observed Luck, cursing her very nature as she did so.

*"I think,"* observed Fate, *"that we've reached the end of the road."*

Standing over the faltering embodiment of what remained of the planet's sentience, the usually confident and cocky threesome could do little else but wait and watch, their optimism severely dented, the prospects for the future left to only a handful of beings who had pressing problems of their own.


Now, where were we?

Oh, that's right, a nuclear warhead fired from a submarine intent on wiping out not just all life as we know it, but the earth itself. Yikes!


At the test monorail borehole site in northern France, Yoyo, his wife Rose and their courageous charges had managed to wrestle control from the dark dragons that had invaded the complex, all of whom had been in the midst of depositing some way into the tunnel itself a vast amount of stolen laminium the precious metal that enhances dragon supernatural abilities beyond belief. Amongst all the chaos and confusion, Captain Battlehard, one of the bravest dragon heroes on the planet, had taken it upon herself after reverting back to her original prehistoric form, to jump feet first into the tunnel in an effort to buy her friends and allies some more time and prevent the onrushing horde of malevolence from escaping. Moments after that, the brilliant blue magical shield they'd all been working to re-establish at the entrance to the gaping borehole had flickered into being thanks to the ingenuity of Monty, Tina, Trayrin and Zebediah, having finally disabled the giant capacitor. Pleased at dominating the control room of the facility, it was only now dawning on the healer, his wife and the youngsters they'd come to think of as their own, exactly what Amelia had just done and the danger she would now find herself in.

Onrushing pack of malevolent murderers almost within striking range, Captain Battlehard, had let her feelings get in the way of the consummate professional that she was.

'Flash, Oh Flash,' she mused, 'what we could have had.'

Before she could move on to her next thought, they were upon her.

The tables had been well and truly turned, with one friend quite literally at the other's throat.

A firm grip on the futuristic blade's hilt, Mas-crate had been pondering for a few moments now, exactly what this young, blonde human was doing down here in the dragon domain amongst the prehistoric monsters that had inhabited the Emporium he'd so easily blown to smithereens only a matter of minutes ago.

Anger and pain running throughout his prehistoric DNA from having one half of his tail cut off, ironically by the weapon he currently held against the girl's throat, a measure of frustration gnawed away at his insides at not having found the being he'd come here looking for... the master mantra maker, the proprietor of the shop itself, the one he thought would be able to provide answers to the burning questions he had. Queries about the imminent coup his friend Manson should have already enacted and be some way towards taking ownership of the planet. So far though, in every search he'd attempted, his queries had fallen on deaf ears. Hence the reason he was here.

Giving in to his baser instincts, having already killed the apprentice, he made a decision to dispatch this one, seek out the others that had been cowering in the back of the Emporium and send them to meet their maker. Taking a deep breath, he thrust the glinting, frost-covered blade forward with all that he had, anticipating the sick satisfaction he knew would follow as it inundated his pleasure receptors.

Close by, buried beneath tonnes of debris from the former bridge that had spanned Camelot Arcade for centuries, the magical presence imbued within the spectacular ring that had been passed down by dragon monarchs for centuries, was at his wits' end. For'son was holding on to the invisible shield he'd conjured up just in time, by the tiniest of threads, begging his partner... no, friend, Tank, to snap himself out of unconsciousness so they might have a chance to free themselves from the dire circumstances they both found themselves ensnared in.

"*TANK... WAKE UP!*" the ring demanded across the vastness of the telepathic link they would normally share. "*Without you as a conduit, my power is fading. I'm struggling to maintain my grip on the shield. Tonnes of rubble will come crashing down any moment now. Please... I'm begging you... WAKE UP!*"

Much as he tried, the rugby playing, human shaped dragon remained deathly still, blood trickling from a cut above his right eye, both nostrils bleeding, one arm bent at an excruciating angle, a sharp piece of rock sticking out of his monstrously thick left thigh.

Tiny dust particles shimmered like golden fireflies in the air, falling slowly on to his immobile body as the magic from the ring started to shake, before contracting, the mountainous mound of wreckage now only a few centimetres from flattening him like a pancake. Oh for some lemon and sugar.


Halfway between the two sorry sights, propped up against the battered wall of one of the nearby dragon dwellings, concealed by the smoky residue of spent magic, another human sat beaten and bruised having been hurled at the wicked dark dragon by his own request. He had hoped to momentarily buy his friend Janice time to escape, something he'd achieved but at quite a cost. Nursing broken ribs, fingers and a shattered elbow, Hook, the daring rugby player, hero of the 'Changing of the Guard' (the battle against Manson, Earth and their forces at the private residence) and hopeful suitor to The White Dragon, could do little else but listen to what was playing out around him. He was astounded that things had gone to hell so quickly... One moment they were all safely tucked away inside the

Emporium, trying to tackle the future, throwing some banter in for good measure. The next... their worlds had been brutally ripped apart by the concussive force of what felt like a nuclear warhead. How's that for ironic?

Across the capital, still within the dragon domain, buried beneath the realm of the humans, a deathly silence had fallen across the king's private residence with the news of the launch of the nuclear missile from the east coast of Scotland. All aware of the ramifications should said projectile hit its intended target, for most of these brave and loyal primordial monsters it was a time of reflection, about what had happened recently, and exactly how it had all gone so wrong. And for none more so than the reigning monarch himself, George, who'd left the comfort of his personal living room, now standing at a monitor on the first floor of the library next to White Wings, watching in real time as the planet's potential doom continued on its sub-orbital trajectory. He was powerless, unable in any way, shape or form to do anything to prevent it. Totally out of his hands, part of him once again wondered if he should have conceded defeat and let the brute Manson and his evil queen have the planet. With hindsight, it seemed like the right thing to have done. But was it, and just how would this play out, were two questions burning at the forefront of his mind.

A deception to be sure, but a necessary one if lives were to be saved in the stunningly beautiful city of Salisbridge. Like many other places across the planet, it had suffered a devastating attack, destroying both modern and ancient infrastructure, as well as the world renowned cathedral.

Hanging in the balance were the lives of a great many school children trapped under the remains of the iconic southern Wiltshire landmark, some no doubt in dire need of medical attention given how long they'd been confined. With no obvious way to extract them, seven friends reunited from the underground domain, three of whom were dragons, had come up with a ruse which would hopefully buy them not only some time, but also the necessary privacy to use their supernatural abilities. So far it was all going to plan, with Angela, Emma, Sam and Taibul all running around like headless chickens, screaming their hearts out about earthquakes and the imminent collapse of those buildings still remaining intact, their actions designed to encourage those in the immediate vicinity to vacate the area. It was mayhem, but in a coordinated fashion, with Jar Man, DomCon and Steel only moments away from being free to use what they considered their birthright, out in the open on the planet's surface, to rescue those trapped beneath the rubble.

On the outskirts of the small Scottish town of Portknockie, on a cliff top looking out at the captivating rock formation known as Bow Fiddle Rock, a series of momentous events had taken place in an amazingly short space of time, not that any locals had been there to witness them.

Disguised to the hilt, Manson and Earth, the would-be king and queen of this world, had come together at the place where he'd first proposed, to discuss what had happened back at the private residence and how they could move forward together, if at all. Words and feelings had been exchanged, but before anything of substance could be agreed upon, unbelievably, to them anyway, one of their many nemeses had appeared as if from nowhere in the form of the lacrosse playing dragon, Richie. The would-be royalty were completely unaware that she was now known to many as The White Dragon.

After that it all kicked off, the gruesome twosome quickly gaining the upper hand, only for matters to swiftly even themselves out in the form of reinforcements arriving. Flash, Fredric and Vimes landed smack bang in the middle of things with their customary diligence, getting stuck in straight from the start.

There were setbacks for both sides, Flash knocked out by some crippling naga magic he could never have envisaged coming, Fredric, Earth's father, taking a hammering at her hands, a dozen deadly snakes delivering decidedly fatal strikes across his body, all ably provided by his daughter's vicious and unrelenting magic. But by that time Richie had got in on the act, brutally taking Manson down more than a peg or two, pummelling him into the ground in a violent and gory attack that she thought had left him for dead.

At about this time, offshore, just beyond Bow Fiddle Rock, up popped the most advanced nuclear submarine the world had to offer amidst the choppy white waves of the chillingly cold sea. The same one in which Manson and his cohorts had travelled from America to the secluded town of Swanage in southern England on their quest to take over the world. Here and now though, it was on a different mission.

Earth, consumed by madness once again, watched her slithering serpents pepper her father with all sorts of different venoms while the massive python around his neck continued to squeeze the life out of him. The White Dragon, needing to assist her friend, the former Crimson Guard, in one fell swoop, punched what was left of Manson, the cruel, dark hearted leader of malevolence and evil, over the top of the cliff, before rushing off to render aid, sure that she'd finished the job.

Unfortunately for her, she hadn't counted on the crew of the submarine, all loyal and dedicated followers of Manson, who flooded him with all their healing energy, and topped up his depleted supply of magic. And so as he ably touched down on the beach as soft as a feather, with a little help from the commander of the submersible, it was as if he was reborn, his human shaped body as good as new, the innate well of supernatural power that had been there since birth almost overflowing with ethereal energy.

Knowing what needed to be done, his journey over the side of the cliff having bought him a few precious moments, immediately he sprinted into the freezing cold sea, diving straight in once he'd reached waist height, the shock of the chilly water burning his hands and face as he ploughed on stroke after stroke, heading for the submarine where he knew some sort of refuge awaited.

Working together, Vimes and his former favourite student, Richie, used their knowledge and fantastical magic to remove what remained of the vile spell the dark leader had inflicted on their friend Flash, rendering him as good as new in under a minute.

As abruptly as they'd appeared, the lethal snakes encompassing all of Fredric's body disappeared into nothingness, his still body and blue face crashing headfirst into the grass, his immobile cadaver looking done for, the toxins and venom continuing to assault his internal organs. What had caused this sudden change in circumstances? Earth had seen Richie punch what remained of Manson, her so-called love and once-upon-a-time king, over the edge of the cliff. Enough in itself to provoke a reaction, what it also did was bring back memories of the loss of her first husband, Peter's father, in much the same manner, causing her to drop to her knees, inundated with recollections from the past, the emotional pain far worse than anything physical she'd ever suffered.

With Flash looking to help the founder of the Crimson Guards, Fredric, only then did Vimes and Richie realise exactly what had happened, spotting the submarine they'd been hunting for, and the healed and reenergised body of Manson swimming towards it. With the impossible now anything but, darkness threatened to consume all those on the side of light.

Out of nowhere, the past interrupted the present, the wicked and evil swimmer continuing, stroke by stroke, having nearly reached the submarine.

*"My love,"* he urged through their shared telepathic link. *"I'm okay."*

A great shock to say the least, Peter's wicked mother, full of madness, was startled out of her reverie, instantly brought back to the here and now. In no small order, she vowed to return to London in an effort to sow the seeds of chaos while he resumed his plan to tear the world apart. Bounding to her feet, she created a naga portal, similar to the one the Antarctic heroes had used to escape an icy prison and arrive just in time to turn the tide during the escapade that had become known as the Changing of the Guard.

All four dragon heroes back to full fitness, a decision needed to be made. Flash, dragging Vimes along with him, headed straight out to sea, both of them changing into their primordial dragon forms during the drop over the cliff face, their mighty wings powering them on towards the submersible, watching from a distance as both the admiral and Manson disappeared deep within its bows.

For Fredric, compelled to put an end to his daughter's reign of murder and mischief, there was only one choice... to follow her through the portal. Disappointingly, he arrived a split second too late, watching as the last of her disappeared into thin air. The White Dragon decided to throw her lot in with him, as she wasn't able to take her natural dragon form and so follow her friends out to sea because of what the priests had done to her so long ago. Just as she pulled up, and with the two dragons circling the vessel in the air out beyond Bow Fiddle Rock, suddenly the dire situation turned into utter catastrophe.

Unexpectedly, a huge dark hatch exploded open atop the heavily armed submarine. As if that weren't enough, what happened next could very well have implications for every living thing across the entire planet.

As Flash and Vimes dived out of the way, an almighty SLBM (Submarine Launched Ballistic Missile) leapt out of the tube into the air, and with the ignition of its thunderous engines, shot up into the sky aiming for a sub-orbital trajectory that would put its final destination somewhere in northern France.

About to zoom off after it, Flash was suddenly recalled by Fredric, more of an order than anything else. Zipping on back to the cliff, the ex Crimson Guard landed directly beside his friend and Peter's grandfather, his gigantic Nordic blue, silver and gunmetal grey prehistoric frame looking magnificent against the back drop of the stunning Scottish scenery.

Mind whirring with calculations, magic and any number of different scenarios, Fredric placed one hand on Flash's scales and unleashed the words in his mind, imbued with more than a little of his magic and will. That done, he sent his friend on his way whilst hoping against hope that his contact from the north would answer his call for help. As he stood helplessly beside Richie on the grass just back from the cliff edge, so far nothing had happened... but he remained optimistic, because that was pretty much all he could do given the circumstances.

Dismissed, and with all the speed he could muster, Flash attempted now more than ever to live up to his name, dashing off south in an effort to somehow beat the nuclear missile that had been launched towards France, over one thousand kilometres away, in a little over eight minutes. Unfortunately, that kind of speed was impossible for a dragon, even with all the spells, mantras and hexes he knew. On his way, he opened up the telepathic link to Vimes to order him to seal shut the rest of the hatches on the submarine and not to let it out of his sight for one moment.

The former *tor*, that's teacher to you and me, confirmed his willingness to do just that and before he had the chance to wish his friend good luck, Flash was gone.

And that's how we left it... Earth having escaped yet again, Manson rubbing his hands in glee deep within the confines of the floating tin can and a nuclear missile on a sub-orbital trajectory winging its way towards France and the monorail test borehole site, currently partly filled with some of the stolen laminium, the light sided heroes all losing their personal battles, unable to prevent the unthinkable from happening. One way or another, in roughly four minutes from now, the world would experience an earth shattering moment like never before.

Ready yourself for the conclusion of The White Dragon Saga.

# 1 A RISKY UNDERTAKING

Frightened for his life, the ex *tor* and steadying influence on Polkinghorne's rash decision making found himself alone, circling the behemoth submarine poking out of the sea beyond Bow Fiddle Rock, that had just launched one of its nuclear payloads.

Confused, hardly able to take in the entirety of the situation they all found themselves in, Flash's words wouldn't stop ringing in his head.

*"Seal the other hatches so that they can't launch any more missiles at any cost. And whatever you do, don't lose sight of that submarine."*

Afraid for good reason, knowing it wouldn't take much to damage the nuclear reactor aboard the submersible, deep within his psyche he fought off the fear that threatened to overwhelm him. Picturing his love and soulmate at the forefront of his mind, he swooped down towards the upper hull of the metallic monster, spiralling corkscrew style as did so, buffeted by the vicious crosswinds that seemed to wrap themselves around the craft.

'What's needed,' he thought, 'is something subtle, yet powerful, more scalpel than a sledgehammer.'

Hovering to a halt just behind the conning tower of the stationary craft, shielded to some degree from the gusty gales, he gazed down at the one hatch that had already been blown open and expended its load, spying three more beside it, close to the reactor itself, he knew. Mind ablaze with possibilities, memories of teaching the young dragonlings back in the Purbeck Peninsula nursery ring came thick and fast, one of which helped him find the answer he so desperately sought. He focused in on the past, recalling exactly what needed to be done.

The inherent flame tucked away deep inside him is what was required, but not the full-on blazing building version, something more like a wielder's torch. Summoning the supernatural within that he very rarely used, Vimes relished the delicious feeling starting to grow in the pit of his stomach. Pursing his lips, his jaws anything but wide open, he savoured the delectable sensation of the fiery heat nibbling at the top of his stomach, the scorching warmth inside licking his tonsils and throat, his mouth waiting in anticipation for what it knew would come. And it did, with an absolute vengeance, the fearsome fiery mixture setting the inside of his gigantic prehistoric jaw ablaze, the intoxicating sense of burning throughout his teeth, tongue and mouth all encompassing.

'Enough,' he told himself, almost carried away by the chain reaction within that he'd set in motion. He had a job to do, and an important one at that. Using the blustery updrafts to his advantage, and not wanting to actually touch down on the submarine itself for fear of any kind of magical treachery, using his massive wings to stabilise himself, he turned over mid air, his fantastical tail pointing skywards, his jaw only centimetres away from the sealed hatches that he knew to contain the worst of mankind's evil.

Retaining a huge degree of control, slowly he exhaled through pursed lips, aiming at first for the line straight down the middle of where each part of the hatch met, before circling around the entire circumference, watching in deep satisfaction as he did so, the darkened metal turning to yellow and then orange, before taking on the bright red glow of molten magma, sealing the hatch firmly shut. He did this for all three, before letting the breeze take him, allowing his primordial body to be carried higher into the air, not the least bit concerned that by now, the residents along the Scottish coast could all see him. Job done, at least for now, the former *tor* relished the sun beating down on his back as he kept a close eye on the devastating war machine in the sea below him, keeping his promise to his friend who he hoped had conjured up a rabbit out of a hat in an effort to once again save the planet.

*"FREDRIC!"*

*"Of course... who else?"*

*"It's good to hear from you my friend, but far sooner than I would have anticipated."*

*"Vasuki... there's no time to waste. The world's about to be torn apart by that bastard Manson, and I kid you not when I say that. Please... I need your help."*

*"Anything,"* replied the king of the nagas sensing the urgency in his dragon comrade's voice, knowing that he wouldn't be exaggerating whatever was going on.

*"The portal... the one that helped us travel from Antarctica to London in an instant, I need to know how to create it NOW!"*

Under normal circumstances, this secretive, ancient supernatural spell wouldn't be shared with anyone, especially outsiders, but in that moment Vasuki had no hesitation, certain beyond any doubt that he could trust his former cell mate. Immediately he gave his mind over to the link, sharing the guttural sounds and inflections needed to create the magical wormhole, while showing him how and when to move his fingers in relation to the magic and willpower involved. In only a matter of seconds, it was done.

*"Thank you my friend, you've been a great help."*

*"You are of course always very welcome."*

*"Can I ask one more thing?"*

*"Of course."*

*"Is there a way to track the destination of a portal?"*

*"There's a spell that can do such a thing, but the residual ethereal energy of the portal in question has to be reasonably fresh."*

*"Please,"* Fredric implored, *"can you teach it to me?"*

*"Sure thing."*

Much simpler this time, it was in fact only a handful of words and sounds, to be cast on the exact spot the portal had stood upon.

*"Yet more danger?"*

*"Yes... a very different source though."*

*"Things sound perilous?"*

All that happened this time was a kind of mental nod to the enquiry.

*"Vasuki... you've been a great help. Without you, the world would most certainly be doomed... it still might be. But we now have a chance, something that I'm immensely grateful for."*

*"Is there anything else I can do?"*

Hesitant to ask, particularly when the nagas as a race had already paid such a heavy price, the founder of the Crimson Guards couldn't resist making one more request given the dire situation they all found themselves in.

*"There's a nuclear powered submarine, just off the coast of a small town in Scotland called Portknockie."*

*"I know the place."*

*"I figured you would. It's just fired one of its nuclear missiles, something we're trying to stop even as we speak. Manson's on board, looking to escape and no doubt create as much fresh hell as he can. If you can assist with that, while we deal with the other matters, the whole of the world would be in your debt."*

*"We're on our way."*

*"Oh and there's a dragon called Vimes... he's one of ours and watching its every move."*

Through the exhausting long range telepathic link, Fredric showed the naga what Vimes looked like and how to contact him. That done, it was time to go, something they both realised.

*"Good luck,"* Vasuki quipped, his accent strangely different without the impediment he'd carried for so long.

*"To us all,"* his friend replied, before abruptly cutting off the link.


A split second before they hit, Amelia Battlehard, heroic captain of the King's Guard, friend to many, borrowed a trick from the dragon she hoped to live long enough to get to know better, whispered powerful words within the confines of her mind and adding her indomitable will, readied herself for what she knew would be an awkward and savage battle given the confines of the tunnel she now found herself dropping down into.

Without any inkling of the magic involved, momentarily her mass increased over twenty times, dropping her, not like a stone, more like an asteroid made up of numerous different heavy metals, speeding up the encounter. It suddenly caught them all off guard, even Oblivion, and he was the most battle hardened and wisest of them all, if such a thing could be said of any of them. She hit the first three of them HARD, much more so than they were expecting, their bared fangs and faces taking the brunt of the impact, dazing two, forcing the other into an uncontrollable spin that had him crashing instantly into the barren rock face off to one side. After that, the all encompassing darkness, only backlit by the flickering blue of the force shield that had been restored above them quickly became filled with scorching fire in fantastical shades of orange, yellow, red and blue, the surrounding thick air shimmering in the heat, the deadliness there for all to see.

Almost as soon as it had been enacted, the magic wore off, returning one of the king's finest to her normal weight, something she immediately used to her advantage, twisting and turning, battering the oncoming onslaught with her wings and tail, using every part of her lithe and limber body as a weapon, just as she'd been trained to do, scratching, clawing, biting and returning fire. The supposedly coordinated group didn't know what hit it, never in their lifetimes having come across a being so outstandingly ferocious and brilliant, one that parried their pathetic attacks and more than made up for being outmatched and outnumbered with her movement and supernatural abilities.

Spreading out both her wings, their tips nearly scraping both sides of the tunnel, she used her momentum to draw to a halt and swing back up so she was now attacking them from below. Steadying herself with her rugged and yet beautiful tail, brilliant, bright blue forked lightning lanced out of both her spindly hands, arcing its way through the humid and dusty air, illuminating the protagonists as it did so, a vicious crackle echoing off the walls in its wake, causing ears to bleed and headaches all around. Not done, Captain Battlehard, with just two flaps of her giant wings, surged upwards, wanting nothing more than to get this over with, her final conversation with Flash constantly at the back of her mind, the worry of a nuclear missile closing in on her destination niggling at her psyche. Every ounce of will she could spare needed to stop it from overwhelming her.

Head thrumming like a cathedral's bell at the centre of a ringing contest by the most vigorous of competitors, Oblivion dug his talons into the tunnel wall to stop his descent, using his outstretched wings to bring himself to a halt and get his head around what had just happened. It was hard to understand, they were all but upon her and then... what? She'd slammed into the middle of them, with more force than was possible, knocking them aside like pins at the end of a bowling alley. After which she'd moved with all the grace of a gazelle, avoiding both magical and physical attacks, before going on the offensive from below them, something he could see first hand from up above and off to one side. And if the smell of roasted scales and dragon flesh was anything to go by, she was gaining the upper hand with every second that passed, something he knew couldn't be allowed to stand.

Readying the naga magic that only a select few had been taught, brushing away the pain inside his mind, Oblivion pulled his tail up, let his wings drop down by his side, and with a dismissive sneer, dropped headfirst towards the brilliant blue lightning that had his comrades burning and screaming for their lives. Determined to change the outcome and not die in this suffocating tunnel, he set his sights on the damned female that had plunged towards them just as the shield above had been restored.

"What's going on?" asked the admiral to the entire bridge crew of the stolen submarine beyond Bow Fiddle Rock just outside the Scottish town of Portknockie.

"It looks as though the missile hatches have been sealed shut... no doubt wielded together by one of the dragons outside."

"Is there any other damage?"

"As far as we can tell, no!"

"Sire," the admiral ventured towards the cold, wet, shivering being standing at the back of the command centre, "do you have any other orders for us?"

"Not at the moment. I think we're quite safe from attack. They wouldn't dare risk damaging the reactor this close to mainland Britain. How are we with tracking that missile?"

"We can trace it all the way, my lord."

"Good enough. Will we be able determine the exact point of impact?"

"We should be able to. If our uplink to the satellites fails, then our other systems should pick up the blast wave at just over a thousand kilometres away."

"Excellent!" Manson mused, stroking his chin and cheeks with his right hand, still dripping cold sea water from his swim out to the submarine onto the dark, shiny floor. "Carry on," he casually observed, so many facets of what was going on coursing throughout his mind.

With the end of the world only a few minutes away, he reflected to no one but himself deep within his head.

'Who'd have thought that someone born into that icy cold dungeon in Antarctica could come this far? Ha! What do you think of your precious domain now DRAGONS? All your guiding and protecting, more like meddling with your wretched human pets, and this is what it comes down to. How pathetic! So many lost already, but that's nothing to what's on its way. I'd love to see your faces when the world crumbles around you, huge fiery fissures and molten magma cracks spewing out the contents of the core, all turning out to be much more than what they appear, while you try in vain to use your precious magic to overcome what will be the death knell for yourselves and all life on the planet. Good luck with that,' he thought sarcastically, not for one second taking his eyes off the monitor that showed the SLBM's sub-orbital trajectory. Satisfaction at having the final laugh, stealing victory from the jaws of defeat, started to pump through his body, a heightened sense of excitement at his impending death along with everyone else's causing him to momentarily exhale in rapture, much to the surprise of the craft's crew.


Prone on the ground, intuitively he tried to react, move towards her, unleash his magic, give his very life so she could be saved, but both physically and mentally it was like wading through treacle, slow, cumbersome, and incredibly draining with little to show in the way of tangible results, the horrific burns he'd suffered rendering him powerless. Once again, Peter found himself sitting on the sidelines, watching helplessly as events played out around him.

Standing next to Bentwhistle, still mightily drained of the legendary magic that went with the job, feeling as feeble and vulnerable as she could remember, Polkinghorne, or Santa as we now know her to be, could only stop and stare at the events unfolding in front of her, heart crushed at the sight of the glistening blade pressed firmly against the young woman's throat, unable to act as she wished. For all intents and purposes, it looked as though the Christmas superstar's bind might well cost one of the mightiest heroes of them all her life, which could bring a veil of darkness down across the planet, one from which there might be no recovering from.

Confused, befuddled and confounded, throughout all his years on the planet, he'd never once found himself in such a state. His razor sharp mind was normally his biggest asset, something that had served him well during his incarceration, and I'm not talking about all those years trapped in the master mantra maker's secret vault, hidden deep below ground behind a series of deadly traps. Oh no... I'm talking about being confined in the futuristic, frost covered, dragon killing shape that he himself had forged into being many thousands of years ago.

Lost, alone, out of his right mind, not knowing where he was or even who or what had a grip on his shiny hilt, Fu-ts'ang, the master weapon smith that in one form or another had graced the earth for many thousands of years, couldn't form a coherent thought, so muddled was his intelligence from the ancient naga magic that Mas-crate had drilled into him. And so as he was forcefully thrust forward, all he could do was yield to whatever physical presence had him in its grip.

Abruptly the haziness and fog that up until now had encompassed his whole intellect suddenly shattered as a blisteringly white stream of light from out of nowhere scattered everything that had been holding him back. As his wits returned, so did everything embodied in the shining bright stream of goodness... a vast array of feelings, ones that up until recently he hadn't felt for a very long time. Friendship, compassion, devotion, closeness, camaraderie and of course the all defining one, the one on which we all thrive, the one that can conquer all... LOVE! Thoughts of his first true love, Song Jin, the dragon so tragically taken from him by her villainous father in a fit of rage came flooding back. Just the mere image of her beauty bolstered his spirits, feelings awakening from the best time of his life, those spent with her, something he'd been reminded of by the companionship of the beautiful human blonde goddess he'd so recently found himself associated with.

Held in that moment for what felt like an eternity, time stopped as the fantastic blade came to terms with everything... his very being, past acts that had led him to being restrained in this way, his current surroundings, the feelings he'd developed for those around him, in particular one whose throat he could currently feel pressed firmly against the extension of his physical being, something that repulsed and frightened him in equal measure, especially as he could now sense her utter terror through their shared link that had immediately snapped back into existence. Not one to dither and always one to do the right thing, as the pressure on his shaft mounted in an attempt to thrust him forward, he acted accordingly.

Dread and fear filled her, first at losing the connection with her friend, the brilliant blade she'd bonded with almost immediately during their time in the Salisbridge market place rescuing Tank and Flash, now at the thought of her love and soulmate watching her die at the hands of the disfigured primeval beast that had her life in its hands. Locking eyes with the monster, watching its mutilated face contort into a sick and twisted grin, suddenly she knew it was the end. With a grudging acceptance of the inevitable, Janice swept everything inside her out of the way, and gave herself over to the love she had for everyone that had come into her previously very dull human existence, from Peter to Tank, Richie, to Hook and Flash, to the now deceased Gee Tee, to Fredric whose acceptance she'd gained, to George the king, Captain Battlehard, Yoyo, his beautiful wife Rose and their charges full of energy, and all the courageous humans who'd now returned to the surface where they belonged. And of course one other, without whom they, no... she wouldn't have survived, one that she'd well and truly become a part of. Her friend, maybe her best friend (alongside Richie), one without whom she felt lost and alone... FU-TS'ANG! Like the first rays of sun bursting through the sky, swapping light for dark, her love for them all exploded out in every different direction, splintering like light reflecting off a broken mirror, powered by the innocence and good that was the true mark of her soul.

A life, okay only a human one, but still, ripping away a sentience, something that could understand and appreciate being alive, was as good as it got, to him at least, and made him feel not only like the apex predator that he was, but engorged, the bloodlust that remained buried in the genetic code of his makeup. He was after all a dragon, albeit one with a human grounding, one with urges and needs, one whose primal instincts had to be sated, and so with as much force as he could muster, he propelled forward the strange and clearly ancient weapon, relishing the thought of seeing the head of this petite blonde crash firmly to the floor.

Using every last ounce of the supernatural available to him, he resisted to the core of his very being, refusing to be moved any further in the direction something was trying to drive him, hanging instead firmly in mid-air, an immovable object, like one of his former cell mates, Excalibur, the sword so long, stuck in the stone, now firmly contained in the vault beneath what remained of the Emporium.

'What?' Mas-crate wondered, the fantastic blade refusing to yield to the strength with which he pushed forward, even a millimetre. Puzzled that it hung strangely airborne, he tried once more, this time putting all his considerable weight behind the attempt. Still... NOTHING!

Having closed her eyes, made her peace and said her goodbyes, the gorgeous blonde bar worker, heroine, friend and soulmate wondered what the hell was going on, and why she was still in one piece. Without needing to peel back her eyelids, the reason immediately became apparent as a familiar voice echoed around the inside of her brain.

*'I can't imagine how you've gotten yourself in this pickle, little one. I disappear for but a moment and here you are.'*

'FU-TS'ANG!'

*'Of course.'*

*'Thank God.'*

*'NO... thank YOU!'*

*'Uhh...'*

*'Buckle up sweetheart, because he's about to be taught what it*

*means to mess with any of my friends. Dive backwards and out of reach... NOW!"*

With the feel of the cold steel tickling her throat, and knowing not to throw away another chance at life, Janice commanded her body to move like it never had before, ordering it to imitate her friend Richie and the astounding acrobatics she was renowned for in battle.

At best, it could only be described as clumsy. After all, the human youngster had no experience or training in anything like this, nor any magical abilities to bolster herself. Throwing her body backwards, she missed slicing her leg on her friend's blade by about an inch as she tumbled over on top of herself, her shoulder taking the brunt of her landing, the wind well and truly knocked out of her sails.

Peter and Polkinghorne watched wide-eyed as Janice took off, sure the deadly weapon would decapitate her before she completed her retreat. Unbelievably, to them at least, it didn't, and much to the monster's horror, she, for the moment at least, landed out of harm's reach.

Further up Camelot Arcade, the last few emaciated fingers of light stretched out across the face of the sundial, the heavy weight of the not inconsiderable amount of rubble above almost touching the lightened skin of the still unconscious rugby playing dragon, only a thin and faltering invisible shield less than a centimetre thick prolonging the inevitable. In mere moments, what remained of him would be crushed, along with the soul of his friend trapped in the ring, For'son, who'd already done so much to keep him alive. What they needed was some help. Where it would come from was anyone's guess.

"We have to get her out of there NOW!" Trayrin screamed at the top of her voice, running over to where the light blue shield crackled and hissed at the entrance to the tunnel's vertical shaft.

After having transformed back into their prehistoric best, sitting on huge dragon chairs, tails draped through the holes in the back of them, at the main controls in the centre, Rose turned to look at her husband, acknowledging the plea of the desperate youngster across the way, who was hoping to find anything that would help the brave captain they'd all come to think of as one of their own.

It wasn't to be, something Yoyo indicated with just a shake of his giant scaled head, knowing that they just couldn't risk deactivating the shield, not for her, not for anyone.

For the next four minutes or so, the brave captain was on her own. After that, well, what would be, would be.


As the last of the flailing limbs disappeared out of sight, running for their lives due to the earthquake ruse they'd instigated in an effort to be free of prying eyes, the three of them, Jar Man, DomCon and Steel, released their grip on the magic just as their four human friends, Angela, Emma, Sam and Taibul, skidded to a halt in front of them. From the looks on their faces they were more than a little pleased to have been of assistance.

"There's no time to lose," put in Jar Man, the ginger human giant, his false form mirroring his prehistoric alter ego.

"Where do we start?" Steel asked, ready and raring to go.

"DomCon, search beneath the rubble for any life signs at all, no matter how faint they may be," ordered his friend.

Closing his eyes, the smallest of the three of them, with a look of total and utter concentration etched into his human disguise, reached out with all the supernatural at his command, scouring every inch of the debris, both above and below ground, and everything in between.

"As soon as he's pinpointed them, Steel, you'll be

responsible for removing as much debris around them as you can, as quickly as possible. I'll use my abilities to hold in place everything that has the potential to collapse, so there's no chance of any wayward concrete harming the schoolchildren as we attempt to free them."

"Understood," Steel shot back, his laminium ball game face and focus most firmly in place now, despite his newly acquired human guise.

"What do you want us to do?" piped up Taibul from amongst the four human onlookers.

"Spread out," Jar Man ordered. "Cover every way there is for people to come back into this area and warn us if anyone is on their way. We'll do what we can to expedite matters, but we can't get caught doing this. Understood?"

All four of them nodded, before splitting up and sprinting off in different directions, determined to play their part in the unconventional rescue.

"I've got all of them," DomCon announced, his eyes still firmly shut, the ethereal energy at his disposal having located every last source of heat as well as the singular heartbeats of all the injured children trapped beneath the huge amount of rubble.

"Share with us," his friend instructed, opening up his mind, immediately forming an unbreakable three-way telepathic bond with the other two.

DomCon portrayed into their psyche a 3D image of the whole site, viewed from up above, tiny pockets of red signifying the life signs he'd found scattered around one particular pocket, deep beneath the inordinate amount of rock and stone which had once formed houses, the school and of course the iconic cathedral.

"Okay," said Jar Man, still studying the map. "We know where to start and we haven't got much time. Let's get going."

With the kind of precision and coordination of much more experienced magic users, mirroring the actions the king's own dragon clean up squads were renowned for, the three of them, their human friends on the lookout for any unexpected surprises, got down to it, hoping to save as many lives as physically possible.

# 2 A NUCLEAR CONUNDRUM

It felt as though she'd been caught up in a tornado. One moment she'd been back at Stonehenge, standing in front of Polkinghorne, about to be transported the length of Britain in the blink of an eye by the supernatural Santa magic. The next... she'd been deposited in northern Scotland, racing around the coast looking for any clue, no matter how insignificant, in the hunt for not only the missing submarine, but also the terror twins, Manson and Earth. In her heart of hearts, she hadn't believed it possible, figuring that it would just be one more wild goose chase, but on stumbling across the pair of them atop the coastal path... well, let's just say things had got really interesting, really quickly, a fight ensuing, one in which she couldn't gain the upper hand, no matter how hard she tried. Luckily her allies, in the form of Flash, Fredric and Vimes, had turned up in the nick of time otherwise... the prospect was too horrifying to contemplate. And just when things looked as though they couldn't possibly get any worse... they had, with a vengeance, Earth disappearing off through one of those damn naga wormholes to goodness knows where, Manson coming back from the dead, seeking refuge in that blessed submarine, before firing one of the four nuclear missiles it carried. That had been the last hour of her life, maybe even the final hour, if they couldn't turn things around somehow. Stunned and astounded, it was a miracle that Richie remained standing, but she did, next to Fredric, her best friend's grandfather, a dragon with whom she hadn't always seen eye to eye (something of an understatement given what had happened during The Changing of the Guard), but one she now found herself counting on, especially given that he'd cast something supernatural on Flash before sending him away. As well, he was up to something... she could tell by the concentrated look on his weatherworn face, almost certainly a telepathic conversation, but with who?

Snapping herself out of the haze of the recent past, she reminded him of her presence.

"What's going on?"

It took more than a few seconds for Fredric to respond, no doubt finishing whatever he had in mind.

"Stand back," he commanded, surveying the scene of Earth's long vanished wormhole, the one she'd used to escape once again.

"What is it you think…?"

"We're going after her, you and I."

"What about the nuclear missile?"

"That's up to Flash now, there's nothing else we can do there. But we can track that psychopath down and stop her from visiting more misery on the innocents of this world. You're either in or you're out. Which is it to be?"

To her at least, there wasn't really a choice, especially since she couldn't take to what she regarded as her natural prehistoric form, after what the priesthood had done to her. What was odd though, as she stood there considering what she regarded as an ultimatum, was the confidence Fredric exuded, from somehow tracking down and reining in his daughter, to the nuclear missile that might shatter the world into a million pieces. In the history of everything, no one, she thought, had ever remained so composed under such pressure. With little choice but to throw her lot in with him and hope for the best, she gave him her answer.

"I'm in!"

"Good," he replied, running his right hand in a circle in the air around the exact space where Earth's portal had been only a short while before.

"What are you doing?"

"Using some rather unusual magic to track where she went."

"Where did that come from?"

"A friend."

"Vasuki?"

"Of course."

Choosing to remain silent, whilst amazed that in such a short space of time he'd managed to get in touch with the king of the nagas, she watched as he continued, a constant worry about her friends niggling away at the back of her mind.


Royally pissed off, that's what he'd been when Fredric had ordered him back to the cliff top just as he was about to chase after the nuclear missile that Manson had launched from the missing submarine. Valuable seconds that could well have been the difference between success and failure, life and death, had been wasted in those few moments, he was sure of it. But not now, not as his gigantic Nordic blue, battleship grey and stunning silver, majestic primordial dragon body scythed through the air on the most expedient route to northern France, cutting through the molecules in an effort to live up to his name and reach his destination before the deadly, potentially world shattering projectile arrived. Under normal circumstances, even with all the supernatural mantras and spells at his disposal, what Flash was attempting would have been all but impossible. Dragons, even at their fastest, and he was one of the quickest by far, could not exceed the sound barrier, just over seven hundred and sixty miles an hour... despite many trying, it had never once been achieved by any member of their race. And even if it had been possible, it wouldn't have mattered. The one thousand kilometres or so would take the missile about four and a half minutes. Even if he managed to break the sound barrier, he'd still be about forty minutes too late.

So why was he even trying if he was that far out? A good question and one answered wholly by explaining exactly what Fredric had done on Flash's return to the cliff top.

To answer that we need to return to the early stages of Fredric's career, not long after he founded the Crimson

Guards to act as his best friend, the king's, enforcer, back to the days of frequent secret missions before his lengthy imprisonment in icy Antarctica. There was one standout mission which had required him to singlehandedly track down a rogue dragoness who'd embedded herself deep within the Brazilian rainforest, dishing out orders from afar to her human lackeys, organising riots and attacks on embassies with even the odd assassination attempt thrown in for good measure. The beast in question was quite the piece of work. After a long boat trip surrounded by locals, relishing the heat and humidity despite being stuck in his ape-like alter ego, one that had taken him beyond Manaus to a small settlement called Coari, the king's friend and Peter's grandfather had, under the cover of darkness, transformed into his original prehistoric form and flown above the canopy of the jungle to the outskirts of the rogue dragon's encampment. To cut a long story short, after taking out most of the well armed humans, the two of them fought, at first on the ground, after that, in the air way above the trees, the first hint of dawn lighting up their primeval bodies twisting and twirling, biting and scratching, a rainbow litany of magic lighting up their sleek scaled forms as they battled for airborne supremacy. Of all the missions he'd been on, that had probably been the hardest because SHE, a dragon named Atarivenasis, had proven to be a formidable opponent. Eventually he'd prevailed, but only by the skin of his teeth and quite possibly more by luck than judgement. It had however come at a cost... a series of devastating injuries that his magic just couldn't heal. In the end, he'd had to stay all alone, in her lair deep within the rainforest, for ten days before he was fit enough to travel back to civilisation.

Predictably bored after only a few hours, despite needing to rest, he'd done what any dragon in his position would do, something dictated by his training, and started to search the place to see exactly what they'd been dealing with. Of course there were vast stashes of weapons, drugs, alcohol and tobacco, as well as a room full of the remains of tortured souls, which made him angry beyond belief because something huge had taken almighty bites out of the poor wretches, presumably whilst they were still alive, a concept that went against his, and the dragon domain in general's core beliefs.

On the third day of his supposed rest, quite by accident he stumbled upon it... Atarivenasis' secret hoard of supernatural goodies, and boy was he surprised, because it was a positive treasure trove. One-off mantra scrolls the likes of which he'd never seen, were piled high, as well as countless artefacts in the guise of rings, amulets, and brooches, and it didn't stop there. A cotton jacket held what he thought was pride of place, a gorgeous white thing with gold trimmings of outstanding quality. It didn't however take him long to figure out why it was prized so much. You see the buttons were made of laminium, and were of course able to boost the wearer's abilities and mana. On discovering that, he was extremely grateful its owner hadn't been wearing it when he'd first encountered her, otherwise the outcome of the battle might have been very different. Astounded at the incredible find, his attention was caught by a flash of dark blue from the deepest recesses of one particularly dark corner of the room. Alert for any kind of magical trap, Fredric was surprised to find a hidden drawer beneath one of the warped and twisted floorboards. Turning it out onto the ground, there was surely a king's ransom in valuable jewels and strips of precious metal, including more laminium. What garnered his attention though, was a tiny scrap of rolled up parchment, secured in place by a flimsy piece of straggly green cotton. Careful to unfurl the scroll outside the encampment, once again worried at the thought of any treachery, what he found changed his world... It was a spell, a highly mana intensive one that if used correctly, would, for a limited time, reduce a being's mass by about ninety-nine percent. Incredible didn't cover it, with all the possibilities quite mindboggling.

He'd stored it away and had cause to use it twice, up until today, both occasions being absolute emergencies, his life most certainly on the line. Should you be wondering, that was the magic he'd cast on his friend Flash, reducing his mass, making him not quite as light as a feather, but not far off, hopefully enabling him to reach his destination in time.

Flying like crazy, his wings pumping ten to the dozen, Flash, knew that he had to make the most of the unusual enchantment Fredric had cast upon him, given that it would only last about a minute. Thirty seconds in, he was trying to give the abundant array of planes a wide berth, wary of the sonic boom in his wake as he passed above Manchester and Liverpool, the cities' tightly knit urban sprawls instantly recognisable, the realisation of the distance he'd already travelled buoying him somewhat, despite the realisation that he had no idea, should he reach his destination, how to stop the impending nuclear detonation.

'One thing at a time,' he told himself, noticing in the distance a tiny red headed young girl engrossed in a book, sitting next to her mother, abruptly turn and glance out of a plane's window, catching sight of his enormous prehistoric, Nordic blue, gunmetal grey and silver body, all but a blur given the speed he was travelling at. If he could have waved, he would have done, despite the fact that to show his unique and original form broke almost every rule there was. He was done with them... THE RULES!

'Damn them to hell,' he thought, the two northern powerhouses below him now firmly out of sight behind him, Birmingham but a blur, the bright blue of the English Channel in the distance getting ever closer as the seconds ticked down.

'It's strange,' he mused, 'the feeling of being so light.' Normally his legs, particularly his massive thighs, felt heavy and cumbersome, up until he'd gained enough momentum to take flight and they'd been firmly stowed away beneath his aerodynamic body. Right now, even though he knew they were there, he could hardly feel them at all. It felt like his wings were made of tissue paper. They weren't, because he would continually glance over and check that the huge, powerful extremities, still the same as they'd... I was going to say, 'always been', but that wasn't the case, not since he'd gained this much stronger, bigger body, during the course of the Changing of the Guard, a combination of very different magic producing something miraculous.

Steering clear of yet another circling plane below him, he shot over Bristol, noting all the traffic on the bridge to Wales spanning the river Severn, certain now that all the passengers would be looking skywards, wondering what the hell that huge booming noise was all about. No doubt during the course of his flight, he'd inflicted a certain amount of damage despite the height he was trying to maintain. Windows would have been smashed, wildlife terrified as well as any number of other disasters. If he could have made amends straight away, he would have. Unfortunately he had more important matters to deal with, in the form of the impending ballistic missile that he just had to stop, not just for the sake of France, or the planet itself, there was more to it than that. It had become personal, ever since Amelia had told him she was trapped in the test borehole with a horde of Manson's rampaging goons. Just the thought of her helpless and alone focused his mind, drove him on, pushed his burning wings to beat faster, his heart all the time racing, no concern for himself, just those that he loved, a list she was rapidly working her way to the top of.

With no mind of its own, the raging rocket of destruction roared up into the atmosphere, continuing on its pre-planned course, carrying a payload with the potential to not only wipe out a great deal of France, but to possibly shatter the planet itself, if it started a chain reaction with the massive amounts of laminium in and around the test borehole. Setting the air on fire all around it, moving at a speed almost incalculable, momentarily it was a thing of beauty, almost like a comet moving through the night sky, the incredible tail the most tangible thing about it. Death and devastation in the form of the SLBM had now woken up much of the planet, at least those monitoring satellites trained on countries in and around its trajectory, initiating flustered phone calls which very quickly rose to the highest levels of government.

# 3 CHOICES

At that precise moment choices were being made across the planet. Most were mundane... what to add to the shopping list, which film to see at the cinema, which radio station to listen to on the way to work, what clothes to wear, what colour to paint the walls. You get the idea. But some were anything but, lives and much more were on the line and time was ticking down for the best of them, none more so than one particular dragon who'd used all the magic at his disposal to reach out into his surroundings in an effort to fully understand exactly what was going on and how he could defeat the very real threat to himself and his friends. What he found shocked him to his very core.

Watching his love tumble clumsily to the scorched, rubble strewn ground, a wave of relief washing over him, Peter, using everything he had, managed to get a complete supernatural overview of the area, a real sense of doom nagging at him deep within his mind at the realisation that one of his two best friends Tank, and his magical compadre, For'son the enigmatic ring, were almost out of time, the mass of compacted debris about to rain down on them for good.

Most would instinctively act, but not for the first time, he was caught in a conundrum, with the helpless Polkinghorne, bereft of most of her ethereal energy, standing, mouth agog beside him, his love and soulmate sprawled out on the floor, Hook badly injured somewhere amongst all the pandemonium, and the despicable dark dragon, clearly one of Manson's more powerful goons, looking to go another round. In all of the confusion, terror and chaos, his mind just couldn't decide what to do. Luckily for all of them, the choice was made for him.

*"Save Tank and For'son, I'll take care of the situation here,"* a familiar voice resonated throughout his mind.

'FU-TS'ANG!' he thought, genuinely buoyed at knowing he could leave his love and Santa in the care of a being he trusted totally.

Knowing what he needed to do and ignoring the demented dark dragon going absolutely mental somewhere out there in the wispy fog that hung in the air around remnants of spent magic and the destruction of the front of the Emporium. Flooding himself with a considerable amount of his ethereal energy to heal his burns as best he could, Peter brought forth the words he needed at the front of his mind, and with his speed greatly enhanced, set off at a blur, cutting his way through the supernatural mist, heading towards the colossal mountain of debris his friends remained trapped beneath, ignoring the woman he loved, focused solely on his rescue attempt.

Like a hungry toddler that hadn't slept, its favourite toy deliberately taken away, Mas-crate stomped furiously out of the smoky shroud, heading directly for the young human, determined to see her blood spilled, ignoring the statue-like Polkinghorne, regarding her as little or no threat at all, something we know to be far from the truth.

'Why, why, why (not Delila) won't you work?' she thought, angry at herself because the inherent Santa magic had deserted her, at this of all times. It wasn't so much gone, as not being recharged as she would have expected, almost as if it were being diverted or used for something else. Seething at having achieved so little so far when things had gone to hell and the shop front had been blown out, Polkinghorne's natural bravery battered her reluctance and reliance on everything supernatural out of the way as she screamed out telepathically.

*"FU-TS'ANG! COME TO ME!"* she ordered, an edge to her voice that very rarely raised its ugly head.

About to get stuck into the approaching dark monster once again, determined to save his friend at all costs, the dragon killing weapon and hero to one and all didn't hesitate in pulling a huge U-turn, zipped over his friend's prone body and with the delicacy of a butterfly landing on a flower, dropped straight into the Christmas legend's outstretched hand.

*"What are you…?"* was as far as he got, before the alter ego of the big bellied, white bearded, rotund and jolly once a year deliverer of joy leapt into action, bounding up the side of the nearest building, a firm grip on the chilly hilt of the fantastic, futuristic blade.

Eyes centred solely on the extraordinarily lucky human flailing about on the ground, slowly he staggered almost within reach, the missing part of his tail causing him great pain, rendering him off balance and angry as hell. Stumbling to a halt just in range, Manson's mate and confidant, the wicked and merciless Mas-crate, pulled in a deep breath and, feeling the familiar tingle of the magic and fire in his belly combine in absolute rapture, prepared to barbeque this insignificant little speck of a human pet that had irked him so much.

*"Close yourself down,"* she commanded, *"so that he doesn't do what he did to you before."*

*"If I do that, how will I save my best friend?"* Fu-ts'ang replied.

*"YOU won't! We will!"* urged Polkinghorne, using her pent up anger to fuel the desire within to save the young woman.

Pushing off with her feet, using all the physical strength her false human form could offer up, very much aware now of the icy cold blade's weight in her right hand, she backflipped through the wispy grey filaments of smoke that remained suspended in the air, and turning as she did so, used all her strength to bring the weapon around in a mighty arc, just waiting for the faint resistance she knew to be coming.

Sure enough… CRACK! The sound of splintering

bones being simultaneously shredded filled the air as Mascrate's left wing was purged from his body, preceding the agonising howl of horror that somehow combined with uncontrollable coughing, the foul beast almost choking on his own fireball, one that was meant to fry their friend to cinders.

'Good job!' thought Fu-ts'ang, just as he closed himself down, entering in essence a state of semi-hibernation, one that should stop the dreaded dragon from confounding his mind, leaving him in limbo. As his senses shut down and the reality all around him faded from sight and sound, of one thing he was certain... both his physical form and his best friend were in good hands.


Skidding to a halt in comedic fashion, like Tom in the Tom And Jerry cartoons, hands and arms flailing everywhere, almost slipping on the dust and dirt, Peter knew instantly that both his friends were buried beneath the mound directly in front of where he was standing, only about two metres away, but it might as well have been light years. As his mind whirred with possibilities, only then did it occur to him to reach out.

*"TANK... FOR'SON?"*

*"Youngster!"* exclaimed the enigmatic presence trapped within the fantastic jewellery.

*"I sense the urgency of your situation. How can I help?"*

*"I'm struggling to hold onto my grip of reality because Tank is unconscious and I need a living being to maintain a link to reality."*

*"Will I do?"*

*"You most certainly would, if we were in a position for you to slip me onto your finger. As it is, that's simply not possible. I'm hanging on by the skin of my teeth. It's all I can do to sustain the shield that's preventing all the rubble from crushing us both. With every second that passes, my grip diminishes and the barrier gets closer to your friend. As it is, it's only a couple of centimetres away now."*

*"Shall I try and remove the rubble from up here, piece by piece?"*

*"I fear we don't have that long."*

*"Then what?"* asked the desperate hockey playing youngster, starting to tremble ever so slightly at the thought of losing his friend.

*"I think we only have a matter of moments left. All I can suggest is that you get a grip on Tank's body and yank us out with everything that you have."*

*"Won't that cause considerable harm?"*

*"Quite possibly, but of the two options, I'm afraid it is by far the more attractive."*

As pure unadulterated silence returned to the inside of his head, Peter knew that the decision had been made and there was no turning back. With pressure weighing heavily on him, he did the only thing he could and, stretching out with all his ethereal energy and intrinsic magic, grabbed hold of his friend's motionless body, and with every ounce of willpower that he had, began to pull.


Shoulder, knees and back filled with excruciating pain, Janice very gingerly attempted to crawl to her feet, her head spinning viciously from her uncontrolled landing, grateful to be in one piece given her previously perilous position, confused at her best friend's presence abruptly blinking out of existence, their link once again disconnected. About to call out deep within her mind, the need to do so disappeared as the cold imbued blade she'd recognise anywhere came scything through the air, just off to her right, the chill in its wake leaving a glistening, frosty trail, preceding one almighty, unforgiving sound.

CRACK!

The splitting of bones followed by an ungodly choking mewl of pain louder than a speaker at the front of a rock concert had her instantly covering her ears, the intensity almost knocking her back down to the floor.

'What the…?', was all she could think before a familiar figure firmly gripping the hilt of her friend bounded into existence... POLKINGHORNE!

"Go girl, go," she wanted to shout, only actually thinking it instead, watching the Christmas legend sweep effortlessly through the stifling grey air wielding her futuristic pal with all the grace of a Samurai warrior, looking more fierce and focused than Janice had ever seen her. Abruptly an explosion of light and heat almost directly in front of her blew her vision away as the remnants of the fireball intended to toast her into oblivion was vomited up by the severely wounded Mas-crate, now not only missing half his tail, but wingless on one side. For the cruel, cunning and ruthless monster that Manson counted as one of his inner circle, things were going from bad to worse. Speaking of which...

Eyes squeezed tightly shut, glistening transparent beads of sweat caking his filthy forehead, the young hockey playing dragon, who all that time ago had not been able to take his chance to rid the world of Manson and prevent all the subsequent chaos and mayhem, stood stock still, his concentration all encompassing, the supernatural grasp he had on his friend anything but, the fear he felt on the inside threatening to spiral out of control. Still he pushed on, or more accurately, pulled... his rugby playing pal's bulky frame coming up through the mountain of rubble, trying ever so carefully to protect his head at all costs, not so much worried about the rest of his torso.

It was working, after a fashion at least, boulders, rocks and stones tumbling into the vacated space below, some as big as a desk, others more akin to pebbles.

*"Careful youngster,"* warned the voice of the mysterious loop, Tank's new partner in crime, the monarch's former constant companion. *"You're bending his limbs into the most excruciating positions. I think one of his arms is already broken."*

*"I'm sorry... but I'm doing the best I can and concentrating solely on protecting his head and getting both of you out of there as quickly as possible,"* rebuked Peter, trying to maintain his wavering focus.

After a moment or two of consideration, For'son, experienced warrior and magical maestro replied.

*"I'm sorry Peter, I truly am. I understand just how worried you must be about him and how much effort you're putting into rescuing us. Please forgive my abruptness. I care for him too."*

*"I know,"* the youngster replied, the magical exertion almost becoming too much, *"I want him back too, but hopefully we're nearly there."*

And do you know what? They pretty much were.

Mirroring Yoda using the force to lift Luke's X-wing out of the Dagobah swamp, the battered, bruised, broken and bloodstained body of Tank rose up in front of Peter out of the gigantic pile of debris, into the air, floating there all of its own accord, tossing rocks and stones in all directions as it burst free.

As gently as he could, the magic within him wavering just a little, Peter set his friend down on the ground, appalled at the apparent damage to his familiar false human form.

*"Peter, take me from Tank and slip me onto your finger... quickly,"* For'son urged telepathically.

Still trying to get his head around everything, sweat now pouring down his neck and back from the exertion of what he'd just accomplished, a sense of pride lay tucked away inside all the worry. But the ring's words put all that into perspective and so he did the only thing he could and pulled the stunning looking loop off Tank's battered and scuffed chunky finger, immediately slipping it on the largest of his own. Abruptly his whole world changed as a much more powerful and symbiotic link with the warrior presence presented itself.

"Whoa," Peter babbled, more than a little taken aback, both overwhelmed and delighted simultaneously.

But there was no time for that.

*"Kneel down next to him,"* For'son ordered through their newly established, much more personal telepathic link.

Peter immediately complied, laying his hands out flat

across his friend's motionless body, allowing the partner in the band to scrutinise all the rugby playing dragon's injuries, in particular those around his head, narrowing in on exactly what was keeping him unconscious.

Through a mixture of impatience, curiosity and fear, the hockey playing dragon could hold his tongue no more as the magic from the ring flowed through him.

*"Do you know what's wrong?"*

A slight hesitation and an unforgiving awkward silence had the youngster thinking the worst, something his temporary partner could sense. Unable to put it off any longer, For'son, knowing no other way really, just blurted it out.

*"He has a bleed on the brain, and I won't lie... it's quite serious."*

*"Can't you just weave your magic and make it disappear?"*

*"Hmmm... I'm not so sure."*

*"Why's that?"*

*"It's hard to say exactly, but my best guess would be that because all of you spend so much time in your human forms, your dragon DNA, instead of being flexible and extremely agile has over time become 'sticky', would be how I'd describe it. And although his particular brand of the supernatural resides somewhere inside his body, as does the ability to revert back to his prehistoric best, for all intents and purposes, currently he's a human with a bleed on the brain, something I'm led to believe most hospitals and neurological specialists would take very seriously indeed. One wrong move from me could not only potentially make things worse, but could actually end his life."*

*"****!"*

*"Exactly."*

*"So what are you saying... that we need a human doctor down here to take care of him?"*

*"Not exactly... just someone with a little more medical experience in this field than I currently possess."*

*"And where do we find them?"*

*"That, my friend, is a very good question."*

Starting with his upbringing in that unforgiving hellhole of an icy prison in Antarctica, Mas-crate had known pain and suffering in abundance and at a level most beings wouldn't survive, let alone learn to tolerate and use to their own advantage. However, at this moment he was engulfed in more agony and misery than even he'd ever experienced, the removal of his entire wing in one precision strike forcing the rest of him down to his knees, eclipsing the dissection of his tail shortly before, leaving him wailing in anguish, his distress mirroring the torture of his youth.

Some way off, another was suffering, not quite to the same degree, but in distress, nursing some hefty injuries, slipping in and out of unconsciousness, using all his concerted will to rally against what had happened, concerned for his friends, the odd shaped ball of his sport and his newly found love spurring him on, his bravery and courage once again coming to the fore as he tried to defeat the waves of woe that would render him out of the fight.

Landing with all the deftness of a dragonfly, one that had seen the inside of many a chimney, Polkinghorne put down beside Janice, momentarily startling the young human, that is until the comforting sight of her friend, the blade, swam into view.

"Are you okay?" asked the Christmas legend.

"I... I... I'm fine," replied the bar worker, "just landed badly on my shoulder, that's all."

"Here, let me…"

Gently touching the young woman on the shoulder, almost amused at the instinctive flinch, the Santa alter ego dribbled just a tiny bit of magic into the joint, flushing away the damage, soothing the tendons and bone... making everything feel as good as new.

"Thank you."

"You're welcome," she all but bellowed over the howling and growling coming from close by.

"What's happened to Fu-ts'ang?" Janice asked, concerned for her friend. "I can't sense him at all."

"He closed down so that he couldn't be compromised by whatever magic was used on him before."

"Oh."

"It's alright. Just think of it as a deep sleep. He'll be back soon and wanting you to fill him in on all the action."

"How will...?"

Unable to think straight, his ravaged mind bypassed by the agonising hurt, Mas-crate rose up. Fuelled by the darkness of it all he ploughed on, determined not to go out with a whimper, his one true purpose now clear... to leave none of them alive. Certain that he would soon be leaving this mortal coil, he vowed through the wreckage of his psyche, that he would take them all with him to the gates of hell and beyond.

Clumsily, he rose, wobbling about all over the place. A bad idea was the best he could come up with, something his intelligence quickly agreed with. But he was not only stupid, but brave as well and continued, one awkward step at a time, resembling a new born giraffe in an effort to home in on the threat he couldn't see, but could most certainly hear.

Feeling strangely buoyed by the unusual sensation of not being alone, despite the fact that physically he was, Peter, crouched over his stricken friend, not knowing what to say or do. Luckily the accompanying presence caught up in the ring that he now wore, did.

*"I'm going to heal all his other injuries. It shouldn't impact the swelling on his brain."*

*"Okay,"* was all the youngster could say, a dread in the pit of his stomach at seeing his buddy just lying there all but contained for now.

Through the heavy dust laden air, a light yellow shimmering started to encompass Tank's bruised, battered, broken and bloodied body, with the exception of his neck upwards. For'son's powerful magic knitted broken bones back together, pulling bright red blood back inside the false human form, repairing skin, soothing muscles and tendons, washing away all the pain from the knocks and jars the body had sustained whilst being pulled abruptly and roughly up through the torrent of debris and rubble.

Fifteen seconds of miracles saw the supernatural do its work, and then it was complete, with the exception of course of the very serious bleed on the brain, something both beings pondered as they watched over their friend.


"How will…?" was as far as she got before a dark purple, tinged with red, gigantic scaled foot punched suddenly through the smoky air behind both women, the filthy yellow talons scything their way across Polkinghorne's back, the power behind the surprise attack smashing her into the floor, her grip on the inert Fu-ts'ang relinquished in an instant, the chilly futuristic blade clattering to the uneven ground, out of reach and most certainly out of the game.

As her friend's exquisite screams of pain echoed up for all to hear, Janice gasped at the monstrous vision dragging itself towards her through all the spent magic, dust, powder and filth hanging in the air... MAS-CRATE, or at least what was left of him, his purple and red menacing dragon form ravaged by what had happened. Left wing totally missing, along with half his tail, deranged didn't do justice to how he looked, his disfigured face screwed up into a ball of never ending anger, scales hanging off both cheeks from his brief encounter with the improvised missile that had been the rugby player Hook. Stomping forward with one foot, the remains of his tail dragging across the various stones and rocks in his wake, the noise from which sounded like a teacher from a previous time scratching his nails down the length of a blackboard, the vicious villain aware that there was now no coming back from what he'd suffered, locked eyes with the beautiful blonde human, the merest hint of a sinister smile wriggling its way across his wicked jawline, intent on inspiring terror. It worked better than he could have imagined because Janice froze in place with shock. Instinctively, she cried out in her head for her best friend, Fu-ts'ang, hoping that once again he'd rush to her aid. But on Polkinghorne's instructions, thinking that the Santa legend had everything under control, he'd closed himself down, become a hermit in his own mind, something of a mistake, looking back on it now. Of course he couldn't answer, leaving her all alone and at the mercy of the crazed, murderous monster before her, intent on having his revenge.

Aware of the fear he'd inspired in her, almost expecting her to drop dead on the spot, Manson's evil associate lashed out with his other foot at the curled up ball of writhing and moaning on the ground in front of him, catching Polkinghorne fully in the stomach, sending her false human frame into the air, off into the distance, a suitably loud CRASH the reward for his wicked endeavour.

Mouth hanging open, stuck to the spot, the courage and bravery she'd become renowned for during her time in the domain having deserted her, all Peter's soulmate could do was watch in utter horror as the almighty dark dragon closed in on her position, his warped and twisted mind enjoying every moment of the torment he knew she must be suffering, determined to make the most of every last second, aware now more than ever that he was a dead dragon walking.

"YOU," he mouthed through his twisted and contorted jaw, "have caused me no end of trouble. Before you go, I'm going to show you what pain really means. You'll watch with your dying breath as I hold your beating heart in my hand, knowing there was no way in hell that you were ever really going to best me. All your dreams and wishes end this instant!"

With the terror infused throughout her body, Janice wouldn't have believed anything could have surprised her in that moment. But it did, the dark dragon monster's face changing in an instant, his eyes opening as wide as was possible, HIS mouth now hanging open, rotting cracked yellow teeth on display, his huge lolling tongue wriggling uncontrollably, dull, gloopy green blood starting to drip from the sides of his mouth.

Had she been able to, now might well have been the point to turn around and run, but fear still had the young woman firmly in its grip, plus there was more than a little curiosity as to what was going on.

Only then did she notice the twisted rusting piece of long jagged metal, the tip of which had just appeared, jutting out of the centre of the beast's chest, more sickly thick green blood gathering around the exit wound, starting to drip forever downwards.

Before she could even question this, a familiar voice cut through the air, washing away all the terror and torment, restoring her faculties and her ability to once again move.

"Blah, blah, blah, I'm going to kill you, I'm so strong, look at me, I'm a scary dragon and absolutely nothing can take me down. Well...," mused the figure stumbling out of the smoky spent magic from behind the mighty Mas-crate, "suck on this you stuck up, moronic, scum sucking piece of filth," mused the rugby player whose heart well and truly belonged to The White Dragon, barely able to walk, looking like he'd be top of the list at accident and emergency.

"HOOK!" Janice screamed, rushing towards him.

"Whoa! Hold your horses," he cried just before she was about to envelop him in one huge hug. "I'm in no state for that I'm afraid."

Now that she'd got closer, she could see he was right. Unfortunately, and much to his disappointment, she had little choice but to grab him and pull him quickly off to one side, causing him an extreme amount of pain, not really the reward he'd expected for once again saving her life.

# BOOM!

And then he understood, as the ground all around them shook from Mas-crate's mountainous form smashing to the floor exactly where they'd just been standing. Despite being doubled over in agony, he just about managed to thank her, the debt now repaid it would seem.

"Quick... we have to find Polkinghorne and Fu-ts'ang and make sure they're alright."

And so they did, rounding the two of them up, the Christmas legend just about having enough magic available to heal her wounds and get Hook back to full health, before nudging Janice's best friend, the fantastical weapon, back to life, something they were all grateful for. It was only then that Janice's thoughts turned to the love of her life, wondering where he'd got to.

*"He's off in that direction,"* voiced her best friend, the blade, pointing the tip of his cutting edge towards what had once been the ancient bridge.

"We need to find Peter and Tank," she urged Polkinghorne and Hook, a real sense of urgency running through her.

Taking two steps in the direction that Fu-ts'ang had indicated, the others following hot on her heels, out of the still smoky air in front of her strode her love, looking as dishevelled and fearful as she'd ever seen him.

"What is it?" she demanded, sprinting up to him, pulling up just short.

"It's Tank... he's been badly hurt and we don't know how to heal him."

"Oh no!"

"Fu-ts'ang, Polks... can you help? For'son believes he has a bleed on the brain."

"I'm afraid youngster, that's well beyond my understanding," replied the bladed dragon killer.

As one, they all turned to Polkinghorne, hoping her unique Santa magic might prove invaluable.

"I'm sorry," she reflected shaking her head, matted blonde strands waving ever so slightly against the backdrop of the spent magic that still hung in the air, "I've done some healing in my time, but never anything like that."

Downcast at his pal's dire predicament, Peter lowered his head in disappointment, wondering what the hell they were going to do next. Luckily someone had heard them from a distance.

"BRING HIM TO ME IMMEDIATELY!" commanded a voice they all recognised... Zarenkesia!

"Can he be safely moved?" For'son, still on Peter's finger asked for them all to hear.

"I would allow the... now what was it again, oh that's right, rugby player amongst you to carry him with as much care as possible while the rest of you return, start putting out the fires and clear a safe space. That should be enough to allow me to ascertain the exact nature of his injury," the presence of the shop added.

As Peter led Hook back to Tank's motionless body next to the humungous pile of rubble, Janice and Polkinghorne re-entered what remained of the Emporium, appalled at the level of damage, the Christmas legend dejected and disconsolate at the very thought of the history and supernatural lost in the attack, from scrolls to magical artefacts, books and tomes in every shape and size including the newly discovered, oh so important journal that could well have held more clues to the fate of the future.

*"Behind the door of the workshop,"* urged the presence of the shop, *"there are human fire extinguishers. They might be your best bet to put out the fires."*

*"Why?"* wondered Polkinghorne, *"would there be fire extinguishers down here?"*, but before she could really wrap her mind around it, an answer was provided.

*"TANK... he thought it wise after some of the previous owner's antics, to take as many precautions as possible. I almost found it laughable when I watched him install them, but now... not so much."*

'Well that explains that,' thought both young women, each hoisting one of the massive metallic red tubes off the wall, before heading back out onto what should have been the shop floor, letting rip with the contents at the base of the many blazing fires, chief of which was at the bottom of the stairs. Sixty seconds later it was done, everything even remotely burning around where the huge counter had stood, doused to perfection, a space to assess the new owner created.

"Are you sure you can carry him?"

Hook nodded as he knelt down to pick up his friend.

"You need to try and keep him as still as possible," Peter urged, his mouth and throat dry, the concern for his pal shining through.

"I know you mean well youngster," For'son's dulcet tones echoed through the air, "but I don't doubt for one second that Hook realises what's at stake and shares your concern."

"Sorry."

"It's okay Pete," observed the rugby player, effortlessly lifting Tank's body up in front of him with all the care of a mother crocodile taking her hatchlings in her mouth down to the river for the first time. "Let's just get him back to the Emporium."

Slowly, they did so, Peter leading the way, pointing out any obstacles across what was once a walkway the size of a road but had now become a debris field. About four minutes later, they entered the remains of the Emporium, Hook placing the body of the new owner down on a gigantic mattress next to what was left of the shop counter, the two women having dragged it down from upstairs.

That done all those there stepped back, not wanting to

get in the way of what Zarenkesia was about to do. Through the darkness, dust and wispy air, one by one, tiny yellow pinpricks of light started to appear across Tank's forehead, the powerful presence that had vowed to look after him attempting to do just that.

Less than a mile away through the all encompassing darkness of a derelict warehouse building that had once housed a charcoal production line belonging to one of the most popular brands in the domain, out of nowhere one single atom of brightness popped into existence, surprising the glum surroundings, shining the tiniest of lights into the interior. It was totally deserted, with no insects, bacteria, life of any sort, which in some ways was good, because if there had been, no doubt they would have scarpered pretty damn quickly given what happened next. The illumination with seemingly no depth to it at all expanded out exponentially, the miniature circle quickly increasing in size, the core of its existence moving in different directions creating dangerous looking eddies, tendrils of orange, green and blue tickling its outer edges, almost attempting to lick their surroundings. From that single atom had grown a whirling mass of a wormhole over two metres in diameter in only a matter of moments, a vision of nightmares. Speaking of which…

From out of the very heart of the writhing wormhole stepped madness personified, make-up long since gone, the bright, crisscrossing purple lines on her face and hands emboldened at the thought of the mayhem and chaos of what was to come and the fact that one way or the other the world would finally get what it deserved. And before it did, she just might get a chance to put that miserable runt of the litter, her weak and pitiful son, and his friends, out of their misery forever. Striding forward into the darkness finally with a purpose, Earth smiled at the thought of her bastard father being left behind, no doubt kicking himself at not stopping her, having not a clue where she'd gone, and unable to get here in time to stop what she was about to unleash on his precious grandson.

'This, old man,' she thought, 'will cause you more heartache and misery than being locked away in that Antarctic prison. I hope before the world finally ends, that you'll get to see the broken remains of the one that means so much to you.'

With her goal only a short way off, she tiptoed out into the inky black desolation of dragon domain London and skulked off into the shadows, latching on to the infinitesimally small smidgen of magic she'd imbued her son with, shortly before she'd bugged out of the fight at the private residence, determined to avoid any of the roaming patrols of the king's dragons, not wanting to give her position away and alert those that she sought to her presence.

# 4 COMPELLED TO ACT

"Majesty... is this really a good idea?"

"Honestly," Vasuki said, his voice echoing around the confines of the chilling set of caves they'd found and started to call home, beneath the largest glacier in Iceland, known to the locals as Anaconda Ice Cave, renowned for its crystallised water, "I really don't know. But I do know that they, and the world itself, are in grave trouble, and given the debt we owe them, turning our back now is not really an option."

"After all that we've been through sire, surely there must be another way?"

"I understand there isn't and that it really is end-of-the-world time. Fredric wouldn't have got in touch unless it was desperate. Now remove yourself, Dalvathon, so we can open up a wormhole."

"But my lord, I really must..."

"BE GONE!" the naga king fumed, angrier than he should have been, but not really at his aide who was only doing his job by expressing his honest opinion, one Vasuki usually found more valuable than not.

Unfortunately, circumstances were anything but usual, something he reflected on as Dalvathon's tail disappeared into the dark blue icy water at the outer edge of the cave system. The courageous naga leader promised to make amends as soon as he got back. He'd already been through so much, including being held captive in Antarctica for decades, used as a pawn so that Manson could manipulate the rest of his race into doing his bidding, as well as seeing a great deal of them magically enthralled, forced to fight before being culled by dragons on both sides of the argument, even those on the side of good not really understanding the situation at all. He slithered forward towards those he'd selected to come with him, contemplating exactly what it was he'd hoped for on returning there, one of their old haunts, so they could live the next hundred years or so in peace and try to rebuild and repopulate what remained of their civilisation. It looked like Fate had other ideas.

"Are we ready?" he asked the three of them as he approached.

"Yes Majesty," they replied as one.

Four didn't sound very much, but they were all accomplished magic users in their own right, and had sworn to protect their king with their lives. More importantly, they were all he could spare, despite the dire straits the world seemed to be facing.

"Good," he acknowledged with what passed for a smile on the scaled faces of the naga race, still barely able to believe the sounds as they slipped from his mouth, now that his speech impediment had been magically corrected. It felt like someone else's words altogether. "What's the plan?"

"If there are magic users on board the submarine, we don't want to alert them to our presence and risk them panicking and doing something stupid," the leader of the three bodyguards announced, his professionalism a credit to his race. "I suggest we create an exit portal deep beneath the waves, east along the coast somewhere between Cullen and Portsoy, in an effort to try and sneak in undetected."

"Good thinking... I concur," Vasuki declared. "Let's do it!"

With that, the four of them gathered up all their unique supernatural power and, combining it to great effect, in only a matter of moments conjured up a raging swirling portal of energy, right there in the middle of the cave. With frightened serpent-like faces glancing out of the shadows at the madness once again seeming to resume, the naga king and his protective detail dived head first into the eclectic mix of never ending colours, the whole mass of magic totally disappearing shortly after their tails. In but a moment it was gone, along with much of the hope of the startled and terrified onlookers.


As the sickly smell of singed scales filled the confined space at the top of the tunnel, turning even strong prehistoric stomachs as well as making noses run, still using the bright blue lightning that had almost been her constant companion since dropping down and getting trapped, Amelia Battlehard continued to defy the odds, blinding her opponents here, piercing wing membranes there, sending the enemy spiralling off in half a dozen different directions, mainly down, momentarily bringing some kind of balance back to the fight.

Reflected by the sizzling electricity setting the air alight all around them, the primarily brown, occasionally dabbed with green and yellow patches of scale on Oblivion's almighty primordial frame had once again lurched into action, desperate to take down this newcomer and pummel her head back into her body for what she'd done... not only trap them all down here behind the sparking and hissing shield that had been resurrected at the mouth of the tunnel above them, but inflict so much pain and damage to the small force he commanded. For that, he knew, she would pay with her life when he got hold of her, something he hoped was all but imminent.

# 5 FICKLE FINGER OF FATE

For about the hundredth time since they'd arrived, the words *"I FEEL SO OLD,"* echoed across the dystopian landscape that had contrived to replace what should have been a bustling blossoming meadow filled with gorgeous blooming flowers being pollinated by an array of insects. Three of the four beings there (I say beings in the loosest of senses because what they actually were, was hard to translate into something that we as humans would understand. More presences and less god-like.) Fate, Luck and Time still had skin in the game so to speak, because like the humans and dragons of this world, if it should be destroyed, they too would cease to exist. They were panicked beyond belief, not only because they'd already disobeyed a fundamental rule of their existence by being there in the first place, but also because of everything else playing out across the planet at the same time, a series of events that, if not stopped, could well result in the destruction of the planet and their reality.

*"I FEEL SO OLD!"*

"For goodness sake," spat Time, like the other two, all but reaching the end of her tether, having heard this over and over again, downhearted and dejected at the fact that the human Manson, the one that could take dragon form, appeared entirely immune to not only her charms, but those of Luck and Fate as well. In the history of everything, it was all but unheard of.

"We have to do something," urged Luck, but lacking any sort of cohesive plan.

And so as usual, it all came down to the other one... FATE!

Striding forward with her usual purpose, Time stuck out an arm in an effort to stop her going any further.

"WAIT! What are you going to do?"

"What needs to be done," the devilish developer of destiny replied.

"We've tried that with no luck at all... no pun intended," she said, glancing across at her friend.

"No offence taken."

Shrugging off the arm, Fate continued, moving forward until she stood, towering over the emaciated, grey bearded old man, curled up in a foetal position, shivering and shaking for all he was worth.

Briefly she wondered about the consequences of what she had in mind. But they'd already come too far to turn back now, flouted so many rules. If they couldn't snap him out of whatever loop he was stuck in then they could all very well cease to exist. She couldn't let that happen, and so did the very last thing the other two expected. Fate addressed him by his actual name, one known only to a few, and only then disclosed as a secret never to be revealed, one never to be actually used.

"NOVUS!" she commanded, "WAKE UP... NOW!"


It hadn't started off as much, with maybe half a dozen of them there at the beginning, all wondering what had happened and how they'd come into existence. A light discussion had over the course of days turned into heinous arguments which as you might expect, had gotten them nowhere. With those involved in the blazing row almost coming to blows, out of the blue a powerful yet gentle voice spoke up from all around, dispelling the disagreements instantly, instilling a sense of curiosity as to who or what had so abruptly awakened.

After much conversation, the realisation as to exactly what they were addressing dawned on all of them. The planet, the one they'd unexpectedly found themselves attached to, not only had a consciousness, but was self aware. None of them saw that coming. Days turned into weeks which quickly turned into months. Finally a resolution was reached, included in which was an agreement for the planet who they'd named Novus (which means 'self-made', something they'd all agreed seemed more than appropriate given that it and they had all come into being at exactly the same time), to be left to its own devices and allowed to thrive, given free range in allowing all its occupants to dwell in peace. It was a bit of a stretch, in effect allowing each of them to go off in the direction of their choosing. Occasionally one or two would hook up, watch from a distance together as events unfolded, trying to predict the outcomes, sometimes having the odd wager or two, which although not against the rules they'd made so long ago, could probably have been considered frowned upon. Across all that time, each had gotten wiser, or at least more experienced, except it would seem Novus, who'd by the looks of things, had grown weaker, more cynical and less caring for those that inhabited his shell. If only they knew.

"NOVUS!" she positively screamed this time. "WAKE UP!"

Still no effect.

"What are we going…?" ventured Time.

Full of desperation, her conscious will spread thin, able to sense a determined Flash hurtling through the skies of southern England, Polkinghorne panicking at her distinct lack of magic, a scared Captain Battlehard trapped beneath the bright blue flickering force shield, an unresponsive Tank surrounded by inky blackness, the overconfident, smirking Manson in the bowels of the nuclear submarine, Earth on the hunt for her kin, a focused Fredric and Richie doing everything in their power to give chase, the dragons under George's command back at the private residence, all praying for a miracle and amidst it all, Peter standing out like a frightened child, confused and confounded, not knowing what to do or how to act to save the ones he loved. It was almost all too much for her... but not quite. It did however compel her to act, in the only way she knew how, taking the situation by the scruff of the neck, something she'd seen others do time and time again.

Leaning down, Fate used one hand to roll him over onto his front and then pulling the other one back, used the palm of the other hand to slap him with all the might she could inject.

# THWACK!

Luck and Time looked on aghast.

"Uhhhhhhhh…"

"Novus, please, wake up."

"You… you… you… you hit me."

"I know. And I'm sorry. But you have to snap out of it. Everything, including all of us and you yourself, are in grave jeopardy. Please…"

As tiny yellow grains of sand whistled around his feet and legs, Novus now appearing at least slightly more compus mentus, sat up and glanced about, taking in the other two for the first time, wondering what the hell was going on, why they would renege on their ancient agreement and exactly what this had to do with him.

Everything, he would soon learn.


Their frantic attempts to destroy the capacitor had paid off, which had resulted in a moment of sheer joy, the plan working a treat, that is until they realised exactly what had happened and the unintended consequences. With Yoyo and his gorgeous wife Rose sitting at the control panel anxiously trying to find a solution to their current predicament, the remaining youngsters leant over the sparking and arcing force shield, glaring down into the cavernous hole that their enemy had so willingly taken to with most of the stolen laminium. Through the myriad of prehistoric bodies visible, one above all others stood out, their friend and the commander of this mission, Amelia Battlehard, shocking, maiming and incapacitating with fabulous fluorescent forks of brilliant blue tinged lightning, making those who would have her head on a platter pay with their lives, cutting off limbs, demolishing wings, tails and hearts, destroying pretty much anything in her path. On current form, she was an absolute legend, something each of Yoyo's charges knew already. Unfortunately, the more opponents she destroyed, the more kept creeping out of the darkness, constantly threatening to overwhelm her, at least that's how it appeared to the youngsters, peering through the translucent blue energy barrier, willing their friend on, sure she could prevail. It didn't look as though she could last much longer. In a frenzied telepathic cry for help, each of them gave a shout out to the healer and his better half working frenetically at the control panel, all but willing them to take down the shield so they themselves could plunge down and add their support. For now at least, that was some way off happening.

Snapping a neck with two hands whilst hovering in place mid-air, Captain Battlehard adjusted her form enough to allow her to bite through a wing that tried in vain to separate her head from her body, its razor sharp edges circling around at a dizzying rate, the attack made all the more difficult because of the confined space all of the combatants found themselves in. Watching in satisfaction as yet one more of Manson's forces lazily spiralled towards the inky blackness of the dark and unerring hole, Flash's love let go of the beast whose neck she'd just broken and, ducking out of the way of a sizzling line of wicked looking green imbued electricity, tumbled head over heels, tucking her wings in above her head, dropping one hundred metres in the blink of an eye, buying herself a split second with a view to assessing the situation.

'Things,', she thought, 'are not good,' as she noticed more enemies rocketing up out of the darkness with every second that passed. She would never have imagined they'd have been down there in such numbers. And that was before they'd even reached their by now, very, very disappointed leader, Oblivion, the feared and almighty dragon that had been personally tasked by Manson to transport the stolen laminium all the way from Russia to its current resting place. Had the beast in question known the ultimate purpose of having the valuable metal in this particular location, then even he might have disobeyed orders from the being he thought of as his commander in chief.

Letting his subordinates throw themselves at the nuisance newcomer with absolute abandon, clearly able to recognise an experienced and well drilled opponent when presented with one, Oblivion knew he'd have to catch her off guard to stand any chance of taking her down. Knowing that the longer this went on, the more it played into her hands, using his cunning mind to craft any number of possibilities, gradually he began moving himself into position behind some of the broken bodies she'd already taken out of the fight.

"It's no good... I can't lower the shield. What the hell are we going to do?" Yoyo declared to his wife sitting next to him.

"We must keep trying. Don't give up. You know better than that. Amelia's life is quite literally in our hands."

Sensible words presented in a calm and composed way by the dragon he loved more than anything else on the entire planet were enough to get the healer to redouble his efforts and reassess everything he'd already tried with regard to the controls.

'There must be something else we can do... there just must be,' was all he could think, his psyche almost overwhelmed with everything going on, despite his prehistoric dragon mind being able to compartmentalise and multitask on an absolute beast of a level.

Gazing down past the transparent shield into the gaping hole, the youngsters were having the same conversation deep within the telepathic link that served as their conduit into each other's consciousnesses. It wasn't going well however, and they couldn't come up with a single plausible idea as to how to overcome the hissing and spluttering energy barrier in order to render assistance to the female dragon who they'd not only grown to love, but to admire and see as something of a mentor and role model.

'If something doesn't give soon,' they all thought, 'she might well be overrun and overwhelmed.' The only good news to come out of it all was that at least for the time being, they'd completely forgotten about the imminent nuclear missile strike. How long before that returned to the forefront of their thinking?

A measure of calm and deep seated satisfaction washed over the cruel and twisted being that had put the world in so much jeopardy in the first place. Standing dripping wet on the dimly lit bridge of the nuclear submarine just beyond Bow Fiddle Rock, Manson ignored the blaring alarms that echoed around the confined space he shared with the other officers, all of whom were dragons and former comrades, instead concentrating on monitoring the nuclear missile that had been launched only a short while ago, imagining what awaited at its final destination. No doubt a stockpile of the valuable laminium, stolen from the Kremlin in Russia under the noses of the stupid dragons there, taken at first to the Black Forest, before Oblivion had hopefully carried out his orders to the letter. Confident in his brother in arms, with every second that passed it became harder to contain his thrill at exactly what he'd done and just how cataclysmic the outcome would be. Desperate to brag about the imminent catastrophe, there was still enough common sense inside him to know he must keep his mouth shut... at least for now. If the submarine's crew cottoned on, they could still abort the launch in one all-out effort to save their own skins, an outcome he wanted to avoid at all costs.

Abruptly the sub lurched forward, the front portion of the ship taking a severe nose dive. Quick as a flash, Earth's evil other half grabbed onto a brace of silver bars surrounding a number of control systems just above and in front of his head, making sure to put one foot in front of the other on the dark metal floor, spreading his weight evenly in an attempt to stay upright.

"Con... report!" yelled the admiral.

"Rudder non responsive, sir. We appear to be heading deeper. Should I change our course to an offshore one?"

Fleetingly the admiral glanced in Manson's direction.

Not really caring one way or the other, only wanting to stay alive long enough to see the world crack open like a fresh egg dropped on the floor from some considerable height, he returned the look with an almost imperceptible nod.

Not needing to be told twice, the admiral issued the order.

"Take us at best speed into deeper water."

Hands a blur across the entirety of his station, the con did as ordered and as the tin can they were all trapped in continued to dive, he turned the sub away from Bow Fiddle Rock and the shore beyond, steering it towards something deeper and hopefully far less treacherous.

From high up in the air mid-way between the coastline and Bow Fiddle Rock, Vimes swore loudly, not caring if anyone heard. I mean... what difference did it make? Not now he was here out in the open, exposed as a dragon for all the local humans to see, of which many now graced the shoreline. He had much more important matters on his mind... life, his love, the universe, oh and of course the impending doom of the entire planet at the hands of the nuclear missile that had only a short while ago rocketed into the atmosphere from the very craft he hovered above, watching, one that had just decided to dive below the surface of the choppy grey water, immediately disappearing from view. Fully aware of Flash's orders not to let the submarine out of his sight, and scared beyond belief, way more than he ever had been, even when Christmas had been in Crisis and his love's life had been on the line, taking one long, deep breath, he angled his tail sharply upwards, and with all the speed he could muster, plummeted headlong towards the murky ocean, bracing himself for impact and the impending assault from the chilling water.

# SPLASH!

Outstanding was the only way to describe the pain from around his head, the mindbogglingly icy sea terrorising his ears, nose and forehead, dozens and dozens of frighteningly cold needles pricking his skin and scales, at least that's how it felt, bringing the urge to open his mighty jaws to the forefront of his mind. He didn't, but not for the want of trying, his fight or flight reflex kicking in with a vengeance, no doubt his time spent hanging around with his friend the former Crimson Guard having something to do with his reaction. Continuing to tell himself he could last for a very long time beneath the waves (at least an hour), Vimes kept reassuring himself that it was just the cold he had to worry about and that his inherent dragon magic would keep him safe for a while at least. All he had to do now was stay close to the sub and keep an eye on its current whereabouts and trajectory and hope he'd done enough to make sure that no more missiles could be launched.

Less than five miles away to the east the tiniest pinprick of luminescence sprang into being from out of nowhere, lighting up the darkness just above the sea bed about three hundred metres offshore, causing small fish to scatter for their lives, frightened lobsters and crabs to scuttle off in search of cover and a mother seal and her cub to dart much further out to sea. In only a matter of moments the radiance expanded out into a swirling, constantly rotating five metre wide flat disc of unusual magical energy. Maintaining its mass for a few seconds, suddenly three dark monstrous shapes shot out of its heart, their silky ancient lines perfectly adapted for this environment, their black as night bodies instantly blending in with their surroundings.

Simultaneously after having spread out, they drew to a halt, swimming in tight little circles, taking everything in, extending the range of their senses through the use of the supernatural abilities granted to them. Sure now that it was safe, an instruction was sent telepathically. A split second later a fourth rocketed out of the ever moving, multicoloured magical circle, their leader the famed king of the nagas, Vasuki, one who'd personally been through so much, and one whose race had given everything in an effort to release him from the grip of primordial evil in the form of the being that now lay at the heart of the submarine only a short way off to the west.

Foregoing the need for words, Vasuki's warrior bodyguards slipped into formation, one in front, two either side of the naga monarch, before the group turned tail as one and headed in the direction that Fredric had suggested the underwater tin can would be, all the time on the lookout for not only danger, but also one lone dragon that was supposedly keeping a solitary watch on the humans' death dealing submerged monstrosity.

As he glided effortlessly through the freezing, dark water, countless images assaulted the naga king's mind, some from the frozen hellhole of a prison that he and Fredric had been held captive in for all that time, others from the battle that they'd dropped right in the middle of at the private residence in the dragon capital, London. Acidic bile flooded his throat at the memory of the filthy, sadistic jailer beating a dragon scientist to death right in front of their eyes, all on Manson's orders, the victim confused and unable to fight back, clearly anything but violent, even in his last throes of death, not able to comprehend what had happened. Keeping his jaws firmly clamped shut as they fizzed across the dark, desolate seabed, the last moments of Bag o' Bones' life span into view, the hacking cough, the epic wheezing and then... GONE with one almighty CRASH! Finally put out of his misery after all that time contained. The pain and heartache these images caused was immense, but that was nothing compared with the extraordinary treachery the wicked leader of the dark dragon force had committed against those of his kind. From the very first day when one of his race had stumbled quite accidentally across their Antarctic prison, to all the pretence about working in exchange for his return... it had all been a lie, one to placate his race, to dupe them into doing the dark leader's bidding, effectively transforming them into puppets, all because he'd been played like a fool, allowing himself to be captured and then used as bait in a magical war that they had absolutely nothing to do with. Anger and desperation threatened to well up inside him at how badly the nagas had been used and exactly how many of his kind had been killed. So many in fact, that as a species they might never recover, going extinct at some point in the very distant future, only then because of their extended lifespans.

Continuing to swim in perfect synchronisation with his three defenders, thoughts of escaping THAT prison continued to haunt Vasuki, jumping in an instant across the world, ending up in the middle of a pitched battle that they simply had no right to slither away from, inundated his consciousness. The cowardice of the man, dragon, whatever-he-was, stood out like a teetotaller on a pub crawl. Not only how he constantly had to surround himself with his troops, or in this case, nagas under the sway of some binding magical agreement, but how he scarpered at the first sign of trouble, leaving his psychopath of a queen all on her own. His spinelessness could only be described as astounding. Fancy discovering an entirely new kind of species... an invertebrate dragon!

With that thought and the fact that he could sense some trepidation from those surrounding him, Vasuki returned his focus to the here and now, wondering if he'd once again have the chance to go head to head with the wicked and vicious Manson.

Shaking off the cold, using his inherent supernatural ability to swirl the flame inside his massive belly around and around, warming him up just a touch, a little flicker of awareness of something unusual off to the east caused him to turn in that direction.

'Oh God... what now?' was all that Vimes could think as four dark shapes materialised out of the deep sea dimness, heading directly for him. Stretching out his wings as far as they'd go, the freezing temperatures of the water bombarding every last inch of them with an ice-like barrage, the kind, caring and selfless former *tor* and Santa's other half, brought forth a sparkling, arcing series of bright red lightning bolts, allowing them to settle atop the fingers of both hands, hoping to hell that he wouldn't need to use them.

*"Whoa... steady on friend. You must be Vimes,"* echoed a voice deep within the confines of his mind, *"Fredric sent us to help out."*

*"And you would be?"* Vimes asked, suckered into maintaining telepathic contact despite the fact that it could have been a trap, something a more experienced warrior dragon would never have fallen for.

*"Vasuki... naga monarch, former Antarctic prisoner and comrade in arms with the aforementioned Fredric."*

Dispelling all his magic, about as certain as he could be that there was no deception here, Polkinghorne's other half did the only thing he could.

*"It's a pleasure to meet you, Majesty. How can I be of service?"*

*"Is he on board that huge metallic leviathan?"*

*"You mean Manson?"*

*"YES!"*

*"He is."*

*"Are you absolutely sure?"*

*"I am. We watched him disappear below decks just before it submerged. After the missile was fired, I sealed all the hatches stopping them from launching anything else. No one has come or gone from that thing. I haven't taken my eyes off it."*

*"Understood! Good job by the way."*

*"Thanks. So what now?"*

That was the sixty four million dollar question.

# 6 BETWEEN A ROCK AND A HARD PLACE

Through their shared unbreakable telepathic link, the three friends, one laminium superstar and the two dragons who each thought of the other as a brother, combined seamlessly in the kind of effort only dragonkind knows. Whilst Steel removed debris both large and small from off the bright red thermal targets that he knew were school kids buried alive, Jar Man held anything with even the remotest of potential to collapse firmly in place, each going about their tasks with all the professionalism they could muster. Speed was critical of course, but so was teamwork. It wouldn't do anyone any good if they tried to recover all the missing children quickly, only to collapse more rubble and debris down on top of them. It was a balancing act, quite literally in places, like no other.

As choking clouds of thick white dust carried through the breezy warm air, DomCon used his intrinsic dragon magic to lift a tiny young child, bent out of shape and covered in blood, high up over the rubble, gliding him steadily through the air, gently setting him down on an open patch of lush, untouched green grass some way from the impending danger of what remained of the ruined buildings. One down, many more to go.

Witnessing that very first child touch down as softly as a ballet dancer's pointe shoe, looking on as he let out a pain filled sigh of relief, was a boon to each and every one of them, not just those of a prehistoric persuasion, but also all four humans who'd helped instigate the ruse that was currently playing out. All they had to do now was hope that officialdom could be kept at bay for a little while longer. If that happened, then just maybe the unconventional rescue would be a success.

Quite quickly they had it off pat, their magical methods

almost flawless. It certainly wasn't text book, that was for sure, but it was efficient and undoubtedly the fastest way to remove those trapped under the demolished buildings. While for the most part things progressed swimmingly, just occasionally the three of them would stumble upon a broken body where the opportunity to be saved had long since passed. Corpses of teachers and children alike littered some areas, causing more than a little dismay through the shared link. Of course it was the ginger giant Jar Man who held the other two in check, steering them back on course, reassuring Steel and DomCon about the greater good, reinforcing the fact that in these circumstances, it was impossible to save everyone. Passions were running high, but his common sense and no nonsense approach was just what was needed to continue to use their magic in conjunction with the subterfuge they were all still buried up to their necks in. All the time the four human friends who'd already been through so much underground in the dragon domain continued to do their part, occasionally glancing round from their lookout positions, pleased to see the still moving bodies of the children gathered together on the grass in the midst of all the chaos. It was a bright spark on a very dark day, one which made the humans proud to belong to this fabulous, ancient city.

*"How many more?"* asked the former laminium ball captain, sweat pouring down his falsehood of a face, the toll taken to maintain his new found human persona almost as great as it was to remove the rubble.

*"Half a dozen,"* DomCon replied robot-like, his mind focused on the task at hand, floating yet one more lazily through the air, this time a young girl dressed in a very smart uniform, bright red blood stains caking her knees and elbows, sickly grey and white grime covering the features of her face making her look more like a ghoul than anything else.

About to speak out into their shared link and congratulate his friends on the epic job they were doing, out of nowhere Jar Man's train of thought was rudely interrupted.

"Uhhhh... guys," shouted Taibul, "You're going to need to hurry. Some of the volunteers are heading this way."

"*******S!" swore the friendliest of the lot, only too aware that they still needed a little more time to finish the task they'd started.

The second fastest moving object on the planet was currently wrestling with the weight of the world on his shoulders as he streaked gracefully above the English Channel, wings burning, his tail quite literally on fire, resembling the fiery exhaust plumes from a drag racing car. Under normal circumstances Flash's Crimson Guard training would have kicked in, enabling him to ooze professionalism, but here and now that couldn't be further from the truth, his thoughts turning to not only his friends and one in particular in the direction that he was headed, but also the greater good and of the potential choices to be made. That was all on top of the damage he'd caused in his wake, the sonic boom trailing behind him destroying windows, wrecking roads, scaring animals and humans alike far and wide.

'How many,' he thought, 'is too many? One life lost? Ten? Fifty? One hundred? A thousand? A hundred thousand? What if it numbered into the millions? Could he sacrifice all of those and most of France in return for saving the planet? When you looked at it logically, there's simply no choice to be made. But what kind of decision is that and just how much of a monster would he have to be to sanction such a thing.' These were just some of the many questions flitting around Flash's brain as he closed in on northern France and the monorail test borehole site, the one in which as far as he knew, Amelia was still trapped.

The good captain... wow, wasn't she something. Not one to believe in love at first sight, there had definitely been some kind of spark between them. It could have just stemmed from the fact that she was a high ranking member of the King's Guards and he was a former member of the much more elite Crimson Guards, their rivalry legendary, many a late night scrap involving the two factions renowned throughout dragon law enforcement. Looking back though, it seemed much more than that, a shared admiration of not only her combat skills, but more so of how she'd fared protecting the king, something that he thought of as solely his responsibility. It wasn't of course, but ever since sharing accommodation with the monarch after his little change in bodily circumstances, Flash had come to take George's welfare and safety as something of a personal mission. To see the way Amelia dealt with her responsibilities in that regard was almost like looking in a mirror, the same passion and sense of duty glancing back. Two kindred souls dedicated to saving a being they'd pledged their allegiance and lives to. And what a fighter she was, more than a match for him if everything he'd witnessed during the Changing of the Guard was anything to go by. In the air, on the ground, one on one, bravely battling multiple enemies at any one time... her speed of thought, extraordinary reactions and compunction to do what needed to be done were qualities he admired more than ever. She was... perfect! And that was before he'd had a tantalising glimpse into her personality, one that despite all the mayhem and chaos going on around them, he'd well and truly fallen for.

'Amelia,' he thought, 'please... hang on, I'm nearly there.'

But here's the thing. Despite all his brains, brawn and magic, he had absolutely no idea what he was going to do once he got there, not with regards to the good captain anyhow. The rocketing nuclear missile heading their way though, that was a different matter entirely, because you see, Fredric had given him an option in that regard. All he had to do was beat the blessed goliath of destruction to the site and then in theory, all would be well. It was going to be a close run thing, especially if he was going to save the dragon he'd fallen in love with.

With all that in mind, the almighty gun metal grey, silver and Nordic blue prehistoric monster that was the former Crimson Guard moving like a blur across the sky, opened himself up to all his primordial magic and reached out in search of a particular someone, a being he'd recognise anywhere on the planet.

Furiously studying dials, power conversion charts and rows and rows of buttons that numbered into the many hundreds, Yoyo felt under more pressure than he ever had in his entire life, and that was saying quite something especially given everything he'd been through in the last few months. That burden was made all the worse knowing that Captain Battlehard was trapped beneath the flickering transparent blue energy barrier and there wasn't a damn thing he could do about it, despite the expectation radiating off not only his young charges, but his wife as well. Just as he was about to swear profusely, a familiar nagging at the back of his mind caught his attention. Using just a fraction of his intellect to explore exactly what was going in, it took him but a split second to realise that his friend, the former Crimson Guard, was vying for his attention.

*"FLASH?"*

*"YOYO!"*

*"My friend. It's so good to…"*

*"How's Amelia?"*

*"Sh… sh… she's trapped beneath the energy shield that protects the top of the test borehole. We're trying everything to switch it off in an effort to get to her, but so far nothing has worked. Flash… you have to believe me we're doing all that…"*

*"Get clear… all of you. That's an order. INCOMING!"*

High up in the atmosphere, the air was being set alight not as usual by something falling back to earth but by an object doing its very best to escape the considerable forces trying to hold it in place, quite successfully as it turns out. The SLBM (Submarine Launched Ballistic Missile) had almost reached the apex of its journey and would soon be about to let gravity provide it with a very welcome boost... but welcome for whom? That was the question.

# 7 CONVERGENCE

The emotional turmoil currently ravaging her body was on a par with anything she'd ever known and that included losing her husband over the side of a Welsh cliff on a dark and dismal night all that time ago, an event which had taken a huge toll, what remained of her soul toppling into the deepest, shadow filled abyss never to be seen again, the madness that occasionally showed its face instantly becoming all consuming. Lost never to return, the being Earth had become was unrecognisable from the kind, caring and considerate daughter Fredric still fondly remembered.

Having taken off at a sprint after fleeing the derelict warehouse, it soon became clear that speed needed to be swapped for stealth. Visible through the continued fires and thick acrid smoke that could be tasted on the air, teams of light sided dragons scoured the skies for as far as the eye could see, some searching the rubble in the immediate vicinity, others heading towards the outskirts of the capital, no doubt intent on securing every last suburb before extending out across the country and then no doubt, the continent.

That it should have been theirs, was just one of the many gripes which continued to eat away at her. How they'd lost out, she just didn't know. Right up until the point he'd disappeared like a big old coward, they seemingly had everything under control... outnumbering the opposition many times over, as well as having a superior supernatural advantage. How all that had changed and so quickly was still a mystery to her. Her bastard father turning up had of course had an effect, along with the allies he'd brought with him, but their fighting force was so insignificant, it just wasn't true. They should have trampled them like the inconsequential insects that they were in the scheme of things. But... NO! It had all gone wrong and now here they were, just the two of them, using all their considerable knowledge to destroy everything those bastards had left, including of all things... THE WORLD! Other grievances included not having yet killed her father, despite her having given it her all on a number of occasions and the fact that her weak and feeble son still roamed the planet, a situation that she was on her way to correct. Looking back, she couldn't believe she'd tried to persuade him around to her point of view, to run away with her... just the two of them. PATHETIC! What she should have done was kill him there and then, but before that had become obvious, reinforcements had arrived in the form of the runt of the litter's friends, making it all but impossible. The only choice she was able to make was escape. But not before she'd marked the little twit with just a smidgen of her supernatural, enabling her to find him wherever he was on the planet at any given time. And guess what... surprise, surprise, right at this very moment, he was at that bloody Emporium, no doubt with some of his pals and that human girl. Huh... she was just another objection. Her son, cavorting with a fully fledged human... DISGRACEFUL! What would his father have said? The exact same thing, no doubt, disgusted for sure, contaminating their pure lineage with the blood of what were extensively only PETS! There... she'd said it in her own mind, that's what she and a great number of others thought. Guiding and protecting them... for goodness' sake! What an absolute waste of time that was. They should be hunted for sport, chased down and killed, before being eaten and washed down with a nice glass of Chardonnay.

Momentarily she stopped, pressing herself firmly up against the only remaining wall of what had once been quite a large house, shrouded in dark shadows, all the time reining in all her supernatural, a squad of eight gigantic dragons soaring overhead some way off to her right.

Watching as nigh on a swarm of her enemies banked hard left, remaining in a tight formation, instinctively Earth let out a long, slow deep breath, the relief at not being spotted palpable. Being careful where to tread through the debris strewn dystopian landscape, using everything available as cover, with the grace of a well trained ninja, Fredric's wicked daughter moved ever forward with all the haste she could muster, knowing the Emporium and her prey were only a stone's throw away.

Staring off into the distance, lost in thoughts from the nursery ring and of their time together, Peter watched as tiny pinpricks of yellow light zipped and zapped across the top of Tank's forehead, some sparkling briefly before disappearing altogether, others bouncing off their counterparts before splitting apart and multiplying. It was a different magic from anything they'd witnessed before.

Abruptly the youngster was startled out of his thoughts of his friend, a slender hand gently caressing the small of his back.

"It'll be alright. He's as strong as an ox," Polkinghorne suggested, a nervy smile etched across her beautiful pale face in an attempt to put her pal at ease.

Unfortunately it was never going to be that simple.

"Is that what your magic tells you?"

"I'd like to say yes, but for whatever reason it's not recharging at nearly the rate it should. My observation is based purely on experience rather than anything else. Tank's tough, as tough as they come in fact. And he'll fight with everything he has, right down to the very last second."

"Of that I have little doubt."

"Then what is it?"

"The entry in Artorius' journal."

'Ahh... yes,' thought Santa, 'the elephant in the room, or more appropriately, the dragon in the flagging flames of what remains of the Emporium.'

"The seer," Polkinghorne reflected, "was renowned for his accuracy with prophecies."

Bentwhistle turned to face her, opening his mouth as he did so.

Immediately she stopped him dead in his tracks by holding up one finger to his mouth.

"However, these things are never quite that simple. Take it from one who has an extraordinary amount of experience with THE most powerful magic."

Mouth as wide as a wizard's sleeve, the hockey playing dragon continued to listen.

"No matter how consistently right Artorius was, there's simply no way he could have predicted what's unfolding here and now. Not with the amount of variables and supernatural involved. Could he have somehow glimpsed the future? I don't know... maybe! But for everything to have come to pass across this amount of time would be outrageously unlikely at best, all but impossible at worst. I would suggest that what's written in the journal are just words and you should pay them no heed. Take it from someone who knows more than most, we each forge our own destiny, make our own decisions for better or worse and can't be boxed in by preordained nonsense. It just isn't possible."

"But..."

She hadn't finished there, however.

"And don't forget, prophecies themselves are THE most complicated of things and can be translated in any number of different ways depending on all sorts of variables. There's no telling if there's even an ounce of truth in any of it. I certainly wouldn't count on there being any magic involved. My advice to you is to ignore what you've read, trust your instincts which I know are usually spot on, and your friends. Right at this moment, you're surrounded by some of the most courageous and wise beings ever to have lived. Trust in that and you won't go far wrong."

As they were designed to do, Polkinghorne's words had the desired effect, metaphorically slapping Peter out of his daydreams, forcing him back into the present and the reality of the situation. It may not have been perfect, but it was just what he needed. With just a look and a nod, he thanked his friend the Christmas legend.

Replying with more of a smile and a dip of her head, she watched as the young dragon sauntered on over to his human other half and wrapped his arm gently around Janice's shoulder, pulling her in tight, both of them watching over Tank who remained prone in the middle of the hastily set up mattress. Maintaining her smile for appearance, something very rare started to niggle away at Santa's insides. Can you guess what? You probably can... GUILT, and not just a little. Whilst what she'd told Peter was true from a certain point of view, most of what she'd said should have come with a warning, one about what applies to especially powerful magical beings, something that Artorius was absolutely considered to be. Although she had definitely meant everything she'd said, she knew there were always exceptions to the rules and this, she feared, might well be one of those. But she had to do something to distract her young dragon friend, otherwise he might be on the end of a self fulfilling prophecy, and she just couldn't have that, not after everything they'd all been through. All she needed now was for Zarenkesia to weave her magic and bring Tank back to the realm of the living so that the prophecy could be nullified... simple really, or at least that's what she hoped.

The experience of returning to the dragon domain had been unnerving for Hook, to say the least. Back to his physical best for now, only a short while earlier he'd been convinced that all that beckoned was death. Relieved to still be alive, reuniting with Richie at the top of his 'to do' list, he felt torn up inside standing watching over his rugby playing teammate, hoping that whatever unusual magic was currently being cast would be enough to see him recover. They'd all been through too much for tragedy to strike at this late hour.

That sentiment was echoed by the heroic sentience

trapped in the enigmatic band, For'son. For the very first time in what seemed like forever he felt as helpless as he could remember, looking on as yet one more supernatural entity attempted to give their all in an effort to save one of their own. And not just any one, but the being he'd found the most pleasure in uniting with, full stop. What they'd achieved... the cohesion, the unity, the teamwork had been nothing short of astounding, surpassing even his wildest dreams, and believe you me, he'd had some of those. For but a moment he considered their shared union and exactly what it had meant to him. Okay... so there'd been some disagreements right at the very start, like any relationship, but they were overcome pretty much straight away, moving forward at pace, their skill and ability, knowledge and experience combining in extraordinary fashion to not only perform the most outrageous of acrobatic antics, offensive fighting and outlandish magical mischief making but also keeping alive themselves and the exceptional group of friends in which they were embedded. Taking a moment to consider everything that had happened, the presence trapped in the inscrutable loop came to the only conclusion that he could. Thrust together out of necessity, they'd become the best of friends. If he'd been able to shed a tear at that realisation, he would have.

*"What do you think his chances are?"* a perfectly innocent voice whispered across the private link she shared with her best friend.

The fantastic futuristic weapon known as Fu-ts'ang hovering in a darkened corner of the empty shell of what remained of the devastated Emporium, took a moment to consider the young human girl's question weighing up what sort of answer to provide... the truth, the whole truth or just a partly digestible variation of the truth? Not wanting to visit any more heartache on the youngster than she'd already suffered, the former weapon smith from times gone by had his work cut out as his decision making attempted to come to a conclusion. Before he could answer though, she tried to keep him honest.

*"Your hesitation is a dead giveaway."*

*"I'm not sure what you mean,"* he blustered.

*"You know only too well. The reason I asked is because I want an honest reply. Your experience with magic is second only to For'son in these matters. Would you prefer that I ask him?"*

*"No..."*

*"Then please... give me your honest opinion."*

A brief silence ensued, one in which the dragon weapon smith trapped in the fabulous blade he'd created had a decision to make.

*"I can sense you want me to reassure you that he'll be okay. Simply put though, I don't know if I can. Zarenkesia's supernatural strength is on par with that of For'son and I. And I get the sense she's a competent healer. But there's more to it than that. Dragons nowadays can replicate their bodies to appear human in so much more detail than even a hundred years ago, almost down to the cellular level, which means the problem might well be more of a human issue than a dragon one. If that's the case, Zarenkesia's hands might be tied with regard to exactly how much she can do. Tank might well be better off in a human hospital surrounded by the best specialists."*

*"But..."*

*"You wanted the truth, and there you have it. On that matter there's not much more that..."*

*"Fu-ts'ang!"*

Sensing his short-lived distraction, the brave and courageous bar worker gave him a moment. But when his focus on her didn't return, she began to wonder if his consciousness had once again become lost or even appropriated just as it had with Mas-crate.

*"FU-TS'ANG!"*

A heavy dark blanket encapsulated by a shadow strewn cloud all wrapped up in a parcel made from the blackest of nights was how it felt, less than two hundred metres away and closing. How whatever it was had got past his senses was anyone's guess, but now it was approaching he could feel not only the gaping hole that it created in the surrounding scenery, but the malevolence and evil, hell bent on revenge, that lay at the heart of it.

About to answer his best friend Janice and simultaneously raise the alarm, he was just beaten to it by a flea's belly button.

"EVERYONE!" announced For'son out loud, "ready yourselves! It would appear that EVIL is inbound."

Instantly they all backed up against the far and only remaining wall of the fantastical Mantra Emporium.

"W... w... what is it?" Peter stuttered, his arm still wrapped around Janice's shoulder, his fear of another attack obvious.

Knowing that now was not the time for beating around the bush or being cryptic in any way, shape or form, Fu-ts'ang spat out the answer for everyone to hear.

"Your mother... she's nearby and heading this way."

"****!" interjected the hockey player, his fear doubling, causing his hands and fingers to shake.

"How the hell did she find us?" Janice wondered out loud, deeply disappointed that this wasn't over yet.

"A good question youngster," a silky smooth voice whispered from out of the infrastructure of what remained of the building. "Peter, take your hands off Janice and step forward."

Shocked at the tone the Emporium's mysterious presence had used to speak to him, more of a command than a request, instinctively he obeyed, taking four steps towards a bright light that had flared into existence amongst all the debris.

Clueless about what was happening, Janice made to go with him, that is until her best friend the blade zipped in front of her, blocking her path.

*"Leave him be. He'll be okay. I think she only wants to examine him."*

*"Think?"*

*"Trust me."*

She did.

About to open his mouth to speak, abruptly Peter was startled into silence as a beam of much brighter light started to scan him from head to toe. Swallowing nervously, he didn't know what to do. A few moments later though, it was all over.

"Just as I thought," announced the embodiment of the Emporium.

"What is it?" asked For'son.

"There's some kind of magical marker on tail bearer here."

This, thought practically everyone there, was no time for jokes.

"WHAT?!" exclaimed Peter, angry and mortified in equal amounts that he may well have led his mother straight to them.

"STAND STILL!" Zarenkesia ordered.

He did as commanded as the others looked on.

The same beam of light as before ran itself up and down him before blinking out of existence.

"There... it's done," voiced the Emporium, sounding more than a little pleased with herself.

"You've removed the magical tracer?" For'son enquired.

"I have, for good. She'll no longer be able to get a beat on him."

"That's all well and good," put in Polkinghorne, "but she's close by and on her way here. What on earth are we going to do?"

Yet one more multimillion dollar question.


In an almost identical approach to what had happened only a few minutes earlier, the tiniest pinprick of light burst into being out of nowhere, illuminating the inside of the abandoned warehouse, before expanding exponentially into a huge, wafer thin, constantly moving multicoloured disc whose roaring eddies circled slowly clockwise, the mysterious supernatural energies as frightening as they were mesmerising.

If anyone or anything had been brave enough to stick around, they would have witnessed two sets of legs simultaneously stroll out of the middle of the aperture, of course attached to the rest of their bodies. One... a giant human, or at least appearing that way, well muscled, a no-nonsense look on his face as he scoured the depths of the building, ready to ignite his magic at a moment's notice. The other, smaller in comparison, curly dark brown hair sitting atop a pale freckly complexion, looking no less down-to-earth and ready to fight. It was an unusual and epic pairing, one on the hunt for the wicked witch both had tangled with before, one more than the other.

"Can you sense where we are yet?" Richie asked.

"Give me a moment," Fredric replied, his exquisite mind working overtime in an effort to work out their location, having jumped here all the way from Scotland in the blink of an eye.

Whether or not they had a moment was debateable. However, it didn't take too long to find out, Richie's inherent dragon senses in the human body she'd become trapped within all but screaming out to her. She could sense them... all of them, well nearly. Peter, Janice, Fu-ts'ang, For'son, Polkinghorne and the one that stood out above all the others... HOOK! And they were close by, really close by.

Simultaneously both the dragon warriors who had so much in common and yet had found themselves on the opposite side of things in the midst of the Changing of the Guard turned to face each other.

"THE EMPORIUM!" they both yelled.

Powered by their intrinsic primordial supernatural abilities, both took off out of the abandoned warehouse at mindboggling speed, Fredric in the lead desperate to find and stop his daughter, the need for revenge pumping through his false human form, vowing to himself on the run that he'd finish what he'd started and once and for all put her body in a hole in the ground. Richie, superstar lacrosse player and The White Dragon hot on his heels, was as desperate as her partner to get to the wicked witch known as Earth but for very different reasons... to save and protect those that she loved, the ones who were now in the line of fire, no doubt Manson's other half on her way to finish off Peter in much the same way Fredric wanted to finish her off. And so as fast as their legs and innate magic would carry them, they sped off towards the renowned Mantra Emporium for what would prove to be the scariest and most troubling game of 'Happy Families' ever.

"THE VAULT!" commanded Zarenkesia, the voice of the essence of what remained of Gee Tee's beloved Emporium.

"What about...?" put in Peter.

"CLEAR OFF THE DEBRIS AND GET TO THE VAULT. I'LL HOLD HER OFF FOR AS LONG AS I CAN!"

"What about Tank?" Peter persisted. "We'll never get him down there in his state."

"Leave him with me... I'll protect him," reassured the invisible voice of everything surrounding them.

"I'm not..."

"PETER!" Zarenkesia all but screamed, "she's coming for YOU! Not Tank, not anyone else here, but YOU! By heading down to the vault you keep yourself and your friends safe as well as putting all the defensive measures in that place at odds with her. If you want to do something to help everyone here, including Tank... you must head to the crypt full of treasure at great haste. Deep down, you know it's the right thing to do."

"I can't leave him!"

"YOU MUST! If we're to prevail, then you must go and

let me do my job which is to keep him safe. I cannot protect all of you here on the surface against the oncoming threat of your mother. As well... if we confront her here and now, she'll leave no one alive. Escaping to the vault and buying more time is the only option. YOU MUST TAKE IT!"

"My love," observed Janice.

"Peter," urged Polkinghorne, "I think you should do as Zarenkesia suggests."

"W... w... what if this is what the entry in the journal referred to? What if…?"

"I assure you, youngster, I will do everything in my power to keep him safe. I promise!" assured the shop's presence.

"And don't forget," added Fu-ts'ang, "I'll be here as well. I have a score to settle with that she-witch, one that will involve removing her head from her body. Sorry... no offence intended."

"None taken," Bentwhistle replied, wanting nothing more than to see his mother dead and his friends to a being... SAFE!

"I..." piped up For'son out loud.

But before he could continue with what he had to say, another much more powerful and passionate voice interjected.

"I'M STAYING!" Hook declared defiantly, much to everyone's surprise.

"Hook... you have to…" Janice started.

"NO! He's my friend and I'll make my stand alongside him. Given where we are and who we're up against, I don't think facing off either here or down below will make much difference to me. It's not up for debate. I'm sticking with Tank and I'll do everything I can to stop her from harming him."

To a being, they believed him one hundred percent.

"In that case," interrupted the voice from before, "you should hand me over to Hook," For'son directed. He'll be better able to defend Tank and buy more time under my guidance."

"*But…*" Peter whispered into the shared telepathic link with the enigmatic loop, not knowing what was for the best.

"*Take Janice and Polkinghorne into the vault. I'll use everything at my disposal to keep the others safe, including Tank and Hook. If nothing else, our efforts might buy more time. I think that's all we can hope to do.*"

"*I'm scared,*" Peter confessed.

"*I know, but make the choice that you know is right and get a move on. Time is running out for all of us.*"

Slowly, Bentwhistle started to gently pull the unfathomable band off his finger. Before he'd finished, he whispered two words.

"*Good luck!*"

"*To us all,*" was all that came back before their connection went dead.

Nodding his head in Santa's direction, knowing that there was nothing more he could do up here and that HE was the target of ire for his incoming mother, the hockey playing dragon tossed the ring to Hook and with absolutely no alternative springing to mind, grabbed Janice's hand and headed off towards where he knew the entrance to the vault would be.

Already ahead of him, once again Zarenkesia illuminated a brilliant shaft of light, this time cascading down on a huge pile of rubble that included bricks, wooden support beams, what remained of the bookcase that could spin on its axis and split casually into two, and of course the tomes themselves.

"You'll need to totally clear this area to allow me to open up the entrance for you."

Still low on ethereal energy, but not caring one iota, Polkinghorne flicked one finger in the direction of the pile of debris that blocked their path. Instantly the entire mound flew off towards the back wall of what remained of the Emporium, a loud CRASH echoing around their position. If Earth hadn't known where they were before, she most certainly did now.

Standing over Tank's prone body lying peacefully on the worn, stained mattress, Hook slipped For'son on the smallest of his fingers and waited to see what would happen.

As the area beneath the rubble became exposed, soft words rang throughout Janice's head.

*"I'll take care of them, youngster. This'll all be over before you know it. Stay safe and we'll reunite on the other side."*

*"Thank you, Fu-ts'ang. You're the best friend anyone could ever have. You know I love you dearly."*

*"I do and I hope you realise that sentiment is returned with interest."*

*"Of course."*

*"Go... be safe. I promise to destroy that witch so you and your love can have the future you so desire."*

*"Only if you promise to come and live in the annex in the house specially reserved for you."*

*"I do."*

*"That would make me very happy."*

*"NOW... GO!"*

Hanging onto Peter's coat-tails, Janice waited to see exactly what they were getting themselves into.

As one, Peter, Polkinghorne and Janice stared down into a dark, evil feeling hole, the very top of a shiny metal pole just visible through the blackness.

"Is this it?" asked the blonde bombshell bar worker, expecting something much more magical.

"It is," assured Peter, swallowing nervously at just the thought of going back down into the vault, a place which had given him nightmares after his first visit with the master mantra maker.

"I assume you know how to navigate the safeguards and traps?" Polkinghorne asked.

Mouth agog, resembling a surprised inflatable doll, the hockey playing dragon was momentarily lost for words. It was Zarenkesia who interrupted.

"There's no need to worry about any of the vault's

defences. I'll nullify all of them until you reach the treasure trove. Just make sure you enter the left hand tunnel to start with. Now go... hurry!"

Somewhere inside his mind, Peter was totally blown away.

'If Zarenkesia could nullify all the tricks, traps and death dealing potential that existed en route to the vault, why the hell didn't the old shopkeeper demand she do just that on my first journey? It would have made things much easier and would have...' Briefly his thoughts tailed off as he recalled the adventure they'd had, at first working out how to position the dragon statues by moving the noses in correspondence with the days of the week so they could choose the right tunnel and not end up in one of the two wrong ones that were unending, self replicating labyrinths and completely impossible to escape from. That had followed on from a narrow escape with Olgoi the Mongolian death worms, transplanted from the Gobi desert. Recalling that part of the journey brought back the smell of the poison they'd sprayed him with, causing bile to start racing up his throat. It had taken all his willpower to swallow it back down. Just as he'd done so, one of the most amazing sights he'd ever seen crashed back down into his consciousness. Trailing off into the distance for as far as he could see had been a vista to behold. Four or five metres in front of him was a stream, two or three metres across with shallow, crystal clear water that disappeared over a tiny waterfall, before it rippled, tickled, tumbled, swirled, flowed and lapped at grassy banks on either side. Never before had he seen water move in such a magnificent way. And then out of nowhere had come an overwhelming urge to touch the stuff, dip his hand into it, drink from it even. That was, as Gee Tee had gone on to explain, just one of the many traps woven into that part of the tunnel which somehow defied every law science had to offer, including... GRAVITY! The stunning stream, scattered with tiny weaving bends, waterfalls measured in centimetres and thick twisting branches looking like they'd fallen perfectly across it in places, was really something special, particularly if you looked up, because an exact copy of the watercourse in every last detail also ran along what was considered to be the ceiling of the tunnel, its water glued there somehow, defying belief. Between the two impossible streams running up the curved walls of the circular tunnel sat a stunning layer of perfectly mown lawn interspersed with the most beautiful wild flowers. The flawless grass was besieged by swathes of daisies, most of which had a shield of Goldilocks buttercups surrounding them. Towers of pink and yellow snapdragons stood up proud from the river bank protruding from the ceiling and the bowed walls of the passageway. Ironically, yellow dragon's teeth blooms were dotted about everywhere, almost splattered like paint from a brush. Pink evening primrose, creeping forget-me-knots, bluebells, snowdrops, daffodils and cowslips melted seamlessly into the picture perfect landscape. Honeysuckle and clusters of stunning red poppies beset the curved, enclosed rock walls. Common spotted orchids plagued sections of the river bank, tormenting pockets of the surrounding stone, almost covering it in a jacket, their white petals imprinted with perfect patterns of purple, resembling some kind of textbook tie-dye production. It was a visage of absolute beauty and one he could remember almost getting lost in, that is until the brilliant and yet often grumpy shopkeeper had snapped him out of it. If he hadn't, Peter might well have remained transfixed for all time. Only then did he recall the most deadly trap of all... the dandelion seed heads that from a distance appeared so harmless, but zooming in with the right dragon vision showed them to be death dealing monstrosities with razor sharp barbed stalks, some of the heads looking as though they were coated in an ominous, oozing liquid of some sort. No doubt a type of poison.

"Peter!"

"PETER!"

## "PETER!!!!"

"Uhhh…"

"Are you okay?" Janice questioned.

"I was just thinking about…"

"The vault's defences and your trip there with my former master," the personality of the Emporium cut in.

Peter nodded.

"I've disarmed all of them. You have to go now. Get to the trove of treasure as quickly as you can so I can re-arm all the safeguards. Good luck!"

Finally appreciating the tough, dangerous and fruitless situation they all found themselves in, the young hockey playing dragon prepared to jump.

"Cling to the pole," he quipped to the other two. "Make sure to stay tucked in and I'll meet you at the bottom. Let's go!"

And with that he jumped into the darkness, hoping not to get sprayed with Olgoi's poison or experience their electric shock. Gripping the shiny silver pole for all he was worth, he shot off like a rocket, bright orange and yellow sparks flickering around his shoes.

Extending out her arm, Polkinghorne indicated to Janice that she should go next. Falling back on the bravery that had served her so well during the course of her time underground, the young bar worker and Peter's soulmate followed her love, leaping into the shadow filled fissure, seizing the pole as she did so, a tiny little screech accompanying the start of her journey. Without any fuss or further ado, Polkinghorne followed, eager to see the renowned vault that she'd known for many years was secreted deep beneath the shop, but had been unable to get a glimpse of, even with all her supernatural Santa abilities.

*"Well hello my young friend. It's a pleasure to get so overly acquainted. I'm sorry it's not under more favourable circumstances,"* For'son reflected across the link that had formed between

himself and the rugby player, Hook, the moment the stunning ring had slid down the end of his finger. *"This'll be a new experience for both of us because I've never been paired with a human before. In fact, I think it's safe to say it might not even be a thing. Whether or not my magic works, we'll just have to wait and see."*

Of all the things Hook didn't want to hear right now… that was probably it.

*"Groovy,"* he replied sarcastically, his fear at facing the onrushing storm that was Peter's mother and Fredric's daughter barely contained.

*"Groovy indeed,"* For'son replied, not taking even the vaguest notice of the sarcasm the comment was laden with.

This was about to get very interesting.


Through the haze of what remained of the dust and smoke ravaged Emporium, a sparkling, bright yellow containment field materialised around Tank's prone body situated on the mattress. That done, it was almost time.

"She's nearly here," Zarenkesia announced. "I can sense the she-witch weaving in and out of the debris from the other end of Camelot Arcade, the opposite end to where the bridge used to be. You should all ready yourself. I'll do as much as I can, but my main goal here is to protect my new master."

"Understood," asserted Fu-ts'ang drifting tip down towards what would have been the front of the shop, ready to face head-on the threat of Manson's wicked other half, the deadly coating of icy white chilling frost rotating around his futuristic blade at quite some rate now.

Unable to do anything else, the big, butch and brave rugby player strode forward, putting himself and For'son between the exponential threat posed by the psychopath known as Earth, and Tank. Hook was willing to lay down his life for his teammate in a heartbeat, though he hoped it wouldn't come to that, not with his new found friendship with The White Dragon only just starting to blossom. Through the sickly black smoke against the light of the powerful, still raging fires, the magical collection of ragtag heroes and Xususi (beings revered throughout history for their potential to battle evil on the darkest of occasions, dispersed across space and time in preparation for such cataclysmic events) stood their ground, ready to face the madness and mayhem that was almost upon them.

# 8 THE THREE AMIGOS

"W... w... what on earth are you doing here?" Novus stuttered awkwardly.

"There's no time for that... not now," Fate spat, fear getting the better of her for once, which was odd because she'd done a disappearing act.

"I... I... I don't..."

"We don't have time for all this," Luck blurted, her inability to do anything to control the situation they currently found themselves in, freaking her out beyond belief.

"W... w... what has all this got to do with me?"

"Novus," ventured the third of the god-like trio, "it has everything to do with you. Can't you see... time's running out and I can't do anything about it. We're all about to cease to exist. Is that what you want?"

'Slightly harsh,' thought Luck, still reaching out with her entire essence in the hope of influencing just one tiny detail, however small, in an effort to turn darkness into light. Just like before though she had no... well, you know.

"My mind feels like it's on fire and for the life of me I just can't concentrate," ventured the fundamental nature of the planet, looking and feeling about a thousand times older than he actually was, which in itself was saying quite something.

"Novus," Fate mused in a much softer voice now, willing to try a new approach, "what's wrong with you? You appear much weaker and more out of sorts than when we last met. I know that was an awfully long time ago, when we agreed to leave you alone, but surely natural aging alone hasn't done this to you?"

Surrounded by the three Providences had Novus on edge, more so than he'd been for as long as he could remember, which in itself was extensive. Combine that with his rambling, and his sorry looking state and you had all the makings of a disaster in waiting instead of the powerful entity he should have been, one capable of helping to defeat the darkness that was looming over all of them. Using all the concentration he was able to muster, Novus attempted to pull back the curtain of murkiness and explain what had happened.

"T... t... the essence that makes me what I am, my l... l... lifeblood, it's nearly gone. Without it I can't function, can't watch over those who inhabit me. I'm lost, alone and have no way to influence events as I have in the past. I'm... dying!"

The three Providences were aghast to hear this unexpected revelation. To a being, they were all reeling, because they'd broken all the rules to get this far, only to find that what remained of the planet's essence was in no position to help, even one iota. What they were going to do now was anyone's guess, especially as they'd already exhausted all options. Was there any way back? Would everything depend on the heroes already engaged in trying to save the world, human and dragon alike? Or was it possible for the three of them to nudge things in the right direction, and give those in need a helping hand? Stick around to see.

# 9 A TIGHT SPOT

One way to look at it was considered chaos with attacker after attacker throwing themselves and their despicable dark magic at the courageous and plucky captain. Another and more accurate depiction was of absolute pandemonium, with not one single dragon knowing what the hell was going on beneath the sparking, arcing translucent blue energy shield that had them all trapped in the aperture of the monorail test borehole in northern France, a location that looked set to become synonymous across the course of history with death and destruction on a scale never before matched in this universe or any other.

Falling back on her wealth of training and acting purely out of instinct, Amelia Battlehard continued to give as good as she got, lashing out with thunderous bursts of brilliant luminous blue lightning bolts, shredding wings, tails, chests and jaws, sending opponents crashing into themselves, smashing into walls and spiralling clumsily to an agonising death. Lost in the majesty of the magic and fighting, nothing else existed for the ingenious, gutsy and daring defender of good, her continued focus on surviving spurring her on to greater deeds, thoughts of anything else and a life she might have outside of her job all but forgotten.

Whilst gut feeling and character alone continued to prolong the good captain's life, a sense of fear and the need for retribution and revenge flooded through the course of one dragon opponent's body, pushing him further and further into the darkness despite the fact that he was near enough to the translucent energy shield to be able to taste the daylight. Oblivion had surreptitiously managed to sneak closer and closer to the mind bending supernatural action, skulking behind the corpses of those previously dispatched, using all his innate dragon abilities and some naga taught gifts to mask as much of his presence as he could. So far it was working a treat, having almost gotten into not quite arm's length, but certainly close enough that surprise could lead to a killing blow. Knowing that his adversary was better than good, he took pride in the fact that she would be dead in only a matter of moments now.

Slamming his fist into the main stay of the control panel, the kind, caring and considerate healer made his frustration known.

"DAMN! It's no good. There's simply no way to remove that shield."

"Darling…"

"NO! Not darling. She's overwhelmed and if we don't get it down she'll die. As well… Flash is on his way… how, I just don't know. But he'll want to get to her and I'll have to tell him it's not possible."

"What did he say?"

"Just that he was incoming and for everyone to get out of the way."

"Then we should… RIGHT?"

"I don't understand how he could possibly…"

"YOYO! We need to move… NOW!"

Suddenly realising that he might have made a catastrophic error in thinking that his friend the former Crimson Guard didn't have a plan, instantly he leapt to his feet and grabbing Rose by the arm, pulled her away from the control panel, over towards where the youngsters were situated beside the huge capacitor.

*"Everyone,"* he stressed throughout the confines of their shared link, *"you need to take cover NOW!"*

Barely staying on top of the situation, her movements an absolute blur even to herself, Amelia continued to do the only thing she could… FIGHT! Slicing a wing from one that had breached her defences and come in too close, the King's Guard captain used magic to enhance her weight and drop out of the way of a vicious volley of toxic bright green shards intent on cutting her head from her body, landing atop another whose teeth were bared, intent on taking a chunk from out of either leg. Bending her knees, she raked her talons down the back of his neck, tearing five huge almighty lines into his scales, severing an artery in the process, thick, bright green blood spraying like a lawn sprinkler all over the place in the process. Igniting more luminous blue crackling forked lightning ready to dispense with yet one more oncoming threat, out of nowhere a stunning pain mushroomed out from the centre of her back, instantly winding her, causing the offensive mantras she'd conjured up to be dispelled straight away, leaving her ears ringing and her vision going double. Frightened beyond belief, the first thing she did was try and box up all that fear so that she could assess the threat and get on with the job. However, her opponent had other ideas, which might see her life measured in seconds rather than years, decades or the centuries it was supposed to be.

After the astounding head-butt straight into the middle of her back, Oblivion sent three lines of sparkling orange flame flying from his fingertips, each piercing a crucial part of Captain Battlehard's right wing membrane, causing her to cry out in pain, or at least it would have done had she not just had the stuffing knocked out of her. The noises were more like muffled thwumps.

Not content with the damage he'd already done, the deranged dark dragon didn't stop there. Bringing his left wing around with such force and speed that it was barely visible, he slammed the outer bones against the left side of Amelia's head, destroying her left ear, rendering her unconscious, a thick trail of viscous green blood dripping down onto her neck before leaping off into the shadowy abyss of the borehole. Supporting the entire weight of her body with his, Oblivion knew exactly how to end the life of the opponent that had caused him so much bother. Forcing her head back as far as it would go, with a perverse grin etched across his prehistoric features, he barred his incisors and eyed the exposed throat with much glee, prepared and almost salivating at doing the unthinkable and separating this apex predator's head from its body.

Huddled behind the capacitor out of sight of the shield and the top of the borehole, with the exception of Rose, all of them wondered what the hell was going on and exactly what they were supposed to be doing. This, they all thought, was an utter waste of time, particularly as they were supposed to be destroying the energy shield and getting to their friend. It was at that point Rose had the forethought to command all of them to raise their personal shields. They did so straight away, still remaining as confused as ever. About to voice their concerns, the need to do so was batted away in an instant.

Strangely, the air itself was just kind of sucked up and spirited away, leaving Yoyo, Rose and their crew of forward thinking youngsters gasping for breath. About two milliseconds after that it felt (ironically) as though the world itself had been viciously ripped in two, a blast wave with the brute force of a downed aeroplane pounding the facility, flattening the capacitor, collapsing buildings, destroying the entirety of the controls, pretty much decimating the whole epicentre. That, however was nothing compared with what happened when the speeding bullet hit the immovable object that had been its target all along.

Despite his enhanced dragon intelligence and aptitude Flash was struggling to comprehend all that was happening. It had only been a matter of minutes since he'd been standing on the shore above Bow Fiddle Rock in Scotland and now here he was in northern France, his mass temporarily having been reduced by magic, two huge problems on his mind, one obviously much bigger than the other, though the smaller one measured almost as much in his mind given his relationship with her, as if such things could be weighed. Determined as always to give everything he had and wrest the outcome of both dilemmas away from the likes of Fate and back under his control, after warning his friend the healer, he did the only thing he could and smashed headlong into the translucent sparking and fizzing blue energy shield atop the monorail test borehole, bracing himself for the mother of all impacts, not knowing the resultant cost or even whether he would survive. For both their sakes and the world at large, he hoped he would.

Within moments of reaching landfall, Flash had extended his most powerful shield out in front of him in an effort to contain the massive overload of kinetic energy he knew would result from his assault on the top of the borehole. Praying he'd get it right and be in the nick of time, the selfless former Crimson Guard closed his eyes and lay his destiny at the feet of Fate.

# BOOM!

Savouring the moment, the taste of his own kind's flesh, a delicacy he loved to partake of on occasion, his almighty scaled stomach rumbled in anticipation as he hovered there taking the weight of his deserving enemy with both hands. Oblivion craned his head forward to slake his desire and finish the female off once and for all, when the world around him exploded, arms, legs, wings, torsos and concrete blasted in every direction, as well as the most resounding and brutal noise he'd ever heard causing his and every other being's eardrums to implode. Forced to drop his prey, the treat he'd been looking forward to tucking into, all he could do was hold out his hands in defence as he was smashed violently into the nearest wall, the reinforced concrete breaking his nose and shattering his forehead, causing him to tumble uncontrollably downwards, which given what had happened could actually have been in any direction as far as he was concerned. Hell had just been unleashed onto all those in and around the top of the borehole. It would have to be seen what kind of apocalyptic nightmare would follow in short order. For now though, the incumbents in the tunnel were well and truly out of control, most unconscious, those that remained alive and alert cowed by fear and dominated by the physical force of whatever had just struck and destroyed the protective force shield.

Total turmoil existed across Flash's eye line as he tumbled out of control, breath knocked out of him, a series of tiny bones in his left wing broken, exquisite pain emanating from the tip of his tail, why... he had absolutely no idea, but that wasn't the focus of his attention. Amelia... he had to find Amelia and make sure she was alright.

Brutally ripped out of unconsciousness, Captain Battlehard found herself spiralling dangerously out of control, having just crashed head first into the drifting corpse of a dragon thug missing most of one wing. Pushing her tail down as far as it would go, she spread out both wings in an effort to regulate her flight and gain some height. Predictably, given what Oblivion had done to one of her wings, it didn't work, the three shredded holes causing distress and stopping her from getting a grip on her flying, plus her hearing was non-existent, viscous green blood dribbling from her remaining ear, her usually exceptional balance shot. With all the other obstacles in the confined darkened space, the courageous captain couldn't find the focus to start healing her wounds with a view to recovering the situation. Bumping and smashing into bodies, limbs and in particular, the reinforced concrete circular wall that surrounded her, the love of Flash's life dropped further and further away from the surface and any help her friends might have offered.

Feeling as though the world had just ended (ironic given what was to come), through the unerring silence Oblivion flooded his forehead and what remained of his nose with as much healing magic as he dared, all the time tumbling head over heels further into the borehole's darkness. One moment he'd been about to satisfy one of his many perverse desires in the form of eating one of his own kind, only for everything to implode to the backdrop of the biggest explosion he'd ever encountered. Rallying against pain the likes of which he'd never known, through the mass of bodies and limbs that littered the monorail test borehole, somewhere in the distance he could just make out the female, the one he'd gotten so close to devouring, the one who'd made so much trouble for him and his crew. Sights set, just about able to fly, in a world where any noise was now completely suppressed, the boss beast from hell slammed his tail upwards and then nosedived in the direction of his prey, looking to finish what he'd started and satisfy that rumble in his belly.

Effectively floating somewhere towards the top of the tunnel, dazed and severely concussed, it was only an emergency Crimson Guard mantra set off automatically after the collision which had stopped Flash dropping like a stone alongside everything else. Returned to his normal mass, the spell that Fredric had cast in Scotland having worn off, the former Crimson Guard had quite literally had the stuffing knocked out of him. Not many would have been brave or stupid enough to ram the shield like he'd just done, and believe you me, most would not have survived. He had, but only by the skin of his teeth, his suffering reminiscent of his short confinement in Antarctica. It was almost more than he could take, but one thought and one alone kept him alive and alert, determined to succeed where others would no doubt fail... AMELIA!

Pushing aside the pain whilst flooding himself with as much healing magic as he could spare, shaking his huge primordial head in an effort to regain just some of his balance, the very first thing he did was roll over so that he was facing downwards. After that, it was all about using his exceptional vision, switching instantly to the type that could zoom into anything from long range, absolutely certain of what he was looking for. It took but a moment to find her, there in the depths, spiralling out of control, beyond corpses, wings and limbs, the three massive puncture wounds in her wing standing out like a fox in a hen house, her predicament obviously dire. About to give chase as only he could, suddenly in his peripheral vision he noticed something that sent a chill up his spine... an almighty, desperate looking dragon whose sights also looked set on Amelia. Ignoring the absolute agony coursing through him, with one flap of his giant wings, Flash shot down into the shadows powered not only by what was right, but this time, by... LOVE!

Only a short distance away on the surface amongst what remained of the test borehole facility, (which wasn't very much... it well and truly resembled a waste refuse site, flattened in almost every way), brave warriors in the form of Yoyo, Rose and their group of heroic youngsters continued to stagger to their feet, like their counterparts in the tunnel, all having suffered burst eardrums, each enduring the effects of the concussive blast and the energy wave it had created. Luckily Rose's well timed advice about igniting their personal shields had saved each of them. Only now were they shaking off the effects, attempting communication through their all too familiar telepathic link.

*"What the hell was...?"*

*"FLASH!"* announced Yoyo in a very wobbly voice indeed.

*"Uggghhh..."* sighed more than one of them.

*"It was Flash crashing through the barrier."* concluded Rose almost up to full steam, *"Now all of you need to snap out of it. Or have you forgotten about our perilous situation? Two of you go check on the borehole and see if you can assist Flash and Amelia. The rest of you focus your minds on what's heading our way. Needless to say, we're going to need a miracle of some sort to wriggle out of this. And since that's generally your speciality, I suggest you all get your thinking caps on."*

Wings and legs firmly tucked in, the gunmetal grey and Nordic sky blue blur that was the former Crimson Guard shot bullet-like down the test borehole, having switched his vision to the infrared kind that would allow him to see in the pitch black. Gaining steadily on both his targets, Flash decided it was time to slow one down, even up the odds, the much bigger picture hanging over him at the back of his mind. With just four words that harked back to his early training in the exclusive Crimson Guards, he directed three invisible tendrils of high powered healing energy at Amelia's damaged wings before adjusting his course ever so slightly, his sights now firmly set on the monster deep below him, the one he rightly assumed had inflicted said wounds in the first place. It was, as far as he was concerned, about to be payback time.

Giving all that she had, without a great deal of success, in an effort to stabilise not only her flight but also the fear and anger threatening to overwhelm her mind, out of nowhere an intense tingling sensation started to nibble away at the abrasions on her wing. Afraid that the beast that had bested her once already had her in his sights, once again using unusual magic to finish the job he'd already started, Captain Battlehard was flabbergasted when all three of the tears in her appendage instantly healed up right before her very eyes. Finally getting a grip on her ragged breathing, knowing she had everything she needed to come out of the crazy death spiral that had taken hold of her huge primordial body, she sought the composure she was renowned for and in an epic feat of aerial acrobatic trickery, slammed the caudal spade on the end of her tail down with as much power as she dared, whilst simultaneously extending both wings out as far as they'd go, each acting as an air brake, steadying the bulk of her being, slowing her descent, all the time instilling the confidence she needed to survive. Feeling something familiar prickle her psyche, about to open herself up, a quick glance upward all but paralysed her with fear as the almighty frame of Oblivion closed in from above, jaws wide open, a sickening grin etched across the scales of his antediluvian face. Too slow to ignite any of her magic or defensive options, the brave and courageous captain, one of the heroes of the Changing of the Guard and the monarch's fierce protector, very calmly, in the middle of the tunnel in total and utter darkness, came to accept her fate. As the hulking primeval fiend of a dragon breached her defences and she was able to smell his sickly scent, Amelia accepted the inevitable with the kind of good grace she was renowned for, regrets flooding through her mind about letting down her friends, the king and Flash, as well as not being there to help stop the impending threat of nuclear doom. Eyes closed, expecting the kind of impact that would kill her in an instant, as the moments ticked by, her curious and calculating mind began to wonder why it hadn't arrived yet. Still unable to hear, as she hadn't had an opportunity to focus healing energy on her one remaining ear, slowly she opened her eyes, almost too afraid at what she would find. Fortunately for her, it wasn't the kind of nightmarish scenario her imagination had run riot with, quite the opposite in fact.

There, hanging precariously in the air, head not two metres away from hers, was the depraved brute of a dragon that had caused her so much harm, wriggling about like a baited worm on a hook, knowing what was about to happen next. Glancing past the squirming fetid fiend, a smile the likes of which had rarely crossed her face shimmered into being at seeing who was grappling with the tail at the other end. Of course... none other than Flash himself. Over the moon at seeing the dragon she could now admit to herself that she loved more than anyone she'd ever met, the true Captain Battlehard finally returned to the fray. Adding a dab of wickedly powerful lightning to both hands, in an instant she was on him, carving through his hugely muscled neck with her talons, looking on in delight as the beast's head parted from its body, both sections tumbling away into the shadow strewn depths leaving just the two of them hovering there. About to reveal all her true feelings and throw herself at him, without warning the former Crimson Guard grabbed her hand and in a turn of speed only associated with a fighter jet, surged upwards towards the tunnel's entrance, dragging her kicking and screaming in her wake. Not the romantic reunion she'd expected.

One by one Yoyo used his exquisite abilities to heal everyone's eardrums. Rose first, then his own and after that, each of the youngsters who he thought of as his own kin. It didn't take long before they were all back to full fitness.

"NO... that won't work. It's moving too fast," admonished Monty.

"What if we all combined to form a shield using all our magic?"

"It has waaaaay too much velocity and power. It wouldn't even slow it down, let alone stop it," put in Tina.

"Is there any way that we can supernaturally grab the thing and stop it from making contact with the surface?"

"Not at that speed," added Rose, normally the most optimistic of them all, but here and now feeling as though they'd all failed spectacularly.

"I think," ventured Monty, "that we're well and truly out of ideas and hope."

"Well it's a good job I'm here then," yelled Flash over the almighty BOOM of both himself and Amelia landing amongst the crowd of friends.

"FLASH!" Yoyo bellowed, hugging his pal for all he was worth.

"My friend."

"Amelia!" the youngsters all exclaimed, crowding around their impromptu leader, glad to see she was okay.

"ENOUGH!" yelled Rose, instantly instilling silence. "Whatever your plan is, Flash, you'd better implement it now," she announced, tilting her head skyward, looking straight up.

As one all the others did the same. Just visible in the distance, many, many miles away, was the scorching tail of the SLBM (Submarine Launched Ballistic Missile) getting bigger with every second that passed.

"Flash...?" Amelia asked.

"I'm on it," replied the confident former Crimson Guard, sure he could nullify the onrushing nuclear threat.

Closing his eyes, surrounded by the dragon he loved and a great number of friends, Flash sought out that which had been passed onto him in a hurry, hoping against all odds that it would prevent the end of everything everywhere.

# 10 INFORMATION OVERLOAD

"White Wings... report!"

"American satellites are tracking the trajectory of the missile, Majesty, and there's no deviation from its current course."

"Is there any news on a self destruct of some sort?"

"Apparently the only way the missile can be destroyed is from the sub itself, and that comes straight from the American intelligence agencies."

"DAMN!" swore the king, slamming his fist onto the huge wooden table with enough force to make a huge dent. "Can you think of anything we've overlooked, my friend?"

"I'm afraid not, sire. We just have to hope those on the ground can play their part and somehow snatch victory from the jaws of defeat."

'No truer words,' thought George, wondering exactly what those he loved were doing right at this very moment.

Throughout the private residence, dragons who'd been working furiously slowed on hearing the news about the nuclear missile launched from the missing submarine, all too aware of the impact the attack would have on mainland Europe. What they didn't know, because the monarch hadn't actually revealed the whole picture to them, not wanting to cause a panic, was the fact that not only would most of France be destroyed, but likely the world would be split in a dozen pieces, representing the end of everything. As groups gathered together across the different levels of the residence, a resounding hush swallowed them all up. It was unnerving, but then it should have been given all that was happening and the dire consequences if they failed.


Communication across the planet increased exponentially as the alarm was raised, warning of a potential nuclear menace rising precariously into the atmosphere. Chatter within and between intelligence agencies was off the chart, allies querying allies, enemies accusing enemies, whilst all the while threat levels increasingly put the world at risk in a totally different way. Trust was a hard commodity to find anywhere.


Dripping wet, still soaked to the skin, Manson clung tightly to the overhead handles as the submarine started to dive, not once taking his eyes off the scope continually tracking the path of the weapon of mass destruction they'd launched only a short while before, his ego massively proud of getting this far especially since it had looked as though his race had been run, back on the top of the cliff. For the crew to have saved what remained of his body and give him a chance to get aboard was truly remarkable and a testament to all their courage and supernatural abilities. Whether or not they would have helped had they known the full extent of what he had planned, well, that was another matter entirely. Of course he had no intention of revealing that to any of them. Their thinking, to a being, was that a statement was being made by attacking the northern part of France with a nuclear weapon in the hopes of subjugating those who'd stubbornly refused to surrender, when in fact it was actually all about retribution. Revenge for overturning certain victory, the settling of a score for taking ownership of the planet away from him, reprisal the ultimate act of betrayal and petulance from a being clouded by madness, steeped in shadows, having long since lost any sign of love. Bathed in a ghostly red glow encased in the futuristic tin can, those under Manson's sway continued to do his bidding believing that their future depended on it. How wrong they were.

As the super advanced electric submarine nose-dived ever deeper, its darkened hull blending in more and more with the much chillier, darker water, five archaic shadows followed in its wake, their profound magic ready to be set free at the first sign of trouble. What that looked like, who knew? Vasuki's thoughts focused on the being he hated most on the planet, one now trapped inside the submersible they were tailing, no doubt celebrating having unleashed death and annihilation in the form of the nuclear warhead, with no idea he was being followed. What to do now though, that was the question. Should they pounce before the sub got any deeper or would waiting until it reached greater depths provide a measure of safety given the nuclear reactor within? A tough call to say the least, it was on Vasuki's head to decide. Much as he wanted vengeance for all the naga deaths caused by Manson's mischief, there was still an element of wanting to protect the sea, the planet and those remaining inhabitants. If he got it wrong, it would spell disaster.

# 11 CONSEQUENCES BE DAMNED

Caught between a rock and a hard place, knowing they were there to save lives, the dragon trio of Steel, Jar Man and DomCon had a decision to make, one that couldn't be put off. Be discovered and continue to rescue more children from beneath the rubble in Salisbridge's renowned Close, or pack up and go home. As dragons, it was deeply ingrained in them not to be exposed, so normally any course of action involving unearthing the truth seemed an impossibility, no matter how noble and righteous the cause. But here and now, everything was upside down, chaos ruled instead of order. The humans needed the help they could provide using their supernatural gifts. To do anything else would be counterintuitive, against all their instincts as a sentient race... wouldn't it? With dozens of men and women in high viz jackets sprinting towards them, it was the leader who'd spent so much time captaining his teammates in laminium ball matches across the world who stepped up as the other two continued to debate what they should do.

"**** *this!*" Steel reflected through their telepathic link.

Momentarily Jar Man and DomCon paused, not sure what their friend's rude words meant. It didn't take long to find out.

*"We continue, and to hell with the consequences. No more lives lost through deception. Save everyone you can, and then we're gone. Best possible haste."*

By now, Angela, Emma, Sam and Taibul had sprinted back and surrounded their three dragon friends in human form, all of whom had their eyes closed, fully focused on their assigned tasks, Jar Man holding everything in place, Steel removing debris in an effort to reveal the location of the bodies, DomCon carefully removing those alive, floating them out of the gaps created, before gently setting them down on the adjacent luscious grass.

Leading the pack, a wiry, middle aged man drew to a halt in front of all the friends, not even breaking a sweat or remotely out of breath.

"What the hell's going on here?" he demanded in a tone of authority.

More than a little cowed and taken aback, the young sports men and women struggled for an answer, that is until Angela stepped up and forward, ready and willing to show some backbone, just as she'd done during her time in the domain.

"I'll tell you what's going on," she stated, prodding her index finger into the middle of the man's high viz vest, "these three are saving lives and bringing children back to their parents. I suggest you get the emergency medical teams in here as fast as possible. All these children will need to be checked over, right NOW!"

It was an odd turn of events that's for sure, a gaggle of humans all standing there with their mouths hanging open, looking on blindly as things they couldn't possibly begin to understand unfolded right before their eyes, namely small bodies floating unhindered out of the rubble and through the air. To some it was just ungodly.

"But..." started the man who appeared to be in charge, the one on the end of Angela's finger.

"Just one minute," put in a well dressed woman in expensive wellington boots and an even more costly dress under her luminous top.

"What is it you want?" Angela asked, her temper flaring. She had no time for all this nonsense, knowing just how important it was not to interrupt the concentration of her dragon friends.

"Uhhh..."

"These three are saving those kids. I suggest you all stand back, be quiet and let them get on with their jobs if you know what's good for you. If you don't, the one thing I can assure you of is...TROUBLE! Don't say you haven't been warned."

With that, Richie's friend and teammate crossed her arms and plastered her face with the most terrifying stare her arsenal had to offer. In that moment, it was enough to stop the group of do-gooders in their tracks. On the periphery of their collective, Steel, Jar Man and DomCon listened to what their human friend had just done and in their minds at least, applauded her brave actions in standing up to be counted.

As time ticked by, and the supposed miracles continued, one by one, more small figures were recovered, most caked in blood, nearly all breathing raggedly, their distress even in an unconscious state, apparent to all.

With a huge sigh of relief from the dragon trio, the last of those alive buried beneath the debris was set down gently on the picture perfect grass with enough precision to barely disturb any of the blades. What they'd set out to do was accomplished, with consummate professionalism and a dash of remarkable guile. Multiple lives had been saved.

Right on cue the emergency medical teams came charging through in a series of vehicles with their blue lights flashing ten to the dozen, sirens blazing, the eerie tranquillity of the disaster site brutally interrupted. As one the volunteers all turned to watch the medics sprint from their transports and attend to the children, their duty of care clear, along with their specialist skills.

Given the ready-made distraction that had just presented itself, the three dragon heroes who'd just shown off their inherent supernatural abilities in all their glory above ground, decided through their telepathic bond that now was the time to vacate the area. Not even saying goodbye to their human allies and friends, Steel, Jar Man and DomCon charged themselves with as much magic as their false human forms would allow and, enhanced by a little known mantra that the sometimes furious pocket rocket had picked up in an elicit game of poker deep below ground many decades earlier, scarpered at super speed back up over what remained of the rubble. Leaping over part of the retaining wall of the Close that had somehow remained intact, all three disappeared into the human population on the other side, before coming together to decide on their next course of action. Buoyed by their success, the trio were well and truly buzzing.

# 12 RELATIVELY SIMPLE

Reaching the turn, the earth's pull added to the nuclear missile's terrific speed, dragging it back towards the ground and northern France, its flaming tail terrifying against the dark backdrop of space, the roar of its intense engines heard by no one, the death dealing human engineered masterpiece locked onto its destination, with only those inside the sub able to abort a catastrophic calamity, a decision none were willing to make. The four horsemen of the apocalypse galloped furiously alongside the potentially planet busting projectile, sickly sweet smiles barely noticeable from beneath their cowls, the race well and truly on, the finishing line getting ever closer with every second that passed.


It wasn't subtle, sneaky, crafty or stealthy. In fact, all she did was turn the corner and stroll straight into what was left of the Emporium amongst a few roaring fires that hadn't been extinguished and a haze of thick black smoke, something that ensconced most of the underground capital.

Despite having one of THE most powerful magical beings for company, Hook, brave and fearless rugby player and one of the stars of the Changing of the Guard swallowed nervously as the feral nightmare from hell, Peter's mother, strolled casually around the corner, a sadistic grin ingrained across the shocking purple lines that crisscrossed her haunted and psychotic face.

*"FOR'SON…"*

*"Stay calm, my boy, and we might yet prevail,"* was the strongly worded reply that played out across the bond that had been forged between their minds only moments before.

In an example of her quick thinking, seconds before the wicked she-witch Earth had rounded the corner, Zarenkesia had used her magic to turn over the tattered and torn mattress which Tank had been lying on, flipping him onto the cold, hard floor, the most powerful force shield she knew fully extended around him, his body now covered fully by the mattress, any hint of his existence all but hidden, the hope being that he would be ignored fully, any thoughts of healing his bleed on the brain forgotten momentarily, this brand new threat taking full priority.

Surrounded by an ever moving coating of frost, Fu-ts'ang hovered next to the back wall, tip facing down, standing proud, the futuristic, impossible, rounded lines of his body glinting from the light of the small raging fires, the former dragon weapon smith taking a considered approach in this the second round of going up against an enemy who'd nearly destroyed them all and taken the planet the first time. Every ounce of his experience would be invaluable in the coming moments, of that there could be no doubt.

"Ah... yet another sickly human pet, no doubt one of my son's so called friends. I'll take great pleasure in tasting your underdone pink flesh before your heart stops beating," Earth's gravelly voice echoed as the raised purple lines of her face jostled for position.

Hook would have swallowed again nervously had he not been too terrified to do so.

*"I won't let it happen,"* For'son urged, *"don't let her paralyse you with fear before things even kick off."*

"You've run your race, you vile creature. You'll not harm another living being here today, on that you have my word," Fu-ts'ang voiced out loud, floating forward, putting himself just to the side of the plucky rugby player.

"Ahhh... the fortunate blade back from the dead! A neat trick for sure, but not one you'll get to repeat, I assure you. Even your kind are no match for my magic," she vowed, two spheres of black as night twisted tendrils appearing out of nowhere in both her hands, resembling despicable, shadowy, bunched up balls of wool. If only they could have been that lucky.

*"HOOK!"* For'son demanded using all his indomitable will to get the strapping rugby player's attention. *"All you have to do is let yourself go. I know it sounds counterintuitive, but that's it... I'll do the rest. Please... don't put up any barriers or rally against my presence. Understand?"*

*"I do,"* he squeaked with as much courage as he could muster.

*"Good."*

Presiding over all this was the Emporium's presence, Zarenkesia, a powerful magic user herself and one who, under normal circumstances would certainly be able to give Earth a bloody nose at the very least. Unfortunately, given she was currently caring for Tank and doing her utmost to keep him stable in the very dubious position he found himself in, for her it would have been like fighting with one hand tied behind her back, only able to hop on one leg whilst having the mother of all itches in her nose that just couldn't be scratched. Overwatch was the best she could manage at the moment.

Using her supernatural gifts to spin frightening looking shadowy orbs of constantly wriggling vines in the open palms of her hands, Peter's vile mother took two steps forward, trying to intimidate those in front of her even more. It worked for one, the other two... not so much. Recognising that the time was at hand, only in that moment did she get the sense of three more beings which she hadn't accounted for somewhere in the immediate locale. Not her son of that she was sure, or his pet human girlfriend, but there were others, two strong magic users, with the other feeling as though it were... ASLEEP!

"'How odd,' she thought. Pushing all that to one side and without the usual snakes writhing around the top of her head, she POUNCED!

Neither elegant or understated, the attack was effective, Earth's exceptional hand eye coordination allowing her to toss two tightly packed magical explosives, made up of a particularly wicked shade of naga magic, at both Hook and

Fu-ts'ang simultaneously.

The master weapon smith trapped for an inordinate amount of time in the shining, sleek, futuristic blade held his ground, absolutely certain that despite the unusual nature of the magic he was more than a match for it. In a deft display that would have had most cricket fans firmly on their feet, instead of running, hiding or simply moving out of the way, Fu-ts'ang batted the supernatural incendiary menace straight back at the wicked witch with the top part of his icy blade, watching enthralled as the expression on her face changed from overconfidence to manic panic.

Briefly it reminded him of the high-speed journey he'd been dragged on by the woman, well okay, dragon he'd fallen head over heels in love with, nabbed from his doorstep, surrounded by an almighty bubble of magical energy and then in what felt like an instant, transported the fifteen or so kilometres to Stonehenge, whereby he was thrown unceremoniously into the battle from hell against God knows who, only a short while before. It was all of that, only with the added bonus of the most excruciating pain he'd ever known across every inch of his well honed body. Most humans wouldn't have fared well, but luckily Hook was a supreme athlete, something his sport demanded in order to play at the level he did. That was all that saved him as For'son the enigmatic, charismatic and millennia old dragon warrior presence trapped within the stunning band, used his inherent abilities to control every aspect of Hook's body. Never in his life had the rugby playing champion moved so fast, and that was saying quite something given the heroics he'd performed on such a regular basis at his chosen sport. Muscles burning, expanding and contracting to the maximum, he tumbled off to one side cartwheeling out of the way of a smouldering fire, dancing around one of the remaining stanchions that still supported what was left of the building, bounding up to his feet, having avoided the threat now ready to go on the attack.

*"Whoa... steady on there tiger, I'm not sure how much of that my body can take."*

*"You'll be fine, I promise,"* For'son replied. *"I'm fully conversant with how fragile you bipeds are."*

*"Oh thanks... I think."*

Momentarily, a strange chuckling echoed across their telepathic bond, more haunting than anything else, something Hook found rather chilling.

Caught off guard by the magical blade's defiance, Peter's mother reacted instinctively, igniting a powerful purple shield all around her, hoping it would be enough to contain the dark naga mischief she'd instigated. With a booming

CRACKLE that shook what remained of the structure, causing wood, stone and dust to litter the air once again, the constant wriggling shadowy orb exploded against her supernatural armour, causing a cascade of luminous pink forked lightning to spread out in every direction, hissing and spluttering as it did so, sparking off the floor, what little remained of the ceiling and everywhere in between. Much to Earth's surprise her own magic completely overloaded her supernatural defences, causing her shield to come crashing down.

Not resting on his laurels, immediately recognising what had happened, Fu-ts'ang acted, seizing the opportunity knowing that it might be the only one they got. Frost fizzing around the length of his cutting edge, the fantastic blade arced up his tip and dived for the she-witch, his aim set directly for her heart, should she even have such a thing.

Noting their comrade the weapon smith snatch his chance at taking out their opponent, For'son made a split second decision to help as only he could see how... a distraction was what was needed. Using the Hook shell he'd been provided with as a conduit, the inscrutable hoop unleashed what to anyone else would have been a devastating salvo of luminescent green poisonous bolts, each one locked on and heading straight for the wicked woman's head, sure at the very least that he'd provided the mother of all disruptions.

Attack, in the blink of an eye, had morphed into defence, underestimating the blade a costly error, one Earth had only now come to recognise as she scrambled to recover. Bad enough that her shield had failed, spluttering completely out of existence, the formidable naga magic proving far too punishing for what she considered her staple defence, one that had saved her life on many an occasion. Wrapping her mind around that and wondering how to repair what had been undone, out of the corner of her eye she glimpsed a speeding bright white blur closing in on her position.

'The blade,' she thought, followed quickly by, 'the cheek of it,' the deep source of anger that fuelled most of her being nearly all the time welling up.

Sure that the frost imbued weapon was no match for her, and totally forgetting her recent lesson about not underestimating said enemy, she was about to conjure up yet another bout of depraved dark magic and go massively on the offensive when a smidgen of lush jade green off to one side caught her attention. Irked beyond belief now, temper in full flow, she responded as only her make-up would allow, backflipping twice, slicing her right hand open on a twisted shard of dark grey metal sticking up out of the smouldering remains as she did so, but continuing anyway, unable to see any other way out of her precarious predicament.

All the while keeping a sharp eye on her charge, making sure his unresponsive body was not only shielded by all her supernatural, but also secreted by the giant mattress that had been recovered from upstairs, Zarenkesia would have smirked at how quickly the tables had been turned, had she had the face to do so. Instead she continued to watch, urging her allies on, hoping they'd dispatch this clear and present threat as quickly as possible so she could get back to tending to Tank.

Sensing the poisonous projectiles in his wake and thankful for the assistance from his friends, Fu-ts'ang sliced through the air, his super cold blade negating any resistance, the mistress of evil his only focus, wanting nothing more than to remove her head from her miserable body, in his mind his wrath fully justified after everything that she'd done and the misery she'd inflicted on not only her son, but Janice, the young human female who he thought of as his best friend.

On the back foot now, Earth, as troubled as she'd been in some time and wanting nothing more than to get her hands around her son's scrawny neck, tried desperately to compose her thoughts, knowing that now was not the time to lose her nerve or focus. Bounding up a small pile of rubble, before launching herself backwards, somersaulting head over heels onto yet one more of the surviving columns that had supported the upper storey of the Emporium for centuries, she pushed off and in doing so avoided two toxic projectiles heading straight for her, watching as they splashed unceremoniously into the debris behind her. Only during her mid-air tumble did she recall exactly what her other half had set in motion, the most despicable plan in the history of plans, one that should with just a little luck, destroy the entire planet. For an implausibly short amount of time, barely measurable in nanoseconds, it gave Fredric's daughter, Earth, pause for thought, which went something like this. She was just a distraction, a minor irritation in the enormous scale of things. All she had to do was keep them occupied for a little while longer and maybe with just a little luck, she might just manage to end her son and his precious human pet of a girlfriend before the biggest bang of the lot ended them all. An interesting take on things, of that there could be no doubt, and one that freed the shackles of fear and trepidation from the monstrous murderer, allowing her battle hardened senses to take over, knowing that whatever happened, none of them would have very long left on the planet. Unchained, at least within her psyche, in that moment a decision was made to reverse the state of things and turn cowardly, running away into something much more aggressive.

Hook's poorly designed body (in this regard) had been taken over by the puppeteer For'son, forcing him to give chase at dragon-like speed to the object of their rage and indignation, the female dragon that had caused so much pain and chaos in the murderous spree she'd been on with her mad-as-a-hatter other half, Manson, the would-be king and newly crowned leader of this world, or so they'd hoped. Stopped at the very last second, their plan would have succeeded if not for the intervention of a group of unlikely heroes, dragon, human and inanimate object alike, some from the here and now, others returning from the scattered snowflakes of time itself, known only to a select few as Xususi, thrown in place by an unshakeable force more powerful than anything either past or present for just such an eventuality.

Limbs burning from the exhaustion of moving at super dragon speed without any of the inherent magic that such a thing usually required, the gallant rugby player could barely summon up a thought, let alone articulate it. Closing in on the primeval princess of pain, For'son used both of Hook's hands to shoot off magic in all its supernatural varieties, from brilliant copper coloured forks of fantastic lightning to fabulous orange and red shaded streams of nefarious looking flame, as well as the continued barrage of poisonous bolts, all of which ripped up the ground in the wake of their so far, ever so lucky prey. All the time giving chase, their ally, the frost enshrouded blade ever so slightly out in front of them, to each it was just an inevitability that the devilish creature would be caught and slain in short order.

Inexplicably, the female fiend did the last thing all three of them expected... she turned around to face them, in one silky smooth motion batting away all the offensive magic cast at her with massive waves of shadowy spectral supernatural fizzing out of her purple topped fingertips. No doubt it was naga in nature given its unpredictability and the fact that neither For'son nor Fu-ts'ang had seen it before.

Instinctively Hook attempted to skid to a halt mid-chase. Luckily for him For'son had other ideas, throwing the young lad's athletic body screaming to the floor off to the left, ploughing through a whole pile of broken wooden beams that had come down in the aftermath of Mas-crate's dastardly deeds. Although it sounds painful, and don't get me wrong, it was, the enigmatic ring's actions saved the fearless human's life, because waves of sickly evil cut through the very air that he'd occupied only a split second earlier. The weapon smith trapped in the advanced and ultramodern cutting edge did not fare as well, taking the full force of the darkness meant to destroy. Fu-ts'ang's saving grace was the fact that he'd faced it head on, his profile as slim as possible in the face of the wave of destruction. At once the supernatural coating of frost that he held a great affinity towards, an outer layer that made him feel safe, secure and fearless all at the same time, was brutally stripped away, cast into oblivion, not to be recovered any time soon. The anguish in that moment was catastrophic for the former smith, a searing ripple of exquisite agony cleaving at his soul, rendering him all but out of the fight as he spun uncontrollably off outside the Emporium, smashing firmly into the remains of the footpath before slewing to a halt against a raggedy pile of rock.

Glancing across at the wrecked, human shaped body that had been shooting an array of magic in her direction only moments earlier, lying there amongst a pile of broken wooden beams, briefly Earth wondered whether or not to finish him off. Tempted, (well you would be wouldn't you if you were that sick and twisted,) instead she decided to make sure he wouldn't present any more of a problem. With a casual flick of a finger, the wicked she-witch brought down the remaining section of ceiling onto the already defeated body, filling the air with dust and debris, an overwhelming urgency nagging at her to get on and seek out her son and his friends. Scanning the immediate vicinity of the ruined building through burning fires and thick black smoke, evil personified struggled to understand why she couldn't find any trace of the supernatural stamp she'd sprinkled her kin with.

'Odd,' was all she could think, standing amongst her dystopian surroundings.

Aghast at the startling turnaround of events, sure that only a second or two earlier her allies and those friends of her charge, who still remained protected and hidden beneath the well used mattress somewhere in the middle of all the wreckage, had things well under control, the presence imbued into the very shop itself discovered a new found respect for the disgusting being that stood amongst everything she considered hers. Stomach churning might well have described her actions, but the display of magic and dexterity was nothing short of outstanding, characteristics of truly one of the most capable magic users Zarenkesia had ever come across in her over extended life. With that in mind and not wanting to be discovered, Gee Tee's partner for so many years reined in her essence, hoping not to be detected, using only the faintest sliver of magic to keep the new owner of the Emporium as safe as she possibly could. Metaphorically holding her breath, she waited to see what would happen next.

Something or someone, she concluded, had eradicated any trace of the magic she'd marked her son with. It was the only possible explanation as to why there was no sign of him. Cursing her bad luck, her temper flared wanting nothing more than to lash out. A rare bout of sanity encouraged her not to, instead instilling a sense of urgency, partly because time was ticking down, providing her insane other half had fulfilled his part in their dastardly deal. Getting no sense that her traitorous and weak offspring had scarpered in any direction and absolutely certain that he'd been here shortly before she'd turned up, Earth knew there must be another explanation. But what? Some type of escape route... it could only be that and nothing else. What would it look like, that was the question.

And then she had it. Underground, of course... there was simply nowhere else to go. Pissed beyond belief, striding about, Fredric's crazed daughter kicked out at everything, booting rocks, books, remnants of bookcases and even the odd fire or two, causing bright red, orange and yellow embers to ignite the smog filled air, tiny cinders floating like feathers back to the ruined floor.

It didn't take long for Zarenkesia to realise exactly what had happened and that evil incarnate had discovered their ruse. Okay, she might not have known exactly where the others had disappeared to, but there was some comprehension that it was underground. And unfortunately, as she circled the smouldering surroundings, she was coming precariously close to discovering Tank's hidden position, which was something the Emporium's essence just couldn't have. Making the toughest choice of her hugely long life, Zarenkesia took the only course of action available to her and let the magic disguising the entrance to the underground vault slowly drift away, revealing its location in all its glory, in an effort to protect her seriously ill young ward.

Kicking yet one more blasted mound of burning wood into submission, taking minor comfort from the shimmering heat and roaring flames licking the bottom of her boots, extraordinarily, from out of absolutely nowhere, an opening the likes of which she'd never seen became apparent in an area she'd already traversed. Immediately it set alarm bells ringing deep within her mind... well, it would, wouldn't it, especially if you're that paranoid. But what it did do was keep her well away from a discarded old mattress that appeared both unloved and lost. Once again pressured by time, Peter's mother and queen of all things immoral, strolled casually across to said access point, momentarily hovering over the darkened, shadow soaked hole that had appeared as if from nowhere. Sure that this was where her prey had gone, with all other thoughts banished from her psyche, wanting nothing more than to end her weakling son's life and that of those he loved, Earth did the only thing she could and leapt into the obscurity below.

Mortified at the course of action she'd taken the Emporium's magical presence could only comfort herself with the fact that she'd already reactivated the vault's supernatural defences in the wake of Polkinghorne, Peter and Janice's mad dash for survival. In theory it should stop the princess of pain in her tracks... IN THEORY! Practice though, that was another matter entirely.

# 13 AS LUCK WOULD HAVE IT

In an effort for a little privacy, the three had not so much stepped back, as floated off to one side, their demeanours bleak, optimism in short supply.

*"What do you think he means by lifeblood?"* Luck whispered, although why, who knew given that Novus had the capability to listen in to everything going on across the planet.

*"I'm not really sure,"* Time put in, her distress at discovering just how battered, bruised and run down the sentience of the earth itself had become clear for the other two to see.

*"I have some thoughts on that,"* Fate interrupted, the cogs in her mind spinning faster than a supercar's tyres on launch.

*"Do tell,"* begged Luck, keen to hear her associate's take on things.

*"The metal... the one the dragons use to bolster their supernatural abilities and the strength of their telepathic connections... what was it called again?"*

*"Laminium,"* Time interjected.

*"That's right... laminium. I think it's all to do with that."*

*"Really? I thought Novus' magic was tied up in the ley lines that crisscross the planet."*

*"It is,"* Fate continued, *"but hear me out. The mana flowing through the ley lines has across millennia gradually seeped into the ground where it winds up being attracted, for whatever reason, to the laminium, steadily building up in high enough concentrations that it offers these wonderful ability enhancing properties to any and all that live in the domain. Across time they've thrown life, limb and a serious amount of wealth to get their hands on it. Throughout their reign dominating as the apex predator, I would surmise nearly all that metal has been mined, in fact I would guess very little still resides in its natural form in the earth itself. What if the laminium is the lifeblood Novus is talking about?"*

*"But…"*

As a three, still watching the weary, wiry old form of the planet's sentience from a distance, they considered what had just been said. Was it possible? Could the extraction of the laminium across the course of the world's history have removed so much of his intrinsic magic that it had weakened Novus to the point of no return? Not only could he not perform the parlour tricks he'd been renowned for in his early days, saving animals, humans and dragons alike with his god-like powers from potentially fatal mistakes through no small fault of their own, but he now found himself at a critical point, one from which there might be no coming back.

*"Do you get a sense that's what's happened?"* Time asked, looking Fate directly into what passed for eyes.

Luck listened in intently.

Stretching out using all her mysticism, Fate attempted to absorb the entire planet, quite a feat even for one as influential and dominating as herself. Rolling across grassy hills and craggy cliffs, wriggling sublimely through deserts and snow covered plains, scouring ocean floors and white hot summits of the highest mountains, in an extraordinary exploit like no other before it, for but a brief moment she was everywhere all at once.

Sensing what was happening, Luck and Time gave her all the room she needed.

It felt like her essence was dough and had been over extended when it had been rolled out, thin to the point of being almost non-existent. Dangerous couldn't begin to cover what she was doing. Still she pushed on. It felt really strange, especially since she supposedly knew everything. Okay, not quite everything, because from a celestial point of view, that just wasn't possible, Novus's dilemma being a prime example of that, but everything else earthly and otherwise she should have known. But not about the laminium and she supposed that was because it was intertwined so closely with the planet itself. Okay… it might have been because previously she'd have been more concerned with the everyday struggle of humanity and dragonkind, looking on as individuals battled precarious circumstances, wagering whether or not they'd bitten off more than they could chew or whether they would overcome adversity and whatever plight they were facing... enjoyable times to say the least, but very far from the here and now.

Blanketing the entire world, Fate slowly let herself sink into its mass, through lava flows, mighty wild water rapids, gorgeous green sunlit prairies, blossoming wild flower meadows, murky swamps, glistening snowdrifts, tropical rainforests and everything in between. Absorbing all that beauty, from the splendour of the sounds to the sumptuousness of the exotic scents, was a wonder to behold and in that moment changed the way this particular Providence would view the world from here on in, however long that might be.

Pinching herself, metaphorically speaking, Fate pushed aside her momentary lapse and got back to the task at hand, searching for the metal so precious to every dragon on the planet.

There... microscopic sparkling nuggets in a remote hillside in deepest Siberia.

Again... the tiniest sliver in a far-flung part of the Amazon.

More... minute chunks in a remote, blazingly hot part of Australia.

There... a handful of bits atop a mountain in coldest Norway.

Aha... miniscule pieces beneath a Fjord in Argentina.

And so it continued, a sprinkling of laminium discovered across the remotest destinations throughout the globe beneath the ground. However, there wasn't nearly as much as she'd thought there would be, as her expectations had been well and truly tempered by Novus' dire condition. Buried deep across the entire planet, there couldn't have been much more than a couple of hundred kilograms, which in comparison with what would have been there at the beginning was just a drop in the ocean. Only now was it becoming evident where the issue really lay and just how sizeable the problem was.

About to gather herself up and return to the other Providences, Fate realised there was one thing left to do. It was all well and good knowing how little laminium remained within the earth itself and the constrictions of the ley lines, but for her to appreciate the true scale of things and just maybe come up with a solution, they had to know where the remainder of the metal resided. And so allowing her essence to slowly drift upwards, the decider of destinies and fickle finger of fortunes settled at first throughout the dragon domain, and then across the human occupied surface. Of course it didn't take a genius to realise just where the bulk of the mineralised magic lay... the dragons' underground world! There were deposits in secure sites such as Cropptech throughout the earth in the hands of the developed apes, but not on the scale of that in the underground domain of the prehistoric protectors. The balls for their favourite sport alone accounted for over eighty percent of the entire planet's worth of the stuff and that was before you even got down to the trinkets, trophies and artefacts like Fredric's dagger. Dragon kind had well and truly plundered the globe and could well be considered responsible for its demise, and that's without the nuclear missile heading towards the monorail test borehole in northern France and Manson's obscene objective. Without a moment to lose, Fate returned to the others.

*"It's the laminium,"* she stated.

*"Are you sure?"*

*"Almost certainly."*

*"Almost?"* enquired Time the most sceptical of the three.

*"Why don't we ask him to be sure,"* suggested Luck, the most pragmatic of them.

Across their shared bond they reached a consensus and

as one glided back over towards the broken apparition that represented the earth's awareness.

"*Novus,*" Fate whispered softly not wanting to startle the once gentle giant. "*Novus... please answer me. We need your help in confirming something we suspect to be true.*"

"*Uhhhhhh...*" he continued to whimper, looking as though the life had been entirely sucked out of him.

Starting to lose her patience, never a good sign, on that I think we can all agree, the purveyor of prophecies and deliverer of doom abruptly became overwhelmed. "*NOVUS!*" She barked. "*Snap out of it... NOW! WE NEED YOUR HELP!*"

Metaphysically rolling over and sitting up, having been lying face down before, the pained presence looking and feeling gaunt turned to face that which had scolded him.

"*I feel so...*"

"*NO!*" she commanded softly, "*you don't. Being what you are, you want to help, we know that. Now please, answer this question. It might save us a great deal of time and all of us in the end.*"

Figuratively his essence nodded.

"*The lifeblood you talked about... is it the metal the dragons and humans refer to as laminium?*"

"*Yes,*" he murmured in a low voice.

Having what they feared confirmed, the Providences all looked across at each other, before Fate reeled off another question.

"*Novus... is it possible to restore you back to full health?*"

"*M... m... maybe,*" he stammered.

"*What's the quickest and most efficient way?*"

Silence.

"*NOVUS!*"

"*Laminium... earth's core!*"

Momentary delight flooded across the small tight knit group that is until they realised the magnitude of the task before them.

"*How the hell are we supposed to...?*" started Time, more than a little negatively.

But she was beaten to it by Fate, the by now de facto leader of this impromptu gaggle of god-like individuals.

*"Unbelievable,"* she smiled, turning to face lady Luck.

*"What is it?"*

*"There might just be a way."*

*"And?"*

*"I would suggest it involves one of your favourites."*

*"Favourites!"* spat Time. *"I thought we weren't allowed favourites."*

*"We're not supposed to,"* added Fate, *"but that's never stopped this one."*

*"Oh come on, you know you favour him too. His courage, selflessness and outright refusal to die matched with the most extraordinary of daring deeds that could well be his signature, make him stand out... one being amongst billions,"* ventured Luck in a soft honeyed voice, her demeanour now slightly gooey, the thought of this brave adventurer almost a little too much.

*"And just how is he supposed to help?"* Time cried, her worry at their apparent impending doom now all too clear.

*"Because,"* Fate chipped in, *"right at this very moment he finds himself in exactly the wrong place, and if you'll excuse me... at exactly the wrong TIME."*

*"Yes... but he's renowned for doing the impossible."*

*"The impossible is one thing, but this is something else altogether."*

Impossible, improbable or just downright unlikely... for the Providences things were just about to get very interesting, especially now they had skin in the game.

"The missile," reported the weapons officer dispassionately, "has engaged in re-entry. Time to target... three minutes ten seconds."

Still clinging on to the overhead bar, feet spread firmly apart to counteract the angle at which the futuristic submarine was plummeting towards deeper water, somewhere within his wicked and evil psyche Manson chuckled manically, icy cold water running down his spine making him feel ALIVE, something he and everyone else inhabiting the planet wouldn't be for very much longer.

Abruptly he was startled back to reality by one of the dedicated crew whose only job it was to use his inherent supernatural abilities to search for and detect threats outside the submarine itself. Not sure who to report the anomaly to, the relatively inexperienced youngster instead just blurted it out.

"Sir, sir... I'm sensing some kind of magical irregularity close by. Uhhh... no, hang on... not just one abnormality, but... two, no three... four actually."

That got the attention of the entire command crew, especially their despotic leader and all round psychopath.

Ignoring the overhead handholds, he strolled purposefully across the grated metal decks until he reached the officer.

"Identify!" he ordered.

Eyes remaining closed, swallowing nervously, this his first time in the presence of the main man himself, Jones, the name he'd been allocated for this particular mission, steadied himself and using a burst of his internal supernatural senses, stretched out from the confines of the revolutionary weapon they all found themselves trapped in, through its reinforced metal hull and out into the millions of square kilometres of dark watery matter that cast a huge weight on the submarine in every direction, the icy sense of it through his mind feeling both strange and tempting at the same time. Strange of course because of his deep down dragon DNA that due to their current circumstances had to be warped into the form of a human so that he and all the others could fit inside the overly ambitious tin can. Tempting because some of the magic he'd been using was naga in origin and linked in a most visceral way to the ocean itself, the primordial snake-like beings' home from home for tens of thousands of years, a connection of sorts shared from the very beginning.

"Beings... five of them. None human."

"Can you be any more accurate?" Manson asked, his tone all business like, any anger and rage quenched, flattened at the bottom of his stomach, all his senses overwhelmed at having gotten so close to his sick and twisted goal, the thought of anything getting in his way absolutely catastrophic.

Groomed for exactly these circumstances, to perceive other magic users at a distance, Jones was good at his job. Wanting nothing more than to be as certain as possible, after a couple of awkward moments he delivered his opinion.

"If I'm not mistaken there are four nagas close by and one dragon."

"Interesting..." Manson murmured.

"Sire?"

Recognising that he wouldn't be able to do it to the same standard himself, the dark and twisted leader piped up.

"Is there any way to share with me what you can sense?"

"Better... I think," Jones replied grabbing the would-be king's hand, much to his surprise.

Instantly Manson's mind was filled with a deep inky blackness that extended out in every direction. Shaking off the panic that tore through his intellect at the momentary thought of some kind of trap, the conniving king of criminality took a long slow breath and opened up all his being in the hope of gaining some insight into what was happening only a short way away.

*"Did Fredric leave you with any instructions?"* a strange but compelling voice whispered through the mind of Vimes.

It took him a moment to realise the words belonged to the naga king.

*"Uhhh... it was Flash actually."*

*"My saviour during the battle at the dragon king's private residence... what did he say?"*

*"To seal the hatches so that no more missiles can be fired and to keep an eye on that metal monstrosity wherever it goes."*

*"Wise words!"*

*"Indeed. What are you thinking we should do?"*

*"Flash's advice is fine for now, but we do need to come up with some way to contain the magic of those trapped inside, and also any and all nuclear material belonging to the submarine. If any of it escapes even by accident, it would be a disaster for the marine life, humankind and the planet itself, something we just can't let happen."*

Across their link Vimes added his agreement, although what they were going to do about it was anyone's guess. That, however, wasn't the only thing on his mind. There were two others... his love, Polkinghorne, what she was up to and whether or not she was safe. And more importantly, a problem that could have catastrophic consequences for each and every one of them, as well as the world itself... the nuclear missile that had already been launched, the one his friend, the former Crimson Guard had gone chasing off after. Logic, common sense and the laws of plain old physics told him that Flash didn't have a hope in hell of getting to the impact point before the weapon exploded, but that didn't stop the former *tor* from believing. If there was one being on the planet who could outrun Fate and give Destiny a bloody nose, it was his pal, the one who'd gone above and beyond when Christmas had been in crisis some years before, saving not only Santa, but the festival and even hope itself. If anyone stood a chance of stopping the devastating destruction destined for the planet, it was the brave, courageous and inventive dragon agent.

Standing out like the Millenium Falcon in an armada of Starfleet ships, Manson instantly recognised the aura of one of the four nagas swimming someway off the forward bow of the submarine... VASUKI!

'Damn that blasted naga,' he thought, trying to maintain his composure, desperate for the crew he shared the confined space with to think him cool and calm under pressure. After all, he was their supposed king. If it were any other being out there, he wouldn't have been nearly so panicked, but he was more than a little flustered. Well... you would be, wouldn't you, especially if you were the one responsible for them being captured and then imprisoned in that icy hellhole for over eight miserable decades. You'd be thinking that they might just be harbouring the tiniest of grudges. How that would manifest itself was anyone's guess.

"Sire?"

"Sorry White Wings. What was that again?"

"Should we not tell those stationed here exactly what's at stake? They deserve to know the full scope of what's happening."

Lost deep in thought, staring up at the different levels of the newly rebuilt private residence that he thought of as his own, George, trying to put aside his concern for all those that he loved, considered his colleague's question as his mind pondered the future and just what that vile, disgusting projectile crashing into northern France would mean for the entire populous of the planet.

"What difference would it make?"

"They'd know the truth, maybe have time to contact their loved ones, send out a warning..."

"Spread panic you mean!"

"Majesty?"

"You'd like me to tell them all what we suspect to be true... that the planet itself is in danger? Stop them from doing their jobs, just as those we have out there are doing theirs, trying desperately hard to find a solution, even, if I know them, ready to lay down their lives in an effort to stop this once and for all."

"Si..."

"NO!" hissed George. "Not happening, not now, not on my watch. Spreading the word about a truth that we're only guessing about anyway will do no one any good, least of all those here. To a dragon... we work! Continue and give those trying to deal with this as much information as we can, as well as a chance. It's what we're here for and all that we can do. If we don't stand firm and work together, we might as well have handed that BASTARD the planet anyway."

"Sire... I'm so sorry."

Letting out a deep sigh, George tapped into all his experience and training, disappointed with himself for losing his rag with his friend at this crucial point in proceedings.

"It's me that should apologise to you, my friend... I'm sorry. The pressure of what's going on... it's taking a toll on all of us. Please... let's just do what we can to aid those on the ground. Our support might be the difference between winning and losing, destruction and survival."

"I understand, Majesty. I'll make sure they're all on it, right to the very last."

"Good dragon. We might prevail yet."

White Wings bounded up into the air, disappearing off behind the balcony on the third floor within a split second, determined to rally his troops and get the most out of them right until the very end.

# 15 A HOLE LOTTA PRESSURE

Standing proud amongst a landscape of debris that up until a couple of minutes ago had been the infrastructure of the test bore hole site in northern France, Flash had his eyes closed. His head was tilted towards the sky and the incoming threat of the nuclear missile that had been launched less than ten minutes earlier from Manson's sub from the cool, choppy waters off the coast of Scotland. To one side, Amelia stood looking on at the dragon she loved amongst Yoyo, Rose and their group of talented, out of the box thinking youngsters who'd assisted in no short order in getting them this far.

Throughout the entirety of his life, from his difficult upbringing, to finding purpose in the King's Guards and ultimately reaching the pinnacle of servitude, in his mind anyhow, by becoming a leading light in the elite, shadowy force that was the Crimson Guards, founded by George's best friend, Fredric, all those years ago, Dendrik Ridge, Flash to his friends, had never found himself under as much pressure as right at this very moment. Literally, he had the weight of the world on his shoulders.

Moving faster than any dragon ever had on leaving the gorgeous glens of Scotland, due in no small part to some unusual magic appropriated by George's best friend, before he'd gotten out of range, Fredric had passed on a series of supernatural equations that might just help him to get ahead of the nuclear menace that threatened to tear the planet apart. Naga in design, Flash could only assume that his ally, Vasuki, had freely given over the secret details of his race's ability to transport themselves halfway across the world in the blink of an eye. More interesting was the fact that the naga leader had included how to calculate the destination coordinates to a point well outside the earth's atmosphere. That meant that if he got it right, it might be possible to open up a wormhole in front of the approaching missile and transport it to a point in space, negating not only the danger from the nuclear fallout, but from the explosion that combined with all the laminium in the test borehole had the potential to rip the world apart. IF HE GOT IT RIGHT! Currently his extensive and brilliant mind was grappling with how to do just that, a challenge given the millions of calculations required, the unfamiliar type of magic involved and the sheer amount of mana needed to pull off such a thing. The title of one particular Queen song played over and over deep within his head as if to emphasise everything threatening to spiral out of control.

"Is there anything we can do to help, my boy?" Yoyo shouted from off to one side, concerned about interrupting his friend's concentration but well aware that he might need assistance.

NOTHING! The former Crimson Guard was too lost in what he was attempting to do.

"FLASH!" echoed a familiar voice, one that finally had enough gravitas to pull him from his work.

Stuttering back to reality, intellect still full of workings out and equations, he turned to face his friends and the dragon he'd only recently realised he'd come to love.

"What's going on, Flash?" the more than capable captain asked as dispassionately as she could, given the circumstances.

With all the others watching eagerly, he tried to explain as best he could.

"There's a way... to stop that thing. I just have to get my head around all the information I've been given in order to do just that."

"How?" Yoyo was first to ask.

"A naga wormhole, hopefully transporting it into outer space."

Surprise and hope spread amongst them all.

"What can we do?" Amelia asked softly, her tone reflecting her love for him.

"If I need to borrow some mana, you'll all have to open up to me. But honestly, I don't think that'll be the issue."

"Then what is?" stated Tarko this time.

"The calculations are off the chart complicated. I've never seen anything like them. If I don't get it right, if I can't get the wormhole to open at exactly the correct time in the direct flight path of that thing, then…"

"Let us help," urged Rose more cheerfully than she had any right to be, especially with everything going on around them.

"I…"

"Send us what you have, Flash," Monty insisted, his confidence and smile infectious.

Running out of time and really not sure this was a good idea, it was the slightest of nods from his pal Yoyo that convinced the former Crimson Guard that he was doing the right thing. Extending out his consciousness, he shared everything he had with them all, from Yoyo and Rose to Amelia and the youngsters. In but a few moments it was done, and now there was no going back.

Individually they all stood stock still, resembling statues at a prehistoric theme park, each processing what they'd just learnt, using all their extraordinary intellects to try and wrap their heads around the nagas' complex, mysterious and normally guarded supernatural spells.

For Amelia, Yoyo and Rose, just like Flash before them, the math and magic involved appeared mindboggling to say the least, four or five steps above even the most complex mantras they'd ever seen, because of the moving target and weather conditions involved, and that was saying quite something given their collective experience. The thought of conjuring up a wormhole with a diameter only a few centimetres bigger than the projectile itself, in mid-air, somewhere on the same trajectory as the nuclear missile travelling at over 21,000 kilometres an hour, was a damn sight more than daunting, particularly when they would only get one shot at it. One shot to save not only themselves and their loved ones, but also every single living creature on the earth itself. If you thought revising for that test, prepping for that job interview or applying for that promotion was stressful, show a little compassion for these heroes in this moment. Things don't get any tougher.

Unlike their more mature counterparts, the band of young dragons that included Tina, Monty, Trayrin, Tarko, Zebediah, Essie, Bullhorn and Thadeous were absolutely buzzing within the telepathic link they shared. Not only had their curiosity been piqued, but they'd been truly wowed by the information flashing before their eyes, the complexity of the naga spell beyond fascinating to each of them, their minds and pulses racing despite looking like figurines in a diorama.

*"I've got my head around the destination coordinates,"* Tarko piped up, the first to say anything, startling at least a couple of the others from the majesty of what they were seeing for the first time.

*'I know how to efficiently channel the ethereal energy to maximise the diameter of the wormhole,"* added Zebediah.

*"Precisely locating the aperture in the path of the missile should be a breeze,"* Essie contributed, *"with all of us working together."*

This is how it continued, together able to exceed the sum of their parts by some considerable margin.

"What are they doing?" Flash asked, his concern evident as time continued to count down, the flaming trail of destructiveness above their heads getting ever closer.

About to answer her new found love, Amelia was beaten to it by her friend.

"They're brainstorming," Rose put in, "and if you know what's good for you, you'll let them continue."

About to respond in a very undiplomatic manner, out of the corner of his eye Flash just caught Yoyo shaking his head in warning. It was enough to render him silent for the time being.

Across the youngsters' familiar bond, Tina had stepped into the role of leader, breaking down tasks individually, assigning duties and making sure those with specific skill sets were placed where they could be most effective. Decisions taken, all the well oiled parts of the machine were put firmly in place, whilst the others continued to dream about any number of added variables, the young dragon leader knew she had to separate herself from them momentarily in an effort to inform the others of what they'd come up with. Cutting off her mind from the mental clutter and noise, Tina approached Yoyo and Rose, looking for all the moral support they could offer.

"And?" asked Rose, sure that as a group they would have by now worked the problem and come up with the most effective solution.

"We've got it!"

"What?" Flash exclaimed incredulously.

"As a team," the youngster declared, "we've come together to understand everything you've passed on. I've assigned individual roles so everyone knows what they're doing. We've got this."

Staggered, the former Crimson Guard didn't know what to do with this information. Luckily his love was there to reassure him.

"Flash... I've seen what they can do together. They're unconventional, perhaps even a little immature, but above all they are... BRILLIANT! If they say they can do this, then you should believe them wholeheartedly."

Knowing that with time running out, he'd struggle to even attempt such a complicated rescue on his own, Flash had little choice but to acknowledge what he'd just been told and let the youngsters take charge. There were, however, some conditions, something Yoyo could see right through straight away.

"You'll have to include all of us in your link," the experienced healer announced.

"Of course," Tina responded.

"And... you'll have to show us what you have planned before you implement your scheme," Rose insisted.

"Okay."

"Let's do that now, shall we?" suggested Amelia with a wry grin spread out across her prehistoric face.

Closing her eyes, Tina informed her brothers and sisters what was going to happen, before extending out the link to the other four more sage members of their small team.

As each one joined, the shock on their faces became ever more apparent and increasingly intense.

'What the...?' was all that Flash could offer on seeing the plan floating about in the ether. It consisted of all the information he'd passed on about the naga spell, but it was now broken down into tiny little parcels of data, ripe for each individual to use in their own way.

*"See... I told you,"* a soft, reassuring, full of love voice, one he hoped to share a future with, whispered across his consciousness.

*"They certainly seem to know what they're doing,"* he replied to Amelia's private correspondence.

Concerted chuckling from an array of different voices echoed around the shared mental space.

*"Uhhh... you do know that they can hear you, don't you?"* mused Rose, stifling a laugh.

*"Uhhh..."*

*"It's nice to know we have your full confidence,"* joked Tina, trying to lighten the mood.

*"I meant no disrespect."*

*"We know,"* chimed Thadeous still chuckling.

*"I think that's enough,"* echoed Yoyo, trying to get things back on track, like the others only too aware of the roaring engines overhead getting eminently closer with every second that passed.

*"Tina!"* beseeched Rose, *"can you explain to those of us struggling to wrap our heads around all this, how you plan to proceed?"*

*"Sure."*

She outlined each individual's part in the process, expanding on how they'd calculated the precise coordinates for not only the outer space destination, but more importantly placing the wormhole directly in the path of the nuclear monstrosity. Resembling a kindergarten class being taught maths by a university lecturer, Yoyo and Rose beamed with pride at just how far the ragtag bunch of supposed misfits had come. With them in charge, the earth's fate was in safe hands, as far as the married couple were concerned.

Flash and Amelia couldn't find anything to contradict that.

In a deserted, bin littered back alley behind a row of huge expensive family houses, three speeding blurs skidded to a halt, surrounded by a hail of miniscule bright blue forks of lightning, their appearance a surprise, not least to each of them.

"Are we far enough away?"

"I think so," replied Jar Man to his diminutive friend.

Steel fought to catch his breath, the appropriation of his new human form taking a toll both magically and physically. Standing tall, spine arched as far back as it would go, he interlocked his fingers behind his head in an effort to pull in the biggest possible lungful of air.

"Aren't you supposed to be one of the top tier athletes on the planet?" quipped DomCon, sarcastically.

"Bite me!"

"Only if I can transform back first."

Jar Man stood there shaking his head, wondering just how the other two could joke around at a time like this.

"I think that's probably enough guys, don't you?"

The glares disappeared as both Steel and the pocket rocket turned to face their ginger friend.

"What now?" the laminium ball captain asked, his concentration split between controlling his breathing, maintaining his false human form and trying to decipher a way forward.

"Back to the domain?" enquired DomCon, sure that was

the best course of action.

With his pals looking to him for a definitive decision, the gentle giant considered the possibilities. Should they disappear back underground or was there still more to be done here? After all, they'd managed to successfully pull all those children from the rubble, getting them the medical attention that they so desperately needed, effectively saving their lives. Alright, they'd displayed some of their supernatural in doing so, but needs must when lives are on the line. And that was the crux of the matter... LIVES!

"How are you doing with your new form?" he asked Captain Fantastic.

"I'm devoting a whole lot of my concentration to keeping it stable, perhaps more than I'm comfortable with, but I'm okay. It's an interesting experience to say the least."

"Good to know," observed Jar Man.

"What are you thinking?" DomCon asked his friend.

"I'm wondering if we shouldn't stick around on the surface and see if there's anywhere else we can ply our supernatural trade and help out."

"Is that wise?" Steel wondered out loud.

"The devastation in some places is nothing short of horrific. If we can help, then we probably should. I know there's the case about revealing our magic, but I say that be damned! What do you say?"

Simultaneously, they both replied,

"I'm in!"

# 16 CHASE THE ACE

Killing their magically enhanced speed, sliding to a halt on the debris laden path just outside the Emporium, Fredric, laminium dagger tucked into the back of his pants, and Richie entered side by side, both on edge as you'd expect given who they were hunting, tempers quelled fleetingly by common sense. How long that would last was anyone's guess.

Doubled up as a team out of necessity, each individually stretched out with their inherent supernatural abilities, both different in nature due in no small part to their previous experiences. Richie, now The White Dragon, was stuck in human form, but was still a more than capable magic user although clearly lacking the ability to transform into her old primordial state or take flight. Fredric was the more knowledgeable, his know-how and improvisation skills second to none, his past recklessness tempered to some degree by his time imprisoned in Antarctica, but as you can probably guess, not necessarily when it came to this subject... hunting his daughter Earth. He wanted nothing more than to end her life for all the pain and misery she'd created across her time roaming the planet. And that was the rub you see, because they were close, DAMN CLOSE!

Sharing a glance through the twisting grey smoke that swamped what was left of the underground capital, the two allies who'd had their share of disagreements, (well, humdingers actually) stalked deeper into the remnants of the shop, utterly gobsmacked at the damage, each wondering how on earth their prey could have done this in such a short space of time. After all, they'd been right on her tail. This kind of devastation was... unimaginable.

Abruptly both were startled by a small, low groan coming from beneath a pile of wood in one corner of the wreckage.

"Uhhhh…"

Turning to face in that direction, supernatural defences at the ready, the brown, curly haired superstar lacrosse player glimpsed part of an arm and a hand sticking out through the tiniest of gaps in the timber. Even in the darkest pitch black, she'd have recognised it, or at least who it belonged to anywhere... HOOK!

With the agility and guile born of her chosen sport, she was over there in an instant, pulling off twisted remnants of the structure that had for so long kept the Emporium in check.

"Oh my God! My love... what the hell happened?"

With parts of his body on absolute fire, an exquisite agony coursing through bone and muscle alike, the courageous rugby player managed to flutter his eyes on hearing the voice of the being he loved most on this planet. At first fearing it was a dream, he dismissed what his eyes revealed as reality, but as she leaned in close and he could just make out the sweet smell of her breath, only then did he know for certain that she'd arrived not quite in the nick of time.

"R... R... R... Rich," he gasped.

"My darling... what are... why... what…?"

Struggling to swallow, Hook tried to find the words he needed to explain what had happened. Due in no small part to his injuries, he could not. However, his temporary partner could, despite still reeling from the magic used against him.

"Boy am I glad to see you," announced a well-known voice, one that instilled both optimism and fear at the same time.

"For'son?" Fredric questioned from just behind where Richie had knelt down to deal with her other half.

"Of course."

"What on earth are you doing with Hook?"

'A good question,' Richie thought, still unburdening her love of all the considerable debris, 'and perhaps one I should have asked sooner.'

"I... I... I... Zarenkesia, please can you tell them what went on?"

About to ask what the hell a Zarenkesia was, Fredric and Richie both jumped back against what remained of the far shop wall as the dull yellow image of a full sized dragon sprang into being not far from Hook's position.

Fearing they'd been led into a trap, the formidable pair ignited their defensive shields and let their offensive magic thrum to the fore. Sickeningly sparking forks of blood red lightning appeared atop Richie's fingernails, crackling away ready to fulfil her wicked desires whatever they should be, whilst thick, acid green tendrils of poison snaked their way from wrist to fingertip on both of Fredric's hands, waiting patiently to be dispatched towards the nearest enemy.

"Ahhh... the father and The White Dragon!"

Within touching distance, Fredric didn't bother to waste any of his ethereal energy, instead instinctively choosing to lead with an almighty roundhouse kick imbued to the hilt with supernatural energy, a formidable attack and one that would have downed almost any opponent.

But of course he wasn't facing an opponent. Whistling through the smoky space, his foot, instead of making any sort of contact, found only thin air, forcing him off balance and dumping him unceremoniously on the uneven floor.

Agog, it took The White Dragon a split second to react, launching a furious barrage of sparkling branch-like salvos directly into the midriff of the entirely dull yellow dinosaur lookalike. Surprisingly, to her at least, the attack travelled straight through its target, sparking and arcing, rebounding and bouncing around against one of the few remaining stone pillars left supporting the building in a kaleidoscope of rainbow reds and sumptuous salsas.

What the...?

"Desist!" shouted For'son, over the crystal clear crackling and ricocheting of ethereal energy.

"But..."

"She's a friend," insisted the enigmatic band, from the still buried hand of the rugby player.

"And not real," added a melodic voice from every direction. "At least not in this particular form anyway."

After yet one more glance in each other's direction, both Richie and Peter's grandfather turned to face the dull yellow depiction of a dragon that on closer inspection appeared to be hovering about ten centimetres off the ground. In the rush and their concerted efforts to attack, they'd failed to notice that. Slowly the beast, or rather, hologram in question, turned to face them. It was most disconcerting.

"My name," continued the depiction, "is Zarenkesia, as you've already gathered and my presence has been imbued within the walls of the Emporium for over one hundred years, my undertaking to protect the proprietor and those he or she deems worthy."

'Wow!' thought Richie, seeming to recall Tank mentioning the name now that she came to think of it.

"If you're designed to protect the Emporium and everyone in it, then how come this is what's left? If you don't mind me saying, you don't appear to have done a very bang up job," Fredric criticised, his temper threatening to get the better of him.

Common sense prevailing hadn't lasted very long at all.

"We were taken by surprise," the shop's magical essence replied wistfully, recalling the events of the last hour, "by a brute of a dragon, Manson's second in command if I'm not mistaken, a veteran magic user by the name of Mas-crate, a being who'd accrued a whole host of ancient and unusual enchantments."

This told them about the assailant, all that remained now was the how.

"His abilities were like nothing I've ever faced in both the magnitude of power and the unusual type involved."

'NAGA!' both Fredric and The White Dragon thought at the same time.

"Long story short... we faced off, he decimated the shop

before we'd even had a chance to recognise the threat, after which he proceeded to try and kill everyone inside."

"Who was here?" Richie asked, full of fear and worry.

"Tank, Tail bearer, Hook, Polkinghorne, the human... Janice, Fu-ts'ang and For'son," she stated very dispassionately.

"Tail bearer?" Fredric remarked.

"Sorry... Bentwhistle!"

"Peter, Tank, Janice and Polks... where are they all now?" the lacrosse player asked frantically.

"Peter, Janice and Polkinghorne escaped into the depths of the vault in order to outrun the one known as Earth."

Richie breathed a sigh of relief, before remembering to ask.

"And Tank?"

Fredric and The White Dragon turned at the sound of rubble and debris being shaken about, stones, rock and splinters of wood thrown off the dirty and covered mattress, as it slowly twisted around to reveal a yellow shrouded supernatural shield beneath which lay... TANK!

"Oh my God!" exclaimed the lacrosse player, bounding over, forgetting all about Hook who was still trying to extricate himself from everything that had fallen on top of him.

"Tank," she whispered, stretching out her hand towards his face, only to find it blocked by Zarenkesia's unique blend of magic.

"Remove the shield!" she demanded.

"NO!" came the reply, ringing out across what remained of the Emporium.

About to explode, the anger and rage at seeing one of her two best friends so near to death almost too much, the presence of the shop stopped her in her tracks, its voice this time a much more comforting and softer tone.

"After being trapped under what remained of the bridge outside by the monster Mas-crate, he was diagnosed with a bleed on the brain. With no other choice, I had to put him in an induced coma to keep him safe and prolong his life. That's where we are now. To remove my protective measures would significantly increase the chance of him dying, something I won't allow at this time. I would have thought you of all people would respect that. My primary directive is to keep the owner of this place safe at all costs, no matter what it takes and who it affects."

Gazing down through the tinted yellow glow into her best friend's ashen, lifeless face gave the lacrosse superstar pause for thought.

"Oh... Tank," she murmured in a low voice, a tear slipping seamlessly from her left eye, passing across a number of the freckles on her beautiful pale face before diving to the rubble strewn floor.

"I give you my word, vixen of righteousness, that I will do all in my considerable power to keep him alive and safe in an effort to rally against the prophecy."

"PROPHECY!" declared Fredric from the back of the shop aghast at the use of that bloody word, more than a little aware of just how misleading and troublesome such things could be. "WHAT PROPHECY?"

From somewhere outside a quivering voice interjected.

"We discovered a new prophecy related to The White Dragon in a diary cast aside within the Emporium," Fu-ts'ang quaked, hovering into view, his normal coat of glistening rotating frost missing from the outskirts of his shining blade.

"Fu-ts'ang!" Richie exclaimed, instantly jumping to her feet. "Are you okay?"

"I suffered some damage but I remain able to function to some degree."

"Tell us about the prophecy, weapon smith," Fredric commanded.

"Tank wanted some help in tidying the shop. Janice consented to do just that with a few stacks of magical volumes, knowing she couldn't trip any of the supernatural inside them. I acted as a buffer and translator. All proceeded as planned, that is until she found a totally blank tome that she wished to keep. Putting it to one side, shortly afterwards she cut her hand, the blood from which dripped onto the blank pages of the book which she hoped would be hers. That contact sparked a chain reaction, instantly revealing the full text from a bygone era."

"And?"

"The book in question was a diary, one that had belonged to Artorius the Seer."

"CRAP!" blurted George's best friend.

"Indeed," Fu-ts'ang put in.

"Am I correct in thinking that he's never made a prediction that hasn't come true?" the lacrosse player asked.

"As far as it's known, that's correct," ventured the timeless weapon smith.

It was left to Fredric to ask the question on everyone's mind.

"What did it say?"

"It talked of a great battle, humming birds, the loss of power, the appearance of a conjoined two and how after a devastating loss, The White Dragon steps up to save the day, which I think we can all agree refers to what we all experienced and the death of Tim."

Just the mere mention of his name set her off, goose bumps riddling her arms, a cold chill settling down her spine, memories of their brief time together flashing across her subconscious, from making out in the cold cellar just before the explosion that destroyed the clubhouse, their illicit encounter on the Swanage railway, to their almost picture perfect romantic get away in the stunning city of Florence, Italy. The recollections cut like a knife twisting in her gut. It took all The White Dragon's strength to remain standing and still in the game.

Fu-ts'ang continued.

"After that it goes on to say that an even greater loss awaits, stating that when The White Dragon walks the glens and confronts the dragon with three skins, the time is close at hand. One of two 'amicorum' must be sacrificed if the planet is to be saved. Still there remains no guarantee."

"Amicorum?" Richie queried.

"It means best friends," answered Fredric thoughtfully.

"So what you're saying," The White Dragon mused, wanting to be totally and utterly clear on the subject, "is that because of my trip to Scotland you think that either Tank or Peter are destined to die because of what's written in the diary belonging to Artorius?"

"It does all appear to fit," observed the former weapon smith trapped in the futuristic blade.

Closing her eyes whilst rubbing her forehead, Richie let out a huge despairing sigh, more than a little hacked off with everything they continued to face, Fate appearing to throw a spanner in the works at almost every turn. This one though, felt like the final straw. One of her two best friends set to die because of... because of what? Because of her, because of something she'd done. Had she not travelled to Scotland and tracked down Manson and Earth, would the prophecy have been voided? But... that didn't make any sense. If she hadn't gone then the evil twosome would have gotten away undetected. It was all so confusing!

A few metres away, Peter's grandfather was thinking much the same thing. Prophecies, in his experience, were just the worst, pushing and pulling at people's intellect, tugging on their heartstrings in order to get them to do what you want them to. Most terrible of all though was the fact that in most cases, they could be twisted in just about every direction to suit the needs of those who'd created them, fitting a particular point of view, a distinct lack of facts normally an industry standard, should such a thing exist. Mind games on an epic scale, that's generally what they all boiled down to.

In one humungous effort, Hook, ably assisted by For'son, extricated himself from all the rubble and debris without any assistance at all from the love of his life who stood only a short distance away, dust, stone and splinters of wood spiralling in every direction as he did so, blood trickling from numerous wounds, any number of bruises starting to blossom. Most in his position would have resented her reticence to free him and turn instead towards Tank, but not him, selfless to the very core, his concern for the rugby playing dragon who was his teammate mirroring hers. Wanting nothing more than to envelop her in his huge, well muscled arms, his sense of decency and a nagging urgency compelled him to do otherwise.

"Rich," he begged, "you need to forget about everything to do with the prophecy and all that you see around you."

In a fit of feisty frenzy she whirled around to face him, her face flushed bright red, her ire tested to its max, her affection for him momentarily quashed, the love for both her best friends shining brighter than anything in her universe in the here and now, her inherent instinct to protect both of them with every last molecule of her body.

"How dare you say…"

Stepping forward in a move that showed not only how much he cared but just how much courage he possessed, Hook placed his index finger over her lips, something I think you can agree in the circumstances and given her history, could well warrant the kind of response that might see him physically hurt. All the beings there, from Fredric to For'son, from Fu-ts'ang to Zarenkesia, watched in not only fascination, but awe at the rugby player's bold move.

"Listen," he stressed softly, "you've misconstrued what I mean. You need to ignore all this and set your focus on what's happening below us. Janice, Polkinghorne and Peter in particular need you more than ever… RIGHT NOW!"

Eyes wider than they'd ever been, distraught that she'd misjudged him so badly, her bottom lip trembled briefly against his huge sausage-like finger as her whole body shivered just slightly, all the time gazing passionately into his eyes.

"I mean it, Rich… you need to go after them now. With Peter's mother hot on their tail, their lives almost certainly depend on it."

"Uhh…"

The two sports obsessed lovebirds only had eyes for each other, a declaration of love passing between them with just a look. They truly were meant to be soul mates, something this moment confirmed beyond belief.

"The vault… tell me about it!" demanded Fredric, glancing over at the dragon hologram, expressly addressing Zarenkesia.

"It's below ground and protected by the most intricate and powerful supernatural defences on the planet."

"Really?"

"Yes."

"Expand."

"On reaching the lower level, should you make it past Olgoi, you must choose to enter a particular tunnel, one of three. If you fail to pick the correct option, you will spend the rest of your short lifespan in an unending, self-replicating labyrinth."

"Olgoi?"

"Mongolian death worms! I can protect you with a mantra that'll neutralise their poison. You must select the left hand of the three tunnels. That's the only way that leads safely to the vault proper."

"Is that it?"

"No… there's far more to it than that. Open your mind, I'll send you the details."

"Much appreciated," Fredric offered up, doing just that.

In a matter of moments, he fully understood the intricacies and magnitude of what he intended to charge head first into.

"Can I ask, what will we find when we get there?"

"Some of the former master mantra maker's most valuable possessions, the likes of which the world very rarely gets to see."

"Really?"

"YES," interrupted Fu-ts'ang, slightly more harshly than

he'd intended, his memories of what he considered an unwilling incarceration still as vivid as ever given his eidetic recall. "I was constrained there for quite some time. The artefacts and valuables are like no other collection on the planet."

"Will our friends be able to use them to defend themselves?"

"I see no reason why not."

"Good."

"You are of course assuming that your daughter gets that far," Zarenkesia chimed in, her voice echoing throughout what remained of the shop.

"That's correct!"

"The defences are exceptional, let me assure you of that, and on par with anything, anywhere else on the planet."

"I believe you."

"Then…"

"She's shown herself to be full of not only unusual magic, but a whole host of surprises, escaping situations that should be virtually impossible. I think it unwise to take for granted that she can't make it there, not full of vitriol as she is with the head of her son the prize at stake. I think we should assume that the defences might only slow her down."

"Understood. I'll keep as close an eye as I can and see if there's anything else I can do in that regard."

Focus firmly fixed on a final confrontation with his bitch of a daughter, the founder of the Crimson Guards and former Antarctic prisoner declared,

"I'm going after her right NOW!"

What he was hoping for as a response, even he didn't know. But he got one.

"I'm coming," Fu-ts'ang voiced angrily, "there's no way in hell that I'm letting that witch harm my best friend."

And that left... SILENCE!

Balanced on a knife edge, her decision was perhaps the toughest of her life. Leave her new found love, Hook and the gentle giant of a dragon, the kindest, most caring and considerate being she'd ever known and one she owed a whole lot to, Tank, in a precarious position, maybe even on death's shortlist, or go and rescue Peter, a dragon who'd been there when she'd hatched in the nursery ring all those decades ago, one who'd been her best friend across all that time, inseparable for the most part, their bond irreplaceable and more than skin deep. It broke her heart to have to choose, but in the end it came down to HIM. NO, not Bentwhistle, but Hook, the altruistic words he'd spoken, his thoughts as always centred on others, just one of the many reasons she loved him so much. Tears now streaming from her eyes, she gave him one last look before turning away for good.

"I'm in. Let's do this!" she positively roared, strolling over to join Fredric and the weapon smith trapped in the futuristic blade who appeared unusual to say the least, going into battle without his icy white coating, reminding them all of the private residence after the Changing of the Guard when he'd so nobly delivered food to all those stationed there at the kind of speed still unheard of today.

Standing on the edge of the shadowy hole that would take them all to their immediate destiny, Fredric turned to face Hook and For'son, knowing that the Emporium's enigmatic presence would be listening in.

"Look after him," he observed, nodding in the direction of Tank prone on the rubble strewn floor, still surrounded by the dull yellow magic. "And secure this place as best you can. We'll be back!"

And with that, gigantic muscles bulging, Peter's grandfather slipped seamlessly into the darkness, followed ably by the weapon smith's blade and then The White Dragon herself, not once looking back over her shoulder, the very thought of the heartbreak it would bring almost too much.

The chase was well and truly ON!

# 17 LIFE… ON THE RUN

Landing had sent a shuddering, debilitating pain rocketing up both legs, stinging both knees and forcing her down to the uneven ground. Glancing up, she found her love glaring back down at her. About to make a pithy comment or two, abruptly Peter pulled her up and away from the slippery silver pole she'd just slid along so keenly. Right in the nick of time too, because exactly then another pair of feet touched down, this time as light as a butterfly kissing a leaf, knowing exactly where the ground was from out of the darkness. Polkinghorne used the pole like a dancer, swinging around effortlessly once before somersaulting through the air and landing between the two of them. Before a word could be said, the Christmas legend extended her arm out past Peter's head, reached up behind, grabbing something neither of the other two could see.

"Well," she said, "aren't you a cutie?!"

"What the…?" stammered Peter, taking two sharp steps back in quick succession, away from the beast that now hitched a ride in one of Polk's outstretched hands.

"Oh my," gulped Janice, bravely standing her ground.

"Stroke the back of his neck. They're really quite harmless."

"Uhh… no thanks."

"Suit yourself," Santa quipped, giving the gargantuan spider a little tickle behind his head for good measure before placing him back on the rocky wall.

"I really don't think there's time for all that," Bentwhistle objected, still slightly shaken from the ride down.

"A few moments for a common courtesy is never wasted, mark my words," Polks pointed out, standing her ground.

Not wanting to argue, the hockey playing dragon

pointed at the left hand supernatural channel and with urgency in his voice suggested they needed to go. Following in his wake, they set off into the shadows. As they did so, the other two tunnels faded into nothingness.

Out of nowhere the most eye-catching vista Janice had ever seen lit up in front of them, forcing her skin to prickle and instantly taking her breath away. Trailing off into the distance, the tubular passageway was a sight to behold.

Four or five metres in front of them, a shallow trickling stream full of brilliant crystal clear water rippled, tickled, tumbled, swirled and flowed around tiny narrow bends, lapping at perfectly mown grassy banks on either side, occasionally stumbling over minute waterfalls measured in centimetres, washing over the odd strategically placed dislodged branch on the way. If they'd have staggered across it in the wild on the surface, it would have been THE most picture perfect place on the planet, nature at its beautiful best, an iconic scene to be photographed, shared and loved by all. Now was not the time to forget where they were though. For two, it was obvious, the most powerful magic user there and one under normal circumstances of the mightiest on the planet had no illusions about their surroundings, easily able to sense all the traps and tricks for exactly what they were, despite her diminished festive powers. For Peter, the only one to have previously been to this place, twice in fact, once with the former Emporium owner, Gee Tee, on an adventure full of fear and wonder, that had led the master mantra maker to believe him about Richie being The White Dragon, a visit he'd never forget right up until his dying breath. And on a separate occasion when he'd accompanied Tank on his first view in an effort to safely store the laminium dagger that had threatened to fall into enemy hands. Danger was everywhere, something he was more than well aware of thanks to the lessons learned from the former Emporium owner.

Pulling Janice along in his wake, making sure not to let go of her hand for even a split second, knowing from first hand experience just how strong the urge to touch, bathe or even jump into the crystal clear water actually was, giving in to his curiosity for just a second, Peter glanced up certain of what he'd see. Mirroring everything on the ground in front of him, the exact replica of the stream crisscrossed the curved ceiling above his head, its water seemingly glued there, gravity somehow defying belief. Remarkable couldn't begin to do it justice. Tilting his skull from side to side, the hockey loving dragon eyed the flawless grass running between the two streams up the curved walls of the almost circular tunnel, still besieged by intricate swathes of daisies, Goldilocks buttercups, towers of pink and yellow snapdragons, blooms of yellow dragon's teeth, pink evening primrose, creeping forget-me-nots, a carpet of bluebells, ribbons of daffodils, cowslips dotted everywhere as well as a cloak of snowdrops. Honeysuckle and clusters of bright red poppies beset the curled rock walls, a faultless vision if ever there was one, as long as you weren't a hay fever sufferer.

Not keen on seeing any of the many fluttering insects come into contact with the very tempting, ever moving liquid, knowing full well what the end result would be, they continued on, Bentwhistle leading the way, the two dragons in human form often glancing back over their shoulders to see whether or not they were being pursued. So far they weren't, but how long that would last they just couldn't be sure.

Like an itch that just wanted to be scratched, Janice's need to dip her fingers into the slow moving, translucent, enticing water was all encompassing, her body instinctively fighting being pulled along by her love, the compulsion to stop, take a moment and feel the touch of the beguiling liquid overwhelming. Luckily the other two had no intention of letting that happen.

Drawing to a halt, by now panting like an overworked husky pulling a heavy load on the way to the North Pole, Peter figured it was time to stop and yell the words that Gee

Tee had shown him on that infamous trip down here. But before he had a chance to shout, "SPERMA REDIMIO," just like the old shopkeeper had all that time ago, the vista started to warp and transform. Expecting the same transition that had occurred on both his previous visits, the youngster was surprised to see the array of flowers all start to wilt and get guzzled up into the pristine green grass itself. Apart from the dandelions, whose bright yellow flowers twisted and writhed, wriggled and jiggled before doing the most outright amazing thing... to a flower, they uprooted themselves and started to move. Not having the faintest idea of what the hell was going on, the hockey player just watched in fascination, wide eyed and open mouthed.

Marching in formation, the lush yellow plants stalked across the ground in front of them, the ceiling, sides and supposed floor their parade ground, their movements uncanny, all the individuals working towards a much bigger common goal.

Sure this wasn't 'the way', and about to pipe up to Polkinghorne to warn her that something was wrong, two things happened simultaneously.

First... the company of swaggering yellow blooms coalesced into a uniform shape, the outline of a path in fact, one that traversed floor, sides and ceiling alike, twisting off deeper into the distance in front of them.

Second... a familiar voice echoed down the tunnel from somewhere up above.

"It's okay youngster, this is my doing and it's supposed to happen when the security measures are temporarily neutralised," Zarenkesia observed. "Follow the path laid out by the dandelions and that'll take you to the treasure trove. Once there, I suggest you barricade yourself in and take stock of anything you can use in your defence. The considered opinion is that Earth is hot on your tails. How? I'm not sure. I don't seem to be able to detect her by any conventional means. My hope is that by reactivating all the protections they might be enough to stop her for good. But

I've been told that's unlikely, for which I'm truly sorry. That said... you all need to stay strong, fight with everything you have and never give up. Even as we speak, help is on its way. Good luck!"

'Just peachy,' Peter reflected, not relinquishing his grip on his soulmate's hand, striding ever forward, his thoughts centred on all the supernatural goodies in the vault proper wondering if any of them would be enough to save their asses, because goodness knows if his crazed, psychopathic mother was coming for them, then not only would they need a bountiful amount of good luck, but all the ancient and powerful relics they could get their hands on. Gingerly all three moved forward, their nerves apparent, a standoff in the most magic filled cul de sac in the world all but inevitable.

Through the hissing, crackling, splattering and fizzling of overspent ethereal energy and a whole lot of fuss, an outrageously angry package landed with an almighty BUMP on her ass at the bottom of the slippery silver pole between the two mammoth murderous looking dragon statues. Briefly it could have been a fantasy prison line up of the world's most deadly predators, that is until the wicked she-witch Earth, still smarting from being attacked on her descent by a something or somethings unknown of a very poisonous nature, and overzealously bitey to a point of almost ridicule, ignited a fluorescent wave of vicious purple energy above the fingers on her right hand and lashing out as she was prone to do, thrust it immediately towards the statue by her side. Ancient in design and having been one of the guardians of the vault for centuries, the dragon effigy exploded in a magnificent display of light and sound, sending the arachnids that had lived in its shadow for almost as long, scattering in all directions.

Clothes covered in holes and still smouldering from Olgoi-Khorkhol's brutal show of aggression as she slid down through their territory, Fredric's daughter climbed to her feet amongst the stifling smoke and still burning remains of the former prehistoric protector and began looking around to see where she was.

Three dragon sized, gloom filled tunnels sat directly opposite, their insides obscured by cunning supernatural, all appearing almost gothic in nature, each as terrifying as the next with absolutely no way to distinguish between them.

Through her war torn, rage ravaged, anger filled mind, a semblance of sanity accompanied the intrinsic craftiness she was renowned for in some parts of the world, a drive by of sorts, not so much shooting, but a wondering on how best to proceed given the obstructions in front of them, an overpowering desire to get her hands around Bentwhistle's scrawny neck all the time fuelling the intense bonfire currently licking at her soul.

'A choice,' she thought, 'and not one easily made. How quaint.'

With no discernible way to tell them apart, that only left a guess, a chance, a gamble with the odds being one in three. Anyone who knew her and was still alive to tell the tale would know that she preferred the odds in her favour to be significantly better than that. How to go about achieving such a thing here and now though, that was the question.


At not quite a sprint and with Polkinghorne watching their backs, the trio of friends eventually reached the part of the tunnel where the perfectly mown grass met the cold, hard, rocky floor, having left both streams some way behind. Even a genius with the combined intellect of Yoyo's band of brilliant youngsters would have had trouble telling if they were the right way up or not. It appeared so, but they'd doubled over on themselves at least a dozen times, throwing what they thought they knew into a whole lot of doubt. A fleeting look back in the direction they'd come from had them looking on with interest as the dandelions outlining the path that had guided them here scattered randomly every which way, some hiding amongst patches of re-growing flowers, others settling in the middle of the perfectly formed grass, one hell of a blot on the landscape in that respect. That however, wasn't all that happened. Right before their very eyes, the lush yellow petals of the flowers wilted and died, transforming into intricate seeded orbs or dandelion puffballs as they're commonly referred to on the surface, the kinds that toddlers everywhere are familiar with blowing the seeds off. Only these weren't the benign kind that human youngsters would regularly pluck from the ground. Oh no. Despite appearing all fluffy and lovely from a distance, when telescopically examined, real menace was laid bare in the form of razor sharp stems entirely covered in an ominous coating of thick, oozing, poisonous, unidentifiable liquid. They were danger personified and the quickest way to death for both humans and dragons alike. Certain that this stage of the vault's defences had been reset, Bentwhistle and the others turned back towards the main event.

Trepidation now exchanged for wonder and excitement at the thought of what was to come, Peter led Janice and the Christmas legend along the now fully enclosed rock tunnel, around the sharp bend and waited for the reaction he knew would come as the passageway opened out into a huge underground courtyard. He wasn't disappointed.

"Uhhh…"

"Ohhh..."

"Uhhh…"

"Ohhh…"

The two gorgeous ladies both let out tiny gasps of surprise at what awaited them at the end of the blind alley, sounding like a nuisance caller heavy-breathing mouse on the other end of a telephone line.

Stretched out in front of them, terracotta coloured, the gigantic rock vault overflowed with the most beautiful, intricate, gaudy, powerful and frightening things any of them had ever clapped eyes on… and that included Santa who'd visited practically everywhere on the planet. Nooks and crannies carved into the solid stone walls spilled over with amulets, charms, wristbands, rings and even the sparkling tiara that Peter had noticed on his first trip there, each piece oozing raw, unearthly energy in a nod to the now deceased shopkeeper's obsession with collecting only the best from across the globe. The assembly of artefacts was nothing short of spectacular, and that was only on first glance. A more considered approach was needed and would no doubt throw up a whole host of fascinating, rare and valuable objects.

In her quest to determine the truth and the real path forward, the insidiously evil villain Earth had spent more than a few moments mulling over how to reach the right conclusion and not get herself killed in the process. Clearly two of the three passageways would lead to that eventuality, something she wished to avoid at all costs. Still, how to choose eluded her.

Nerves frayed more and more with every second that passed, no matter how hard she tried, the queen of darkness and despair still couldn't get her head around how to pick the correct option. And as she knew better than almost anyone, time was well and truly running out and that was the wrinkle. Patience spluttering out like the morning dew on a car's exhaust, she fell back to her default setting, opting to go with her biggest bargaining chip, sure that it could once again save the day and get her right back on track. And what was that? It could only be one thing... MAGIC! In an overtly extravagant and wasteful display that most other magic users could ill afford or conjure up in the first place, the epitome of evil let rip with everything she had, her cunning plan to unleash enough supernatural to destroy the replicas leaving the one true route left standing. In a wild display of terrifying insanity, crackling purple energy spun through the heavy air towards the trio of tunnels, expanding out from every part of the wicked would-be queen's body. Intense heat, light and cold as well as the invisible effects of magnetism and gravity surged forward in a nightmarish display of what Peter's mother was capable of. Unrefined dragon magic combined with naga spells coalesced, creating the kind of supernatural power evil usurpers across time and space could only dream of. Guided by Earth, whose eyes remained closed, arms outstretched to the sides, ethereal energy in numerous shades of purple circling her body at various different speeds, the directed enchantments battered the three versions of the mysterious magical burrows, waves of pure unadulterated force smashing against them time after time, white hot brilliance exploding against their shells, fierce fire burning them, icy white coldness ripping at their very fabric all at once. Sacrificing all her considerable will and every last ounce of mana at her disposal, something had to give as the torrent of explosive supernatural built to a crescendo. And it did... In a hail of intense, unforgiving light, two of the three tunnels winked out of existence, the ancient spells binding them together well and truly overloaded, the safeguards put in place never meant for this intensity of attack.

Dropping to her knees, soaked in sweat, spent in just about every way possible, the vicious vixen set on murdering her own bloodline continued to breathe hard, the tremendous effort she'd just expended having taken its toll, a short time now needed to recover and replenish. But that was the one thing she didn't have going for her... TIME! It was running out faster than even she knew. And so in the ultimate show of stubborn defiance, she crawled to her feet and headed for the only remaining spectral tunnel, her usual depraved grin having now returned, thoughts of retribution all consuming.


Spell books, layers of parchment, rolled up magical

scrolls, one off mantras, dust covered tomes and elaborately decorated notebooks stuffed nearly all the horizontal shelves that surrounded and overlooked the main vault and its fabulous supernatural contents. Two or three overflowing with tightly wound scrolls resembling neatly stacked log piles from an end-on view, blew the minds of the trio of new arrivals, one of whom was the first full blown human to ever have visited this, one of the most secure and secretive sites on the planet.

"Wow…" sighed Janice, blown away.

"Indeed," added Polkinghorne, who'd popped into the Emporium on Christmas Eve numerous times to deliver Gee Tee his gifts and although realising this place existed, had never breached or even thought about violating its substantial magical defences. It truly was a sight to behold she thought as she scanned the entirety of it all.

Taking a step forward, Peter pulled Janice in his wake. Abruptly Polkinghorne stepped out in front of them.

"Hang on a moment. Aren't there any more defences?"

"As Gee Tee would have said, that's it. That's all there is. If you get this far... then you're welcome to the lot of it."

"That does sound like him," Polkinghorne laughed.

"He certainly was one of a kind," Peter mused.

"This," Janice stated, "is what I imagined the end of the rainbow would look like."

"Don't get me started on those blasted leprechauns," Polkinghorne spat with just a hint of venom in her voice, very out of character.

"Why?" asked the young bar worker inquisitively.

Beautiful, long blonde hair waving across both shoulders as she shook her head recalling a harrowing incident from many decades previously, the Christmas legend wondered briefly just how much she could say. Not much as it turns out.

"One Christmas Eve a very long time ago, not long after I'd started, a group of them ambushed me, set the reindeers free, stole the sleigh and the presents, nearly rendering

Christmas null and void."

Both lovebirds stood looking on, mouths catching flies.

"What happened?" asked Peter, unconsciously leaning forward, his curiosity piqued despite the dire circumstances.

Still shaking her head, more at the memory and how she'd narrowly avoided disaster by the skin of her teeth, Santa knew there really wasn't time for the complete picture.

"I needed help and wasn't sure where to go, so I called in a favour from an old friend."

"Vimes," guessed Bentwhistle, sure that he was on the mark.

"No... another, someone with let's just say, slightly more gravitas."

"That's it?!" exclaimed Janice.

"For now, yes," declared Polkinghorne strolling purposefully forward towards the treasure trove of supernatural goodies, putting an end to the conversation once and for all.

As the two soulmates trailed behind their friend, they gave each other a 'look', one which said they wished to know everything about that adventure once this was all over.

Cautiously Polkinghorne strolled into the mass of terracotta coloured rock plinths at the very heart of the vault, noting the complex dragon runes that dated far back.

'That shopkeeper,' she thought with a modicum of fondness, 'certainly liked his secrets.' Weaving past the raised pedestals, she noted the massive marble bowls in different, colours, shapes and sizes dotted about on the floor. Each was gruesomely filled to the brim with macabre piles of teeth or damaged individual scales in a variety of hues. Briefly she contemplated their origin, imagining battles from many thousands of years previously, a time that For'son might well have experienced first hand, when elements of dragonkind might well have been considered savages, just like the primates that would go on to become modern day humans. History in all its guises hung in the air like a skunk's parting shot.

"What's this?" the calming, soft voice of Janice rang out around the blind alley they'd deliberately chosen to hide in.

Peter and Polks closed in on her position from opposite sides, noting the cracked and twisted length of wood that slightly resembled a staff poking out from a smaller, foot high plinth with a hole in the middle. The sliver of tree was rampant with knots and had clearly seen better days, looking as though it would turn to dust at the merest of touches. And then Polkinghorne picked up on something else, an almost indefinable emotion radiating off it, making it feel... ANGRY! All of this against the background of rampaging supernatural power, lead her to believe that this artefact was much, much more than it seemed, something one of those dear to her confirmed mere moments later.

"Ahh... Merlin's staff!"

"Really?" blurted his soulmate, unable to believe what she was hearing.

"Yep."

"But it looks so..."

"I know, but I think that's somehow the point."

"If there were a thousand staffs to choose from, no matter how bad the others were, this would be the last one you'd pick."

Peter couldn't argue with her, in fact thinking about it, those might have been his exact thoughts on his first visit.

"It certainly is unique," Polks offered up, admiring everything about it.

"I should say so. But the question is, do you think it's going to aid in our defence against that...?"

He didn't have the heart to say it, not about his own... well, you know.

"It probably wouldn't be my first choice in 'go to' weapons that this place is rocking," the Christmas legend quipped, in an effort to get a smile out of the couple.

No such luck.

"Then what would?" Peter asked.

From amongst all the valuables, Polkinghorne, using not only some of the inherent Santa magic that had slowly started to recover as well as her aeons of experience, did a full three sixty, studying every single aspect of each and every item, all the time assessing how useful it might be in the upcoming battle that now appeared inevitable.

Glimpsing past the stacks of human armour piled high in all its shapes and sizes... shiny and positively rusty alike, boots, bracers, chest plates, gloves and helms, some splattered indiscriminately with dried, ancient blood all towered high which, together, could have been mistaken for a modern day work of art, her focus homed in on the rows of worn metal hooks that adorned the back wall. Dangling precariously, dozens and dozens of worn leather belts, some with dog-eared swords hanging off them, others with bejewelled masterpieces sheathed, others old, weathered and rusty, some positively tattered and worn out. Moving along, belts with shabby holsters housed pistols ranging from Wild West six shooters to sixteenth century, single shot, muzzle-loading flintlock ignition variations, something she could well imagine in the hands of mutinous bands of pirates. It was an antiquities collector's dream!

And then something intrinsically supernatural vied for her attention, giving her a little nudge in the direction of a shabby old, tan coloured gun belt peppered with bullets that hadn't quite lost their sheen, the worn, white grip from yet one more six shooter sticking out of the holster, hanging up above a propped up rifle from the same era. Even though she was eyeing the weapons from a distance, a faint smell of leather and some of the oils associated with it assaulted her nostrils, conjuring up images of horseback pistol fights across wide open plains, chasing outlaws against an overriding sense of... betrayal. The past had just revealed itself in extraordinarily vivid detail.

Returning her attention to the weapon at hand, Polks recognised it for what it was... a Colt .44 and once the gun of choice for a consummate professional, but a professional WHAT? Gunslinger? Thief? Rustler? Sheriff? All of the above?

Unable to help himself, having also been obsessed with it on his first visit with his now deceased friend, Peter had cottoned on to exactly where Polk's attention was focused, and the history associated with said revolver.

"It once belonged to someone special," he whispered in her ear, hoping to tantalise her briefly, just as Gee Tee had done with him.

Instead he got somewhat of a shock.

"Billy the Kid... yes I know."

"How? Surely that was long before…?"

"It was, and don't ask me how I know. The Santa magic seems to have a history with that particular individual and has just given me a brief recap."

"Wow!"

"Hmmm…"

"What's so special about…?" Janice piped up.

"Given how much time we don't have, I think we'll have to save the full story for later. Let's just say that history rather badly misjudged 'the Kid' and played down some of his rather extraordinary exploits."

"That's funny…" Peter cut in.

"Why?"

"Because those are almost the exact words Gee Tee used."

"I get the impression that they were both friends."

"They were."

"That explains a great deal."

"His weapons... can we use them?"

"Quite possibly," Polkinghorne replied, handing the rifle to Janice and the gun belt to Peter. "Keep hold of them anyway, you never know what might be needed." And with that she moved on, her attention focused on the furthest corner away.

Trailing in her wake and recalling his first visit with the

master mantra maker, Peter couldn't help thinking about all the differences. Back then he'd thought throughout the entire adventure that his life, their lives in fact, had been on the line, but what he knew now about Zarenkesia, her presence watching over them, able to switch off the vault's defences at the drop of a hat, gave him a whole new take on the episode, much more fondly in fact knowing that Gee Tee would never have seriously put him in harm's way, something that couldn't be said about what they potentially faced now... his own bloody mother of all creatures, a being that had no compunction about killing and from everything he'd seen first hand, probably even quite liked it. That gave him pause for thought, wondering why indeed he'd let Janice and Santa come with him knowing that Earth would come for him no matter what. Why did she hate him so much? Was it all tied to the battle at the residence? And what were those moments all about... the ones in which she'd had the opportunity to take his life but had at the last second, failed to do so? Were they lapses in judgement, a change of heart or the first sign of mental instability? Either way, at one point it had almost appeared as though she'd hoped to... what? Reconcile? Make up? Leave for some quality mother and son time? All of the above? It was all so confusing. Here and now though, he wished he'd sprinted off out of the burning remains of the Emporium and into the dystopian landscape of the capital, leading his mother away from those that he loved, stopping her from getting her grubby hands on them. Why hadn't he?

"You can't think like that!" assured the voice of calmness in the middle of the storm... SANTA!

"I should have…"

"You didn't have a choice, as well you know. We wouldn't have let you go and that would just have put all of us in more danger."

"What's going on?" Janice asked, confused as to why they'd stopped.

"Your love here was just wishing that he'd run away into

London somewhere before we'd come down here, certain that he'd have saved us all by dragging his mother off in another direction. Tell her!"

"I…"

"TELL HER!"

"I just thought that…"

"There was no thinking involved, that's the problem Peter," Polkinghorne spouted, more harshly than she'd intended. "Backed into a tight corner, it was the right decision with the information we had at the time. As well… it can't be undone, so buckle up buttercup, for good or bad, this is all we have. Now… tell me about these bows," she ordered, pointing down to the huge pile of weapons stacked in the corner, pretty sure the youngster knew more than he was letting on.

Taking three steps forward, the hockey player reached down and picked up a specific bow from many, a gorgeously smooth wooden creation and stood it up next to himself. Standing on the floor, it came right up to Peter's neck. Polks reached out and ran her index finger down the almost taut string, able to sense the resonance of a great deal of magic somewhere deep beneath the weapon's primitive outer layers. This, she knew, was something special.

"It belonged to Robin Hood," he stated matter-of-factly, which given the revelation was totally out of character.

"THE Robin Hood?!" Janice exclaimed.

"Yep!"

"That would explain a great deal," Polks confessed, now running her fingers along the bow itself.

"Apparently he had a much smaller one for hunting. This one he used when fighting the Sheriff of Nottingham's men."

"Someone," whispered Polkinghorne, "made this one especially for him."

"You can't know that," cautioned the hockey playing dragon, shaking his head.

"But I can…" the Christmas legend replied, her eyes now firmly shut, her own unique blend of supernatural combining with that imbued into the bow.

About to speak up, more than a little irked now, Peter thought better of it on seeing his friend Santa slowly immersing herself into whatever the exquisite weapon had to offer.

"And better still, it was a magician or maybe a wizard, not a fletcher, who designed this one."

"And why is that better?" Janice asked.

"Because, if I'm not mistaken, and I don't think I am, the yew from this bow derived from the churchyard at Papplewick."

"Gee Tee mentioned something about that… the wood proven to have possessed medicinal, spiritual and symbolic qualities for dragons and humans alike, making it special beyond belief."

"That's right, and I do believe that this is probably the finest example of its kind ever to be made, when all that's taken into account."

For a few moments, the three of them stood in silence, each studying intently an iconic weapon, one used by the legend Robin Hood in his fight against injustice and deprivation, the epitome of selflessness, giving back that which had been so brutally taken away to many, many thousands of people, fighting the good fight in and around Sherwood Forest.

What most, including these three would never have known, is that Billy the Kid and Robin Hood before him, were, in much the same vein as For'son, Fu-ts'ang, Fredric, Flash, Yoyo, Rose, Peter, Tank, Richie and even the two heroic humans, Janice and Hook, Xususi, revered throughout history for their potential to battle pervasive evil, called upon during the darkest of instances, dispersed across space and time in preparation for an earth-shattering event such as the one taking place all around them right NOW!

Orphaned at an early age, using the alias Henry McCarty at a point when he should have been enrolled in the nursery ring, the dragon known only as 'the Kid' would extricate himself to the surface, immersing fully in Wild West culture. After only a few visits he'd become a prolific thief, renowned for taking risks robbing saloons, stage coaches, trains, laundries and undertakers alike. This very quickly got him noticed, not only by those upholding the law, but also by more otherworldly forces that did their best to placate the rashness of his actions and temper his need for adrenaline filled action, guiding him in a slightly different direction in the hope of using his unique skill set for good, one that would have him cross paths on his journey with the legendary master mantra maker and store owner. Whilst his exploits with those in the west had become infamous for all the wrong reasons, few if any knew his true purpose. The conspiracy that he'd ended up thwarting at the cost of his own reputation was one that could have led to the whole of the planet taking a wrong turn and ending up soaked in shadows and depravity. Thanks to his courage and bravery, the narrative had been changed and put back on the right track, something his friend the Emporium owner could perhaps have guessed at. To this day the name Billy the Kid remains highly regarded across the pantheons of time and throughout the annuls of history, more whispered than rushed, he was one of the most self-sacrificing Xususi ever to have roamed the earth.

Robin of Locksley in many ways couldn't have been more different from the Kid. Yet one more dragon who'd loved to roam the surface in human guise, albeit on a much more local level, he'd been brought up both above and below ground in anything other than poverty. The offspring of wealthy dragon parents who owned opulent castles across the dragon domain throughout Europe, Robin wanted for very little, his time in one of the most renowned nursery rings supplemented by private tutors and expensive overseas vacations. From the outside it appeared a privileged version of perfection, one that dragons would fight to attain, but not for the individual concerned because despite his upbringing, he rolled another way. Kind, caring and sometimes described as over sensitive, he was a stickler for the 'right thing' and often during his sorties to the surface disguised himself in peasant attire so as not to be teased and picked on, but more in an effort to blend in and gain access to everywhere his normal persona wouldn't be welcome. He wanted to see the world from the other side of the fence, from the view of those downtrodden and struggling in an effort to understand the problems of the land and to work out how to put them right. Whether through noble righteousness or his selfless work ethic, know this... he didn't succeed in what he'd set out to do. Indeed, how could he, not with so much stacked against him? When that became apparent, to him at least, and let's just say it took a while, other schemes and machinations took hold, ones that ultimately led him to lead the band of outlaws based in the forest of Sherwood. A powerful uprising to be sure and one that had Fate on the edge of her seat, not just because of what he was achieving on a day to day basis for those poor subjugated souls who were the constant victims of the Sheriff's cruelty and viciousness, but one that unknowingly had turned the tide of something much bigger and potentially much more oppressive. Being in the right place at the right time to do the right thing every moment of every day had paid off in terms of keeping not only a small section of England away from brooding malevolence and wicked criminal intent, but it had stopped the rot from spreading across the planet. Yet one more crisis averted by the unlikeliest of Xususi. The term outlaw had never been so misappropriated across the course of history.

"I'll have the bow," said Polkinghorne, taking the stunning weapon off Peter's hands and grabbing four quivers of arrows while she was at it. "I'm not sure quite how much use it'll be, but it would be stupid not to take it given its history."

And with that, Janice carrying the rifle, Peter with the Kid's gun belt firmly fastened around his waist and the once a year legend, four quivers strapped over her back, supporting the almighty bow that almost eclipsed her in height, the trio scoured every last inch of the vault, picking out the best defensive positions knowing that a last stand was all but inevitable.

# 18 A HOLE'S A HOLE'S A HOLE'S A HOLE

*"So this is what you're reliant on,"* Time asked Luck incredulously as all three Providences homed their extraordinary abilities in on what was happening in northern France.

*"Well…"* Luck swallowed nervously, *"I know it's not a done deal, but he's where he should be in the nick of time and armed with formidable supernatural knowledge that if used creatively in his normal manner, could well do the trick."*

*"A gamble then?"* Time scoffed, barely able to believe the risks involved with the stakes at hand.

*"Of all the beings at the centre of this, let me assure you,"* interjected Fate, *"that this is the one you'd want to be at the sharp end of things. More often than not he's turned things around when the universe seems to have conspired against him."*

*"More often than not… that's what you're basing this on,"* Time chided in an almost child-like outburst. *"Do you realise what's at stake? Not only every living being, but the planet itself and our very existence! MORE OFTEN THAN NOT! The two of you have lost your ****ing minds!"*

If they'd have had physical bodies, Fate and Luck would have shared a look, one that would have gone something along the lines of, 'she's not wrong'. And to some degree, she wasn't. But having nudged one of their favourite adventurers into a position where he just might make a difference, all they could do was sit back, watch events unfold and hope that with his usual aplomb he managed to pull a rabbit out of his hat, so to speak.

And who was this beloved first choice of a swashbuckler? Ridge… Dendrik Ridge! Or as he prefers to be known… FLASH!

Less than two minutes... that's how much time they didn't have. In theory it wasn't a problem, because if what they had planned worked, it could go right down to the very last second, opening one of the nagas' supernatural wormholes directly above their heads and transporting it in the blink of an eye up and beyond the atmosphere, as far into outer space as possible. It was a unique solution to a problem that could, if not dealt with correctly, shatter the earth five ways to Sunday, bringing about the extinction of every living creature on the planet in but a moment. To a dragon, the fearless group of intrepid opportunists used the pressure of the moment to fuel their intellects, all coming together as one cohesive unit, Flash now having taken charge despite him not fully understanding the complex magical equations involved in making such a thing happen. Interestingly though, he didn't have to, now with all the tasks broken down into much smaller pieces, overseen to some degree by Rose, the youngsters' mother in all but name, a role she'd taken to like a dragonling to charcoal.

Maintaining his composure, garnering strength from having the being he'd so recently fallen in love with standing next to him in this, the biggest crisis he or anyone else in the history of everything had ever faced, the former Crimson Guard shook off the fear that threatened to incapacitate him and sweeping aside what passed for adrenaline in his false human form, sought to move things along.

"How's it coming?" he asked, the telepathic link now assigned purely to share information, swapped for talking out loud given they all stood within ten metres of each other.

"Nearly there," put in Tina, who was doing a magnificent job at not only rallying her siblings but in keeping them focused, calm and on task.

Breathing deeply, his mind constantly aware of the apocalyptical projectile racing towards them all at over 21,000 kilometres an hour, Flash sought out the very special single-mindedness he'd used to such good effect across the decades. Adding all his considerable heart into the mix, he readied himself to pull off what at first glance appeared unachievable. In all his life, he'd never been so motivated and highly charged.

"Got it," announced Tina, "we're ready to go!"

And that was the signal to begin.

With Flash and Amelia standing at the centre, the youngsters making up the main part of the concentric circle, Yoyo and Rose hovered around the outside, Rose's job to very calmly make sure that each individual did their part, whilst Yoyo remained on alert for anyone too stressed or devoid of ethereal energy, instantly ready with a healing touch or some spare mana. In theory they were set, well... as much as they were ever likely to be. As death and destruction on a massive scale hurtled towards them, their minds merged and the magic began.

Slowly the pieces started to come together. Masterfully watched over by Tina, Monty and Trayrin began calculating the missile's trajectory starting with its course, after which the speed was taken into consideration. Variables such as wind shear and atmospheric interference had to be accounted for, no easy task given the circumstances, not when you're trying to create a hole out of thin air directly in its path.

Tarko, Zebediah and Essie focused their efforts on conjuring up the necessary magic, speaking the words across their shared link, putting all their willpower behind each, making sure to pronounce the guttural syllables correctly, the nagas' alien sounding tongue ancient in origin and difficult for a dragon to replicate so precisely. Fredric had managed it on the cliff top in Scotland only because he'd spent all those decades incarcerated alongside Vasuki. If not for that, then even he would have struggled to conjure the wormhole that had allowed him and Richie to give chase to his murderous daughter.

And that left Bullhorn and Thadeous with the

nightmarish job of combining all the data with the sum of the magic invoking the naga inspired wormhole into the onrushing path of the monstrous nuclear missile, their computations checked by Tina and then Rose, before everything was put together, using Flash as the conduit that would ignite the wormhole into being. Ethereal energy from them all passed through him to its source for the matter of moments the event horizon had to burst into being and maintain its position, for just long enough, they hoped, to gobble up the apocalyptic threat and spit it out somewhere beyond the atmosphere.

From his position on the outer edge of the tight knit group they'd formed into amongst the wreckage of the control centre directly at the heart of the monorail test borehole site, Yoyo paced, not quite anxiously, but definitely on edge, his intrinsic magic splayed out beyond his body, encompassing all the youngsters he thought of as sons and daughters, their rescues pride of place in his list of achievements across his considerable lifespan. Scanning for anything out of the ordinary, he knew that the hopes of the entire planet's population rested with his charges and friends at this spot, not that most of the world knew that. Had they, then panic would certainly have ensued, a state that on its own would have caused hundreds if not thousands of casualties. While a smidgen of him thought every being deserved to know that their fate was well and truly on the line, a much larger part envied their ignorance, knowing that if things did go wrong, there'd be no time for the populace to realise what had happened, let alone feel the barrage of death and destruction. Offering up a few wise words of calm and encouragement to all the youngsters in turn, the wise and caring healer remained aloof and off to one side for the most part, letting all the others do their thing without interruption or distraction. It was up to them now, he knew, and he had total and utter confidence in their ability to prevail when evil and doom had teamed up in an effort to thwart them all.

The ground beneath their feet started to shake, that's how close the incoming missile was, its searing tail of orange and yellow flame streaking across the brilliant blue sky no doubt having revealed itself to the whole of France by now.

*"CONCENTRATE!"* commanded Tina, her voice spurring the others on, forcing them to fix their legs one in front of the other for fear of falling over and becoming distracted. Now was not the time.

With considerably less than a minute before impact, all the imaginary pieces came together through the shared link that had originally belonged to just the youngsters. In that moment a cascading flow of ethereal energy sought out Flash, and using his almighty dragon powered body, channelled itself through him before surging up into the sky above them, homing in on the destination that had been calculated to within an inch of its life. Magic, might, fury and intellect were about to combine to stunning effect high up above the French countryside.

Bathed in the sinister red glow from the submarine's internal lighting, Manson watched like an excited kid spotting his presents under the tree on Christmas morning, well... on the inside at least. His stoic facade gave nothing away on the outside, not wanting any of the crew to realise the real extent of his machinations. Wiping out half of France was one thing, annihilating the entire planet was something else altogether.

"Forty five seconds to impact," the weapons officer announced robotically from his station.

Barely able to contain his giddiness, the evil, failed emperor slipped into an empty seat, the ominous smirk reserved for moments like this threatening to come out and play. Instinctively he turned his head away, covering his face with one hand as if to scratch an itch.

'So close... tantalisingly so... in just a few moments more, the dragons and their oh so precious human pets will get exactly what they deserve, and so much more.' Lapping up every second, he sat back and basked in what he knew would be the world's ultimate end, content that he'd finally repaid all of them for the pain they'd so heinously inflicted on him. As petty resolutions go, it was the ultimate revenge.


Knowing that they were only thirty seconds or so from being incinerated in the most violent way possible did little to quell Flash's anxiety as their plan bloomed into fruition. Recognising Amelia's stunning beauty through the chaos, he etched all her traits onto his soul just so that he could get better acquainted when this was all over. Sure the life he sought and deserved was just around the corner, all he wanted to do was return to the capital, hand in his notice and live happily ever after with her. If ever one being deserved all that, then it was HIM given everything he'd sacrificed across the decades in keeping peace and world order both above and below ground. He was a true hero the likes of which the earth had rarely seen and one that warranted a long and happy retirement, all of which he could almost reach out and touch.

Unfortunately life is hardly ever that simple.

Right on cue the youngsters' brilliant plan coalesced, the sheer raw energy and willpower combining with naga phrases that had been pronounced perfectly and coordinates, of both the destination and the ultimate goal synching up flawlessly. Computations that a thousand super computers would struggle with whistled through their link, the complex equations checked, doubled checked and then verified once more... nothing left to chance. As teamwork went it was the ultimate example and the pinnacle of the youngsters' achievement so far in their very short lives.

Yoyo, Rose and Amelia, although still entangled in the telepathic link they all shared were far out on the periphery of it, mere bystanders as every last detail merged together, the fulfilment of their extraordinary plan about to save the planet. It was creative, cunning, obnoxiously over complicated and had required the utmost use of all their resources. As a group of enigmatic heroes, they'd given their all and stopped the world from being destroyed. Only they hadn't!

Mid-air, just over one hundred kilometres above the test borehole site in northern France, an unusual circle of swirling, spinning and churning light in a rainbow litany of colours blinked into existence, originating as the tiniest pinprick of brightness before rapidly expanding out past the three metre mark, the wicked looking eddies of the event horizon running parallel to the ground. This was the culmination of everything the heroes had been building towards, the supernatural answer to the question: how could the earth be saved? Resembling the most vicious whirlpool ever seen by either man or dragon, various competing currents vied for supremacy within the magical construct that hung without support, there amongst the clouds, threatening to wolf down every single molecule within kilometres, given the opportunity. It would never have the chance, its existence dependant on a finite supply of ethereal energy from below, one that would cease to exist after only a few seconds at most.

Suspended by nothing and having almost burned through its supernatural power supply, abruptly the snarling growl of highly charged engines caught its attention as the menacing nuclear missile roared towards it faster than a human's eye could see.

Content that they'd done enough to save not only the day, but everything else on top, Yoyo's youngsters mentally patted themselves on the back at a job well done, the celebrations all but started.

More cautious than their young charges, those with more time under their belts held fire, wanting to be one hundred percent sure before heaving a sigh of relief.

Watching from afar with all their enhanced intellect, a sense of collective calm rippled through the group, the inevitability of what would happen clear.

Still raging with the last of its unique and bizarre magic,

naga in design with just a hint of dragon somewhere in between, the mighty wormhole, wanting nothing more than to fulfil its purpose, waited expectantly for the delivery it was destined to make.

Streaking ahead, full of hate and vengeance, the nuclear warhead cut through the air, setting the atoms behind it alight with the astonishing power from its highly advanced engines. Approaching the wormhole as an absolute blur, the strangest thing in the world happened as it got within touching distance. It winked out of existence, only for one thousandth of a second, reappearing three metres off to one side, missing the churning waters of the supernatural sea of the wormhole by a matter of millimetres. The supercomputer that acted as its brain deep within the bowels of the projectile not understanding what had just happened, corrected its course immediately.

Across the ethereal plain they all shared, the three ever watching Providences simultaneously let out the same shout...

# "Nooooooooooo!"

Mouths hung open, hearts fell and hope imploded.


With the jubilation from the most epic success of his life threatening to consume him, Manson, serial killer of dragons and humans alike, failed would-be monarch and husband, a being so psychologically damaged that he was willing to destroy the entire planet in a fit of pique like a spoiled toddler not getting its way, dredged up the memories of first boarding the futuristic submarine. Soaking wet and freezing cold from his brief swim in the North Sea, standing by the entrance to the control room all but reborn both physically and magically given the heroics by the ship's crew out on deck, he looked on as the admiral and the helmsman entered the command codes to enact the launch of the nuclear missile that would bring about the destruction of the entire world, something only he was privy to. Positively bristling with magic, the one thing his unavoidable dip in the icy cold water surrounding Bow Fiddle Rock had done was to heighten all his senses giving him clarity on a number of issues, one in particular now at the forefront of his mind. Grinning like a Cheshire cat that had not only wolfed down all the cream but had taken a family of mice hostage for its own sick desires, the human-dragon hybrid psychopath opened himself up to his restored well of everything supernatural, sure that one last effort on his part was needed to thwart those who would try and stop him.

Leaving the king's private residence in the manner that he had felt like a kick in the teeth, seemingly events beyond his control conspiring against him on a number of different occasions. Paranoid to begin with, after a series of surprising actions like that in quick succession, he'd become fearful, suspicious and positively obsessed, believing that the whole world and even Fate herself had turned against him. And to some degree he'd have been right on the money.

Given his crazed mindset and the refreshing wakeup call the freezing water had provided, you might have thought that he'd sit right back and enjoy anticipating the ultimate victory given that he was about to destroy the entire planet. Deep within though, a nagging doubt persisted, one that said over and over again that 'they' would stop him. As repetitive as a broken record, it spurred him on to use some of the bristling magic that he was now overflowing with. Like a chess grandmaster, thinking many moves ahead, Manson's twisted mind tried to imagine how it was possible to thwart his enemies.

It didn't take long and he could only come up with one possibility. Even that had odds in the many millions to one category. Still, given all that had happened in such a short space of time, it seemed prudent to try and be prepared for such an eventuality. All he had to do now was fathom a way around such a prospect. There were a number of options but a blast from the past and one that carried a certain amount of irony presented itself at the forefront of his twisted and scheming mind, causing his smile to widen quite significantly, which shouldn't really have been possible.

Just as the command codes were entered after the destination had been set, the maniac of madness and mayhem used all his considerable willpower and a great deal of his reinstated mana to cast the same spell he'd used what seemed like a lifetime ago on that damn Astroturf hockey pitch, the one that had moved the hockey ball right at the last second of his fabulous shot, the one that blasted idiot and piss poor excuse for not a hockey player and a dragon had failed to stop, leading to a goal and his side levelling the match. And he didn't stop there... oh no. There could only be one thing left to do, using a spell so ancient in design that he'd had to rip it from a compartmentalised section of the mind of a shaman who'd helped guide him to Earth on the Shetland Isles. He had stolen it in the most brutal and vicious fashion right before she'd died, a secret she'd almost taken to the grave, but one he'd discovered right in the nick of time. And saving the best for last, because it was a rather complicated spell that if enacted correctly, might even thwart the gods themselves. How cool was that?!

'Oh the irony,' he thought, as the very last syllable of both enchantments rolled off his tongue inside his psyche, certain now that nothing could stop his dastardly plan even if the gods once again tried to connive against him.

As the nuclear warhead left the sub, he knew he'd succeeded in everything he'd set out to do.

Unfortunately for you, me and the rest of the world, it looks as if he'd been spot on with his assessment.

# 19 STALKING THE PSYCHOPATH

Clinging on for dear life in the dense darkness, a sense of being spied on through alien eyes clawed at her as vines and leaves rustled against her exposed arms and face from their foothold on the rock face, her descent all the time getting faster and faster, the occasional metallic glint buoying her spirits as she glanced downwards past crossed legs. Futs'ang, the former weapon smith and unbeknown to her, one of just a handful of Xususi dotted through time and space for end of days crises such as this, had zipped tip first into the shadow ridden abyss a moment or so before she'd taken the plunge. Sliding at speed, not knowing what lay in wait, strangely gave her a brief sense of freedom, her complicated mind momentarily unburdened from the pressure put on her by The White Dragon moniker that she'd inherited through no fault of her own. Ignoring the stranglehold on her heart from leaving both rugby players… one her best friend from almost the very first instant that they'd met, the other, she'd fallen so hard for recently, one who time and time again had proved to be a hero amongst heroes, a human valiant enough to stand amongst the most courageous of dragons, a being that should they all survive this, songs would be written about. A more kind and gentle soul, at least as far as she was concerned, didn't exist.

In full flow now, travelling so fast she couldn't begin to calculate the real speed, which was saying something with her enhanced dragon mind, the superstar lacrosse player spent a moment not so much re-examining her choices, more attempting to put them into perspective, and leaving Hook and Tank was just one of them. Would she have done it for anyone other than Peter? That gave her cause to pause because her initial answer was almost a big **** off NO! But that wasn't right, not by a long shot. There and then it dawned on her why. Of the three beings down there, the ones she was on her way to hopefully rescue, she would without a doubt have laid down her life in a heartbeat and gone after all of them, individually or collectively. They were her friends, in the same way Tank and Hook were. (Well... you know, not quite in the same way as Hook, but you get the idea.) To some degree that hit her hard because you see she was someone who had trouble letting others in, past her emotional defences. Of course Peter and Tank didn't count, but even they struggled in that regard at times. But with everything that had happened recently... the world burning both above and below ground, nearly dying in the cellar with Tim when the clubhouse had been destroyed, her dragon-ness being stripped away by the priesthood, leading the charge underground with a ragtag bunch of humans in tow, the cold hearted torture of Casey, watching Tim die at the sadistic hands of Troydenn, defying death in the battle from hell, calling out Fredric when he'd so callously tried to intimidate Janice, facing the reality of Gee Tee's death and Tank's spiral into depression and then stumbling across the terror twins on the coast of Scotland. So much had happened in such a short space of time that she hadn't begun to realise the extraordinary benefits that had so seamlessly slipped into place, until now that is. And by that I mean the relationships. True friendship, as I'm sure a lot of you already know, is hard to find and even harder to hold on to. That rang true for the lacrosse superstar as well. Okay, it didn't help that for so long she'd had to live a double life... the dragon one she shared with her two best friends and the occasional other such as Gee Tee or Vimes, and the human one that almost every day had her surrounded by beings she not only liked, but thought highly of. Still, and this applied to her teammates to a slightly lesser degree, she just couldn't get close, not properly so, not given what she really was, just like most of her kind. But all that had long since gone out of the window, the reality of the dire situation the world currently found itself in taking precedence over everything else. But with all the chaos and confusion had come friendship... real and proper friendship. Those she shared a sporting connection with... Angela, Emma and even Sam and Taibul, had proved themselves brave enough to join her on the mother of all quests, down in the domain, each hugely pivotal in saving Tank and Flash when it looked for all intents and purposes as though their lives were forfeit, and they'd taken the revelation that she was a dragon in their stride. How utterly amazing was that?! Of course it didn't stop there. A budding romance, despite her reservations with one of the others from that crucial night, the eye-opening disclosure when Polkinghorne had turned up about their past antics that had quite literally saved Christmas when it had been well and truly in crisis, and perhaps most significantly of all, the almighty turnaround from a friendship point of view with a human whose bravery easily matched that of her love... JANICE! Their first encounters could only really be described as prickly, teasing Peter in the clubhouse when the beautiful blonde bar worker had clearly showed an interest in him, from the more than awkward encounter at the cinema, one that could easily be described as frosty. And that led back to the momentous night at Taibul's restaurant, when the brooding Janice had tagged along, much to her own displeasure. But from that moment onwards, the blonde bombshell had proved her worth a thousand times over, freeing dragon prisoners in the Salisbridge marketplace to aid in the rescue, bonding with the fantastic weapon Fu-ts'ang's consciousness in a manner that was hard to describe, before proving herself in battle like no other could, saving Peter in the process and standing up in the end to his overbearing and outdated grandfather's views with, of course, a little assistance. All in the name of love. Most amazingly, she hadn't bulked even the slightest when the master mantra maker had revealed that the light of her life was in fact a totally different species. What a woman! Over the course of everything that had happened they'd grown... CLOSE! Best friends kind of close, which in her eyes had almost sneaked up and wriggled its way through her defences. Who knew precisely when it had happened?, Maybe when Janice had handed the laminium dagger back to her after Casey had nearly removed her head from her shoulders with the demonic whip he'd tortured Tank and Flash with, perhaps some time after that. The main point was that they'd bonded on an almost cellular level, now able to glance across some distance and have a conversation with just their eyes. If you've ever experienced such a thing, you'd know the sheer, raw, unadulterated power such a friendship can impart and what it means to have that in your life. How they'd got there didn't matter, all that did was they were now besties, with the young fully human bar worker someone she wanted in her life for as long as she remained on this earth. So there it was, the realisation that not only was she doing this for Peter, but for the best friend she'd so long needed in her life, as well as the Christmas legend who also meant so much to her. In essence, it was all about LOVE for those she surrounded herself with, knowing wholeheartedly that one way or another, she'd lay down her life for those now trapped in the vault by the delusional queen of evil, her friend's mother and Fredric's daughter, a being that she'd have to wipe from existence if everyone else were to live. As her feet slammed hard into the debris of the destroyed dragon statue at the base of the slippery, shining pole, The White Dragon vowed to do just that to save all those she loved in an effort to attain a future that she never thought possible. In some ways it was almost within touching distance, in others... it might as well have been in a different solar system.

Rocking, rolling and ready to go she sidled up to Peter's grandfather who stood next to the former weapon smith, both studying the single remaining tunnel that they could only guess had been left in their prey's wake.

"I'm assuming this would be the left hand tunnel that we've heard so much about?"

"It would appear so," the founder of the Crimson

Guards replied, his voice laced with worry, the concern for his grandson evident in everything he did.

"Time's a ticking," declared Fu-ts'ang, his anguish at his best friend's predicament equally unmistakable.

"I want to make one thing clear before we proceed," Fredric began, turning to face the lacrosse superstar.

"And what's that?" Richie replied, doing all she could to hold her anger in check, knowing how important it was for all three of them to work together to get the desired outcome.

"When we get there... SHE'S MINE! Do what you need to save our friends, but that kid dies here today, by my hand. Understood?"

They did, neither choosing to argue with the formidable warrior, both nodding their agreement, the futuristic blade, remaining tip down, rocking his hilt gently back and forth. That was enough to placate the over burdened dragon weighted down with more baggage than JFK airport had on site during any one day. Leading the way, the seriously 'disappointed off' father leapt into the only available tunnel and set off to find his daughter for the very last time.

# 20 A REAL BRAIN TEASER

For an hour or so the trio had aimlessly wandered the suburbs of Salisbridge on the lookout for anything they could help with. Of course there was residual damage but nothing on the scale of the destruction of the historic cathedral and the buildings located within the renowned Close, including that of the school they'd just rescued the children from. Fully repairing the odd house here, the occasional shop there, as well as clearing out a huge amount of debris from two of the stunning rivers that passed through the city in an effort to stop the flooding that had occurred and get the waterways back on their original courses, Jar Man, DomCon and Steel had come to a grinding halt in a park just off the main ring road, taking up residence on a bench a hundred or so metres from a deserted children's play area, their non-stop activity over the last hour having taken the stuffing right out of them.

"What now?" the tiny terrier of a dragon with a yap to match asked his two friends.

"We haven't done badly," suggested the laminium ball captain, proud of what they'd all achieved on his first outing above ground, finally feeling somehow comfortable in his newly acquired form.

"You're right, of course," put in Jar Man who unbeknown to him had inherited the role of their leader, "but there's just so much more to do. We need to figure out where and how we can be most effective."

"There's so much damage over such a large area, how on earth are we going to work out where we need to be?"

Silence ensued as they all pondered the question. A short while later, Steel, getting used to being an interim part of humanity, piped up.

"Could we use their social media channels to find out what's been hit the worst and take it from there?"

They could, and indeed they did. Twenty minutes later after having all used the phones that were an intrinsic part of their disguises when on the surface, they regrouped having come up with the same answer... THE HOSPITAL!

According to local news reports, wards had been closed, the power supply was only sporadic at best, and part of the main building had been evacuated due to structural safety concerns, all of which meant casualties were having a hard time being treated, the normal steady flow of accident and emergency wounded had to be turned away with anything minor such as broken bones, sprains and twisted ankles just not being dealt with at all. From all accounts it was chaos, a situation mirrored across the planet and one the three friends felt obliged to help out with, at least locally. With that in mind, and at a screaming blur powered by their inherent dragon magic, they took off to the hospital. Ten seconds later they screeched to a halt in the car park, the tread from their shoes leaving long, dark black lines scorched into the tarmac.

"Where do we start?" the fiery pocket rocket asked.

"What about the power supply?" Jar Man suggested. "If we can get that up and running, we might just have a chance of returning the hospital to its previous state."

The other two nodding in agreement, all three set off into the main site to see if they could fix the number one problem on their list.


Leaning in towards his friend and teammate who remained unconscious behind the haze of yellow against what was left of the back wall of the Emporium, Hook felt as helpless as he ever had, watching his new found love, supposedly the saviour of them all, leap into the entrance to the vault without even so much as looking back over her shoulder. Most would have been disappointed on that point but not him... NO! Why? Because he understood just how hard it must have been to turn her back on both himself and Tank and choose to go and rescue Peter, Janice and Polks instead. That decision alone must, he knew, have been utterly heartbreaking.

Gazing down at his hulking great friend, the gentle giant he'd so often shared a pitched sporting battle with, having little idea of the rough and ready rugby player's true character, Hook couldn't help being perturbed by the serious nature of Tank's condition. Not a medical expert by any means, even he knew that a bleed on the brain was bad... really, really bad. More than a little intimidated at the thought of speaking up, only then did he start hearing the distant chortle resonating from the back of his mind.

*"What the...?"*

*"I'm sorry,"* For'son whispered across the landscape of his psyche, *"but I thought you knew that I could hear your thoughts."*

*"Uhhh... no."*

*"Well... you do now."*

*"Good to know,"* replied Hook, with just a smidgen of sarcasm.

*"Don't be like that, I just wanted you to know, especially since more and more of your feelings continue to centre around... HER!"*

*"I can't help how I..."*

*"I know and it's fine. I just wanted you to be aware now that we're linked I can hear everything going on in your mind. Think of it as good manners on my part."*

Hook supposed that kind of made sense.

*"Your concern about Tank is something that I share and does you great credit, youngster,"* the enigmatic band continued.

*"We need to do something for him,"* Hook urged.

*"Zarenkesia said that she'd reached the full extent of her medical knowledge in this regard. I don't see what more we can do."*

*"What about getting him to a hospital where they have the facilities to treat him properly?"*

*"How are we supposed to do that given the precarious nature of our circumstances?"*

*"You're the thousands of years old bright spark with more*

*knowledge than most ever to have existed. On top of which you're loaded with a huge amount of supernatural power that allows you to work miracles in almost everything you do. And you're asking me?"*

"*Hahahahahaha,*" echoed around their consciousnesses in a familiar female tone. "*He's got you there!*"

"*Zarenkesia!*"

"*Of course. I hope you didn't mind my eavesdropping, it was only meant to be a bit of fun.*"

"*Well…*" started For'son.

"*No problem,*" interrupted Hook, certain that his thoughts would never be his own ever again. "*About Tank…*"

"*Yes,*" answered the Emporium's unfathomable presence, "*a conundrum to be sure, and one that I'm desperate to solve and see him return to full health. Do you have any suggestions?*"

"*If the main issue is that his dragon physiology is too human in design, surely we must get him to a hospital so that he can be treated as one of my kind using all the technology at their disposal.*"

"*For the sake of his survival, that would present as the best plan. But as For'son asked, how exactly are we supposed to do that?*"

"*I'm sorry, I have absolutely no idea,*" replied Hook scratching his head, literally and otherwise. "*How would you normally evacuate someone from the domain back up to the surface?*"

"*I have no idea,*" the mysterious loop reflected. "*Across all of my history, I can never recall there being a need to do such a thing.*"

"*Oh!*"

"*What we need,*" Zarenkesia put in, "*is to work out the quickest way possible to the best facility available.*"

"*I can answer part of that,*" voiced the rugby player. "*Our home town of Salisbridge has got excellent facilities when it comes to neurology. I only know this because one of our opponents got badly hurt some time ago in what was a mightily illegal, crunching tackle. Because it was a head injury, he was airlifted straight from the side of the pitch to Salisbridge hospital where he was treated immediately. Apparently, they saved his life. It was all over the papers.*"

"*And does this facility have a dragon emergency plan in place?*"

Having overheard Tank talk about Peter's time after

battling Manson on the Astroturf and Richie's extraordinary recovery from what should have been certain death following the clubhouse's destruction, he categorically knew the answer to that one.

"*It most certainly does!*"

"*Then that's where he needs to go,*" affirmed the presence behind the Emporium.

"*But just how can we get him there?*" For'son wondered, his thoughts ringing out through their three way telepathic connection.

"*Wait a moment,*" Hook stated, trying to keep his thoughts from wandering off in the direction of the woman (alright, kind of dragon) he loved. His willpower let him down in that regard, but it did make him think. "*Weren't Fredric and Richie in Scotland like less than half an hour ago?*"

"*Hmmm…*" mused Zarenkesia.

"*I think they were,*" For'son chipped in.

"*Then how did they get here so fast, and is that something we can use to get Tank out of here and the medical help he so desperately needs?*"

"*Hmmm…*"


Imagine a feral kitten, its genitals covered in fire ants, bounding over hot coals, being chased by the hungriest Rottweiler in the world, and you might be part way to conjuring up a mental picture of the maiden of madness, Earth to you and I, only surrounded by magic, attacked on all sides by the vault's cunning defences, splashing through water that was designed to paralyse, swatting away insects that could kill in one bite, trudging up, over and around the inside of the twisted tunnel that under normal circumstances might resemble a picture perfect smidgen of the countryside. But not here… not right now. The air was on fire, Fredric's daughter burned, the grass and flowers were ripe with raging flames. It was like a scene from an inferno, with rampant magic of all types zipping and zinging all over the place, Earth's reinstated supernatural shield surrounding her as she moved, miniscule gaps occasionally opening up allowing some of the supernatural flames to sneak through, burning her clothes, skin, hair and face. Still... she prevailed, dead set on her mission, that and nothing else, her twisted and deranged mind truth be told, already wringing her weakling of a son's neck, squeezing the last remnants of life right out of him, looking on in delight as his eyes bulged and his disgusting human face turned bright blue. That was what kept her going, one step after another, through a landscape that could well have come straight from the pits of hell.

Although she didn't have direct control over what was happening, only ever able to switch the defences either on or off, she was able to get an impression if anyone stormed the barricades. Zarenkesia had an awareness of what was occurring far below her usual perimeter, instilling a sense of fear that she hadn't felt since Gee Tee's death at the hands of that bitch of a dragon thought of as just 'Red', the one that had so prodigiously tortured Steel when he'd been captured during their efforts to take Fleet Street back from Manson's mass of murderous goons.

Pushing the chaos and mayhem instigated by the she-witch Earth to one side, the presence embedded into the Emporium sought out one of three, not quite their de facto leader, but one easily spotted from a distance due in no small part to the fierce ball of rage wrapped around his very essence.

*"Fredric?"*

*"Zarenkesia?"*

*"Yes."*

*"What is it you need? We're rather busy at the moment."*

*"You should know that she's somewhere just up ahead. But be aware, from what I can tell she's set everything alight, all the traps, tricks and defences."*

*"Thanks for the warning... we'll take that into account."*

*"There's something else."*

*"What is it?"*

*"We need to get Tank to the surface... his condition is deteriorating. Can I ask how you got back here from Scotland so quickly?"*

Leaving the tunnel proper, Fredric stopped in his tracks gazing intently at the firestorm that filled the passageway up ahead, considering Zarenkesia's request. Should he reveal Vasuki and the nagas' secrets and give her the details of the wormhole spell? It wasn't as though his former cell mate had said he couldn't share it, after all he already had with Flash. But the more beings that knew, the more chance there was that the powerful magic would become common knowledge. That said, he knew she wouldn't be asking if Tank wasn't in a bad way. And that took him back to the moment at the private residence when as a force they'd had their magic brutally ripped away from them, on the precipice of death as a group, until that is the rugby loving dragon had appeared out of nowhere and against all odds, alongside For'son, restored all of their mana for each and every one of them. Without him, they'd all be dead and Manson and his witch of a daughter would be ruling the world. As well, he knew without having to ask what his companion The White Dragon would want him to do, as well as his own grandson who they were on their way to rescue. It was a no-brainer really.

*"We used a naga wormhole spell that allows instantaneous travel between two points. It's magically intensive but I doubt that would trouble you."* And with that, he proceeded to pass on the details.

*"Thank you,"* echoed the reply, followed quickly by, *"good luck."*

*"Well..."* asked For'son impatiently, sensing the Emporium's presence return to them.

*"I'm struggling to believe it."*

*"Believe what?"*

*"They used a wormhole spell derived from some very unusual magic that's..."*

*"Let me guess… naga in nature."*

*"That's right. How did you…?"*

*"Fredric and Vasuki's bond is extensive to say the least. Being held prisoner for all that time will form unlikely alliances. They're closer than they make out."*

*"Hmm…"* pondered Zarenkesia.

*"Does that get us our method of transporting Tank to the surface?"* asked Hook, running out of patience.

*"I think it does."*

*"Then what are we waiting for?"*

*"We need to contact those disguised dragons already working at the hospital,"* For'son put in.

*"How do we do that?"*

*"Under normal circumstances we'd just check the database on a local node and find names and contact details. Obviously that's not an option with everything that's going on."*

*"For'son! I can boost your consciousness that far. Do you think you could scan all those on site in an effort to find the right dragon?"*

After a brief pause, he replied.

*"Sounds like a plan. Let's get on with it."*

And so using Zarenkesia's curious and ancient magic as a conduit, For'son's experienced mind set off at first underground before soon rising above and soaring over the exquisite British countryside heading for Salisbridge district hospital in an effort to drag yet one more of their kind into the madness they were neck deep in. Little did he know that three of his staunchest allies were already on site. Perhaps they'd be able to grease the wheels a touch.


Sitting watching everything unravel about him, George in his human form as was his usual wont had the insight as leader not to show how he felt on the inside, instead wearing not quite a grin, more a warm, kindly weathered look of someone who knew everything was going to be alright. Unfortunately that's not how it was unfolding deep inside his mind… quite the opposite in fact.

*"Come on Flash, come on... I know you must have somehow got there in time despite the fact that it appears impossible. Amelia, I know you're there. One more miracle, please... just one more miracle!"*

And so as the control room staff working at the heart of his private residence went about their business with the dedication and professionalism that defined their race to a tee, despite knowing that a nuclear bomb was about to be unleashed in the middle of Europe (of course they didn't know the true extent of what would happen once it exploded), George continued to hope and ask any deity that would listen for that one last miracle, one that would grant the planet a new lease of life. From where he sat and with the countdown to impact sub thirty seconds, it looked more and more unlikely that he'd get his wish.

# 21 ALEA

As the last syllables of their shout of, *"Noooooooo…"* rang out across the spectral landscape where they'd been trying to question Novus, horror at the realisation of what had happened, or not as the case may be, dawned on all of them for the first time. Used to manipulating everything in front of them, being in control, the thought of having none rendered them more helpless than a kitten circumnavigating a lake full of hungry crocodiles. Barely able to speak, let alone string a cohesive thought together, Fate, Luck and Time looked across at each other and then back behind them towards the pitiful remnants of what had once been the most powerful entity in the universe… the planet itself, one that had burst into being from absolute nothingness on a monotonous day much like any other, one that in the blink of an eye had become extraordinary in the inky blackness of space.

Originally it had just been one humungous ball of rock, but as the life essence of the being at the very centre reached out with tendrils of earth magic that would go on to become what we today know as ley lines, slowly everything started to change. As gravity took hold, water developed, from outlandish seas and raging rivers, to freshwater lakes and crystal clear streams. From out of nowhere plants flourished in all their spectacular colours and magnificence. Insects sprang into being, decorating the landscapes, making the newly grown plants their homes, using them as fuel to power their new lives.

By now the supernatural of the ley lines had spread across the surface of the giant ball of rock, bolstered by flecks of laminium directly from the earth's core, the lifeblood of the one that oversaw everything. Enamoured by what had been crafted in such a short space of time, Novus pushed on, letting his imagination run wild and the entirety of his supernatural to follow its instincts. Birds and fish in a million different varieties just appeared, the first taking issue with the second, not quite, the original hunter finding its prey quandary, but almost. And then it was the turn of mammals. Rodents, bats, hedgehogs, moles and shrews integrated themselves seamlessly into the flora and fauna of the lands, followed quickly by primates including very rudimentary humans, pigs, camels, whales, cats, dogs and seals. In what passed for a split second the newly created space sphere had become populated by a hugely diverse ecosystem. Somewhere amongst all of it, a huge nursery of dragon eggs blinked into existence. Notably this huge swathe of eggs had materialised atop the largest deposit of laminium yet formed across the planet, which might explain the inherent magic imbued within their race and their relationship with the rare metal. That was how things unfolded. Sometime later the Providences arrived on the scene. Speaking of which…

*"We need to act NOW!"* Luck urged, her ethereal face screwed up in concentration from the effort she was using to try and stop the nuclear missile.

However, nothing worked, and that included attempting to tamper with the state of the art weapon's insides with a view to stopping it exploding.

Time focused on the area between the nuclear warhead and where the heroes stood on the ground amongst the debris of the test borehole site in northern France, agog at their spectacular failure. Gathering up all of her considerable power she unleashed the whole lot, everything she'd ever had, in the hope of at least slowing the monstrous murdering missile, all to no avail.

Fate, she was the one, their leader by… what? Seniority… maybe. But it was probably more to do with trust. Although fickle by nature, the others, of which there were quite a few, had learned to put their trust in her, especially during the darkest of hours of which there'd been many over the course of their lifetimes. Here and now though, this was the worst of the lot. Never during their combined experiences had they ever faced the possibility of wholesale extinction. It appeared only seconds away.

*"There must be a way out... there just must be,"* the denier of destiny thought to herself, the sum of her magic spread far and wide looking for an answer to the impossible question posed by Manson and his demonic plan that had all but come to fruition. Twisted, ancient and unusual magic had denied them any chance to get involved and thwart such fiendish and nefarious behaviour. How? Goodness knows, but it didn't matter because they were down to the wire, having been thrown out of the last chance saloon for bad behaviour by the bouncers, lying in the puke filled gutter next to the road overflowing with trash outside the 'you're out of time' kebab house. Individually they'd done everything in their power to avert disaster. Nothing could stop the inevitable now.


Crestfallen, their brilliant minds, augmented by magic, could barely believe what they'd just seen. It couldn't be possible... it just couldn't, because if it was the consequences were just too dire to conceive.

It was Flash who managed to break out from under the spell first, his agile and quick thinking mind using all the training he'd been through to offer up an alternative. But with less than twenty seconds to go before the 21,000 kilometres an hour warhead wiped them from existence, even he came up short, the terror plummeting down towards them all encompassing. All he managed to do was faintly call her name, a pathetic gesture given the circumstances.

"Amelia!"

Turning to face him, knowing that's all she'd have time to do, their eyes met against the backdrop of the air being sucked out of the immediate area, their smiles in that moment revealing the love the pair felt for each other. Knowing that it was over, not just for them but the planet as a whole, the sense of failure all encompassing, but with the bravery both had lived their lives on display, their eyes remained glued to each other for the very last few seconds of existence. It was a plucky end for two of the most courageous beings the world had ever seen.

In time honoured tradition, Yoyo grabbed his wife's hand and squeezed it tight, his heart torn apart at not having the time to express his love for her. Rose, grasping his hand for all she was worth had the foresight to open herself up to those all around her, the husband she loved more than ever, the youngsters she'd hoped to somehow adopt in a future now denied, and Amelia and Flash, two dragons she held in the highest regard and who she regarded as her friends. Using all her telepathic ability, she broadcast three words to all of them, the last she would ever utter.

*"I LOVE YOU!"*

As the air dried up and the earth shook, the tip of the missile approached the ground, gleaming in all its magnificence, doing only what it had been programmed to do, fulfilling a purpose no human being involved in its construction would ever have dreamed of. It was over. Once again evil had triumphed over good, mirroring everything Manson had known growing up.


Speaking of down on their luck drunks lying in the gutter, well... close enough, one in their midst, formerly the most powerful of them all, Novus sprawled out amongst them continuing his usual, *"I FEEL SO OLD!"* party piece, his frail appearance matching the fragile words ringing out from his mouth, or at least what passed for it. Suddenly, and in a 'blink and you'll miss it' moment, the message changed.

*"You need to... work together."*

*"I FEEL SO OLD!"*

*"What the...?"* was all that Fate could think before instinctively her reasoning took over. *"Of course..."*

The sound of two sweat soaked towels THUDDING

loudly to the slightly springy surface of the otherworldly boxing ring that had appeared in the midst of the Providences and their seemingly done for guest echoed across the ghostly landscape they inhabited, LUCK and TIME conceding defeat in the only manner they knew how.

*"SNAP OUT OF IT! I KNOW WHAT TO DO!"* Fate screamed across most of time and space, scaring the living daylights out of the other two.

*"What…?"*

*"We need to work together and we need to do it now. There's no, excuse the pun, time to lose."*

In a whirlwind of activity, they got down to it.

Throughout the course of the history of everything it had never happened, and on first contact it felt about as alien as anything the three had ever experienced. Just the touch of another's consciousness in such close quarters was enough to have their minds screaming in terror, the solace that defined them so rudely intruded upon causing them to freak out. However, given it was that or permanent extinction, each fought to override their underlying dread, their trust in Fate hanging on by an increasingly unravelling thread. They continued, each gaining an unerring insight into the others, their perspectives changed forever in that moment.

*"What would you have us do?"* ventured Luck.

*"Combine all that we have and concentrate it on the missile!"*

*"To what end?"*

'That,' thought Fate, 'is a good question.'

She had no idea. Even if they could slow the destructive missile right down, what then? 'Perhaps,' she mused, 'I should just ask.'

Multitasking on an existential level she reached out to Novus, shook him awake and with a great deal of restraint, yet forcefully enough, commanded him to answer her question.

*"What will it take to make you strong enough to avert this disaster?"*

Now was not the time for silence, but currently that was the reply on offer. However, it did look as though the consciousness of the whole world was at least mulling over the question.

Concentration personified and with her eyes closed, Time reached out around the speeding nuclear warhead and using all her intrinsic enchantments, bathed the projectile in a cylindrical dilation field that under normal circumstances would stop time altogether for whatever lay inside it. Once again... NOTHING!

*"It's no use... it simply isn't working!"*

*"AGAIN!"* commanded Fate. *"If you have to, keep spamming it over and over."*

*"But..."*

*"No buts... just do it!"*

Feeling more than a little deflated at their impending doom, Time did as ordered and continued to repeatedly flood the missile with the dilation field, continuing to wonder about that aeons old phrase, "the definition of madness is doing the same thing, over and over again expecting a different result." If that were the case they, and the rest of the planet, were well and truly doomed.

*"What...?"* Luck got as far as whispering.

*"Target every last inch of the time dilation field... try and up the ante and get it to stick. Whatever you can do to increase the odds of it succeeding against whatever magic is being used... do it!"*

Offering up a mental nod, the connoisseur of chance slapped her own unique taste of the supernatural into the mix, overlaying it on top of the dilation field, spamming it again and again and again. Still... NOTHING!

'Work together...' that's what Novus had said, she was sure, even at a whisper. With her two comrades in arms combining to little or no effect, Fate started to have a bad feeling. And when that happens, you know you're probably moments away from catastrophe.

'Why won't it work?' she continued to think, cursing Manson, the ancient, unusual naga magic and everything in between. If she'd understood the how, then just maybe she could come up with a workaround, a wrinkle to get them out of this mess. But nothing they tried appeared to have any effect. And then it hit her like a bolt out of the blue, the most extreme solution to the radical situation they faced.

In that moment, for whatever reason, a specific memory leapt to the fore, one that of all things featured one of the group of heroes who'd fought so valiantly at the private residence, giving Manson and Earth a bloody nose, but not quite vanquishing them for good, a young dragon at the very heart of all this madness... BENTWHISTLE! Strangely it wasn't whatever he was doing now or anything that he'd done during the midst of the Changing of the Guard... NO! It was a private moment with the now deceased master mantra maker Gee Tee, the two beings alone in his workshop, one in which the former Emporium owner had spotted something absolutely bedazzling, to him at least, around the hockey playing dragon's neck. An exquisite piece of jewellery that was in fact far more than it appeared and known according to the shopkeeper as an *'alea'* and in his own words, roughly translated meant 'gamble' or 'last chance'. She could remember it well, but before she had a chance to dwell on that vision, another swam into view, a much darker, more dangerous and foreboding apparition. The realisation of the time and place was made even more obvious than it should have been by the fact that instantaneously she felt... COLD! And not just a little. Accompanied by the fact that they were indoors somewhere and it was quite recent, and when I say that, I mean within the last decade or so which given her unholy lifespan, was like narrowing it down to the last few seconds of a pensioners life. Indoors... cold... bright white surroundings... related somehow to the *alea* and the naive young dragon Bentwhistle who very reluctantly had at least started out at the heart of all of this, it could only be one place that she returned to in her recollections, one that unusually had haunted her for a few hours afterwards, something that given all that she'd seen, never, ever happened. As if to confirm her suspicions, three loud words drifted across her mind on the breeze.

*"Amplificare Magicus Nunc,"* which I'm sure you can all remember means 'amplify magic now'!

Combined with the dainty, pale, strong white hands snapping the *alea* in two and an eerie green glow from the extended personal shield that had popped into existence around them both out of absolutely nowhere about a hundredth of a second or so later, Fate looked on helplessly for the second time as a magically induced hell rained down on the two lovers who'd been hiding in the sports club cellar during yet one more of their illicit liaisons. As hundreds of tonnes of rock, stone and debris in all sorts of fashions crashed down on them, the fickle finger just managed to glimpse the frightened face of the lacrosse superstar before she was crushed into submission.

It had turned her stomach on witnessing it in real time and although she wouldn't admit this to another soul, living or otherwise... she'd tried to intervene but through no fault of her own hadn't been able to. Why? To this day she didn't know. Perhaps it had something to do with the revelations of the youngster in question being revealed as The White Dragon. Maybe it was something else. Either way she'd disobeyed very clearly defined guidelines to interfere where she shouldn't and it had failed spectacularly, but the dragon in question had still defied all the odds and survived. Strange and amazing at exactly the same time and with hindsight, clearly no coincidence.

But what did all of this have to do with the impending nuclear strike they were trying to stop and why would none of their sickly sweet, hugely powerful magic work? Nothing made any sense!

It was exactly at that point she locked eyes with the diluted and despairing Novus who in temporal terms could have been light years away, but in the chosen reality the two of them currently shared, lay just across the way spread out on the grubby floor. In a look that lasted a millisecond, more information was exchanged than a week long chat between two supercharged A.I.s. It took a great deal to blow Fate's mind, her residency somehow comparable, if not in length then perhaps in stature, to that of Elvis Presley's six hundred and thirty six shows from 1969 to 1976 in Las Vegas. She was a stalwart, alright not quite from the very beginning, but not far off. And ever since, she'd basically run the show, well... when it came to the Providences anyhow, not that the others would have admitted it. Surprising her on this scale should have been impossible, but the planet's consciousness, using the last remaining dregs of its supernatural power, had prompted the visions within her for a reason. And now she knew why. One thought and one alone circled what passed for her brain.

*"You've got to be ****ing kidding me! You want me to do...* WHAT?"

It was madness, total and utter madness... wasn't it? But that's what she'd got from the almost too subtle hints that Novus had inundated her brain with. Of all the things, who'd have thought this would be either THE answer or even AN answer.

Taking a breath, metaphorically speaking, Fate wondered if she had it in her to do what he was suggesting. Most beings wouldn't, that's for sure and even if they did, almost certainly they'd spend too long deciding to act. Since there were only seconds remaining, it was literally DO or DIE!

Rallying against every instinct she had, DO it was then!


As one, the group of dragon heroes at the test borehole site in northern France, Flash, Amelia, Yoyo, Rose and the youngsters faced their inevitable demise with all the courage they'd shown previously, each glancing up at the sky, the murderous missile of annihilation only five kilometres or so out now, a mere moment away at the tremendous speed it was travelling at, its shiny metallic surface carving its way through the atmosphere, a bright orange tint from the heat enveloping the whole of its body. In doing so, they were lucky enough to witness a miracle in the making, one that sent a shiver throughout their bodies.

Reaching three kilometres out, the unlikeliest thing in the world happened... the death fuelled missile stopped, just hanging there in the air. It took more than a moment for each of the dragons to get their heads around what they at first thought might be a dream.

"What the...?" Amelia exclaimed.

"Flash... what's going on?" Yoyo asked the former Crimson Guard.

"I... honestly, I have no idea."

"Are we... saved?" Trayrin squeaked.

"I very much doubt it," Rose put in, bursting nearly everyone's bubble. "That thing is still close enough to ignite the laminium in the tunnel if it goes off."

"Is there anything we can do with it?" Monty enquired, all the youngsters revelling in being given another chance at life, their cunning minds starting to work through the possibilities, each wondering what could be done to the almighty projectile that still had a huge orange, yellow and red tail as its jets continued to fire furiously.


On another plane all three Providences were blown away that their efforts had actually succeeded by working together, Time constantly spamming her dilation field atop the death dealing projectile, luck overlaying that again and again, Fate adding her magical abilities to the mix whilst continually multitasking, keeping an eye on Novus, hoping for an answer to the question she'd posed whilst readying herself to do the unthinkable, hoping that the other two who'd been following her lead would understand. She didn't think they would.

Tearing her thoughts away for but a moment, she

repeated the question again, this time a little more forcefully in the hope that her words would get through.

"*NOVUS, what will it take to make you strong enough to avert this disaster?*"

As she'd expected... still nothing.

Knowing it was now or never and still continually throwing her magic on top of the missile just like the other two, she knew she'd better at least offer up some sort of warning lest they freak out and stop what they were doing altogether.

"*You're not going to like what's about to happen, but you need to hold your resolve, not panic and continue with what you're doing. Get ready!*"

Glancing across the ethereal plain, one that could allow them to see every last scrap of the planet, both opened their mouths to speak. Before they could... IT HAPPENED!

In the biggest gamble of her life, and that was saying quite something, and without the assistance of her comrade-in-arms, Luck, in this perhaps their final escapade, with every single living organism on the planet at stake, using all her supernatural ability she ripped apart every last piece of the missile hanging in the air, causing it to explode outwards in every direction in a rip-roaring nuclear blast of outstanding devastation that had just doomed the world. Momentarily the combined magic of the three Providences faltered, but it was only that, momentary, the three spectral entities once again applying their abilities over and over again across a now slightly expanded area around the projectile itself barely containing all the concussive force, kinetic energy and radiation released in the time dilation field at the very heart of things.

"*OH NO... WHAT HAVE YOU DONE?!*" Time cried utterly bereft.

"*WHAT THE...?*" Luck whispered, shell-shocked.

Royally dejected, depressed and deflated, Fate, just about to explain her reasoning behind such a thing had no time to do so as the answer she'd been waiting for was suddenly forthcoming. Or at least, that's how it appeared at first.

"*Good girl,*" were the words whispered across the barren plains of her mind in a voice she vaguely recognised as that of the planet. Not sure whether to be offended at just how patronising the language was or to be upset that he hadn't in fact answered the question she'd been hanging on tenterhooks for in the middle of the biggest crisis the earth had ever faced, mouth wide open she was about to give him both barrels. However, he beat her to it.

"*What you've asked, it can be done but I'll need the help of your favourite and his friends to achieve any semblance of what I need to become in order to avert this disaster.*"

"*My fav... oh, you mean... the one known as FLASH!*"

"*Yes... and now you must hurry, we don't have much time.*"

Which was odd given one of their current allies should have had all the time in the world and a hell of a lot more.

"*What do you need them to do?*"

"*Find all the laminium placed in the borehole and get it to the core.*"

"*Get it to the core?*"

"*Throw it down the borehole... gravity will do the rest. You do realise you'll have to reveal yourself to them?*"

"*Yes... won't that be fun?*"

"*Now go... there's no time to waste.*"

Still keeping an eye on Novus, still spamming what was left of the exploded missile and its surroundings with all her magic on top of that of the others, whilst continuing to listen to their concerns, Fate gathered all of herself up and just by closing her eyes, wished with everything that she had to be in northern France. In the blink of an eye... she was!

# 22 THE WORLD ON FIRE

Desperately 'disappointed off' at the extreme amount of effort and magic she'd had to use to get this far, let's just say Earth's downright anger that was her normal, run of the mill base level, had shot well up past one hundred times that, the further her incursion into the vault continued.

Being attacked on all fronts from every direction did little to quell the boiling rage that usually remained pent up inside her... not here though and not now, every ounce of supernatural essence being burned up as quickly as it recharged deep within her false, medusa-like human form, the ancient dragon DNA that had been altered over time by enchantments taken by force from those dumb nagas, having to work overtime, the sheer energy consumed colossal in comparison to even the best of her enemies, and I'm thinking of legends like Fredric, Flash, Amelia and of course The White Dragon.

Reverting to type, the wicked she-witch that was Fredric's daughter and Peter's mother fell back on only one course of action… her inherent supernatural powers. As usual she decided to use little in the way of defence, her personal translucent purple shield flickering and sparking, arcing and wavering in and out of reality in places because of the pummelling it was taking. Mostly though, as you would guess, she'd gone on the offensive, using bright bolts in a variety of colours to scythe down anything that got close enough, from a variety of realistic looking insects that had been pre-programmed to attack at a moment's notice, to the hell spawn of those dandelion seedlings with their razor sharp barbs and the coating of thick, toxic poison that would render her dead in an instant. Fire, lightning, ice, magnetism and deadly shadowy naga enchantments surged forth from her fingertips, setting plants, animals and even the air behind her alight, the tunnel resembling the worst kind of blazing inferno, one even the bravest of firefighters would baulk at. It was bedlam, chaos, mayhem and instantaneous death all rolled up into one. But she continued to prevail, to move ever forward, footstep by footstep, crushing what had been lush green grass, stamping the life out of flowers that would do her harm, getting ultimately closer to the dead end that was her goal, her prey not far off being in sight. God-like, with a supernatural plague in tow, the countdown to the finale had all but begun.

It felt like a cross between a dream and a drug induced hallucination as his consciousness spread out like an oil leak in the ocean, leaving the relative safety of the dystopian underground world that he regarded as his, before filtering upwards, reaching the surface and heading in a south westerly direction. Drifting lazily past urban sprawl after urban sprawl, the occasional smidgen of countryside thrown in for good measure, For'son was surprisingly familiar with his intended mental destination, coincidentally having been there twice in recent memory, both times accompanying the dragon king, George. Firstly in the aftermath of the battle between Peter and Manson on the Astroturf on that chilling bonfire night (in more ways than one) and secondly in the hours following the brazen attacks across the world, one of which was the attempted bombing of the entire city of Salisbridge, a part of the scheme thwarted by Tank and Peter's brave efforts that sadly led to the loss of the sports clubhouse, though thankfully no loss of life. Fulfilling his customary duty as the monarch's constant companion and advisor, on that second occasion he'd been there to be greeted by Peter, Tank and Flash outside the underground ward in which contained two surprises... Tim, who they'd thought at the time to be The White Dragon from the renowned prophecy and Richie, alive through some freak magical accident, a combination of her own unique supernatural abilities with breaking the *alea* that had originally belonged to Mark Hiscock, one that her best friend had bequeathed her. And honestly, that was as much of the above ground world as he'd seen in roughly twenty thousand years, since dragon kings are forbidden to leave the security of the domain, his and their only real connection to the human world on the surface the high level reports from those of their own kind disguised amongst them, guiding, protecting and empowering choices from desperate individuals to governments of the most wealthy and biggest nations. And unfortunately for him, he'd been tucked well away from prying eyes when George the dragon king had escaped his post and skulked off on an illicit holiday, otherwise he might well have had a better insight into what he was witnessing now.

Flying free, well... in his mind anyhow, allowed him to take in a small portion of humanity. Their motorised vehicles were everywhere and on consideration, it was a shock to see their sheer numbers. The variety of buildings in which they lived, from huge castle-like mansions surrounded by acres of open ground, to cramped looking flats and terraced homes that almost appeared as though a giant had squashed them together with both his fists, was staggering and he supposed, a testament to how well, despite the recent devastating events, that they as a race were thriving. To some species, a blow like that would have them on the edge of extinction, but not this lot. Time and time again they got back up, okay, sometimes on the count of nine, but that didn't matter. What did was that they staggered to their feet and met their fate head on with gusto, using their hope to counter fear, their ingenuity to oppose destruction, their good deeds to defy even the tiniest splash of evil amongst them. It was testament to their character as a race and perhaps a glimpse into the past and why they'd been chosen to be protected by his kind, a tenet that had become ingrained in dragon way of life from their earliest days in the nursery ring.

Spotting the characteristic landmarks of what he knew to be the remains of a royal castle and cathedral housed within an Iron Age fortification known as Old Sarum situated on the outskirts of the city of Salisbridge, the enigmatic essence contained within the fabulous sparkling band was brought back to reality with a bump, a timely ethereal updraft throwing him up in the air before twisting him around three hundred and sixty degrees, causing him to feel mildly nauseous for a moment. Back on track, he continued on towards the south westerly side of the city and the gigantic settlement that looked almost like a town in its own right, the… HOSPITAL!

He didn't so much touch down as spread out, the intricate workings of his mind expanding far and wide across the medical site, probing and searching, his keen instinct on the lookout for anything dragon related that could lead him to some place to start. Not easily surprised given his twenty thousand years residing on the planet, in this moment he instantly was. Why? You can probably guess. That's right... in one of their biggest moments of need he'd just stumbled across three of their major allies, here at the hospital of all places. How they'd come to be here he didn't know. But what he did was that they could prove vital. Without wasting a second, he got on with reacquainting himself.

Appearing as nonchalant as possible, the three friends and dragons in disguise worked their way steadily closer to the off limits electrical sub-station on the outskirts of the grounds of the hospital, having found out that's what had taken the most damage and that currently all the facilities were being powered by one automatic uninterrupted backup generator, which could fail at a moment's notice leaving a lot of people in a great deal of strife. With the time factor hanging over their heads, it took all their courage and mental fortitude not to run and give the game away. Almost within sight, the unintended leader of the trio suddenly found the defences around his mind breached as a voice echoed around its confines.

*"Jar Man, can you hear me?"*

*"For'son?"*

*"Who else?"*

*"What are you doing here?"*

*"I'm of course not actually here, but at what's left of the Emporium in London."*

*"What's left?"*

*"There's no time to explain that now."*

The strawberry blonde leader chose to remain quiet, just giving a mental shrug of his shoulders and nod of his head. His friend continued.

*"Tank's been hurt... badly! The assessment is that he needs human medical help... urgently! So I was sent here to weigh up the situation and I stumbled across the three of you. What on earth are you doing here?"*

Clearly and concisely, Jar Man explained.

*"I see,"* was the enigmatic band's reply.

*"What would you have us do?"*

*"Find one of the dragon medical professionals, one that has access to the emergency backup plan that our kind use here. Get them to give you access to the facilities and then we'll try and get Tank to you."*

*"How?"*

For'son explained about the naga wormhole spell and waited for the agreement from his friend that he knew would be forthcoming. It was, but there was a caveat.

*"I think we need to repair the electrical sub-station first,"* Ginger chipped in.

*"He's hurt badly and needs attention straight away."*

*"I understand that, I do, but if the backup generator goes down when he's being worked on, then he, like a lot of others, could well end up dead."*

He made a good point, thought the inscrutable presence within the shining band.

*"Are you near the sub-station?"*

*"Yes."*

*"Show me."*

Before things could go any further, Jar Man realised that as a disguised human trio, all three of them had stopped, the other two, DomCon and Steel standing staring at him, perplexed looks ingrained across their faces.

"What's going on?" asked the fiery pocket rocket of a dragon and human.

"I'm conversing with For'son."

"Really," mused Steel intrigued.

Briefly he shared the details of their conversation.

"I agree with you," Steel put in. "Fixing the sub-station generator should be our top priority, and that in the long run will work in Tank's favour as well."

"For'son says he might be able to help with that if we can get within sight of it."

Breaking into a jog, with fewer people around now they were on the periphery of the site, they rounded a corner of some evacuated nurses' accommodation and pulled up sharply at the sight in the distance. There, surrounded by a plethora of workmen and their vans was the sub-station, all cordoned off.

"How are we going to…?" spat DomCon, his irritation getting the better of him.

*"I'm pretty sure I can help with that,"* For'son's silky smooth voice echoed this time across all three of their minds.

*"What can we do to assist?"* offered up Steel.

*"A distraction of some sort would be great."*

*"Leave it to me. I could do with a break from holding on to this form. I'll get you what you need."*

*"You're going to revert back,"* DomCon asked incredulously.

*"Why not? It'll get them scarpering in every direction."*

*"But…"*

*"It'll be fine,"* urged Jar Man, putting his hand on his friend's shoulder in an effort to calm him down.

*"Jar Man,"* ventured the powerful presence some way off in the ring.

*"You want us to find one of the dragons that work here?"*

*"Tank's really struggling. But there's something else… a prophecy*

*about him and Peter, the details within suggest one of the two of them will die. We need to prevent that at all costs. If you could help and expedite the process that would be great."*

Sharing a glance, the two friends were instantly on exactly the same page.

*"We're on it,"* replied the gentle ginger giant. *"We'll let you know when we've found one of the dragons in charge."*

*"Good luck."*

*"Right back atcha!"*

*"Steel... you ready?"*

*"Absolutely! Let's do it!"*

As the renowned laminium ball captain freed the bonds holding his DNA in this particular shape and the change started to happen, boosted by their inherent supernatural abilities, Jar Man and DomCon shot off back in the direction of the main hospital facility on the hunt for one of their own kind, in the hope that they could get their friend the help he so desperately needed.

# 23 THE CALM BEFORE THE STORM

In a whirling blur that no human would have been able to see, the dull silvery metal of the gun shot out of the brown, worn leather holster, spun five times around the index finger that nestled against the trigger before settling on a target some way back against the terracotta wall in the distance. No shot was fired because just like the previous fifty times it was just Peter practising with Billy the Kid's six shooter.

Seamlessly slipping the pistol back into its housing on his right hip, the hockey playing dragon readied himself to go again.

"Having fun?" enquired Polkinghorne, her beautiful face framed by a fabulous smile despite their desperate circumstances.

"I... I... I was just... practising."

"Don't panic, I didn't mean anything by it. You just looked for a moment like you were enjoying yourself."

"Part of me was imagining what Billy the Kid must have felt like chasing down all those criminals across the Wild West."

"I'm led to believe it was a rough time for both dragons and humans alike. And while he generally gets a bad rep both above and below ground, as you and I can attest to, the truth is always incredibly difficult to suppress and in this case is there to find, if you look hard enough."

Peter nodded his agreement.

"What's going on?" Janice asked, wandering over carrying the rifle slung over her back. It was almost as tall as she was.

"Your other half was just showing off his cowboy skills. Go on John Wayne... show her."

Dropped right in it and recognising the look of astonishment and wonder in his soulmate's eyes, after giving Polks his best 'look', once again he drew the revolver at speed, spun it around his finger, pretended to fire at the far wall and re-holstered at his hip. It was pretty impressive even in dragon terms but to the heroic human who'd done so much to get them all this far, it was absolutely astonishing, making her go slightly weak at the knees, much to Polkinghorne's amusement.

"Anyhow," Santa remarked, "much as all this is fun I think we should ready ourselves for the approaching storm."

The expression on both youngsters' faces dropped immediately, both tinged with more than a little fear at the thought of what was to come.

Sensing not only the downturn in mood, but the genuine terror both her friends were trying to hide, Polks knew that now was the time to use her unique blend of Christmas, and I'm not talking about anything supernatural per se, more the spirit that anything is possible, to try and instil some sort of hope that they could indeed prevail against what they knew to be a considerable threat.

"Both of you... listen to me NOW! What's coming won't be easy, but that doesn't mean it's not possible. Focus on the here and now if you want to have any sort of future together. I know you both do. A house, a life, a family... all these things are possible, but... we have to get through this. It'll be difficult for all of us, but especially for you, Peter. A mother trying to kill her son is almost unthinkable, but that's the situation we find ourselves in. I'm sure you've got questions, my young friend, because I know I have. But I'm guessing today you can either have answers or a future but probably not both. Don't be distracted by her taunts, don't respond to any mind games and do not let her get a rise out of you. Succumb to any of those and you'll make failure more likely. Stay strong, stay together... I shouldn't have to tell you about teamwork, a concept I know you believe in wholeheartedly. Work with each other to fend her off, keep her guessing, off balance and unsure... if we can do these things, we have a chance, of that I can assure you. We might have no way to counter her despicable and unusual magic, but if I'm right, and I usually am, I would guess even as we speak our allies are on their way here perhaps with the answers and the solution that we seek."

Powerful words I think you'll agree, but whether they would be enough you'll just have to wait and see.

"You really think they're coming?" Janice asked, timidly.

"I know it!"

"Are you just saying that to make us feel better?" Peter queried calmly.

"Do you really think that your grandfather and best friend won't come for you? If you do, you don't know either of them as well as you should."

"But they're in Scotland, you said so yourself. There's simply no way they could get here in time," the beautiful blonde bar worker reflected.

"Where there's a will, there's a way, or at least that's what I've always been taught. All I'll say on the subject is that I wouldn't count them out. Your grandfather is now, and has been for a considerable amount of time, one of the most resourceful and powerful dragons on the planet despite his Antarctic incarceration. And Peter, as for your best friend, how many times have you seen her defeat the odds and not only prevail, but rocket straight to victory?"

Smiling to himself, quite an odd thing to do given the circumstances, he knew Santa was right. He'd all but lost count of the number of times Richie had defied probability, kicked chance in the 'fork' and brushed off likelihood only to go on and win in style. If anyone being on the planet would come for them, it was her. Closing his eyes, he whispered a short plea to his friend, asking that she get there in time.


Against the backdrop of the eerie red glow that encompassed the entire command compartment, the weapons officer, to Manson's delight, continued the countdown.

"Five... four... three... two... one... IMPACT!"

Depraved desire fulfilled, the leader of all things dark put his hands behind his head and lifted his feet onto the control board in front of him as he sat down in the empty chair at that particular station, adrenaline at the thought of what he'd just accomplished running riot through his body, making his heart beat ten to the dozen, eliciting a thrill like none he'd ever experienced in his entire life. It was done, the denizens of this planet, in all their shapes and forms, were doomed. It wouldn't be long now, he knew.

"Uhhh…" mused the weapons officer, garnering everyone's attention, in particular the tempestuous dragon leader.

"What is it?" demanded the admiral, trying to keep things as shipshape and Bristol fashioned as if the regular crew were still in charge, irked at the lack of professionalism from one of his men.

"T... t... the missile…"

"What about the missile?"

"I'm... still tracking it."

"And?"

"It should have exploded by now."

"I thought it had," interrupted Manson, his tone downright threatening.

"The impact should have occurred right when I stated. But we're continuing to track the missile from the data coming over the link, which absolutely shouldn't happen."

"And what does that mean exactly?"

"That for whatever reason, the missile has failed to explode."

## SMACK!

Manson slammed his fist in frustration down onto the control panel, crushing backlit buttons and making a huge dent in the outer metal casing.

"HOW IS THAT EVEN POSSIBLE?" Manson

screamed, his voice positively ringing around the confined space they all shared.

"I... I... I... don't really know. From the telemetry and the data it's transmitting, the missile is in the right place and should have already impacted. How it's still transmitting and why it hasn't exploded yet is a... mystery."

"BLOODY MAGIC!"

"My lord?" questioned the admiral, about the only one there with the station and balls to do so.

"That's all it can be."

"But who or what would have the ability and power to stop that?"

The million dollar question.

"What exactly does the telemetry tell you about its position?" Manson asked a little more calmly now, sauntering over to the weapon's officer's station.

"From what I can tell, the missile is within a couple of miles of its destination."

"Is it moving?"

"Supposedly... I mean the jet engines are at maximum thrust but its position relative to everything else just doesn't change."

"Hmmm..." mused Manson, his despicable and desperate mind working overtime in an effort to try and understand what was happening and how he could rectify it in order to achieve his required outcome.

"Can we detonate it from here?"

Swallowing nervously, not understanding anything at all that had happened since their leader boarded, the weapons officer considered the question.

"Currently it's set up to explode on impact. Remote detonation might be possible, but it won't be either easy or quick."

Running the calculations through his expansive mind, his entire intellect working the problem, the death dealing dark lord knew that the detonation might be too far from the laminium to have the desired effect and split the earth down the middle. But with few other options he was also well aware that time was running out and this might be the only opportunity to detonate the warhead. France would be a start and taking out the magic users there trying to thwart him would be something of an added bonus.

"Get working on the remote detonation. I want that thing to go off as soon as is humanly possible."

"Yes sir," the weapon's officer replied, his fingers moving like a blur across the keyboard in front of him, his highly advanced mind, just as his leader's had done only moments before, working the problem with a view to finding the ultimate solution.

As the sub continued to dive into the inky blackness, all things were still on the table, for now at least.

Cutting through the icy water like torpedoes homing in on their target, the four shadowy black nagas swished their tails effortlessly from side to side, easily able to keep up with the futuristic nuclear powered monster they were stalking. For Vimes, swimming through the brutally cold sea water which turned chillier with every stroke was anything but easy, and it took all his courage to continue and do as his friend the former Crimson Guard had instructed... don't lose sight of that damned submarine. Determined to do just that, wanting nothing more than to be with his legendary other half, he ploughed on, plunging deeper and deeper, the arctic feel to his surroundings burning his body like nothing else could, cold being a dragon's kryptonite. This was quite possibly the worst case scenario for him particularly given he could be regarded as one of the few peace loving, non violent members of his race. Redoubling his mental fortitude, fighting off the freezing temperatures with everything he had, Vimes considered that Fate had treated him rather cruelly today. If only he truly knew what his friends were involved in across the globe.

"*STOP!*" a voice commanded across his consciousness,

sparking him out of his revelry, bringing him back to reality with a jolt.

*"What is it?"* he instantly replied to the naga king's instruction.

*"Hold still."*

He did.

Vasuki, who since his incarceration and the Changing of the Guard had regained some of the attributes that had previously gotten him elected as king of his race, with renewed confidence recited the words, or more like guttural sounds, to a little known enchantment, one passed down to him from his mother. It took hold almost instantly.

'Oh my,'" thought Vimes, as the harsh contact of the sea water disappeared completely, his body now enveloped by a skin of air, one warmed to room temperature, one that would enable him to take a breath should he need to.

*"How's that?"* the naga monarch asked, more than pleased with his work.

*"I can't begin to tell you how good that feels,"* Vimes replied, feeling absolutely ecstatic after being immersed in the icy water for so long. *"Thanks."*

*"You're welcome. Sorry... I should have thought of it earlier. Anyhow, back to the hunt. Try and keep up."*

And so he did, the nuclear powered monster of a submarine continuing to dive, so deep now that it was difficult to tell which way was up, the shadow strewn darkness closing in around them all. It was only by keeping within fifty metres of the futuristic tin can that they could continue to follow and track its movements.

Only then did Vimes think to ask,

*"Should we try and block its communications?"*

*"Although we, like your kind, have studied the humans closely, I have no idea how such things work aboard a vessel like that, and neither do any of my guards. Do you understand its inner workings?"*

*"No,"* Polkinghorne's other half answered honestly, not really having thought much about it, assuming that his underwater allies would know the ins and outs of the sub.

*"Do you have anything supernatural in your arsenal that would stop electronic communications?"*

There was a brief pause whilst Vasuki consulted the other three. Quickly though, he got back to his dragon comrade in arms.

*"We have a great deal we can do to contain and constrict their magic, but nothing like that I'm afraid. And without knowing the exact details of how these things work, we'd only be guessing at best and I don't really want to waste any of our ethereal energy on a hunch right now."*

*"Understandable,"* Vimes replied sympathetic to what he'd just been told. *"So what do we do?"*

*"Monitor what they're up to, keep following and if they get to deep enough open water, try and take them out."*

*"I'm happy to follow your lead. Let me know if there's anything I can do."*

*"I will do. Stay in our wake and don't drop back. We'll follow them for a while longer and see what they're up to. If they take any direct action against us we might well have to take them out here and now. It's not ideal, not with that nuclear reactor on board, however it might be our only option. The further we can get them away from the coast, the less environmental impact their destruction will have, but it could still be catastrophic."*

*"Understood."*

With that the five prehistoric shapes faded into the dark blue and green shadows all the time keeping the submarine in sight, desperate to try and find a solution as to how to destroy it and the crew without damaging the surrounding underwater landscape, the nearby coastline and all the animals in the immediate surroundings. It was a puzzler that's for sure.

In a nearly identical conversation to the one that had begun on the sub, George, dragon king, courageous leader and would be uniter of races had just asked for an update. What he got in response initially mirrored that of the weapon's officer.

"Uhhh…"

"What the hell does that mean?" he admonished the King's Guard monitoring the projectile, barely keeping his temper in check.

"I… i… it should have impacted and exploded already Majesty, but…"

"Yes… but what?"

"We're still able to track it, which is odd and it's still sending telemetry back to the submarine."

"So it hasn't reached its target yet, is that what you're saying?"

With all the cool efficiency of a seasoned warrior, White Wings leant over the youngster and studied the data on the screen for but a moment or two before coming to his king's rescue.

"It's odd, that's for sure sire. The warhead should already have impacted and decimated half of France."

"But…"

"It hasn't. It looks like it's reached its destination, but so far there's been no explosion."

In his mind George leapt ten metres in the air, screaming with joy at the news of what had happened, smart enough at least for now to not show his true feelings out in the open, not in front of his subordinates, and especially as nothing had been truly confirmed either way. Instead, with his best stoic look, he turned to face his friend and comrade.

"It has to be them… doesn't it?"

"I can offer up no other explanation, Majesty."

"Well, they must have the situation under control. That's a good thing… right?"

"From what I'm looking at here, the engines appear to be at full thrust despite the object in question not moving."

"And…"

"I would suggest that things aren't quite under control just yet. Perhaps they've bought themselves time to act."

Rubbing the bridge of his nose with one hand whilst

sweeping the hair on one side of his head back behind his ear with the other, George considered what he'd been told. A brief respite, if this is what had occurred, was welcome to say the least, but what did that mean for them and the planet as a whole? Had Amelia and her friends got things under control enough for them to celebrate having thwarted the earth's demise, or was there still an ever present danger that could rear its ugly head at any second? They'd tried to get in touch with both her, Yoyo, Rose and of course Flash who, as far as they knew, was nowhere nearby. Sinking back down into one of the luxurious leather seats next to a wall full of computers, the king focused all his thoughts on his friends, hoping that for one final time they'd all come through.

# 24 A TWIST OF FATE

As a group they stood, necks craned, mouths agog, studying the impossibility that lay absurdly in the air above them, the remains of the exploded missile just hanging there, seemingly stock still, metal tearing itself apart, minuscule flashes of scorching fire just visible through the tiniest of gaps, screws, cogs, washers, wires, springs and fragments of housings having parted ways with the main fuselage, the start of the blossoming nuclear reaction almost upon them. It was both terrifying and fascinating in equal measure.

Without warning the sound of footsteps trampling over rubble from behind where they all stood set off alarm bells in their heads. Almost as one, Flash, Amelia, Yoyo, Rose and the youngsters turned, ready to face yet one more threat in a day of unprecedented ones. Expecting survivors from Oblivion's crew, the surprise at what greeted them almost outweighed the half exploded SLBM hanging over their heads.

"PETER!" exclaimed Yoyo, both shocked and delighted to see the Bentwhistle boy traipsing through the debris towards them. So much so that the healer started heading his way, determined to envelop him in a huge hug.

"STEP BACK YOYO!" Flash commanded with just a touch of magic added to his voice to make sure his friend obeyed.

Yoyo complied instantly.

"What are you doing Flash, it's…?" Amelia interceded, before cutting herself off, sensing something similar to her other half.

By now the whole group had got the gist of what was going on and had formed up behind Flash, Amelia and Yoyo.

"I DON'T KNOW WHAT YOU ARE BUT LET ME ASSURE YOU TH…" was as far as the former Crimson

Guard got before being interrupted.

"Please let me assure you all that I wish you no harm," whispered the voice of the young hockey playing dragon, in a perfect replica of the being who was currently tucked away in the Emporium's vault, quite some distance away.

"WHO ARE YOU?" Flash demanded, one hundred percent sure it wasn't his friend and hugely offended that something would choose Peter's form to reveal themselves.

"I…" started whatever it was, before stopping abruptly to think.

Not having had much time to contemplate all this, and still multitasking on an epic level, Fate carefully considered what she was doing. Revealing herself presented many challenges, but was also a massive risk should they ever get past today's dangers. Still, she could come up with no other solution and so chose to continue.

"I've selected this form in the hope you will see it as a friend. Clearly, I underestimated all of you in hoping to gain your trust that way. Please may we start again from the beginning? I assure you our goals are aligned and I want nothing more than to help you get through this crisis in one piece."

It sounded genuine, but something impersonating one of their allies in order to gain their trust was not only baffling but set alarm bells ringing across all their minds.

"Who are you?" Yoyo asked, his momentary misstep now behind him.

"You would possibly know me as… FATE!"

"WHAT?!" spluttered Flash, caught off guard.

"Fate?" Yoyo enquired sceptically.

"That's right."

"But…"

"How is that even possible?" put in Amelia, concerned about not only what was going on in front of them, but above them as well.

With Rose about to butt in and the youngsters looking more agitated than a mother chasing her toddler who'd just broken into her bedside table, around the room at a party, shouting, "I've got mummy's ear cleaner, I've got mummy's ear cleaner", the imposter in front of them piped up.

"I'll try and explain if you let me. But I'll have to be quick and you'll have to be patient. Currently it's all my friends and I can do to hold that thing," she nodded upwards, "in place."

"Please…" said Yoyo.

"You'll have to take me at face value for some of this because it would take too long to explain, but I'll do my best to break it down for you."

And so she did, describing how the planet had been born out of nothing, almost self-made, enlightening them about its sentience, the relationship with the ley lines and the laminium, as well as giving them some clarification about herself and some of the other Providences. The looks on their faces only went on to prove that even favourites could be surprised.

"And so all three of you are working together to hold the remains in place?" asked Rose, wanting to be absolutely certain about what she'd just been told.

"Even as we speak."

"Why did you have to break it?" pondered Tina out loud. "Surely it would have been easier to keep it intact."

"You have a point youngster, but I believe by breaking it, we've managed to negate some unusual and ancient magic that helped it avoid your very cleverly placed wormhole that would, had it have worked, saved the day and dropped the warhead up into outer space."

"This is all very interesting," sighed Flash, starting to get a little frustrated, "but you still haven't explained why you're here and revealing yourself now."

'Straight to the point as always,' thought Fate, more than a little in awe of the former Crimson Guard who was another of her favourites, which was stretching the rules to say the least, because like teachers, you weren't allowed to have favourites… it just wasn't done!

As briefly as possible she laid out what kind of state Novus, the planet, was in now and how he could be helped.

"Let me get this straight," observed Amelia, "you want us to round up all the laminium the dark dragons brought to this site and then toss it down into the core?"

"That's correct."

"In the hope that will be enough to spark Novus into some semblance of his former existence with enough power that he could supposedly deal with... that?!" Yoyo queried, looking up towards the already exploded SLBM hanging in the air above them.

"Yes. I believe that's the only way to prevent the all out destruction of the planet."

Collectively they let out a breath they hadn't realised they'd been holding in.

"That's quite the tale," Flash added.

"It is, and not something we particularly wanted to reveal with all our hopes pinned on the lot of you opening the naga wormhole in its path."

"I have a question," put in Thadeous, clearly having given some thought to what he wanted to say.

"Go on."

"Couldn't you have just obliterated the submarine that fired the missile and all those in it?"

"One... it doesn't work quite like that. And two... that blessed vessel is shrouded in powerful, unique and primordial magic. Even as we speak, I can't sense it, not anywhere in the vicinity of where it was."

"I have someone there... a friend," Flash put in.

"Vimes... Santa's soulmate."

"That's right!"

"I can no longer track him I'm afraid."

"DAMN!" Flash raved, worried for his pal.

"He's probably okay," Fate offered up, "just a little bit too close to the enchantments surrounding the sub to find."

"I do hope so."

"Anyhow," interrupted the healer with some urgency,

"back to the here and now. What would you have us do?"

"You and Rose should coordinate things from up above while all the others round up the laminium. You could use your little electromagnetic trick from the hillside. Because what we're looking for is in a confined space, it should be relatively easy to locate every last ounce of the metal, now that you know what to look for, and guide all your friends to the laminium. Once the rest of you have found some, take it as low as you can at speed and then release it once you've given it as much momentum as possible. That should give it the best start to the journey it can have and hopefully get it to the core pretty damn quick."

"RIGHT... what are we waiting for?" demanded Amelia, immediately taking control of the situation much to Flash's surprise and admiration. "Let's get to it. All of you now, down the borehole."

Without needing to be told twice, they changed their DNA, momentarily shimmering before reverting to their prehistoric best, and then bounding into the air, each of the youngsters flapped their wings, put on as much speed as they dared before turning over and diving into the perfectly circular cavity that was the opening to the borehole.

Following suit, the two soulmates, Flash and Amelia, transformed into their primordial, I would say alter egos, but obviously that's not true, natural forms, and with just a nod towards Yoyo and Rose, leapt up into the air, spectacularly backflipped, before corkscrewing down into the darkness of the test borehole on the hunt for the stolen laminium that had been placed there at Manson's direction.

Eyes closed, reaching out with all his magic, his mind fully open to the telepathic link they now all shared, Yoyo, brilliant healer and one of the heroes that had saved the planet twice over already, started searching for the nearby eddies and ripples that formed the patterns created by the planet's electromagnetic field, knowing exactly what he was looking for this time unlike the last, ready to guide the group to the exact location of the precious, magic enhancing metal.

Mirroring her husband with her eyes closed, Rose, very subtly at first, started to lend him some of her ethereal energy, aware this time because of the close proximity of the laminium, that Yoyo wouldn't need to draw on nearly as much magic as previously. Hopefully he could drill down with exact precision, find what they were searching for and guide the others to it. Still... she stood by to assist in any way possible, deeply aware that things could change or go wrong in an instant, all the time wondering about the strange encounter with the being that claimed to be the Providence known as Fate. Never in all her time had she dreamed of a day like this.

Looking on as the heroic dragons strutted their stuff and disappeared over the edge of the test borehole, a completely different part of Fate continued to spam the entirety of the exploded missile with her unique blend of supernatural, layering it in on top of what Luck and Time were already doing, holding every last atom in place, giving it her all in an effort to contain the potential disaster. Whilst maintaining all that, she switched her focus over to the segment of her that resided with her friends, the other Providences and of course the bedraggled and befuddled Novus, a creature who currently looked a long way short of being able to save them all.

*"Novus,"* she whispered, moving in close to his spectral presence, *"I've done what you've suggested. Even as we speak Flash and the other dragons are searching for the laminium with a view to getting it into the core. Please... hang in there."*

A resounding moan was all the response she got.

About to blink back to her facsimile of Peter, she changed tack, instead moving across to Luck and Time.

*"I don't know how much longer I can keep this up,"* Time stressed, appearing slightly gaunt and sweaty which was unusual given that she could technically be referred to as an essence, but it demonstrated the kind of effort she was having to expend.

*"Keep going, just a little while longer. We've got a plan to boost Novus' magic and hopefully bring him some way back to his old self. If we can do that, then he can take care of that car crash of a nuclear missile."*

*"Is what we're doing working?"* asked Luck, the concentration on what passed for her face making her look like a statue.

*"It is,"* Fate replied, *"to some degree at least. Looking deep into the time dilation field, I can see individual particles moving, but incredibly slowly. It would take a month or so for parts of the missile to reach the edge of what we're doing. Good work, keep it up. Hopefully for just a little longer."*

Both Providences vowed to redouble their efforts.


Prepared this time for such an eventuality, Yoyo, tapped into nearly all his magic and watched as the invisible eddies that the laminium gave off sprang to life, creating long, dull yellow lines, starting well above ground before flooding up and over into the borehole itself, swallowed by the darkness, resembling a long exposure photograph of cars travelling along a road at night. It was exceptionally beautiful, both looking at it and getting his head around the concept that what he was seeing was the super valuable metal being moved through time, a little slice of its history as it travelled from the vehicle they'd been tracking down into the test borehole, some deposits clearly placed lower than others, but all giving off the same resonant frequency. Reaching out across their telepathic link, he shared what he was seeing with his companions, using the long, dull yellow lines to lead each of them to their prize, laminium in all its shapes, forms and sizes.

Smashing open a light coloured wooden crate that she'd been guided to by her mentor and father figure, Essie, having touched down on a narrow rocky shelf beside it, picked up what remained... a tiny bar of the precious metal. Surprised at how heavy it felt, taking all her strength just to lift it up, she bounded out into the centre of the huge vertical shaft that essentially led straight to the core. Sending out a telepathic shout out to all the others, letting them know the first batch was on its way, with all the might she could muster, she drew back both arms and enhanced by as much magic as she dared, threw the bar straight into the centre of the pitch black abyss. Almost immediately she lost sight of it, and that was with all her enhanced dragon senses. One down... plenty more to go.

At first what they were doing had appeared straight forward, but as time moved on it got more and more complicated, especially since the stolen laminium that had originated in Russia had been broken down considerably, some into ring sized nuggets, others into fist sized chunks, the occasional one or two turned into bars... no mean feat for even the cleverest of supernatural beings, but all had been separated and hidden in and about levels around the twenty kilometre deep mark within the borehole. Finding all of it had become a treasure hunt indeed, even under Yoyo's guidance. Quickly though, all working together, they'd formed a system, following the light trails in the healer's mind in pairs, mostly because the dragons who'd dropped off the precious metal had done so sloppily, heading towards a single point whilst just throwing what they had on the ground on the way there. With that in mind, pairs made perfect sense.

Yet one more problem was the falling laminium and so they'd countered that by magically attaching a horrific screeching noise to their prizes, (child's play for any second year nursery ring student) as well as a bright, blinking red light, both of which together should have been enough to stop any of the team below from getting hit. So far it had worked a treat with none of the deeper pairs venturing out into the middle of the tunnels unless they absolutely had to and even then, the other of the pair would keep lookout, yet one more reason to team up.

Throughout it all, the haunting Bentwhistle duplicate

continued to watch, Fate's concentration split between venues, both earthly and otherworldly, akin to juggling swords, swords that were on fire, swords that would occasionally turn invisible and sometimes turn to water. Nightmarish for even the most experienced of jugglers to toss into the air.

# 25 A BLESSING IN DISGUISE

"Afraid of a little fire?" Richie quipped, attempting to goad her partner into action, absolutely certain that time was of the essence.

It was, but Fredric was still proceeding along the supernatural tunnel beneath the vault with unerring caution, displeased by everything he saw in front of him.

"Fire... NO!" he replied. "Whatever those dandelion seed things really are... YES!"

"And just why is…?" she muttered, glancing through the wall of bright orange and yellow roaring flame that extended out as far as they could see down the tunnel, burning grass, plants and insects with impunity, off the charts heat spikes in the confined space, roasting the two of them on the inside and the outside.

Wiping a long line of salty sweat from her brow, The White Dragon attempted to finish what she'd started, her telescopic vision allowing her only now to see the contemptible dandelion spores for actually what they were... lethal, poison coated traps that could kill a dragon in the blink of an eye.

"I'm sorry... I didn't realise."

"That's okay," laughed Fredric, taking one tiny step closer to the nearest edge of the living wall of flame that tickled and prickled, darted and ducked all around the circumference of the tunnel in front of them. "I confess to never having seen the likes before. I assume they were part of the defences guarding this place."

"I think I've heard Tank and Peter mention them, yes."

"I'm no expert, but from the looks of things it would appear that at some point they might have been imbued with the tiniest smidgen of sentience in order to outwit anyone that might trespass. I'm guessing that our prey came through here all guns blazing, not only setting every last inch alight, but throwing her magic about all willy nilly which looks to have disrupted any connected to this place. What that means for us, who knows."

Richie knew exactly what he meant, still spying a group of twenty dandelion seed heads all hovering off to one side together just beyond the barrier of fire, their outer skins ablaze, the poison on the microscopic razor sharp barbs bubbling and steaming, looking more vicious than it ever had before. Fredric was wise to be cautious, despite the need for urgency.

"Couldn't we just follow her lead and throw all our magic at it?"

"I do like your thinking and the gusto with which you live your life, as well as the fact that you're prepared to do absolutely anything to save your friends. However in this case I think throwing more of our supernatural at it would be a mistake."

"And just why is that?" asked the lacrosse superstar, purposefully reining in her temper at the thought that he might be patronising her.

He wasn't.

"Because that's not just any fire that's been left behind in her wake... that's demonic fire, which might explain why the so-called defences have gone a bit haywire. Not only will it burn straight through any of our magical defences, but the slightest touch would almost certainly incinerate us."

'Wow,' thought Richie, 'he's not messing about.'

"How can you tell?" she asked.

"If you look deep within the tunnel and try not to focus on any one point, you'll catch flashes of occasional pink. That's the giveaway and means there's more at play here than meets the eye."

Momentarily she did just that, astounded that she hadn't noticed the significant change in colour before.

"How do we defeat it?"

"A good question, and one I'm not sure I can answer."

"Really?"

"I've only ever come across it once before and that was in some freak accident over one hundred years ago. Then it was allowed to burn itself out, something that took over two months to happen. Clearly we don't have that kind of time to waste."

Nodding her head, Richie couldn't have agreed more, her shoulders weighed down more heavily with every second that passed.

"Fu-ts'ang... do you have any ideas about how to counter the demonic fire?" the lacrosse superstar asked, hoping the experienced weapon smith within the blade might be able to help them out.

Transfixed briefly, the sound of the young woman's voice snapped the futuristic blade back to the stark reality of the desperate situation they found themselves in.

"I..." he started, but stopped abruptly.

"What is it?"

"I don't know for sure."

"But…"

"No... it's nothing."

"Fu-ts'ang... it's important. Tell us, please."

There was a pause whilst the weapon smith considered what he knew.

"From time to time, back when I resided in my prehistoric body, occasionally smiths from certain regions would meet up. It wasn't really my thing, but I did attend on a couple of occasions, mostly finding the whole thing too gregarious for my liking. Anyhow, at one of these events a little known artisan from what would now be known as Thailand started to explain to a group of his peers about a longsword that he'd once crafted. He was upbeat and joking around at first, but very quickly the talk turned serious as the story evolved. It turned out that he was something of an innovator, always experimenting with different ways in which to forge and apply magic to his wares. Staggeringly, he went on to recount a time when he'd created a demonic circle around his particular forge when crafting said sword.

Now, even an untrained novice would have reservations about such a thing, but he was as broad minded as they come, an experienced magic user and had stringent supernatural safety measures in place. What could possibly go wrong? Everything, as it turned out, because as you can probably guess, the sword ended up being imbued with, that's right... demonic fire!"

Fredric and Richie stood before the supernatural carnage of the tunnel, hooked on their friend's every word.

"He went on to describe his elation at what he'd created, a sword to envy all swords and a dragon killer at that. In fact there probably wasn't a magical being in existence that it wasn't capable of destroying. Certain that he'd found a way to make himself wealthy beyond belief, he made a big fuss about the weapon, looking to auction it off to the highest bidder. A dragon did indeed buy it for an exorbitant price, one that made him rich overnight. Lying awake that evening, in his mind he planned out future exploits with the forge surrounded by the demonic circle, sure that he could create armour and weapons the likes of which no one had ever seen. About to doze off in the very early hours of the morning, cries of panic started to emanate from across the city he was located in. Not one to shirk responsibility, he bounded out of bed, leapt out of the nearest window and headed towards the source of the commotion. What he found broke his heart!"

"And what was that?" Fredric asked, enthralled but all too aware of the time they were wasting.

"The dragon... the one he'd sold the demonic fire infused sword to, was smack bang in the middle of things, cutting down all comers left, right and centre, decapitating the most powerful amongst them with a single strike, no scale too hard to deflect a killing blow."

"WOW!" reflected The White Dragon.

"Indeed," continued the weapon smith.

"This is all very interesting, but how does it help us?" ventured Peter's grandfather and founder of the Crimson

Guards.

"After having exhausted his array of offensive spells in an effort to take out the deranged dragon, the smith settled on the only course of action left... healing. A powerful healer with extensive training, at first he attempted to restore those who'd been struck down. However, the sword and its wielder were far too efficient in their madness, nearly every blow a killing one... piercing the heart, taking off the head or even penetrating the brain. It was cold hearted lethality at its very best, or worst in this case."

"What happened next?" asked the lacrosse player, entranced.

"Out of options, he went on to explain that all he could think of was to apply an obscure blessing he'd picked up in the remote jungles of his country in an attempt to honour those already fallen, supposedly sending the remains of their souls to a better place. After letting the blessing roll over what remained of the casualties on the ground, getting slightly muddled, he applied exactly that just as the blade was about to strike its next victim. But instead, for whatever reason, he ended up directing the supernatural blessing directly at the imbued sword. Startlingly, it had the most bizarre effect, temporarily nullifying the demonic fire instilled within the blade and shocking its wielder and owner out of the demonic stupor he'd been befuddled by."

"And?"

"Sensibly, the dragon that had gone on the rampage dropped the sword, severing whatever supernatural connection had been there, and becoming no threat at all. Apparently he remembered nothing of the carnage he'd instigated once that link had been cut."

"And the weapon?"

"Left on the ground with everyone too frightened to go near it. After the dragon responsible for all the killing had been taken into custody, the smith rounded up those left. Understandably they weren't happy, most blaming him for this calamitous course of events. Through much diplomacy, he managed to placate them enough to get them onside with what he had in mind for the sword. Surrounding the weapon lying there all alone on the cobbles, the smith having already shared the blessing with all those there, simultaneously they applied their magic, fortified by the strength of their combined wills and applied the blessing. Not only was the demonic fire destroyed, but so was the blade, disintegrating right there before their very eyes, disappearing into thin air."

"And that was that?"

"Almost. The smith, after a short trial, was banished for his part in events, his forge and the surrounding area levelled completely. The city and its denizens learnt a harsh lesson that day, something that is remembered in its history."

"And the point of all this?" Fredric asked.

"Just that a potential remedy for the demonic fire must exist."

"Do you know the blessing?" the superstar lacrosse player asked, hoping to address the elephant in the room.

"I'm sorry... no!"

"DAMN!" declared Fredric.

"I'm sorry!"

"It's not your fault and you were right to let us know that a solution exists."

"That doesn't help us much now though, does it?" the futuristic weapon replied.

"Oh I don't know," a familiar voice echoed throughout the destroyed landscape they stood amongst.

"Zarenkesia!" Richie exclaimed. "You know the blessing?"

"No... but I might know someone who does. Be right back."

And with that she was gone, leaving the three of them together watching the demonic fire filled tunnel in front of them, each wondering how dearly the delay would cost them.

Still wrapped around one of Hook's chubby fingers in case Earth decided to show her face again, and having healed all the rugby playing human's injuries from the brief spat with the demented she-witch, the presence confined within the stunning band was surprised to hear his name called out loud by the guardian of the Emporium.

"For'son!"

"What is it?" replied the ethereal spirit within the ring, most of his focus still bolstered by the Emporium's magic firmly at Salisbridge hospital about to aid his allies, Jar Man, DomCon and Steel in the hope of restoring main power back to the site.

"Fredric, Fu-ts'ang and Richie are trapped by what appears to be an almost solid wall of demonic fire. Do you know of anything that can help them out?"

Wracking his brains, Zarenkesia summarised the weapon smith's story about the blessing back in what now would be known as Thailand. The mere mention of that place sparked a memory within the enigmatic band, taking him back many thousands of years, briefly what was happening all around him at the hospital all but forgotten.

At a time when they'd been under resourced, his friend the king had called on his assistance with a matter of the utmost urgency, sending him and him alone to the southern coast of Thailand after reports had emerged of savage dragon raiders looting and pillaging settlements in the area. After a journey of over five days, exhausted and starving, he recalled touching down in a jungle clearing in Rayong province, twenty or so kilometres from the coastline. Spending the night recovering, filling his belly with spit roasted wild boar and foul, allowing the hissing, spitting and crackling flames from the fire to rejuvenate not only his body but his soul as well, at first light he set off in search of some of the local villages that had been tormented by these so-called outlaws.

It didn't take long to reach the first, or should I say, what was left of it. Even back then and in the depths of the jungle, dragon villages and the houses within them were built not only to last, but also to be relatively luxurious. What had transpired there looked as though the mother of all tornados had come sweeping through, levelling pretty much everything.

'If this was done by a group of dragon desperados, then I genuinely fear for the inhabitants, all of whom appear to be missing,' he'd thought.

With no clue to their whereabouts, For'son swiftly moved on to the next village and then the next and the one after that, each one resembling the first in terms of the scale of destruction and the missing occupants.

Arriving just before nightfall at the final village on his list, only a short way from the sea, the charismatic warrior and king's right hand dragon scoured every last inch of what remained, searching for a clue of any sort that would help him in his quest to track down the missing villagers and find the brigands responsible for all the terror and destruction. As he combed his way through the wreckage and broken personal belongings it suddenly dawned on him that he was being watched. Going about his business, pretending not to have cottoned on, he reached out with every last ounce of his magic, detecting at first just a few of his kind, but as the minutes ticked by it became obvious there must have been over one hundred beings beyond the nearby foliage. Given that he was alone, very quickly he had to choose. If they were the bandits then he was already in a world of trouble, but if they were the villagers seeking refuge then they probably desperately needed his help and were almost certainly the ones who'd contacted the king. It was, he knew, about to become a sheer test of nerve.

Continuing his investigation of the scene, all the while still acting as if he had no idea they were even there, very gradually he worked his way towards the edge of the foliage, his super enhanced senses all the time alert for any kind of trap or ignition of magic. So far it hadn't come but maybe they were luring him in.

Close enough now that he could see an array of vertical, slits, the luminous pupils peeking through the branches and detecting only fear and trepidation instead of arrogance and overconfidence, stretching up tall from a kneeling position, he turned to face where he knew the crowd to be cowering and projecting as much calmness as he was able to in the situation, addressed those watching.

"I mean you no harm. I'm here by order of the king and have come to investigate the despicable deeds going on in this region. Please... show yourselves."

A spike of fear ran through all those hiding at the thought that their attackers might be back and attempting to trap them.

Convinced that these were indeed the residents of this and the other surrounding villages and knowing that he had to get them onside and quickly, their terror almost palpable now, in a show of astounding bravery, For'son did something utterly extraordinary. Taking probably one of the greatest risks of his life, he lowered his mental defences and properly opened himself up to all and sundry in an effort to convince them that he was who he said he was.

One huge collective gasp rang out from the confines of the jungle as they got a sense of him. For his part, once he'd proved his worth, it felt like an ever increasing cascade of water pummelling him almost senseless with a variety of information that it was hard to either delve into or resist. But he wasn't the king's number one for no reason and so with the kind of mental fortitude he'd become renowned for across the ages, For'son very slowly managed to sift the data flooding through him, discarding most of it instantly, his keen and curious mind attracted as it usually was by anything related to the supernatural. And let me tell you, there was plenty of that. There were spells for partitioning water used primarily to catch fish. There were mantras to manipulate the trees and enchantments that encouraged crops to grow twice as quickly as they would normally. And so the list went on. The supernatural diversity was on an enormous scale, but what was fascinating was there was very little in the way of offensive magic... it was all about managing the land for the betterment of everyone.

There were, however, two spells that caught his eye as a collector and connoisseur of such things, neither of which he'd ever seen before. One was a rather innovative hex for defending against serious squalls of wind and the other, well the other was ancient, unusual and as unique an enchantment as he'd ever come across. Curious, he caught hold of that particular thread and instead of tugging, followed it back to the source, in the process stumbling into the most passive and peaceful mind he'd ever come across. Introducing himself with as much diplomacy as he possessed, he pointedly asked about what he'd just discovered. The priest (wow, that was a shock initially, because dragon clergy were rare in the extreme, especially so far from civilisation) explained that the magic in question was a supernatural blessing passed down through dozens of generations of dragons, one meant to ensure a being's soul was delivered to a better place and used infrequently given the long lifespans of their kind.

All of this transpired in but a blink of an eye.

Accompanied by the rustling of branches, a wondrous dull green example of their race, slightly taller and thinner than the average dragon, pushed her way out of the foliage and into plain sight.

Holding his nerve, For'son did his best to smile and look unthreatening. It must have worked because the middle aged maiden strolled right up to him and introduced herself as Moxicilla, the de facto leader of one of the destroyed villages and the individual whose idea it had been to get word to the king. After greetings were exchanged, what had happened was explained in great detail to the king's emissary and the meagre food they still retained shared around a series of rather smoky camp fires.

Needless to say For'son, with the villagers' help, went on to prevail, beating back the rogue dragons, forcing them from the small forested island to the south that they'd taken over, regaining everything that had been stolen before burning the bandits' camp and possessions in one unholy inferno. From then onwards, a constant line of communication was kept open with the dragon capital in London via a regular series of messengers, giving the villagers a feeling of belonging, a sense of protection and the impression that they were part of something much, much bigger. All in all, For'son's mission was a total success, with the added bonus that he'd discovered some new magic, which he was excited to tell Orac about and eager to add to the capital's library at the earliest opportunity.

All of this came flooding back to him at Zarenkesia's mention of the word 'Thailand', his eidetic memory serving him well, the faces of the villagers, some of whom he'd ended up calling friends, there right in front of him in exquisite detail, especially the priest. Brushing off the melancholy that threatened to overwhelm him at the thoughts of those long dead dragons, focused, he turned his attention back to the Emporium's mystical presence.

"I know the blessing they need to use."

"Excellent! Recite it to me now and I'll pass it on."

It took only a moment, after which he returned his attention to the sub-station back at the hospital with a view to bringing the main power online.

# 26 HOLEY MOLEY

Where scorched grass met solid rock, Earth dropped to her knees, choosing to rest her forehead on the ground, wispy dark grey smoke rising from across her body, clothes either on fire or littered with holes from the attacks she'd sustained so far. Blood oozed down her arms and legs, pooling around her ankles, dripping off her fingernails, slicking up the floor. Over the roaring rage of the demonic fire she'd used to set alight the magical defences now behind her, a sporadic, crackling hum from tiny forks of bright purple lightning assaulted her ears as what remained of her shield sizzled across her limbs and around her face, the protection that had saved her life on numerous occasions now gone forever, the vault's defences having done a job on her in that regard. Of course she'd tried to reignite the mantra that had been hers since youth sure that it would simply be a case of recasting, but not so, tendrils of insipid magic having crept past her mental defences, seeking out and permanently destroying her most formidable form of defence. If she'd been paying attention, Peter's mother and Fredric's daughter would have been mortified, but she wasn't, in too bad a state to think of anything other than survival and her goal... to destroy HIM!

Using all her formidable strength of character and mental fortitude, the wicked she-witch fought off the intense waves of pain that threatened to set off tears and would by now have destroyed almost any other being, her breathing ragged, probably the only thing keeping her going the adrenaline pumping furiously around her body and her misguided need for vengeance.

Almost totally consumed by madness, on top of the exquisite agony that coursed through her, it was a wonder she didn't just drop to the ground and die. But that wasn't her nature, not after everything she'd been through, and so determined to finish things off before her would-be king destroyed the entire planet, deep within her mind she boxed up the pain, cast it aside and with every ounce of her indomitable will, staggered to her feet, the whole of her body still smoking. Focusing on putting one foot in front of the other, Earth gathered up all her supernatural and sensing that those she was seeking were nearby, set off to end this once and for all. Evil incarnate with nothing to lose was about to make all that was good pay for her mistakes.

It felt fantastic... no, better than that. It felt unbelievable, extraordinary and a relief after being confined in what to him felt like the smallest of boxes, and that was before he'd fully reverted back. As the shimmering blur about the size of an average human expanded out in every direction, the heroic laminium ball captain revelled at the familiarity of the prehistoric within him coming to the fore.

# BOOM!

He was back to his primordial best, returned to the form he belonged in, the one that although pretty much brand spanking new, could perform miracles above the sizzling hot lava, the one that always had his teammates back, the one that had thrilled and entertained fans for decades across the dragon domain.

Familiarising himself with his surroundings, and more than a little muddled, tentatively he scraped the talons of his left foot across the concrete he stood on, cutting the paving slabs in two with just the faintest of touches, marvelling at how such a small action could do so much damage. Only then was he startled from his thoughts at the sound of distant shouting.

"Oh my God, oh my God!" yelled one.

"Run, run for your lives," belted another.

"I... I... I can't... let's get out of here," boomed yet one more.

With the kind of coordination that rarely showed its face

during the working day, the group of engineers attempting to repair the electrical substation on the outskirts of the Salisbridge hospital grounds tore off as fast as they could move, one or two of the more overweight ones bringing up the rear as the fittest of the group disappeared out of sight.

'Well,' thought Steel, 'that was far easier than I thought it would be.'

*"You were of the opinion that turning into an almighty dragon wouldn't have them running for their lives?"* For'son questioned across their telepathic link, one that Steel had forgotten he'd left open.

*"Not so much that, more…"*

*"I'm just kidding. Trust me… they were always going to be terrified beyond belief and sadly, that's probably the only way to get this done. Now stay here and look mean for a little while longer, while I take a gander at the intricacies of the substation."*

*"Understood,"* the laminium ball captain replied, deciding to have a little stomp around for good measure, in an attempt to keep anyone and everyone as far away as possible.

Still boosted by Zarenkesia's unusual magic, For'son's consciousness drifted on over to the electrical substation proper and began to take in the scale of the problem. His very first thought was that things were a mess. The connection to the primary power lines had been damaged as well as the lightning arrester, part of the control building and at least one of the circuit breakers by the look of things. These guys didn't need magic, what they needed was a miracle. Hopefully he could provide it.

Strolling casually across one of the main car parks, trying their best to blend in and look like part of the scenery, Jar Man and DomCon knew that heading towards the main hub of the hospital was the only way to go if they wanted to find one of their own amongst all the humans buzzing around, not quite a needle in a haystack but not far off. They entered the café on the ground floor, which was all but deserted, before taking the stairs to the main level, reaching what should have been the busiest part of the hospital that included the main lobby, a series of restaurants, a charity bookshop and of all things a sweet shop. Given the time of day, it really should have been alive with people heading to outpatient appointments, visiting relatives and arriving for operations. Unfortunately this was not the case although there were still a few people around. This, they both concluded, was where they were meant to be and should give them the best chance to scan as many beings as possible as most filtered through that part of the building at some point. Hopefully one of their kind would show their face sooner rather than later. So sitting on a bench directly beside the main thoroughfare, the two friends, looking as inconspicuous as possible, opened themselves up to their inherent dragon magic and began searching, in the hope of getting Tank the treatment he so desperately needed.

Mirroring those nurses nearby doing an outstanding job, the formidable warrior trapped in the enigmatic band had a little triage of his own to perform, in an attempt to work out what order to try and repair the damage to the substation. Having already decided very deliberately to leave the main connection to the grid until last, he set about restoring the lightning arrester, thinking that safety should probably be put first. Imagining how the wires deep within should be connected, it was a case at first of replacing some of the copper beneath the outer layer of plastic for some, stripping others out entirely before using his dizzying array of supernatural to revamp the circuit boards and check they were working. After that the outer casing was fully mended. Simple it wasn't, but it was effective. After merely a matter of moments, the first part in a chain was completed, and being bolstered by the Emporium's protective essence meant that he wasn't drained of any ethereal energy. Moving swiftly on, he attacked the next part of the puzzle, the circuit breakers, which on first inspection all looked to be totally shot to hell.

Monotonous on an almost industrial level, the two friends perched on the bench just inside the main entrance had taken to reading papers, spending time on their phones and just chatting casually away in an effort to conceal their true purpose. With fewer people about than normal, they supposed it was possible that some smarty pants might notice their over long stay and so each had come up with a back story in case they should be quizzed. Both supposed godfathers to two of the children recently rescued from the school within the renowned close, they were awaiting any news on their condition, unable to get through to the parents of each child themselves. Of course the tall tale was full of plot holes, but they hoped it would be enough to buy them some more time and pass tentative scrutiny if necessary.

*"Got anything?"* DomCon enquired through their shared invisible link, whilst reading the sports pages of the paper.

*"Don't you think I would have alerted you if I had?"* his friend replied a little too testily, their roles reversed for once.

*"I just thought that…"*

*"I know, and I'm sorry for snapping. But none of this is getting us anywhere. There must be something else we can do."*

*"What about heading towards the basement? After all that's where the emergency dragon command centre is located."*

*"It's risky on so many levels especially…"*

*"What is it?"*

*"There's…"*

*"What?"*

*"I think I've just found what we've been looking for. Follow me!"*

Both standing up simultaneously, a little too eager, Jar Man started to stroll with his typical good grace after a white coated medical professional in the distance, following him out into the murky main corridor, all the lights away from the main entrance running on emergency power, before trailing him at a distance as he headed towards the different array of departments located on this level.

"*What's the plan?*" the diminutive pocket rocket asked.

"*We need to nab him before he gets anywhere near his destination.*"

"*How the hell are we supposed to do that?*"

"*I have absolutely no idea. We'll just have to wing it!*"

Picking up the pace and keeping their inherent magical abilities fully reined in, both pals, all the while gaining on their target, started to scout about for an opportunity to get their prey alone and make sure he was what he appeared to be. The distinct lack of main lights down the main hallway was one advantage in their favour; however the options were limited, to say the least.


On closer inspection, the circuit breakers were never going to be repaired, the damage being far too substantial. Discarding them effortlessly over the security fence which had been torn asunder in numerous places, For'son created a series of new ones from scratch. It took nearly five minutes in all, but the results were so totally worth it. The replacements were well crafted and designed, definite upgrades, which he knew would be noticed eventually, but he wasn't willing to budge, knowing that the king would want the place to be as safe and efficient as possible even if there were one or two telltale signs of interference by someone or something slightly more advanced in nature. Yet one more piece of the puzzle complete, For'son, mind working feverishly, knew that from now onwards it would get increasingly difficult. Steeling himself for what was to come, he moved on to repairing the outer wall of the control building, knowing that no good would come of it if people could gain entrance willy nilly, or that the decidedly poor weather could get in and attack all the electronics. Ignoring the giant dragon skulking about close by, very slowly and carefully he began hovering the individual bricks that lay scattered on the ground next to the main transformer back into place, using his powerful magic to create a super strong mortar from thin air with which to bond them. Slowly the damaged outer walls started to take shape.

Up ahead the two of them could just make out a sign that read 'Scanning Department' off to the right of the main drag, its interior marked by being especially dark, computers and lights at the reception turned off, the generators running on backup making all but the essential scanners in accident and emergency redundant, this one currently the quietest of departments and an ideal placement for a potential ambush. With just a look this time, the two friends sped up, determined to catch their target, trying to discover if he really was something other than human and that he had access to the emergency dragon contingency area in the basement of the main building.

Timing their progress to perfection, they caught up with the white coated medical professional just as he was about to walk past the entrance to the scanning department. Taking the initiative, Jar Man leapt into action.

"Excuse me, my friend," he said, "you couldn't possibly tell me which way to the paediatric department could you?"

The dark haired doctor turned around to face them, standing off to one side of the nearly deserted main thoroughfare, the name on his badge stating that he was Doctor Tomlinson, the head, unfortunately for them, of the department that they been pretending to search for.

"Of course," he replied, both eloquently and professionally, although slightly suspicious, "perhaps you could tell me who you've come to see?"

Both stumped momentarily, with the good doctor's attention firmly focused on the gentle ginger giant, DomCon did a quick recon of the corridor they stood in.

Briefly it was clear of anyone looking in their direction. Without even bothering to ask his pal, instinctively he acted.

Gathering up all his magic, he encased the three of them in a huge sound proof bubble before grabbing the doctor and Jar Man with all his supernatural and thrusting them through the darkened entrance, sliding to a halt some twenty five or so metres in.

Taken completely by surprise, it took Doctor Tomlinson a second or two to realise that all was not okay and that he might well be in danger. About to ignite the most powerful offensive spell he knew, he was once again caught off guard when a giant pale hand slammed firmly over his mouth accompanied by a voice that said,

"Please don't do anything rash. We don't want to hurt you. We just need your help."

Still on guard but sensing no duplicity and in all honesty having no other choice, the good doctor gave the slightest of nods, which was all he could manage with Jar Man pinning his head up against the wall with his hand over his mouth.

"I'm going to take my hand away now. Please... hear us out. We're on a mission from the king himself and have a comrade who's in a dire state and needs the facilities here to stand any chance of recovery."

As the big fella's hand slipped aside, the first thing the doctor did was take a breath, an encouraging start as far as the other two were concerned.

"Y... y... you could have just revealed yourselves and asked for help," he muttered nervously.

"I'm sorry Doc," Jar Man put in, "but the mission we're on would be regarded as top secret at best, and who knows what at worst. Trust is currently in very short supply."

Their new found friend nodded his agreement.

"Will you help us?" DomCon asked, attempting to move things along.

"What would you have me do?"

"One of our own, a friend who's saved the king's life

half a dozen times over, has a traumatic brain injury and needs treatment immediately."

"Surely he needs to be taken to a dragon facility in the domain?" whispered the doctor, now certain of the need for privacy.

"Unfortunately it's not quite as easy as that," noted Ginge. "Our friend spends much of his time in his human guise and that's the form he was in when the injury occurred. Best diagnosis is that he needs to be treated somewhere that has excellent human medical equipment available and since he's a resident of Salisbridge, that's here."

"I... I... I see."

Well, he didn't actually, but perhaps he would at some point in the near future.

"Where is he now?"

That was the question they'd both been dreading because the explanation, something neither totally understood, was quite confounding.

"He's in the domain, the capital actually."

"And you want to bring him here from THERE?! If he's in as bad a shape as you suggest, the journey alone might kill him."

"It's quite complicated," suggested Jar Man with as much tact as he could muster, realising he was slowly starting to lose the doctor's cooperation and trust, "but let's just say that he could be here in the blink of an eye if conditions were right."

Puzzled, the medical professional tried to get his head around the concept.

"Please doc, will you help us?" DomCon pretty much begged, a huge turnaround in attitude from him.

With little other option and able to almost sense the honesty, pain and misery of the two strangers standing before him, what else could Doctor Tomlinson do but comply?

Quickly he agreed, telling them that for all of this to

work they needed to head down to the basement through a series of stringent checks that would allow them access to the emergency dragon medical facilities.

Absolutely delighted, the two buddies followed in the doctor's wake as he led them through a maze of wards and back rooms, followed briefly by the odd secret entrance on the way to their final destination.

He was immensely enjoying being back in his magnificent primeval body and above ground in his natural form, a first for him as it broke every rule he'd ever been taught, as laminium ball players are strictly forbidden from doing just that. Steel inhaled a huge breath as he gazed lovingly at the sun up above in the clear blue sky as wispy ringlets of light grey smoke flitted into the air from around his nostrils. Feeling the radiant rays beating down on his humungous dragon body was special beyond belief and something he'd only ever dreamt about before. Still plodding around the periphery of the electrical substation in an effort to cause the mother of all distractions, the courageous captain, his mind on his surroundings, turned a corner only to be confronted by...

It was an unspoken, filthy secret, yet known to many, an area behind one of the buildings furthest from the hospital itself. Covered from all three sides, staff and an occasional patient in the know could walk out into the grubby courtyard and enjoy a cigarette, something that had been banned site-wide a few years earlier because of the health implications and the destructive nature of the addiction. That hadn't stopped those with the compulsion for a smoke finding a way to fulfil their detrimental craving. And so as per usual during the day, a group of thirty or so men and women, doctors, nurses, orderlies and secretaries, with the odd patient thrown in for good measure, gathered in the midst of a cloud of smoke so thick you could almost cut it with a knife, surrounded on the ground by hundreds of flattened cigarette butts that nobody gave a damn about. All were chatting with friends and one another, bonding over their illicit infatuation, each puff giving them that brief and immediate buzz. Out of nowhere their informal gathering was rudely interrupted when, of all things, an almighty dragon stomped casually into the courtyard, his gigantic head tilted skyward, his attention seemingly elsewhere for the time being. Every single human being stood stock still, hoping against hope to escape the monster's attention, still smouldering cigarettes hanging from pursed lips and forked fingers.

Relishing not only the delight of basking in the sun but the cool breeze and the taste of the fresh air, suddenly Steel realised something was happening off to his left. Craning his neck around slowly, he immediately came face to face with the staggered group of human statues, all of whom looked as fearful as any could.

*"Uhh... For'son, I've got a bit of an issue here."*

*"What is it?"* the enigmatic essence in the ring remarked, disappointed at having his concentration interrupted.

*"I've stumbled across a group of humans... they're just standing there like statues looking at me. I think their insides might be on fire."*

Reluctantly splitting his focus, For'son said,

*"Show me!"*

The brave laminium ball captain did so.

*"Ha ha."*

*"What's so funny?"*

*"What you have there is an assembly of smokers."*

*"Huh?"*

*"Those things in their mouths... they're called cigarettes and they inhale the contents wrapped up within them."*

*"Why?"*

*"A brief high."*

*"Oh."*

*"Generally speaking though, they're bad for you."*

*"Why do they continue to...?"*

*"They get addicted to all the nasty chemicals."*

*"What should I do?"*

Still repairing parts of the control building at the substation, For'son smiled, or at least would have if he'd had a physical body. The general gist of what he felt passed between the two allies as he told Steel what he thought he should do.

Up for the challenge, the laminium ball player instantly got on with it.

Stomping forwards, he stopped just short of the group, and stood gazing straight at them. One or two had bladder control issues.

Leaning his giant scaled head in towards them through the sickly harsh smoke that made his eyes itch and water, he eyed them all before carefully considering his words.

"Smoking," he articulated, "is very bad for your health. Ditch it immediately!"

Lit cigarettes dropped from hands and mouths onto the grubby, lichen covered ground.

Deciding it was time they left, Steel let out a huge stream of flame directly above the group's heads and with as much authority as he could muster, commanded,

"BE GONE!"

Like rats racing out of an aqueduct, the humans ran back through an open door into the building as fast as they could move, some getting stuck in the entrance itself, all of them kissing goodbye to the last smoke of their lives after what could be described as the most bizarre encounter any of them had ever experienced.

With For'son's chuckling echoing in his mind, Steel let out a huge belly laugh, one that threatened to resound throughout the entire hospital site.

# 27 EMERGENCY INTERVENTION

*"Can this possibly work?"* Zebediah reflected across the telepathic link in the direction of those he considered his siblings.

Momentary silence abounded as the individuals continued to hunt out every last scrap of laminium in an effort to get it as expediently into the core of the planet.

*"Who's to say it won't?"* replied Tarko, corkscrewing through a small gap in the rock off to one side of the borehole about fifteen kilometres down, following one of Yoyo's streams of light, closing in on a small amount of the precious metal.

*"All of this... Fate, and the planet having some sort of sentience seems odd and unlikely at best,"* Zeb answered, hanging out in the midst of the tunnel watching up above for any stray packages heading their way.

*"What other choice do we all have?"* Essie piped up whilst wheeling around in a tight circle heading for the next target her healer mentor had picked out for her.

*"It's just that..."*

*"We get it, we do,"* Tina chipped in, *"but what's not to believe? Did you see what was hanging over us at the top of the borehole?"*

A few mental nods of agreement flourished through the shared connection.

*"Who or what else could wield the kind of power to hold that in check for such a long time? If you have another explanation, I for one would love to hear it."*

Of course he didn't. I mean what other explanation could there possibly be?

*"I understand what you're saying, but... this! It's wacky beyond belief."*

In a sense they all agreed with him.

*"I suggest,"* ventured Tina, *"that we keep our heads down and concentrate on the job at hand. Who knows how much time we have*

*before the grip on what's remaining of that missile is relinquished? The sooner we get all the laminium into the core, the greater our chance of survival."*

Agreeing with more mental nods, Yoyo's youngsters continued to go about their business with consummate professionalism.


It felt to Fate like swiping between apps, when she flitted between different realities. One moment she'd be overseeing the delivery of the precious metal to the core, the next she'd be giving Luck and Time a pat on the back for their efforts with the nuclear warhead, after that she'd be throwing all her magic at the already exploded missile before trying to communicate with the increasingly erratic and exhausted Novus, the being who lay at the heart of their scheme to defeat the evil that would demolish the entire planet.

Pleased to have co-opted the dragon heroes to help with their plan, metaphysical eyes closed and with just a thought, Fate found herself beside her two partners, the other Providences, checking in to see how they were doing.

Before they'd even become aware of her presence it was clear that both were struggling, the toll taken by the constant spamming of the missile and its surroundings by their inborn magic tremendous at best, epic at worst, each close to faltering if she wasn't mistaken. And that led her to believe that she had to do something, but what, that was the question. Almost as if her thoughts had been read, the tiniest voice in the world resonated around her subconscious, suggesting a course of action.

*"Let them see a fate in which we prevail and they go on to thrive. Make them think that all their efforts now will lead to a successful outcome."*

*"You mean... CHEAT!"*

*"Is it cheating? You don't know that won't be the upshot anyhow so how can it be cheating?"*

*"But it's just... wrong!"*
*"Not if it redoubles their efforts and pinpoints their focus."*
*"But..."*

It was only then that Fate recognised the voice... it was Novus! What the hell?

Turning her attention back to her struggling... what? Friends, yes she was pretty sure that was it... friends. Turning her attention back to both of them, watching the sweat dripping in droves off Luck whilst Time stood there shaking almost uncontrollably, in that moment she knew the planet's presence was right and that she really had no choice.

*"Only bad things can come of this,"* her conscience, if that's what it was, told her. It was, however, too late to do anything else and so she acted as only she could, showing each a glimpse of the future, one in which they all survived, along with humanity and of course the dragons, one that they once again could influence and watch over. Allowing the visions to drift away, she went on to hint that it was all dependent on their current struggles, whispering in their ears for them to intensify their efforts once again and continue to spam the exploded wreckage of the warhead over and over. Observing closely, taking no pleasure in the deception she'd just initiated, Fate could see that Novus' cunning ploy had worked, with Luck standing tall and strong, and Time now the personification of confidence.

It had been a gamble, but it had paid off big time. Shaking her head, wondering what the hell would happen next, she instead turned the main part of her attention back to events in and around the borehole, hoping that the being who'd become their favourite and his allies were up to the task of getting Novus firmly back on his feet.

Back in France, Flash and Amelia having teamed up in much the same way as the others had, tasked themselves with going for the laminium hidden in the furthest depths of the borehole. Okay... it wasn't all that deep, but it was still taking some finding because those who'd deposited it clearly had orders to hide it all over the place. Even under Yoyo's guidance using the resonating frequencies of the earth's magnetic field, it was still tough going for the dream team King's Guard and the former Crimson Guard. Still, they ploughed on and on, not daring to even think about the already exploded missile hanging twenty five or so kilometres above their heads, because if they did, even they'd be frozen by fear.

*"Do you get any sense of how much we've completed?"* Captain Battlehard asked the dragon she'd totally fallen head over heels for.

*"If I had to take a guess I'd say comfortably over half, maybe even more than that."*

*"Good to know."*

*"Amelia."*

*"Flash?"*

*"Do you really think we can wriggle our way out of this one?"*

Sighing out loud, which didn't come across the link as they were separated by about two hundred metres, the good captain considered her reply.

*"All I can really say is that I hope so. Although the future I see seems bleak and short, I've got so much to live for now... you, these fabulous friends, more than I've had across the whole of my lifetime, and all that I wish is to share a long and happy life with each and every one of you. Whether that comes to pass depends on the actions of so many in the here and now. I suppose all we can do is our best, give it our all, and hope that good conquers evil once and for all."*

Of course she was right, Flash knew, but that didn't stop the sinking feeling he had in the pit of his stomach from exerting itself hugely.

*"How are you doing, lover?"*

That made him smile and almost forced him to lose his focus... ALMOST!

He knew she could be playful at times, always knowing the right thing to say and how to illicit a smile even on the darkest of days.

*"You do realise all the others are attuned to what we're thinking, lover,"* Yoyo teased his wife right back, ready and waiting for some witty comeback.

*"I'll be sure not to mention your fascination for rubber then,"* she quipped, almost holding back the tears now.

A series of yucks, ucks, ughs and owwws came ricocheting back throughout their telepathic connection.

*"SHE'S JOKING!"* the healer exclaimed, having been thoroughly rinsed.

*"I can't tell you the number of times I've come home only to hear the sharp TWANG of rubber on scale as I enter the house,"* Rose giggled rather inappropriately.

*"I'm a healer... some of my work involves wearing rubber gloves. That's it!"*

*"Me thinks thou doth protest too much,"* interjected Flash imitating a Shakespearean voice, playing along with the momentary distraction.

*"Ugh... ugh... ugh... ugh and double ugh,"* ventured Monty.

Throughout the borehole every dragon shook their head apart from Amelia who, with a wry smile on her face, burst out laughing.

The hilarity felt like a fleeting ray of sunshine in the darkest of times.

A familiar voice brought the husband and wife team back to reality with a bump.

"How much laminium has been returned?" Peter's perfect facsimile asked in exactly his voice, only slightly more stone cold.

Sharing a look with his wife and conferring telepathically before answering, Yoyo took this one on the chin.

"If I had to guess, I'd say about sixty percent of what is here is on its way to being sent back."

"That little?"

"That, my dear, is a considerable amount, especially when you take in to account that it's dotted about all over the place within the borehole. They're working as fast as they can."

Glancing overhead at the partly exploded nuclear warhead hanging there above them with one partition of her mind, whilst taking in the effort that Luck and Time were having to exude with another, Fate's response was rather blunt to say the least.

"Work faster! We're nearly out of time!"

Vacating the Bentwhistle duplicate on some level at least, the mistress of mischief and flayer of fortunes ordered the part of her with most control to return to Novus. Immediately it did so.

*"NOVUS! NOVUS! Snap out of it. We need you and your abilities NOW!"*

NOTHING!

Very naughty words in a variety of different languages ran through the Providences' de facto leader's mind, all with the same theme. Her patience balanced on a knife edge, and struggling to hold herself in check, she decided on a change in tack.

*"Novus,"* she whispered this time, across the ethereal realm between them, *"I'm assured the laminium is on its way, please... come back to us."*

Looking for all intents and purposes as though he was out for the count, the sickly looking old man laid out prone on some kind of invisible floor began to groan and grumble, his arms and legs twitching like he'd just peed up against an electric fence.

Injecting just the tiniest smidgen of her rare and curious magic, all that she could spare in fact, Fate sent the slenderest of threadlike tendrils off in his direction, hoping that perhaps she could kick start him into being that way. At the merest touch her supernatural exploded in a way unlike anything she'd ever experienced. Expecting to hit a dull wall of absolute resistance, the connoisseur of chance was astounded to be inundated with not only a staggering array of emotions but also of varying degrees of what could only be described as raw power, some humungous in scope, others minute, all growing incrementally with every moment that passed and although she couldn't find the keen and caring mind of the being she'd once known, she was absolutely certain that a reaction had started, one she hoped would have the outcome they all prayed for. Fingers crossed!

*"Flash,"* Yoyo prompted across their shared connection, *"I thought you should know, Fate's just implied that we're running out of time."*

*"It's impossible to work any faster with all the laminium being spread out as it is."*

*"I know... that's what I told her, but reading between the lines it can't get to the core quick enough."*

'Quick enough,' he reflected, his eidetic dragon memory recalling every last syllable of the words only recently spoken by his friend and someone he, for the most part, thoroughly admired. 'Quick enough,' there... he said it again.

*"Yoyo... pull Amelia and I off laminium duty."*

"FLASH!" exclaimed Captain Battlehard.

"DO YOU TRUST ME?" he asked, turning to the prehistoric beauty beside him, the female he thought of as his soulmate, wanting nothing more than to live out the rest of time entwined in her wings.

No pause, no hesitation, just an immediate instinctive response.

"WITH MY LIFE!"

"And everyone else's?"

"YES!"

"GOOD!"

*"Yoyo! Do as I've just instructed. Amelia and I are about to speed up the transfer time of our special metal deliveries. Flash out!"*

With that the former Crimson Guard grabbed the good captain by the hand, dragging her in his wake out into the middle of the tunnel proper and explained exactly what they were going to do. To say it blew her mind didn't really do it justice.

# 28 SUB-SISTENCE

"Anything?" George asked Whitewings, as the general touched down with all the deftness of a marine's perfect parachute landing right beside him.

"An oddity, sire."

"Go on."

"A couple of the satellites are picking up traces of radiation from the site of the borehole in northern France."

"But I thought it hadn't exploded."

"That is the considered opinion from those working on the problem. There's been no discernible shock wave, no damage to the surroundings, no catastrophic reaction as far as we can tell. That's what I mean by oddity."

"Then where has the radiation come from?"

"A leak from the missile? A remnant left over from whatever our dragons on the ground have done to avert the crisis? It's very difficult to tell from this distance," reflected the general.

Shaking his head softly and rubbing his eyes, the dragon monarch let out a sigh as his thoughts turned to those he considered friends, the heroes who'd given so much, supposedly already having vanquished Manson and his villainous queen, the wicked witch and daughter of his best friend, turning around a dark dragon invasion, repelling an army of nagas caught under a dastardly supernatural spell, saving so many in the process. But had all that, and the heartbreaking death of the former Emporium owner, been for nothing? Radiation from the nuclear warhead being detected over the test borehole was more than a concern and signalled, in his mind at least, that this emergency was far from over.

"Whitewings," directed George, the seriousness in his voice nothing short of deadly, "task a satellite over that area that will give us an image of exactly what's going on. I don't care how you do it, just get it done, and quickly!”

“As you command, Majesty,” the general replied, darting up into the air before doubling back over on himself, disappearing behind the second floor balcony on his way to do as his friend had just asked.


“Uhhh…” groaned the weapons officer busy at the computer trying to bypass all the safeguards with a view to remotely detonating the warhead.

“What is it?” Manson demanded, picking up the concern that was evident to all those in the command centre of the sub.

“T… t… the missile my lord…”

“Yes?”

“I… I… it appears to have already… exploded!”

“WHAT!”

“I… I can’t explain it.”

“Then why are we not reading an atomic explosion and mass devastation?”

“I’m sorry,” the officer submitted, “I don’t have any detailed answers. All I can tell you is that the missile has detonated and… that’s all.”

Restraining himself from lashing out once again and smashing another console with his enhanced supernatural senses, the failed would-be king considered what he’d heard. Nothing made sense. Surely if a detonation had taken place, they would have known about it by now, even if it hadn’t reacted with the laminium that he was certain would have been correctly placed within the confines of the borehole. How had the death and devastation he’d planned so carefully, not occurred? It simply wasn’t possible!

Anger coursing through his veins, barely containing his ire, all he wanted to do was visit annihilation and mass casualties on both dragon and human populations, the searing need to do evil overpowering each of his senses. Fed up with running away, absolutely certain that none of them were escaping the super expensive tin can they all found themselves trapped in, not with dragons and nagas outside working together, his keen and malicious mind decided on a new course of action.

"Helm! Set a change of course!"

"Destination, my lord?"

"Take us east and then south. I want us as close to Edinburgh as is…", he nearly said "humanly possible," but that single word, the one that described the dragons' pets, felt so repulsive that he couldn't bring himself to even utter it. "I want to be right on the city's doorstep... as quickly as possible. Get on with it!"

"Course laid in," replied the officer, his mind working overtime wondering why the hell they were now heading towards the Scottish capital.

It was a common question running riot throughout the heads of all the other beings trapped in there with him.

Barely able to see through the black, shadowy water, it came as something of a surprise to all four of them when quite abruptly the state of the art submarine made the sharpest possible turn it could, heading back on itself eastwards, parallel to the Scottish coastline.

*'That's odd,'* Vimes expressed across his constantly open link to Vasuki.

*'Unusual... yes,'* the monarch replied, *'but not unforeseen. I think we have to assume they've come up with a plan, one in which they think they can shake us off their scent and maybe inflict more misery.'*

*"And that would be what, exactly?"*

*'Impossible to say I'm afraid, without being privy to their clandestine conversations. But I think we have to assume that all the local populace are in grave danger.'*

That, thought Vimes, really went without saying.

Grateful for the borrowed spell that defended against the chilling cold of the icy sea and allowed him to breathe should he need to, the former *tor* and Santa's other half effortlessly swept back on himself using his gigantic tail as a rudder, pursuing his allies, all of them continuing to track the nuclear submarine, still following his friend Flash's orders to the letter.

*"Should we try and take it out?"*

*"Easier said than done,"* shot back the snake-like monarch in an instant, pondering the same question himself. *"A nuclear leak, implosion or explosion in these waters would be a disaster of epic proportions, not only for the human inhabitants nearby but for the sea and the wonderfully diverse ecosystems it supports, recovery from which would take many, many generations."*

Vimes could see his point, but was more than slightly distracted by the word 'explosion' which started him thinking. What had happened to the missile that had already been launched?

*"We'd know in an instant if the warhead had exploded,"* Vasuki assured, not quite reading his mind, *"even inland and away from the oceans."*

*"And it hasn't?"*

*"Not so far."*

*"That can only be a good thing... right?"*

*"Let's assume so, but there's no guarantee."*

*"The longer this goes on, the more it makes me think we should finish them, one way or the other, right NOW!"*

*"On many levels it does make sense. But aside from the questions we've already explored, there's the very real issue of how we achieve that. Not only because of the state of the art human defences the ship possesses, but because undoubtedly it's protected by magic, some of which I can feel is naga in nature, some of which is anything but."*

*"It's dragon based,"* the former *tor* put in.

*"So, how to defeat human technology combined with ancient naga and dragon supernatural spells, that's the question."*

*"I wouldn't even begin to know who to call,"* Vimes added sarcastically, going on to mimic an ordinary human. *"Is that planet annihilation assistance, I'd like to speak to a specialist please."*

Strangely though, that gave Vasuki an idea.

# 29 BLESSED RELIEF

"Do you want me to do it?" The White Dragon asked, eager to get on with it.

"I'll get it done," Fredric asserted, all the while trying to control his breathing and slow his heart, the thought of what was to come and exactly what his grandson might be facing almost overwhelming, but not quite.

"If you need extra support, we're here," put in the weapon smith trapped in the fantastic blade.

"Your backing is very much appreciated," announced the founder of the Crimson Guards, turning to face his comrades in this crazy escapade, his huge, well muscled silhouette outlined by the raging demonic fire filling the entirety of the tunnel blocking their way behind him, "both of you!"

With the tiniest nod of her head, Richie acknowledged Fredric's well intentioned words, their past disputes all but forgotten.

Fu-ts'ang mirrored the gesture, tipping his hilt forward ever so slightly from his upright hovering position.

Plucking up all his indomitable will, long, unkempt hair flapping about wildly in the raging gusts produced by the devilishly frolicking flames, the father of the psychotic dragon they were stalking turned to face the most immediate obstacle in their path. Clearing his mind, bringing all his innate supernatural to the fore, the sound of rushing water ringing in his ears, his concentration intense, applying all his remarkable resolve, deep within his consciousness, Fredric, eyes now closed, repeated the ancient blessing Zarenkesia had passed on from the enigmatic presence For'son.

*"Utilising the power of the land, grant us the magical counter to snuff out the wickedness of the fiendish fire and favour a positive outcome. Reflect the malevolence back to whence it came and strengthen*

*our outer shells in this time of uncertainty."*

Arms spread as wide as they'd go, biceps bulging through his clothes, feeling a gargantuan gale of magical mana surge out of his body, he opened them just in time to see the primeval blessing hit its mark.

The taint of evil in the form of the demonic fire resisted, well... for but a moment, but after that it had little choice, overcome in every aspect by not only superior magic, but by an impeccable sense of righteousness and good. In a matter of seconds every last scrap of it was expunged.

Fixing her eyes on the dystopian panorama ahead, truly appalled at the total obliteration of the magical landscape that had previously existed within the confines of the supernatural route to the treasure trove of ancient artefacts, the blackened, smouldering and smoking remains making her want to cough up a lung, fighting back her disgust, the superstar lacrosse player spoke just two words.

"Let's go!"

With Fredric by her side, the mystical weapon smith trapped in the futuristic blade at their back, enhanced by all the supernatural speed their magic could muster, they set off at a blur for a date not only with family, but with destiny.


Deep underground, well... for the human world anyway, two ape-like shapes, one small and squat, the other much larger and ginger haired, followed an apparent doctor in a long, flowing, off white coat down a dark and dreary corridor lined with blue plastic seats mainly made up of holes, ones that not long ago had cushioned the butts of Peter and Tank as they'd awaited news of their friend Richie, supposedly back from the dead. This as it turns out, was the exact place in which George the monarch had turned up to see what they thought at the time, was The White Dragon in the form of Tim, the hockey player who'd so brutally died at the hands of Troydenn at the very start of the Changing of the Guard.

Negotiating the swinging double doors that led to the ward that both Richie and her illicit lover Tim had been contained behind, Doctor Tomlinson drew to a halt before opening up his arms to indicate his surroundings.

"This," he announced, "is the best we have. A human-dragon hybrid facility that's jam-packed full of the latest cutting edge technology... if your friend needs medical attention, then he won't get better treatment than what's on offer here."

Glancing around, both DomCon and Jar Man could see the good doctor spoke no word of a lie. It was indeed both impressive and advanced.

"What do you think?" short stop asked his strawberry blonde buddy.

"It looks perfect. I'll get in touch with For'son and let him know what we've found."

Closing his eyes, the gentle giant reached out towards an entirely different part of the hospital site.


Making the most of the opportunity provided to him by Steel's dramatic change in bodily circumstances, For'son, never one to look a gift dragon in the mouth, pressed on with all the professionalism and speed he could, his mind a whirring blur, having to switch between his instinctive use of magic and his understanding of technology, which although diverse and competent, did slow him down a little. Determined to restore the main power to the hospital not just for his partner in crime Tank, but for all the humans that now more than ever needed its services, the mysterious former warrior dragon proceeded with less caution and more haste.

Seemingly from out of thin air the current transformer inside the control building began repairing itself... at first the circuit boards, multiple layers of copper rebuilding themselves, old schematics thrown out for something much newer and eminently more fantastic, a feat that might come back to haunt him at some point in the future should the humans notice, but not today. Damaged capacitors and their flimsy connectors simply disappeared, replaced in the blink of an eye by much smaller, more efficient, new ones, designs beyond cutting edge, some might even say from the future itself. And so it continued with the resistors, the fibreglass base and the wires running off them, total re-fabrication completed in seconds, the entire transformer rebuilt from scratch in less than a minute.

On a roll now, the moment that was finished For'son moved on to the busted security fence surrounding the perimeter of the electrical sub-station, fully aware of just how important it was to keep members of the general public out and maintain a degree of safety with such dangerous equipment. Reinforcing the concrete terminal posts of the surrounding fence with just a thought, the damaged sections of the chain-link barrier disappeared into complete nothingness, replaced by brand new wire, fence ties, tension bars and top rails. To round it all off a gate frame and gate was added, after which For'son used the previous combination padlock to secure the lock, sure that those in charge would appreciate not having to break into the good as new facility. And that only left one thing... to reconnect the primary and secondary power lines to the current transformer. That should, in theory at least, get things back up and running across the site, which would change everyone's disposition and situation.

Using a great deal of the borrowed mana from Zarenkesia, a vast array of his magical knowledge combined with his deft touch at telekinesis, addressing the problem with the intricate workings of his psyche, he allowed his consciousness to step back in the ultimate out of body experience and watch on as the power lines were reattached just as they should be. Display screens inside the control building sparkled into life as row upon row of brightly lit buttons burst into being. Fans whirled as servers came online, newly rebuilt overhead lights blinking on to offer some illumination. That familiar process started to repeat itself across the entire hospital site, rows of neon tubes shedding light on dimly lit corridors including those in the hidden basement section known only to a highly selective group of prehistoric beasts whose job entailed constantly blending in with the humans in the facility. Air conditioning thrummed instantly into life simultaneously providing some comfort for all, none more so than in the maternity ward where dedicated nurses and midwifes continued to do their utmost to support all those mothers in varying degrees of labour. Throughout the main building a muted cheer rang out, mostly from the patients, the doctors and dedicated medical professionals too utterly exhausted to even raise their voices, let alone applaud.

Job well done, the warrior dragon presence trapped in the peculiar loop, deep underground back in the capital breathed a sigh of relief, well... metaphorically anyhow. But his work was far from done. About to reach out to DomCon and Jar Man, a nagging telepathic manifestation from the two of them just about beat him to it.

*"You have news?"* he queried, sensing the pair somehow basking in satisfaction.

*"We do,"* the larger of the two replied. *"We've found what we need."*

*"Go on."*

*"We're here with Doctor Tomlinson, a dragon who's in charge of the emergency dragon protocol plan. There's a ward that Tank can be transported to immediately, one with the very best in technology and resources. In fact, we're standing in it right now."*

*"Excellent! I'm about to reintegrate myself back into the ring. Once I've done that, I'll get in touch and we'll send his body via a wormhole directly to you. Stand by."*

First though, he had something else to take care of.

Steel was pleased and yet concerned that he'd frightened the hell out of the smokers and made them seemingly run for their lives despite the fact they weren't in any real danger. The unstoppable laminium ball captain and one of the many heroes of the taking back of Fleet Street, continued to stomp around part of the hospital grounds adjacent to the electrical sub-station, not knowing that For'son's ingenuity had since got it back up and running.

*"Enjoying our little jaunt out in the open in your natural form?"* echoed the voice of the engaging former dragon warrior throughout the confines of his mind.

*"For'son!"*

*"Of course!"*

*"Is it done? Have you restored the power?"*

*"Yep. And that's why I'm here. You'd better shift back into a human pretty damn quick because company in the form of half a dozen security guards are right around the corner. I'd suggest hightailing it back to the main hospital building after that. Your companions will be able to guide you to their position in the secret basement level."*

*"And you?"*

*"Back to the capital to help induce the wormhole so that we can transport Tank down here."*

*"Thanks for your help,"* Steel ventured, truly happy to have assisted in even a small way.

*"It was my pleasure. Now... get changed, quickly, they're nearly upon you."*

Across the entire hospital district, lights flickered into being, servers buzzed into life, computers booted up, air conditioning units hummed with newly found power as doctors, nurses, orderlies, secretaries and porters sprinted towards where they would normally be, the order having come down from upon high that as soon as the electricity was fully returned the hospital would be up and running as normal in an effort to plough through the backlog of patients who'd waited throughout the crisis. Missing medics and staff who were in fact dragons treating those of their own kind injured locally, based in the cloak-and-dagger basement, had as usual been stealthily rotated into position in a manner that none of the humans would notice, the practice tried and tested across many, many decades. In all but an instant, the underperforming, partly functioning facility had returned to its fabulous best, a boost not only to those waiting to be treated, but to the dedicated staff also, knowing that they could once again fulfil their purpose, treating the sick, incapable and injured.

# 30 RALLYING CRY

Oceans across the globe are a dog eat dog environment. The biggest and meanest apex predators usually come out on top, the global food chain all but set in stone, different species knowing their place and never straying from it due to their size, ferocity and how well equipped and adapted they are to their locale. The key word here is USUALLY because going back hundreds of thousands of years (and no one knows exactly how) a supernatural contingency of sorts was developed and bred into the DNA of everything living beneath the surface of the sea. Ninety nine point nine percent of the creatures going about their daily lives would be classed as receivers and/or conduits, even then not realising they were so. The other point one of the top percentile were those capable of ruling their individual species, the kings and queens if you like, those chosen in whatever way... by birthright, some form of democracy or occasionally dominating a constant series of fights to the death. Each of these were classed as broadcasters and had the ability through their tweaked DNA, should circumstances call for it, to give a shout out for help on a very specific frequency, one answered and adhered to by all, one only to be used in the most dire need. The last time it had been used was well over twenty thousand years ago when a rogue group of leviathans (that's sea serpents to you and I) had used their innate shadowy supernatural abilities and threatened to annihilate the entire world by colliding a series of tectonic plates under the Pacific Ocean. Briefly a violent war was waged, one unknown to all land dwellers including the dragons, one in which many perished, including whole seafaring species. Whilst good had prevailed over malicious malevolence, the victory came at a cost, one now known as the Pacific Ring of Fire, a horseshoe-shaped belt roughly forty thousand kilometres long, about five hundred kilometres wide, a series of subduction zones created as a result of the magic used, allowing the volcanoes conceived to blossom and erupt, and earthquakes to occur on a regular basis threatening both marine and land life on an unprecedented scale, up to and including the present day. Back then, the shout out had been instigated by a gossip of mermaids who, handily, had been accompanying their queen on a hunting trip deep within the Japan Trench off the coast of Honshu. Completely by accident they'd discovered some of the dastardly work by the villainous sea serpents. If not for that advance warning by the mermaid monarch, the resulting consequences would have been much, much worse, a valuable and poignant lesson passed down throughout generations of marine majesties across the globe.

Recalling that lesson, the casualties and consequences almost as if he'd been there himself (of course he hadn't, it was just the magic woven into his DNA), Vasuki, king of the nagas, friend of the dragon race and one of so few survivors of the betrayal of his kind by the fiend Manson, swam to a halt in the wake of the futuristic submarine they were all tailing, the one that had so abruptly turned eastwards deep below the chilly Scottish waters only a short while ago.

Doubling back, both his concerned bodyguards drifted to a stop beside him as Vimes flailed and flustered in an attempt not to plough straight into the back of him.

*"What's wrong?"* asked the former *tor* and Santa's soulmate, desperately wishing she were here.

*"We need a moment."*

*"A moment to do what? Shouldn't we continue to track the sub? What if we lose it for good?"*

A series of chilling chuckles echoed across the mind of the reluctant dragon hero. It took him a moment to figure out that it was multiple beings laughing all at the same time.

*"What's so funny?"* he quipped, indignantly.

*"We mean no offense,"* Vasuki remarked wholeheartedly,

*"it's just that the thought that we could lose that monstrous metal beast in such a small pool of water is quite frankly ridiculous. I'm sure you understand."*

Looking at it like that, knowing they were well and truly on the nagas' home turf, he kind of did.

*"I'm sorry to even suggest such a thing. I wasn't thinking straight!"*

*"Whilst your apology is welcome, it's far from necessary. You are quite correct, we really shouldn't stop. But there's something I have to do, an act that's not only become necessary, but I feel will be essential in what is to come. Please bear with me. It won't take long, but I might have to scrounge some of your supernatural off you if all doesn't go to plan. Is that okay?"*

'What the hell,' Vimes wondered, 'is so important that he needs to borrow some of my mana, and is such a thing even possible?' Not knowing the answer and sure that he was up to his neck in things deeper than he could ever have imagined, fighting off the fear on an almost industrial level, the valiant former nursery ring teacher replied with a mental nod of acceptance, knowing that there really was no other choice.

'Oh Polkinghorne,' he reflected, 'I miss you so much. I hope you're faring better than I am.'

Opening himself up to his three bodyguards, knowing they'd share all they had in an instant for him, Vasuki, tapping into the intrinsic knowledge captured within his magnificent DNA followed its instructions to the letter in order to broadcast the exceedingly high pitched shout out that he knew would travel most of the way around the earth within a matter of minutes. Far beyond the scale of what domesticated household pets could hear, the signal, after leaving the naga monarch's snake-like lips, infiltrated every strand of connected water, travelling through race after race, species after species, from crustaceans to anemones, from the largest of mammals to the smallest of fish, to those bound with ancient supernatural abilities to those possessing little or no magic at all. The message was simple. It carried no words to be twisted or misunderstood, no context or background, only acted as a warning and of course what its sender had hoped for... a rallying cry. In essence it was a shout out to those nearest their position, asking... NO, demanding... assistance in this, a potential end of days scenario.

Throughout the oceans, thousands upon thousands of different types of animals all received the supernatural memorandum, some passing it on, others trying to understand its meaning and pinpoint its whereabouts. Across shallow tropical waters, fevers of stingrays wriggled and writhed, their long barbed tails dancing about like a human parent late at night inadvertently stomping on some misplaced Lego. Just off the coasts of both the Atlantic and Mediterranean, smacks of jellyfish squirmed and twisted, their translucent bodies momentarily flashing brightly, trying to discern the coded alarm, their long flimsy tentacles blown this way and that by the offshore currents, not that you could tell because their prevalence made them look like one all encompassing floating island of weed. Shivers of sharks in all shapes and sizes swimming in much deeper water across the oceans saw individuals going crazy with fright, their world rocked by something not experienced in their lifetimes, their unbridled intelligence questioning who or what could be the cause of the extraordinary signal, most agreeing almost straight away that it must be down to surface dwellers, already the bane of so much of their existence. Herds of seahorses on the Dorset coast in southern England chattered away to one another, the pregnant fathers choosing to seek protection rather than stay out in the open amongst the seagrass meadows. Across coral reefs and turquoise depths, batteries of barracudas abruptly changed direction, terror the likes of which they'd rarely known buzzing their miniscule brains, reminiscent of being caught on a line and reeled in, a lucky escape in those very last moments, only this time shared collectively, the same abiding questions haunting all their minds about what had already happened and what was coming next. It was a wakeup call for every living thing that thrived beneath the waters of the world.

As all five drifted lazily in the depths of the dark and disturbing freezing cold water, not a sound could be heard, not even the minute thrum of the advanced electric motor that drove the submarine, whose audacity had led to the nuclear warhead being fired. It was eerie, especially to a dragon whose body might well not have survived this far down but for the borrowed, powerful spell. Not called upon to loan any of his mana, Vimes could clearly see that something had happened, all four of his allies appearing spent, floating there in the darkness, the effortless currents rocking them back and forth in the vertical, their tails dangling precariously towards the seabed, looking like a tempting snack for a predator with teeth should any be brave enough. About to ask whether they'd achieved what they'd set out to do and how they should proceed, the need to do so was swiftly taken out of his hands.

*"It's done!"* observed Vasuki matter-of-factly. *"All we have to do now is wait and hope that some allies are close enough to assist."*

*"Assist with what?""*

*"Taking down the submarine. You do remember that's what we were talking about?"*

*"I do,"* insisted Vimes, *"but how on earth are they supposed to help out with that?"*

*"I don't know,"* put in the naga king. *"It rather depends on who shows up and exactly what their skill sets are, so we'll just have to wait and see."*

Shaking his head, Santa's other half trailed after the four others as they turned and hightailed it off in the direction the submarine had been travelling in, east if he wasn't mistaken, all the time fearful of what his friends across the planet were experiencing, his hope that they were somehow prevailing tempered by his understanding of Fate's cunning and sleight of hand when it came to such things as the destiny of the entire planet and its denizens. Terror started to unravel his composure despite his confident and heroic travelling companions. As he pushed on after the naga king and his cohorts, Vimes began to fear that he'd never again get to tell his dragon soulmate that he loved her more than life itself. Ironic really!

# 31 INFUSION

Resembling a modern art sculpture hanging flawlessly in mid-air above the industrial test borehole site in northern France, the nuclear warhead, less than a millisecond into its detonation, continued to be contained by a combination of powerful ancient magic, full on stubbornness and a refusal to give up by three of the most formidable incorporeal beings the universe had ever seen... Fate their ringleader, Time and Luck her willing cohorts.

Continuing to spam the dilation field across, around and outside every piece of exploded debris, making certain that even the tiniest trace of invisible radiation didn't escape her grasp, Time, mustering all her concentration, felt as weary as she ever had, the effort required on her part phenomenal, the struggle as real as anything she'd ever encountered, her strength of will tested to the limits of its endurance.

Similar in no small regard, the Providence that was Luck followed suit, continually bombarding the same area as her immortal sibling, overlaying her unique primordial magic, the same toll exacted, the exertion felt beyond any she'd ever experienced, the drain on her soul exquisite and all encompassing. Running on fumes, she could have done with dipping into her own well of good fortune. That, however, was never an option, not because it had been forbidden (it had) but simply because it wasn't possible. The Providences' distinctive, one of a kind abilities could no more affect each other than you or I could squeeze a single atom with our finger and thumb. Not only was it beyond comprehension, but the practicalities of such a thing were far outside ridiculous.

Multitasking on a god-like level, Fate was well aware of what her co-conspirators were going through, able to feel their anxiety, fear, pain, and trepidation as well as their doubts about any sort of future existing at all. Recognising the value of a few kind words, the incorrigible dealer of destiny whispered across their minds, telling them what good jobs they were doing, praising their abilities, marvelling at their strength, murmuring that they were legends in their own right. Although clearly able to see straight through her little ruse, her encouragement was enough to bolster their flagging wills and give just a little more impetus to their labours. For the time being they continued to hang in there. How long that would last was anyone's guess.

Following Yoyo's imaginary bright lines developed from using the planet's electromagnetic field that continued to trace the path the stolen laminium had taken when transported into the borehole itself, the youngsters applied all their physicality and mental resourcefulness to the problem at hand, flying at super speed, pinpointing the exact position of the invaluable metal all but instantly, before using their inherent love of teamwork to send it on its way towards the earth's core. Still it wasn't sufficient. What they needed to transpire wasn't happening fast enough.

Understanding all that and trying to grasp the bigger picture, the heroic legend that by the Providences' own admission had become one of their favourites, had used his out of the box thinking in an effort to get things back on track.

*"Listen up!"* Flash commanded across the telepathic link.

As one, they all did so, whilst still continuing to hunt down the precious metal.

*"We're running out of time and seemingly not getting the laminium to the core fast enough!"*

*"But we're working as hard as…"* protested a few of them simultaneously.

*"I know… and it's not your fault. What we need is a way to speed things up and I think I've come up with something that'll work."*

To a dragon, they were all ears.

Sensing a general chorus of approval once he'd passed on the mantra he'd selected, it was time to see if his untried method would have the desired effect. The general idea of what he hoped to achieve went something like this.

He'd selected a mantra developed in the Crimson Guards, one designed to massively increase an object's mass, one he'd used back at the king's private residence during the Changing of the Guard to great effect. It was similar to the one Amelia had used in her initial foray against Oblivion's dragons when she'd first become trapped at the top of the borehole, and they would apply it to the laminium as it was cast into the tunnel on its way to the core. The individual responsible for looking out overhead for any of the approaching metal would apply the spell, whilst their partner flung it with all their might and magic down towards the unending darkness. Hopefully the enchantment would decrease the time it would take for the laminium to reach the core and in turn get Novus back up to speed much quicker. Speaking of which…

The untangling of an intellect was how it felt, seeing clearly after the rain had gone, able to zero in on details and brush aside the brain fog that for so long had kept him at death's door and his thoughts and good natured personality subdued. With every ounce of laminium returned, Novus' fiery core grew exponentially hotter, HIS flame burning brighter, the planetary presence the Providences once acquainted with starting to return with a vengeance. As ley lines across the globe pulsed with raw, visceral energy, primary earth magic was drawn in from their locale. Would his power be restored in time to take care of the ever looming threat presented by the suppressed nuclear warhead explosion?

# 32 SIRENS! (AND NOT THE NEE NAR, NEE NAR KIND)

Globally, below the sea, the message continued to be passed along, the one that simply said something catastrophic was wrong, that an approaching storm of epic proportions was nearly here and that everything should be afraid. To a being, it was.

On a local level, creatures started to gravitate towards the north eastern coast of Scotland, dragged there under the sway of deeply buried magical DNA, the pull, despite their fear, utterly irresistible. Crabs scuttled sideways, their pincers clacking anxiously, whilst their distant cousins the lobsters scampered between rocks, occasionally leaping into the deep sea current, allowing it to assist them on their journey. Shoals of herring, haddock, mackerel and cod ignored their basic instincts, all turning as one, heading inland in both brave and desperate measures, although what use they could be was anyone's guess, not least theirs. Skates and rays skimmed the seabed, flicking clouds of sand up in their wake, the urge to get to the source of the mysterious signal overwhelming, as monkfish darted through the dark, frozen water above, all on the same mission. This part of the ocean had never been so crammed full of life and it was about to get even busier as species never before seen near the coast headed that way at full tilt. Help comes in all different shapes and sizes.

After their brief sojourn to send out the antediluvian message, Vasuki, his guards and the dragon ex-*tor* Vimes, once again caught up with the futuristic metallic beast of a submarine cutting through the water at somewhere in the region of sixty kilometres an hour, not quite a record for that type of vessel, but not too shabby either. Keeping its stern in sight, looking on as the huge propeller silently cut through the chilling salt water, from out of the gloom below them a series of dark shapes suddenly appeared. Fearing the worst, sure that reinforcements for those trapped in the exotic submarine had finally arrived, it came as a relief when finally the darkened outlines resolved into something vaguely familiar... MERMAIDS! And not just one or two but over a dozen.

Momentarily Vimes' heart skipped a beat, but with the realisation of what had just arrived came an acceptance that help of the right sort might just be at hand. Could it be that easy or (excuse the pun) would there be some sort of twist in the tail?

Leaving the sub to go on its merry way, the four nagas, with Vimes bringing up the rear, spun around to face the new arrivals, Vasuki all smiles, attempting to look as non-threatening as possible.

"Welcome, my friends," he boldly announced through the icy cold dark water that encompassed them all. "In the name of..."

"STOP!" demanded the lead mermaid, a gorgeous redhead with picturesquely long hair down past her pale, naked waist, a twisted grimace warped across her face in stark contrast to the sheer beauty she exuded.

"I..."

"WHAT HAVE YOU DONE?!" she barked, her words deformed ever so slightly by the volume of water in which they all lounged.

"We've done nothing," the naga monarch replied, more than a little put out given the situation and what was on the line, "but there's a very real threat that endangers us all and I wanted everyone to know."

"So once again you've meddled in affairs that have nothing to do with you!"

Vasuki shook his head from side to side, the gills on the side of the snake-like hood almost at a standstill instead of pumping furiously as they'd previously been.

Not the most adept at reading others, even Vimes could tell that something unspoken was going on.

'Do they have previous?" he wondered, "or is there more to it than that?'

"Listen, let's not…"

"Dredge up the past?" the red headed beauty spat, interrupting what sounded like the start of an apology.

Cowed before the group that outnumbered them over three to one, the naga king looked as though he'd thrown in the towel. About to press forward and give his side of their story, the chance was completely taken away from Vimes before he'd even started to open his mouth.

"ENOUGH!" bellowed Vasuki, startling each and every one of them, causing the mermaids to shrink back ever so slightly and his guards to adopt a more defensive posture. "This is beyond serious."

"How so?" screeched a brunette towards the back of the mermaid pack, one with a seductively coloured rainbow tail.

About to explain the finer details of exactly what they were facing, just then lots more shapes glided out of the darkness.

'Oh my,' thought Vimes, picking up even more hostility than before from the gossip of mermaids in front of them.

"What the **** do you think you're doing here?" spat the red headed vixen in charge, addressing the even newer arrivals.

Given that shoals of fish numbering well into the hundreds had taken up circling their little impromptu gathering, it was starting to get not only a little tense, but quite choc-o-block.

"I don't think I've had the pleasure," ventured the naga king, effortlessly gliding forward to greet the leader of these latecomers.

"I am Ajahn of the Abgal," stated the tall, chiselled jawed, bare-chested, prime example of what definitely looked like a supreme specimen of a merman, accompanied by well over a dozen of his people.

'Ahh… descendants of the Sumerian empire, if I'm not mistaken,' thought Vimes, well versed in the history of supernatural races.

"Ajahn, it's a pleasure to make your acquaintance," the monarch replied with all his practiced diplomacy. "I'm Vasuki, king of naga kind and swimmer of cold waters."

"I…"

"I'm tired of all this bullshit!" exclaimed the brazen copper topped leader of the mermaids, clinging on to her temper by a thread, clearly having some sort of beef with both the nagas and the abgal. "You had absolutely no right to issue that damning call to one and all across the ocean. That signal is meant to warn of an end of days scenario, not some naga mischief making gone wrong."

About to try and put her in her place yet again, this time Vimes could no longer hold his tongue and so in a very out of character eruption, decided to well and truly make his presence known.

"We've not met, I'm afraid, or been introduced, but my name is Vimes and as you can all see, I'm a dragon and about as far away from my comfort zone as it's possible to be."

About to rudely interrupt his diatribe, the lead mermaid thought better after a pointed finger and a withering look from the former *tor*, some of Santa's attitude clearly having rubbed off on her partner.

"I'm not a king, queen, monarch or royalty in any way, shape or form, just a lowly dragon mixed up through no fault of my own in something that, if we're all not careful, has the potential to destroy the planet."

"Ha…" more than a few of the gossip of mermaids smirked.

"What I tell you is one hundred percent true and could quite possibly be regarded as the darkest chapter in this world's history."

That gave all of them slight pause for thought, but it looked as though the crimson haired, fishtailed vixen still wasn't buying it. In an effort to win their trust, the former *tor* decided to plough on.

"A dragon of... curious origin, in conjunction with a vengeful witch of a monster, again one of my kind, have over many decades plotted to take control of the earth. Across the course of the last week or so, their scheme has come to fruition. Working in unison with both nagas and humans," Vimes continued, conveniently forgetting to mention Vasuki's race's magically enforced role in said events, "dragons from all spectrums have come together like never before to thwart the conspiracy."

"You expect," interrupted the mermaid leader whilst everyone else continued to listen quietly, "us to believe that dragons have been working side by side with both nagas and of all things... HUMANS?! You must think us simple!"

"IT'S TRUE!" Vimes protested.

Taking a turn for the worse, and do you know how they all knew... the warped grimace on her face having transformed into something that vaguely resembled a smile, the copper haired chief of the mermaids wriggled on over and put herself right in the former *tor's* face, flickers of wispy blue magic sparking off her blue bikini top and down the entire length of her light green tail, dissipating into the lonely, dark blue sea, an imminent threat if ever there was one.

"I've never taken a dragon's soul before," she announced menacingly to all and sundry. "What's to stop me taking yours here and now?"

'NOTHING,' he thought absolutely terrified, 'NOT A DAMNED THING!'

But you see... that wasn't strictly true.


Magic can mostly be regarded as both strange and unfathomable. Strange because even the purveyor at times doesn't know what the exact outcome will be, and unfathomable because it can have a whole life of its own, under the will of no one person or being, despite appearances. It can be playful, obstinate, wayward, cagey, surreptitious, downright insubordinate and on occasion it can very much live up to its name... MAGIC!

None more so than with the exceptionally powerful kind, the type that only legends with a sympathetic heart and a good conscience can wield, the sort rarely seen at all nowadays, except on few defined days. One of which belongs intrinsically to Polkinghorne, used sparingly throughout the year before inundating itself across the globe in every nook and cranny, sprinkled generously over every ocean, sea and river, traversing every known landmass, touching almost all sentient beings on the planet. What has this got to do with Vimes about to have his soul stolen by a particularly grumpy mermaid, one who most definitely had a grudge with not only the nagas by the look of things, but with either Ajahn himself or the people of the Abgal as a whole? A great deal, as it turns out.

Microns of unique supernatural were strewn everywhere, not just from her yearly trips as the inimitable once a year superstar, but from her predecessors as well, infiltrating absolutely everything across the earth, from the simplest of rocks and plants to the genetic material of most living things. Scattered far and wide, there was barely a part of the world that hadn't been touched by the one of a kind ethereal energy that was her trademark and despite it having long since been freely given away, the tiniest infinitesimal speck embedded within still remembered, recalled the generosity, the smile, the verve she had for life and the love and kindness shown for each and every being. It was infectious, never ending and a debt unpaid, up until now that is. You see, despite being spread so thin and lacking a singular mind of its own, each tiny morsel could easily distinguish her taint, something the soul of the being threatened right now, was absolutely smothered in. Acknowledging their chance to pay back, the uniqueness acted as only it could.

Reaching the end of his tether, Vasuki, seemingly with few options, chose that moment to act, bringing forth his most powerful enchantments, ordering his guards to do likewise in an effort to assist the ally that had been nothing but helpful. They did so without hesitation. Unfortunately it was all for nothing, their mighty magic no match for the gossip of mermaids who'd acted as one, snuffing out the slippery, snake-like supernatural in an instant, binding each of the nagas in place with the precision charms they were fabled for. With the Abgal looking on and hundreds of circling fish having now turned into thousands, Robyn, as this little group's leader liked to be known, prepared to show these interlopers exactly who was in charge.

A little over seven hundred kilometres south, deep underground in a vault full of the most wondrous and magical treasures ever to have graced the earth, three beings, two dragons in their preferred customary ape-like forms and one actual human, stood ready to face their destiny. For one of them it presented a traumatic chance to relive his only previous encounter with the mother he'd never known. For both of the others it was a prospect more fearful than anything they'd ever experienced in their entire lives, which for the most powerful of the trio was quite something indeed.

Facing the only entrance to the vault, the barrel of Billy the Kid's rifle rested on the empty plinth that had in the past been reserved for the scruffy looking, but anything but, 'Boots of Fleeting'. The same boots that Flash had borrowed to travel from Salisbridge to meet up with Yoyo and his band of youngsters in Australia before heading on to Antarctica in an effort to save the imprisoned Fredric. Janice, despite their differences of which there had been many in the past, wished for nothing more than to have the extraordinary form of Peter's grandfather here by her side right now, sure that their chances of success would be enhanced by his company. Thoughts of the founder of the Crimson Guards, the secretive and successful specialist group of dragons that worked exclusively for the monarch himself, got the young woman thinking about her friends and their fates as she quite literally stared down the barrel.

Almost able to sense her best friend firmly embedded in the futuristic blade that had saved them all on a number of occasions, she knew that he would have done all he could to stop the demonic witch Earth from coming after them. The resounding echo of crackling, hissing and spluttering magic off around the corner in front of them revealed that her allies up above, amongst the burning wreckage of what was left of the Emporium, had been unsuccessful in stopping Peter's mother once and for all. She just hoped that somehow they'd gone on to survive and not become yet more names on Earth's long list of victims.

Mulling over her extraordinary friendship with the supernaturally imbued blade turned her thoughts to that single drop of blood, one that had led to the discovery of that damned prophecy, the one all three of her friends were supposedly caught up in. Never having heard of 'The White Dragon', which astoundingly turned out to be Richie of all beings, Janice didn't put a lot of stock in such things, even though others around her including two she considered the wisest of them all, For'son and Fu-ts'ang, remained adamant there was a very real chance it would come true. Given the stakes if it did, she just couldn't face that prospect, the one that involved either losing her soulmate and love, or Tank, the kindest, most gentle being she'd ever met. It was all so confusing and downright frightening.

Still staring down the sights of the rifle, unable to make use of any of its supernatural enhancements, her attention wandered off task momentarily. Images came to her of a nice house in a tree laden road, weaving a pushchair around all the cracks and potholes in the pavement, her love and soulmate, the dragon she now sheltered down here with, smiling happily as he held her hand and strolled along beside her. It was all she wanted, all she'd ever dreamed of and was about to be brutally ripped away from her, if the odds were correct, by a being she supposed could potentially have been called her mother-in-law. How sick and twisted was that? Wiping her clammy hands on the front of her tee shirt, the courageous young woman stood firm and prepared to meet whatever destiny had in store, head on.

The dragon at the heart of everything stood off to one side of his love, close enough to assist should he need to intervene, just far enough away to use the cover of yet another empty plinth, appearing, it had to be said, remarkably calm and collected, unusual for him at the best of times, which this most certainly wasn't. Just like his soulmate next door, he'd had his share of thoughts about exactly what the future held in store for them, should they be able to weather the incoming storm. Unsurprisingly, their dreams were for the most part almost identical... a home, car, family, the usual... for most humans anyhow. Whether it was possible for a dragon to share those things with an out and out human remained to be seen, not just whether the biology would or could work, but whether or not the rules could be bent enough to allow it. Even with the king as a staunch ally and assuming his grandfather's support, he supposed there would still be insurmountable opposition. Truthfully, it didn't bear thinking about, but you know what it's like when you're in love, these things generally don't leave you alone. But that wasn't all. His focus dipped between those he cared for, from his grandfather, who he hoped with all his heart was on his way here right now in an effort to turn the tide, to Tank, seriously injured in the remains of his shop somewhere directly above them. Choosing for good reason to ignore the contents of the prophecy they'd stumbled across, well aware the words could be manipulated to suit many different outcomes, eventually his overactive imagination settled on the other of his best friends, the one who over the previous days had lost and, he supposed, gained so much, the one those of his kind across the domain referred to in hushed whispers as 'The White Dragon'.

'Damn prophecies,' he cursed deep within his psyche, recalling the moment he'd seen the disfigurement on his friend's pale back, scarring that had revealed the shape of a mighty dragon, one that had led him to believe wholeheartedly that she was THE one from the story that had been foretold for thousands of years and passed down throughout dragon generations via the very nursery rings themselves. UNBELIEVABLE!

Sadly, at least from his perspective, it had turned out to be true. Who'd have thought... his friend being the saviour of both dragons and humans? Looking back on their time together growing up and with the benefit of hindsight, he supposed it wasn't that outrageous a concept, not with everything she'd gotten up to and achieved. Still, it was utterly radical and as far as he was concerned, totally undeserving, not because she wasn't worthy of the title or adulation, but simply because she didn't deserve the pain, pressure and unrelenting attention that the claim brought with it. Whilst she'd been doing a sterling job of hiding the toll it was taking from the others, he'd on occasion glimpsed into her very heart and seen the eternal darkness she constantly had to rally against. Wishing she could be here for the coming battle as Santa had implied she would be, Peter fingered the dull metal trigger of the Kid's pistol, knowing that the inevitable was only a few moments away. Casting aside all other thoughts, he glanced across at Janice, buoyed briefly by her infectious, out of this world smile. For an instant, all was right in his world.

Running her bright red fingernails down the glue soaked hemp string of Robin Hood's yew longbow, having already attuned herself magically to it just as Peter had done on a previous journey to the vault what felt like a lifetime ago with the aged master mantra maker and shopkeeper, Polkinghorne, one of the apex magic users on the planet at any given time could feel the fickle finger of fortune fast approaching. Eying up all four, full to the brim quivers lying next to her feet on the cool terracotta floor and having already done the maths, the Santa legend was sure she could rattle off one shot every two seconds with the magnificent weapon that stood a little taller than her head, making thirty shots a minute. With fifteen arrows to every quiver, that gave her two whole minutes of consistent fire. If that wasn't enough in combination with Janice and Peter's efforts, then she had no idea what would be. About to check on her two accomplices, abruptly her whole body started to tingle uncontrollably. Thinking it a distanced supernatural attack by their loathsome enemy, she was about to shout out a warning to the mismatched loving couple she'd accompanied down here, but before she could do so everything behind her eyes went dark. As the fabulously famous longbow clattered off to one side, Polkinghorne's pale skinned, blonde haired, beautiful body slammed full force to its knees before tumbling hard onto the ground. For the time being at least, the Christmas legend was out of the fight.

Imagine a scream so very terrifying and powerful that it's capable of not only knocking you off your feet, but throwing your intellect some hundreds of kilometres distant, slashing mind from body, opening up a rift through which you'd just been plucked. That's what happened in an instant, the residue of past Santa magic lashing out, simultaneously forging a link between where they knew her to be and the trouble at hand. The timing was inauspicious to say the least, because going one down at the vault could only really be described as catastrophic, at least for the other two there.

As quickly as the dark had appeared and taken her, an all encompassing light burnt her eyes from every direction. Of course it was all in her mind, but it felt as real and intense as anything she'd ever experienced. Applying her vast knowledge whilst extending her considerable senses and know-how out as far as her limits would allow, it took but moments for her to get a grip on the situation, one which momentarily rocked her to the core.

Without her physical body, which wouldn't have done her much good right now anyway, because it had become so drained during the day from the horrific magical injury she'd unknowingly sustained at Stonehenge, Polkinghorne was in somewhat of a pickle as to how to save the dragon she adored as much as the festival she'd done her utmost to serve. Born of a split second decision and recognising that time was of the essence, in that moment she decided to bring her card playing skills to the fore.

Unlike the brilliant white molars he'd imagined, the bad-tempered leader of the mermaids, Robyn, opened her mouth in an imitation of a smile to reveal an unnaturally chipped set of dull yellow and dark brown teeth, to Vimes who was frozen in place only a hand's length away. If there'd been a thicker layer of air around his prehistoric flying form, he might well have thrown up. As it was, there really wasn't room, unless of course he wanted to choke on it.

About to dine on a soul that felt from the outside as though it might well be harbouring more good than she'd experienced in decades, before the twisted mermaid could apply her unique supernatural enchantments, whisper the words and reinforce them with her indomitable will, a soft, persuasive and ultimately powerful female voice rang throughout the chilling dark water, scattering the shoals of circling fish in every different direction and scaring the bejeebers out of all the other beings there.

*"THIS ONE IS MINE AND HAS BEEN MARKED AS SO! IF ANY HARM BEFALLS HIM OR HIS NAGA ALLIES, I WILL PERSONALLY SEE TO IT THAT YOU ROAST OVER A FIERY SPIT IN THE BOWELS OF HELL AND THAT ALL YOUR KIND CHOKE ON*

*THE SCENT OF YOUR SMOKED TAIL AS YOU'RE DOING SO! DO I MAKE MYSELF CLEAR?"*

# YIKES!

Totally dumbfounded as to the how of the matter, Vimes had never been so grateful to hear his lover's voice. However, he'd never in his wildest dreams imagined it sounding anything like that. There was nothing veiled about that particular threat.

As the mermaid leader skulked (a hard thing to do deep underwater but she managed it) back to the rest of the gossip, she telepathically acknowledged what had been said, passed on her sincere apologies for the supposed mistake and vowed that the group would do all that they could to support the cause that had upturned the underwater world and presented such a threat to life globally.

Satisfied as much as she could be and burning through the surrounding magic at an astonishing rate, before the consciousness of the once a year legend disappeared back to whence she had come, there was just time for the briefest of personal messages.

*"Vimes!"*

*"Polks... it's so good to hear your voice. I'm astounded that..."*

*"I'm sorry my love, but we have to keep this brief,"* Santa interrupted. *"At the rate I'm burning through magic, I only have a few seconds left at best. Know that I love you with all my heart and will do until the end of time."*

Keeping her words in mind and referencing a running joke, the former *tor*, stoic friend to the fantastical heroes of this piece and a giant among dragons replied with,

*"Ditto!"*

Through the smouldering microns of invisible magic, Vimes chose his words carefully.

*"Are you safe?"*

Polkinghorne replied not quite instantaneously which, given their distinct lack of time would have translated to a huge indecisive pause on any other occasion, making him worry more than ever.

*"Not really,"* she eventually replied, her voice, usually full of confidence, now laced with just a hint of fear, which sent his concern totally off the charts.

*"Wha...?"*

*"We're about to face Earth, just the three of us. Wish us good luck!"*

*"Good..."*

And then she was gone!

Treading water surrounded by an assembly of beings nearly all of whom were total strangers, there and then the kind, caring and dare I say it, courageous former *tor* of the three friends, Peter, Tank and Richie, felt more lonely than he ever had in his entire life. He would have given anything in the world to be with his soulmate for just a few seconds more in the standoff she was about to face. Circumstances beyond his control, however, dictated that he remained here at one of the three epicentres of potentially the end of the world.

# 33 FIFTY SHADES OF CRA!

Against the backdrop of unmistakable raging magic resounding from somewhere out of sight just around the corner, the courageous human woman that had done so much since joining her friend, the lacrosse player, after leaving Taibul's family's Indian restaurant on that fateful Saturday evening, took a step in the direction of Polkinghorne's prone form, desperate to help the Santa legend, a being that had well and truly infiltrated her close circle of friends.

Out of the corner of her eye, from behind the nearest plinth the slightest of movements caught her attention, causing her to stop dead in her tracks.

Not wanting to make a sound despite the rising panic he felt at seeing the most powerful amongst them drop to the floor, Peter, gripping Billy the Kid's pistol in one hand frantically waved the other in an effort to get his soulmate's attention. Luckily for him it worked a treat.

Put out at having her selfless action momentarily curtailed, whilst understanding the need to keep quiet, glaring across at him, Janice, in no uncertain terms, mouthed the word, "WHAT?"

Waving his index finger from side to side, the hockey playing dragon warned her off approaching the Christmas legend, rallying against his most base instinct which was doing its best to compel him to help their friend and supernatural ally.

Retreating back behind the plinth she'd been using as cover, barely keeping the spike of anger at being ordered to stand down under control, the young bar worker fell back on a whisper, needing to get her point across.

"We need to see if she's alright!"

Shaking his head, her love replied.

"Leave her be. She'll be okay."

"How can you be so sure?" Janice replied with a defined sense of urgency.

Frustrated and overflowing with fear at what he could sense was fast approaching from up ahead and around the corner, he knew the only way to resolve this issue was to come completely clean with what he'd felt directly before their friend Polkinghorne had so dramatically hit the ground.

"She's not hurt, well... not in the conventional sense," he put in.

"How can you...?"

"Right before she took a tumble, I felt a... kind of calling."

"A calling?"

"What I sensed was a whispered echo of a scream, one that was attempting to get her attention rather than do any harm. It was both unrecognisable and familiar."

"How can that be?"

"The supernatural reaching out, felt identical to the power that Santa wields, that's the only way I can think of describing it. It definitely wasn't unfriendly, merely wanting to get her attention. Despite the fact that she appears unconscious, I don't think any real harm has befallen her. For now, the best bet would be to leave her alone and focus on what's about to come our way."

Fighting her natural instinct to rush to her friend's aid, Janice realised from everything Peter had said that he too was doing exactly the same thing. Knowing how hard that must have been for him helped alleviate some of the anger, frustration and terror that currently circulated throughout her body at the situation they both found themselves in. Acquiescing, the youngster nodded her approval, once again hefting the rifle belonging to the supposed infamous outlaw whose magical enhancements she was unable to use, atop the plinth, directing its aim at the furthest point out in front of them. After that and using all her considerable will, she slowed her breathing and tried to stave off the overarching dread that threatened to consume her. It was as tough as freeing the hostage dragons back in the Salisbridge, dragon domain market place when their small force led by Gee Tee had been trying to save Flash and Tank from the makeshift metal gallows that had been used to torture them.

Partners, lovers, soulmates... MORE! The two companions readied themselves, the raucous, penetrating sound of fierce and formidable magic only a few steps away from revealing its nightmarish origin, the air growing heavier with every stomping step, revulsion causing stomachs to rumble uncontrollably, bowels balancing on a knife edge.

Smouldering from every limb, fluorescent orange glowing embers burning away across her torso, a paragon of purple pain and suffering staggered ever forward, desperate to fulfil the quest she'd set herself, the one that culminated with the death of her only son and those he loved. Driven forward by madness and any number of voices deep within her psyche, all of whom screamed injustice, betrayal and unfairness, each rallying against a profound wrongdoing by those she should have been able to trust, the mark of two deaths having exacted a heavy toll, one she was still paying the price of even today, many decades later. Firstly that of the death of her mother, an intensely traumatic event at the best of times, let alone when you're smack bang in the middle of being manipulated by a cult of Nazi sympathisers who were determined to mould you into the tip of their spear, using your arcane abilities for nefarious ends with a view to shaping the world in their image, using their undue influence to isolate you from your loved ones in the process. Heartbreaking for no other reason than her young age and breathtaking naivety, the pain and misery didn't stop there.

Eventually breaking out from under their spell, you'd have thought hooking up with a likeminded kindred spirit might have tempered the melancholy, buried grief and wretched despair. For a time it did, their experiences together almost bordering on happiness and some semblance of normality. Fate, as we already know, can be a fickle mistress even at the best of times, something that could never really be attributed to the dragon female in question. Responsible for murdering many humans and dragons, as well as turning her back on and her magic fully against her father, some might describe the tragic turn of events as either retribution by some higher power or karma in all its magnificent glory. Whichever way you looked at it, things did not go well, their illicit cover story destroyed in a moment of heroic madness, one that would go on to cost them both dearly, him with his life, her with the burden of guilt, a heavy weight to be sure and one that over time would only go on to stoke the flames of madness that continued to run riot throughout her cunning, devious and wicked mind. Some would say she'd been forged into the ultimate incarnation of evil long before crossing paths with the personification of malevolence in the form of Manson, others would cite circumstances beyond her control and outside surrounding influences. Either way she'd long since become lost, her sanity shattered like a mirror into a thousand pieces, the occasional reflection providing the odd glimpse into the life she could have had, one that couldn't have been further away. You or I might attribute much of the blame to the outpouring of grief on both these occasions, and those that had tried and in some cases succeeded in taking advantage of her. Not her I'm afraid, her vicious and wanton nature directing her vile bloodlust at the world in general, the dragon race as a whole and one specific individual who, mourning the loss of his wife had only tried to do what he thought was right and had played no real part in her spiral away from reality. Of course the party in question was Fredric, her dad and Peter's grandfather, a being steeped in history, one renowned for doing the right thing, always putting others ahead of his own needs, best friend to George, defender of the realm and long incarcerated Antarctic prisoner.

Messed up was an apt description of not only the she-witch Earth's mindset, but of the family dynamic she'd long since tried to leave behind. Through no fault of their own, Fredric, Peter and to some degree Janice, had all gotten caught up in her psychotic orbit, with two of them now about to pay the ultimate price.

As the personification of lunacy lurched into view, it was all the naive couple could do to contain the shaking of their hands holding the weapons they'd chosen to defend themselves with, having gone for something ranged rather than allow Peter's demonic mother to get up close and personal, against which they had little or no chance.

The purple tinged personal shield that had been her saviour on hundreds of previous occasions was now non-existent alongside the trademark snakes writhing across the top of her head, and with a familiar sneer etched across the amethyst crisscrossing lines that divided her face up into different levels of madness, Earth took a moment to survey the terracotta cul-de-sac, almost able to smell the fear emanating from within. Victory appeared to be well within her grasp.

"Ahhh…" she mused, struggling to catch her breath after everything she'd been through to get this far, "if it isn't my wretch of an offspring and his filthy, ragtag human pet. Don't the two of you make the perfect couple?"

Swallowing down the bile that threatened to fill not only the top of her stomach but the entirety of her throat, Janice ignored the sarcasm, tried to stay cool and not react, knowing that they were effectively sitting ducks for a magic user this powerful, having seen the extent of her abilities on more than one occasion already across the past week. As well, she thought it really was up to her other half and soulmate to reply, especially since it was his kin they were facing out there.

If ever there was a time that he needed just a smidgen of composure, it was here and now. But guess what… that's right, it had deserted him big time, his right hand, the one hanging over Billy the Kid's holstered pistol, now shaking like the deck of a gold recovery wash plant, his terror at just the sound of her voice forcing him to relive the moment outside the council building when she'd delicately run the long, sharp, purple nail of her index finger down the side of his exposed throat, enabling his blood to flow freely, right before she, and that son of a bitch Manson and their formidable army, stormed the entrance. It was outlandish and a recollection that had haunted his dreams on many an occasion since, waking him up in a cold sweat, choked to the brim full of panic, the stench of Tim's urine fresh in his memory.

With the exception of the involuntary shaking, paralysis began to set in, his legs immovable, his feet feeling as though he were wearing massive clown boots forged from lead, chest barely able to rise, head stuck facing the direction of his misbegotten mother, eyes watering as they locked firmly on her, blinking an ever increasing impossibility.

Sensing the effect his mother's presence was having on him, Janice, rallying against the sheer terror of the situation and dismayed to still see Polkinghorne's prone form slumped on the floor, did the only thing she could think of, something only one of earth's mightiest heroes would consider under such circumstances. Lowering her head atop the barrel of the exquisite rifle, the young woman countering overwhelming magic with unerring logic and bravery lined up the shot with the devilish monster's head in the centre of her sights and with her delicate, pale index finger poised, pulled on the trigger.

A splintered CRACK reverberated around the enclosed space of the vault, causing shelves to shake, one of a kind imbued jewellery to tumble helplessly to the orangish floor, bandoliers and swords to crash to the ground, one-off scrolls to flutter into the air, and sending the occasional giant arachnid scuttling for its life.

Deep within the renowned rifle, the firing pin created a small explosion which in turn ignited the gunpowder contained within the bullet. This rapid combustion generated a significant amount of high pressured gas which rapidly expanded within the confined space of the bullet casing, reaching several thousand pounds per square inch in only a matter of milliseconds. Pushing against the walls of the casing, the base of the bullet expanded to seal the chamber, preventing gas from escaping backwards, directing all the energy into propelling the projectile forwards. As the ever expanding gases built up pressure, they exerted an intense force on the bullet, pushing it into the barrel, sliding it along the rifling, the spiral grooves on the inside of the barrel used to promote stability and accuracy during flight. Continuing to accelerate, finally the bullet reached the barrel's open muzzle. At this point, the pressure dropped as the projectile exited.

Parting air atoms at three hundred and seventy nine metres a second, the dull, silver tipped, rounded bullet fired from the magnificent Winchester '73 rifle, (which in its own right would almost have been considered a work of art, and that was without taking into account the magical enhancements Gee Tee had added and keyed to the Kid's DNA all that time ago) homed in on its prey in only a matter of milliseconds, no emotion attached, purely function and form working in unison, enabling a swift and decisive death to whoever should find themselves in its sights. In this case, the usual magic that Billy the Kid would have drawn on wasn't required, that's how accurate the young woman's shot had been. Her strength of will and determination to end this NOW, not only for her sake but for that of her soulmate, were nothing short of outstanding. In fact it's fair to say that the Kid's magic might actually have proved a hindrance, the wicked she-witch huntress being attuned to such things, almost certainly able to detect and deflect at a moment's notice, something that was simply not possible without a magical touch. Following the straight trajectory it had been set off on, the blur of a bullet closed in on the purple crosshairs it had been targeted at, dead centre. If the

Providences had been paying attention, (which they weren't) they'd probably have had a bet on the predicted outcome. They'd have been wrong!

# 34 TUNNEL VISION

"You want me to do what?!" Hook ranted, referring to the instruction he'd just been given out loud instead of deep within his mind which is how they'd communicated up until now.

"I understand your hesitation, but it'll be alright. The others will catch him at their end."

"Just tossing him through in his condition seems unwise at best," the heroic rugby player stated, verging on disappointment, his concern for his friend evident from the tone of his voice.

"It'll be alright, youngster," assured the soft, smooth tones of the Emporium. "We've been assured that he'll get the best care possible. That's all we can hope for."

"I don't doubt for one minute that he'll get looked after, it's just that…"

Despite both magical presences residing in inanimate objects, through time honoured vast experience each had some idea of what the courageous rugby player was going through… his worry for Tank obvious, his frustration at not having accompanied The White Dragon, the female he loved so much, on her quest to save three of her best friends, not so much, and that was on top of the realisation that the planet could cease to exist at a moment's notice. All things being equal, both former dragon personalities thought the valiant human was dealing with things pretty well. If they could just get him to acquiesce on this one sticking point about throwing Tank's broken body through the naga wormhole they were about to create, then their goal would be advanced considerably.

"What if," Zarenkesia started, "you could see what was happening at the other end, make sure that those there had indeed caught his body as it came through?"

"Zarenkesia?" the enigmatic presence inside the ring

queried.

"I still don't understand why I can't just take him through myself," Hook mused, disappointed to have been told that this scenario simply wasn't an option.

"Hook," ventured For'son as neutrally as possible, "we can't risk leaving this place for even a moment, something you know in your heart of hearts. What if Richie and the others need us? What if the murderous miscreant mother makes it back up here? Zarenkesia is in no condition to do anything about it and I, despite all my considerable magic, need a host through which to channel it. You are the glue that binds us together, without which we wouldn't stand a chance. Please... try and understand."

He did, he really did. The mention of the woman, no wait... was that right? The mention of the dragon that he'd fallen head over heels in love with focused his resolve more than any of the mystical presences could, no matter how rational their arguments. It was just that he cared about his pal and teammate immensely, worried what would ensue, especially given the prophecy Janice had stumbled across. If anything happened to Tank from here on in, he'd never forgive himself, and that led him to wonder whether his prehistoric other half would exonerate him either. He didn't want that to happen, or to have to deal with the consequences afterwards. And that made him think that Zarenkesia's offer might be the best of both worlds, if such a thing existed in the here and now.

"Is it really possible to get a glimpse into what's going on at the other end?" he asked sceptically.

About to butt in, only then did For'son realise that the question wasn't directed towards him, but also he didn't know the answer anyhow, and so he chose to stay silent.

"I... I... I could try and expand the accretion disk after Tank's body has gone through," stated the ancient intellect of the Emporium, doing her best to disseminate the unfamiliar naga spell in her mind, the one she'd only recently learnt of.

"Would that do the trick?" Hook's new partner in crime asked dubiously.

"In theory it might grant us a small window to peer through, although how long it would last I really don't know."

"Hook? What do you think? Would that be enough to satisfy your curiosity and negate some of your worries?"

Knowing he wasn't going to get a better offer than that, the strapping rugby player replied, his mightily muscled neck nodding his huge head as he did so.

"I think it would."

"Then what are we waiting for?" suggested For'son, eager to get his former partner and one of the few beings he'd come to think of as a true friend, the treatment he so desperately needed.

"You contact the others at the hospital," Zarenkesia urged, "and I'll get started on the wormhole."

Aware that his was the most basic part of the whole procedure by far, Hook bent down and scooped up his friend's huge, lifeless human body, taking his weight in both arms, ready to do as he'd been instructed, whilst reciting a small prayer for his safe return, hoping that the technology at the hospital, in conjunction with the dragon magic available, would be enough to cure Tank of the his ailments.

Moments later, it was on and they were ready to enact the unconventional plan. All three focused with everything they had, setting the scene for a most unconventional transport, one only possible due to some very unique and unusual naga magic.

At Tank's destination, preparations were at an advanced stage, the ward set up for anything he might need, a human sized bed of all things ready and raring to go. Coincidentally it was the same one that Richie herself had been placed in when recovering from her injuries sustained when the sports clubhouse had been blown apart and she and Tim had been caught out in the cellar, only saved by a combination of luck, quick thinking magic and the breaking of the *alea*. The dragon physicians here were some of the best across the world at successfully treating their own kind, both in their primordial natural forms and in their disguised ape-like get-ups, and had the finest equipment to match the unsurpassed supernatural enchantments. The ward, getting on for the size of a football pitch at a rather large stadium, had everything they required to treat any sort of brain injury, from industrial sized X-ray equipment to computer assisted tomography (CAT scanners) and magnetic resonance imaging (MRIs). It was the complete set up, one barely used in the past, the equipment pristine. The more Doctor Tomlinson was updated on his patient's condition though, the more he worried that what they had might not be enough. Only time and the superior abilities of the staff would tell.

Steel had fought his way to them through the maze of corridors and surreptitious entrances, guided mentally by one of the dragon staff members, the brave laminium ball captain stood next to both friends as they waited patiently in the middle of what could only be described as a mountain of empty space within the white walled and floored ward. With all three sharing the same mental connection, they found themselves executing the hardest thing of all... WAITING! Each would have preferred a fight to the death against overwhelming odds to this, something attested to by just how quiet they'd become and the lack of banter between them. Even in the most serious of situations they'd continued that little act, but not now, not with Tank's life at stake. Abruptly, the silence they shared was interrupted.

*"Are you set?"* asked the familiar voice of the former warrior dragon trapped in the unknowable band.

*"Everything's set up here and ready to go,"* Jar Man replied taking charge.

*"Good. Zarenkesia's about to open up the wormhole. Stand well back. We're also going to try and sneak a peek through after we've sent Tank on his way."*

About to ask why, something For'son could sense, the

need to do so was suddenly made redundant.

*"Don't ask. Just be ready to catch him. Understood?"*

They did.

Zarenkesia continued to ignore the considerable damage to her outer structure and some of the still blazing fires, the result of the fights with Mas-crate and Earth. Attempting to put behind her the heartbreak of the destruction of all her treasures within, from the long forgotten one off scrolls, the ancient and elapsed spell books, tomes and unique relics from across the globe spanning the course of dragon history, to just the odd ordinary trinket or two that still reminded her of the genius master mantra maker, Gee Tee, she gathered up all her considerable will and, perfectly replicating the guttural sounds and inflections of the naga tongue, cast some of their most powerful magic right in the midst of the store. Immediately a pinprick of light burst into being out of nowhere, shining the tiniest white glow throughout a plume of choking dark smoke onto one of the remaining upright wooden beams about halfway down its vertical structure.

Standing as far back in the furthest corner as it was possible to be, Hook noted what was happening, his bulging biceps now starting to ache from the constant weight of carrying his teammate and friend. His thoughts concentrated on what he was about to do, worry for the beautiful lacrosse player he felt destined to be with until the end of time cast to one side momentarily, the importance of getting this right paramount in his mind. Losing the giant dragon rugby player was really not an option, not now, not ever!

Fearing the worst and that she'd somehow incorrectly misinterpreted the foreign (to her at least) spell, Zarenkesia continued to watch the singular point of illumination, wondering why nothing else had changed and exactly what was supposed to happen. Knowing that disturbing Fredric was not an option right now, feeling him and his companions traversing the magical, trap laden tunnel at speed some way below them, closing in on their quarry, the exotic presence of the shop considered her options. Right about then, rainbow rings of outlandish colour sprang into being to surround the original pinprick, all the time swirling and whirling, a rampaging torrent of foamy sea cascading around an underwater sinkhole, only upright in mid-air, the thick, supercharged atmosphere within the remains of the shop now tickling with the taint of supernatural, a distinct low pitched THRUM bouncing back and forth off all the debris and rubble, suppressing and altering the course of the occasional lick of flames here and there.

'Aahhh,' she thought, 'patience must be the key.' Clearly some sort of delay was a different aspect to their underwater allies' enchantments, unlike the immediate effect she was used to.

Watching intently as the wormhole expanded with every moment that passed, it was clear that it would soon be able to accommodate Tank's mighty frame. And that's when it occurred to her, something that perhaps they should pass on because it could prove vital.

*"For'son! Should we not inform them of Artorius' prophecy about the two friends?"*

*"I don't see why they would need to know the exact details."*

*"But…"*

*"If anything, I would suggest it might make them second guess any decisions that need to be made and muddy the waters with regards to Tank's treatment. Keeping it vague could prove to be a blessing in disguise, allowing them to focus by applying all their considerable medical knowledge without any background interference from something that may or may not be relevant."*

That was enough to make her think that his judgement was spot on.

*"I concur wholeheartedly. I'm sorry to have brought it up."*

*"Don't be sorry for trying to cover every angle. Sometimes it all seems mindboggling and overwhelming. I always appreciate another considered point of view."*

And with that she withdrew, nodding her thanks as she

did so.

*"It's nearly time, my friend,"* For'son whispered across Hook's consciousness, well aware of the importance of what was about to go down and the relationship the young human had with the Emporium owner.

Huffing out the deepest of breaths, about to ignore what instinctively he thought was the wrong thing to do and put his trust in two magical prehistoric beings he couldn't even see, let alone understand, the gutsy rugby player stepped towards the ever expanding and circling array of just about every colour imaginable, trying hard not to become captivated by it all, the bulk of his pal causing the muscles in his arms to bulge, causing slight pain which provided the concentration levels he needed. Approaching the intense, esoteric, wild and uncontrollable circle of rainbow light, Hook stood about a metre in front of it in all his glory, the reflection of the multiple hues reflecting off his pale white skin, making him look as though he'd been transported in time back to an 80's nightclub, disco ball and all.

Looking on, contemplating the intricate details of the magic they were about use and what the resulting consequences would be, sending a living, breathing being more than a hundred kilometres away in just the blink of an eye, on closer inspection, Zarenkesia noticed that the portal had opened up to what she'd been assured would be its maximum diameter, signalling that it was time. Not knowing how else to phrase it, she went with what she thought might be right. It was unusual to say the least, and fitting in the sense of the 80's disco theme.

"It's time," she announced, "to get the party started!"

Not appreciating the humour but understanding the meaning behind the words, the one rugby player extraordinaire, carrying another, stepped forward and with all the strength he could muster, threw the bulk of his pal through the direct centre of the furious looking multicoloured churning and spinning eddies, watching intently, more than a little dismayed as every last molecule of him was gobbled up by its seeming viciousness. Waiting on tenterhooks, it felt as though it took an age for the apex to open up behind Tank's body... but it did, showing a brief glimpse of the bright white ward at the other end and Steel using all his magnificent reactions to catch the unconscious form of their friend. Buoyed beyond belief at witnessing what had happened, abruptly the shop was pitched into near total darkness, only the occasional remaining fire providing any kind of illumination. It was done, and was about as far out of their hands as it could be. Tank's life now rested in the hands of those hidden deep beneath Salisbridge district hospital.

Accompanied by a rush of air and a resounding WHOOSH, the ancient and unusual naga magic folded in on itself before disappearing completely with a harsh POP, leaving them all in the brightly lit, white, sterile ward.

"Where do you want him?" Jar Man asked, not taking his eyes off Tank's lifeless body cradled in Steel's prodigious arms.

"Over here," Doctor Tomlinson replied, "in the MRI scanner."

Trailing the physician, the rugby playing dragon's unresponsive mass was laid down gently onto the patient table, the laminium ball captain acting as respectfully as possible knowing full well the deeds the young dragon had accomplished. Without him, the world might very well be under Manson's control already. To say he'd had a huge part in countering the darkness and horrific evil that had threatened to overwhelm the planet, was something of an understatement.

"What now?" DomCon enquired, the sadness at seeing one of their own in such a ghastly state almost too much to bear.

Giving the order to the computer operating assistant behind the glass adjacent to the ward they stood in, with just a wave of his finger, the four of them watched as the scanner started to whirr into life, Tank's inert form slowly sliding into its darkened confines.

"Once his head is positioned in the exact centre of the magnetic field, we'll do a detailed scan of his brain to see what we're dealing with. After that, decisions will have to be made as to whether we operate and if we do, how we go about it. Magic might be required given that his current form is a facsimile of his true self. None of that, however, can be done until we've completed this part of the process. And I'm afraid, for the scanner to operate properly, we all have to leave. Should you wish, you can observe from behind the glass of the computer monitoring room... gentlemen," the doc suggested, using his arm to usher all three of his guests towards the exit.

"Sire," whispered his friend the general, having crept up on the king who, through a combination of lack of sleep over the previous days and quite possibly the most stress and worry in the world, had fallen asleep in his chair hunched over his laptop, no doubt trying to get some answers.

"Fuuuzzzlephmph," George muttered as transparent ribbons of slobber dribbled down either side of his mouth and onto his clothes, his aging dragon consciousness taking a moment to get to grips with the return to reality.

"My friend."

"Majesty."

"Uhhhhh..." groaned the monarch, rolling both his shoulders simultaneously whilst twisting his neck side to side, trying desperately to get rid of the kinks that had set in whilst he'd unknowingly grabbed forty winks.

"My lord," Whitewings stated, "I've done as you've ordered. We've found a satellite that can get us an image of the situation in northern France. It'll be on site in mere moments."

As George attempted to come to terms with that, the

general moved the king's tiny laptop to the far side of the desk he was sitting at, replacing it with a much larger dragon version, some four or five times the size, opening up the screen right in front of his friend.

"Who does the satellite belong to?" the monarch asked, assuming the answer would be one of the most powerful countries on the planet... USA, China, Russia, United Kingdom, Germany, France, etc. But that wasn't it at all, far from it in fact.

"We've coerced it out of a globally renowned company."

"Who and how?"

"I think, sire, that it's far better if you didn't know."

That got George's attention and under normal circumstances would have led him to delve microscopically into what was going on. But right at that very moment, he was tired, exhausted in fact, right to his very bones, oh and don't forget stressed with worry for not only the world as a whole, but every single one of those that he loved, and so some shady deal for a satellite that might get him the answers he needed, strangely, just didn't bother him.

"Keep your secrets, my friend, oh, and good work by the way."

Smiling at the complement and the fact that he didn't have to divulge the deal he'd cut, Whitewings leaned over and switched on the laptop. After a moment or two of whispered whirring, the screen flickered into life. A few taps of the oversized keyboard later and the live link appeared.

"****!"

"Oh my God," mused the king, using slightly less fruity language than his friend.

"That... just can't..."

"I thought you said this was a live link, General?"

"Uhhhh... it is, Majesty," Whitewings replied quickly, checking the telemetry down the side of the screen.

"So you're telling me that what we're seeing, an exploded nuclear warhead just hanging there mid-air, is actually what's happening over the borehole in northern

France right now?"

Scrutinizing the data from the satellite running down one side of the screen at super speed and then rechecking to make sure he had it absolutely right, the puzzled general's huge prehistoric head turned to face his friend and commander in chief.

"The feed is live... the data confirms that. What you're seeing is a real time depiction of what's happening right there on the ground, or not, so to speak."

"How is that even possible?" George mused, more rhetorically than anything else.

"I don't know, Majesty," Whitewings put in.

"Extraordinarily powerful magic... that's all it can be."

"But who?" the general questioned, "Flash, Captain Battlehard, Yoyo and his group of misfits or maybe all of them together?"

For more than a few moments the king of everything dragon and human pondered all he'd seen and heard. The images coming in over the satellite link couldn't even be regarded as improbable, they were totally and utterly impossible. Nothing, absolutely NOTHING, as far as he was concerned, had the supernatural ability or propensity to perform such an audacious, clever and cunning feat of magic. Not a single dragon, or even a group of a hundred or more. Even some of the other outlying magic users across the globe coming together could not have achieved something so outrageous as to hold the warhead of a nuclear missile in place once it had detonated. It simply wasn't possible for any number of reasons and yet here he was, supposedly watching it unfold live. Reality, he knew, could very often be stranger than fiction, but this... this was something else altogether. As his mind tried to seek out answers to impossible questions, both he and his friend continued to watch, unable to avert their gaze, knowing full well what was on the line should that thing unleash its devastating potential.

# 35 IN EVERYONE'S INTEREST

With Robyn their leader and the gossip of mermaids as a group quelled by Polkinghorne's off the cuff intrusion, the undersea gathering had settled down, especially now Vasuki and his guards had been freed from the magic that had been cast to restrain them.

With a vast array of different species of fish returning to circle the gathering, some in shoals, others acting as lonely individuals, Ajahn of the Abgal, any housewife's merman dream, glided over, powered by one swish of his almighty grey scaled tail, his long, dark flowing hair pulled this way and that by the cold water currents, both his matching beard and pointed moustache making him look about as regal as any being could.

"My friends... I apologise for any misunderstandings with my long lost cousins of the sea. It would seem," he ventured glancing back across his broad, well muscled shoulders, "that the centuries haven't blunted their edge or their tongues."

Robyn glared in his direction but continued to remain silent, knowing when to speak and when to shut up, just as any good leader should. Polkinghorne had clearly put the fear of God into her, which given the corrosive attitude of the soul stealing underwater maidens, was probably only a good thing, particularly as their assistance might well be required to avert the disaster that currently threatened them all.

"Whilst I don't agree with the sentiment and the tone in which the query was expressed by the delightful leader and her gossip, I do," Ajahn put in, "require an answer to that same question. What have you done?"

'Fair enough,' thought Vimes, his huge dragon body treading water in the chilling dark waters of the North Sea directly behind Vasuki and his guards, not wanting to face the wrath of the mermaids one more time.

"Perhaps it would be best if our dragon friend here explained, after all, he has considerably more knowledge about what's happened than I do," Vasuki stated.

Vimes gulped, never one to take well to the pressure of speaking in front of other beings, even back when he'd been a *tor*. Standing up in front of the class to address them all on some subject or other had always been nerve wracking for him.

About to try and wriggle out of it, before he had the chance, the four nagas whom he'd sought shelter behind all turned tightly, effectively doubling back on themselves, putting him front and centre, all four of them at his back.

'Oh crap,' he thought, now with no way out of addressing the entire gathering.

With all eyes on him, he wondered if there wasn't a more expedient way of getting things done.

"Are you all open to letting me show you what I know?" Vimes asked, sure that they'd understand he meant telepathically.

After much muttering, mainly from the mermaids, they all agreed to open themselves up to him.

Closing his eyes, trying to filter out what felt like bleak surroundings at best, especially given the cold that he was protected from by the thinnest layers of magic, scouring his memory, he began.

Visions of the battle at dragon domain Singapore flashed through his consciousness, the one in which Polkinghorne had finally ended it using the out of the box Singapore Sling, throwing a great deal of the resistance at unerring speeds into the tunnel enabling the heroes to outflank and outgun those that would wreak death and destruction down upon innocent civilians of all persuasions.

Moving swiftly on, the scene cut to their unexpected arrival at the king's private residence and their dalliance with all the dragons there who, caught off guard, had at first believed that their appearance was an attack. After that, events revolved around some of their allies and friends reporting what had happened during the Changing of the Guard. Even as it replayed in the former *tor's* head, it sounded far-fetched, details of fabulous battles, epically heroic deeds from the most courageous of dragons, with oodles of bloodshed, gore, treachery and betrayal all thrown in for good measure. That was before they'd even got to the point where Manson and Earth had brutally snatched away all the light sided magic in one fell swoop, about to end it all there and then, but unable to due in no small part to For'son and Tank. After that came Fu-ts'ang's return from the dead, more gutsy fighting, the revelation that Earth was Peter's mother and the standoff between them, Manson's cowardly escape and his wicked she-witch bride's last minute disappearing act. To cap things off, he showed the emergence of the mythical creatures, just when the heroes had thought they had things under control and finally the melancholy, woe and grief of the master mantra maker's death. Everyone from Ajahn himself to the entire gossip of mermaids heaved a sigh of relief, not just from the emotional strain of seeing what had happened, but from the audacity of it all, unable to comprehend beings willing to spend so much time planning such diabolical deeds before attempting to bring them to fruition. As they were about to find out, things were far from finished.

Vimes' visualisation moved swiftly towards their outing at Stonehenge when they'd tried to boost the ley lines and enhance their search potential for the gruesome twosome, embellishing just how quickly things had gone wrong. Recounting his brush with death, the deadly naga assassins waiting for them, all the humans witnessing the most unusual of events, Polkinghorne getting her ass well and truly kicked, until the well timed arrival of the only two beings capable of turning things around... THE WHITE DRAGON and the fearless human rugby player, Hook!

Wow... it was all that those experiencing these events second hand, including Vasuki and his bodyguards, could do to keep their composure. An emotional rollercoaster didn't quite do it justice. More like an emotional theme park.

Then came the realisation that their leaders had been played and the fearsome submarine wasn't anywhere near where they'd been led to believe, but on its way to Scotland instead. And so they did what they had to, splitting up, Polkinghorne and Hook returning to the dragon domain capital whilst he, Fredric, Flash and The White Dragon herself set off towards the very north of the United Kingdom in an effort to find a needle in a haystack and stumble across the wicked would-be rulers of the entire planet.

A shudder ran down the spines of all those assembled at the thought of those two despicable beings becoming crowned owners of the planet, not only without their say so, but without their knowledge, not even an inkling that any of this had happened. Resisting the urge to shy away from the rest of what Vimes had to offer, they delved back into the imagery, hoping to ascertain how events had come to this, a nuclear submarine so close to the coast with rogue actors aboard intent on grievous amounts of harm and supposedly the destruction of the earth itself.

Richie's accidental discovery of the evil pair rolled on like a movie and of course her subsequent all or nothing fight against them. Before the terror twins could end her for good, the viewers saw those who'd flown so far north in such a short space of time, including Vimes, arriving to even up the odds. What had happened next was both extraordinary, and unbelievable... some of the mermaids thinking it complete and utter fantasy. But the rest knew it to be true, having already scanned the former *tors'* mind for any sense of deception or trickery. They'd found none.

As father and daughter had tried desperately to kill one another, Flash was taken completely out of the battle by wicked, subversive magic. Cue The White Dragon. Just as Manson had thought he'd won, the superstar lacrosse player succumbed to her baser instincts and the need for revenge given what had happened to both Peter and more importantly, the master mantra maker. In a fit of rage and using all her customary strength both mental and physical, she'd only gone and done the one thing others had been unable to... she'd beat him to a pulp. Certain that she'd extinguished his flame for good, when Vimes came calling, needing help with Flash's precarious position, she didn't hesitate to help, possibly the gravest mistake of her life. Because through a combination of luck and extraordinary timing with the sub and its crew now being so close at hand, the murderous protagonist was able to be fully restored in an instant (even though he'd been at death's door) escape and board the futuristic vessel. With the fighting still raging, Earth getting the better of her father before surprisingly fleeing through yet one more naga wormhole, the very last thing any of them expected would happen, had done: the launch of a nuclear warhead from the submarine in question, one designed to not only cause devastation and loss of life on an unimaginable scale, but one with a purpose like no other. To fracture the planet itself in conjunction with a vast amount of stolen laminium already in situ at the test borehole site in northern France.

*"And that,"* Vimes announced through the shared telepathic link, *"is where we are right at this very moment."*

Cue the start of one almighty quarrel, mermaids bickering amongst themselves before choosing to squabble with any number of the accompanying mermen, whose demeanour had changed somewhat after learning about recent history. Ajahn and the red headed Robyn went at it hammer and tongs in various different languages, some so ancient that neither Vimes nor Vasuki recognised them. It was underwater bedlam with even some of the shoals of fish snapping at each other for no apparent reason.

*"I thought they were here to help."*

*"They're supposed to be, or at least that was the idea. Clearly it wasn't one of my better ones,"* Vasuki ventured rather miserably to his new found dragon ally.

As the disputes got even more heated, a faint tinge of magic flickered brightly into life against the dull, dark background of the chilling depths. It soon became obvious that everything had travelled full circle, the fall out now about what the nagas and dragons had done to instigate the aforementioned events.

Fed up with the squabbling, tired, deeply disappointed, scared for his life and that of his supernatural soulmate and of course his friends, who were out there right now risking life and limb to put an end to all of this, in an unlikely fit of pique, the former dragon *tor* let his temper get the better of him.

"SHUT UP... NOW!"

Stunned by the outburst, the gossip of mermaids, the group of mermen and the shoals of fish, as one turned to face Vimes, their anger at being addressed like that more than apparent. Unfortunately for them, he just didn't give a damn.

More composed than he had any right to be, Polkinghorne's soulmate tapped into all his classroom experience, in particular that involving unruly and childish behaviour.

"Whilst I understand your dismay at what you've just learned, the shout out that attracted your attention in the first place wasn't designed to send you all into a full on hissy fit."

A look not so much of daggers, more... rapiers and broadswords tore across the inky, icy waters from the soul stealing red head, the vicious vixen almost willing to ignore the overt threat from one of the most powerful magic users on the planet and pick up where she'd left off. It was, however, never going to be that easy.

Dismissing the rather alarming and more than a little threatening stare with the wave of one hand, Vimes continued.

"The shout out, as some of you have already emphasised, is only to be used in cases of the most dire emergency. It was dispatched in the hope that we would find allies to help with our most immediate problem, that of the submarine, not so that we could take our mind off the situation by watching a bunch of whining toddlers hurl insults at each other."

Boy... none of them liked being compared with that, each looking more than a little 'disappointed off'. Their telling off, however, hadn't finished yet.

"So if all you can do is bicker and fight with one another, you'd best leave us to our assignment, which is stopping that submarine at all costs and doing so whilst containing the very evil and very powerful magic users within, beings that think nothing of destroying not only all of you, but the earth itself. It's a fat lot of good you've all been in helping to seek the answers to questions that might affect every living organism on the planet."

Totally and utterly flabbergasted, the mermaids and mermen exchanged a look, one to end all looks, each and every one of them, including their leaders, ashamed at their actions in the world's greatest time of need.

"What is it you would have us do?" Ajahn queried.

"I'd hoped," put in Vasuki this time, "that between all of us we could come up with a plan to safely dismantle that sub and everyone inside it, so that no one gets hurt and there's no damage to the environment. I shouldn't have to tell you about the risks of the reactor inside that thing overloading. So obviously magic of any sort is out of the question, given the catastrophic consequences should it go wrong, otherwise we'd have already dealt with it by now."

He didn't have to overegg the part about the nuclear power the vessel thrived on. They all knew about the humans' advanced technology and the jeopardy associated with it. So here they were, the quietest they'd been, all supposedly wracking their brains as to how they could securely disable or destroy the submarine with the tools at their disposal.

Still bristling from being suitably chastised, it was a

turquoise haired mermaid from the back of the gossip that flitted forward, a youngster by the look of things.

"What the hell do you think you're doing?" Robyn barked, scaring the living daylights out of almost everyone there. "Get back to your position NOW, before I consider stealing YOUR soul."

With a swish of her bright brown tail, the youngster turned to leave.

"WAIT!" Vimes commanded, his words continuing to be slightly garbled because of the thin layer of air they had to traverse before slamming into the water.

"Just one damn…"

"NO MORE!" Vimes bellowed, his words and intentions very clear to all of them this time. "If this one," he said, referring to the youngster with the turquoise hair, "has something to say, then she should be allowed to. Please... go ahead. What's your name?"

"Llottie," she announced shyly, more than a little startled after the telling off she'd just gotten and to now be the focus of attention.

"Llottie," Vimes repeated, "what a lovely name. Please, if you have something to say, some idea of how we might proceed, now is the time to speak up. You won't be in trouble for doing just that, I give you my word."

Vimes and Robyn locked glares for but a moment before the mermaid leader, knowing what was good for her, backed down.

"I... I... I think I know what we should do," stuttered Llottie, like a bunny in the headlights.

"And what's that exactly?" asked Ajahn, addressing somebody he clearly thought of as beneath him.

"First we need to get the vessel out into much deeper water."

"Easier said than done," Vasuki added, urging the youngster on, hoping she had what it takes to go above and beyond.

She did!

"We use a siren to lure the craft's navigator into making small, unnoticeable changes to their heading towards a much deeper part of the ocean."

"And where would we find one of those at such short notice?" sneered Robyn, looking down her sweet little nose at her underling.

"There's one out there, somewhere beyond the five mile marker, no doubt answering the call as we have. I can just about feel her at the very edge of my supernatural perception."

The leaders of both the mermaids and mermen shared a piercing glance this time, one that showed their derision for the youngster, one that agreed that she just couldn't be right. But on extending the range of their supernatural abilities, they found, to their utter astonishment, that she was indeed correct and that a siren, ancient in origin, was indeed floating somewhere just beyond five miles away.

"I take it from the look on your faces that young Llottie here is correct in her assumption," Vimes mused, his instincts about the juvenile mermaid spot on.

"She is," admitted Ajahn, somewhat perturbed that he'd been outmanoeuvred by someone so youthful.

"Excellent!" asserted the former *tor*. "And for the next part of the plan, Llottie, I assume you have something in mind to safely destroy the submarine, after it's been hoodwinked into deeper water?"

Smiling in almost the exact opposite way to her leader, a purely innocent grin that at the edges showed glimpses of her sparkling, bright white teeth... a ray of sunshine on a cloudy day, Llottie knew what they should do next.

"The perfect answer to that conundrum could be found using only one word."

"And that is?"

"Kraken!"

"Are you insane?" Robyn ranted, her voice an octave or two higher than normal.

"I have to concur," added Ajahn, the other mermen behind him looking absolutely aghast, "kraken aren't to be trusted, their tendencies are far too violent to go anywhere near."

"Llottie?" Vimes ventured, wondering what the youngster had to say for herself on the issue, sure that she would have some sort of retort.

"Kraken get a bad reputation for no apparent reason," put in the dazzlingly beautiful mermaid, "and I know of a breeding pair whose grotto is located not far from here. If I can explain the situation to them, I'm sure they'd be up for helping."

Vimes turned to Vasuki to see what he thought. From the crazed serpent-like smile and the slight nod of his head, it looked as though they had some sort of plan.

Vasuki and his bodyguards zipped off in the direction of the futuristic submarine in an effort not to lose sight of it, while the mermaids and mermen, under the joint leadership of Robyn and Ajahn, sought out the secretive siren in an attempt to compel her to help them lure the vessel back out into deeper water. Vimes followed Llottie further out into the ocean looking for an encounter with two ever elusive krakens that were renowned for their short temper and unerring violence. Once again, the former *tor* had got the short end of the stick.

# 36 BULLET PROOF

As the bullet's epic momentum launched it from the muzzle of the rifle directly towards its intended malevolent prey, the pressure difference between its wake and the surrounding atmosphere caused air to flow in from the sides to fill the void left by the projectile, creating tiny vortices, spiralling patterns of movement in its trail. Unseen by the human eye due to the sheer speed and scale, only a magic user of epic proportions would have any chance of detecting such a phenomenon. Unfortunately in this case, the target was exactly that.

As simply as you or I would reach out and snaffle a snowflake on the breeze, the vicious tormentor stretched out her hand towards the direction the bullet had been fired from. Using just her index finger and thumb, with god-like timing and dexterity, she plucked it casually from the air, much to the bewilderment of the young human bar worker who'd just pulled the trigger, convinced she'd done enough to end the wicked dragon's reign of terror.

If Peter's hands hadn't been shaking before, they most certainly were now, witnessing one of the most impressive feats of supernatural mastery performed in quite some time, all of which had been accompanied by his mother's usual psychotic smile. Knowing they were in trouble was one thing, knowing just how much was quite another. It really was a pee your pants moment. Neither did when most would have.

In a brief moment of clarity, or should I say sanity, Fredric's daughter marvelled at the audacity the young human had shown in firing the ancient weapon towards her. If she'd been paying slightly less attention, if her magic hadn't been a combination of both dragon and naga and some of the most unique and extraordinary on the planet, the attack might well have succeeded. Who'd have thought a mere human could have gotten that close when everyone else had failed so spectacularly? Not her, that's for sure. In a strange way she'd gained a new found respect for a race she absolutely abhorred, humans in general being a long term bugbear of hers.

Crestfallen that her attempt to put her love's wicked mother out of her misery forever had failed, Janice felt the icy grip of malicious evil squeeze the confines of her heart, everything good within, and her inherent positive attitude threatening to implode. Glancing sideways at the still lifeless form of her friend the Christmas legend, strewn out across the cold, hard terracotta floor nearby, caused her to swallow nervously, the super powerful, unique magic user the one thing that had bolstered her faith and optimism in coming down here, now rendering her anxiety at fever pitch levels, the hope she'd had of coming out of this alive all but evaporating, her spirit crushed just as Earth had meant it to be. So far villainous vengeance had gotten the upper hand. Whether or not that could be wrestled away was anyone's guess, but it wasn't looking likely.

Startled, akin to a teenage boy pulling back the shower curtain to discover his grandma there wearing nothing but her beard, Peter could barely believe what he'd seen his soulmate attempt. His enhanced dragon senses had followed the trajectory of the bullet and the vortices trailing it, sure in the same way Janice had been that the shot was nothing short of perfect and would fulfil its ultimate purpose by murdering their nemesis. But to see it so easily plucked out of the air was all but a killing blow, devastating any faith he had in destiny and fate being on the right side of good, causing his already quaking hands to shake just that bit more uncontrollably. As the insides of his stomach continued to perform somersaults and his legs turned to jelly, the naive hockey playing dragon attempted to follow suit, drawing the Kid's pistol from the frayed holster at his hip and pointing it in the direction of his bitch of a parent. Trying to use his left hand to steady the gun in his right, he glanced down the barrel at what he hoped would be an unsuspecting target. As it turned out, it was anything but.

Mind abuzz, half a dozen different voices at loggerheads as to what to do next, abruptly the supernatural danger sense that had so often saved her life kicked into overdrive, sending an icy chill down her arms, raising her hackles. Simultaneously her inborn magic flared into life, the most wicked of enchantments ready to be used in anger directly at the front of her mind, only a couple of words and a smidgen of will required to recreate hell down to the finest of details. Alert to any threat and poised to act, as if on autopilot, Earth turned in the direction of her spineless son who she knew to be cowering behind one of the plinths closer to the back of the dead end vault. Across the confines of the intricate, mystical lair, their eyes met, his as wide as they'd go, the dread and alarm evident, hers resembling two pitch black holes, swallowing up everything good about the world, the lunacy that was her base setting encapsulated in both. Holding the gaze, Peter froze, unable, unlike his heroic lover, to even pull the trigger. In that moment his mother knew not only that she'd secured victory, but also that his death couldn't come soon enough. In her mind at least, he was a disgrace, a runt, one that needed to be put out of its misery for good.

Facing her fear head on just like she'd done on any number of occasions since being dragged down into the domain of the dragons by her now best friend, The White Dragon, Janice, chose not to be defined by the terror so categorically set off by the wicked she-witch that was Fredric's daughter and her soulmate's mother. She resisted the urge to curl up, instead deciding to duck back down behind the plinth she was hiding behind, but not before barking at her transfixed other half.

"Peter! PETER! Snap out of it. I need you now more than ever!"

Those last few words seem to do the trick, metaphorically slapping the face of the naive young dragon, pulling him out of his stupor and the horror which he was currently experiencing.

"I... I... I'm sorry," his whispered words carried across the gap. "I... I... I don't know what to do. She's just too strong. My magic won't even make a dent against her. We're doomed!"

Not exactly a rallying cry or ringing endorsement, I think you can agree.

Appreciating his words on some level, having been deeply involved in the Changing of the Guard, she fully understood the storm that was his mother, having seen her best Fredric more than once as well as George, Vasuki and Flash, together four of the most powerful beings ever to have drawn breath. For just the two of them to defeat her here and now probably depended a great deal on luck and having a fully fit Polkinghorne by their side, neither of which seemed plausible currently. Sure that the wicked woman's arrogance wouldn't last long and that she'd become bored very quickly and want this over in a heartbeat, the beautiful and courageous young human woman reflected on the choices that had led her here, and any available to her now that could buy time for a rescue she didn't think was coming or catch her love's miserable mother off guard. Surprisingly, nothing sprang to mind other than to slide over and try and shake Santa awake, something she vowed to use only as a last resort, not wanting to expose herself to the wicked witch's magic. Lacking the promise of any kind of way out, Janice resolved to try and calm Peter down in the hope that somewhere inside him was the answer to their current predicament, either the intrinsic power to match his mother blow for blow, or an alternative in the form of deeply buried knowledge about the vault that could help them thwart the misery their enemy had planned.

The rags that remained of her clothes still burning furiously, wispy tendrils of dark grey smoke curling up into the air all around her, for the first time in what felt like hours but was more like only half of one, Earth drew in a long deep breath, savouring the moment, having achieved what she'd set out to do, well aware that at any second the world could be wrought in two thanks to the machinations of her despicable other half. Giddy at the thought of payback for everything the dragons had visited down upon them, almost to the point of being drunk, oddly she did a little skip followed by a shimmy, a dance of delight if you will, content in the knowledge that she'd be the one to end her easily led and cowardly son, seeing him off with a flourish into the next world, should such a thing exist. Feeling almost playful now, and with the pressure off to some degree because there was simply no hope of escape for either of her prey and not a cat in hell's chance of them being rescued, determined to satisfy her sick desire for retribution and to somehow avenge the deaths that had caused her to endure so much, in that moment she swore to herself to make their suffering stupendous before she snuffed out both their life forces forever.

# 37 FALLOUT

It felt terrifyingly tragic and yet apocalyptically exhilarating, working as they were in the shadow of the already detonated nuclear warhead hanging mid-air over their heads, to Flash, Amelia and all Yoyo's innovative youngsters, as they continued their undertakings with the utmost professionalism, selflessness, dedication and a sense of purpose like none of them had ever experienced. What was on the line was simply life or death, not just for them but for every living organism on the planet. There were no two ways about it... they had to succeed. There was no other option.

Rushing around at super speed, enhanced by their magic, the pairs continued their quest to find every last gram of laminium in order to send it back to where it had originated from and restore the consciousness of the world to some semblance of greatness. It was a huge ask for such young and inexperienced dragons and yet, just as they had since meeting up with Flash on that runway in Perth, Australia what felt like another lifetime ago, they'd committed to travelling to not only one of the most hostile environments on earth, but a dragon's worst nightmare. To a male and a female, they'd stepped up... BIG TIME, not only with their fighting back at the private residence when they'd lost some of their own, but in the Black Forest using their initiative to track down the stolen laminium and garner leads that nobody else would have a hope in hell of finding. In short, they were nothing other than amazing, their teamwork, sense of belonging and love for one another shining through in these, potentially the last few moments of their lives. Of course it didn't go unnoticed, Yoyo and Rose as proud as punch, even Flash and Amelia taking note of how exceptional they were. Perhaps that might lead to something in the future, should such a thing even exist.

In their pairs, Tina and Monty, Trayrin and Tarko, Zebediah and Essie, Bullhorn and Thadeous, not to mention Flash and Amelia, continued their work at speed It was organised chaos but somehow, thank goodness, it continued to work, right up to Flash and Amelia discovering the very last bar of laminium and sending it on its way. After that, as a group, all the youngsters, the good captain and the former Crimson Guard gravitated towards the surface, a reunion with Yoyo and Rose the only thing on their minds, their part done, with nothing else to do but wait and see if it was enough to revive Novus and avert utter disaster. Zipping up and out of the borehole, each landing with an effortless THUMP next to the healer and his brilliant wife, it was difficult to ignore the elephant in the room in the form of the already exploded warhead hanging mid-air directly above their heads, now ever so slightly expanding outwards, something they all considered didn't bode well at all.

A spooky reminder of what they were all doing here stood statue-like nearby, a perfect replica of Bentwhistle, unblinking, with a dull blank look etched across its humanoid face, gazing out across the top of the shadow strewn test borehole. Some of the youngsters recoiled at seeing the flawless facsimile of their friend as they dropped down to the ground next to their mentor and his wife. For Flash though, it just gave him the willies knowing that something so powerful could create a construct so picture perfect and accurate. He didn't like it one bit. Powerless to intervene in any other manner, the ragtag group of heroes sidled up to one another determined to extract every last ounce of affection they could, knowing it might be their last opportunity.

Behind the faultless brown eyes of the hockey loving dragon imitation, some degree of multitasking was still going on despite the heroes having returned all the laminium available, playing their part to a tee. Novus was pretty much on his own now, a transformation of sorts taking place already. Whether it would be enough to solve the almighty conundrum that was the ever expanding (albeit at the microscopic level) already exploded nuclear warhead hanging in the sky above, they'd just have to wait and see.

Fate was bursting with pride at what the dragon heroes had accomplished in such a short space of time. She let that part of her compartmentalised brain drift into nothingness, diverting her remaining attention to her siblings, or more like cohorts, Time and Luck, both of whom were struggling, each sweating profusely, unable to find the words they needed to communicate, their supernatural wearing thin due to constantly spamming it over and over again across the entirety of the missile debris, Time with her dilation field, Luck trying to bless it with all the fortune she could spare. Despite their best efforts, the remains were expanding with every moment that passed. The Providences' grip on the wreckage, the kinetic energy and the devastating radiation was slowly starting to slip away.

Focusing now on only the other two and the magic all three of them needed to constantly apply in an effort to keep the already detonated missile in place, and having left the conscious will of the planet to it, sensing a change of some magnitude having already kicked off, the Diva of Destiny, Fate herself, continued on the only course of action she knew... to keep encouraging them both. If that didn't work, then they'd all probably be dead in only a matter of moments.

*"I know it's difficult,"* she whispered across their shared connection, *"but please, keep going. Our efforts are all that contain that thing. And it won't be much longer, I can assure you. Even as we speak, Novus is getting close to being his old self once again."*

I probably don't need to tell you that the last part was a lie. Fate didn't know the state of the planet's sentience, having relinquished her grip on that part of the multitasking some time ago. But she considered it one of those, little white lies, you know the type. The ones you tell your children to get them to bed on time, to brush their teeth, to get them to eat their vegetables. Or maybe those that you tell your other half in order to build up to a surprise, wanting to enhance the fun and enjoyment of that very special day. Either way, it was done in order to help them focus, give them a little boost right at the very end, to know that they weren't alone, and that their preferred outcome was close at hand, helping them inch across the line. But whether it would or not was dependent on one thing, and one alone... NOVUS!

Akin to the sun bursting through parting clouds and hitting you straight in the eyes, washing away any semblance of darkness and gloom, this was what it felt like for Novus to have the fog around his brain lifted, the memories rushing back in at pace, filling his consciousness with experiences from long, long ago. Lush jungles full to the brim with wildlife, the varying shades of green a reminder of the tranquillity back then. Turquoise oceans atop bustling reefs where fish and sea creatures of all shapes and sizes thrived and lived in peace with one another, flashed into being behind what passed for his eyes, followed quickly by untouched snow capped mountains, ecologically diverse river systems, picture perfect prairies, scintillating scorching deserts, epic estuaries, luscious lakes, majestic meadows, the cool tang of crisp, clean fresh air, outstanding orchards bursting with epically ripe fruit, wicked woodland, heaving hilltops, crystal clear trickling streams, wondrous waterfalls, icy plateaus and glistening glaciers, as it had been at the inception. For a moment he thought he'd been cast back in time, to the beginning when things had been simpler and he'd understood everything. But as his mind remembered what the planet looked like in the here and now, he got more of a shock than ever. The devastation from Manson's recent attacks was huge, but by no means all of it. There was an overall maliciousness clouding everything from the basest pettiness, to the wanton disregard of others. The taint of selfishness spread out across the globe. How was that even possible? How had everything changed so much in so little time? It was a mystery, to him at least, but whether it should have been was a whole other question, one that perhaps would have been more relevant.

There are two things about the sentience of the planet that I should point out. Firstly, it was exceptionally childlike and naive, in the mould of a certain hockey playing dragon that Novus had already forged a somewhat tenuous bond with. Secondly, although Novus preferred to be known as 'he', he was neither male nor female, more the purest form of both combined together for all time, taking everything that's good from each and welding it together to produce something exceptional. He knew the humans had advanced more rapidly than he himself, and some liked to call themselves 'they'. Perhaps he would get to that point one day, but just not yet.

But for now, there were no boys' nights out, no leaving the toilet seat up, no late night curries or kebabs, no drinking too much, no listening too little. No screaming at the ref, no changing room banter, no wolf whistling, no backstabbing, no threats of intimidation or violence and no lunatic driving. You might think it would end there, but... NO! Dancing around handbags was definitely out, alongside yoga retreats, the bottling up of feelings, emotional immaturity, gossiping on the phone, all day shopping trips, snide glances, cheating, psychological mind games, whispering behind backs, rejection, hurt and body shaming. None of that in Novus' world had ever, or would ever exist. You might think that a bad thing, until you discovered what did.

Sitting under endless starry skies, glorious sunsets with colours to die for, perfect kisses that lasted an eternity, picture postcard walks along infinite sandy beaches, dolphins surfing across beautiful breaking waves, that thrill of holding hands with a lover for the very first time, getting lost in comforting cuddles until nothing else exists, soothing foot rubs, unexpected compliments, sumptuous dinners, playful picnics, everlasting love, perfect moments, unerring friendships, the delight and excitement of a newborn baby, pure joy, resounding laughter and a contented heart.

Essentially, the best bits of both worlds, all rolled into one kind hearted, perfectly innocent, wondrous and inquisitive soul that had nothing but good intentions, but had through no fault of his (there it is again) own, become lost along the way. Maybe his return, should such a thing be possible, could provide a platform for humanity and dragonkind to forge ahead, work together, come out of the darkness and into the light, forgoing all the malice, vengeance and pettiness that had swept its way in whilst his back had been turned. In some circumstances hope could be a terrible thing.

# 38 KRAK-ON

Despite the angst between the two factions born of any number of historical disagreements, Ajahn and Robyn, leaders of the Sumerian descended mermen and the soul stealing mermaids respectively, swam silently side by side, heading north beneath the chilling dark blue water, homing in on a being whose help they desperately needed, one feared by nearly all sea dwelling creatures, one whose infamy had throughout the centuries spread not only across the world's oceans but onto the land as well. Few and far between, it was a surprise to both leaders that a siren, of all beings, would be located so close by. It would appear that Fate had given them a helping hand in providing what they needed at just the right time. Whether the nightmarish horror could be persuaded to help was something else altogether. Not known for their cooperation with any other species and feared by all, even getting close to a siren presented a very real risk of falling under its spell. That said, there seemed little alternative but to try and cajole the creature into helping, almost certainly their best bet in tricking the disguised dragon helmsman on the sub in an attempt to guide it into deeper water.

Powered ever forward at speed by their huge, swishing, scaled tails that, unlike fish, moved up and down instead of from side to side, both tightly knit groups passed beyond the point at which they figured they were vulnerable to the siren's supernatural abilities and opening themselves up, projected a united front of peace and friendship outwards in front of them, hoping at least that she would take the hint. Squeaky bum time underwater was much less fun than on the surface, and that was saying quite something.

Bemused by a call so ancient and fundamental that it had

stopped her in her tracks, all but forcing her to navigate in the direction of its origin, Aglaophonos, which roughly translated as 'beautiful voice', managed to control herself and pull up about five miles short. That had been a while ago and, puzzling even herself, she'd remained stationary trying to figure out what was going on, something of epic proportions no doubt, otherwise the shout out wouldn't have been used. Figuring that no situation, no matter how dire, could benefit from her unique skill set, she was surprised to sense a delegation on their way in her direction. They seemed to be a cross between fish and the ones up above, many of whom she'd lured to their deaths across the decades, but whatever they were, they were swimming quickly towards her. Momentarily she wondered if they perceived her as THE threat, the one the cry for help had been about. Very quickly she dismissed that idea wholeheartedly. Nothing in its right mind would come for her, not knowing the ease with which she could overcome even the mightiest of defences, able to get anything or anyone to do her bidding at a moment's notice. Intrigued, she waited to greet the newcomers, eager to hear what was so important and how they thought she could figure in their plans.

The bad feeling that felt like a constant companion nowadays had intensified beyond belief on leaving Vasuki and the others, despite being accompanied by Llottie. From what little he knew, she was the kindest of the gossip of mermaids and quite possibly the only being as shy as he was. It was all Vimes could do not to laugh at that, something he was sure would offend if he did.

Trailing in her wake, his humungous dragon form struggling to keep up with her lithe, nimble, half fish, half stunningly beautiful human body which was perfectly suited to swimming underwater, the former *tor* didn't know what to say or do, only to follow, already having been assured that the youngster knew where to find the home of a mating pair of kraken. It had all sounded so straight forward when she'd thrown it out there and the others had agreed to him accompanying her. That is until he remembered overhearing the fantastical blade, Fu-ts'ang, recount a story from his past, long before he'd been incarcerated in the fierce and formidable blade, a master weapon smith at the time, forger of all things futuristic and incredible. In a whispered hush involving some of the mightiest heroes to have survived the Changing of the Guard, he'd detailed a bounty being posted, thousands of years in the past, for of all things, a... KRAKEN!

Allegedly a group of three dragons had gone into an inshore lake, in which one of the alarming and redoubtable octopus-like creatures had been known to reside, their minds clouded by not only the hefty reward on offer, but by the leader's omission when it came to THE most important fact about the terrifying creature. Just like now, kraken are immune to any sort of magic... it simply doesn't affect them, well, not directly anyhow, something the leader of the three finally used to his advantage against the beast, but not before it had inflicted considerable pain and damage.

Here and now, that wasn't something Vimes particularly wanted to dwell on. Of course his mind had other ideas, to the point of fixating on that very trait and just how helpless they'd be should things go badly for them.

Unable to tell up from down with the darkness of the chilling sea having closed in all around them, he concentrated on keeping an eye on the very ends of Llottie's tail. A real fear of losing her in the darkness ran through him, especially as he figured they were some forty or so kilometres further out to sea from where the meeting of minds had taken place. It was only then that Vimes could sense they'd started to move down towards the seafloor. As nervous as he'd ever been (and that included the time that his soulmate had been kidnapped by the Easter Bunny,

Cupid and The Tooth Fairy) the former *tor* opened up his mind and sought that of his partner in all things Operation Kraken.

*"What's going on?"* he asked.

*"We're nearly there,"* she replied instantly.

He gulped nervously. Luckily the surrounding pocket of air that Vasuki had cast kept him from swallowing anything salty.

*"Are you sure you can trust them?"*

*"As sure as it's possible to be."*

*"What does that mean?"*

*"It means they've let me swim alongside them on occasion, something practically unheard of."*

*"And that's a good sign?"*

*"I should hope so,"* she answered with all the naivety of youth.

'That's what we're basing this on,' Vimes thought to himself, now closed off from his mermaid partner, 'they've let you swim alongside them on occasion.'

Shaking his head, he blew out a long breath, the madness of what they were attempting now all too apparent.

'Perhaps, they thought you were an aperitif or just cute like a kitten and they let you go. Either way, I don't have a great feeling about any of this.'

Right as that thought crossed his mind, the sandy bottom swam into view, a desert of yellow occasionally punctuated by typically huge boulders shrouded in seaweed. More on edge than ever, he continued to follow in her wake, unable to do much else, far too scared to turn around and go back on his own. Just as he thought it couldn't get any worse, a huge rocky structure punctuated by a gigantic overbearing arch in the middle swam into view. Littered on the seabed beside it were the discarded remnants of ships... wooden beams, algae covered sails, intricate ropes, lines and nets all tangled up, damaged wooden barrels, unopened chests of all descriptions, cannon balls and cannons, glistening silver cutlery, slivers of china plates and from behind it all, two pairs of very wide open and very alien looking eyes, watching their every move.

# GULP!

So fast that it was one stretched out sound echoing out into the furthest reaches of the king's private residence, spindly prehistoric fingers tapped keys on a specially designed dragon keyboard in a blur, almost impossible to see which individual character had been pressed even with enhanced supernatural senses, the accompanying monitor still showing a detailed downward view of the already exploded nuclear warhead, the kinetic energy from the detonation all but visible through the initial discharge, sparks of fire and broken components. It was a mess, but a recognisable one to those who knew what to look for.

Holding his tongue, something of a novelty given his usual gung ho attitude in demanding answers from those around him, George sat quietly watching the image on the screen, curiously reflecting on what had gone wrong, or quite possibly right in this instance. Who knew what was happening right now in northern France and elsewhere across the world, without more information and context? He was still perplexed at the level of magic involved in keeping what he'd been assured was a live representation, fully in check. Not only was it puzzling, but the intrigue on top of that was off the scale, rousing all his curiosity like nothing else ever had. What a time for that to happen! So he sat and waited, pondering possibilities, none of which made any sense, searching for the answers across the length and breadth of his eidetic memory, hoping to come up with something, anything that might shed some light on what the hell was going on. So far nothing had been uncovered.

Fifteen minutes, that's how long it took for Vasuki and the two accompanying nagas to catch up with the super quiet, futuristic submarine and slip back effortlessly into its wake, trailing at a distance of about two hundred metres in the cold, dark, harsh waters that reminded all of them of home.

Suffering the kind of mental scars from his Antarctic incarceration that might well never heal and could possibly, if he were any lesser a being, affect every decision he made, it was only the resolve and fortitude that had earned him the position of monarch in the first place that kept the overwhelming darkness at bay, his mind making a conscious decision to focus on the here and now in an effort to make amends for all the atrocities those under Manson's wicked spells had committed in his name, and the misery and deaths his race had suffered, due in no small part to his confinement.

Once again he was assisting the dragons, all his trust put in the one known as Fredric, hoping to unite some of the ancient undersea creatures in an effort to put a stop once and for all to the monster that had haunted a great many of his dreams... MANSON!


You could have cut the tension with a knife, along with the surrounding murky water, as both the mermaids and mermen under Robyn and Ajahn's respective leadership cautiously approached the waiting siren. Neither leader knew what lay ahead, having never before encountered one of the fabled creatures, but both were slightly encouraged by two things. One... they hadn't had to sneak up on it, a course of action both considered the kind of mistake that would have gotten them killed in an instant. And two, she, and it was a she, that much they could sense with just a tiny dribble of their supernatural power, hadn't attacked yet. They were certainly in range and would have little in the way of defence if she had. Taking inspiration and some tiny comfort from both these things, they anxiously continued, their minds abuzz, wondering how they'd win over the mythological monster.

The trepidation wasn't a one way street, the siren herself having not physically spoken to anyone in over three centuries… outside using her song to lure others to their deaths. Even then that was only a passing merman, a European, Nordic by nature, a well muscled, long blonde haired monster of a beast, a creature that had surprised her by enquiring about her wellbeing. Nobody, not even her parents, had ever done that before. It was quite something at the time and a moment she recalled with great fondness. Could those approaching arrive with the same attitude, she wondered, or would she have to use her vocal chords which had saved her on so many occasions.

Gliding to a halt, the mermen and mermaids inched forward, allowing the undersea current to edge them just that little bit closer, all encompassing fear rife amongst the gossip's shared telepathic connection, the mermen faring about the same.

Slowly the gloom of icy cold water parted to reveal the creature they'd all been searching for, the one they'd been able to sense for some time, one of the most elusive throughout any of the planet's seas.

Strange didn't really do her justice. Let's start with the lower half. Legs akin to a human, but scaled… a gentle light brown around her waist getting progressively darker the closer it came to her feet. Speaking of which, they had three long, bony toes with webbing in between, in the same overall dark tone as her legs. Put that together and you had a combination that was unusual to say the least. But that wasn't what seemed most odd on first impression. From her waist to her neck lay feathers, silvery grey in colour, preened to perfection. Now you might think there'd have been wings, and it looked as though there might once have been, as the feathers around her back and shoulders looked… bedraggled and damaged, almost as if covering up an horrific injury from an attack by something much more powerful. What that could have been was anyone's guess and probably worst nightmare given the individual floating before them. And that left what? Long, pale arms covered with the same intricate scales as her legs, sharp nails carved to a point residing on the ends of her gangly fingers. But most impressive of all was the exquisite beauty atop all that. The pale scales from her arms and shoulders continued on an upward trajectory, changing gradually in colour, tinged with just the barest hint of green making her face appear slightly lizard-like, but not in a bad way. Gorgeous would be the only word to describe her, from the cute button nose, the perfect pursed lips to the mane of long, brown, curly hair. She was a vision alright and it was hard to see how, combined with her song, sailors could resist her. One more foible to mention was the necklace precariously washing over the top of her chest, moving this way and that in the current, made up of at least two dozen bleached human finger bones, no doubt taken as trinkets from sailors who'd been lured to their deaths in the depths.

More awkward than an actual standoff, both sides fearing the other at least a little, it was Ajahn who plucked up the courage to speak first.

"Greetings... legendary one. It's a pleasure to meet you. Would you do us the honour of listening to our plight?"

Who's not going to be bowled over by that introduction?!

Being the shining example of the social outcast that she was, the anomalous siren was taken aback at all those looking on and at how politely she'd been addressed by what she'd be the first to admit, was a smokin' hot example of any merman on the planet, his bare, hairy chest alone provoking thoughts about all sorts of inappropriate comings together, causing her to blush profusely for the first time in many, many decades. How crazy was that?!

"I would be happy to," Aglaophonos replied, her voice a little wobbly, more to do with the peculiar feelings she was experiencing than the thick, gloom laden, salty sea water that flowed between them.

Before the tale could begin, introductions were made, not everybody there you understand, just the leaders, and then it was story time.

It took about fifteen minutes to recount everything... their meeting with Vasuki and Vimes and the mission they'd become embroiled in. For the most part Ajahn passed on the details, with Robyn occasionally interrupting, much to Aglaophonos's indignation, the siren much preferring the merman's undivided attention. They went on to explain why they needed her help and how critical it might prove. When all was said and done, the groups of mermaids and mermen waited for an answer.

For as long as she could remember she'd craved company, having even on occasion imprisoned captured sailors, holding them for as long as their tiny lifespans would allow. But it wasn't the same, their fear evident from the disgusting stench they gave off, a constant reminder that they weren't there of their own free will. This though, this felt different, like she could be part of something bigger, recognised not for the frightening things she was capable of, but perhaps for herself. It was a risk, one she wouldn't even consider taking under normal circumstances. But here and now, gazing across at the expectations on everyone's faces, especially HIS, she felt it worth taking a gamble.

"I'd be happy to help," she announced, much to everyone's genuine pleasure.

With no further ado, as one combined band of brothers and sisters, they set off back towards the Scottish coast to find Vasuki and that damned submarine.

*"What do you mean, you've never had any actual contact with either of them?"* Vimes blurted across their shared connection.

*"I just project peace, tranquillity and kind thoughts and they take it upon themselves to come and swim with me,"* Llottie replied, all

sweetness and light.

'*Brilliant!*' the former *tor* thought sarcastically to himself at the realisation they had no real way to communicate with two of the most dangerous creatures ever to grace the oceans.

"*Oh... it'll be alright,*" piped up his mermaid cohort, "*they know I'm friendly and mean them no harm.*"

"*That they might,*" Vimes replied sceptically, "*but that doesn't get us any closer to acquiring their help or even explaining exactly what we want them to do.*"

"*Hmmm...*" mused Llottie, pondering the problem.

But her contemplation would have to wait.

From in front of the overbearing rocky arch and out from behind the mass of tangled nets, splintered masts, algae covered sails, decomposing wooden barrels, unopened chests and smashed china, rose a colossal, misshapen set of yellow and green tentacles over eighty metres in length, each flailing about independently of the others, probing the deep dark blue, for... what?

Two thoughts above all others ran over and over in Vimes' mind.

'Oh crap, oh crap, oh crap,' was one of them. The other went something like, 'Don't use magic, don't use magic, don't use magic,' figuring that if the monster was immune to everything supernatural, it would surely be able to sense when something of that nature was instigated. It was a good call because he'd have been spot on.

Without any regard for Vimes or his thoughts on the subject, Llottie, being the childlike and pure mermaid she was, never having seen a soul being stolen let alone taken one herself, swished her tail twice and torpedoed through the chilly water on a direct collision course with the kraken that had come out of hiding.

Vimes' anxiety erupted like a cork from a bottle of champagne, Santa's soulmate wondering what the hell he would do should the thing attack.

Bright brown tail having stopped swishing, the

gorgeous, turquoise haired mermaid drifted closer to the unfamiliar octopus lookalike, the kraken by now having reversed itself completely, tentacles wafting lazily behind it, bulging eyes clearly hiding a razor sharp intellect standing out atop a rippling head, the beast's burgundy beak barely visible, now only a few metres from Llottie.

In that moment Vimes feared for both their lives.

Out of nowhere an intense pressure exploded behind both Llottie's and Vimes' eyes causing the kind of pain only a chronic sinusitis sufferer would recognise. Instantly the former *tor* was rendered helpless, floating on his back, unable to form any kind of defence or shout out a warning. For her part Llottie appeared to cope with it better, remaining upright, massaging her forehead ever so slightly.

Abruptly a deep throaty rasp echoed across the confines of their minds.

*"Visually pleasing Vixen of the seas... it's good to see you again. If you've come to swim with us, why have you brought this strange looking creature?"*

Llottie, now rubbing her rosy red cheeks horizontally as well as the bridge of her nose due to the intense pain, tried desperately to formulate a reply.

*"This creature is a dragon and my friend,"* was all that she managed to get out on first try.

*"A... DRAGON, you say..."* repeated the kraken, the shock in his voice hard to mistake.

Both the new found allies had the same thought, 'Uh oh,' which was immediately made all the worse by the other kraken swimming out at speed from behind the sunken debris to join her mate.

*"Ingrained in our DNA, are tales of dragons past,"* observed the newly arrived female, a scowl of epic proportions crossing her face, at least that's probably what it was, it was so difficult to tell.

About to suggest a run (well, swim) for it, the chance to do so disappeared as the newly arrived female slinked her way behind them both, the two sets of eight tentacles now surrounding them.

Working the problem and bereft of any magic, Vimes did the only thing he could think of... ignoring the splintering pain behind his eyes, he used one of his strong suits and engaged them in conversation.

*"These tales,"* he continued, *"could you give me some examples?"*

That was the last thing the kraken expected.

*"Our kind were hunted as sport long, long ago,"* the male ventured.

*"Mothers,"* put in the female, *"were ripped apart, their young wolfed down as part of a gruesome initiation. Wicked and evil can't begin to describe it."*

Vimes, not knowing what else to do, just shook his head as he continued to tread water.

*"There were, however, some good encounters,"* the female's voice continued, monosyllabic.

That piqued Santa's soulmate's interest.

*"Some of your kind ventured into the depths at great risk to themselves to save us from the merkind revolution, losing many in an undersea battle that lasted weeks, cost much and caused the water to run every different shade of red, green and blue, the seabed for hundreds of miles in all directions littered with the corpses of kraken babies."*

*"Really..."* Vimes commented, staggered at the brutality, having never heard of such a thing despite being a history know it all.

*"Supposedly under secretive orders from the dragon monarch of the time, his very best warriors were sent to assist after a chance meeting with kraken royalty on the eastern edges of England... More than that I do not know, other than they fought valiantly and proved a credit to your kind, selflessly assisting us in our time of need."*

*"Who'd have thought?"*

*"And that's what we have here and now,"* Llottie observed, recalling having learned about the battle as part of her schooling, *"a time of need!"*

Silence abounded between the mermaid and dragon, only the chilling water sloshing around their very different bodies. But it was clear from tiny changes in colour around the sides of the krakens' heads that each was continuing to communicate with the other. This went on for some minutes.

All the while attempting to figure out an exit strategy, should they need one, through the writhing mass of surrounding tentacles, Vimes hoped they could explain the peril the planet was currently facing and how the two octopus-like creatures could play their part in helping out. Exactly then, both of the gigantic beasts parted from each other, allowing their heads to drift closer to the former *tor*, their tentacles now having created a bubble surrounding both of the newcomers entirely. Any sort of exit strategy now involved fighting their way through the mass of muscled tendrils, an action that was never going to go well for anyone.

*"YOU,"* the female suggested referring to Vimes, *"have an unusual taint. Explain!"*

*"Uhhh…"* was all that came to mind, his psyche drawing a total and utter blank.

Fortunately for him, Llottie picked up the baton.

*"He's the mate of the one the dragons and humans know as… SANTA!"*

'That's never going to work down here with them,' Vimes mused, still wondering how to extricate themselves from the ever growing sticky situation.

Without warning one of the huge, sucker covered crimson coloured tentacles started to wrap itself around the bottom of Vimes' right leg.

'Oh crap, oh crap, oh crap,' he thought once again, figuring this was quite possibly the end.

And then a sharp but not too unpleasant tingling sensation surged up from the tentacle's grip, causing his whole body to convulse. Moments later it was gone, the tendril's grasp released, suckers and all retreating back to where they'd come from.

Exhaling the biggest breath he ever had, Vimes

wondered what the hell was going on and what would happen next. He didn't have to wait long to find out.

*"She's telling the truth,"* voiced the male, with a tone of incredulity in his voice.

"Hang on," *ventured the former tor,* "you know of Santa?"

*"Oh yes,"* cried the female kraken excitedly, *"she visits us once a year, dropping off shipwrecked junk for us to fortify our home with. Quite often she stays for a drink and a chat."*

'WHAT?!' he thought only to himself, followed quickly by, 'how in the hell is that even possible?' Vowing to ask her when they next met, should the crisis they found themselves tangled up in ever get fully resolved, Vimes turned his attention back to both of the monstrous looking sea creatures.

*"Will you help us?"*

*"For the mate of the once a year legend? Of course... how could we possibly refuse?"*

Yet again his connection to the dragon he loved more than life itself had not only saved him from a watery grave but had garnered the assistance of the two strange beings just when they needed it most. Was there simply no end to Polkinghorne's magic, even when she wasn't around? Marvelling at her influence across every aspect of the planet, Vimes, with a little help from Llottie, went on to explain what they had in mind and just how both kraken could play their part. Agreed, in principle anyhow, it took only a couple of minutes for the pair of octopus lookalikes to be ready to move out. As a foursome they headed back towards shallower water and the northern cost of Scotland at speed, in an effort to hook up with the others. Very slowly, their plan was coming together.


Abruptly he realised that the sound of the super speedy tapping had stopped. Glancing up, the spell of his daydream well and truly broken, George found himself gazing into a primordial face that he was all too familiar with, his friend and time honoured general... Whitewings.

"Sire!"

"My friend, do you have something for me?"

"I do."

"And?"

The pause alone was enough to reveal it wasn't good news.

'Spit it out, and don't sugar coat it... not at a time like this."

"Using the telemetry from the satellite and the computing power here, we've been able to calculate that the already exploded warhead isn't quite as stuck in time as we'd hoped."

"What on earth is that supposed to mean?"

"It's moving, Majesty."

"Moving?"

"Expanding outwards, albeit at a snail's pace, but the kinetic force, explosion itself and the radiation are all spreading out. Whatever force stopped it dead in its tracks is slowly losing its grip."

Looking as down in the dumps as it was possible to be, his educated and cunning mind still trying to examine the problem from every possible angle, George had nowhere left to go, no cards up his sleeve.

"How long?"

"My lord?"

"How long until the explosion reaches the laminium in the test borehole?"

"Impossible to say, I'm afraid."

"And why's that?"

"Because it's not expanding uniformly. Who or whatever had a grip on that thing is losing it at an exponential rate. It could be five hours or five minutes, there's simply no way to know."

'Brilliant,' thought the king, 'just brilliant!'

Cutting through the water beneath the dark, chilling North Sea waves, the futuristic submarine emitted little noise or anything else to give away its position, its electronic footprint almost zero, heat and sound insulated to such a degree that even the most advanced satellites couldn't pick it up. It was the ultimate stealth killing machine.

So inside the ultramodern tin can full of prehistoric dragons disguised as humans, things continued as they had been, their new course set for Edinburgh, all the crew wondering what this new and illicit plan was, sure that their leader was dead set to rule the world, each waiting to bask in his glory and claim the rewards on offer. Little did they know the chance for that to happen had long since passed, the need for revenge and retribution now the only thing driving Manson, no thought at all given to others, even his beloved queen who he'd tasked with causing as much mayhem and damage in London whilst they waited for the world to burn, something that hadn't happened yet, much to his disappointment. There was still time though.

Within the eerie red glow of the command centre, those in charge continued with consummate professionalism, all focused on the work at hand and not getting on the wrong side of their leader whose demeanour continued to deteriorate with every minute that passed. Nobody knew why and nobody wanted to ask, all leaving him to his brooding, each member of the bridge crew finding tasks to consume their time, no matter how small.

With all those around him appearing both busy and full of expertise as they carried out their duties, it would never have occurred to Manson that something untoward was happening right underneath his nose, even if he hadn't been distracted by the darkest of thoughts about the destruction of every living being on the planet.

In the sweat infused confines of the command centre the helmsman, a dragon by the name of Dianstagous, was having what felt like an out of body experience. Hotter than he'd like (which was saying something given the natural coding of his antediluvian DNA) tiny beads of water were dripping down the forehead of his filthy human disguise. He'd been trained to within an inch of his life on how to operate all the navigational systems onboard the futuristic vessel, but for some reason he kept forgetting whether their heading was correct, and so over and over again began to make tiny course corrections, some so minute it was impossible to feel any discernible change within the submarine itself. After having lost any sign of a tail, the dragon and naga cohorts totally out of the picture, they'd been on an absolute bearing of ninety degrees. Over the last twenty minutes or so, that heading had altered and was now much closer to seventy degrees, meaning that instead of travelling parallel to the coast towards Fraserburgh, they were now on a route that would take them slightly further north and into deeper water, much to the delight of the assembled allies supernaturally hidden someway in their wake. Aglaophonos was doing a sterling job of intentionally using her abilities to interfere with the helmsman's mind. So far, so good... in fact, you could probably say everything was going... swimmingly!

In a contrast to his cohorts, Vimes was struggling to keep up with the pace they'd set, his huge prehistoric form not designed for swimming, unlike his companions' superb aerodynamic bodies which cut through the cold, dark water with ease. Muscles quite literally burning with effort, wings on fire, Santa's other half gave all he could in an effort to stay with them, but he was severely lagging behind, now barely able to see the dull white suckers on the tips of the kraken tentacles in front of him. Wondering how far they'd travelled, his normally keen awareness of his surroundings having long since deserted him beneath the ocean, he hoped there wasn't too far left to go to meet up with the rest of their ragtag contingent.

Luckily it didn't take long, the four of them relying on

Llottie's connection and sense of direction to home in on the gossip of mermaids. Slowing right down, much to their surprise, the water changed abruptly from shadowy and downright freezing to something much warmer and almost turquoise in colour, the golden seabed they'd stumbled upon littered with glistening rocks. Amongst it all the mermaids and mermen had briefly set up camp, tearing themselves away from following the sub, some of the rocks having been arranged as fortifications and others tipped over to make seats. Seaweed in a variety of brilliant, bright colours had been stripped from the ocean floor and was now either being combed or lay basking atop some of the spare giant stones. What was this all about? Vimes couldn't be sure, but if he had to take a guess, it resembled a meal being prepared for all parties. In the middle of everything they faced, those present had put in the effort so that all the different species could break bread together, so to speak.

Floating to a halt, introductions were made, Robyn and the rest of the mermaids utterly flabbergasted that the youngest amongst them, Llottie, had managed to secure the help of both krakens, her reputation greatly enhanced amongst the gossip.

With the siren, Aglaophonos, still connected to the helmsman's mind, managing to slowly guide the submarine in their direction, all that was left to do was come up with a scheme for once it arrived, not only to break it in two, but to contain everything supernatural and radioactive as well as make sure those inside were sent to a watery grave. It would take some planning that's for sure and so they got started straight away, Vasuki taking point, explaining how he thought they should proceed. Ideas and food were exchanged as the danger from the futuristic sub got ever closer.

# 39 A DISTRESSING DIAGNOSIS

Watching through both the small window of the booth that looked out into the room with the MRI scanner in it, and on the monitor in front of them that gave a top down look at the entire length of their stretched out friend's body, Jar Man, DomCon and Steel hoped and prayed that the rugby playing youngster would be okay, his heroics more legendary than Steel's laminium ball antics and that was saying quite something. Sitting in chairs in front of them, two technicians continued to monitor all the information and the scan's progress. Out of nowhere, things went straight to hell!

Abruptly, Tank's well muscled, human shaped body started to convulse erratically, his head twisting from side to side, his huge arms flailing about, smacking into the sides of the scanner, his legs and feet trembling uncontrollably.

"DOCTOR!" one of the technicians shouted urgently at the top of her voice.

"What is it?" the physician answered, appearing as if by magic through the door behind the three pals looking on in horror.

"He's having a seizure!"

Jar Man, DomCon and Steel had little in the way of medical experience but it was plain to see that whatever was going on was bad on an epic scale, something confirmed in that moment as they turned to look at the medical professional's face, greeted with an expression that would forever be ingrained in their eidetic memories, one that said that the situation could not have been any more dire, one that denoted that Tank's life was hanging in the balance. All three simultaneously had the same one word thought.

'****!'

"WE NEED TO GET HIM OUT OF THE SCANNER... NOW!" yelled the doctor.

Both technicians bolted up out of their chairs, pushed past the three friends and sprinted into the ward. In a few moments the machine had been stopped and Tank's still shuddering body had been pulled out on the patient tray, the three medics now trying to restrain his involuntary movements, with little luck it would seem.

"Need a hand doc?" ventured the giant, ginger haired human form of Jar Man, slipping into a gap between the two technicians.

"If you can hold him down I'll try and sedate him."

"No problem," declared the trio's impromptu leader, putting one firm hand on Tank's forehead and the other in the middle of his chest, whilst the two technicians continued to struggle with a leg each. Steel and DomCon watched anxiously from beside the control room, there not being enough space for them to get any closer.

"Keep him as still as you can," urged the doctor, grabbing a syringe out of black bag he'd brought into the room with him.

Jar Man used all his strength to do so, trying not to hurt his friend in the process. Five seconds later it was done and Tank almost immediately became still after the injection in his neck.

"What was that all about, doc?"

"I don't know," sighed Doctor Tomlinson, "but probably nothing good. I need to examine the data we got from what little of the scan we managed to complete."

"Can't you put him back in right now?"

"No... not with what I've just done. That sedative in his bloodstream would knock out a herd of elephants and keep a concert audience of humans quiet for weeks. Scanning him now will only impede us and muddle the information."

"Doc?" Jar Man pleaded, desperate to know what the professional was thinking and why he'd phrased it like that.

"I'm sorry," Doctor Tomlinson voiced, "but I won't lie to any of you. Tank's situation can at best be described as precarious."

"And at worst?" put in Steel, he and DomCon having stalked over from their position beside the monitoring room.

"Whatever's going on inside him, it's serious, deadly so. I can't tell you any more until I've looked at the data which I'm going to do right now. It might be that we have to operate and do it sooner rather than later."

"You're going to cut him open?" the most diminutive of the three asked, the fear and in trepidation in his voice obvious to all those there.

"Going in to look at his brain is the worst, last option, but the more I've seen of this, combined with everything you've already told me, it's looking like that's what we're going to have to do. Now I'm sorry... but I'm going to have to ask you all to wait outside in the corridor. Excuse me."

Heads bowed, the three of them were escorted from the ward by the two technicians, their emotions a mess, wondering what the hell they should do now, each feeling totally helpless and lost, a moment in time returning to haunt them all. And which one was that I hear you ask? Gee Tee's last fleeting seconds, of course, where all three had been powerless to intervene. Bugger!

Could it be that part of Artorius' prophecy was starting to come true?

Just down the road in the city centre, four extraordinary human beings trudged along an uneven path through a weathered stone arch that had once been part of the defensive wall surrounding the cathedral, each of them breathing a sigh of relief at the outcome they'd had no small part in achieving. Whilst those inside the renowned Close in charge of the hunt for survivors scrabbled around to find answers as to how so many of the missing children had just turned up on a patch of grass out of absolutely nowhere, the four friends had sloped off into relative obscurity, not wanting to reveal either what they knew or their part in events.

"Wow... that was quite something," Emma sighed, absolutely exhausted but chock-full of adrenaline.

"Imagine being able to attain that result in such a short space of time. You'd be able to do almost anything," put in Sam, still barely able to believe what had happened, not for the first time.

"I want to be a dragon!" announced Taibul in a hushed voice.

Momentarily they all chuckled.

"I think we all do," Angela volunteered, putting her arm around the youngest of them, "but to have contributed like we have to maintaining world order... You, all of us in fact, should be extremely proud."

"Not only that, don't forget the powerful new friends we've made," murmured Sam, punching his young pal playfully in the ribs.

That made Taibul smile.

"Yes," Emma added, "and I don't doubt for one minute that when this is all over, they'll want to repay us for all we've done."

"Whilst you're unlikely to be transformed into a dragon, I'm pretty sure you'll get to visit their realm again and be rewarded. That," observed Angela, "is the kind of opportunity that well over ninety nine percent of all humans on the planet will never get to have. Be content with what you've helped accomplish and knowing that you're one of the few trusted with such a fantastic secret."

The youngster nodded, knowing that his friend was spot on.

"So," Sam reflected, "anyone fancy a coffee, or something a little... stronger?"

They all did, the four of them ending up in one of the city's renowned pubs, Taibul sticking to soft drinks only whilst the other three drowned their thirst with the first of many lagers, blissfully unaware that the planet itself was far from safe, their futures for the most part undecided.

Resembling a dystopian landscape, what remained of the famed Mantra Emporium once owned by the renowned shopkeeper Gee Tee, continued to burn despite the best efforts by those that had defeated Manson's despicable lieutenant, Mas-crate, only a short time before. Having cast his teammate reluctantly through a naga based wormhole, Hook, now guided by For'son, the ancient dragon warrior presence trapped in the ring on one of his huge sausage-like fingers, set about some damage limitation and putting out some of the roaring fires that were still engulfing mysterious one off spells, lore filled tomes and any number of supernatural artefacts.

*"Over in that corner... be quick,"* For'son urged.

*"Here?"*

*"Yes... hold out your hand in the direction of the fire!"*

Lost in thought about his friend with the brain injury and the love of his life who right now was about to risk everything in an effort to save one of her two best buddies, the rugby playing human did as instructed.

*"The other hand... the one with me on it! Concentrate!"*

Immediately Hook swapped hands, suitably chastised by the dragon inhabiting part of his mind, more than a little intimidated.

Sensing all this and more, the unfathomable presence did something that could be considered a rarity. He apologised.

*"Hook... I'm sorry, I didn't mean to be so harsh. It was no reflection on you and I know how troubled you are about your friends. You're doing a fantastic job, one I doubt any other human could do. And that's not me being patronising when I say that, I'm only telling the truth. The loop I'm contained in was only designed to be worn by dragons. The fact that we can communicate so well and use you as a conduit for my powers is a credit to your courage, bravery and intelligence. In fact, if I didn't know better, I'd swear there's more than a little dragon in you."*

*"I know you're trying to brighten my outlook and I appreciate that a great deal, but until I know that they're all safe and well and that wicked bitch has been sent to hell, I think my outlook will remain the same... sorry!"*

*"Don't apologise, youngster, I fully share your sentiment. Despite having no physical body, I still count all of them as friends, as well as yourself of course. And my time linked to Tank makes my bond with him extra special. There's nothing I want more right now than to be at his side and use everything I have to heal him. But that's not within my gift at the moment. We have to believe he's in the right place and in the best hands, getting unsurpassed treatment. That was the whole point of sending him there."*

Both physically and mentally, the hulking great form of the rugby player nodded his agreement.

*"Hold still,"* For'son commanded.

Arm outstretched, fingers pointed towards a raging, crackling fire giving off the darkest cloud of black smoke it was possible to imagine, Hook relaxed just slightly knowing what to expect next. He wasn't disappointed. Pins and needles was how he imagined the sensation as a surge of thick, dark blue energy built up behind his wrists, the potent magic gushing forward, releasing tiny, intricate forks of what looked like lightning towards the base of the ever expanding fire.

With a loud, hissing POP, what remained of the flames and the shadowy smoke cascaded in on itself leaving just the glowing orange embers of a wrecked wooden support strut. That fire extinguished, the pair, guided by the ever present spectre of the shop, Zarenkesia, moved on to the next, doing their best to save all that they could, especially those considered the most dangerous, powerful and valuable. It was an unrelenting task and quite possibly ideally suited to Hook because of his humanity, which for the most part acted as an impediment between the supernatural energy flitting about and For'son's inherent dragon abilities.

Having commandeered the tiny waiting room along from the main ward where Tank had just been scanned, DomCon and Jar Man set about raiding the vending machines of all the drinks and confectionary they held, returning to Steel with huge handfuls of goodies, their faces lit up with guilt like a tiny child having successfully scoured their home for Christmas presents, but having to keep up the pretence in front of their parents. Their haul had distracted them from Tank's serious state of affairs, if only for a moment or two. And then it happened.

Out in the corridor, all hell broke loose!

White coated disguised dragons in their human forms began shouting with great urgency. Not too bad or unusual you might think given where they were, but for two things. One... the three friends had already been informed that Tank was the only patient currently down in the depths of the hospital being treated by the secretive medical professionals. And two, and this was really when alarm bells started going off deep within the psyches of all three... everyone they could see making a fuss was running. Again... so what?! They were, however, doing so using their enhanced dragon senses and magic, zipping through the surrounding bright white corridors at a blur, the kind of speed an actual human would never have a chance of registering let alone actually visualising. Things had clearly just gone pear shaped.

Dropping his treasure trove of unhealthy goodies on the pristine white floor, Jar Man made for the door. In an instant DomCon stood in his path.

"MOVE!"

"What ya doin'?"

"I said MOVE!"

"We were told to stay out of the way and wait, my friend," Steel offered up in a somewhat cheery voice, attempting to be more positive in an effort to diffuse the tension between the two best mates. From the looks on their faces it hadn't made a blind bit of difference.

"I won't tell you again," the ginger giant murmured with menace.

"You can't go in there," the diminutive pocket rocket replied, in as soothing a voice as he could muster.

"NO... YOU can't go in there. I go where I please."

"Buddy..."

"Jar Man..."

Both friends tried to cajole. But their pleas fell on deaf ears, instead they were rewarded with a small piece of his mind, almost certainly ramped up by his frustration at the situation that had now almost boiled over, the look on his pale, freckled face one of absolute roaring thunder.

Before Strawberry Blonde could fully explode the laminium ball captain managed to sneak in a question, one he hoped might buy enough time to calm things down a little.

"What is it you hope to accomplish?"

A brief pause consumed them all, probably not long enough to siphon off all the friction, but a lull in proceedings nevertheless.

"I'M DONE! NO MORE! NO MORE DEATH, DESTRUCTION, MURDER, MAYHEM AND MADNESS! I WANT WHAT WE HAD BACK AND I WANT IT NOW!" he positively roared.

"But..."

"That's not it, not why I'm going in there!"

"Then what?"

"They don't know," uttered the gentle giant of a dragon disguised in his human persona, "they don't know what he's done."

About to butt in again, the two were stopped with just a look from their de facto leader, the words clearly not having finished welling up to the surface.

"I don't know him... not that well anyway. We've all spoken to him briefly, in particular about the death of his mentor, the shopkeeper who will always remain in our hearts given we were there at the end, something he understandably took worse than ever given their relationship. But we know in intricate detail about all his daring deeds, the fact that combined with For'son HE saved everyone during that battle and in turn not only the three of us, but the entire planet. If not for Tank, we'd all be dead and Manson and his murderous queen would be ruling the world. Take a moment to think about that."

They did, his spiky words doing the trick.

"How does that…?"

"DAMN IT!" Jar Man yelled.

The other two jumped.

# BANG!

The big fella smashed his massive fist through the glistening white wall, which was slightly less tough than it looked,.

"Jar…"

"NO! He's in there all alone. They don't know what he's done. They won't take care of him. It's not right!"

Steel and DomCon shared a look, one that transferred a whole host of information in just a moment, mainly that they agreed with their pal's sentiment and that they were both worried as to where his loss of control would lead.

"They're professionals Jar, some of the best around, my friend. Tank couldn't be in more capable hands," Steel said softly, marshalling all his experience and diplomacy.

Sad to say it wasn't enough.

"I'm going in there to see what's going on. You can come with me or stay here. Frankly I don't give a damn. But I can tell you with absolute certainty, whatever that young dragon's going through, you can be damn sure he's going to have at least one friend by his side. And that's as it should be. CHOOSE!"

# YIKES!

Not so much an ultimatum as a glimpse into the nature underpinning the ginger giant's gentle soul, I think you'll agree that standing side by side with him was not only the right thing to do, but the only thing.

There were no words. DomCon simply stepped aside as Steel slipped into Jar Man's wake as he walked through the hulking great door frame that could potentially cope with one of their kind in its natural guise, the diminutive pocket rocket following, all three determined to get some answers and stand shoulder to shoulder with the kind, caring, plant and animal loving dragon whose best friends couldn't be with him at the moment due to extenuating circumstances.

Choosing to maintain human pace, it took the trio thirty seconds or so to reach their destination, the door to the main ward, through which they could see a flurry of activity around a single bed at the far end.

"That's far enough!" commanded a voice off to their right, a fierce looking nurse stomping over, appearing as though she might be readying her intrinsic dragon magic.

"We need to see what's going on," Steel suggested before either of the other two could show their tempers.

"I'm sorry... but that's just not possible. The doctors are doing all they can to treat the youngster, but as for all of you, going in there is totally off limits. Return to the waiting room... NOW!"

It doesn't take a genius to figure out how that's going to go.

What the other two hadn't spotted on the thirty second walk to the entrance to the ward, was that they'd passed a series of trolleys loaded with a variety of medical equipment and medicine, atop which had been a disused scalpel. Using all his sleight of hand, Jar Man had purloined said item, slipping it up his sleeve. Why? Who knew, almost certainly it was a moment of madness. But could it have been a split second of clarity? Hmmm... we'll see.

Standing stock still, waiting to see if the nurse would challenge him directly or call out for some of her colleagues who were rather busy at that moment, Jar Man wasn't surprised when the female in question strolled forward and attempted to twist his arm behind his back in an effort to physically guide him out of there. It was a surprise not only to her, but to both Steel and DomCon, when with the speed of a dragon half his age, he deftly, twisted her around and simultaneously with his other hand, produced the procured scalpel, holding it softly against her now exposed throat.

"Whoa…" mouthed the laminium ball captain.

"Uhhh... what ya doin'?

"Whatever's necessary!"

"You don't want to…" started the nurse, only to be immediately shut down by the normally gentle giant.

"We're going in to see our friend one way or another. Any stupid moves on your part would be a mistake. I don't want to hurt anyone, I really don't, but I'm guessing by now you can see just how passionate I am about this. No sudden moves or magical endeavours. Understood?"

She replied with the tiniest nod in the world, well... you would, with something that sharp at your throat.

With Jar Man and the nurse leading the way and DomCon and Steel following reluctantly in his wake, wondering how the hell this had all gotten so out of hand, slowly they traipsed into the ward, heading towards the far end and all the action and excitement.

The fact that they'd had to wait for so long to be noticed went some way to stating just how dire Tank's situation must have been.

"What the ****?!" declared one of the junior medics, looking up from trying to strap Tank's human body in place across a huge metal table that had been wheeled out from somewhere.

This got Dr Tomlinson's attention.

"WHAT ON EARTH DO YOU THINK YOU'RE DOING? DESIST AT ONCE AND RETURN TO THE WAITING ROOM BEFORE I HAVE SECURITY CALLED! YOUR FRIEND NEEDS HELP, NOT A HOSTAGE SITUATION!"

"That's right," Jar Man replied calmly, "and we're here

to make sure he gets just that."

"Why would you think he wouldn't?"

"It's not so much about the quality of your care, more about him having some friends watching over him."

"Listen... you really can't..."

"Not happening. You can choose how this plays out, doc. All we want to do is stand in the corner and watch over Tank. His very best friends can't be here at the moment, but we are and we're not going anywhere. Didn't you understand when we tried to tell you who he was and exactly what he's done?"

That got the rest of the medics looking around, wondering what the hell was going on and what was so special about this one.

Picking up on that, and with the situation still on a knife edge (see what I did there) Steel, ever the leader, decided to use all his captaincy skills to explain. Very quickly, he let them all have the abridged version.

"I'm so sorry... I didn't know," whispered the nurse with the scalpel at her throat, a single translucent tear running down her pretty, pale face.

Sensing a tipping point had been reached, Jar Man removed the improvised weapon and let her go. Expecting her to run off towards the other staff, the gentle, ginger giant got the surprise of his life when she turned around and threw herself into his huge arms, hugging him for all he was worth.

By now the rest of the staff had turned to face Doctor Tomlinson, their faces full of uncertainty, worry and disappointment at only now finding out that their patient was responsible for saving the world.

"I just thought he should be treated like any of the others we get in here. We always give our best, no matter what. I thought revealing all that might turn things into a circus and act as a distraction. I'm sorry."

"So whadda ya say doc," chirped DomCon, "are we alright to stay, watch and support from a distance?"

"Of course, of course. Stand over in that corner there," the good doctor pointed, and we'll attempt to give you a running commentary on what's going on."

"Which is what?" Jar Man asked politely.

Turning to face all three of them, Doctor Tomlinson attempted to explain.

"The partial scan revealed that there's something magical attached to the inside wall of his brain. Thank God he didn't try and revert back to his natural state... that would have been a catastrophe."

"How bad is it and what's the plan going forward?"

"It's serious, calamitously so, hence all the running around like headless dragons."

"And?"

"There's simply no option other than to open him up and try and remove whatever it is. If the supernatural tumour or trauma expands any further, it could end his life in an instant."

"Can you remove it?"

"Quite possibly... yes. But the risks are severe to say the least. His chances of survival, even if we're successful, are about fifty, fifty at best."

That wasn't the news they, or the world at large, wanted to hear.

So the trio of friends stood back in the corner allowing the medical professionals to continue their work in the hope that one of earth's mightiest heroes, the kind, caring, animal and plant loving rugby player who everyone owed so much to, could be saved from the magical malady that had him at death's door.

Delving through his skin, holding the blood back with just a few chosen words, splitting his skull came next, supposedly the easy part in all this. Continuing at pace, a dull white triangular section that seemed to the friends to represent about half of his cranium but was actually more like a fifth, was removed and placed gently on an adjacent sterilised metal tray. So far so good.

It was at this point that the pesky little... let's call it a globe, about the size of a ping pong ball, revealed itself, a sparkling combination of striking cyan morphing into a deep electric blue around the outer edges, framing fluorescent forks of crackling tangerine and apricot crush lightning within its centre, embedded in the wall of Tank's brain.

All the medical staff had but one thought. You can probably guess what it is so I won't waste any stars and exclamation marks.

Through the very private connection that had served them so well up until now, the trio of pals commented on what they could see.

*"That thing looks diabolical,"* voiced DomCon.

*"Is it some remnant from the fight or just a natural dragon infection that's somehow caught him out in his human guise?"* Steel wondered.

*"I don't know,"* Jar Man answered, *"but they all look like they've seen a ghost. Nothing good is going on here."*

On that they could all agree.

Casting off their surprise at the discovery, and under the guidance of the superb Doctor Tomlinson who was indeed one of the foremost dragon physicians anywhere on the surface of the planet, as a team they started the delicate procedure of trying to remove the magical growth that threatened a dragon who'd unselfishly given so much, all under the watchful eye of the three friends, each of whom were wishing Tank luck in their own inimitable way.

Enchantments were carefully cast to probe to what extent the supernatural swelling had delved into the youngster's brain. After that, the tiniest of shields was cast around the outer edges of the growth, sure to keep it well away from whatever unnatural magic had occurred. It was tricky stuff, but what they were doing wasn't slow. In fact quite the opposite, which was essential given that the size of the unknown object was increasing exponentially with every second that passed and was now bigger than a table tennis ball.

A telltale sign of just how unusual and difficult this procedure was showed itself in the good doctor swallowing nervously on more than one occasion, picked up of course by the trio who continued to take it all in and support the good hearted rugby playing hero as best they could, hoping that not being alone in his time of need gave him some sense of support and comfort despite him having been unconscious for quite some time.

"What do you think?" the doctor's assistant asked, a grey haired woman resembling a kindly, experienced grandmother.

"I don't think we have any choice... it's got to come out and now, otherwise it'll edge further into his brain and..."

"I concur."

"Well... let's get it done!"

And so they did.

Through a combination of precision engineered spells, some that made sure to contain his mind, others surveying and investigating the anomaly, after careful consideration and tried and tested mantras, the wicked looking tumour was slowly splintered into a dozen or so fragments before each was carefully vaporised, leaving absolutely no trace. It was exhausting work and for the most part went unseen, some of the complex patterns, defensive shields and salvos of shots, darts, bolts, call them what you will, all being invisible in nature even to those with enhanced magical senses. The skills used were mindblowing. Doctor Tomlinson had performed miracles in removing the invasive, quite frankly, vicious globule of magic, but on replacing part of the skull that had been removed and then supernaturally sealing the skin that in effect was still part of a disguise, once again he swallowed nervously, letting out a huge sigh, before turning to face the trio of friends who'd stood silently in the corner for so long.

As he did so the technicians alongside him used some of their supernatural gifts to raise Tank's body into the air, gently floating him across to a clean and comfy bed that had been prepared for him earlier.

"Doc?" Steel asked, worried at what the prognosis would be.

"As you've just witnessed, we've successfully removed whatever it was that was inside him."

That made all three of them smile for the first time in what felt like an age.

"But…"

There's always a but!

"He's not out of the woods yet… far from it in fact."

"What does that mean?" a concerned Jar Man asked, his hostage taking days well and truly over.

"Tank remains in a coma and it's not one we've induced. If he can't somehow pull himself out, well… all the magic in the world won't save him. It's truly up to him now. I hope he's as strong as you've said, because he's going to need to be to battle this."

"So… that's it!" DomCon declared, more than a little frustrated.

"It is, I'm afraid. All we can do is hope and pray that he can fight his way out of wherever his mind is currently at. Stay positive!"

With Tank very firmly tucked into the bed especially provided for him, the cardiac monitor displaying his heart rhythm and electrical activity in real time, alongside the highly advanced (ICP) intracranial pressure monitor, measuring the pressure around his brain after the difficult and complicated surgery, giving the staff a constant insight into his vital signs, the good doctor turned and walked away with a few parting words.

"I'm sure you want to remain with him. Pull up a few chairs. You're welcome to stay as long as you like."

# 40 TEMPER TANTRUM

Her whole body smoking like a spare, overcooked burger left on a barbecue, Earth, blocking the only exit of what was left of Gee Tee's once precious vault, smiled delectably, her victory now assured, nothing and nobody in the way of stopping her snuff out the life of the son she'd so unwillingly given up and never really known, aside from the battle back at the king's private residence. Across that short space of time she'd witnessed his cowardice on numerous occasions and gone from wanting to take him with her to vowing to end his life. In a few moments that would come to pass. But before it did, she had some things she wanted to get off her chest.

"Your father would have been so disappointed," she announced, enhancing her voice with just a touch of magic to make it carry that bit further. "He was a powerful, resourceful and courageous sorcerer... we both were. Clearly you didn't inherit anything of any value from either of us."

The words of the bone chilling voice brought Peter back to earth with a bump. There was nothing she had to say that he wanted to hear. However, his better half, the plucky and fearless Janice, had other ideas.

"Keep her talking," she mouthed silently towards the dragon she'd gone through all this for.

"Why?" he mimed back.

"To buy us some time," she replied, shaking her head at how extraordinarily dumb he could be sometimes.

"Oh... okay," he said, realising his mistake, quickly thinking about a retort, any retort.

"When you say sorcerer, you clearly mean... psychopath!" he yelled.

That got her attention as well as sparking just a little ire behind those maddened eyes. With the tiny rational part of her mind choosing to ignore it, knowing that she was about to have the last laugh, the very last thing she needed to hear echoed out from behind the plinths.

"Given your propensity to kill everything and everyone in your life, I suppose you killed him as well, did you?" the hockey playing dragon ventured, matter-of-factly.

Janice, ducked down behind her particular plinth smacked herself hard in the forehead with the palm of her right hand, the noise from which resounded across to her lover.

"WHAT?" he mouthed.

"You're supposed to keep her talking, not get her so enraged that she comes for us here and now!"

Only now could he see his mistake. DAMN!

Self control hanging by a thread, temper threatening to erupt like Mount Vesuvius on that fateful day, goose bumps spontaneously burst into being down both arms as her inherent, wicked magic started to course through all her limbs. About to set the world straight, concerning both her husband and her child, the need to do so was abruptly put on hold as a series of words resonating across the distance between them stopped her in her tracks.

"Why did you just drop me off and leave me, never to be seen again? What kind of callas parents would do such a thing?"

Sitting back against the plinth with her eyes closed, Janice marvelled at her love's ability to turn things around in just the blink of an eye, sure that this would get his devilish mother to take a moment and think. She wasn't wrong.

Heart pounding, head thumping, mind in a spin, suddenly she was transported back, to the best time of her life many, many decades earlier, to Swanage in Dorset, of all places.

Their lifestyle could hardly have been described as decadent, not with her working as a waitress and him on the railway, but they had a house they called their own, and although officially on the run, they hid in plain sight off the beaten track and were for once absolutely, mind bogglingly happy. They'd even gone as far as to make friends with some of the humans, a thought that now repulsed her beyond belief, but back then it had seemed something of a boon. And then they'd decided to try for offspring. Of course there are no guarantees when it comes to such things, with not even dragons being above the mischievousness of fate. But they'd been blessed and she'd become pregnant quite quickly and all that had entailed, apart from the obvious, was curtailing their social activities to some degree which in their eyes was a small price to pay.

And then there it was... an egg of all things, brilliant bright white on the outside, imprinted with what looked like a darkened smudge but she now knew it to be the markings he'd been born with, the ones that from a certain angle very much resembled a bent whistle. Much to her dismay at the time, a decision had to be made, one that the whole of her DNA had rallied against, but one she supposed made sense given that they were still on the run from the dragon authorities for war crimes committed in aiding the Nazis during the whole of World War Two. In a huge gamble, they'd snuck back down to the domain in the middle of the night and against all her baser instincts dropped the egg off at the Purbeck Peninsula nursery ring, before quickly darting back up and resuming their everyday disguises. Not long after that they were discovered and forced to go on the run once again, later ending up in North Wales where they decided, not for the first time, to settle down. At the time, giving away the egg caused her more pain than she ever imagined possible, gut wrenching at best, catastrophic torture at worst, the sorrow and anguish she felt in the aftermath tearing her up inside for years to come, despite the support of her then husband. Throughout the whole of her life that consisted of a litany of one bad decision followed by another, this was the one she'd have changed should it have been possible to return and do so. Back in the present, those feelings and the exquisite agony behind them returned with a vengeance, as though a knife were twisting in her stomach. Most other beings would have dropped to the floor there and then. Not her, not now, not with so much at stake and the closing curtain approaching. Using all her considerable strength of will and mental fortitude, for one last time she put the past behind her and focused on what was in front... HER WEAK AND PITIFUL SON! But not for much longer. With desire burning like the fuse of some dynamite, the anger inside her topped out, turning her previously playful demeanour into something far more vicious, unpredictable and packed full of retribution. In essence, she'd snapped. Falling back on both habit and instinct, Earth lashed out in the only way she knew how. Across the vault... brilliant, bright colourful magic abounded!

It felt homely, comfortable and familiar, sensations that would make any of us feel safe and secure, but doubly so for her given the seasonal nature of her job and the power and responsibility that came with it. Not wanting to leave... (well, who would?) on the outer edges of her consciousness noises so loud they felt as though they might shake her skull loose erupted into being, accompanied by an awareness of potent, heinous and nefarious supernatural energy being used for fiendish and immoral reasons. Much like her evil doppelganger, this powerful magic user couldn't ignore a slight, affront or her friends being in any sort of danger. Casting off the invisible shroud that felt like a heated blanked imbued with all things good both past and present, one of the single most powerful entities ever to have graced the planet commanded her psyche to return to the present, and taking solace from having spoken to her soulmate one last time, readied herself for the nightmare that awaited. She wasn't disappointed.

A terracotta torrent rained down from above, shrapnel from the walls, ceiling and even floor zinging about, burying themselves into everything, the plinths, the bows, guns, jars, the artefacts and scrolls hidden in the ancient hidey holes, bouncing and deflecting off armour and the magical items remaining including Merlin's staff, the Kid's rifle and Robin Hood's bow that lay discarded on the floor.

Picture a shop full of fireworks set ablaze by an arsonist. It was very much that sort of thing. Soft, fluttering whistles crescendoed to high pitched piercing screeches whilst snaps, crackles and sizzles pummelled the thick, smoke laden air. Concussive bangs and booms resonated throughout the terracotta cul-de-sac causing the ground to shake, the plinths to wobble and piles of armour to come tumbling down. Deep, resonant roaring similar to the rumble of thunder or the growl of an engine accompanied multicoloured bolts of bright, brilliant magic, predominantly purple, filling almost every spare space. Forceful hisses and crisp, loud pops ricocheted across the floor, the vile, unique supernatural exploding throughout the vault, brilliant bursts in varying degrees of size and intensity putting on a show like no other, one that any youngster would immediately been drawn to above ground. But this deadly combination of sparkling and shimmering lights carried any number of dynamic threats from straight up poison, cutting edge forked lightning to wavy trails and streaks of the filthiest shadowy filled naga enchantments. In short, it was a breathtaking display encompassing the most stunning of visual elements, a multisensory experience like no other, one that if not for the underlying wanton death, destruction and murder with which it had been instigated, would have captivated pretty much anyone.

Waking to all this was almost a perception overload, but she hadn't been chosen for her job for no apparent reason. With cat-like reactions, the once a year Christmas legend scrambled to her feet and, using all the power she could muster, leapt for cover behind what remained of the nearest tall plinth, having the awareness to dangle her arm out on the way and grasp hold of Robin Hood's bow and four quivers' worth of arrows.

Back firmly pressed into the sides of the earth coloured plinth she continued to cower behind, hands covering both ears against the brutal sounds detonating all around her, pure, good natured Janice swore using the worst word she knew, stunned at the turn of events that had led to such an almighty outburst from the she-witch that was her lover's mother. She shouldn't have been really, not having witnessed the murderess' base nature on a number of occasions, but she'd thought Peter's change of subject might have done the trick and bought them some more time. Not so!

Spotting something a little bigger moving against the backdrop of all the glowing bursts, trails, streaks and explosions, the gorgeous blonde bar worker glanced sideways, rewarded with not only a smile but a smidgen of hope, on seeing Polkinghorne awake and sitting there nocking the giant bow under her command. In a moment that she'd remember for the rest of her life however long that should be, the two shared a look and a nod, subtle gestures that echoed their friendship and affection for one another.

Shying away from everything coming, much like his soulmate, Peter had his hands pressed firmly over his ears, the outrageous noise from the attack very much part of the assault his mother was sending their way, as well as his eyes firmly shut, the nightmare of what was going on all around him too much to take. It was a shame because if he'd seen Santa roll back into the game, it might have given him the confidence and faith to stand up and fight back. As it was, he looked like the most timid of dragons, lacking any sort of courage as per usual, fear having trapped him in place, waiting for the sweet embrace of death that his parent was intent on delivering.

As the barrage of noise accompanying the rainbow array of magic continued to blast everything around them to smithereens, Janice, now buoyed by Polkinghorne's awakening, instinctively fiddled with the long, sleek silver necklace that hadn't left her, the one she'd been presented with by her soulmate back at the private residence, the one with the matt green triangular shaped scale on the end. Just the touch of it gave her some crumb of comfort as she glimpsed a fleeting look to her right towards her love. She wasn't surprised to see him almost curled up in a ball, what was going on all around simply too much to bear. Deep down she continued to will him to get up and fight, use just a little of the inherent magic she knew he possessed like every other one of his race, and make some sort of stand. But he looked broken, utterly bereft of any sort of retaliation and to some degree she could understand why. Not having known either of his parents, especially his mother, and having spent so long trying to find out what had happened to them only for the tragic reunion to take place in the circumstances that it had, was nothing short of catastrophic and had no doubt shattered him psychologically. Add to the fact that she'd already tried to kill him and his grandfather on any number of occasions and you could see why any sort of riposte on his part was out of the question. There and then the young human didn't see Peter's cowardice and refusal to act as any sort of weakness, but found it understandable and a credit to his kind and caring underlying nature. Knowing it was her and Polkinghorne versus the psychopath that was Fredric's daughter, Janice did the only thing she could, the only thing love would allow her to do. Removing her hands from her ears, she picked up the Kid's rifle, reloaded and prepared to face the epitome of evil.

The very last vestiges of sanity that had been hanging on by a thread were in the wind now, Earth having well and truly snapped, waiting for the world to come crashing down around her from Manson's evil machinations. She'd decided to end it once and for all and kill both her son and his lover. Interestingly, she had no idea there was a third presence inside the vault. For her, there was no more, no more anything. With her sick, twisted nature taking over, she figured the best outcome was to kill the human girl in front of her weak and pitiful son, wreaking havoc and heaping shame upon him before she ended his life. Utterly taken by this idea, stoked from all the supernatural coursing through her, gradually she started to curtail the bombardment, showering them both with just enough magic to keep them contained, as slowly she attempted to stroll forward, grey wisps of smoke rippling through the air in her wake. Images started to run through her mind of raising the girl above her head with one strong hand, strangling the life out of her as the Bentwhistle freak looked on in horror, the pale human flesh of his lover turning bright purple, a fitting end to say the least. Full to the brim with confidence, brilliant luminescent magic crackling from her fingertips, the end she knew was nearly at hand.

Sprinting full pelt through the hellish nightmare that was the only remaining supernatural tunnel leading to the vault, on a rescue mission to end all rescue missions, the futuristic blade, the tip of the spear out in front now, swatted away deadly dandelion seed heads by the dozen, carving a path for both Fredric and The White Dragon, who both used their innate magical abilities to enhance their speed and defences, not wanting to let their guards down on any level, as determined as they ever had been to reach the dead end crypt that contained the kind of fabulous treasure most could only dream of. Far off in the distance the most spectacular light show could be seen in the reflection of the rock wall exactly at the point the passageway turned ninety degrees, the ground transforming in an instant from scorched grass into solid stone. All of this was accompanied by a series of echoing booms, snaps, crackles, sizzles and bangs as well as the strong scent of spent magic. They were close, but were they close enough?

# 41 ONE LAST ROLL OF THE DICE!

Not missing a beat, Yoyo positively sprinted towards his pal amongst the wreckage at the top of the borehole, the dragon he'd saved from a very unsavoury death at the hands of the naga poison what felt like a lifetime ago.

"My boy!" he exclaimed, hugging Flash tight.

"My friend," replied the former Crimson Guard, returning the affection.

"Your timing is second to none. How in the hell did you…?"

"If I told you, you'd never believe me!"

"But you were in Scotland only moments before. Correct?"

"I think," Amelia put in, now that there was a lull in the action, "we'd all like to know how that came about."

"Agreed," Rose added, as all the youngsters nodded their concurrence, the spectre of the already exploded nuclear warhead above them in the sky most certainly getting larger with every moment that passed.

"How's our representation of FATE doing?"

"You don't believe it's her?" Trayrin enquired.

"I… I… I don't know who or what else could be holding that thing above our heads in check and produce such a worthy duplicate, so, perfectly honestly… I really don't know. At this point I suppose it's worth opening our minds to any possibility."

"Well… that's a relief," the Bentwhistle lookalike concurred, much to their surprise.

"You're actually Fate?" Amelia asked.

"It's a little more complicated than that," replied the denier of destinies, "but that would probably be an apt description and one all of you can understand."

"Couldn't you have just willed it not to explode?" Essie solicited.

"That would have been nice," the Peter duplicate replied with just a hint of sarcasm, "and might have been possible under normal conditions. But as Flash here found out by trying to open a wormhole in its path, before it left the submarine the missile was imbued with some pretty complex and utterly malicious magic to prevent such tampering. The only way to circumvent all that supernatural nastiness was to detonate the warhead."

"Wait a minute," put in Tarko incredulous, "you're telling us it was you that exploded the damn missile?"

"Yep."

"To what end? What the hell's supposed to happen now?"

"Well…" Fate responded sceptically, "if we hadn't done that to negate the attached supernatural, the earth would already be shattered into a million tiny pieces and all of us would have ceased to exist."

"Oh."

"And as to what happens now… that's out of our hands. The others and I are slowly losing our ongoing magical battle in holding the remains in place. Sooner or later we'll be defeated and in that instant the warhead will do what it's designed to do and explode, channelling all its energy into the borehole. Without the laminium there to ignite, hopefully the blast will only destroy a fair part of France and not the entire planet, but I can't be sure that will be the case."

"I thought you said that…" Rose ventured.

"I did," the Providence interrupted, knowing what the intelligent and beautiful dragon was about to say, "but all we've done by tossing the laminium into the core is give Novus a chance, perhaps nothing more than one in a thousand, to somehow regain enough of his natural abilities in the hope that he can deal with the situation. There are no certainties. It never was a done deal!"

"I see…"

"Is there anything else we can do?" Amelia asked, the

captain in her reluctant to just stand by and watch, let everything else play out around her, and have no say in the matter.

Unfortunately, that's all that was left.

"NO!" Fate replied a little too forcefully, still multitasking with her sisters, constantly spamming her magic on top of theirs to hold what remained of the warhead in place. "It's out of our control. My siblings and I will attempt to constrain the explosion for as long as we can. After that, well... let's just say we're all in the hands of the gods."

'Good to know,' thought Flash, 'good to know.'


The sensation was like waking from a daze, only on a larger and more powerful level, which was to be expected given how long he'd been deprived of the lifeblood that was so pivotal to his existence. But the first few grams returning with a vengeance in the manner that they had, started a transformation of epic proportions, one which saw the foggy curtain of uncertainty and dim-wittedness pulled back to reveal fragments of the startling intellect that had been there in the beginning when this had all started. Revelation couldn't do it justice. It was a shock, a surprise... the ultimate eye-opener for a consciousness that had for so long been constricted and suppressed through no fault of its own.

As stunningly beautiful images from across every part of him continued to assault his perception, Novus started to become aware of... other beings. No, not the Providences, although he almost certainly knew on a subconscious level that they were close by, but some of the other inhabitants of the glorious landscape on which they thrived... there were plants in hundreds of thousands of different guises, all of which he could feel, yes... FEEL! Their essences and general wellbeing, their surprise and wonderment at recognising him on some existential level was a marvel to behold and one equal in spectacle to Novus himself. He would have been bowled over by this if he'd had time to think, but unfortunately he hadn't, because events were now unravelling at speed, including the astonishing revelation that there were animals in all their spectacular guises dotted far and wide throughout every last corner of his surface. They could feel his presence and wonderment at their very existence, the link simultaneously travelling in both directions. Every different emotion flooded through him in a matter of moments. It was ecstasy and a turning point in his recovery. But that was nothing compared with what was to come. Why? Because then he started to sense the others... dragons, humans and all the other supernatural beings dotted about far and wide, in the sea, underground, on the surface, in all their majestic shapes and forms. If it were possible, which of course it wasn't, Novus would have cried there and then, the splendour of it all feeling overwhelming to say the least.

With each moment that passed, more and more laminium tumbled into the borehole's core, stoking the lifeblood within, making Novus eminently stronger and more capable. But capable of what?

Mind free of the restraints that had bound him in place for so long, the ancient sentience started to drill down into everything he could feel, in particular the individuals involved. Lives flashed by in an instant, revealing the most intimate details in crystal clarity. After only a matter of moments he had an astonishing list of questions, all of which needed answers. But things were moving too fast for all of that. Love and life quickly became intertwined with one another. The importance of family stood head and shoulders above everything else, washing away fleeting glimpses of darkness that encapsulated all things negative and bad, from the lies to the cheating, from scandal, deception and stealing to the base human nature of jealousy that continued to cause so much harm, even in this enlightened age. Advances, he marvelled, had been made on so many levels, but not when it came to these attributes, the same afflictions causing all the so-called highly developed races to rot from the inside out. It was mesmerising and intoxicating to take in, as well as being quite repulsive at the same time. But what he'd experienced in those first few moments was only a brief glimpse, the smallest of samples if you like. Only now, as more of the precious metal was added to the mix, was it possible to see the good that clearly outshone everything bad. But that was somehow tempered by... what? Searching frantically, finally he found something... recent devastation.

'That's right,' he thought, recalling part of a plot, one that would... ahhh, there it was again, the fuzziness, the overriding gloom that prevented him from thinking clearly, the overall picture starting to swim into focus, but the all important pivotal points tantalisingly out of reach. DAMN!

Curbing his frustration he sought to find out more, delving deep into both the underground world of the dragons and that which had occurred on the surface. SUFFERING! That was the underlying sensation he felt, a shiver of epic proportions inundating his psyche, causing him to briefly shake his metaphorical head. But how had this been allowed to happen? Tugging further on the thread he'd already had a go at, hoping to unravel much more, only then did fleeting snippets of insight start to reveal themselves.

What felt like a hugely distant memory but couldn't possibly have been, returned in a vision of shimmering whiteness. SNOW, of all things, gigantic, intricate, crystal clear flakes falling at pace, an absolute torrent inundating an unusual surface, bright green in nature, but not natural at all, in fact it was... ARTIFICIAL! That word! It meant something, to the humans at least. But what was it?

He could have cursed, should have cursed, the annoyance at not being able to think straight overpowering. But that wasn't in his nature, either back then or in the here and now. And so he did what he'd always done, he fought back but with logic, trying to think through what he knew step by step, hoping to gain a better insight and reveal more of what was missing.

There was sport, but it wasn't being played. That didn't make any sense. There was the colour of grass, but no grass at all... yet another conundrum. And snow when none was forecast. Somehow he got the impression that he'd had something to do with that, but why? That was the question he just couldn't shake or get out of his head.

Bright fluorescent colours, brilliant dazzling lights exploding across a chilly night sky gave him pause for thought. There was... now what did they call it? That's right... MUSIC! Loud music playing in the background and what was it again that the dragons so loved? FIRE! One huge almighty fire bursting into being after a countdown being cheered along by... youngsters! And just the thought of those kids and their happiness at being part of the pomp and ceremony on that bonfire night was enough for it to all come flooding back.

A sick and twisted scheme had been instigated far in the past, a major part of which was ready to come to fruition. And that's right... his lifeblood in vast quantities about to be stolen away and used for nefarious purposes. He recalled the utter devastation and sadness he felt on learning this, but because he'd been in such a weak and pitiful state he'd been powerless to intervene. But wait, what was this? A thorn in the side, a spanner in the works in the form of a young boy, no... dragon! A juvenile dragon meddling where others wouldn't dare, following tenuous lead after tenuous lead, trusting his gut instinct against all odds, even defying his friend's thoughts on the subject. All of that led to the... ASTROTURF! That's what it was called, the artificial surface the humans used to play the game of hockey on, a kind of false lawn designed to make the tiny ball run truer than it would on actual grass. Recollections of a showdown abounded, one in which the adolescent had been captured and presented to the leader of the scheme by some of his lackeys. There was an explosion in which humans died, followed by a confrontation, one that in all likelihood would end the young dragon's life. Unable to do very much at all, Novus could remember watching from a distance, willing on the disguised teenager, hoping that against all odds he'd vanquish the murderous monster known as Manson and stop his lifeblood being used for the immoral and reprehensible purposes planned. Given the disadvantages from the cold and being trapped in human guise, the youth fared better than expected, that is until the deranged dark dragon transformed into his prehistoric best. After that, all bets were off as far as Novus was concerned. Staggeringly though, Bentwhistle ploughed on, whether through luck, judgement or a helping hand from the one known as Fate, and managed to defy the insurmountable odds and continue to survive, once even going on the attack himself, something that turned out to be a feint from the wicked would-be ruler of this brand new world order. In that moment, Novus could remember being impressed by the naive, human loving dragon, his resilience and fortitude outstanding in the face of adversity. And so using every last ounce of magic he'd had at the time, tapping into the ley lines running through the Salisbridge sports club, he'd done the only thing he could think of, one of the few things he had control over. He made it SNOW! And not just a little either, intricate flakes like those toddlers would cut out of paper under the supervision of their teacher, accompanying almighty hard packed balls of frozen ice pelting the artificial pitch that held the valued laminium already packed away in a gigantic dragon harness, the escape planned down to the finest detail, with the exception of the young dragon who by now had suffered wounds that would have killed any other of his kind. Through the bright white hail of the localised snow storm, he could remember watching the humungous black primordial beast just about take to the air, shrieking in agony with every flap of its wings from the horrific pain of the pounding frozen flakes. That, he recalled, had given him some sense of satisfaction. Afterwards there was a brief period of nothingness.

Time had passed. How much? He didn't know, not for sure, but quite possibly, many of what the humans and dragons referred to as months. Slowly he suckled on the remnants of whatever ley lines he could find, laminium all but impossible to reach, not now it was so close to the surface. Slowly his strength and resolve returned, but to nothing like the level it once was and should have been. In effect he'd become something of an outcast in his own psyche, too weak to do much but observe, certainly not able to interfere on the kind of level he had before. And so that's what he'd done, picking tiny pockets of humanity and dragonkind at random, watching over them, seeing if there was anything miniscule that he could do to make a difference. The odd subconscious word of encouragement here when needed, the tiniest nudge in the right direction there when appropriate. For a being of his standing and potential power it was pretty pathetic and a far cry from what he'd once been, the planet, HIS planet, the crowning glory of everything. But that's how low he'd sunk, barely able to function and so he meandered along. Until the fateful day his attention had been drawn once again to the boy dragon who'd so narrowly, through luck rather than judgement, saved them all on the Astroturf on that cold, fateful bonfire night. Inquisitive about how the youngster was faring, on one of his infrequent visits he found the adolescent dragon and one of his best friends in quite the pickle, trying frantically to diffuse what could only be described as a supernatural bomb, one of many and primed to go off shortly. Wracking his brain for a solution or some way to help, he'd remained powerless to act because he still wasn't anywhere near strong enough. What made things worse, was that now he knew what to look for, he could sense similar devices dotted around about his surface, their wickedness about to cost beings their lives in the tens of thousands, both above and below ground. At first he'd panicked, his consciousness trying to expand out everywhere all at once. But that failed spectacularly, nearly causing him to pass out. Reeling himself back in, he sought to find any way, no matter how small, that he could affect events playing out across the entirety of the planet. Unbelievably, he found one by helping disperse the results of the two dragon youngsters' unique approach to solving the problem that they faced, conjuring up a series of strong currents in the atmosphere above the channelled explosion that would have caused outlandish damage from the fallout had he not done so. In the scale of things, given what had happened worldwide, it was nothing, nothing at all, but it had, in conjunction with both of the dragons' quick thinking, saved any number of Salisbridge residents. A small crumb of comfort given the devastation and lives lost.

Whilst that act alone hadn't caused him to black out, it had left him in a state, one where he barely knew who he was, let alone his origins or what he was supposed to be doing. Most frustratingly of all it left him feeling his age, like when Polkinghorne had recently caught up with him on trying to use the ley lines in an effort to discover the missing nuclear submarine's actual location. But he'd had one more part to play in all of this, having become quite fixated by now with the developing plot to take control of what he regarded as his, by the malicious actors involved in what he knew was a rather a sick and twisted play.

Ignoring some of the major players in events surrounding the subversive takeover of the planet, due in no small part to the supernatural power they wielded or had the potential to do so, the likes of George, For'son, Fu-ts'ang, Fredric and Flash for example, knowing that their experience and the magic within them would most likely resist his efforts to lead them down any one path, Novus instead focused all his efforts on the two friends. I say two when actually all along it had been three, but very quickly he'd deemed Richie, whether because of the legacy that was yet to be written or simply what she'd achieved up until now, in the same category as the others... too powerful in a supernatural sense with an unbendable will to match, the lacrosse playing superstar far from suitable for his purposes.

Novus concentrated his attention on Peter and Tank after witnessing their heroics at the sports club, curtailing the damage from the Salisbridge bomb. He rapidly became engrossed with both mates, following them wherever they went, either together or separately, something that proved tricky because it consumed more ethereal energy than he generally had to spare. Still he persevered. And a good job too, otherwise the rugby player might well not have been around to unite with For'son further down the line and save the huge band of intrepid heroes during the Changing of the Guard.

Keeping both of them under observation, that is until Peter, alongside the imposter White Dragon, a former human known as Tim, got themselves captured by the dark forces in question, Novus had switched all his attention to Tank, hoping that he might stop the same thing happening. As he pondered all this, he witnessed from afar the youngster disembarking from one of those bullet shaped silver carriages that their kind used to travel across the globe, with the former Crimson Guard Flash at his side, both full of high jinx, an odd shaped ball the centre of the comedy for some reason. Before he could fathom what was going on and the doors to the monorail had finished whooshing shut, they'd bounded up a huge set of stairs, reaching the main plaza of the station. Exactly at that point the two dragons started to get pulled along against their will by the massive crowd that had almost come out of nowhere. And then he could remember experiencing the pair's total and utter dread as the realisation of what was happening hit, the former Crimson Guard's biggest nightmare coming true in that moment, the fact that somewhere close by there were... NAGAS! After his experience in Antarctica who could blame him for reacting like that.

Unsure of what he could do to help the pair, he'd

watched as Flash had instinctively responded to the situation. Determined to find out what was going on and as usual confront it head on, the more experienced of the two grabbed Tank by the elbow and began pulling him through the crowd towards the front of whatever crisis was playing out.

Metaphorical goose bumps raced across Novus' consciousness at the memory of what the two of them found. Resembling a giant flare going off, thick, matt green smoke streamed forth from a most unusual object. At the middle of the mass, a shimmering, deeply hypnotic shadow drenched, swirling, all encompassing blackness reached out almost as if to suck you in. Immediately, just like the other two, he'd recognised the danger from what the dragon authorities would have described as a very unstable 'heavy element'. A bomb of sorts, one that could unleash carnage on an industrial scale, normally only used by the most crazed of terrorists or fanatics, the effects of such a device ranging from murderous concussion and sonic blast waves to deadly area of effect explosions and everything in between. Flash, throughout his time in the elite Crimson Guards, had come across these weapons on a number of instances, but never had he seen either one so big or so powerful. There and then all his nightmares were coming true at once.

Unable to fathom a way to intercede, the world's underpowered psyche watched in horror, too captivated to turn away and too invested in both individuals to want to do so. Willing them on from a distance, incapable of seeing how they could prevail, pity and sadness filled his figurative stomach causing the kind of ache he'd never known before. Staving off his mind's overwhelming desire to just pass out, Novus fixed his awareness on them and waited for events to unfold.

Reacting as only he could, Flash had flown into action, sprinting towards the hazardous danger instead of away from it like the hordes of dragons surrounding them. To say it was foolish was something of an understatement but his training, inherent selflessness and wicked instincts had taken over. Mirroring his pal in that moment, Tank dropped to his knees, opened his mind like he'd never done before and reached out to the former Crimson Guard, offering up all his mana and magic in the ultimate noble gesture.

Close enough, or at least that's what he'd figured, Flash had bounded into the air using all his physicality and supernatural to power forward towards the diabolical threat that would within moments kill all the innocents nearby. Mid-air he erected the strongest shield he could around his body and almost certain it wouldn't be enough, let his momentum take him closer to the heavy element.

In that instant Novus with all his experience could tell that the former Crimson Guard was going to die, knowing that he didn't have nearly enough magic to withstand the blast from such a device. But what he hadn't counted on was his friend and the teamwork he so vehemently believed in. And so he looked on in sheer disbelief as the rugby playing dragon shared every last drop of mana and supernatural that he had in quite possibly the most unselfish act he'd ever witnessed. At the time, it was utterly astonishing.

Mind all of a flutter at the possibility that something extraordinary was about to happen, Novus had fought with all he had to stay awake and in that moment with the two courageous dragons, determined to see what transpired.

The malicious device designed to do the maximum amount of harm had reached its tipping point, the circling, shadowy negative energy folding over on itself before transforming into the merest pinprick of wicked bright light, resembling a distant star on a space strewn background. Having fulfilled the purpose it had been created for and hit the apex of its critical reaction there was only one thing left to happen.

And happen it did! The resulting explosion had been all encompassing, or at least would have been if not for the close proximity of Flash and his surrounding personal shield, the one now reinforced by a shed load of magic from his friend, the gentle giant known as Tank. Because of this, the surrounding invisible magical barrier took the brunt of the deadly kinetic energy, absorbing and deflecting in equal measures, tossing Flash high into the air in the process, his body constantly spinning on every axis, a rag doll thrown by an unruly child.

Everything and everyone across the plaza was knocked to the floor with the force of the most violent storm, including Tank who'd just reached the only conclusion he could... every last one of them was supposed to have died!

'And they still might,' Novus could remember thinking at the time, the deadly, matt green, noxious gas continuing to flood out of what little remained of the device at the epicentre of the explosion, potentially filling the enclosed narrow passageways, the food court and the monorail tunnels themselves with the murderous, foul smelling fumes. It was in that moment, witnessing all the vulnerable, unconscious dragon bodies scattered across the ground, that he decided to act and be damned with the consequences. So he did all he could, depleting every last ounce of magic in the process, using all his abilities to conjure up a fierce breeze that brushed through every last inch of the Salisbridge dragon domain monorail station, dissipating the airborne poison, giving those there at least another chance at life further down the line. Shortly afterwards, blackness had gripped him once again.

Those memories brought him back to the present and quite possibly the biggest quandary he'd ever faced. You see with every last smidgen of laminium returned, so did more of his supernatural abilities, one of which was the ability, should he choose, to glimpse just a little bit further ahead into a particular being's future. Not normally something he would opt for, even back when he was at full strength, instinctively he'd done just that only moments earlier with the juvenile dragon who'd gone through so much to get them this far, his suffering nothing short of immense on the way, and one of his two best friends, the one referred to as Tank. And now he wished with all his being that he hadn't because there was an impossible decision to make. Well... it wasn't, not impossible that is, because what kind of idiot puts one life ahead of either millions or potentially billions? Not him, that's for sure. In fact, nobody in their right mind would. But that didn't stop the sting of failure from puncturing what both the dragons and humans would refer to as his heart, causing him immense pain at what doing the right thing would lead to. Shattered, Novus took a moment to compose himself, using all his newfound confidence and power, drawing on his recently returned memories and intellect to bolster his resolve. Just to underline how far he'd returned, he was able to recognise the situation as being straight out of a Shakespearean play. DAMN!

Since his formation he'd witnessed billions of sentient beings dying, but only on occasion would any be regarded as significant. Monarchs across the supernatural divide from all the varied races throughout the ages might be looked upon as such, along with sporadic fabled individuals: Artorius the Seer, the being responsible for the renowned prophecy, or the Santa legacy were both good examples. With the death and rebirth of each Father Christmas came an underlying sadness because age can only be defied for so long, even with a lifespan measured in so much good.

Never in all his time had he become so attached and invested in two individuals as he'd become recently with the dragon sporting the bent whistle markings and one of his best friends, the gentle, kind and caring rugby player. Something about these adolescents had gotten under his skin and shown the best in what the primordial race that lived underground and the humans, of all beings, had to offer. Despite Peter being terribly naive, immature and lacking worldly experience, notwithstanding all the obstacles put in his way, especially in the form of his wicked mother, he'd triumphed at almost every turn, overcoming his inherent fear, natural reluctance and cowardice, spurred on for the most part by the love for his friends. It was a testament to the clandestine courage the youngster kept under wraps, only bubbling to the surface when most needed or in times of absolute crisis. Perhaps subconsciously it was a particular facet of his introverted and bashful nature, or some kind of split personality that trumped all others when calamity struck. Who knew? What Novus had come to realise was that he and Peter were very much alike, kindred spirits if you will. And maybe that's why the decision, the one not to save either youngster's life against those of billions, was so especially hard.

Screaming through the shadow soaked darkness on the ultimate downward trajectory, tiny fragments of the gold coloured precious metal tore their way homewards towards the planet's core, attempting to return what had once been lost in a global effort to expand an understanding of those that he cared for and had vowed to protect. With every split second, more laminium was gobbled up by the fiery focal point, the very heart of Novus himself, making him stronger, acutely more aware and instinctively ready to act. But to pull off what needed to be done required not only a fair degree of tenacity, but almost certainly the return of every last molecule of the stolen Russian laminium that had been placed within the test borehole by Oblivion and his despicable crew, some of which was still some way off. As things stood, Novus was short of the ethereal energy needed in order for his Harry Houdini escape act to work. As my gorgeous younger daughter would say... it was balls o'clock!

Exhausted, worn out, all but running on empty in regard to mana, the supply of ethereal energy each of them took for granted, all three Providences had reached the end of their tethers and in turn, the road. Constantly spamming the ever expanding wreckage of the already exploded nuclear warhead had taken its toll. Each allegorically sweating, Time and Luck shook like leaves during a howling gale, their minds frazzled, barely able to separate present from past and future realities. They were moments from losing their grip on the floating field of debris and radiation that had the potential to destroy everything and continued to hang over all their heads.

The stronger he got and the faster he recovered, the more regret and despondency ate away at his metaphysical insides about not being able to prevent one of the two young dragons from dying, their fate sealed like a Swiss bank vault. Now, with his memory returning, able to recall Artorius the Seer's prophecy and the reasons behind the truth in that regard, Novus couldn't help but think that there had to be a better way. What that was, short of sacrificing the entire population of the planet, he had absolutely no idea.

Continuing to revel in the homecoming of the precious metal that was an integral part of his very existence, his hunger for the return of his magic sated with every ounce that got reabsorbed by the molten magma packed core, Novus turned his attention to the elephant in the room, or the weapon of mass destruction hanging in mid-air. Back when he'd met Polkinghorne not so long ago, he'd have had absolutely no chance of taking on such a challenge, let alone contemplating the idea of winning, a thought now at the very forefront of his mind. Figuring it was going to be a close call as to whether or not he had enough magic when the Providences finally, through no fault of their own, called it a day, he watched intently, readying himself to act.

Amidst the wreckage adjacent to the gaping black chasm

that was the entrance to the test borehole, twelve magnificent dragon forms stood contemplating the nature of events they'd all played a pivotal part in.

Flash, one gun metal grey wing wrapped around Amelia's well defined shoulders, had the broadest of smiles etched into the prehistoric lines of his quite frankly intimidating jaw line, supposing that he, like everyone else there, had done all he could. If they were to die here, then at least he would go out surrounded by friends and the dragon he'd fallen head over heels in love with. Much more than that, he really couldn't ask for.

Mostly, they all agreed with the sentiment, none of them actually wanting to die, especially the youngsters who still had far too much life left inside them to offer up. But even they'd made their peace, all now enveloped in one almighty group hug with the two adults, both of whom they'd come to think of as parents, one for so much longer than the other, but by no means any less loved.

Tucked beneath one of her love's fabulous wings, as contented as she was ever likely to be given the cruel circumstances that had led them to this point, Amelia had a slightly different outlook. Of course she knew that they'd gone above and beyond to save the situation and mirroring those all around her, she certainly didn't want to die. But unlike the others, she was full of guilt at not having stopped Manson and his vicious queen once and for all during the Changing of the Guard, back at the king's private residence. Replaying the battle as many times as she had, if she could have gone back in time she would have willingly sacrificed her life to kill them both, assuring the future of the planet, including those she'd learned to love and call friends, even THE most unlikeliest of beings, humans in fact. Head bowed, she pulled in tighter to Flash's hulking great body, hoping he wouldn't pick up on her shame and lament at not having done more, sooner. He didn't, figuring her actions as a sign of affection, which of course they were. Standing gathered together for what might well be the final time, all twelve of them craned their necks skyward, glancing up at the intricate and damaged innards of the previously detonated nuclear warhead that hung there as if by magic, which of course was exactly the case. Using their inbuilt specific supernatural vision, simultaneously they zoomed in to get a better idea of what they were facing. To a dragon, they immediately wished they hadn't.

Slipping like the sands of time through an hourglass with no bottleneck, the Providences' grip on the wreckage of the exploded nuclear missile and all that it entailed finally came to an end, with a whimper rather than a flourish, all three spectral beauties flopping clumsily to the ghostly floor of their realm, spent beyond anything they'd ever experienced. In that one single moment the world, balanced on a knife edge, teetered towards extinction.

Pure, raw, untainted magic raced through what passed for veins, filling a void that had been barren for too long, igniting all of Novus' senses in one hit, not exactly returning him to his prehistoric best (there was too much laminium missing to do that) but boosting all his innate abilities to the point where he felt able to try his luck, realising it was now or never, with never looking like the more probable outcome. Taking a leaf out of Flash's book, using all the indomitable will he could muster and with a never say die attitude, he caressed the words across the far reaches of his mind and watched them soar high and far, all the while applying every last ounce of the inborn ethereal energy the laminium had returned. The spell was a beauty, one that in every conceivable universe and timeline was built for exactly this purpose, but it needed an awesome amount of fuel in the form of mana and resolve. Would what he had to offer in the here and now be enough?

The moment in time we're talking about could have direct correlation with a micron in length, considerably less than ten thousandths of a second, the supernatural hold from the Providences' continually rehashed enchantments finally broken.

With all the kinetic energy released, the missile's detonation continued just as it should have done in the first place. But not for long! Think about a tenth of the time from the moment described previously. After that…

# SNAP!

Every last associated molecule of the warhead, the missile's outer structure, all the kinetic energy and the released radiation was instantly… GONE! It was quashed from existence, the threat of the planet breaking apart annulled once and for all.

The only thing more rare and valuable than a dragon's tear was that of a mermaid. Today in northern France against the backdrop of the top of the test borehole, they were widespread and for good reason. Joy abounded at the bloodied nose evil had so rightly been given. But was the happiness a little too premature given the events unfolding across the rest of the world and the potential for the prophecy to come true?

# 42 CHRISTMAS CRACKER!

Deafeningly loud magic crackled across the thick, heavy air, accompanied by successive shockwaves, creating a chaotic and disorientating soundscape, one that all but rattled her brain despite the supernatural protection her legendary status afforded. Taking a breath, only the second since she'd been so rudely awakened by the hellish events playing out around her, Polkinghorne, clutching the renowned bow in one hand and the worn leather straps of four quivers of arrows in the other, did her best to ignore the deep vibrating thunderous rumble that continually rolled across the terracotta coloured ground of the vault, her brain feeling as though it were rattling around inside her head with the sounds of shattered armour, splintering rock, crumbling debris, high-pitched crashes and reverberating cracks. All she needed was one eye wateringly small moment of time to gather her composure, an oasis of calm in the middle of the storm. Unfortunately the wicked she-witch Earth had no intention of letting up her diabolical bombardment, determined to end the lives of her son and his human lover.

Holding on to the lungful of air for a few moments longer than normal, trying to ignore the pandemonium playing out through the vault, shaking some of the tangles out of her beautiful, long blonde hair as she did so, instinctively she glanced sideways along the row of plinths. Furthest away she could just make out Peter, looking absolutely terrified as fragments of stone shattered all around him, not even attempting to put up any kind of defence or offer anything in the way of a fight back. He appeared done and dusted, resigned to his fate, only a matter of time before his mother got her fiendish way.

Between them though was a beacon of light and a flagship of hope, a rugged beauty with thick, matted, blonde hair and an attitude to die for (well... let's hope not), without anything even vaguely supernatural which made her courage, audacity and daring all the more impressive, especially given that her usual partner in crime and best friend, the former weapon smith trapped in the futuristic blade Fu-ts'ang, was nowhere to be seen. It was of course Janice, sitting there reloading Billy the Kid's rifle, a look of sheer determination ingrained on her young, flawless face that should, given everything that she'd been through, have appeared much more weathered. The fact that it wasn't, was yet one more testament to her sparkling personality, strength of will and love for those around her, especially the dragon she'd fallen head over heels for.

Sensing movement amongst the mayhem of roaring fire, hissing enchantments and whistling projectiles, no small feat in itself, Janice glanced over, absolutely delighted to see who sat across the way smiling at her. The Christmas myth herself... SANTA! Both women exchanged a thumbs up, each delighted to be allied with the other again.


Through the fiery rage stoked by the perceived injustice of her life up until that point, Fredric's disillusioned daughter caught a fleeting glimpse of the barest hint of movement through the torrent of nefarious naga enchantments she continued to unleash in a part of the vault she assumed was empty.

Paranoid, delusional, wracked by half a dozen different voices all offering up assorted opinions, sometimes simultaneously, the evil, failed would-be queen tried desperately to quell the noise in an effort to be able to think straight, still unleashing offensive spells the likes of which the vault had never seen in its hugely long life.

Was there something there, she wondered, another person, an ally of the two of them or perhaps yet one more of the place's defences?

Sure that she'd seen something, Earth changed tack ever so slightly, directing a few blasts of brilliant purple forked lightning in that direction with one hand, hoping to flush out who or whatever may have been hiding there.

'Ahh... so you've seen me,' Polkinghorne mused as the top of the plinth she sat behind exploded into a hundred little pieces under a constant onslaught from the branched purple electricity, stray bolts from which passed straight over her head smashing into a pile of discarded, rusty, worn armour in all shapes and sizes, causing an absolute racket as it did so. And that was when she spotted it... a huge gleaming glass jar sitting on the floor, tucked away against the corner of one of the other pedestals. What was clearly visible through the shining outer glass set Santa's heart racing, and not in a good way.

'Oh crap,' she thought, against the hail of noise and destruction that simply refused to give up.

What was she so concerned by? The huge jar jam-packed full of laminium rivets, the one Gee Tee and Tank had used in their late night illicit splicing escapades which ended up creating the mantra that had freed all the nagas from Manson's hold over them, turning the tide for the better during the Changing of the Guard, almost certainly securing them victory.

'If any of her despicable magic hits that thing,' the Christmas legend reflected, 'not only are we all dead, but it'll destroy everything up above and a whole lot more, including Hook, For'son, Tank and Fu-ts'ang as well as the consciousness of Zarenkesia. Things just keep getting better and better!'

Finished inserting into the rifle a dozen or so .44-40 cartridges taken off the gun belt beside her on the floor, readying for a flurry of action once the opportunity to poke her head above the parapet presented itself again, Janice took a moment to glance across to the blonde haired Christmas miracle worker. The look on Polkinghorne's face gave the young human woman huge cause for concern.

It was at that point she really looked around, only having given the renowned vault a cursory glance when they'd first arrived, picking up on Robin Hood's longbow almost straight away, attracted not only to its design and the supernatural power imbued within but also of course the legend associated with it. Now though, after the scare with the huge jar of laminium rivets, it was starting to dawn on her exactly what they'd taken shelter amongst, by the look of things some of the most extraordinary and powerful magical artefacts she'd ever seen in one place, which was saying quite something. And whilst that might have sounded like just the ticket, a variable smorgasbord of weapons and armour to use as they all saw fit, in reality it wasn't quite so simple because that outright power in the form of mana and supernatural potential might well blow up in all their faces... quite literally. Bugger! Spiralling very quickly into the depths of insanity rather than just inhabiting the upper echelons as usual, all the voices now shouting at once, the peace and tranquillity of a calm, unshakeable mind far removed, Earth, all the time expending more of her indomitable magic than was absolutely necessary, sure the world was about to end at any second, continued to focus on the one thing those in her head could agree upon... that she needed to kill her traitorous son. Guided by them, she stepped up the intensity and viciousness of the enchantments she was using, sure it would get the couple's attention and maybe even provoke whatever threat continued to go unseen, all the time oblivious to the danger her abilities presented to the ancient relics stored there for so long.

Ready for a little payback and about to go on the offensive herself, Polkinghorne couldn't shake the feeling that here and now she was meant for something else, the memories from Stonehenge fresh in her mind from when the Santa magic had rebelled at her attempt to use it to take down the nefarious nagas stationed there. That episode was a constant reminder of the good that resided behind not only all that she was, but every last drop of supernatural available to her. With that in mind, fearful that once again she could be removed from the fight by her own hand so to speak, she'd taken a moment to really think things through. The conclusion she'd reached was a little left field to say the least. But in her mind it felt like the best way forward and one in which she could make the most valuable contribution.

Sitting with her back against the terracotta coloured podium, shrapnel raining down on her, the fabulous Christmas legend fluttered her eyes closed and, ignoring all the explosions and the volley of intensive noise ricocheting around the small space, reached out with her intrinsic magic on the hunt for THE most powerful items and artefacts. There were many... too many to count, but it was only the apex pieces she was after. Why? Why do you think? In an effort to use her unique blend of the supernatural to protect them and stop the whole place, and all three of them, from being blown to smithereens.

First and most obvious was the massive jar of laminium rivets, almost close enough for her to reach out and touch. Using the tiniest circular movement of her index finger, a dab of her unconquerable will and a splash of her, one of a kind supernatural, immediately just the faintest of magical blue glows became visible deep within the thick, transparent outer glass. Moving swiftly on, her consciousness picked up something hidden towards the back of one of the cubbyholes high on one side of the walls. Delving deep inside past all the trinkets including tiaras, necklaces, rings, and dozens of one off mantras written on parchments all rolled up into tubes and tied up neatly with different coloured twine, Polkinghorne stumbled across her prey in the form of a dust encrusted, worn spell book, the front cover an old, thick, weathered, leather thing that had clearly seen better days. Although it appeared as though nobody should give it a second glance, like many of the objects Gee Tee had collected and then gone on to store in the vault, it was a one of a kind masterpiece and something no magic user should ignore. Briefly wondering what was so special about the decaying ancient tome, in a fit of curiosity that was odd given all the fighting going on around her, Santa flicked through the first dozen or so pages, the sheets fluttering open atop one another at speed as if turned by an invisible hand.

'Ahhh…' she thought suddenly understanding the significance of the object. 'Leonardo da Vinci, of course.'

It made sense from an all encompassing power point of view because the book was full of mantras, hexes, enchantments and spells that the great man himself had crafted, his work being some of the foremost and finest of its time, still futuristic even today. Slamming the book shut, sure that it wouldn't be heard over the continued bombardment, she applied the same protection as around the jar, the wrinkled leather cover now sporting just a hint of blue.

Strangely, after that her attention was drawn towards a flimsy, brown, leather belt hanging off the back wall, a blade sheathed around its circumference, a long, grubby strip of linen wrapped carelessly around the hilt just visible, the very ordinary looking, dull, blunt blade, unloved, uncared for and hidden away. But it was special in no small measure and carried the weight of history, which made it dangerous in more ways than one, certainly worthy of Santa's protection. She didn't know why it was exceptional, only that it was. If she'd have been able to ask Peter in that moment, he'd have known, having handled it during his first visit with the master mantra maker Gee Tee. Alas he was lost and afraid, his mother and her tendency for violence scaring the living crap out of him. What he knew and Polks didn't, was that the sword in question was the one George had used to incapacitate Troydenn during their one on one battle in the city of Salisbridge, the one that coined the renowned tale of George and the Dragon and had in some ways started all this off. If the former knight had killed the despicable monster responsible for so much murderous mayhem, then Manson would never have been conceived, and the world wouldn't be where it was right now. Unfortunately there was no going back. In the blink of an eye exactly the same protection was offered up to what most certainly wasn't a run of the mill weapon, coating it and the belt in a shimmering haze of blue. And speaking of renowned swords, there was the mother of all surprises tucked away amidst a jumble of very dull, blunt rusting blades in one unloved far off corner... EXCALIBUR! Polkinghorne was momentarily shocked... The intrinsic magic inside her was briefly buoyed, recollections of long ago adventures with the sword once trapped so famously within a stone, flooding her memory. In that instant she thought about swapping the bow for the famed blade. But it was a no brainer really, for her at least, certain that getting up close and personal with Peter's mother and Fredric's daughter in such a confined space was never going to go well. In the end she chose to stick with a ranged attack.

Good as she was, well... better than that in actual fact, even Santa wasn't infallible, something proven by her overlooking a relic that might well have been considered the most wondrous of them all. First, the Traveller's Bag of Capacity, the one Gee Tee had taken with him to Salisbridge when he'd intercepted Richie and her daring group of humans before saving Flash and Tank from the clutches of Casey's wicked torture. Inside he'd hidden goodies for all of them, from all sorts of magical grenades to the heavy water backpack Hook had used to immobilise numerous guards, to Peter's, nay... Fredric's laminium dagger that Richie had used to such extraordinary effect. Don't forget, it had also contained quite possibly THE most important of all... Fu-ts'ang, combining to such stunning effect with the heroic human now famed throughout the domain itself... JANICE! And then there were the Boots of Fleeting, without which Flash would never have made it to Australia in time to reunite with Yoyo and provide Fredric with a rescue of such epic proportions. The artefacts gathered by the former Emporium owner had saved the world time and again, helping them get this far. But one of the most unique and treasured items hadn't left the vault. For whatever reason, only the deceased Gee Tee would know, a secret if it was such, taken to the royal bereavement grotto adjacent to the king's private residence. And what was that particular relic I hear you cry? A cracked and twisted length of wood, rampant with knots, vaguely resembling a staff of some sort, appearing as fragile as a child's blown bubble, ready to crumble into dust at any moment. Poking out of a hole in the middle of a foot high plinth, just behind and to the right of Janice, if there were a thousand staffs to choose from, no matter how bad the others were, this would be the last one to be taken, that's how ghastly and inferior looking it was. But that was probably the point... hidden in plain sight, but still it shouldn't have fooled the experienced Santa. What was so special about it? Many centuries ago, it had belonged to a dragon sorcerer called MERLIN and was unfathomably powerful. Given everything playing out around her, Polks could probably have been forgiven for her lapse in judgement. But that oversight, no matter how small it may have seemed, might possibly cost them dearly at some point in the very near future.

Metres away, through all the supernatural banging and bedlam, the naive and innocent some would say fool, the young dragon who completely by chance had stumbled across Manson's reprehensible scheme in the first place, setting nearly all of this in motion, shied away from it all, hidden behind one of the many pedestals designed to show off the former shopkeeper's prized possessions. Head in hands, his dragoness, if that's what it could be called, was nowhere to be seen, his personality genuinely more human-like with every second that passed, his desire and propensity to fight barely there at all. He was unlike the majority of his race in this regard, with even the most timid of their kind relatively easy to provoke into action when push came to shove. Occasionally he'd shown the odd glimpse of something fierce but only when he'd thought those he loved were in mortal danger, understandable really. But that only made the here and now stranger because you'd think with his love and soulmate's life on the line as well as that of his friend Polkinghorne, that he'd come out swinging, determined to risk it all if not for himself but for them. The pity party continued however, tears now streaming from his buried face, bypassing his hunched knees, plunging straight down towards the cool terracotta, forming tiny little lakes resembling oases in the desert. Most perplexing of all though was the fact that in his own unique way, once again he did have those he loved at heart, his body wracked with sorrow at what he'd got them tied up in. In a million years he'd never have wanted to inflict any of that on the two he loved like brother and sister, Tank and Richie. To leave his friend upstairs amongst the debris of his Emporium had torn his heart asunder, not wanting to take refuge down here at all, only spurred on by the love of his life and the brilliant Polkinghorne, both of whom had constantly reiterated that he was doing the right thing, whatever that looked like. To think that the kindest, most caring being he'd ever had the good fortune to meet, one he'd shared so many great times with across the years, had been put in peril because of his actions destroyed him on many different levels. Not knowing the fate of his pal felt like having barbed wire slowly pulled out of every orifice. It was torture.

Like a broken record skipping a beat, it didn't take long for his thoughts to refocus on the other of his two best friends... the lacrosse playing superstar with whom he'd shared so many adventures, been dragged kicking and screaming into too many daring deeds, one who'd changed his life immeasurably for the better from the day she'd hatched right there in front of him in a darkened part of the nursery ring. From that moment forward they'd been almost inseparable, her strength showering his lily-liveredness, the boldness with which she made decisions a stark contradiction to everything faint-hearted that all but defined him. They were chalk and cheese, polar opposites, but the best of friends, him even for some time yearning to be her mate despite the underlying feeling that he was never actually good enough. Whilst that might have been true to some degree, them not hooking up had more to do with what she was searching for, something unique, challenging and irreplaceable, a special kind of love that she'd found only recently in the midst of all the anarchy and madness with quite possibly the second bravest human being on the planet. Boy did he wish she were here now, but Santa's false promise that she would be, stung more than ever. Given the doom and gloom infesting him from head to toe, I doubt very much whether even Richie could have shaken him out of his stupor.

There had of course been two major upsides to the recent disastrous events, from the young hockey playing dragon's perspective.

The first was discovering more about his grandfather, the king's best friend, confidant and founder of the Crimson Guards, the elite fighting group answerable only to the monarch that Flash had been a member of up until his bodily change in circumstances. And as if hearing about his relative wasn't good enough, supposedly back from the dead, Fredric had actually showed up in person through a naga wormhole of all things, straight from Antarctica itself alongside a whole host of allies, changing the course of what had looked like a losing battle. Wow... what an introduction that had been! Things between the two of them had gone from strength to strength with the exception of the odd blip preceding the fight with the released mythical creatures, something The White Dragon herself had gone some way to sorting out in her own inimitable way, standing up for the young, human woman who'd, become her best mate practically overnight. Speaking of which...

Not quite matching the surprise return of his grandfather, Janice at least took equal status in Peter's mind when it come to the plus sides of everything that had happened to lead them to this point. She'd grown from bar worker to one of the most courageous warriors, having easily eclipsed many of the top dragons with her heroics and daring deeds that would no doubt go down in the annuls of history, should the planet still be there for the tales to be told. Kind, caring, gorgeous, gutsy, audacious and with a smile that would melt anyone's heart, perhaps the true measure of the woman was the fact that she'd managed to bond on a level practically unheard of with the most fabulous of weapons, one ancient in design, the personality of a dragon weapon smith contained within it. That alone should indicate the measure of the plucky young human. Her importance hadn't stopped there though, the reason in the first place for her entering the underground domain of the dragons still shining bright... PETER HIMSELF!

That's right, everything she'd accomplished against all odds was down to... LOVE! The outstanding sacrifices she'd made and selflessness shown on multiple occasions was all for him, originally to save him, but then her extraordinary willpower spurring her on to greater deeds so that THEY could have a future together, the connection between them characterised by mutual respect, trust, kindness, compassion and generosity, their bond all encompassing, one of true soulmates. Of course there'd been the odd challenge or moment of conflict, but they'd passed like a grain of sand on the wind, fleeting, over in the blink of an eye.

Most would have thought him lucky... to have found such happiness, warmth and tenderness at such a relatively early age with a being so spirited, brave, bold and beautiful. That's how it should have been, but for one single thing... his MOTHER!

Through a fluke like no other, he'd fallen into her dastardly clutches after being captured by the would-be king of this world, a being he hated more than any other after their numerous humiliating encounters at Cropptech, the misery he'd inflicted on Al Garrett and then finally the chillingly cold showdown on the Astroturf on that fateful bonfire night that had nearly cost the world so much. Crossing paths with his mother though hadn't been straight forward, neither of them recognising the other for who they truly were, Peter given no choice but to witness her vile malevolence close up, through the monstrous murder of the wickedly corrupt Councillor Rosebloom, a dragon who was certainly due a fair amount of karma, but not what had happened, never that, and the torture she'd inflicted on both Tim (who at the time presented as The White Dragon from the prophecy) and himself. Her actions had caused him to feel terrified, intimidated, inferior, unworthy, resentful, almost but not quite creating divisions between him and those he loved more than life itself. Only their hard work, patience, understanding and love for him had saved the day on that front.

Those feelings... all the negative ones, the overarching sense of dislike, intense aversion, animosity and hostility that his grandfather's daughter had shown and continued to demonstrate towards him in the most spiteful, vengeful and sadistic way, weighed not only on his consciousness, but on his personality, staining his soul, ruining him, rendering him pretty much ineffectual and inept, just as it was doing right at this very moment. And no matter how hard he fought, how much he rallied against the negative emotions and psychological damage he'd already suffered, he couldn't seem to overcome the lack of understanding that haunted his every waking moment as to why his mother would want him dead. It was that simple!

And so here he was, not for the first time, letting down those he loved, out of the fight, relying on others to do the dirty work and take his mother out once and for all, the magic blasting away all around him, inciting both dread and panic in equal amounts, his consciousness just wanting it to end one way or another. Without some sort of miracle, Peter was about to get his wish.

Unlike her father but much like his grandson and best friend, Earth had long since thrown off the shackles of her almighty prehistoric natural dragon form, the one she'd entered this unjust world in, preferring instead the more adept, athletic and dextrous guise of the humans she so hated, sacrificing flight for nimbleness, quick thinking and the ability to hide and blend in something that had served her well from the shadows she so liked to stalk. Bizarrely, it felt less contrived and more... organic, unpretentious and inherently right. Given her loathing for the bipeds, it was indeed an odd stance, but then she was a being full of contradictions. Vowing to stick to the shadows after the incident atop the cliff in Wales all that time ago, she'd worked hard in recent years to get close to Manson with a view to becoming his queen, fulfilling all his needs and requests, doing his dirty work when required, even staying out of sight until right at the very last moment before walking out into the sunlight to take the starring role, somewhat going against her nature. And then there was just the simple act of marrying again. Okay perhaps she'd been momentarily swept off her feet by his charm, sophistication and sickly scheme to take over the world. But was that truly what she wanted? Not really... NO! Of course there was the attempt to turn Peter back at the Changing of the Guard in an effort to persuade him to go with her. One moment she wanted to be a mother to him, the next she'd vowed to wipe his sorry ass from existence. A great many inconsistencies, mired in ambiguity, dressed up as a paradox. Combine all that with being a more than competent magic user, acquainted with some of the darkest spells and supernatural enchantments ever to have existed, alongside her decades old experience dishing out vengeance and retribution to anyone that got in her way, I think we can agree that not only was she one sick and twisted individual, but a match for practically anyone else, a fact that Fredric her father could most certainly attest to.

As raw, visceral, supernatural energy surged through her,

dopamine, serotonin and an endless array of endorphins, neurotransmitters associated with euphoria, caused her hands and feet to tingle, her heart rate to spike, heightening her mental and physical arousal. Overwhelming joy, accompanied by a sense of pure and utter bliss at being at the top of her game, an unstoppable force of nature, and on the cusp of achieving her long term goal of wreaking havoc on the dragons as a whole and the personal satisfaction of wiping her offspring from the face of the planet, had the wicked she-witch in a state of awe and wonderment. Never before had she experienced the like. Even the crisscrossing purple lines chiselled into her demonic face looked happy, having foregone their usual psychotic undertones, appearing more than a little 'Joker' like. A side effect of this heightened perception was that the negative emotions bottled up inside her started to melt away, which in turn caused her to momentarily reconsider the reckless and evil path she trod. For a brief instant her bombardment of the positions in front of her stopped, the magic instantly recoiling back inside her, halted dead in its tracks.

Tapping into all her patience, having hooked her defensive magic around everything she considered a threat from the sheer power that it possessed, Santa sat, eyes closed, back against the terracotta platform that had just taken such a hammering from the fiendishly capable enchantments Peter's mother had been throwing their way. Polkinghorne, or at least the unique magic inside her, sensed an opportunity, one that wasn't likely to show itself again. Having already used just the tiniest tendril of her supernatural abilities to merge with her weapon of choice, a bow so epic that it could well have featured in a thousand songs up until that point, the one, the only... SANTA CLAUS did the last thing any child would imagine. Faster than a speeding bullet, she opened her eyes, rolled over, bounced up to her feet, and manhandling the bow like

Robin himself, pulled back the hemp using all the considerable muscle in her right arm, nocking the arrow at the same time after retrieving it from the quiver attached over her back. Taut for a miniscule moment, she allowed the inherent ethereal power of the weapon to guide her aim. It did so in a heartbeat, her vision zooming in and locking on to the evil hag whose assaults had been pounding their positions for what felt like hours. With a twinkle in her eyes, she let go and watched with immense satisfaction as the crudely made arrow imbued with more than a little ancient magic cut through the very molecules of the air itself, homing in dead centre onto its target.

Brushing aside the absolute ecstasy igniting every cell in her false, prehistoric body, an abrupt, shrill, all encompassing alarm startled Earth back to the present and the unusual threat that had presented itself from behind the pedestal in the direction she'd sensed the movement. Initial fury at being caught off guard was briefly replaced by that twisted smile again, a brief hint of amusement rearing its head at the fact that whoever or whatever this was, it was using a weapon so archaic that it couldn't possibly breach her impassable defences and cat-like reflexes. Caught in two minds as to how to proceed given the rudimentary nature of the attack, a wry smile settled on her face as the decision was made.

About to heft the legendary rifle belonging to the Kid atop the plinth in an attempt to rattle off a few shots, Janice, having witnessed Polkinghorne's extraordinary transition from contemplative hiding to full on, out and out attack in just a moment, couldn't resist watching the arrow scythe through the thick air, which was heavily laden with spent magic, on its way to a date with destiny.

Even from this distance, she could see the half cocked smile, overloaded with superiority, the one that reflected everything you needed to know about the villainous murderer.

'Huh,' Polkinghorne mused eyes locked fully on her target despite already having nocked another arrow, 'underestimate me at your absolute peril!'

With what should have been the most casual uneventful episode ever, leaning back and attempting to expend as little thought and effort in an attempt to avoid getting hit, Earth suddenly had the shock of her life when right at the very last moment the fast travelling arrow adjusted course fractionally, keeping its tip fully in line with the movement of her head. If she could have cursed she would have, but there simply wasn't time to even think the filthy word she would have used, let alone brandish it out loud. In a testament to all her fabulous instinctive reactions, unseen even through eyes of a magical nature, Peter's mother lifted her right hand up in front of her face in one last chance gamble.

'DAMN!' Polks swore in the recesses of her mind, keeping it much cleaner than she'd have liked, the innate righteousness deep within still triumphing even at times like this.

"AAAAARRRGGGGHHHHH!!!" Earth shrieked at the top of her voice, causing the ceiling to rattle and relics in all shapes and sizes to fall to the floor from the pockets and cubbyholes cut into the vault's walls.

Conquering the fear stemming from facing her love's mother, a being she'd witnessed murder in cold blood on countless occasions, crestfallen that Polkinghorne's first arrow hadn't quite hit its mark, Janice, braver than ten men twice her size acted on instinct, determined to seize the opportunity. With Earth hopping about enraged and distracted, Santa's first arrow buried deep in the palm of her right hand, taking a long, deep breath, the gorgeous blonde haired beauty slowly exhaled before swinging the Kid's rifle atop the plinth, once again taking aim, the purple crisscrossing lines on the witch's face standing out like a crosshair on the modern day version of what she had in her hands. Squeezing the trigger like a Wild West veteran, she started letting off round after round. Gunshot after gunshot reverberated around the tiny vault against the backdrop of the hopping mad, deranged psychopath who was only just coming to terms with the tables having been well and truly turned.

'Oooooo... so close,' Polkinghorne mused, sure she'd been within a gnat's genitalia of hitting the depraved dragon disguised as a woman right between the eyes.

However, there was no time to reflect or contemplate that possible outcome. Acting as only she could, nearly all her legendary magic scattered about the vault offering up the most potent of defences to the relics and artefacts that she'd deemed the most powerful and dangerous, with just a tiny tendril of ethereal energy bonded to the longbow, the weapon now attuned to her every wish when it came to firing it, Santa, spurred on by the thought of missing her love, Vimes, set about the task at hand. In a whirring blur of spectacular agility and fortitude, arrows were pulled from quivers, nocked without delay and then fired directly towards her prey's head, the longbow's intrinsic enchantments locking the projectile onto its target. In conjunction with her extraordinary focus, indomitable will and unique blend of supernatural, Polkinghorne was managing to rattle off one shot every two seconds, a feat no other magic user on the planet could have achieved. With fifteen arrows in each of the four quivers that gave the dazzling blonde, once a year Christmas legend about two minutes of sustained fire against the murderous butcher that had throughout her relatively short life, killed so many... if that couldn't turn the tide, then she didn't know what would.

# 43 SUB-DUED

After the brief lull and sit down to share some food, Vasuki's slick and efficient enchantment had the entire group trailing in the wake of the futuristic nuclear submarine disguised both from a supernatural and physical point of view. Simply put, there was no way in hell that any being inside that tin can, no matter how advanced it was, could detect they were being followed. And they were, by a whole armada of creatures. Four nagas, the king and three of his bodyguards, one very tired and frightened dragon in the form of Vimes, the gossip of mermaids led by the now slightly subdued Robyn after her little run in with Santa, Ajahn and his cluster of mermen, Aglaophonos the siren who they'd all come to like and appreciate, both the male and female kraken who in their own way were friendly enough, and about ten trawlers worth of fish from two dozen different species... never had there been a greater mishmash of living things under the sea tasked with such an important mission, which they all recognised.

So far their plan was working a treat, Aglaophonos having long since infiltrated the helmsman's mind, now having a constant hold over the sub's direction of travel. In tiny increments the vessel had changed course from a ninety degree heading to around seventy, pretty much as they'd hoped, now cutting through much deeper and darker water, further away from the coast and ideal for what they had in mind.

The plan put forward by Vimes, who was the only one with any real knowledge when it came to the design of this class of submarine, was simple... to break it in two between the sonar room and the missile tubes thus separating the weapons, nuclear reactor, turbines, generator and propeller from the control room, conning tower, torpedo tubes and the officers' wardrooms. If they could achieve that, a radiological event of epic proportions could hopefully be avoided, averting a disaster both under the water and along the Scottish coastline. Saying it was one thing, but getting everyone to play their part was proving to be quite something else.

"What is it we do again?" the leader of the mermen asked, swimming alongside the former dragon tor, able to speak freely because of the naga spells cloaking their presence.

"Hang back," Santa's soulmate asserted, "until the kraken have done their thing. Once the sub's been split in two, move in and deal with any stragglers. The shock of the attack might surprise them so much that they drown in an instant. But we have to assume they're all competent magic users and so may be able to form a defence of some sort. Leave no one alive, especially the being I've described to you, their leader... MANSON!"

Ajahn nodded before using his huge tail to power the rest of his body back on itself, swimming off to tell those under his command the details of what they'd been tasked with.

It was then that Vasuki sidled up, if such a thing were possible at that depth.

"Do you think it'll work?" he asked.

"I think it's our best chance," Vimes replied. "But there are so many variables that it's hard to predict an exact outcome."

"What worries you the most?"

The former *tor* and one of Flash's best friends after their epic adventure together during Christmas in Crisis, paused for a moment to think.

"It would have to be their leader," Vimes stated wholeheartedly.

"MANSON!"

"You're familiar with him I take it?"

"Oh yes. Alongside Fredric, he had me imprisoned in Antarctica for decades, the smug, murderous bastard, as well as being directly responsible for the deaths of thousands of my kind."

'Wow!' thought Vimes, wishing he'd never asked.

"I'm sorry to hear all that."

"My kind and I need to put all that behind us and start anew, something I'd hoped we'd gone some way to achieving. But the call to arms from Fredric couldn't be ignored and so despite the dire circumstances, I'm glad to be here. But I totally agree... of all the beings on that vessel, Manson is almost certainly the most dangerous. Give him an inch and he'll take a yard. The only thing I intend on giving him is the death he so deserves and a one way trip to a very watery grave."

Vimes smiled at that thought, agreeing in principle with everything his ally said.

Right then Llottie, the youngest mermaid of the lot, swam up to both of them looking radiant despite the gloominess of the water surrounding them, her turquoise hair glistening as she moved, a better suited model for a shampoo advert it would be hard to find.

"Glorious Llottie," greeted Vasuki, his diplomacy as smooth as ever.

Knocked ever so slightly off balance, all the youngster could do was bow in return, a gesture appreciated by Vimes.

"How fare you, young mermaid?" Vasuki enquired very politely.

"I... I... I'm okay I suppose."

"You suppose?"

"I'm just worried that something might have got lost in translation with both the kraken, and given that they're the most important pieces of this jigsaw we're trying to put together, well... let's just say I'm on tenterhooks."

"It'll be alright," stressed Vimes. "Don't forget that as well as your instructions, I've shown them where they need to split the craft in two. Right between the furthest missile hatch, the one I sealed down straight after they launched the warhead, and the conning tower. I'm certain they understand what they're supposed to do, so don't fret on that front."

W... w... what if it somehow goes wrong? What do we do then?"

'A good question,' both Vasuki and Vimes thought simultaneously, and one they had no real answer to.

"It'll be okay youngster. It's not our first rodeo."

"What's a rodeo?" the naga king asked.

"Riding about on a bucking horse to see how long you can hang on for."

"Oh…" Vasuki answered. "What's a horse?"

Santa's squeeze shook his head, wondering where to start.

"Just kidding!" put in the sovereign with a chuckle.

"Good one," Vimes quipped, enjoying the moment of humour before the main event started.

And then it did!

With every single one of them still shrouded in Vasuki's remarkably bizarre magic that the naga race had been using for hundreds of years to get close to the boats of human fisherman and steal a significant portion of their catch, slowly they all began moving into position, each knowing their roles in the upcoming performance.

The mermaids and mermen paired up, much to Robyn's disappointment, one of each together dotted around the sub, the thought being that their different magical powers might well complement each other should they end up facing dragons that were familiar with many of the nagas' unique and varied spells, thus giving them more chance of defeating their foes. Ajahn and his red headed mermaid counterpart swam together around the halfway point, figuring that if their enemies somehow got an inkling of what was going on, that was the place they'd come streaming out from once the two kraken got on with their party piece.

Vimes, Vasuki and his three guards slinked through the water just above the conning tower at what was effectively the top of the submarine around about midpoint, ready to act if necessary, the former *tor* wanting nothing other than for all this to be over.

Aglaophonos trailed the vessel, continuing to ply her trade from a distance, absolutely buzzing from having made new friends even though the circumstances could be described as less than ideal.

The whole craft was surrounded by shoals of fish made up of thousands of shiny individuals, their ever moving scales glistening and glinting as they swam despite the lack of direct sunlight, some wanting to witness the outcome, others thinking their services might somehow be required although how, it was difficult to fathom.

Swimming amongst the shoals on the starboard side of the nuclear submarine, Llottie ran her slender, pale hands across the translucent tops of the kraken's heads, reassuring them through their telepathic bond that everything would be alright and that all the others were there with them together. If anything went wrong, aid would be but a moment away. It was a tough concept for both leviathans to wrap their brains around, help from another being such an alien idea for each. Llottie, through her ongoing friendship, had done her best to make them understand. A bizarre kind of thank you in the form of a rainbow luminescent light show down the side of each of their bodies was her reward, at least that's what she thought it meant. But without further ado, it was time for the opening under sea act.

Charging out of a silver shoal of Atlantic mackerel without warning, approaching the futuristic submarine at ninety degrees, side on, both wide eyed kraken, as sleek as you like, tore towards the vessel at speed, the female's crimson tentacles trailing behind her, the white suckers lining each looking like spots that needed popping, the male mirroring her every move directly by her side, his yellow and green tentacles flailing about just a touch more, showing, if Llottie was any kind of judge, just how anxious he actually was. At the very last second before crashing head first into the silent craft's bulkhead spearheading its way through the dark, murky water, both kraken, with the kind of agility only really able to be shown off beneath the sea, doubled back on themselves so that their eighty metre long tentacles were now dangling precariously close to the sides of the ship, both in exactly the agreed positions. Llottie, Vimes and Vasuki sent them positive messages of encouragement through the telepathic link they all shared, all of which were returned with interest. If the unusual aquatic species could have smiled it would have lit up the sea right back to the Scottish mainland.

Travelling along in tandem with the sub, slowly, both kraken started to use the suckers on their tentacles to probe the outer casing of the hull, tentatively at first, just using one or two before going on to use them all. It was their way of testing out what they'd been tasked with breaking, getting a feel for what was to come.

"Won't they know?" Vimes asked Vasuki, travelling side by side with the naga monarch from a much higher vantage point.

"I very much doubt it. But even if they suspected something, they'd be hard pressed to prove it. And even then... what would they do?"

'He has a point,' Santa's squeeze reflected.

Familiar with the cold, metallic touch of the futuristic vessel that could potentially cause so much harm, the female octopus-like creature spoke through the link to Llottie who they'd come to think of as their point of contact between the rest of the group.

*"We're ready. Do you want us to proceed?"*

Looking up and over towards Vimes and Vasuki, the youngster got what she was looking for... two separate head nods, both of those in charge eager to get on with things.

*"Proceed at will and please... be careful!"*

*"Of that you can be assured, young one. Make certain to take care of yourself."*

And then their connection was cut off.

Done querying the outer skin of the vessel and eager to show their new found allies and friends exactly what they could do, both kraken slid effortlessly into position on the starboard side of the submarine, in exactly the spot that had been explained to them, the main body of the male over the missile tubes themselves, the female in turn directly below the conning tower, her eighty metre long appendages snaking around the torpedo room and up as far as the periscopes and radio masts, each tiny white sucker gripping on to something, ready for her to leverage the hold she had when the time was right. It was an impressive sight for sure and one that sent a shiver of fear up many a spine of those that called the undersea watery realm their home, glad that for once they were on the same side.

What happened next was an all out battle between the most advanced technology developed by humans and two of nature's mightiest monsters. Who or what would win was not assured by any means, but all those watching from the surrounding, chillingly cold, gloomy waters had come down on the same side... their own!

Initially both kraken applied external pressure creating a compressive force along the length of the futuristic submarine, the muscles in their tentacles bulging with the effort exerted, each doing their darndest to inflict maximum damage. Despite this, there was barely even a scratch on the paintwork.

Abruptly against the eerie red glow illuminating the command centre, a judder the likes of which the crew hadn't known since taking over from the humans back in America, rocked the vessel from side to side causing nearly everyone there to grab on to something, even those sitting down. Most put it down to some unexpected current or turbulence in the ocean outside, but not Manson. He had but one thought... TREACHERY, and probably of the highest order. He'd have been right of course.

Closing his eyes, shoving aside the disappointment that the world hadn't yet split into a million pieces, still holding out hope that it would at some point in the near future, the cunning, crafty and practised magic user extended his supernatural outwards from the sub attempting to determine what the hell was going on and just how they could neutralise it. The shock on his face was a sight to behold at discovering both of the humungous kraken wrapped around the midsection of the craft he was now trapped in. And that's all that he happened upon, Vasuki's inimitable spell still shrouding them all from the prying eyes of the dragons contained within.

'This,' Manson mused, 'can be no coincidence. There has to be magical mischief at play.'

Considering an appropriate course of action, briefly he wondered if they should dive deeper, seemingly realising that the kraken wouldn't be affected by that at all. If not that, then what?

About to order the magic users to take up arms and use their supernatural against the beasts, hoping that the damage they'd already done was minimal, only then did he wonder what on earth they were doing there in such relatively shallow water.

"HELM!" he positively screamed across the glowing red of the confined space they all shared. "HELM!"

Still no answer and so he turned to see the helmsman sitting at his station, sweat pouring down his face, eyes wide open, mouth agog. DAMN!

There and then he knew, well... not what was going on and the forces surrounding the sub, but he knew that they weren't where they were supposed to be, instead somewhere with much deeper water, a place more suitable to the base nature of both creatures currently attacking the ship.

Scurrying across to the helmsman's station, Manson drew back one of his hugely muscled arms and without hesitation landed the mother of all punches with one of his gigantic, pudgy fists, sending the dragon disguised as a human, named Dianstagous, flying out of his seat and into a bulkhead, the sickly sound of his neck snapping as it hit the metal echoing around the chamber, causing alarm to all those trapped inside as well as a fair degree of panic, most jumping immediately to their feet.

"STAND DOWN!" he commanded. "THAT'S AN ORDER!"

Reluctantly they did so, despite being confused and afraid, not understanding what the hell was going on after seeing one of their own summarily executed.

"They're here."

"Who, sire?" the false admiral enquired.

"Those who would defeat our plans and kill us where we stand."

"The dragons…"

"Yes."

"How do you…?"

"Can't you sense it? They're attacking the sub even as we speak."

To a being they all directed their supernatural energies outwards, instantly recognising the threat of the two colossal octopus-like fiends.

"But I can only sense…"

"KRAKEN, yes I know, but they're being controlled by other magic users somewhere close by."

"How can you be so sure?"

"Because this is what they do. Somehow they must have followed us from Portknockie."

There was a brief pause while everyone caught their breath, the tension in the air thick, like the smell of fear running throughout the command centre. If they could have popped a window, they would have. It would most certainly have freshened things up.

"What are your orders, my lord?"

And there it was, the toughest question of the lot, given

that he had no idea of the strength of the opposing force or even where they were, the cowards once again using proxies to do their dirty work, too afraid to come and get him themselves. What to do, what to do?

*"You're doing great... stick to the plan, stick to the plan,"* Llottie's voice echoed across the link and throughout the confines of both kraken's minds.

Redoubling their efforts, channelling every last ounce of strength they possessed into their almighty tentacles, both octopus-like aquatic beasts started to sense a slight deformation in the hull, the vessel minutely starting to bend, a tensile force now in effect on the opposite side of the compressive force that had been applied before. Their plan, albeit rather slowly, was starting to work.

Hope, normally so hard to find in these situations, had appeared out of nothing in abundance as those all around looked on at the extraordinary efforts being applied by both kraken. Scary as it was for most of them, to the fantastic shoals of fish, the mermaids, mermen and even Aglaophonos, to a being they were in awe of what both leviathans were in the middle of doing. Travelling alongside the sub itself was no small feat, let alone wrapping yourselves around it in an effort to snap it in two.

Falling back on his default setting, slamming his fist down hard onto the helmsman's control panel, Manson gave the order, the only one that he figured would get them out of this mess and back on track to Edinburgh.

"ATTACK!"

Bound through confusion, dread and a genuine fear for their lives, although not from whatever was going on outside their ride, all those inside did as commanded, each having been handpicked for their unswerving loyalty and supernatural ingenuity. With their allegiance being put to the test like never before, each of them leapt into action, directing their most powerful and spectacular spells towards the kraken entwined around the outer hull.

It was utterly bizarre attacking something underwater at that depth. Of course everything fire related was instantly snuffed out, and that had nothing to do with the kraken's natural resistance to anything remotely magical, something none of the disguised dragons inside the submarine had any clue about. Under the cosh from their leader, and feeling the pressure like never before, the astounding assaults instigated ranged from potent poison, luminescent green tendrils exploding one by one against the monsters' bodies, eyes and tentacles to absolutely no effect, to vicious streaks of continuous forked lightning in every conceivable colour, hammering every inch of the octopus lookalikes' forms, zapping suckers, tentacles, eyes, heads and even their beaks, all as you've probably guessed, to no effect. The kraken shrugged off the bombardments, the sensations involved akin to you or I being tickled. Given the beasts' immunity, the efforts from those inside the sub were nothing short of pathetic.

Manson tried get the blasted controls from the submarine to work and get them back on the right heading, without much luck it had to be said, Aglaophonos having done a great job at not only confusing the helmsman but getting him to lock down the computer at his station with a code so diabolically long, nobody would have been able to crack it in less than a week. The leader's extended senses took note of what was happening around the outskirts of their craft and sensing the less than effective actions from his crew, decided momentarily to devote himself to the task at hand, certain he could prevail where they had failed.

Reaching out with the sheer overwhelming power of his mind, he went straight for the jugular, which in this case was each of the kraken's brains, a brute force strike if ever there was one, his attitude and temper worsening with every moment that passed, determined to execute one last act of vengeance before he was neutralised, realising now that it was nothing short of inevitable, still nurturing a tiny bit of hope that the nuclear warhead they'd launched what felt like a lifetime ago would do what it had been tasked to and destroy the entire world and every living soul. So far no luck on that front, but he continued to wish and dream.

Finding the outer edges of their primitive minds was child's play. After that it was just a case of launching his raid which he did at full pelt, no more messing about. Using all his indomitable will combined with much more mana and supernatural power than he would under normal circumstances, the wicked, failed would-be king threw practically everything he had at one all out simultaneous assault on both brains at once, sure that their corpses would be floating off into the distance in the blink of an eye. Staggeringly the harm he'd just tried to visit upon the kraken was reflected straight back at him inside the futuristic vessel within which they'd all taken shelter, temporarily blinding him and causing no end of pain, the creatures' imperviousness proving to be all encompassing and of no small regard.

"Aaaaaarrrrgggghhhhh…" he bawled, the noise resounding around the small space all but deafening, forcing those in the command centre to cover their ears.

Despite the magic only really tickling and the fact that the others had warned them beforehand there might be some sort of retribution for what they were about to attempt, both kraken had become riled at the audacity and very thought that someone would think to lash out at them in such a manner. Inspired and more than a little angry now, their grip around the supposedly impenetrable metal increased tenfold.

Aware that both kraken had probably reached the outer edges of what they could do physically, Vasuki, chosen as king by his race for many reasons, his logic and presence of mind yet more of them, stepped in and through the telepathic bond shared with all the creatures there, encouraged everyone to feed just a smidgen of their supernatural towards the two tentacled trouble makers, wondering if that might somehow make the difference and bring about the result they were all hoping for.

Renowned for their resistance throughout the ages to any form of supernatural, kraken have rarely been troubled by magic users of any kind, with perhaps the one exception that saw one of their race living peacefully in a landlocked lake captured by three desperado dragons desperate for the bounty on offer, nearly losing their lives in the process. So it was something of a surprise for the mating pair trying to tear the submarine apart to feel a very different kind of power flow through their muscles and veins, engorging their brilliantly coloured tentacles, causing their bright white suckers to swell past twice their normal size, providing them with an edge that in all their time alive they'd never had before, adding a crucial one percent to their attack.

When compressive and tensile influences reach their limits, the object in question ultimately snaps, shear force coming into play, acting parallel to the cross-section causing the two halves to separate. All that you need to know is in that moment the super silent, state of the art submarine succumbed to the irrepressible will and unconquerable force of the two supernaturally resistant kraken, snapped in two, the top heavy front half encompassing the torpedo tubes, control room and the conning tower tumbling uncontrollably downwards towards the ocean floor, whilst the rear section containing the remaining warheads, nuclear reactor, engine room, generator and propeller, flat spun out of control, still spiralling towards the depths just vastly more slowly and in a more southerly direction to its counterpart.

As a huge cheer resounded through the shared telepathic link, Vimes let out a sigh of relief having completed the unspoken mission his friend Flash would have him do... making sure the sub was taken out of commission. However, before the applause and merriment had begun to diminish, shadowy figures could be seen escaping from the front section of the broken vessel as it plunged uncontrollably towards the seabed, shapes that would have been very difficult to distinguish against the background of the gloom if not for the light produced by the frictional forces of the surfaces of the broken halves of the submarine briefly rubbing together. Instantly recognisable because they'd all been primed about that very trait, a fully matt black dragon, something out of most magical beings' nightmares, could just be made out swimming away at speed towards the darkened depths... MANSON!

Simultaneously the same nasty expletive echoed around the link, all of them disappointed he hadn't drowned during the sudden influx of icy cold sea water, having been previously warned what would happen should that particular psychopath escape the vengeance of the sea and their off the wall alliance that had vowed one way or another to put him down for good.

With Llottie's comforting words of a job well done ringing in their ears, both kraken, absolutely spent, let their tentacles interweave with one another, effectively enjoying one big hug, their part in this once in a lifetime caper played to perfection, the finishing touches now down to the other members of the ragtag group.

A burning fury the likes of which he'd never experienced before coursing through every molecule of his being, Vasuki with one swish of his giant snake-like tail set off in pursuit of the murderous monster Manson, who'd done so much damage not only to the planet at large, destroying humans and dragons in vast quantities, but also to the naga race in particular, something he, their elected monarch, still felt responsible for. Determined to gain justice for all those deaths he carried with him during every moment of every day across his consciousness, the naga leader knew the time for revenge and retribution was close at hand, especially since he had his own personal grudge to settle... his incarceration in Antarctica for all those decades. Never truly believing an opportunity like this would present itself, Fredric's close friend and ally, the naga sovereign, pushed the emotions pulsing through him to one side and, tempered with an ice cold edge, set about imposing the ultimate naga justice onto the sickly schemer and murderous monster, certain that the spirits of his dead would approve.

It wasn't even a decision... not really. Of course he didn't want to go, every atom in his body rebelling at just the thought, but Vimes had come too far to dip out now, a build up of gritty resolve that had never reared its ugly face before encouraging him see this through to the bitter end. So in the wake of Vasuki's bodyguards, he swam off after the naga king, hoping to see the main protagonist in all this finally get what he had coming.

To an individual, the mermaids and mermen were amazed to see as many as a dozen human bodies tumble out of the shattered submarine into the icy cold water, nine from the front half encompassing the command centre, three from what would have been the back end taking in the engine room. Hoping to see them all drown one by one, a fitting death for such duplicitous and despicable beings, they suddenly got the fright of their lives when a familiar transformation started to take place across the board.

*"What's...?"*

*"THEY'RE TRANSFORMING BACK INTO THEIR NATURAL DRAGON FORMS,"* Vimes screamed through their shared link, continuing to head off in the opposite direction after Vasuki and Manson. *"TAKE THEM DOWN BEFORE THEY CAN FULLY REVERT!"*

Recognising the urgency with which he spoke, Ajahn and Robyn simultaneously gave the command to attack. Following their leader's instructions, they did just that!

Each of the mermen had various different bracelets around the wrists of their dominant arm, some brightly coloured, others much darker in nature, but all with the same purpose. In chorus, each member of the troupe whispered a personalised, closely guarded spell across the confines of their minds, adding a touch of mystical willpower along the way. It was instinctive, something they'd done tens of thousands of times before, an act of both defence and attack, second nature to the individual concerned. Unfurling of its own accord, each bracelet, seemingly with a life of its own, slithered up their pale wrists, wrapped around their palms and the back of their hands, weaved in and out of their agile fingers, before extending upwards in the most magical of fashions to form an array of different blades, mostly dagger-like, every one razor sharp and deadly, some serrated, others oozing with puffer fish poison, one or two generating tiny waves of electricity in a variety of different colours around their edges, enough to stun practically anything at this depth from a distance of one or two metres. As a fighting force, they moved in for the kill.

Some of them died before they'd finished slipping back into their original skins, that's how fast the mermen were enhanced by their particular taint of supernatural, speedily swimming in before ruthlessly dispatching each individual, the dark dragons' scales and enchantments no match for their perfectly balanced weapons that, like Fu-ts'ang or Fredric's laminium dagger, sliced through them as an ordinary knife would through butter. For about half their contingent, it was that easy. The other half though, that was a different story.

In the kind of time it would take to click your fingers... it was over, the submarine, THEIR submarine, stolen from directly under the noses of the United States Navy what seemed like a lifetime ago, had been ripped apart by whatever those creatures were, tens of thousands of litres of bone chillingly cold sea water flooding into every compartment, short circuiting every electrical component in an instant, plunging them into darkness and danger, giving them only one option... to swim out into the open ocean in their human guises and attempt to transform once there, precarious under the best of circumstances, something this most certainly wasn't.

And so that's what they'd done. At the start there'd been an element of coordination, a telepathic link opened by the falsehood of an admiral, the idea being that they would be able to organise their defences thus standing a much better chance of not succumbing to the enemy whose real strength and force they knew nothing about. But with the vicious chill from the water and the absolute bedlam in evacuating the sub, the connection quickly failed, each dragon relapsing back to their self centred, prehistoric selves. All for one and one for all it most certainly wasn't. And that's when they'd been struck, in the middle of the change, nearly half their force wiped from the board in an instant by... swimming fish men! Those remaining, disgusted at the outlandish ambush that had caught them off guard, incensed and infuriated, brought their superior supernatural to bear after they'd applied the naga breathing enchantment, exactly the same one which currently enveloped Vimes, allowing him to breathe easily, and keeping him warm as well. After that, let's just say that revenge became a priority, each forgetting about where they were (one of the most inhospitable locations on the planet... especially for a dragon), that their leader had deserted them and exactly what the hell was going on across the rest of the world. If they survived, which looked doubtful at best, they were in for the mother of all shocks.

Arms tucked in, gleaming dagger clutched firmly by his side, one of the mermen kicked his tail out and like a silver bullet homed in on his prey ready to make a swift, merciless kill, by now having chosen the target after that. But don't forget, these were dragons, some of the mightiest magical beings ever to have stalked the earth, underestimated at the peril of others down the ages and no slouches when it came to wielding mantras and enchantments.

Storming forward, head on, the merman in question

wrestled his dagger out in front of him, fighting against the pressure and momentum of the water he was travelling so fast against, only to run into the most potent, fierce and formidable stream of ice that quickly enveloped him in its grasp, much to the delight of the brute who'd so spectacularly unleashed it. Sensing a moment of victory, savouring every second, the brown hued beast used all his momentum to pirouette as fast as he could with his wings wide open, reinforcing their edges with a very specifically designed enchantment. The merman captured by the ice was decapitated in an instant, much to the horror of those allies looking on. Glancing around in every direction, his apex predatory instincts kicking into overdrive, the dragon in question, the chief engineer aboard the submarine, flapped his wings against the harsh sea water he found himself surrounded by and kicking out his tail, using it as a rudder, set off towards what women of all ages across the surface would no doubt consider an absolute dreamboat. A scintillating scaled grey tail that shimmered as he moved, long dark hair flowing back behind him as he torpedoed through the murky cold water, his matching beard and pointed moustache made him look regal to say the least, all of which was kind of appropriate because after all, he was the leader of this outlying faction.

From a distance Llottie let out a heartfelt squeak, her body keen to throw up, her mind rallying against the natural desire stemming from the calculated gore and cruelty that she'd just witnessed, her inexperience causing untold anxiety. That, however, couldn't be said of Aglaophonos the siren who across her time roaming the oceans had seen more than her fair share of death and wanton destruction. This was somehow different. Never having had any allies to speak of, even any of her own kind, it had been a big ask for her to speak to the strangers that had sought her out only a short while before, let alone join them on a quest to put the world to rights. But here she was after agreeing to team up, remarkably one of the best decisions of her life, totally invested in what they were doing, enjoying not only some of the banter between the mermaids and mermen, but loving every second of the glances she was attracting from Ajahn himself. It was all a very new experience. And then the sub had been ripped in two and she'd figured their jobs were done. Not so, and now this!

'Oh no you don't!' she thought watching the merman murdering dragon circle around, setting his sights on a different prey this time.

Closing her eyes, Aglaophonos tapped into her distinct and unnatural magic, casting it out in front of her with just two guttural sounds deep within the confines of her psyche, think Klingon stepping on Lego, that's how harsh and abrasive they were. In but a moment the field of movement spread out ahead of her lit up like a Christmas tree, the minds of each individual the sparkling or not so sparkling baubles, each different, some much darker than others, the occasional one a positive lighthouse in a storm offering up clear direction.

It took a split second to find the one she was looking for, a shadow strewn cesspit of filth travelling at speed towards the aforementioned beacon of light... Ajahn! Vowing not to let the primordial assassin anywhere near a being she'd developed a great fondness for ever since he so politely introduced himself, Aglaophonos pinpointed her intended target, the former fake chief engineer and directed all her ire in his direction.

Confident of yet another quick kill, this one by the look of things of significantly more substance, the dark dragon's egotism and superiority would have been there for all to see had they been looking, his conceit towards all the enemies dotted around the ambush overwhelming, something that might yet be his undoing.

Normally it would be subtle, infiltrating a consciousness a slow and considered exercise, gradually taking control over a substantial period of time, letting the individual in question go about their business in a timely, productive and ultimately normal manner until all the invasive tendrils were well and truly established and there was simply no way back. Not this time! It was one sudden assault with all the mental fortitude that she possessed, letting loose with all she had in the most direct manner possible, akin to a sledgehammer cracking open a walnut. It was brutal, cruel, vicious and violent, but that's what was required to keep Ajahn from being next on the monster's hit list.

On breaching what could best be described as pitiful defences, Aglaophonos wasted no time and very little energy, deciding that, 'to the point' was best. In one fell swoop, she crushed the swine's consciousness, wiping him out of existence there and then. With one final flap of his wings the fiend's magic spluttered into nothingness, seawater instantly gushing past his sickly yellow teeth, battering the back of his throat, the swirling white water filling his enormous bulging stomach until it could fill no more. Floating lifelessly, the cadaver was a reminder to them all of the unconditional power of the ocean.

Twirling around as gracefully as a ballet dancer, only then did Ajahn recognise the threat, the monster having got well within range of a potentially devastating attack. Glancing first at the corpse and then across to the siren, realising she'd just saved his life, the merman chief offered up a respectful nod and for good measure added the most coquettish of winks, a gesture that made Aglaophonos blush profusely. With no time left to lose, Ajahn rejoined the fight leaving the hot and bothered siren to her very inappropriate thoughts.

Whilst all that was going on, Robyn and two of the more senior mermaids had taken down three of the remaining dragons, stealing their souls in a ritual as ancient as the dragons themselves, watching merrily as their antediluvian bodies, now just vessels without consciousness floated listlessly amongst the chilling gloom of the open ocean.

Able to function much more effectively and swim that bit faster not only through experience but because his body had been designed over millennia to do just that, Vasuki trailed Manson's every move from about three hundred metres away, directly above, between him and the surface, his ultimate escape route. If he reached fresh air, he'd be gone, just like that, able to reset and revisit a whole world of pain on yet more unsuspecting fools in the future. That could not be allowed to happen again. Full of angst and rage that the evil villain thought he could once again slope off into the sunset so to speak, his cowardly custard act now almost becoming a signature move, suddenly the tiniest movement in the water gave away the presence of four others, all three bodyguards who'd had no trouble at all in keeping up as well as the perfectly affable and good-humoured dragon, Flash's pal Vimes, who due to his much larger frame and cumbersome shape was having no end of trouble. Still, he persisted, something the naga king gave him credit for.

With the bodyguards remaining quiet, it was the dragon who broke the silence between them.

"I'm sure I don't have to reiterate that he's as dangerous as they come. How the hell are we going to take him down with just the five of us?"

And that was the crux of the matter, Vasuki thought, having already gone head to head with the murderous monster back at the private residence and lost more than once. Even if you added all three bodyguards and Vimes into the mix, the odds were probably still not in your favour. How best to even them up, that was the question.

There was something... a summons if you like, one that only his race could answer. Never before had he been in a position to use it. Twice though, he'd thought about it. Once during his captivity in Antarctica, bound opposite Fredric for all those decades. Of course the magically constraining chains had prevented that, just like Manson's dark grip on a great deal of his kind during the Changing of the Guard. Again he'd tried to use the enchantment to summon help, but to no great effect, not with such stupendous shadowy supernatural involved. Okay... he'd rounded up all he could after the two main protagonists had fled like the cowards he took them for, ignoring any plea to help deal with the mythical creatures that had shown up on a whim. After which they'd escaped back to their natural environment in an effort to regroup, repopulate and start again. And before that could happen, here he was, facing the one being on the planet that scared the living daylights out of him and he was seriously outgunned at that. In this moment, surveying one of the most sadistic, cunning and despicable creatures to ever stalk the earth, from a distance, hoping to prevent him from fleeing, he was seriously contemplating using it. The only issue? Many more of his kind could die and that was a price his conscience just couldn't handle.

Cutting through the miserable, murky and depressing water as fast as his primordial matt black form would allow, he was enhanced, not only with regards to speed, but surrounded by the same naga spell that allowed Vimes to breathe and resist the cold. Still he could feel the constant pressure of the ocean pummelling his supernatural defences, just waiting for any sort of weakness, ready to flood in and overwhelm, a consequence he truly dreaded and would do anything to avoid. A cold, watery grave was any dragon's worst nightmare, his in particular given how he started out, in Antarctica, his home in the midst of the most inhospitable place on the planet, one surrounded by freezing seas, all the time incorporating biting winds, icy chasms, deadly snow storms, potentially lethal stalagmites and stalactites and run by a leader only interested in vengeance, his father... TROYDENN!

In that regard they were very much alike, his son's traits mirroring those of his parent after being tricked into killing the only other person he'd ever really loved, his... MOTHER! The change in him after that had been brutal and unforgiving, making him become almost a polar opposite of the being he'd been. And if he could have killed his father he most certainly would have, but the ancient magic used by Troydenn when he'd been hoodwinked was powerful to say the least and there were absolutely no loopholes… goodness knows he'd tried to find one. Thankfully the lacrosse player had done the job for him, ridding him of the intimidation, bullying, physical and mental violence and the torture that he'd suffered for years. He should have been delighted, and part of him was, but he'd spent so much time planning his father's murder that watching someone else take up the mantle and do it right before his very eyes was an anti-climax, leaving him full of regret at having not tried harder to circumvent the supernatural and finally find a way.

Almost certainly imitating what his father would have done in the situation, epitomising everything he'd become, Manson, stressed beyond belief and bone weary tired despite having been fully replenished physically and magically only a short while before whilst falling over the Portknockie cliff, slowed to a halt and turning over onto his back, began to tread water, all the time facing the four sickening nagas and a dragon he was unfamiliar with, up until he'd boarded the now destroyed sub that stood in his way to the surface and the freedom he so craved.

Echoing his actions, Vasuki, Vimes and the three naga bodyguards reduced their swimming speed, pulling up directly above the matt black monster they couldn't take their eyes off.

"What do you think he wants?" Vimes asked.

"Our heads on a silver platter," Vasuki replied sarcastically, sorry that he had, no sooner had the words left his mouth. "I'm…"

"It's okay… it was more rhetorical than anything else. Do you think we can defeat him?"

"Not on our own," came the naga king's honest assessment.

"Then…"

"I think," Vasuki interrupted, "that we need a little help from our friends."

The former *tor* was speechless as he continued to tread water.

Determined now to get out of this situation and find somewhere off the grid to recover and plan his next move, Manson's thirst for retribution and settling scores only stoked the fire and madness within, causing him to partly take his eye off the ball, focusing momentarily at least on the four beings sitting firmly in his way. One hundred percent certain that he could destroy all of them in less time than it would take for him to grill a human with his flame, smother its entire length in ketchup, shove it into a massive bun and devour it in one bite, the failed would-be ruler mustered all his mind's madness, flooded himself with his unique and rather strange ethereal energy and offering up the sickest of smiles, prepared to proceed.

He, however, wasn't the only one to have chosen a course of action.

With the ice cold water barely circulating throughout his gills, Vasuki, former Antarctic prisoner, fierce warrior, loyal friend, mentor to many, renowned secret keeper, the conscience of his kind and naga sovereign, chose to discharge his duty as only he could, knowing that the summons he'd tried to invoke previously could well be the answer to all their questions, not only in defeating Manson but in gaining some measure of justice and closure. In an act only he was capable of, the supernatural shout went out, straight forwardly stating the reasons, beckoning all to his point in space and time with the greatest of urgency. It was magic used on an epic level, perhaps even on par with what the Providences had done in containing the already exploded nuclear warhead over northern France, and an enchantment not seen in his lifetime. Whether it would work, and on what scale if it did, was anyone's guess. Depleted of every magical resource he possessed, the naga monarch slumped forward, letting the pressurised water take hold of his snake-like form, his eyes still firmly open, keen to see the outcome of what could be considered his biggest ever gamble and that included teaming up with a ragtag bunch of misbegotten dragons and jumping halfway around the world with them in the blink of an eye. Here's hoping!

'What the hell?!' Manson mused, looking on from a distance as the king of the disgraceful, lying and cheating, vile nagas drooped over, looking for all intents and purposes as though he were out of the forthcoming fight before it had already begun.

'You snivelling, cowardly piece of...' was as far as his train of thought got before being rudely interrupted.

Singular pinpricks of light only a few millimetres in diameter abruptly began to appear all around him, on all sides, below and up above, between him and the five enemies he was about to so effectively destroy. First one, then two, five, ten, twenty, thirty, fifty in all, his gloom ridden surroundings now resembling the landscape of an alien sky.

Puzzled, trying to take it all in, abruptly an excruciating memory from back in the private residence from a time when he'd seemingly had everything under control and looked for certain to be the new incumbent world leader, returned with a vengeance.

'But it can't possibly...'

Manson couldn't finish the thought because it was just too terrifying to contemplate if it were true. But it was, you see.

Each manifesting as a giant, blindingly green wormhole, stomach-churning dark energy, a swirling, twirling vortex of hatred rolling around their circumference, thick tendrils of charged bright blue energy tried to snake free from the outer edges of each of the fifty underwater supernatural portals that had sprung to life out of absolutely nowhere. As their accretion discs effervesced and writhed and tiny concentric bubbles echoed out from their centres, almighty crashes of rumbling thunder reverberated across that part of the ocean causing water molecules to crash into each other, rocking and rolling everything and everyone there. Manson wanted to be sick.

Vasuki watched with incredible pride, knowing what was about to come next.

Simultaneously, a blossoming yellow sparkle sizzled around the outside of all the rings, whose centres now looked more liquid than either solid or gas, their violent arcs fizzing, jumping and buzzing, preceding what was to come. Without further ado, come in all its magnificence, it did!

The gooey fluid that was the middle of all fifty rings parted, allowing nagas of all different shapes, sizes, ages, sexes and colours to slither out into the darkened ocean, at least a dozen in most cases, occasionally even more than that.

Across all his extended existence, he'd been touched by panic and dread numerous times, mainly in the form of his father's torture and intimidation, but he'd only known true terror on one occasion... in the moments surrounding his mother's death! What had happened then had crushed his spirit, torn his soul apart, neutered the individual he'd once been. It had been catastrophic, agonising and relentless, crushing all his hopes and dreams forever in an instant. Nothing he'd thought up until now could match that moment for trepidation and anxiety. Oh how he was about to be proved wrong.

Borrowing just a little supernatural, freely given by the guards who'd accompanied him on this most crazy of quests, Vasuki found enough resolve to address all those who'd answered the summons and used their supernatural to track him down. Maybe now the darkest chapter in their chequered history could finally be put to rest.

*'Every single one of you here has lost loved ones... brothers, sisters, mothers, fathers, sons, daughter, friends... all memories in the tide, gone but not forgotten, most taken too soon, before their time, before they*

*had an opportunity to make their mark on our world."*

Deliberately pausing, despite the fact that the incarnation of evil was floating in the middle of them, no doubt wondering what the hell was going on, he took a huge mental breath before continuing.

Using all his focus in an attempt to maintain his composure, sweating profusely despite the freezing ocean cooling the surrounding air from the naga spell he'd cast on himself and lowering the temperature around his scales, Manson's mind was focused on one thing and one alone. And what do you think that was? Surprise, surprise… running away! Now that he'd calmed down enough to think straight, he had just the thing, the enchantment that had saved him back at the private residence, naga in design, the teleport spell that would allow him to put some distance between himself and his would be attackers, those that would have their revenge for what he'd done to pretty much their entire race.

Closing his eyes to centre himself, the villainous protagonist that had harmed so many, son of Troydenn, dark destroyer himself and perish the thought, would-be ruler, surrounded by over five hundred pissed off nagas, gathered up all his mana, applied all his considerable will and extending his mental capacity out as far as it would go, whispered the words to the spell he'd used to such great effect last time, knowing all he had to do was get to the surface. After that he could bound up into the air and be off in the blink of an eye, those soppy, flightless naga idiots standing absolutely no chance of catching up with him. Expecting to feel the faint tingle of magic around the entirety of his prehistoric body, he was more than a little surprised to find that NOTHING had happened.

'Uhhhh?'

Holding back the alarm that threatened to consume him, realising that due to whatever was going on all around him he had a few moments to double check things, Manson did just that and finding nothing untoward, tried again, this time applying every last ounce of his indomitable will, convinced that what he had in mind would work. And what was that? To teleport away using the secret, ancient magic so unjustly ripped away from some of their finest shaman for their entertainment and selfish plans, just as he had in two short hops back at the private residence when events had become a little too hot to handle. Back then he'd applied everything perfectly, the first relatively small teleport depositing him in a brightly lit stairwell of the council building on the eastern side, all but deserted and ideal for his purposes. He'd taken a few moments to marshal his mind and collect his thoughts, pushing away the darkness and anger knowing that right now they wouldn't serve him well, very quickly he had been on his way once again, this time flitting into being out of absolutely nothing in the middle of a dark, foul smelling sewer. From there it had been a quick sprint on foot to a little known, mysterious entrance to the surface. Given that he'd repeated everything right down to the exact detail here and now, surrounded by a huge enemy force deep beneath the ocean, he was still stumped as to why it wouldn't work. He was sure it should have.

The supernatural in question, as Manson already knew, was draining in the sense of the use of mana required. That wasn't currently in question because he was topped up by the submarine's crew. If he'd had his wits about him and used the exceptional intellect he so often relied upon, he would have come up with the answer in short shrift. But the danger surrounding him had blunted his edge, throwing him off his game, denying him the one thing he sought now above all others... an ESCAPE!

There was only one difference between both events in the past and his attempt here and now in the present... the target location. Simply put, he'd visited both the exact points, the stairwell in the council building and the sewer and ingrained their images into his eidetic memory, something the magic from the naga spell used to teleport him to those precise points. Here and now all he was really doing was trying to pick out a point on the ocean above somewhere where the sea met the air, just a general, run of the mill image, nothing specific. And that was the problem and the reason the enchantment in question wouldn't function. The target location wasn't locked inside his mind, which was made a little more ironic by the fact that even the youngest of nagas present could have picked out a precise point in the ocean, down to the nearest square inch. They are taught to do so shortly after birth by any number of means, sight, smell, taste, sound, experience, animal behaviour and memories, all of which allowed them, should they need to, to use that particular spell if its knowledge had been passed on to them. For Manson to lose out on an escape simply because he was hundreds of miles from the nearest coastline and surrounded by sea was the ultimate irony, one currently lost on him, but not on Vasuki who, even in his weakened state had sensed his nemesis once again try and flee. Instinctively he smiled, Vimes and his guards wondering what was so funny given the dire circumstances they all found themselves caught up in. He was too exhausted to tell them, choosing instead to use the last of his energy to address the elephant, or in this case, dragon, in the room.

Able to positively feel the anger and outrage rippling through the new arrivals, its overbearing mark polluting every individual with a dark, shadowy stain, only then did the naga sovereign hark back into the past, his thoughts centred on what they'd been, wondering if that was their destiny as a race once again.

The advent of so many all arriving at once reminded him of a time long forgotten, an era that might genuinely be considered their darkest hour. Who or where it had stemmed from was anyone's guess and a great many of their finest scholars had done just that... guess, but that's all it had been, no rhyme, reason or actual evidence to back up any theory, instead casting away facts, basing their findings on pure speculation. Of course that didn't matter to most, not with so-called trusted names attached to such conjecture, but what it didn't do was allow them as a race to forget the heartache, troubles and mistrust with a view to healing and moving forward. Instead the animosity and resentment lingered, for decades, if not centuries, causing violence and subterfuge to bubble to the surface, inflicting pain on themselves and occasionally others who'd stumbled across something they weren't supposed to. What had the hypotheses had to offer in a way of explanation as to when and where this had all started and who was to blame? Believe it or not, the shadow cast supposedly went as far back as the prophecy, the one the dragons believed in wholeheartedly, the one they'd almost developed their entire civilisation around, teaching it in their nursery rings, making sure their leaders were constantly on the lookout across the course of time for anything that could be related to it. Of course the nagas, during that alignment of races leading up to the signing of the agreement relating to the prophecy, had been deliberately excluded by not only the dragons, but also the Basilisks, the Manticores, the Heretics of Antar and the Hydra queen herself. This, most naga academics believed, was the true reason for all the guilt, remorse, lament, unhappiness and grief that had held them back as a race for so very long, their leadership not able to put the past behind them and move on into the future with optimism and a new set of goals, instead hiding away like the magical outcasts they supposedly were, plotting, planning and scheming petty ways to get back at the others. It was still this way many, many thousands of years later when he'd acceded to the throne, becoming the youngest monarch in the history of their kind. There and then he vowed to change the attitude of every single naga under his rule, from the youngest to the oldest, from the most set in their ways to the most open minded of individuals. Instigating that change was top of his priorities and something he knew could be achieved, in the long term leading to a much more productive and meaningful life for them all, swapping darkness for light, pessimism for hope, revenge, loathing and hatred for a life full of love. That was his mission, a promise he'd been elected on, one that at the time made him popular beyond his wildest dreams and expectations. But then what do you think happened? That's right... BLOODY MANSON! Or more precisely, his wickedly evil father, tricking them, or rather him, into going to Antarctica to meet them in a false promise, backed up by one of his own kind, an explorer who himself had been fooled along the way. And so started what had felt like a lifetime's worth of incarceration and subjugation for all his kind under threat of never seeing him alive again. He couldn't blame them... not really, it was his own stupid fault for getting hoodwinked, forced into becoming a pawn in a much larger game, one whose end goal was total world domination, not that he'd known it at the time. But it all came back to virtues, or lack of them and more likely debauchery, depravity, cruelness, wickedness, shamefulness and vicious amounts of hate for any number of reasons. These were things his kind were going to throw the shackles off, but before they'd had the chance with him at the helm leading the way, they were sucked back into a circle of violence, one that was never ending with no discernible way out. That is until the dragons under Flash's command had mounted THE most unorthodox of rescues, one that offered up just a chance of redemption and a smidgen of hope, until he'd found out the level, complexity and sheer brutality of what had been done to his race all in the name of getting him back in one piece eventually. That had been enough to crush his soul at the time, a deed so dirty and underhand that he'd never thought he'd seen the likes, until so many of them were murdered by Manson's almighty dark force of dragons after they'd been freed of their magical constraints by the master mantra maker and his spliced together spell. In one fell swoop so many of his kind had been murdered, decapitated or just downright marked for death. It was heartbreaking and a burden he carried with him every waking second of every single day. On sensing all those who'd arrived here, some five hundred or so, he could feel all the darkness that had crept in over the short period of time that had elapsed since they'd been freed and had retreated out of the way to somewhere considered to be one of their last natural homes. The olden times and everything dark that went with them had returned with a vengeance and were, as far as he could tell, determined to have their revenge on a being that had done so much harm to so many, an individual trapped here below the water with them, one whose matt blackness not only defined him, but the attitude of those towards him. Everything he'd vowed to put right so long ago was coming unravelled and would, if he wasn't careful, send what remained of their race spiralling towards its doom.

It had started as a question...

*"Why have we been summoned?"* But soon a realisation ripped through the open telepathic link like wildfire, some of the naga arrivals having survived the magical subjugation and fought for the wicked and malevolent would-be dragon ruler of this world, the huge matt black monster currently trapped amidst them all, before being freed and able to rejoin the rest of their kind. But here they were about to pronounce judgement on the being that had visited genocide on their race, all in the name of taking over the planet. There could of course only be one verdict and in that regard one punishment... GUILTY and DEATH!

Quickly reaching that conclusion, the five hundred or so very swiftly decided which of their vicious spells they would use to dispatch the cruel, homicidal villain into the next life. Choosing something entirely appropriate, an enchantment that would inflict as much pain as was nagaly possible, the combined might of the snake-like beings all in conjunction with one another closed their eyes and set about bringing forth the words that would elicit the supernatural consequences, ones leading to an agonising departure from this plane of existence for the being Manson that deserved nothing less.

Exhausted from the summons and everything else that had happened since first being called into action by his former fellow captive, Fredric, Vasuki, naga king and friend, mentor and astonishing ally, an instant too late realised exactly what was about to happen. In an extraordinary feat of defiance and stubbornness, he resolutely shook himself awake and commanded all those that had mustered to his summons.

*"NO!"* he ordered in a tone jam-packed full of authority and clout, his, the final say-so on the matter.

Five hundred simultaneous *"buts"* resounded through the mental connection. However he wasn't finished there.

Almost able to sense their weakness despite not understanding their language even though he'd had the opportunity to learn it on a number of occasions, but never having bothered. His only interest had been in subjugation and bending them to his will, making certain they did as he ordered, using only his tongue and that of the dragons and humans, kowtowing to all his demands, Manson willing once again to bet that he could spot the Achilles' heel of these pathetic nagas set about hatching a plan, one he hoped would turn the horde against their king for a moment or two, leaving him with a suitable distraction that could allow an escape.

Certain of the road he travelled, truly inspired by his beliefs, the vows he'd made so long ago and convinced of the virtue in those he represented, the very last thing Vasuki expected was any sort of backlash. Unfortunately that's what he got, in spades. Outrage undulated throughout the shared connection, desperate thoughts of revenge and retribution spilling out of individuals' minds, clouding all the uncertainty that abounded about the fate of the one who'd visited so much harm on them. They had him here NOW! Why on earth should they not do the world a favour and wipe him from its very existence?

The fever pitch of darkness and malevolence flooded through him. If he'd have been on the surface he'd have dropped to his knees and lost consciousness, but down here in the gloom of the freezing cold sea water, it was different. This was his home... all their homes. This was where they belonged, where they could recuperate, recover, rest and hopefully rebuild after the devastating events that had befallen them all, none more so than he. As five hundred individual, shouting voices screamed their animosity in his direction, his unconquerable will and well developed mind started to crumple under the irrepressible weight of popular opinion. Tapping into all of his heart and soul, he tried to hold on, he really did, but all that hadn't yet untangled was a thread so tenuous it resembled the finest spider silk. On the edge of becoming unravelled, Vasuki became drowned out by the cacophony of irate voices all directed at him.

Physically pushing away the glee that threatened to escape and show itself off across his gigantic primordial, matt black face, Manson gave it a quick slap, immediately forcing it back from whence it came, outwardly determined to remain stoic and resigned until the one opportunity he knew would present itself arose. And it appeared as though the start of something that might well bloom into exactly that, was playing out right at this very moment. Eager to take advantage of the chaos and mayhem, hoping it would somehow lead him back to the surface and away from this potential watery grave, very subtly the mischievous murderer started using his shadowy, underhand magic to very gently probe the minds of all those present, sure that none were capable of detecting what he was doing, hoping to gain some sort of influence when the time came.

It hit him like the wakeup call from hell, the harshest alarm in the world ringing around the confines of his mind, startling him out of his resigned stupor, putting him on full alert, the recognisable foul reek of those under his command once again being defiled. He'd recognise it anywhere and would lay down his life to stamp it out in an instant. What monarch wouldn't?

Preying on the weak, innocent and vulnerable was despicable at best, shameful, loathsome and vile at worst, quite possibly the sickest and most contemptible of acts. And that's what was going on under the noses of most there right this second, without any of them even knowing, apart from their king who just wouldn't stand for it. But it did present a quandary of sorts because what he was trying to avoid was the entire party of five hundred all lashing out and murdering the monster in cold blood, figuring that might be the catalyst to send them as a race back towards the dark old times, a fate he wanted to avoid at all costs, not for him you understand, but for those few of their kind who remained, so that repopulating could became a real possibility. Contemplating all this in less than a blink of an eye, an answer, one that solved all his problems, presented itself so long as he could persuade those who'd answered the call to follow his lead. Gills pumping furiously with swishing white water now he'd been shocked out of his daze, he gathered up all his regality and tore open the mental link through which they all continued to yell.

*"OBEY MY COMMAND!"* he asserted applying all the supernatural at his disposal to the words.

SILENCE!

*"DO IT... THIS INSTANT!"*


Magic spread as thin as it could possibly go, well... it would be wouldn't it with five hundred of them to penetrate, using everything he had, Manson continued with the miniscule dark supernatural tendrils he was using to invade all the newcomers' minds, sure that in a moment or two he would have infiltrated their consciousnesses to the point where he could act and kill a great many of them, hopefully enabling him to slope off in all the elicited confusion. Time ticking down, he knew that it was any second... NOW!

In that instant he acted as only HE, the would-be destroyer of worlds, could, unleashing devastating murderous mayhem on the entire group of nagas, no compunction about killing hundreds in but a moment just to serve his underhand purposes. Unfortunately, he hadn't counted on their king.

Not wanting all of them to feel the unashamed festering guilt that accompanied murdering yet another being, no matter how well deserved, Vasuki, extraordinary leader that he was, decided in the moment to take the choice out of their hands, very much hoping that would be enough and that their consciences could at some point be wiped clean. What command had he insisted they obey? One ancient in design and learnt by the very youngest of their kind.

Up until his unfortunate capture derived from treachery of the highest order by the wicked monster they now had surrounded all that time ago, schooling of their youngsters mirrored that of their dragon counterparts, taking place across the globe usually in far off, out of the way caves or grottos, locations that even the hardiest of human adventurers would struggle to accidentally stumble across. Magic was a mainstay, the teaching of which was instigated after only a couple of years. One of the very first enchantments that both male and female youngsters learnt was a deflection spell, one that if used correctly could be wrapped around their minds, stopping almost anyone or anything from accessing or corrupting it in any, way, shape or form, sending the attack back towards the aggressor. In its own way it was hugely powerful despite requiring little in the way of resources and because learnt at such a young age, became instinctive throughout a youngster's developing lifetime, defending themselves against opponents in that manner without even realising it. It was like human adolescents learning a hymn or a prayer, so deep-rooted that even decades later it would still be there if required. That's what he'd asked of them all, and that, to a male and a female, was what they'd responded with, a defence, pure and simple... nothing else!

Letting loose with everything he had, it was the last act of Manson's long and traumatic life, his vicious, powerful magic reflected back at him at over five hundred times the strength, his dark and deceitful consciousness torn apart without him even knowing, his huge, almighty, lifeless, matt black dragon body drifting into a spiral almost as if lazily floating amongst the clouds up above, slowing corkscrewing towards the ocean floor before in one sudden furore, its entirety exploding from the extreme pressures the ocean presented due to its all but disappeared magical defences. The greatest threat that the world had known in quite some time had been gobbled up by the gods of the sea, watched by over five hundred attentive nagas and one relief filled dragon.

For the second time in quick succession the world managed to take a breath, the danger passed. But Death, scythe over his shoulder, still stood shrouded on the horizon.

# 44 DIRE, DIRE, PANTS ON FIRE

Her normal impenetrable purple shield a busted flush, Earth continued bounding, cartwheeling and somersaulting at speed across the main threshold of the vault, just where the terracotta landscape started, swearing loudly as she did so in three different languages, human, dragon and naga, the worst curse words she knew drowned out by the constant

TWANG of arrows and the harsh CRACK of gunfire.

She was barely able to believe she'd gone from having control over absolutely everything to bouncing about the place in an effort to remain in one piece and even that had been hairier than a middle aged man's nose, ears and back. She'd been grazed on the neck and shoulder by two arrows speeding faster than the eye could see zinging her way from what she had to assume was some sort of accomplished magic user given that nobody else on the planet, even her father, had come close to inflicting those kind of wounds with something so basic. Of course what she didn't know was that the bow firing the arrows was beyond special, a magically enhanced weapon used by one of the most renowned figures in all human history and one that was not only a dragon at heart, but an actual dragon himself... ROBIN HOOD! But that was only half of it because on the other end, utilising the supernatural imbued within, was a magic user of epic proportions and one nearly every human and dragon on the planet would be familiar with. I do of course mean Polkinghorne, or rather the Christmas legend that is SANTA CLAUS.

Not quite at her all time best, still depleted somewhat in magical terms, she'd recovered enough to extend her magic out and around most of the powerful artefacts within the vault that looked as though if touched by any of Earth's uncontrollable violence, could explode on contact bringing half of London down on itself, in essence vastly lowering that risk. That aside, Polks had applied a morsel of her inherent abilities to link up with the longbow, and in conjunction with her natural skills was able to rattle off a shot every couple of seconds, and not just an ordinary one at that... oh no. One that had the arrows homing in on her target, something Peter's mother was finding out to her detriment, having to use all her treachery and deceit to stay one step ahead of being skewered like a stuffed pig at a hog roast.

So far she'd used every trick in the book, conjuring up supernatural gusts of wind that had slammed the projectiles into the wall and floor at the very last second, creating time dilation fields right in front of her face that continually allowed her to pluck the frozen arrows out of the air and snap them with the pure physical strength that would normally be part of her formidable arsenal. On top of that, sizzling streams of superheated fire had vaporised wooden shafts and tail feathers causing deadly, enchanted, white hot metal tips to CLANG to the stone floor in a hail of pointed purgatory. But she was running out of ruses, constantly having to fall back on last moment dodges and unorthodox limbo-like feats of inexplicable flexibility that even she didn't know she was capable of. And that was all in between sidestepping the bullets her runt of a son's female partner continually blasted in her direction from what looked to be a rather ancient rifle, one that was more suited to being hung on a wall in an out of the way antiques store in a desert town surrounded by tumble weed. What the hell was all that about?

And her son's part in all this? As far as she could tell the snivelling Bentwhistle, yellow bellied, piss poor excuse for a dragon had reverted to some lost, alone, tearful and afraid human facsimile that appeared to want to be anywhere but here, once again shying away from a fight, leaving others to defend those he loved. A more disgraceful example of a living being it was hard to imagine, at least in his mother's eyes.

Rolling once, twice, three times out of the way of arrows clanging against the floor all around her, she leapt to her feet, focusing all her energy, leaning slightly forward, picking up speed, sprinting straight towards the nearest terracotta wall, her intent clear, unbeknown to the projectiles in her wake, her pounding footsteps echoing through the air. Mustering all the remaining strength in her legs, muscles tightening with each powerful stride, putting on a brief burst of momentum and feeling something tickling the air just behind the centre of her back, Peter's wicked mother bounded for all she was worth, her body soaring upwards towards the immovable dirt coloured barrier in her way. For a brief moment she appeared suspended, defying gravity's pull. Fingers splayed wide, instinctively her outstretched hands reached for the wall, looking for any surface to latch on to. Momentarily her palms connected, sending agonising vibrations up her fingers and throughout her arms, the pain instigating a surge of determination from her indomitable will that had got her this far. Contracting her core muscles, with an agile twist she propelled herself up and away from the wall. In that instant, she tucked her legs into her chest forming the most aerodynamic shape possible. A sense of weightlessness enveloped her as she executed a full rotation, the most graceful of somersaults. In one fluid motion Earth's body uncurled and in an astonishing display of agility, she twisted her torso and extended her legs, tracing a reverse arc through the air. Gravity once again took hold, dictating her descent back towards the floor, her legs and feet reaching out for the stability and balance that touching the surface beneath her would provide. Absorbing the impact, her nimble landing resembled that of a world class gymnast, her body quickly adjusting to the change in direction and momentum. As yet more arrows clattered against the wall, a tiny voice inside her celebrated the heroic display of athleticism and spatial awareness, having performed the most daring of manoeuvres amongst the mayhem and chaos of the fight for her life in which she'd firmly pushed the limitations of physics to their max.

Physically, magically and mentally Earth was slowly becoming fatigued, her thoughts focusing on how many arrows the mysterious well honed archer had left and what would happen after she (yes... even from here through all the turmoil, against the deafening explosions, the thick, matted long blonde locks of her current nemesis stood out, a lookalike of the human girl who'd fully attached herself to her offspring) had run dry. Would the attacker resort to using her supernatural and if that was the case, why hadn't she done so up until now? Question after question jangled around her brain, the main ones including how to extricate herself from her current predicament and just how things could get any worse.

The timing of the last one could prove to be a killer!


In the ultimate display of human and dragon physicality and all conquering strength of character, Fredric and The White Dragon, the superstar lacrosse player Richie Rump battled for supremacy in their sprint to the finish line, or in this case, to reach the former master mantra maker's vault in an effort to save those they loved, in no particular order... Peter, Janice and of course Santa herself who'd so selflessly decided to accompany the pair of soulmates in a perilous escapade that would see them trapped and at the mercy of the psychopathic would-be queen. With the futuristic blade containing the renowned weapon smith's soul, Fu-ts'ang, now bringing up the rear, defending both from what remained of the vault's supernatural defences, all three presented just a vague impression, rolling mist in a storm, too fast to focus on, an indistinct smear... that's how quickly they were travelling in an effort to outrun two of the three what we now know to be Providences, Time and Fate.

At the rate they were moving the vault was coming up fast and so both individuals presenting as human but each actually very different dragons slammed on the brakes, skidding to a halt where former lush green grass, now burnt to a crisp met a decisive, shiny stone floor, twenty metres in front of the sharp rocky bend they'd been warned about by Zarenkesia, the Mantra Emporium's spectral guardian. Sure that they'd arrived at their destination, not only from the directions passed on but from the barrage of sound and the superlative, music festival light show reflecting off the stony meander up ahead, Peter's grandfather shared a sideways look with the pale skinned, curly haired woman that had gone so far to bring them back from the brink of annihilation and total assimilation by Manson and his dark forces. Ready to make the ultimate sacrifice to save those they loved, both warriors, one the founder of the Crimson Guards, the other the myth from the prophecy that had been predicted millennia before, ignited their personal supernatural shields and tore off towards the bend in the passageway, not quite at the same speed as before. As rescues went, this one was right up there with the unsuspecting human sports players stumbling into the domain, encountering Gee Tee, before going on to save Tank and Flash from an agonising death. Whether the same positive outcome was possible remained to be seen.

Ducking, diving, bobbing, weaving, jumping, running up walls, bounding behind plinths, throwing everything supernatural she had at defending herself from the bullets and arrows desperate to take her life being flung at her by the bucket load, the murderous mistress Earth continued to tread the tightrope of oblivion, staring into the void as she did so, acting and reacting on instinct, fuelled by adrenaline or what passed for it when dragons disguised themselves as humans, on the cusp of having her resistance broken, no chance at all of going back on the attack.

Using all her innate abilities to move as fast as she had been, concentrating perhaps like never before, Polkinghorne, in a flurry of movement, having fired off arrow after arrow all with the intention of taking down

Manson's queen and Peter's witch of a mother, once again reached into the last of the four quivers for another arrow, desperate to continue the volley of projectiles and keep the mistress of evil ever occupied and on the run. Crestfallen could barely describe the emotions running through her on discovering what she held in her hand was the final one. Nocking the arrow, she glanced down the sights, locked onto the fast moving blur that was her target and wishing with all her heart to end this now, let go of the hemp, a satisfying TWANG ringing in her ears. The shot itself was nothing short of awesome, Santa taking into account her prey's movement, anticipating her every last action. Unfortunately a last moment flick of the finger from Fredric's unhinged daughter saw some powerful magnetic madness redirect the head, slicing the tip off one finger of the deranged dragon's left hand instead of piercing her eye and destroying her brain as intended, leaving Polkinghorne standing holding the longbow, looking and feeling bereft of ideas.

As Janice stopped to reload the Kid's rifle the noise and bedlam calmed down. As you might expect, Earth took a moment to consider the situation, a sickening grin crossing her grisly face.

'So,' she thought, positively reeling with satisfaction, 'you're out of arrows and your partner there is struggling to reload her ancient gun.'

Knowing exactly what to do and now mad beyond belief at having had to expend so much energy and magic just to stay one step ahead of being cut down by two filthy females, one clearly an extraordinarily capable magic user, the other nothing more than one of the dragons' grubby little pets. Closing her eyes, stretching out her arms to the side, allowing the anger to flow throughout every synapse of her brain, the strength, fury and power bubbling up from the usual far flung place inside her, Earth, cackling like the insane psychopath she'd long since become, focused all her ire and readied herself to act, knowing it would all be over in a moment. Engorged, about to be fully sated and overflowing with the worst kind of supernatural ever to have existed, what happened next was not only a surprise to her, but to the three targets she'd so carefully set her sights on killing.

About to unleash hellish, dark, destructive, murderous magic in the direction of the unknown assailant that had been so able in tracking her movements with the arrows, nicking her flesh in over a dozen places across the course of a couple of minutes, knowing that she had to be taken out first, abruptly her sense of danger exploded out across her mind, screaming the mother of all warnings, causing her to rein in all her supernatural and in one swift move, turn to face in the opposite direction. It was a good job she did because those actions most certainly saved her life.

One nightmare metamorphosed into relief and the possibility of prevailing whilst another resolved in the form of the very last three individuals she was either expecting or had hoped to see ever again. In the blink of an eye, assured victory had been traded for devastating defeat and an agonising death. Earth's day had just gone from bad to catastrophic.

Standing tall like a not so bronzed Adonis, long straggly mane twisting down past his shoulders, the occasional tresses rubbing against the top of his superbly crafted chest, the muscles of which had been diligently honed to within an inch of their life, Fate, had dictated that it would be Fredric standing there at the front of the queue, ready, willing and more than able to put his misbegotten assassin of a daughter out of her misery in this cul de sac of treasure, one that would fittingly act as her tomb.

Next to him, her thick mop of curly brown hair not having anywhere near the same length as her sidekick (at least that's how she viewed him) but looking at least as formidable was The White Dragon herself, prophecy fulfiller, superstar lacrosse player, warrior queen, friend, confidant and... in the future, should one exist, something much, much more than all of that combined.

As if that wasn't a terrifying enough sight in itself, behind both beings a third in the guise of the most fantastic, fabulous, fatal and outlandish weapon hovered into view, its mesmerising, ever-moving coating of delectable frost missing from around the entire length of its shiny blade, after previously having gone one round with Earth as she passed through the Emporium. Fu-ts'ang, sights set on the wicked she-witch that had killed so many and destroyed so much raised his tip in her direction, ready to attack at a moment's notice despite having already been warned off by the founder of the Crimson Guards, her father and life giver.

Trapped smack bang in the middle of six individuals all of whom wanted her dead, Earth had some timely decisions to make, not so much about how she was going to escape with her life, but how many of them she could take with her on her journey to hell. Let the games begin!

## 45 FATAL FAMILY FINALE

"Daughter…" Fredric ventured, exceptionally calmly under the circumstances and given their recent history, and what I mean by that is each trying to kill the other on a number of different occasions.

"Are you hoping that I'll respond in kind, that you'll build some rapport and then from there you can go on and redeem me? Fat chance, you sick old man!"

That might have been his goal at some point in the not too distant past, but not today, not here, not now. Too much had passed between them both, and that was before her role in all the deaths and wilfully trying to destroy the entire planet. Beyond genocide, there wasn't even a word to describe exactly what the terror twins had contemplated and attempted to carry out. THE ENTIRE PLANET for God's sake!

NO! There was no redemption, no deliverance from evil after what she'd become. No return to the family she'd deserted without a moment's thought. One way or another Fredric knew, matters would be settled over the next few minutes. And after much soul searching during the time since their last encounter on the cliff top on the outskirts of Portknockie, he'd come to the only conclusion available. That he was, and always had been, ready to trade his life to save that of his grandson Peter. If that's what was needed to end this, then that's what he'd do without hesitation or regret. She'd been his responsibility since birth and so it was about time he stepped up in that regard and remove one of the two biggest threats to the world's very existence.

Too terrified to even have got off a single round with the Kid's pistol, Peter's heart leapt at seeing the three new arrivals glide to a halt at the threshold of the vault, knowing now that everything would be alright and that all their futures were assured, his fate inexplicably linked to all those present... his best friend Richie, Fredric his grandfather, Janice, the being he loved most in the world and his forever soulmate, Polkinghorne with whom he shared an unconditional friendship and even Fu-ts'ang, an ally and friend. But what was absent? Or rather should I say who? The missing member of the trio, the kind and caring dragon Tank, who'd always been there for him, the friend he most definitely shared an unbreakable bond with, something that had become overcomplicated and more than a little eerie when Janice had nicked her finger allowing a droplet of blood to fall on the blank diary, back at the Emporium. A book as it turned out that belonged to none other than Artorius the Seer, author of dragonkind's most famous prophecy. The particular titbit revealed by the tenuous drop of blood was astonishing: either Tank or Peter had been marked for death. Supposedly it was impossible for them both to survive past the final act of the harrowing play they'd all been living through. Peter's assumption that all their futures were assured appeared premature to say the least.

'Thank God!' Janice thought only to herself on seeing the new arrivals storm the castle.

Absolutely delighted that reinforcements had arrived in the form of the trio, (although the sight of Fredric still, understandably, made her a little nervous) just seeing her new best friend, the superstar lacrosse player and The White Dragon herself looking as formidable as ever, buoyed her spirits. That was even before the other being she loved like a brother hovered into view, a millennia old, former dragon weapon smith with whom she shared a unique bond. The stunningly futuristic blade without his normally harsh coating of pure white frost decided to nibble at her consciousness.

"*Fu-ts'ang!*"

"*Of course youngster, who else?*"

"*I'm so glad you're here. Polks has just run out of arrows and Peter, well... let's just say he's not really been himself.*"

*"But you've managed to prevail up until now. Good job! We're here now so keep your head down and stay out of the way. Goodness knows how much magic will be flying around during her last stand. Take cover. I'll let you know when it's safe to come out. Understood?"*

*"Understood! Give her hell!"*

*"I intend to send her directly there without further ado!"*

Then the natural silence between them returned.

As relieved as the others at the reinforcements standing at the entrance, Polkinghorne had but one thought before things well and truly kicked off, which was to continue to reinforce all of the epically powered supernatural artefacts within the vault, deciding to redouble her efforts knowing that if any wayward magic came into contact with the objects themselves, the consequences would be dire. Sliding back behind the plinth, her pert little bottom gently hitting the floor, Santa closed her eyes and allowed her inherent abilities to flow.

Throughout the buried, dead end catacomb, some of the more prominent relics took on a much brighter and stronger shade of eerie blue, all but one in fact, the gnarled and knotted staff that had belonged to a certain wizard from King Arthur's court.

Standing proudly one step behind Fredric, the superstar lacrosse player, The White Dragon herself, Richie Rump felt... INVINCIBLE! Physically strong, brimming with magic, mentally sound, although still disappointed to some degree at having let Manson escape when she'd had him on the ropes atop the cliff back at Portknockie, absolutely certain that she'd punched the living daylights out of him and that he'd died straddled beneath her on the cool grassy ground. Seeing him somehow recovered and swimming towards that blasted nuclear submarine had sent a shiver down her spine, knowing what he was capable of with such a weapon, and if she could have, she'd have gone after him in a heartbeat. Unfortunately that option was taken out of her hands by the simple fact that she was unable to revert to her natural dragon form, a supernatural side effect from the laminium bomb planted at the Salisbridge sports club by the evil fiend, Manson himself. How ironic… not being able to give chase to the murderous monster because of his previous wicked actions, ones that were meant to kill tens of thousands, fortunately thwarted by both her best friends, one of whom she looked straight across at right now. Unusually for her at least, Richie felt a little bit of shame staring across the vault at the young dragon who'd been there when she'd hatched on that day in the darkness all those decades ago. Why shame? Because Peter had suspected the inherently malicious Manson's evil intentions some time ago, voicing his concerns to her on a number of occasions. If she'd believed him at the time, then maybe all the bloodshed and violence that had cost many thousands of dragons and humans their lives could have been avoided. For that she was deeply sorry, quite a new experience for the normally overconfident lacrosse captain, something she was only just starting to get to grips with. That was only compounded by seeing the very real pain now etched into Peter's face, no doubt caused by his malevolent mother's malicious acts of magical mischief, the remnants of which could be tasted in the air of the vault itself. It positively stank of spent supernatural.

Glancing away from her sorry looking friend for whom she had a great deal of sympathy and pity, The White Dragon turned towards the blonde haired human who'd so bizarrely, given their original feelings for one another, become her best friend. Talk about judging a book by its cover. Never before had she been so wrong about anything in her entire life. The exceptional human, mild mannered Janice had proved herself not only a capable warrior, far outstripping any originating from the domain, but had gone on to show glimpses of a dragon heart beneath that pale, delicate outer shell that belied who or what she really was. Following her down into the domain in the first place was no mean feat, and should have at the time provided an insight into the girl... no, make that woman, herself. But her actions over the course of the impending crisis, from proving integral to saving Flash and Tank back at the Salisbridge market place under the guidance of the master mantra maker, Gee Tee, to her heroics in conjunction with the sentient blade, Fu-ts'ang with whom she'd formed some kind of symbiotic relationship, at the king's private residence had given all of those around her a peek into her very soul. Only now could Richie understand the young woman for who she really was, having witnessed her selfless bravery and courage first hand on any number of occasions. For a dragon to have achieved any of the feats Janice had would most certainly have earned them a place in the history books, but a human... wow, that was another level of legendary altogether. Songs would be sung, books written, her name spray painted across slums in all quarters of the world for everything that she'd achieved, and all I might add in the name of love.

Speaking of renowned and well regarded characters... out of the corner of her eye, the lacrosse captain just managed to see a familiar mop of bedraggled, but otherwise beautiful, instantly recognisable, blonde hair disappear behind the pedestal just along from Janice, a friend indeed and one who'd delicately altered the course of her very own existence, without whom her own path through this treacherous drudgery called life would be very different. Why? For one simple reason... a Christmas present from long in the past, had altered the course of her very nature for the better. I would hope it would be obvious by now, but if you don't know, then I'm sure you can take a guess. It has to, of course be her very first, prized lacrosse stick, one that so far had led her down a route that encompassed action, adventure, friendship, team spirit, bonding, the will to win, the desire to do what was right and to never, ever give up... all traits that had unknowingly led her to fulfil her destiny and become The White Dragon, the prophesied saviour from many thousands of years ago. How strange that the one simple action of gifting a lacrosse stick could lead to something so epically awesome!

'Did she know?' Richie wondered in that moment. 'Did Polkinghorne know that's what she was supposed to do to play her part in the famous foretelling or was it a complete fluke, one randomised by Fate herself?' If they got out of this in one piece, the lacrosse player vowed to ask the once a year Christmas fable exactly that.


Flustered, perhaps like never before and she'd been through some ****, the spiteful and mean dragon that was Peter's mother and Fredric's daughter cursed the bad luck that had once again found her like a sniffer dog discovering drugs at an airport.

It just simply wasn't possible, she kept telling herself over and over.

But it was. Again her bastard of a father had turned up at precisely the wrong moment, for her at least, costing her the advantage that she was about to capitalise on, killing all three of the vault's current incumbents. To be thwarted at the very last second was aggravating beyond belief, compounded by the fact that the world hadn't been set alight yet by the being that over time she'd grown to love, the one she would have willingly sat beside and called king. Supposedly he'd assured her that taking apart the planet was a done deal, all but signed off on, but so far she'd seen no mark of it happening, none of her supernatural senses picking up anything out of the ordinary, something she assumed they would, should such an event come to pass. Once again he'd gone and let her down in the most disappointing of ways. If the world was on its way to imploding then she could have stood there righteously lording it over them. As it was, her enemies appeared to not only outnumber and outgun her from a magical perspective, but they also appeared what she could only describe as... SMUG!

'Well,' she thought, 'it's about time I wiped that grin of

all your faces.'

Without any further ado, her madness soaked mind absorbed all the repugnant anger running through every molecule of her body and channelled it into one vicious, outright outburst, concentrating her disgusting naga magic towards the one being whose death would devastate them all, except for her of course... BENTWHISTLE!

Abruptly the silent melancholy of the shiny white surroundings was interrupted by a cacophony of ruthless, penetrating sound, startling all three friends, each of whom had been lost deep within their own thoughts. In a manic moment of madness the cardiac monitor's displays had all turned red, a sure sign that the patient it had been hooked up to had flatlined. Likewise the indicators of the intracranial pressure monitors had shown up as critical, both machines responsible for the piercing electric sounds which were now drowned out by more human varieties.

"GET OUT OF THE WAY... NOW!" ordered one of the nurses sprinting into the ward at enhanced supernatural speed, scaring the living daylights out of the trio.

Immediately they did just that, Steel and DomCon dragging their impromptu leader and the three chairs out of the way, much further into the depths of the pristine white palace of a place, as yet more staff appeared at quite some rate, all surrounding Tank's bed where only a moment or two before the three of them had sat patiently.

"What's happening?" Doctor Tomlinson demanded, sliding to a halt on the shiny white floor beside the nurse first on the scene.

"He's gone into cardiac arrest," she replied ominously.

"Do you want the defibrillator?" asked one of the other white coated professionals from the other side of the bed.

A pause to think ensued, because this was unlike anything they'd ever dealt with... a dragon stuck in human form suffering from traumatic brain injuries of an unknown supernatural origin. All they had was a defibrillator for one of their own race in its natural form. What the hell would that do to him?

"DOC?" Jar Man ventured from well back, knowing that the medical professional had quite a lot on his plate but still wanting to know what he was thinking.

"His heart's stopped. At a guess and that's all it is, I'd say from the injuries he's already sustained. The only thing we have now is a defibrillator that we'd normally use to treat one of us in our prehistoric guise. Using that in this instance might well kill him outright."

"What about magic?" Steel ventured.

"Given everything he's been through, there's nothing I can think of that'll work. We removed every last ounce of whatever unnatural magical architecture was lodged inside his brain. There was simply nothing left and what remained at least appeared undamaged. I'm... at a loss."

"Use the defibrillator!" Steel ordered, the laminium ball captain in him shining through.

"Are you mad?!" DomCon exclaimed.

"I'd rather he died with the good folks here giving their all and using everything at their disposal than explain to Zarenkesia and For'son that we held back and could have done more," Steel remarked forcefully. "Doctor... DO IT! I'll take full responsibility."

Shaking his head, still in about three minds as to what to do, the good doctor made up his.

"Nurse... get the defibrillator."

"Doc..."

"NOW!"

Turning on her heels, she scuttled off at super speed, quickly returning with the giant yellow apparatus, bigger than the largest human backpack jammed to the rafters with hiking supplies.

Working efficiently as a team, one of the medical staff quickly turned the unit on and pulled back the sheets to expose Tank's naked chest. One by one Doctor Tomlinson ripped the plastic backing off the electrode pads and firmly pressed the sticky side of each onto the young rugby playing dragon's exposed torso, one on the upper right side just below the collar bone, the other on the left, slightly below his nipple. After that he plugged each of the leads from the electrodes into the appropriate ports of the defibrillator making sure each was firmly connected and seated. With that done, there was only one thing left to do.

"CLEAR!" Doctor Tomlinson yelled.

The staff all moved back from the bed as the trio of friends watched from a distance. Rather reluctantly the doctor pressed the shock button on the defibrillator designed to jolt a dragon in its natural form back to life. Unsurprisingly, the result was rather epic even on the lowest setting.

Tank's well muscled, man mountain of a human body arced up into the air, the only contact points remaining with the bed his heels and fingertips, fizzing forks of brilliant blue and white electrical energy surging across his motionless form, every single hair on his body disintegrating instantly, tiny plumes of wispy acrid smoke rising towards the ward's ceiling.

# BUMPFFFF!!!

His body crashed back down to the bed with a bump, the giant, plump pillow taking the brunt of the fall, preventing any more damage to his already fragile cranium.

NOTHING!

"AGAIN!" ordered the doctor. "CLEAR!"

The exact same thing happened again... and again, and again. Still the displays of both monitors remained in the red, the alarms still blaring for all they were worth, none of the staff thinking to turn them off. Four times in all before the crestfallen doctor flicked the switch on the defibrillator to off and turned to face the grief stricken friends, all of whose faces had turned ashen on witnessing how events had played out.

"I'm so sorry," he said shaking his head in disbelief, "I'm afraid there's nothing else we can do."

Utterly bereft and heartbroken, as one the trio of friends dropped to their knees and let out the mother of all cries.

# "NOoooooooooooooooooooo..."

Manson's latest victim and one of earth's mightiest heroes had left this mortal coil on his way to 'the gloom' to join his mentor and friend.

Against the background of pungent, bitter smelling smoke, Tank's well honed, human shaped rugby playing body lay unmoving and finally at rest. Artorius' prophecy, it would seem, had been fulfilled at long last.

From the moment they'd glided to a halt she'd been ready, the words at the forefront of her mind, the indomitable will that had served her so well ever since she'd hatched was a split second away from kicking into action, targets selected, her friends having already been warned off the offensive spells you might have expected her to lead with. As the very first hint of magic filled the air, Richie Rump leapt into action, producing the most powerful shields in her arsenal around Peter, Janice and Polkinghorne simultaneously, their protection her highest priority.

Across the preceding moments logic and sanity had battled through Earth's madness, attempting to come up with a plan of action, one that would satisfy her base desires and achieve the outcome she so very wished for. With the planet still disappointingly in one piece, one thought above all others stood out across her devious and cunning mind, everyone's worst nightmare, the murderous monstrosity that had visited so much harm on so many.

'How can I hurt them the most?' It was clear there was only one way to do such a thing... to kill her son in front of all of them. With that in mind, and forsaking all thoughts of living to prevail another time, the wicked she witch unleashed everything she had, directing it all towards Peter.

Thinly veiled translucent supernatural shields sprang into life around the three beings within the deepest confines of the vault, The White Dragon using all her focus and concentration to produce the most powerful versions of each, determined to protect her friends at any cost.

Splintered forks of crackling purple tinged, pink edged lightning flickered forward from every single one of her fingers all of them directed towards her son, the cowardly Bentwhistle, who hadn't lifted a finger to defend either himself or any of his friends since she'd been there, Earth's entire body still facing the recently arrived reinforcements.

Using all his physicality, enhanced by the magic of his birthright, Fredric was on her in an instant, crossing the distance between them in the blink of an eye, one almighty fist already pulled back, spring-loaded on the end of an arm reminiscent of Sylvester Stallone in his prime, the Rocky punch ready to be let loose.

Sensing him more than seeing, Peter's mother backflipped twice, the luminescent lightning ceasing momentarily as she did so, narrowly avoiding a blow that would well and truly have downed her forever.

Cursing his daughter's luck and he supposed, skill, Fredric, by now full of rage and venom at what she was trying to do to her son and his grandson, went full berserk, allowing the restraints buried deep within his false form to dissipate, the anger now matched with a seemingly unlimited amount of magic, the taste of which wanted revenge for all she'd done and closure on that part of his life. In a whirling blur of sparkling blue electricity, he bounded after her, determined to wrap his huge hands around her tiny neck and throttle the life out of her.

Only too aware of what he'd been told by the founder of the Crimson Guards and one of the two he'd just travelled through a typically eerie hell to get here with, Fu-ts'ang, concerned for all three of his friends trapped in the very same prison he'd been confined in for decades, made a split second decision, the only one he could make. Tilting his hilt upwards so his entire length was horizontally parallel to the ground, he shot forward faster than the eye could see, desperate to get to his best friend's side, forging the most direct route to her, cutting the molecules of the air apart as he did so. Fortunately, the mischievous mistress of mayhem had just cartwheeled directly into his path. Ignoring the instructions that had been positively hammered into him by Fredric, and without deviating course, sure that if she just happened to be in his way then all bets were off, he surged forward straight towards the sickeningly purple lines that crisscrossed her foul and revolting face, certain he was about to end things once and for all, his blade perfectly willing and able to pierce from one side of her head to the other.

Her intrinsic magic born of many decades of experience caused her to abruptly lean forward mid-jump, tuck herself in and roll off to one side, slamming unbelievably hard into the cold, terracotta surface, her elbow taking the brunt, shattering into a dozen different pieces. The agony from that was put completely into perspective by an exquisite pain emanating from the right side of her neck, her carotid artery severed in an instant, brilliant bright false red blood having sprayed down her arm and onto her legs. In an absolute panic Earth applied more of her ethereal energy than she could really spare, flooding the site of the wound ten times over, her mind briefly a little woozy from the loss of blood.

'That ****ing blade!' she cursed in her mind, rolling sideways half a dozen times in quick succession, avoiding spectacular strikes of brilliant blue electrical energy that left deep black marks scorched into the orangey, mud coloured rock. Bounding to her feet, remaining constantly on the move so as not to become an easy target, Earth sucked up a great deal of the mana within and with just five naga words, unleashed a devastating concentric ring of peculiar black energy, exploding out from her waist, cutting through everything it came into contact with.

Losing herself in a hundred thousandths of a second, Richie recognised what was coming, well... not what exactly, but knew it was something outrageously harmful. In a moment of clarity, she commanded the almost invisible shields around her friends to the floor, the mixture of magic and her inexplicable will pinning them down to the terracotta rock. That one deed saved their lives, the circular naga spell carving through anything at waist height in its way, including most of the plinths, destroying amulets, bracelets, one off mantras and any number of more run of the mill weapons and armour stored there. Through sheer luck Merlin's staff avoided contact with the decidedly wicked naga based enchantment, a singular rusting armour breast plate taking the brunt, exploding on contact, showering the vault with fragments of molten metal. Richie and Fredric simultaneously invoked the same defence, leaping up and over the dark magic of the supernatural concussion wave, whilst Fu-ts'ang shot skyward before swiftly doubling over on himself and shooting back down to the ground, drawing to a halt beside his best friend who was pressed to the ground... JANICE!

*"Uhhhh... get it to stop will you?"* the human youngster urged, barely able to breathe, not realising that her life had just been saved.

*"I think you're pressing them rather too firmly into the deck,"* the futuristic blade berated The White Dragon through their shared connection.

'Oops,' Richie thought, ever so slightly releasing the grip her will had on all three of them.

Each was able to breathe a sigh of relief and inhale a full lungful of air with the pressure released from their backs.

Despite the shock of being thrown unceremoniously to the ground, Polkinghorne had managed to keep her defences up and around all the artefacts she knew were too powerful to come into contact with Earth's shadowy supernatural spells, for the moment at least keeping this part of the country's capital intact. How long that would last though, who knew?

The waking dream that had been Peter's existence for as long as he could remember kept getting worse, as he stumbled to his feet, glad to sense the strength and subtlety of the barrier that had been erected around him, still there. Wondering if there was truly any way to stop the wanton recklessness that his mother so casually tossed around the crypt they now all found themselves confined in, too scared to speak or act in any responsible manner, he ducked back down behind what was now half a pedestal and clutching his head in his hands, glanced briefly across at his soulmate to see how she was faring. Better than him, that's for sure, Fu-ts'ang now hovering by her side, batting away stray darts of wayward magic, the translucent shield around her just visible against the backdrop of colourful, exploding supernatural that was everywhere. It was akin to being trapped inside a chemical factory that had just been torched by a group of unruly teenagers.

In an effort to get his hands on his wayward daughter, Fredric jumped from podium to podium, bounded up walls and skidded across floors, a desperate game of cat and mouse taking place against the backdrop of the supernatural light show from hell, one that could very well cost him his life. Still he persevered, gaining ground inch by inch, using that as a measurement of his success, knowing it was inevitable that he would catch her at some point in the very near future.

'This is not how it was supposed to be,' Earth reflected, narrowly ducking out of the way of a line of bright red bolts elicited from Fredric's incredibly large palm, each of which slammed into the wall behind where her head had just been, sending shrapnel in the form of orange coloured stone exploding out in every different direction. Even on the run and using all the tricks from a lifetime's worth of experience to avoid being enveloped by any of the magic thrown at her, she still cast her evil enchantments in the direction of her cowardly son, hoping to put him and his comrades out of their misery once and for all, certain that should be her very last act.

Crazy might have been an apt description of what was going on, with so much supernatural zinging about in such a relatively small space. It was chaos on an epic scale, some of the world's most legendary magic users going at it hammer and tongs hoping to put this to bed once and for all. Of course no one there had even the faintest inkling that the threat of breaking up the planet from the missile fired by the submarine off the coast of Scotland had been negated or that Tank's body had given up the ghost after the battle with Mas-crate at the site of the Emporium. If they'd known, maybe anger would have gotten the better of them, especially Richie Rump who was renowned for throwing caution to the wind and being ruled by her fierce and incredible temper. But at the moment they were holding back, seemingly letting Fredric do his thing and rein in the daughter responsible for so much slaughter.

Only just coming to the conclusion that she was fighting a losing battle and that her plan of murdering her slow witted and spineless son was a bust, Earth, as was her wont, started contemplating a very different course of action.

'If not him... then who?' she mused.

Against all this, somewhere buried deep in the background of her psyche, troubling thoughts stemming from the past started bubbling towards the surface, centring on the breakup of her family and the unmitigated disaster that had led to father and daughter wanting to kill one another.

Words can easily be sculpted to anyone's desire, nicking here, cutting there, torturing for days at a time in some of the most serious cases, their intent wounding differently depending on the lips they're spewed from and with how much venom. Even from an early age she'd had a mouth on her, not so much in front of her parents, but at the nursery ring... hell yes, her classmates taking the brunt of her frustration and anger. But for the most part she was cunning enough not to do it in front of any of the *tors*, knowing full well exactly how much trouble she'd be in. That had only been the start on the long road to delinquency, one that could have been nipped in the bud but had eventually, through manipulation, led her to be in the company of the Nazis. And it had all gone downhill from there, spiralling out of control on the killing front, before being sought out by Manson and joining his shadowy forces in an effort to rule the world together.

Mostly dark, deranged and full of danger, there had at least been one highlight... the husband she'd met and fell in love with along the way, their collaboration throughout the course of the second world war truly meaningful, both to each other and in changing its course, up until that is, they were each captured by the Allies. Events and more importantly, their despicable connections had them free in no time, after which they absconded into obscurity, living the life they'd always dreamed of, despite most of the time it being in human form, something they both despised at first but soon started to appreciate. In the midst of all of it, a beautiful, all encompassing egg was created by the love the two of them shared, the outcome of which lay someway in front of her, shying away from all the magic and destruction flying around the vault, emphasising clearly the yellow streak that ran through him, top to bottom. Recalling that fateful night, all that really stuck out was the feeling that she didn't want to part with their creation, didn't want to hand it over to the Purbeck Peninsula nursery ring. But he'd talked her round and at the time it appeared the right thing to do. Looking back now with such clarity and hindsight, it felt like the last thing they should have done. I mean where on earth would THEY raise such a thing given that at the time they were both wanted criminals above and below ground, but still... she should never have parted company with that egg. If she hadn't, just maybe things would have been... different! Barely able to see the long black wavy locks perched atop his head, in that moment her heart sang... NO, cried out in the most maternal way possible. Okay, briefly she'd tried to convince him to go with her during the battle at the king's private residence, but truthfully, her efforts hadn't truly been in it back then. But now... she could see the LIE, the one she'd been telling herself over and over, across all the time she'd done her best to forget about him. She... LOVED him, like the son that he was, unconditionally, and so it didn't matter that unlike her he shied away from the action, adventure and danger she so often craved. In fact, part of it in that moment felt like a boon, something she realised in a flash of revelation, she should have been proud of. But she continued drowning in the madness of every perceived slight and wrong that had befell her along the way, the culmination of which was having the dragon she'd loved more than life itself cornered on top of that Welsh cliff on the cold, rainy night, so brutally having his life stripped away by those sent from the domain to bring them both in, his death fuelling her descent into lunacy, transforming her into the being that had wound up by Manson's side, the one here flitting from pillar to post, avoiding death by the smallest of margins, wreaking havoc, attempting to hurt all those there like never before. It turns out that the insidious lies that we tell ourselves are as all corrupting as those that we tell others. Who'd have thought?

And in that fleeting split second of lucidity, it also dawned on her that just maybe her father wasn't the monster she'd made him out to be, but if not that... then what? It was all so confusing, compounded by being smack bang in the middle of all that murderous magic which threatened to end her life any time now. Okay, she'd instigated it all, but the time had long since passed for forgiveness, or had it? If she reined herself in and quit all the psychotic behaviour, was a return possible? Could she be pulled back from the precipice? It appeared unlikely at best, an impossibility at worst. But that was one of the thoughts running through the confines of her extremely unhinged mind.

As was the way with these things, it was never going to be that simple, some of Earth's memories dredged up from the past in a complete and utter jumble. A pervading feeling that her childhood was happy and complete, both parents doting on her, especially Fredric when he returned from extended periods away, underlined everything. They'd had days out, just the two of them… to the most amazingly exotic places, her father passing on fascinating snippets of information, both magical and factual, the youngster that she was back then hanging on his every word, with his every waking thought centred around exactly what he could do to improve his daughter's life and give her a better future. It was a kinder, much simpler time, one which as a family each of them lapped up thinking that it would be this good forever, nothing else standing in their way. But along with attitudes, times change and pressures from being away took their toll on the heroic founder of the Crimson Guards alongside the amount of time and work Earth had to dedicate to her studies. Fractures in their relationships started to appear and that's when things very subtly started to diverge. She went off the rails seeking attention, something she got in spades from her illicit dealings with the Nazis, he for the most part stopped being around so much, even when able, whilst her mother stood imperiously strong, holding things together, the kindest and most wonderful of dragons, attempting to be the glue that would continue to bind them all together. But it wasn't to be, her rebellion long since having passed that of a normal teenager, committing atrocities that just couldn't be shrugged off or excused by her age and inexperience.

Just then a recollection of Fredric following her to a bar in Barcelona of all places, filled to the brim with those of the supposed German super race. The betrayal she felt at the subterfuge that he'd employed on that night was almost certainly the final nail in the coffin. She could remember hoping that the machine guns produced by the crowd would cut him down, tear him in half so that she could watch his broken body bleed out on the cobbles. They hadn't, and he'd escaped by the skin of his teeth, jumping head first through a plate glass window at the very last second, like a cat exercising one of its nine lives. That incident had forced her further into Hitler's hands, compelling her to take more risks and even on occasion reveal what she really was. It was the beginning of the end.

And then a soul sucking well of darkness and pain rose up from somewhere deep within her midriff as she continued to bound about the vault, spraying her own brand of magic in every different direction, all the time trying to avoid being hit by her father's own intrinsic supernatural.

Discovering that her mother had died when she'd been away on a mission for her evil taskmasters had cut like a thousand knives. Not wanting to listen to her father, their relationship by now far too damaged to rebuild, there and then she blamed him for the death, not willing to listen to anything he had to say, too full of rage to see how heartbroken he was. As dysfunctional a family as ever there had been, a point proved ably by current events, the two of them once again trying to murder one another.

Through all the insanity a dozen different voices pulled in two dozen different directions, one or two urging her to surrender and throw herself on the mercy of those who truly knew the meaning of the word, while the rest encouraged violence in all kinds of forms, the blood lust pounding in her ears at their excitement, thoughts of being sated by taking yet another life beyond stimulating. Leaving a wispy trail of thin grey smoke in her wake, the wicked villainess continued to dance up walls, hop from plinth to plinth and hurdle those relics and artefacts in her way, all the time peppered by a spray of sizzling salvos that nibbled at her heels, the converging lines of crackling ruby energy getting ever closer to taking her down.

As superheated shrapnel shot overhead, the only full-on

human there covered her ears, wanting nothing more than for it to be over. Not quite used to it all... and I mean almighty magical explosions, dragons, nagas and a ramped up level of evil rarely visited on anyone, let alone little old her, Janice, despite having become as familiar as any human ever had with the fantastic impossibilities playing out around her, continued to stay down low behind the pedestal where she'd originally taken cover, well aware that her love's mother was once again on the rampage. Where would it all end?

Through her epically advanced dragon brain, The White Dragon looked on, not quite bored but restless and uneasy, knowing that the longer this went on, the more chance someone other than the protagonist priestess of peril would get hurt, and she just couldn't let that happen. Left in no doubt by Fredric about getting in the way of the blood feud with his daughter, all she wanted to do was put an end to it. With that in mind, she decided to give things a little nudge in the right direction.

Staving off the different voices and their diverse opinions, cutting through all the brain fog and madness that so often controlled the decisions she made, Earth, having far too late recognised the lies she'd been telling herself throughout the decades about her family, came to a snap decision and in that moment truly felt at peace with herself. However the moment would play out, she was certain of one thing and one thing only... that love would win out in the end. After all, that's what all the others believed, her enemies... she'd seen their confusing antics up close back at the king's private residence. The only love she could ever remember truly feeling was that of her one true husband, Peter's father. With that experience resounding throughout her mind, in what some might regard as a very different fit of madness to the usual murdering psychotic behaviour, she readied herself to give up and be judged, knowing that the odds weren't quite in her favour, but believing that just maybe redemption was a possibility and that her life and those of her family could be turned around. Still moving at speed to avoid being skewered by any of the flurry of bolts let loose in her direction by her angry as hell father, in her psyche she wondered where she should pull up and try to capitulate, her mind momentarily free from her trademark lunacy, the whole of her completed at the thought of liberation from this life in exchange for a reunion she felt she thoroughly deserved.

Settling on sliding to a halt behind the biggest podium, raising her arms in the air and turning to face them all, one last bound halfway up a terracotta coloured wall saw her change direction and head towards what she hoped would be sanctuary, sure that in only a few moments her submission and deliverance would be a done deal. For the first time in decades, a smile encapsulating true happiness creased its way, in, around and over what were normally the terrifying crisscrossing lines of purple that covered her face. With innocence restored, the lies washed away and the madness conquered, she leapt, somersaulted and cartwheeled across the vault for what should have been one last time.

Ignoring the headache inducing noise of the constant magical bombardments that posed so much danger to everyone present, the superstar lacrosse player, eyes firmly shut, acted as only she could, tracing the path of danger, sensing its every movement until that is, she found the right opportunity. And then she did. As Earth bounced between two of the plinths, her footing totally assured, using just a smidgen of supernatural, Richie, with just the pull of her finger and a couple of whispered words, dragged a rusting metal breastplate along the rocky floor, the sound screeching like fingernails down a blackboard but barely audible over the constant detonations of magic in the confined cul de sac. Earth's dainty foot dropped towards the orange stone, abruptly finding quite a large metallic object in its way. Unfortunately, even with her astounding dragon reactions, there was simply no chance of avoiding contact or altering her trajectory ever so slightly to retain her balance. With her full weight already on one foot, her sole slammed down onto the rounded front and slipped like a buttered pig through a crowd of people. With no time to counter what had happened, her momentum threw her abruptly forward and in very short order smashed her face full on into the remains of a pedestal that had once been the perch for one of the former shopkeeper's prized possessions.

# CRASH!

Cue mashed nose, broken left eye socket, dislocated jaw and almost as much pain in one instant as she'd ever experienced in her entire life as she hurtled to the ground.

Like a raging furnace stoked to beyond safe limits, Fredric's already raised ire exploded exponentially, having been quite specific about what should happen once they got here. It was supposed to have been just the two of them, no interference from the others, but he'd felt what Richie had just done despite the magic involved being the tiniest little sliver, a bullet picked out amidst a full on war... nothing really, but in reality EVERYTHING! Redirecting his anger at what The White Dragon had just done and already hot on his daughter's tail, he was on her in an instant.

"No... wait," was what she was supposed to say, all but ready to surrender and make good on a redemption story that was meant to be. But as the first giant fist, one of many, came raining down, all that came out was...

"Nnnnnwwummppphfff".

For the most part delight rippled around the vault full of treasure at the sight of Fredric finally catching up with his prey and that even included Peter who just wanted all of this to be over, having long since put his obsession about finding his long lost parents well and truly behind him. Richie smiled with glee, sensing the conclusion was close at hand. Janice, still ducked down, raised her head over the parapet, recognising the relief flowing through her link with the fabulous blade that was one of her best friends, not exactly keen, but thinking it the right thing to do to take in the wicked dragon's last living moments.

Polkinghorne... not so much. She instead decided to focus all her concentration on protecting the most powerful relics residing inside the vault, only too aware of what could happen should even an ounce of magic collide with theirs.


Fresh from averting an epic disaster beyond anything in the history of everything, from the spectral realm that so often hosted them, all three Providences had their attention pulled in the vault's direction, sensing a moment in history about to unravel, one that needed their full consideration.

Novus, having expended all his new found power in one overarching action by vaporising the already exploded nuclear warhead, curled up into a foetal position and instantly fell asleep, assured that for now at least, the threat had been negated.


Punch after punch slammed into what remained of her face from her father's formidable fists.

In her mind she screamed.

*"NO... NO... NO... NO... NO!"*

Still the beating continued with no let up, no mercy shown, no quarter given, Fredric desperate to fulfil the vow he'd made to himself about sorting out his progeny once and for all.


With the wicked she-witch's life nearly extinguished, Time, Luck and Fate breathed an ethereal sigh of relief. It was nearly over, crisis averted, the birth of a new dawn well and truly on the horizon. But what about one last parting shot? Had anyone considered that?

All the wicked, shadowy, dark supernatural magic that had gathered inside her over the decades pooled together in the place where dragon magic lurks. Bizarrely it was frightened, something of a new experience and one it didn't much care for. With that in mind, it did what any of us would do in that situation. It lashed out in the only manner it knew how.

# BOOM!

The mother of magical explosions tore through the secret vault shredding everything in its way, sending bodies flying in all directions, Earth's inherent evil having the last laugh.

Fredric, having been squatting over her, took the brunt of the impact, his huge athletic frame tossed like a rag doll forty metres into the air, crashing unceremoniously into the ceiling, instantly knocked unconscious, his body landing in a twisted heap atop a pile of assorted armour in one far off corner.

Santa, through her legendary generational dragon magic stuck firmly in place, the only one to do so, still managing to protect the artefacts and a good job too. Had that explosion come into contact with any of them, then most of the capital both above and below ground would have been a pile of smoking rubble.

Richie, along with Fu-ts'ang, was thrown firmly into an outlying wall, not knocked unconscious but winded and very badly shaken. For the moment she was of no use to anyone.

Clanging first against one shelf that had been carved into the orange rock wall before smashing callously onto the floor, despite his superior surroundings, the essence of the weapon smith shook like never before, causing him briefly to lose all sense of where he was and what he was doing.

Face a broken mess, one eye missing, slathers of skin that had covered her cheeks hanging precariously down towards her neck, blood positively oozing everywhere, what remained of Earth fought to stay alive, a baser instinct it would be hard to find. Fortunately the many voices had been well and truly quashed. Unfortunately it wasn't by the one who'd hoped to be forgiven and reunited with her family. This one had the intonation of true, raw, untapped evil, everything inside her that had festered for so long. Worse still, was that it recognised that it was dying. Before it was lost forever, it wanted to leave its mark on the world.

Showered in dust and debris, lucky to even be alive, Janice stood up, trying not to choke on all the filth that had been kicked up into the air. Four metres away, a vision from hell mirrored her every move, a battered, bruised and ultimately broken, walking cadaver, soaked in blood, face broken, a huge chunk of her head missing.

After all that she'd been through, all that she'd seen, done, been part of, this was something else altogether... epically malevolent, disgusting, stomach churning and so absolutely terrifying that the young human hero remained rooted to the spot, unable to act in any way, shape or form.

With the ear splitting sound of that one explosion still resounding around the treasure filled cul de sac, the air thick with the smell of spent magic and charred flesh, with absolute impunity, what remained of Fredric's daughter and Peter's mother stalked forward towards the nearest target it could find, the human pet that its son had become obsessed with, determined to make it suffer before ultimately snuffing out its life.

Terror, fear, anger, fury, wrath, rage, revenge and retribution joined forces, their twisted malice binding them together in one form, that of what remained of Manson's would-be queen, on one last mission to inflict the maximum of hurt. The planet might not have been destroyed, but somebody's world would be. GET READY!

Stricken with horror, panic coursing through his false veins, Peter could see from off to one side exactly what was about to happen, his soulmate, his future and the being he loved most on the planet about to be torn apart by some shadow remnant of his inherently evil mother. Rallying all his will, driven by love, THE most powerful of emotions, the young hockey player put one foot in front of the other in an attempt to intervene. Unfortunately his body had other ideas and he, just like the blonde haired beauty he'd so desperately fallen for, remained stuck to the spot, unable to do anything.

Searching within, the monster found the most vile and diabolical magic that it could and with one eye (the only one left) on the prize, stretched out its right hand, arched back its neck and let all the supernatural loose, relishing the thought of taking one last life.

It was the one time that he'd ever felt it, which was strange really, but for whatever reason, the revolving coating of ice around his blade, out of absolutely nowhere, returned with a vengeance, prickling his mind back into the present like a cold bucket of water being thrown over an unsuspecting sleeper. Startled back to reality, the fantastical blade, former weapon smith and, with the exception of the Providences and Novus himself, the oldest of them all, acted as only he could. Faster than the eye could see Fu-ts'ang zipped across the distance separating them, his horizontal body cutting through all the spent magic and wispy smoke like a jet fighter on a mission, his pointed tip glinting as he travelled. With a wave of continuous, jet black, forked lightning charging out of the beast's fingertips, it was impossible for the fantastical blade to go on the attack, certain he'd never reach what remained of the horror that had been Fredric's daughter in time. So in an instant he switched to defence, dropping down in front of his best friend, the one who'd been plucked from the surface to come and save them all, the one Gee Tee had handed him to on that fateful day on the outskirts of dragon domain Salisbridge, the one he loved unconditionally. Tip hovering just above the floor, his wickedly white restored edge started batting away every streak of shadowy evil that forked its way through the air towards the young woman, knowing that if only one so much as scratched her, she was as good as dead.

Shaking off the ringing in her ears, Richie just about managed to sit up, a feeling of deep seated nausea washing right over her. It took her a moment to realise what was going on, that one of her best friends was in extreme peril, being attacked by whatever remained of the evil empress that had already caused them all so much pain. Instigating her indomitable will and swearing inside her mind at her body's inability to act, gingerly she tried to get to her feet, knowing that she might well be her pal's one and only chance at survival.

"Ugggghhhhhhh…" Fredric groaned from amidst the pile of tarnished armour, recognising that something bad was happening but unable to see what from his prone position.

There was danger everywhere, something her senses were screaming out at her to recognise. She did, of course, but there was nothing she could do, not without relinquishing her grip on the protection she clung so firmly to around all the powerful relics she was trying to defend. Unusually sidelined, all Polkinghorne could do was watch in horror at the unscrupulous and ruthless attack directed towards one of the few humans she could truly call her friend.

DAMN!

Batting away corrupt branches of debauched shadowy evil that intended to inflict an agonising amount of pain on his best friend before taking her life in the most ghastly of circumstances, Fu-ts'ang, powered by his knowledge, experience and all the magic within his fantastical form, moved as fast as he ever had during the course of his extended lifespan. His blade was practically invisible, even to the magic users looking on, only a thick trail of constant icy whiteness appeared in front of Janice, like a toddler waving a sparkler about on bonfire night. Magnificent didn't do him justice. Unfortunately the supernatural evil continued to come, with no let up in the pounding punishment it was willing to dish out. Very soon, all his resources would be spent, the thought of which sent a chill down a spine he didn't have, knowing that if she died on his watch, he'd simply never forgive himself. It was Song Jin all over again!

In that small arena, three events occurred simultaneously.

Fredric sat up.

Richie stood up.

Peter slid out of view behind the pedestal he'd been sheltering behind.

Sitting here writing all this, one song and one alone won't leave me alone. Wet Wet Wet's 'Love Is All Around.'

Why? Because in this instant it truly was!

Think of all the love there is in that moment for Janice, one of earth's mightiest heroes, about to have her life snuffed out on a whim by such staggeringly vile evil in a wicked act of revenge from deep rooted malevolence born of the dragon known as Earth.

Peter's love for the woman he wanted to spend the rest of his life with, a being he truly regarded as his soulmate, one who completed him like no other could. It was an all encompassing passion and he couldn't imagine a life without her.

And then there was Richie, the lacrosse superstar who not to put too fine a point on it, had not really got on with the blonde bar worker at first, just the barest hint of jealousy rearing its ugly head at the relationship she'd struck up with one of her two best friends. Somewhere in the dragon domain, deep beneath the human world on the surface, that had all changed. Was that down to Janice's inherent kindness and the selfless bravery she'd shown in facing overwhelming odds whilst trying to save the one she loved, or something else? Who knew? But somewhere along the way the two of them had bonded and become the best of friends which was an odd thing for a dragon and a human to do. But was it? Two women... no, two likeminded warriors with a shared love of the dragon called

Bentwhistle, both of whom had given their all, ready and willing to lay down their lives. They were similar beyond belief.

Even Fredric had learned to love Janice purely as a friend, which left Fu-ts'ang who was currently giving everything he had to save the life of the one he loved like a daughter or a sister, a being who reminded him of his past and the turn of fate that had left him trapped in the futuristic blade, the one created by his own hand over twenty thousand years ago. Whirling, twirling, buzzing, batting, his mind was ablaze not only with the sheer audacity and number of attacks being hurled in Janice's direction but by the underlying wanton need within the magic to destroy the young girl. It was like nothing he'd ever experienced in all his considerable time on this planet. His vow to protect her was running out of steam through no fault of his own, the dark, destructive magic burning through the ever revolving ice around his cutting edge, searing his outer casing, causing him great pain. Still he persevered, his unrelenting love for his friend powering him forward.

So... what do you think?

Here it is! Love conquers all, always! It's the strongest of emotions that, yes, can on occasion make us act both childishly and stupidly, but it can at its best spur us on to better things, making us bigger than the sum of our parts, providing courage when we're bereft of it, hope when there is none, ultimately enhancing our lives and those of others to another plane. A life without love is no life at all. It does, however, come at a cost and doesn't stop bad things from happening. Will love save the very epitome of innocence, purity and good?

Do you know what... I think it just might!

The onslaught continued pummelling Fu-ts'ang's defences, destroying his icy encasement, peppering his blade with its vile, naga based wickedness, wreaking havoc on the metal used in the weapon's creation so long ago. Still he continued to protect his friend.

Shaking his head, for the first time noticing what the hell was going on, the founder of the Crimson Guards and Peter's grandfather shook off all the ancient armour he found himself wrapped up in, sending individual pieces scattering through the air. The sound of metal on rock sang across the vault, a fanfare of his imminent arrival on the scene.

Clearing the hazy mist from her mind, back to her best, The White Dragon, superstar lacrosse player, righter of wrongs, fierce friend, warrior queen and love of Hook's life could see even from as far away as she was that the fantastical blade that had done so much to get them this far, was about done. Acting with impunity as only she could, she took one step forward, about to put herself in between the ravaging darkness and the brightest of lights.


Amidst uncontrollable wailing and heartbreak some one hundred and forty kilometres south west of the treasure laden vault in a bright white ward, abruptly a breath was taken, startling all those present, who had considered a life forfeit.


Time slowed as tragedy unfolded.

Tapping into all his experience, Fredric whipped out the laminium dagger that had been tucked behind his back into his belt and moving at a speed Flash would have been proud of had he been there, set course for what remained of his daughter, his huge muscular shape all but a blur.

Charged by the prophecy that had been foretold so long ago, the one all dragons are taught at an early age, the one their race positively lived by, The White Dragon, having made her peace and sorry not to have found solace with the heroic rugby playing human that had so subtly stolen her heart, mirroring Peter's grandfather, moved faster than a streak of light, about to save her friend and in doing so, fulfil said prophecy. It was a done deal, in that moment assuring the future of every single being on the planet.

Typically though, courage had chosen a rather unnerving time to intervene.

Having spent the last ten seconds truly contemplating the meaning of love and exactly what she meant to him, the most unexpected hero of the lot acted before any of the others could, energised by devotion and passion, having finally exorcised all the terror and fear that had clamped him in place. As the shiny, futuristic form of Fu-ts'ang was brusquely cast off to one side by the insidious shadowy, unscrupulous supernatural, at last getting its way, Peter powered by all his dragon magic leapt with all he had, and in doing so, managed to get himself between Janice and what remained of his mother.

He didn't last long... maybe a split second or two. But he didn't need to, because an instant later Fredric carved what was left of his daughter in two, to the accompaniment of a blood curdling scream, the dark magic being cast ceasing to exist. But not what had already been unleashed at the young woman, a dozen or so sticky black tendrils edging ever forward.

Sprinting for not just her life, Richie dived full tilt, attempting to intercept the cruelty that she knew could destroy any and all living tissue with just one touch, certain that she'd been put on this world for exactly this moment, not only to satisfy the renowned prophecy but to save both her friends and allow them to live long, prosperous, satisfying and ultimately loving lives.

She didn't get there in time!

In one fell swoop the remaining shameless tendrils of shadowy magic spat from the vile creature that would have considered itself his mother carved into his chest, disintegrating every last atom of Peter's living tissue.

Split in two, both halves of the toxic dragon, Earth, crashed to the cool stone ground with a THUMP!

The tiniest tinkle resounded close by.

Janice stood gobsmacked!

Richie lay heartbroken.

Fredric... just broken.

Off to one side, the once a year Christmas legend whose powers were on a par with any being ever to have walked the earth relinquished her grip on the shields surrounding the artefacts she'd been protecting, fighting off the devastation of what she'd just seen. Deep inside her mind, something stirred.

*"NO! NO! NO! NO! NO! NO! NO! NO! NO!"*

This wasn't it! This wasn't how it was supposed to be!

Initial surprise very quickly became overrun by the whole lot... sadness, anger, fear, disgust, anxiety, guilt, shame, embarrassment, relief, frustration, loneliness, all of it boiling up inside her, fuelled by a roaring rage at the injustice of it all. In that moment she made a decision, one to act like she never had before. Dropping to her knees amongst all the spent magic, full-on blood and gore, Polkinghorne, or better yet... SANTA reached out, or rather in and brought it all forth.

The air snarled with the sound of thunder as the ground beneath their feet quaked. The ceiling shook. Stones fell as the rock cracked. The United Kingdom and continental Europe shuddered. Novus was startled awake. All three Providences took cover, figuring they'd missed something in Manson's devious plan.

Deep within the recesses of her clever, calculating and kind mind, she focused solely on him and their time together. From his part in saving Christmas when it had been so fully in crisis, to giving him a just a glimpse of his grandfather before having to wipe the memory totally, to his joy at seeing both her and Vimes arrive so abruptly at the king's private residence, to helping him create the perfect gift for his soulmate from one single scale. Using all her love, tapping into every last ounce of magic she possessed (which was saying quite something) she did the one thing she never had, she wished for something for herself: for his safe return.

It didn't quite stop, but it did slow right down... the earth, that's what we're talking about. Novus was shocked. Nothing or nobody could do such a thing. It was simply impossible. But all the magic and power of CHRISTMAS, combined with unrelenting LOVE was as powerful a force as existed in the entirety of the universe, the proof here and now of exactly that.

Deep beneath the chillingly cold ocean off the northern Scottish coast, Vimes fought against a current he would recognise anywhere and anytime... his soulmate, the one who'd done so much for so many across the course of history.

'What the...?'

Adjacent to the dark opening at the top of the test borehole in northern France, Flash, Amelia, Yoyo, Rose and all the youngsters took to the air, compelled by the quaking and movement of the ground, fear and terror running through them at the unexpected shift of the earth itself.

Back at the king's private residence, dragons took cover as walls and stairways came crashing down, all the books in the private library jiggled from their shelves, crashing to the floor in a constant din. It sounded and appeared as though the world was ending.

In her mind's eye she could see him clearly, the renowned smile shining through, his intrinsic goodness sparkling, all with just a hint of the naivety that made him who he was. Peter was there, all but within touching distance. Focusing all her magic on reaching out to that particular image, certain that if she could just stroke it and apply all the supernatural she'd just brought forth, then he could be returned to them all. She was good, better than that in fact. She was fabulous, magnificent, brilliant, outstanding, wonderful, superb and glorious all wrapped up into one. But here's the thing, and yes... there's a thing. Her powers were unequivocal, all consuming, her abilities matching almost anyone or anything. But as children across the world know, if they've lost a loved one and have prayed for a Christmas miracle, death can't be cheated. It simply isn't possible!

Peter was gone and the best they could hope for was that somewhere after 'the gloom', he might cross paths with his friend the master mantra maker.

Earth had cost them dearly!

Bollocks!

# 46 FOUR MONTHS LATER

A cloying sensation of not being able to take a breath caused her to gulp for air frantically as she strolled towards her destination, a feeling of déjà vu once again playing over her.

'This is how it always starts,' her intelligence managed to think, although what good that did her was anyone's guess.

Slowly she walked forward, her soft footsteps making almost no noise on the shiny white tiles laid out across the floor, the distinctive scent of something medicinal and sterile wafting up her nose. This time her mind confirmed that this had happened before. But she had no choice but to continue.

And there it was, the huge transparent tank, easily the size of a four bedroom house, filled to the brim with a yellow tinged liquid pierced by the occasional plume of bubbles bursting up from the surface. Getting so close that her nose almost touched the glass, she gazed inside, wondering what she would find, hoping it would be different from the previous times, although she still couldn't exactly recall what had occurred. The tiniest bit of movement on the ground in front of her caught her eye. There, on the floor, waving gently in the liquid, a single matt green scale about the size of a fifty pence piece stood upright, looking as though it had seen better days. Just the sight of it forced her throat to constrict, her breathing to speed up and her heart to race. She'd seen it before, of that there was no doubt... and it was IMPORTANT!

Right at that point, just as in her previous identical dreams, Janice, covered in sweat, hair dishevelled and thoroughly dehydrated, woke up startled and in a panic, all of a fluster, not knowing where she was or what was going on. All she could remember was that one single scale in absolute graphic detail, the yellow liquid rolling across its rough surface, a constant reminder of everything she'd lost.

Aware of the early hour, and the significance the day represented, without hesitation and ignoring the confusion the dream had prompted, the young bar worker threw herself out of bed, landing on the floor with a THUD and scurried off towards the bathroom like a starving mouse towards cheese. One thing was for certain, she was going to look her best for history's biggest day, not wanting the cameras to capture anything that wasn't even remotely beautiful. Today she would look perfect, and for that, she had her reasons.

The door tore open so hard it nearly exploded off its hinges. Gingerly he slid to a halt.

"Majesty," he declared.

"Yes," replied two very different voices.

Awkward!

"What exactly are you doing here, pray tell?" interjected George.

"Don't give him a hard time," giggled Janice. "Of course he's come to see his best buddy."

He had.

"Hmmmm…" uttered George under his breath.

Looking more apologetic than he had in a very long time, Tank, having burst through the door, sweat dripping off his brow, panting ever so slightly, composed himself as much as he could, and ignoring George's cold stare, slowly walked across the room to where his best friend stood, offering up a subtle wink to Janice along the way.

Breathing steadied, and reaching his destination, he found himself lost for words in a way he never had before. Knowing exactly what was going on, much like every other being on the planet, he hadn't expected this… never this. But here she was before him, like a perfectly formed rose opening its petals for the very first time.

"You… you… you look absolutely… stunning," was all that he could get out.

"Of course she does, stupid. What else did you expect?" observed the young bar worker.

"I... I... I... mean…"

"I know what you mean," offered up Richie softly. "I'm glad you're here. I wouldn't have it any other way."

"So am I," replied Tank smoothly.

"I'm not really sure it's appropriate for you to see the bride," questioned George from the other side of the room.

"I think you're mistaking me for the best man," remonstrated Tank.

"I thought you were the best man?" declared George.

"I think you mean best dragon," Tank replied smugly.

A smile almost appeared on George's face... ALMOST!

"At least he didn't bring the best man with him," mused Fredric off to one side, before taking a sip of something yellowy and full of bubbles from what looked like a huge glass jug.

"I'd like to have seen him turn up. It would most certainly have been unlucky for HIM to have seen the bride. He'd truly know what a shiner meant," quipped Richie, fiddling with a twisted bright red ribbon that adorned her hair.

That got a few chuckles, mainly from Fredric and Janice who'd both had more than their fair share of champagne, despite the relatively early hour.

"He's a braver man than I," announced the founder of the Crimson Guards to the entire room.

"He's a braver man than most," responded Tank, meaning every word.

"That he is," added George, "that he most certainly is."

"Well... this is all very nice and all that, but don't you all have things to do. It's not as if it's just any other day after all."

"We don't have the faintest idea of which you speak," slurred Janice, hiccupping profoundly.

"As you are all aware, this is probably the most momentous day in history... full stop. I don't want anything to go wrong, not even the slightest detail. With that in mind, please can you take care of your assigned tasks?" announced the lacrosse superstar indignantly.

"Uh... okay," a few of them mumbled to themselves.

"So be off with you, and make sure all of your duties are taken care of. It's important."

With that the two best friends, Fredric and George sloped off out of the room, like two naughty schoolboys conspiring together.

As the door shut, Tank turned to face Richie.

"You look beautiful. The whole world will think so."

Unaccustomed to such words, at least directed straight at her, Richie Rump, superstar lacrosse player and dragon of sorts blushed profusely under the soft lighting of the room.

"I think it's time yoooouuuu left," suggested Janice in a garbled, incoherent way, pointing in Tank's direction.

"I think she's right," added the bride.

Tank bowed mockingly, something he'd only have done in front of a chosen few.

"Until later then," he reflected. "We've all got a big day in front of us."

"And I for one can't wait," the young bar worker put in, unconsciously twisting the nissix ring adorning the index finger of her right hand.

"Of all the things to look forward to today, I think the after party is going to be the most special," observed Richie.

"Of that you can be sure," concluded Tank, before turning around and taking his leave.

"Nice of him to drop by."

"I wouldn't have expected anything less," replied The White Dragon.

"Not very appropriate though."

"He's one of my best friends, how's that not appropriate? I don't recall anything about the best man not seeing the bride on the day of the wedding."

"That's not what I meant." Janice continued. "You'll

have to get used to seeing your friends less in the new role that you've taken on."

'Aahhhhh,' thought Richie, wondering where this was all going.

"I'm serious. From what I've learned, it'll be quite lonely for you."

"I know what you're getting at, and thank you for reminding me. But what you've been told applies to how things have been done in the past. And yes, I'm well aware of all the regulations surrounding what I should be doing. But as you well know, I have little regard for the rules, seeing them mainly as obstacles or impediments that need to be skirted around or broken. My friends will always come first... ALWAYS! And that includes you, young lady. So don't forget it!"

Blushing and holding back the tears, Janice threw herself into Richie's arms, trying her best not to ruffle the stunning white dress which made the young lacrosse player look like a fabled princess. As they embraced, something unsaid passed between them, through the connection that had been forged through fire and flame, adversity and misfortune, danger, menace and death. Human and dragon alike, friends forever... who'd have thought that given the circumstances of their first meeting? Fate had given them something in common to love. Simultaneously, their thoughts turned to Peter and just how much they each missed him. Thoughts of their friendship growing up in the nursery ring ran wild through Richie's mind... the high jinx, the selfless way in which he was always there, to talk to, to help, to offer a comforting word whenever required. Often he did himself down, Richie knew, thinking that he wasn't brave enough, or unable to stand up to the horrific bullying that always sought him out, but she knew otherwise. Kind, thoughtful, loving, attentive, she'd known all along that he'd lay down his life for his friends in a heartbeat, something he'd proven beyond any doubt. As these feelings threatened to overcome her, glistening transparent tears trickled from her eyes, racing down her perfect cheeks, magnifying the soft brown freckles of her face, falling like raindrops onto a snowfield as they leapt from her chin onto the striking white hour glass dress. Instead of wiping or dabbing them away, it seemed appropriate to her at least, that some recognition of her grief and friendship with the dragon who was her best friend, and couldn't be here today, for this, the single biggest attraction in the history of the planet, remained in place. And so she left the damp spots the tears had created, hoping they would serve as a reminder of what was to come.

For Janice though, it was different. Unlike her bestie, whenever she thought of Peter, instead of warm, playful memories, there lurked a dark, despairing hole. The future had been ripped out from under her, the heartbreak and despair she'd suffered eclipsing everything she'd gone through in the battle for the planet, all that time ago. Learning that dragons shared their world, watching Casey's torture, being rounded up by Manson's goons after witnessing the slaughter of her dragon comrades, being brought in front of the psychopath leader and his insane queen, thrust into the mother of all battles and watching her partner and friend, Fu-ts'ang, shatter into a thousand pieces... All of this and more broke her heart, but nothing like the death of the one she loved, the one she'd performed heroic acts to rescue, gone above and beyond what she thought possible, giving everything she had for her true soulmate. And just like that, he'd been taken from her in one last twist of fate. That he should have done it to save her made it all the more unsavoury, in her eyes at least. As she stood there, head buried into her friend's shoulder, watching the tears bound onto the intricately designed dress, the young bar worker turned her thoughts to the big day, if for no other reason than to take her mind off not having the plus one she truly desired. If the tears were ever going to come, it would no doubt be much later on. Little did she know how right she would be.

Meanwhile, not far away in one of the fifty two guest bedrooms of Buckingham palace, leant to them by Her Majesty herself, a hero of a different sort was trying his best not to become befuddled.

"Stand still," commanded Flash, doing his best to rein in his frustration.

"I'm trying to, but it's too tight around my neck. I don't like it."

"You don't like it!" exclaimed the ex-Crimson Guard. "Do you really think this is going to be the worst part of your day... putting on a tie? Believe you me, there's a great deal more to come that's going to irritate the pants off you."

Hook's whole demeanour changed, head hanging limp, puppy dog eyes looking up at his friend, a look of surrender overcoming his face, something very rare in the course of the courageous rugby player's life to date.

"Look," stated Flash. "You've known for a little while what you've gotten yourself into. This is no easy ask and while for most this might be one of the best days of their lives, today will not be like that for you. There will be formalities that you MUST observe. And they will go on forever. And that's before we've even got to the television cameras and journalists. Every move you make will be recorded in some way, shape or form. Whatever you do, continue to smile and don't let your guard down for even a second. Understood?"

Through the dejected look on Hook's face, his mouth just about managed a "hurrumphh!"

Flash clasped his friend's shoulder.

"Okay... so I've magnified all the bad bits. But don't forget about everything good going on today... and there's lots. For starters, you get to start a whole new life with the woman you love. How much have you wanted that?"

That prompted a smile, albeit briefly.

"And don't forget the historical significance of what's going on here. Make no mistake, you will be remembered forever. That's not too shabby either, is it?"

"But... I didn't ask for any of this. All I wanted was to be with her. All of this, it's just too much. I didn't bargain for any of it. I never thought it would be on this kind of scale."

"But you knew what had been asked of you. Did you really imagine it would be any other way?"

"Not like this. Never like this."

"I understand how you think it's too much, I really do. But what's happening here trumps anything that's ever happened in the past, by at least a factor of ten. Not even in my wildest dreams did I imagine such a thing could come about. But it has, and like it or not, you've played a huge part. While Richie might get all the plaudits, all the headlines, pictures splashed everywhere, people and dragons alike want to see you... they really do. Think about that while you're up there."

"Flash," declared Hook, ignoring the opulent surroundings they found themselves in, "all I want to do is be with her. It's as simple as that!"

"I know, my friend, and so does she, and you will be. You just have to get through today first. This time tomorrow, it'll all be all over... well, to some degree, and you can begin your new life. One day, that's all. Surely you can do that?"

Glancing across into the gold edged mirror, the huge rugby player considered his pal's words as he slumped down on the end of the walnut coloured four poster bed. Flash relaxed back in a leopard skin chair that looked as though it had come straight off safari, making it all the more ridiculous. Uncomfortable in their surroundings didn't cover it, but the British monarch had been great, and was one of the first to learn the truth. If only all the other world leaders had dealt with it in the same calm and collected manner Her Majesty had! But of course they hadn't, making arrangements all the more difficult, adding more pressure and administration than anyone would have thought possible, some even kicking up a stink that the event had to be here. Once the president of the United States got behind Britain though, that quickly changed, with nearly everybody towing the line. Thank God for some common sense amongst all the chaos.

He supposed it made sense, and he had agreed to all of this... kind of. But only for her, only because she was passionate about doing it, for all the right reasons of course, the main one being the bond it would forge between the protectors and their charges. In fact, she'd gone so far as to say that just maybe those terms could be disregarded, and at some point the two races could grow to look upon each other as equals. Of course that was some way down the line, but as passionately and eloquently as possible, she'd pronounced that this would be the first step. Who was he to argue? He couldn't, shouldn't and just plain wouldn't. It wasn't how he'd pictured his big day though, that was for sure, but he loved her and would do anything to please her. And after all, he had some idea of what he was getting into given her rather surprising new role which in itself brought some rather big boots for him to fill. But after the battle he'd been a part of from almost the beginning, he felt uniquely qualified to deal with any outstanding issues, either now or in the future.

Turning away from the mirror to face Flash, the strapping rugby player, looking dapper in his three piece suit, gave his response.

"I can do one day, that's for sure. In fact for her I'd do a whole lifetime, something that might well be the case anyway... I know. It's just that I'd rather have something small and personal, with all of you instead of the entire world watching. I can't remember a time when I've felt the pressure more."

Nodding along with his buddy's sentiments, Flash totally understood.

"I... I mean we, your friends, understand totally. Given a choice and without the importance, we would all much rather you had something smaller and more discreet. But that's not possible. So get ready to roll, soul, and let's get you smartened up. Tank will no doubt be back in a minute, and if you're not totally ready by then, I'll be in big trouble, and you know how he can be."

They both laughed, lightening the mood considerably.

Reaching out, Flash began straightening Hook's bright yellow tie, glad that he had an eidetic memory, because there was simply no way he'd have remembered how to tackle it otherwise. He swore humans made life harder than it had to be, for no apparent reason half the time.

Right at that moment the door to the room flung open and in burst Tank as predicted, looking all sweaty and worked up.

"Run all the way have you?" asked Flash, much to Hook's amusement.

"Of course," replied their friend.

"You should have transformed and flown. It would have been all right."

"I think you're greatly overestimating the situation."

"Not necessarily so. It might have been okay. And it's not like it won't happen. They'll have to get used to it at some point."

"I don't think this morning is the time for that, do you?"

"I suppose not. But it would have been cool to have been the first one though. Right?"

Tank smiled.

"Maybe."

"You guys and your dragon antics," quipped Hook. "How about a little help with the tie?"

"You still haven't got it right? What on earth have you been doing all this time?"

"Talking about life, love, the universe and everything," answered Flash.

"Hmmmmm..." replied Tank.

Sheepishly, Hook asked,

"How was she?"

"You know I can't tell you that."

"Not what she looked like. How was she feeling? Keyed up, nervous, apprehensive or... just excited?"

Pausing to think for just a moment, Tank thought carefully before he answered.

"There are a lot of things for her to think about today. I think they may all have been playing on her mind."

Hook's face fell.

"Not you, you big dope!" declared the rugby playing dragon, slapping his pal playfully full on in the stomach.

"OUCH!"

"Ahhh... I barely touched you, you big lug."

"No hitting... it's my wedding day. Today should be sacred."

"It is," interjected Flash, "but not for getting any stick. That stays the same, whether you're dressed up and in front of the whole world, or in here privately with us."

"BOO!" whispered Hook.

Flash and Tank just giggled.

"Come on then slow coach," urged Tank. "Let's get this tie done up. I think it's nearly time to leave."

In an instant it was done, with Hook taking a long look at not only his image in the mirror, but also at their extravagant surroundings. During the course of its history, Buckingham Palace had hosted some notable events, but none more so than what would be transpiring today. With Presidents and world leaders from nearly every country on the planet already here, it did seem like a turning point in not only history, but in the fortunes of the earth itself. As all three of them headed for the door, wondering exactly what the day had in store, they all hoped it would be remembered for making the world a better place, taking it out of the shadows and into the light, quite literally in some senses. Closing the door behind them, Tank briefly checked that the most valuable piece of jewellery on the planet was still tucked deeply away in his right waistcoat pocket, as they all tried to remember the way to the garden and everything that awaited them there.


Security was at a maximum, just as it should have been given the number of heads of state packed in there. Some still thought it a falsehood, that they were somehow being conned, but the fact that the major players... the United Kingdom's Prime Minister and the President of the United States were here, lessened their apprehension and nervousness, although not quite dispelling their concerns totally. Bodyguards numbered in the thousands, all thoroughly vetted by human and dragon agencies alike. It was chaos and minor squabbles had already broken out, some before dawn, most triggered by the accommodations not being opulent enough... well, what could be, especially for the President of the United States? She was, after all, the most powerful human on the planet, but not the most powerful being. That honour was reserved for one extraordinary female, or rather it would be from this afternoon onwards.

Dressed up to the nines, all seven of them skirted the beautiful flower beds and the lush grass cut to within an inch of its life, the two women bedecked in long flowing dresses adorned with subtle floral patterns, the men dapper in smart suits, all paid for by their leader and boss, Al Garrett, who himself looked nothing short of superb in a dark suit, white shirt and metallic blue bow tie. Looking immaculate and as though they all totally belonged, something inside most of them, bar Al Garrett, rallied against the formality of the occasion.

"This is surreal," whispered Owen as they snaked along a perfectly paved path, wriggling in and out of exotic flowerbeds overlooked by tall, wavy grasses that flickered in the breeze.

"The biggest event in the history of the planet, and we're here hobnobbing it with the superstars. How cool is that?" replied one of the men known only as Henry.

"Recall what you did, all those months ago," murmured Garrett softly. "Don't you think your actions during the Changing of the Guard, as it's now become known, deserve a little recognition?"

"I suppose," a few of them responded simultaneously.

"It... it... it's just that it seems odd being here with all the heads of state, people you see on the television but never think you'd meet in real life."

Garrett's smile turned into a chuckle, much to the other's amusement.

"What's so funny?" asked the no-nonsense Owen.

You see them as celebrities, which I suppose to some degree they are or more importantly... WERE! But think how the world has changed over the last few months. Dwell on the course of events that have led us to this monumental day. How do you think they feel now? Confused, scared and much more powerless than before. Things have changed, and not just a little, and you were not only there when it happened, but right at the heart of things. I have little doubt that a lot of those world leaders out there would love to swap places with you, or listen to your story directly, rather than spend time with their kind. You've all earned your place as icons in the context of the stories that will be recorded and told forever. What you did turned the tide at a crucial moment. If you don't want to take it from me, then believe what others say. If we hadn't shown up, if we'd hesitated, slowed down, lost our way, everything we know could well be gone and the planet decimated. So use today to rejoice, mix in with everyone here, as equals no less, and enjoy your day. You all thoroughly deserve it."

With Al Garrett's words, born from long experience, ringing in their ears, the small group split off into pairs, heading off in different directions across the palace gardens, determined to explore and mingle, the I.D. on their lanyards giving them access to absolutely everything and everyone. Watching with pride, a single tear threatening to escape from his right eye, the 'bald eagle' arched his back, pulled in his stomach and stood up straight, taking a deep breath through his nose, savouring the exotic scent of the plants surrounding him, the heady mixture of pollen from roses, rainbow coloured tulips and a wide variety of orchids if he wasn't mistaken, all giving him a heady rush. If this was how the day was going to start, then he couldn't wait for the rest of the festivities. He only hoped he'd get the chance to have a word with his employee who was supposed to be the star of the show. So far, she was nowhere to be seen.

In another corner of the grounds, not so far away, the Dutch Prime Minister and the French President were sipping tea from exquisitely patterned china cups against a backdrop of geraniums. Some were scarlet, matching the tunics of the queen's guards almost perfectly, intertwined with the more standard geraniums, some of which were over a metre tall.

"They say it's possible for them to take the form of a human, and then turn back again with little or no effort," offered up the Dutch PM.

Nodding, whilst placing his teacup back down on its saucer, the French President agreed wholeheartedly.

"I've seen it for myself. It's quite impressive, like something out of a Hollywood blockbuster."

"To think, all of this time we had absolutely no idea what was going on underneath us. To be honest, I feel a little stupid. All the resources at my disposal and nothing... not even an inkling of anything untoward."

"I couldn't agree more. Even with all the combined forces of our European allies, there wasn't the tiniest bit of chatter or wild rumour about any of this. How they kept it secret for so long is beyond me."

"Those Brits... the ones that went into the... now what do they call it again? Oh that's right, the dragon domain. Those Brits and their weaponry, we have a lot to thank them for. Without them, we might still be in the dark, living in denial, surrounded by shadows, perhaps never to find out the truth."

"I don't think so," suggested the French President. "No doubt it would have come out at some point in the future, a case of when, and not if."

"I suppose," added his counterpart.

And so it went on, with these deeply personal conversations taking place across the grounds, in all sorts of languages, all with the same subtext, some more full of doubt than others.

In between it all, raucous, high pitched laughter pierced the morning air, turning heads, causing frowns and withering looks to be cast in one particular direction... a group of women all bedecked in the same shimmering, luxurious, brown, floor-length chiffon dresses, all highly excitable, all having had quite a lot to drink already. It was only to be expected given that they were Richie's teammates and friends, the Salisbridge ladies lacrosse first XI. Emma, Angela, Sue, Joey, Ali, Poppy, Tina, Jan and Harriet... they were all here in their formal roles as bridesmaids, and yes, in the history of things, there had never been so many all at one wedding. But the bride had insisted, and given her status, her wishes were met with little protest. It was quite a sight amongst all the pomp and ceremony, the world leaders and royalty. But the women, as was their wont, always treating others as they hoped to be treated themselves, carried on with little regard for what anyone else thought, each determined to make the best of every second of the most momentous day in history, one they'd all been invited to, almost centre stage. Being with their teammate and leader on her special day was nothing short of a privilege for each and every one of them. In the middle of the girls, as well as Polo in her human guise, the dragon who'd led Garrett's team through the domain so expertly, two stunningly handsome men stood out, the centre of attention for all the females, causing males across the grounds to stare jealously. Both were heroes in their own right and part of the tight knit bond between the lacrosse ladies, Sam and Taibul both looked suave and sophisticated in their smart blue suits, the younger of the two feeling more like his usual waiter role than the guest of honour he was supposed to be. Luckily for him, the lacrosse ladies kept on reminding him of his true status and including him in most of their banter, keeping him grounded whilst at the same time filling him with thoughts of his underground adventure and the hockey with his pals that he loved so much. Occasionally his mind would focus in on his friendship with Peter, the mentor he thought so much of, that is until he'd been so abruptly taken from this world by that demon witch. Controlling the anger welling up inside him as those thoughts threatened to consume, took all the experience he'd gained on his fantastic adventure into the unknown all those months ago. Across that small course of time, he'd matured considerably, and was now able to look back fondly on the memories he'd shared with his friends.

Skulking in the cool dark shadows, exactly where they were supposed to be, each carrying a human sized backpack, a quiet contemplation had overtaken their usual exuberance. It was odd for him to be late, is what they would have thought, had their minds not been elsewhere. As it was though, memories of the not so distant past had them all tangled up, broken inside.

Huffing and puffing, his own backpack swinging from side to side in one of his giant hands, the dragon they'd all been waiting for stumbled around the corner, nearly knocking them all down in his haste.

"How are you all holding up?"

With a few sniffles and the odd whimper thrown in for good measure, the general response was, "Okay."

"Good," he replied. "We'll go to the shrine, which given the early hour should be empty, pay our respects and offer up our heartfelt thanks to Wiz and Hillier, before jumping on the monorail to London. It wouldn't do to be late to the big day, would it?"

All of them shook their heads in response, including his wife.

"And since we're in with the VIP's, we need to be punctual in order to get the best seats in the house. We wouldn't want to miss seeing our illustrious leader in her starring role now, would we?"

Again, more shaking of heads, followed by a few muffled, "no's."

Slowly, one by one, with Yoyo in the lead and Rose following in his wake, the band of fearless, history changing dragons made their way into the shrine with a view to paying their respects and honouring the memories of their fallen friends.

That had been thirteen hours earlier. Right now, they'd just come up into Buckingham Palace through a restricted entrance reserved for VIP dragons from the domain down below, only to be greeted by butlers and waiters all looking immaculate. Of course they'd changed straight after getting off the monorail at the closest station. Having brought suitable (but very uncomfortable) attire in their human backpacks, which had caused them all to get some furtive glances on the cross continent journey, they now all looked as though they belonged at the greatest celebration the world had ever known.


With less than an hour to go before the start now, the attendees were gathering in hordes, making the most of the time before all the television cameras started broadcasting within the grounds and the paparazzi arrived to take their assigned places. It was chaos, only in an organised, official and very royal way.

On an upper floor, George and Fredric had been nabbed by a courtier and told to attend one of the smaller rooms at once. Not knowing what was going on, and both assuming it was some sort of emergency that warranted their particular skill sets, they hurried there as fast as they could, without, in this very unrushed and strictly by the book place, looking as they were rushing. Reaching the correct door, they shot through it at speed, only to be greeted by one single person… HER MAJESTY! Both drew to a halt faster than the roadrunner sniffing out one of Wylie Coyote's traps. Trying to regain the initiative and their manners, both immediately bowed and waited for the response, which was more than a little unexpected.

"You boys! You never change. Enough! No bowing while we're alone… you should know that from our past exploits."

Both stood up straight, suitably berated, each with cheeky smiles etched into their time worn faces.

"That's better," commented Elizabeth brightly. "How long has it been?"

George piped up, which seemed appropriate.

"Getting on for six decades I suspect, Majesty."

"No more of the Majesty either. Come on… play the game. I might be frail, old and a little absent-minded, but the very last thing I would forget would be you two. I always suspected there was something special about you both, but not this… never this."

"Sorry ma'am," observed Fredric. "We never meant to deceive you, only to protect, serve and make sure you made it through the toughest of times. It was our duty. I'm sure you understand that."

"Indeed I do, indeed I do," reflected the Queen, turning to face Fredric. "And while you're here, I'd like to express how deeply sorry I am about your incarceration for all that time. Had I known, which I most certainly didn't, I'd have moved heaven and earth to set you free. I'm sorry you had to endure so much."

For but an instant Fredric's face froze, along with his heart, so magnificent was the gesture. Subduing all the emotion that threatened to force its way to the surface, the founder of the Crimson Guards fought to sync his mouth to his brain.

"Your generosity of spirit never ceases to amaze me, Ma'am. That's why you are not only a credit to the Royal Family and your country, but your race as well. I'm always proud to call you a friend and you should know, if you don't already, that if there's ever anything you need, please feel free to get in touch."

With so much left unsaid, the Queen nodded solemnly before turning to face George.

"So...," she started out, "what can you tell me about her? Is she fit to hold the title?"

Having expected an intense grilling and lots more people present, Peter's grandfather smiled before responding.

"Oh... she's worthy alright. If not for her and the courage against adversity that she's shown, we'd all be dead and the planet would be overrun with evil. And I'm not exaggerating in the slightest."

"I see," mused the United Kingdom's monarch.

"That said," continued George, "she's wilful, has a knack for disobeying the rules, doing her own thing, and can be as stubborn as a mule. She's generous to a fault, kind, considerate and will more often than not put other's needs before those of her own. Combine that with her loyalty, love for her friends and the bravery she's already shown in saving the planet, I would say the two of you have a lot in common and that she's the ideal choice to lead us forward into this bright and open new age."

"I like her already," mused Elizabeth playfully, wishing she herself had had a friend like that, back in the day.

"And so you should," added Fredric, thoughts turning towards his deceased grandson and just how proud he would have been of today's proceedings. "She'll do us all proud, of that I'm absolutely certain."

Abruptly, the door to the room was thrown open, surprising all three of them as a young couple casually strolled in.

"I don't know who you are, but this is a private meeting. Please see yourself out," the monarch declared rather plummily.

"Uhhh…" mused Fredric

"Majesty," urged George.

"What is it?"

"This is… uuuhhhh, you know…"

"You know?"

Not knowing what else to do, George mimed throwing a pretend sack over his shoulder and scratching at an invisible beard.

The Queen took the hint.

"So you're…"

"That's right," replied the gorgeous blonde, her famous smile now lighting up the room.

"I'm surprised," continued the Queen, "that our paths have never crossed before."

"Oh Liz," Polkinghorne replied, ignoring royal protocol, "you have absolutely no idea."

Invading the Queen's private space, getting right up close and personal, much to the horror of the three onlookers, Polkinghorne reached out, bringing her hand to within a hair's breadth of the monarch's left cheek.

"May I?" she asked, addressing the stunned pensioner who'd done so much for the British Isles throughout her reign.

"I… I… I suppose," was all she could stutter, the shock of a stranger getting so near all too much.

As it happened, she had very little to worry about, quite the opposite in fact.

Very gently, Polkinghorne placed her soft white palm against the Queen's cheek and with a single command deep within her mind, removed the magical block she'd placed there more than a couple of decades earlier, opening the floodgates, allowing the memories to storm back.

Out of nowhere, Elizabeth's mind was filled to overflowing with recollections from the past, of running alongside the beautiful blonde goddess, of inexplicable adventures, just the two of them, all of which only moments earlier she'd had no idea about.

Sitting on a dull beige sofa with a bereft Martin Luthor King in between the two of them, convincing him not to give up on his cause, urging him on at the toughest of times, nudging him in the right direction, assuring him that the tide could be turned and that racism could become a thing of the past, came flashing back in crystal clarity. Before she had a chance to dwell on that and her friendship with the renowned civil rights activist, she was immediately whisked away to a rain soaked back alley, somewhere in America if the cars on the surrounding streets were anything to go by. Running, out of breath, sodden to the skin, splashes from dirt filled puddles drenching her socks as she sprinted, once again alongside the stunning blonde, accompanied by a male, a panicked one at that, and... someone familiar. Boyish good looks, an instantly recognisable haircut and... Abruptly a shrill sound echoed down the alley, burning her ears, causing her to wince on the run. And then it came back to her, exactly what was going on. They were being hunted by someone with a gun, a man intent on killing... Paul McCartney, lead singer of the Beatles, about to go the same way as his band mate and friend, John Lennon. Huge chunks of brick on their right hand side exploded out of the wall as more shots were fired. Still they continued to move at speed, both females dragging the renowned singer along in their wake, seemingly oblivious to the danger, determined above everything else to keep him safe.

Exhaling, more from the memories than the need to do so, she plunged back into the detailed images, this time to a crowded bookstore, again, clearly in the United States, full of... women.

'Of course,' she thought, 'the first feminist bookstore, and we were there... helping to set it up, against all the odds.' Pride swelled in her chest at the recollection, being part of something so special and close to her heart. Out of nowhere, a single glistening teardrop glided gently down one side of her face, sliding gracefully towards her chin before leaping off towards the intricately tiled floor.

As she blinked, the images resolved into another scene, this time a crowded bar full of shenanigans, boisterous and loud, the two of them partying with one of their best friends, someone George knew well. Marilyn Monroe!

'Whoa,' the Queen reflected deep within her psyche, barely able to believe that she'd been there. But she had! And with Santa of all beings.

Then a day etched into her memory forever swam into view, but this time with a very different take, so much so it was almost impossible to believe.

Sprinting at full pace down the crawler way towards the launch pads and the ocean, the sun's brilliant yellow rays occasionally reflecting through the light green brush that sat either side of them, the man in the middle of the two of them was instantly recognisable as one of the most famous beings on the planet, especially on this of all days. Heart pounding in her ears from the physical toll of what they were doing, she glanced down at the weight in her left hand, amazed to see the huge transparent helmet held tightly in her grip, before once again checking over her shoulder, fearful that the kidnappers were hot on their tail. Thankfully, they weren't, the only thing in her rear view mirror being the huge white and grey Vehicle Assembly Building, an almighty American flag running vertically down one side sending a resounding reassurance down her back, the huge NASA logo on the other side reinforcing not only the reality of the situation, but the danger as well.

"Not far now," shouted Polkinghorne, the least out of breath of the three of them. "You'll be safe once you reach the launch pad. And we'll make sure those villainous monsters are rounded up and put away."

"Much appreciated, ma'am," belted Neil Armstrong, his arms and legs constantly pumping away, the fitness of the man a credit to his astronaut training.

Moments later all three of them skidded to a halt, a short hop away from the pad and the iconic Apollo 11 space craft.

"If not for you I don't know…"

"Now's not the time," Polkinghorne put in. "We've done our job. Now it's time for you to do yours. We're both incredibly proud of you and glad to have helped out. You'd better be off. History's there for the making."

"I'm sure you're right, ma'am. Thank you… both of you."

"All in a day's work."

Elizabeth offered up the helmet, using two hands this time, barely able to take the weight with just one. He accepted it gladly, but not before leaning in for one giant hug, something that caught the monarch of the United Kingdom more than a little off guard. It was very welcome though.

"Good luck," Liz screamed at a rapidly diminishing Neil Armstrong as he dashed towards his awaiting ride, past the tracked crawler transporters, disappearing into the service structure attached to the monumental rocket.

"Well," Polkinghorne quipped, "that was anything but dull."

"Who'd have thought we'd have saved Neil Armstrong from getting kidnapped by those goons?"

"Who indeed?"

Later that day, Liz, iconic monarch and head of the nation had sat, along with most of the world, watching Apollo 11 take off, a feeling of accomplishment and familiarity nagging away at the back of her mind, but not knowing why, the inherent Santa magic having once again blocked out events from earlier on in the day. Here and now though, she could remember everything. What a revelation!

Opening her mouth, about to speak, a cold chill ran up her spine as one last memory returned in breathtaking lucidity.

"Come on, come on," urged a breathless voice from somewhere up ahead through clouds of wispy smoke. "Keep up! We need to stick together."

Spurred on by her friend's words, knowing that the

situation must be bad if there was so much urgency injected into them, Liz continued clambering up the huge pile of rubble they found themselves atop, smack bang in the middle of one of London's busiest streets, scraping the skin off her hands, fingers and knees in the process.

"OH…"

"What is it?" asked the Queen, unable to see much more than a hand's length beyond her face.

"STOP right where you are," Polkinghorne ordered from somewhere up ahead and down below.

"But…"

"No buts. I've found the cause of our consternation, the reason my sense of danger was quite literally off the chart."

"And…?"

"Honestly, you should be about as far away from this as possible."

"That bad?"

"Oh yes."

"I've seen plenty of tragedy and death across all these continued nights of bombing. What could possibly be worse than that?"

"We have what can only be described as… a live one!"

"A bomb!"

"An unexploded and rather large one at that."

"DAMN!"

"Indeed."

"Can't you use your Santa magic to dispose of it?"

"Ideally yes, but this is another of those imbued by magic from the other side. If I go anywhere near it with anything even remotely supernatural, I suspect it will detonate."

"Oh…"

With the blare of air raid sirens and the rattle of anti-aircraft weapons screeching through the wispy nighttime smog, the two women, one of them a dragon as well as a once a year Christmas legend, the other the monarch in waiting of everything around them, absolutely forbidden from being out here, took a moment to consider their next course of action.

"Couldn't we leave it for the authorities?" Liz ventured.

"I'm pretty sure it would take too long, and that's aside from the inherent risk."

"Why the urgency? All the surrounding buildings appear deserted and it's not like anyone else is stupid enough to be out here in the middle of the road."

"Unfortunately," gulped Polkinghorne, "that's not the issue."

"Then what…?"

"There are hundreds of people crammed into The Elephant and Castle underground station directly below us, sheltering from the raid. If the bomb were to explode, it would undoubtedly kill all of them."

"What can we do?"

"Tread carefully and get down here. I'm going to conjure up some tools and see if we can disarm it the old fashioned way."

"Won't the dark magic it's imbued with prevent us from using those?"

"I don't think so," suggested Polkinghorne, having stepped away to use her magic. "I think the same physical properties and safeguards will still apply. Only magic will trigger whatever spells that beast has attached to it."

"Okay… on my way," Liz replied, carefully making her way down the pile of rubble towards her friend's voice, watching every footfall, devastated that many of her loyal subjects were well within the blast radius, a steely determination to protect each and every one of them blossoming into being right at her very core.

Shrugging off the overcoat of mist and smog that nowadays seemed a permanent reminder of the blitz her country had found itself caught up in, free from the treacherous pile, the British monarch strolled across to her companion who'd just, out of nowhere, produced a small selection of tools including pliers, cutters, various sizes of screwdrivers, a hammer, a saw and a chisel. Resembling the most unlikely plumbers in the world, very slowly the two of them headed for the deadly centrepiece, the hissing and spluttering missile, the top quarter of which was fully buried beneath what was left of the busy main road.

It wasn't often nowadays that nervousness threatened to overwhelm her, not with everything she'd been through and had had to stand up for, from such a very young age. But here and now, it had the potential to destroy her, much as the bomb endangered those sheltering down below.

"Take a breath," Polkinghorne urged, sensing the trepidation coursing through her young friend. "Fear is the response the Nazis are hoping for. That's what they want more than ever. Don't give in! Fight with all your heart and soul!"

Wise words indeed...

It was hard to sweep away her mindset, despite the fact that she was one of the bravest of them all. The word Nazi conjured up all sorts of despicable and diabolical images... Messerschmitts and Focke-wulfs filling the skies day and night, dropping their wicked payloads indiscriminately across the country, killing and maiming chaotically, wreaking havoc on those that would do them no harm. Bone chilling and as wicked as they come, even the pinnacle of royalty was not immune to the terror inducing tactics employed by the enemy, and that was before you got to the violence, bloodlust and pure evil at the front. The once promising and progressive new world had with the Nazis, gone to hell in a hand basket, with absolutely no end in sight.

Watching as the breath she let out froze in front of her face, plucking up all her courage, Elizabeth pushed aside her fear, focused on those who needed her help directly below where she stood, and with the expression on her face as resolute as it ever had been, she extended her hand out towards her friend.

"Let's do this thing!" she declared, much to

Polkinghorne's delight.

"Follow me... try not to make a sound."

Liz nodded, hanging onto the coat-tails of the legend she knew to be not only a dragon, but Santa Claus as well, their friendship across the years having led them on all sorts of adventures together, something the monarch hoped would continue long into her reign. Of course, they had to survive this first.

Creeping stealthily forward, the two approached the unexploded bomb, weary of the smoke and steam given off by the section buried into the ground. Ordering her human companion to stay where she was with just one finger, Polkinghorne did a three hundred and sixty degree tour of the warhead, more than a little concerned with the precarious situation they found themselves in.

"Liz... walk carefully around this side. There's a hatch that appears worth investigating."

Emerging next to her buddy, the Queen viewed the aforementioned access point with trepidation, her mind still with the frightened people below.

"What now?"

"I'm going to insert the smallest of the screwdrivers into the surrounding gap and see if I can lever it open. After that... we'll see."

"Good luck."

"To us all," Polkinghorne replied, a brief flash of her renowned smile boosting the monarch's confidence no end.

Knowing that even she wouldn't survive if the bomb detonated, the Christmas legend inserted the shiny silver blade into the darkened crevasse surrounding the hatch as carefully as she could,, and proceeded to put just a little bit of weight behind it, all the while thinking positive thoughts and hoping that she wouldn't be responsible for getting the heir to the throne killed.

POP!

Much to her surprise, the blackened, still smouldering hatch came away with little fuss, no doubt from the friction of the drop, revealing a litany of rainbow coloured wires in a spaghetti mess, the likes of which she'd never seen.

Deep within the confines of her own mind, Elizabeth did something especially plebeian, something and very unusual for her... she swore loudly, using the worst word she knew, raging at the mess they found themselves in.

Brutally aware of the stakes and all the lives at risk, just when Polkinghorne thought things couldn't get any worse... they did, in spades.

Inside the missile, all the wiring appeared backlit and bathed in a soft red glow... never a good sign. Accompanying that though, echoed a harsh ticking sound, enough to send goose bumps down both females' arms. Things had just gone from bad to worse.

Back in the here and now, Elizabeth took a breath, the all encompassing recollection of that experience with the bomb fading into nothingness as Santa removed the palm of her hand, the thought of what was to come leaving the monarch draped in sweat.

"You... I... you... I... we're... friends."

"Forever and always," Polkinghorne replied, pleased at having revealed their previous relationship and just a few of their exploits from throughout the Queen's reign.

"Oh Polks... I've missed you so much. The fun we had..."

"I feel exactly the same way... you know that, and always have, despite the magic involved with blocking some of your memories."

"I know," sniffed Liz, more than a few teardrops now trickling down her pale face.

Rubbing her eyes and shaking her head, the enormity of it all only just sinking in, Liz glanced across at George and Fredric, wondering if they had any inkling of all this.

As if reading the monarch's mind, George piped up.

"I assure you, Majesty, I've only just found out about Polkinghorne myself. If you've been running around the country with her as well, it's the first I'm hearing of it."

"Really?"

"I can attest to that," added Fredric, "but I am eager to hear about some of your adventures, especially if they can startle YOU like that."

"Perhaps that's best for another time," Polkinghorne remarked, much to Vimes' amusement.

"Your Majesty, you asked to be advised when it was time," echoed an emotionless voice from the doorway of the room.

"Thank you," replied the Queen. "I'll be there imminently."

"Understood."

"It seems I have to go. It was good to catch up with you all. And you should know that if you ever need ME, you can call anytime. May God bless you all and I think I'm right in saying... safe skies and thanks for all your once a year work!"

Cheshire cat grins broke out simultaneously on all their faces. Whoever advised her, they were good, in fact better than that, they were GREAT!

With that, she turned and left the room.

Those remaining glanced at each other. It was as dreamlike a few minutes as it was possible to have. With nothing else left to say, they exited the room and headed outside.


The cameras were rolling, the paparazzi filing into their designated stand, and with even the President of the United States gradually heading towards her front row place, the rest of the dignitaries started to take the hint. With a huge main aisle straight down the centre leading to a slightly raised grass circle at the front and huge amounts of seating either side, in this ceremony there were no separate sides for bride and groom supporters, instead all the guests were mixed up, except of course for POTUS, the United Kingdom PM and the Queen who'd had a big hand in setting up all of this.

As the lacrosse girls scooted rather loudly into their seats next to Yoyo's blushing young charges, Sam and Taibul, both looking very much like 007, snuck in on the end of the row, both sipping alcoholic drinks, against convention in the case of the young hockey playing waiter.

Slipping out of a side door, once again in a rush, doing their best not to appear so, George and Fredric walked around a sharp corner straight into a huge man mountain of dark fabric. CRASH went the king, plummeting to the ground, before an outstretched arm with perfectly manicured bright red nails grabbed him by the collar and hoisted him back to his feet. As the two mischief makers gathered their bearings, Flash, whose well muscled chest they'd just run into, gave them his best wedding day grin.

"FLASH!" both friends gasped, pleased to see the heroic dragon and now head of the current crop of Crimson Guards.

Only then did they notice the stunningly seductive and beautiful stranger that accompanied him, the one who'd stopped George from taking one hell of a tumble.

"Enchanted," murmured Fredric smoothly, grabbing her hand and kissing the back of it before she had a chance to realise what was going on.

'Suave,' thought George, cringing at his friend's attempt to charm.

"I don't think we've had the pleasure," announced George, hoping to hell this wasn't going to be another one of these mixed blessings. As far as he was concerned, there were too many of those already. Rules were there for a reason, whether they were made two days ago, two months ago, two years ago or two hundred years ago. That was it, as far as he was concerned.

It was all Flash could do to contain his laughter. This was going to be good.

Standing there with one of the old men kissing her hand, the other a bemused look splattered across his face was almost too much for her... ALMOST!

"Well if it isn't George and Fredric. What brings you two here?" she stated, straight faced.

"Uhhhh…" stammered George, wondering who this was, and why he didn't remember her. Damn his forgetfulness.

'Oh… this is awkward,' thought Peter's grandfather, having the same kind of moment as his best friend. That is, until he spotted Flash holding back the laughter. 'What the…?' was all that he could think, when in fact it should have been 'Who the…?'

Flash couldn't hold it in any longer, a roaring laugh echoed out of his mouth, making everyone across the grounds turn their head in his direction.

A slightly lighter and melodic chuckle resounded out of the perfectly formed mouth of the accompanying female, much to the annoyance of George and Fredric, who both stood there blissfully unaware.

"I think you'd better tell them," urged Flash, tears streaming down his eyes.

"Tell us what?" demanded Fredric.

Tall, strong, confident, beautiful, if this human female had a dragon counterpart it could only have been one of a handful, narrowed down even more by knowing the two best friends. They should really have been able to work it out, but they hadn't… boy were they in for a surprise.

"Sire," she whispered subtly, with just a hint of authority, in the direction of George.

Something about, not so much the voice, but the way the word was said, lingered in the air. And abruptly, out of nowhere, he had it and now that he knew, could have kicked himself for how obvious it should have been.

"Captain!"

"Amelia?" exclaimed Fredric, more than a little surprised.

"At your service gentlemen."

"You two make me laugh," spluttered Flash, still wiping away the tears from his eyes.

"You know I can have you removed from that lofty new position of yours," stated George with just a hint of menace.

"Try again," chuckled Flash. "I think only the monarch can do that."

"And for almost the very first time, George was left absolutely astonished and speechless.

"He was kidding, of course," declared Fredric, clasping Flash on the shoulder, a huge grin showing up on his face.

"I know," replied Flash.

George looked as though he'd taken one too many punches.

"Sire... I mean George, are you okay?" asked Amelia softly.

"I... I... I'm quite alright my dear, just a little winded from running into your friend there."

"I'm sorry about that," remarked Flash, noticing Peter's grandfather looking out of sorts and feeling rather guilty about his previous remark.

"No... no... no Flash, it wasn't your fault as you're well aware. Fredric and I were in a rush and I wasn't looking where I was going... that's all. It's good to see you both, and I mean that with the whole of my heart."

"You too," they replied in unison.

"I do have one question though."

'Here we go,' thought Fredrick, knowing exactly what was coming next.

"And that is?" asked Amelia.

"King's Guards aren't currently allowed on the surface. What's going on?"

And there it was... the crux of the matter.

"I'm no longer with the King's Guards I'm afraid," mumbled Captain Battlehard, unable to look George in the eye.

"WHAT?!"

'Ohhhhh... this is going to get messy unless I step in,' thought Fredric. And so he did just that, stepping between the two of them, all the time facing his friend.

"I should have told you," Peter's grandfather declared quietly, "but the right moment never seemed to present itself. With age taking its toll, I forgot all about it, right up until now, that is."

"YOU FORGOT?! And how is it that you know about this before me in the first place?"

An almighty pause ensued, one which attracted the attention of nearly everyone in the grounds, including the very on edge security personnel, something all four of them were just coming to realise.

Lowering his voice, Fredrick ventured to answer his friend's question.

"Flash came to me on taking up his new role as head of the Crimson Guards, wanting my advice on a few things, one of them being whether or not he could poach Captain Battlehard to head up a new division within his old unit. I told him that from my experience it would be unique, but with everything that Amelia had gone through, she'd probably be the perfect candidate and that I thought it a good idea."

"Oh..." uttered George, slightly taken aback.

"And as you know," continued Fredric, "Crimson Guards are allowed on the surface, in fact that would be a huge part of their job... am I right?"

"Indeed."

"There... settled. How easy was that?"

Turning to the gorgeous visage that was Captain Battlehard in human form, all the while trying to get his mind around that, having only known the deep thinking, tactically aware fighter who'd saved his life countless times in her fearless and fearsome dragon guise, George had only one thing to say.

"I'm sorry. I should know better. Congratulations on your new role. I don't doubt you'll be a great success."

Leaning in and unexpectedly planting a kiss on the side of his face, she very cheekily replied,

"Thank you, sire."

It was a small moment of relief before the big event.

Then something occurred to George. Turning to Flash, he asked,

"How on earth did you get the monarch to agree to all of this? Losing the finest officer in the King's Guards couldn't have been easy."

"It wasn't, and let's just say I had to call in some favours," replied Flash, sombrely.

"I see," said George. "Well... good luck to you both. I'm sure the Crimson Guards will be on top of the world with each of you charting its course."

"Thank you," answered Flash and Amelia simultaneously.

With that, all four of them headed into the melee in a different way from what they were used to, heading through the crowd towards their assigned seats at the front. On their way, they encountered more human faces, Yoyo and his lovely wife Rose, and after spending a few minutes catching up, they took to their chairs in anticipation of what was to come.


Having arrived through the back entrance of Buckingham Palace in a very nondescript black SUV, the bride and her party of one... JANICE, were guided through the long, winding, opulent corridors in the back of the palace, to an area reserved for them, from which they could just open the doors and be in exactly the right place to stroll up the aisle.

Waiting nervously, both young women held their counsel, not particularly wishing to say anything in front of the many courtiers surrounding them. All of a sudden though, as one, the royal minions subtly scattered, leaving them on their own.

"That's odd," whispered Richie to her friend.

"Not really," echoed a loud, regal, and very familiar voice. "They left on my command."

THE QUEEN!

'Oh my,' they both thought, Janice immediately dropping into a curtsey, despite her stunning brown dress getting tangled on the way. Richie, much slower on the uptake, wondered how she'd get down into that position, given that she could hardly breathe as it was, that's how tight her gown felt around her ribcage. She needn't have worried.

"It's alright, both of you. Please stand, young lady."

Janice stood, straightening all the different parts of her attire, barely able to believe she was facing her actual monarch. Of course eventually she'd found out the importance of the dragon monarch, all those months ago, but not really until after the huge battle with Manson and his estranged other half. This though, was something else, on a completely different scale altogether. She'd grown up watching Queen Elizabeth on the television, reading news about her and her family in the press, admiring everything she did, holding together her family, and sometimes the nation. She was nothing short of a legend, and somebody the young woman admired greatly.

With Richie and Janice standing next to each other, the Queen, looking utterly magnificent and close to showing up today's bride, sauntered over to get a better look. Both young women stayed rooted to the spot.

"Uhhhh... would you like me to leave, Your Majesty?" blurted Janice, more than a little nervous, as well as probably having had a little too much to drink.

"It's fine, child, it's fine," replied the British monarch circling the two of them.

Right there and then, the young bar worker vowed to keep her mouth firmly shut from now on.

Stopping directly in front of Richie, the Queen took a few moments to size up the lacrosse player.

Under no illusions, the bride to be knew that she was being vetted, almost as if some unwritten test was taking place. Allowing her face to remain neutral, she focused on controlling her breathing until she was called to speak. She didn't have to wait long.

"I've heard quite a lot about you," announced the Queen, a tiny glint in her eye that only those that knew her best would recognise.

A little in awe, caught totally off guard, which she assumed was the point, the blushing bride decided on a policy of total honesty.

"Well, that could be either very good or very bad."

"Ha... I like you. You're very forthright."

"Thank you, Majesty."

"Oh please, not while it's just the three of us. Call me Elizabeth."

Both women nodded vigorously, well... you would, wouldn't you, when being given an instruction by the head of the monarchy.

"You're probably wondering why I'm here?"

"Not really, Maj... Elizabeth. It is after all, your house," answered Richie.

"That it is, that is. But that isn't the reason. I thought I'd come meet you myself and offer up a friendly face before we see each other outside. It wouldn't do for our first encounter to be in front of a crowd like that... trust me! Occasions like this can be mightily stressful, even when it's supposed to be YOUR special day... in fact, especially when it's YOUR special day. If you need any advice, support or just a means to escape some of the more talkative of VIP's, then don't hesitate to ask or signal. Everyone needs a get out of jail free card occasionally."

Richie laughed. Janice laughed. The Queen laughed.

"But seriously, let me know if there's anything I can do. If you need a pause in proceedings, a short break, or even a moment just to catch your breath, all those things are fine and I will make it so. Sometimes the governments of this world can be too full of red tape but being who I am, I'm able to cut right through it should the situation arise. If you ever need to circumvent any of that today or at any other time, you can be sure I'm the right person to come to."

"I'll remember that, Elizabeth, thank you."

"So…" the Queen went on, "marrying a… rugby player if I'm not correct. That's going to be… interesting. My granddaughter knows all about that."

"Yes it will," replied Richie, knowing exactly to whom she was referring. "But I love him very much. He's as kind, loving and considerate as he is brave and courageous."

"Yes… I've heard all about what you all did during the adventures underground," voiced Elizabeth, taking note of Janice out of the corner of one eye, something that wasn't lost on the young bar worker.

"They were dark days, that's for sure, but if we hadn't worked together, then it would have been all over, for us and the planet. I truly believe the time has come for humans and dragons to work side by side so that the world and every being sharing it can thrive like never before."

"Wise words, young lady. I hope you truly believe them with all your heart."

"I do," replied Richie.

"Good because I think it's nearly time for the proceedings to start. It's a pleasure to meet you, and as I stated before, if I can ever do anything to aid you, you only have to ask. Have a lovely day, remember your lines and may your coupling be long and fruitful, if that's at all possible."

Richie blushed.

Turning away to head out and take her place at the front of the crowd so that she could perform the ceremony, the Queen paused to take in Janice.

"You don't have very much to say for yourself, child," she commented softly.

"It's a pleasure to meet you… Elizabeth," replied the young bar worker.

"On the contrary youngster, the pleasure is all mine. I know all about you and everything you did, including the loss you incurred, for which I'm truly sorry."

"Thank you."

"If I may offer some advice?"

"Of course."

"Continue to help, advise, and keep your friend's feet firmly on the ground. Your experience, courage, wisdom and view of the world will help her immeasurably. If anyone else were saying this, you could take it with a pinch of salt, but not me. Take what I say at face value and live up to your full potential. You are a credit to all of us humans, after all, who could wander into a secret domain and help save the world...? There aren't many. Make sure you too have a wonderful day, and that's a royal order."

"I will do," squeaked Janice in reply, knowing that not only was this THE most important day in the history of the planet and Richie's big day, but probably one she'd never forget for the rest of her life.

The Queen turned and exited out of the door that they themselves would use in only a matter of a few minutes, when the announcements were made. Things felt surreal, dream-like and just downright strange, but with a day like today, that was always going to be the case.


From a couple of seats much closer to the back, three rather uncomfortably dressed males that nobody recognised, but who all had the proper accreditation, squirmed awkwardly in the late morning sun, fiddling with their ties, kicking off their toe pinching shoes, wiping the sweat from their very unfamiliar hands, wishing that it was all over, keen to get back to the dragon domain, sat alongside one very composed female.

"Sit still," ordered the slightly bigger of the three, sitting on the outside, a mop of lush ginger hair spilling out over his head, setting off his pale freckly complexion.

"This tie is killing me," ventured DomCon, adjusting the piece of clothing for what must have been the thirtieth time since sitting down.

"Leave it alone," barked Jar Man a little too loudly, attracting the overt gaze of all those around him.

"You two make me laugh, whether we're underground on a mission, or up here trying to enjoy the most eventful day in the history of the planet. Why don't you just get a room?"

"Oh... haha," declared the little man from the other side of Jar Man sarcastically.

"Who says I'm kidding?" shot back Steel, a massive grin covering his chiselled human face.

"Knock it off, all of you," commanded Nurse Conscience, Steel's date. "This isn't about us today. It's all about Richie and Hook, and they deserve to have a great time, and not have it ruined by a trio of bickering imbeciles. Okay?"

All three were too ashamed to look up and felt well and truly put in their place by the kind and caring female, the one who'd gone so far in saving the laminium ball captain in the aftermath of his recovery during the attack on the medical facility. The fiery little pocket rocket and his two cohorts managed to return a grumbled, "okay," before turning their attention towards the front of the crowd, each wondering when the festivities would begin. Unbeknown to each other, both Jar Man and DomCon had their eyes on the gaggle of lacrosse women, each imagining the fun they could have drinking with them later. Little did they know the trouble they were asking for, or the hardened reputation of the sports stars in question. If they thought the dragon ladies' sandskimming teams were bad, they hadn't seen anything yet. Setting the Palace alight might be more than just a pun if these two groups got together. Hopefully there were some big ass fire extinguishers on standby.

Waiting patiently, knowing full well that when the music started it would be their cue to exit out onto the lawn, the two women were suddenly startled when the door behind them creaked open. Turning to face the interlopers, Richie's kind and gentle freckled face bore a look of absolute thunder as a being she remembered quite well strolled effortlessly through the entrance, flanked on either side by two fearsome looking bouncers... THE PRIEST!

Thoughts of standing in her living room, undergoing the ritual to remove all her dragon memories, helpless to do anything about it, Peter, her best friend standing behind her, supposedly in a support and care role, knowing now that there was more to it than that, and thank God there had been. This dragon and his suited and booted cronies were beings she held in utter contempt for what they'd done so casually. If not for her long dead best friend, the world would be gone, overrun by evil, and all for what? The outdated religious beliefs that relied more on power politics than on any actual faith itself. It was all a sham, she'd come to realise, something that made the irony of their current situation all the more delicious.

Leaving his two associates standing by the door, their heads facing forward, wearing sunglasses even inside, unmoving, the head of the dragon priesthood sauntered over to the two women.

"Leave us, child," he commanded Janice.

Picking up the bottom of her dress, the young bar worker turned to depart.

"She stays!" ordered Richie, in no mood to mess around.

"I see," observed the priest.

As a stony silence set in, the lacrosse playing dragon who'd only moments ago dreaded the commencement of the music from outside, suddenly wished that it would start so that she could escape being in a room with HIM. Some small part of her was aware that events couldn't get underway until he was outside and up on the makeshift stage. And so with that in mind, she tried to move things along.

"What do you want?"

"I... I... I... I merely came to offer my... congratulations."

"I bet!"

"And just what's that supposed to mean?"

Never having met the being, and not having a clue as to who the hell he was, the tone of the conversation and the menacing air the two goons by the door were giving off was causing great concern for Janice, who wondered if she should sound the alarm and get Flash, Amelia, George, Fredric and the rest of the gang in there. The whole situation tasted of danger, something she recognised immediately from their troubles with Manson. Richie, sensing what her friend must have been thinking, gave a little shake of her head to signal that she had things totally under control.

"You've come to regret wiping my memories," continued the lacrosse playing superstar, "and have come to give me some sort of bullshit excuse and an apology."

Never in his entire life had the head of the priesthood been spoken to in that way. He was absolutely outraged. It didn't matter that she'd perfectly hit the nail on the head, it was the thought that somebody, anybody, even the newly appointed monarch, could speak to him in such a manner that determined his response.

"HOW DARE YOU?!" he barked into her face, causing the two bouncer lookalikes by the door to assume action ready stances.

A ferocious snarl of epic proportions, that any alpha wolf would have been proud of, tore across her face as she moved to within an inch of his.

"I DARE!" she threatened menacingly, "And not just because I'm now leader of this world. I would have anyway, even in my previous guise, something I'm sure you're only too aware of. Never in my life have I shied away from something devious, underhand and dishonourable. You and your kind make me truly sick. That you thought you could walk in here and try and make things right with some sort of lame apology goes to show how self important and untouchable you think you are. Well, I'll tell you now.

You've had your day, all of you. The priesthood is a sham, as you and I well know. If I hadn't been forced to have you here, then I can assure you that you and your followers would have been banished to some far flung corner of the earth underground, to keep your vile poison from infecting the humans. With that in mind, be warned. If I hear of you or any of your kind trying to influence our charges in any way, shape or form, I will bring a darkened fury the likes of which you couldn't possibly dream of, down upon all of you. In one fell swoop, the priesthood will be gone and there will be no one happier than I. Get out of my sight, and behave yourself. I have beings here watching your every move. If you make one false step today, you'll never see it coming, mark my words."

Stunned beyond belief, and more than a little afraid for the first time in living memory, the head priest, quivering ever so slightly, joined by his acolytes, opened the door to the outside and as meekly as ever, slipped out into the gardens.

"What the hell?" whispered Janice, utterly gobsmacked.

Her snarl replaced by a look of smug satisfaction, Richie turned to face her friend.

"In case you're not sure, that was the clown that wiped all my dragon memories. And no, I'll never forgive him, and yes, I think that he and his kind are a bunch of fraudulent charlatans."

"Given that little conversation, I don't think he'll be wiping any more memories."

"I truly hope not. In fact, I'm going to make it my mission to make sure he and his no longer have any sort of platform in or out of the dragon domain to influence those easily swayed."

"Is that what they do?"

"I would have to say so. Don't worry though. I've got dragons looking into it even as we speak."

'Wow,' thought Janice. 'She's going to make the best queen ever!'

Walking down the main aisle, all eyes on him, using all his considerable will not to fiddle with his tie, Hook, muscles almost bulging through his perfectly tailored suit, strolled as casually as he could towards where the ceremony would take place alongside his best man, or rather dragon, he wasn't sure which. He was currently reconsidering all his choices that had led up to this very moment. Was it worth it? He wasn't sure... not about her, he was very sure about that, no, it was this whole ridiculous event. Something quiet and secluded would have been much better, but now, as he strolled past the on-looking faces of world leaders he'd only seen on the television, he knew that whatever his feelings were on the subject, there was no getting out of it now. All he could do was adhere to Flash's advice and suck it up, with a view to simply getting through to tomorrow. If he could just do that, then everything in the world would be fine.

Reaching the front, the two of them nodded knowingly to Flash, Amelia, Fredric and George. Picking out the lacrosse girls, Sam, Taibul, Steel, Jar Man and DomCon slightly further back, Hook fought the instinct to wave to them, knowing that with the cameras on him and in a situation like this, that most certainly wasn't the done thing. He just hoped they knew he was thinking about them.

As Tank took his place, his feelings turned to three of his other friends... one, Peter, so devastatingly taken from them at such an early age and all during the course of Manson's advance, like many other dragons across the world. Quelling the sadness he felt at the loss of his friend, he knew that one day they'd meet up again. His thoughts then turned to the master mantra maker, who'd been so much like a father to him. Of course across their time together they'd had their differences, like any family, dragon or human, but they'd always cared and looked out for each other. Those last few years, despite the odd spat or two, they'd mainly got on like a house on fire, one set alight by a huge brute of a dragon. The splicing stupidity came to mind... what a night that had been. One like no other, and something he would never forget, no matter how long he lived. 'It was a shame you couldn't be here,' he thought, remembering his friend, mentor and... dare he say it, father. 'You'd like today, in fact almost certainly YOU'D be the centre of attention, no doubt stealing all of Richie's thunder. Take care, my friend. I hope you're stirring up a whole host of mischief wherever you are.'

Unconsciously, the rugby playing dragon's huge hands brushed up against the slight bulge hidden in his waistcoat pocket, something they'd done about thirty times already since leaving Hook's Buckingham Palace bedroom. Only then did his thoughts turn to the hidden ring and the presence it contained. Fitting that it should be him to pass it on, especially given everything they'd been through since their initial meeting at the start of the battle in the middle of the king's private residence, something that now required a much needed name change. Just the tiniest touch through the material was enough to spark some sort of contact.

"*You seem nervous,*" For'son's voice echoed.

"*Wouldn't you be?*" replied Tank, deep within his mind, concentrating on not moving his lips, knowing that the world would be watching.

"*Are you totally sure about this?*" asked the presence, for what seemed like the fifty millionth time.

"*I am. She's perfect for the job, you'll get on like a house on fire, and you already have a pretty good idea of her character and personality. Trust me, everything will be fine.*"

"*Easy for you to say, you're not cooped up in a blessed piece of jewellery.*"

"I know," whispered Tank, wondering why the hell he was whispering when the conversation was taking place completely inside his head. It just seemed like the right thing to do, was all that he could come up with.

"*It'll be alright. I've told you all about her, and you've both fought alongside each other. If two consciousnesses were ever supposed to be friends, it's both of you, I'm sure."*

*"I hope so."*

*"Enjoy the world through her eyes tonight and see what you think. We'll talk again soon. Take care."*

*"I hope tonight grants you what you're looking for,"* observed For'son.

*"So do I... so do I, my friend."*

With that, Tank's perception and concentration returned to reality, noticing for the first time the three burly looking humans looking like they'd stepped straight out of a gangster movie. Immediately he knew who they were, or more accurately, where they were from... the priesthood!

'Sidelined,' he thought, 'just as you should be after what you did to my friend. Hopefully you'll never be in a position again to wreak such havoc on another living being.'

That was the point at which all the "ooohhhs" and "aaaahhs" started resounding around the grounds.

'Odd,' thought Tank before turning around, 'I thought the music was the cue for Richie to enter.'

On looking around though, it became obvious what the audience were gushing about, or should I say... WHO!

Queen Elizabeth II, the British monarch in all her majestic finery, was slowly making her way down the main aisle, crown on her head, looking magnificent, regal and beautiful all wrapped up in one, something only a few beings on the planet could pull off. Strangely, there were two of them here today.

Slowly, every member of the audience got to their feet, even those dragons disguised as humans who were unused to such courtesies. With the train of her striking white dress flowing gently over the dark blue carpet that lined the way, it was a fitting start to the most historic day ever.


Hidden away behind a closed door, netted curtains covering all the windows, allowing only the brightest of sunbeams to enter the room, both women clasped hands, each having some idea of how the other felt, their love for their other halves shining through in totally different ways.

"It'll be alright. All you have to do is get through to tonight," whispered Janice brightly, a huge smile playing out across the beautiful features of her face.

"It's funny," stated Richie, "I was just about to say the exact same words to you."

Both of them chuckled, more nervously than anything else, given what was about to happen.

"He'd be so proud of you," mused Richie.

"Unbelievable! I was about to say the exact same thing to you."

Cue more merriment.

And then out of nowhere came the trumpeters and the moment of absolute truth!

As one the audience craned their necks, the music rousing them all. An impressive sight on an individual scale, but here today grouped together, the world's leaders and dragon heroes were even more astounding for today's broadcast across the world, not only above, but below ground as well. Parks, open spaces and stadia across the planet were jam-packed full of beings, humans on the surface, dragons downstairs, all waiting to see what the special occasion would hold and how a union like this would work. Most were well wishers. Some were not. But still they watched, all hoping for their desired outcome... only time would tell whether or not their hopes would be turned into reality.

Important heads turned as the epitome of beauty glided across the cushioned dark blue of the carpet, the radiant white train of her dress brushing along behind her, the thin, matching white veil concealing her mesmerising brown eyes, dappled freckles looking like flicked, soft brown paint on an artist's white canvas. Those that knew her and had followed her naive and inexperienced leadership underground with the earth at its most vulnerable, recognised not only the outward beauty, but all that lay beneath, exposed and defenceless, here and now. For the others, the world leaders and politicians, they only knew what they gazed down upon, a princess looking picture perfect and glorious.

Sitting between Zebediah and Monty, Tarko leaned across to Trayrin and whispered,

"She looks so beautiful."

"That she does," replied the bubbly brunette.

Monty and Zebediah, as well as the rest of Yoyo's young charges, all nodded in agreement.

Gliding along at a constant pace, Janice by her side, the train of her dress trailing in her wake, the blushing bride to be ignored all the turned heads and the well wishes, her focus firmly on what lay ahead, Hook... her soon to be husband, Tank... best friend, man and dragon, and of course the British Queen, looking outstanding and easily the most important being amongst the world's most powerful. It wasn't often that Richie faltered or that her confidence failed her, but right here, right now it threatened to do just that. Until that is she locked eyes with the rugby player... no, not Tank, but those of her soon to be husband, the valiant and courageous human who'd stoically agreed to put up with all this nonsense just so that she could be his wife. Knowing that he deserved more than a medal (more than the one he already had, anyway), their intertwined gaze that lasted a mere fraction of a moment, yet conveyed all it needed to: their love and regard for each other and the deep seated commitments they were about to make. Inside she smiled, just for him. It was perfect, with maybe just one exception... PETER! Briefly her heart stirred, but not in a good way, the tragic loss tugging at her very core, this way and that. Stamping her authority on the falsehood of a body that she now felt trapped in, one that signified so deeply the coupling of human and dragon, something this very union and the newly found openness that went with it was supposed to express without any doubt to every being across the planet, she suppressed the feelings that thoughts of her friend brought to the fore, vowing instead to save them for later that day.

Drawing to a halt, two steps below the British Queen, opposite her love, she let Janice pull the veil from her face and tuck it back behind her head. The young bar worker did her duty before taking two steps back, leaving her facing the rugby player she had unexpectedly found love with over the last few months or so.

"Please be seated," announced the Queen into the microphone.

Quietly, for a group so large, they obeyed, with the exception of the security presence dotted around the palace, all of whom remained standing.

"It gives me great pleasure today to be the one conducting the ceremony we're all here to witness. Never in my wildest dreams could I have imagined being in such a prominent position, and landed with the greatest honour of my life… joining these two wonderful beings together in matrimony. (Note the missing "holy" in front of that. Why? As you may imagine, when this union was announced, there was, from some corners, absolute outrage that such a joining, or abomination as some had called it, could go ahead. Most of the churches vehemently refused to go along with it, presenting not only a real challenge, but a likelihood of it not happening at all. And so the Queen had intervened, not only offering Buckingham Palace as a venue, but to oversee proceedings and give them her own personal blessing. If not for her, the world would still be tragically divided. Once again, she'd stepped up and not been found wanting. If only there were more like her.)

"With nothing like this ever having been done before, the bride and groom have written the vows they wish to make themselves for all of you to hear. The service itself is akin to a civil ceremony, albeit with a smattering of royal blessing, something hopefully everybody... every being, can get behind and agree upon. It won't be drawn out, unnecessarily complicated or convoluted. It will just be the joining of two beings who love each other very much. Of course there's much more to it than that. And so to that end, and in a very unusual and bold move, in what are exceptional circumstances, the bride herself, would like to speak before the formalities start."

"Ohhs," "ahhs," and a multitude of whispers echoed around the gardens from everybody including the press and the television camera operators. This was nowhere near protocol and something none of them had been informed would be happening. All eyes bore down on the stunningly beautiful, slightly nervous, lacrosse playing dragon queen, for that's what she would be as soon as the ring was slipped on her finger. With bated breath, the world both above and below ground waited.

Pausing for effect, her ribs feeling extremely constricted by the tightness of her dress, and well aware that the entire planet was watching, she searched for the words she needed, that would hopefully win over everyone watching.

"First I must say thank you to you all for joining me on my big day. Who on earth ever gets an audience like this? Not many. Secondly, I want to thank you for your patience and understanding. The last few months have been difficult for all of us with everything that's happened, and I know, just like me, a few of you will still be in shock at exactly what's transpired. You'll have lost loved ones in the course of the devastation that took place, homes, businesses, work places, pets, friends, acquaintances and a whole host of other things that no doubt I'll forget to mention. For all of that, I'm truly sorry and on behalf of the entire dragon race, I apologise unreservedly. While it's impossible to make up for those heart wrenching loses, I fully intend to learn from past mistakes and do my, and our, best to try and help. All of you have seen the great effort that's taken place in the meantime. How using a combination of hard work, ingenuity, togetherness, technology and magic, can beat the odds and get the planet right back on track in terms of where we were before any of this happened. While this is all well and good, I hope we can push on and exceed expectations both above and below ground. My... I was about to say my people, but as far as I'm concerned, you're all my people. Dragons below ground have been asked to help with the way forward, to share their knowledge and resources, ideas and information in an effort to sustainably live side by side with all of you. To that effect, from tomorrow onwards, the dragon domain will open up to human visitors in certain places across the world. As I say, not all sections will become immediately available, and not because of anything sly or underhand, but because we're still rebuilding from some of the destruction that was caused by Manson's dark forces and we have to know that you'll be safe underground. An example of this would be the monorail. While quite a lot of it has been repaired and would be okay for dragons to use, safeguards have to be put in place for humans, otherwise after the first few twists and turns, you'll end up like bugs splattered on a windscreen, but on the inside instead of the outside."

Cue a few subdued laughs.

"And we certainly don't want that, do we? Especially the poor monorail cleaners. Can you imagine the mess?"

More laughter, slightly louder this time.

"Anyhow, I digress. Over time, we'll be working below ground to open everything up to the whole world. There'll be monorail trains specifically for humans, restaurants, tours, exhibits, museums... everything you can imagine. But it will take time. So please bear with us. Our hope, just like yours, is a world where we can co-exist side by side, dragons soaring through the skies, humans living amongst us underground. One in which we can share our technology and magic with a view to solving some of the planet's biggest problems... climate change, pollution, over population, economic hardship and many other issues. All of these can hopefully be solved now that everything is out in the open. My biggest wish is to work together, reside together, live, eat, drink and play together, for the benefit of all. And so with that in mind, and to signify the start of what I hope will be a beautiful and prosperous friendship, I have a little gift that," turning to the British Queen before continuing, "Her Majesty has said I may put in her garden."

She gave Janice the signal. Immediately the young bar worker closed her eyes and reached out for her very special friend. In the blink of an eye, she got the response she was looking for.

Off in the distance to the north, a boom reverberated across the sky. Immediately the security guards throughout the Palace became alert. The British monarch, one of the few who knew exactly what was going on, waved away their concerns with a white gloved hand and a smile. All heads turned in that direction, wondering what on earth was going on and whether or not they were about to see their first dragon carving its way across the horizon. The world was about to be disappointed on that front, but they were going to get a glimpse into the magical and unusual.

Over the course of the last few months, MOST of the details of the epic battle for the planet that had played out beneath ground had come out, some in the immediate aftermath, others leaked piece by piece over the course of weeks. The public, both dragon and human, were intrigued and captivated, all hooked on the stories the press continued to feed them. One such tale, something never confirmed or denied by anyone that had been there, was of a bladed weapon rampaging on a killing spree, helping the light sided heroes significantly reduce the number of enemies in the sky and on the ground, seemingly one of the most valiant fighters there. Rumours ran riot about it being controlled by a human host, whilst some said that it had a mind of its own and did no one's bidding. Magic was touted as an explanation for its very being, while others discounted it as some sort of technology. Any way you looked at it, it/he/she was something unusual and an oddity that had captured the public's imagination. More information about anything related to the fabulous weapon was never released. Nobody knew anything more. That is, until now.

Reluctantly chained to his cargo, Fu-ts'ang felt like a cheapened freight train on its regular late night journey... nobody paying attention, barely any recognition, not a single soul familiar with the important job it was doing. All that was about to change in one fell swoop. And although he hadn't wanted to be part of all this, he'd acquiesced to the request from the soon to be new monarch, especially after speaking to the one true friend he felt he had... JANICE! Once she'd explained the thinking behind it, and how it would give him the stage all to himself on Richie's special day, albeit for only a brief time, his mind had been changed. Then of course there was the cargo he carried. Part of him didn't want to do it because of that, but on reflection, he supposed it was a deserving tribute and, because without him the planet would be lost and almost certainly he'd be committing heinous crimes under the command of that psychopath if the right side hadn't won. But still, it wasn't as simple as that. After all the being in question had kept him locked up for a huge amount of time, very rarely visiting and even then not choosing to interact. And that was the crux of the matter... being detained against his will. Brushing aside his thoughts on the subject, figuring the past was best left behind, the feeling of tension increasing on the chains around the object he carried through the air caught his attention. Looking down beneath him, just to be sure, he checked to see that nothing untoward had happened, mainly because of how important today was. It hadn't and he was sure there was no way it could, given that he was practically unbreakable... PRACTICALLY! Course set on his eventual target, his lithe bladed body shivered uncontrollably, and that had nothing to do with the effervescing frost that continually circled his entire length. It was more down to the thoughts of being shattered into a thousand pieces by the diabolical Manson and then having to be saved from extinction in the deepest darkest part of 'the gloom' by Tank and For'son. Across his history, he'd suffered badly in so many different ways, many too unspeakable to mention, but being destroyed and then brought back was perhaps the most harrowing, with the exception of losing Song Jin.

Brilliant yellow sun beating down across the perfect blue sky, the beams of radiant heat and light reflecting like a glitter ball at a disco, doing their best to negate the cold from the frost, Fu-ts'ang wondered how many of those down below could see him effortlessly gliding through the air, carrying the triumphant masterpiece that many had spent so long creating. He'd been told that few would witness his approach, because nearly all of them would be watching events playing out on their televisions, whatever the hell they were. Anyhow, it didn't matter, because he'd almost reached his destination, and could feel his best friend, the idealistic human girl, standing by to greet him.

Slowing his approach, the fantastical weapon lined up the object with the area he'd been told to deposit it in and slowly descended towards the open ground just to the left of the seating as he looked at it, taking in the gasps of shock, awe and wonderment as he did so.

'I could get used to this,' he thought, noting the respect and longing in the eyes of some powerful beings. It was then that he caught sight of her, dressed from head to toe in brown, looking a lot like an upside down soufflé, which interestingly enough, he could remember eating, many thousands of years ago. With a sharp CLUNK, it was done, the statue, as that's what he'd been delivering, landing perfectly in place.

Over fifty metres tall, created from some kind of metallic glass that had a light matt rainbow sheen running through it, the carving depicted a dragon hunched over, holding the hand of a young woman, the dragon's expression one of hope and help, a wide eyed look of wonderment buried in the human's eyes. Startlingly, although not to the few that had seen the statue already, the magnificent looking dragon in question had a pair of square spectacles perched atop his nose, making him look a lot like someone quite familiar, something that Tank felt was a fitting tribute to his mentor and friend...

Catching the bride's eye amongst all the commotion of the statue and Fu-ts'ang's arrival, the young rugby playing dragon mouthed a huge, "Thank you," to his pal, incredibly proud of what she'd done. In fact, they all were. Everyone who'd been part of the epic battle, or even known the shopkeeper for any length of time, found it a huge mark of respect to a dragon who'd always given his all, took no prisoners and said what he thought. Everyone, humans and dragons alike, could learn from the way the master mantra maker had conducted himself (most of the time). Without his contribution, none of them would be alive to witness this special day. The gold embossed plaque sunk deep into the bottom of the statue said pretty much this.

**MASTER MANTRA MAKER AND EMPORIUM OWNER EXTRAORDINAIRE**

**GEE TEE, WITHOUT WHOM NONE OF US WOULD BE HERE.**

**MAY HE HAVE FOUND PEACE IN THE GREAT RIVER OF LAVA.**

Ignoring protocol, Richie left her place beside the Queen and Hook, leaving mouths agog in the audience, as the onlookers wondered what on earth she was going to do. Strolling casually over to the statue, her intricate white train fluttering in the breeze behind her, the soon to be dragon queen knelt down, placed her hand on the plaque and in the quietest voice possible, told the old shopkeeper that she loved and missed him. Lost on all the humans, not a single dragon had missed a beat, hearing every single word. If this was how the day was going to start, they all thought, then there would be tears aplenty before it was all over.

Rising to her feet, she beckoned Fu-ts'ang down

towards her. Hovering closer in an upright position, Richie removed the chains from his frost enshrouded body, all the time aware of the ever present cold circling him. With the enigmatic magical weapon in mid-air in front of her, almost everybody was caught off guard by what she did next. Mirroring Gee Tee's actions on that fateful day underground in the Salisbridge market place in an effort to get the dragons to accept her as their leader, with a view to then freeing the planet from Manson's tyranny, the young lacrosse playing dragon dropped to one knee and bowed her head solemnly. Gasps rang out across the grounds from everybody, with the exception of those who'd been present at the nursery ring. As one, they all shed a tear, so poignant was the soon to be queen's tribute to her friend and comrade. Frozen to the spot, the groom and best man had no words for what they'd just seen. In fact in Tank's case it was a good job he hadn't known what was going to happen, or he'd never have agreed to be here. Not because it wasn't right or deserved, but because he knew just how much it would tear him up inside and cause him to fully face some of the emotions he'd become conflicted by ever since the old shopkeeper's death. Standing there with a stream of teardrops rolling down his face, unable to react in any way at all, was tougher than anything he'd ever done, and that included losing his best friend Peter. One single being didn't deserve so much sadness and pain, particularly one as kind and thoughtful as Tank. Fate, however, gave no ground or favour, and was no doubt lurking somewhere close by smiling. She was, but not at Tank's visible heartache.

Admiring the gesture, especially since he'd been at the market place when the master mantra maker had pulled the quick witted stunt and given cude lacrosse playing dragon virtually no choice but to lead, Fu-ts'ang tilted the whole of his body forward, acknowledging her actions, something that caused the audience to erupt in applause. Once things had quietened down, the soon to be dragon queen resumed.

"This statue is dedicated to all those who lost anything

in the dastardly fight for the planet. Whatever it was, this is dedicated to you. A human and dragon holding hands signifies hope for a new beginning. And this isn't just any dragon depicted here... NO! You've all heard the stories, listened to the songs, read the reports in the press. As the plaque reads, this is the legendary Gee Tee, master mantra maker and possibly the best friend ever," she said, glancing across to Tank.

Turning back to the audience and of course, all the cameras, the young woman continued.

"This is our gift, and my hope is that it will inspire a spirit of cooperation between our very different races. I'm sure on this long, wild and new journey, there'll be bumps in the road, but together, and this is one of the things Gee Tee taught me, we can overcome almost anything. Nothing is beyond our grasp. In concert we will always make things work."

"BRAVO," shouted one dignitary at the back, standing up and clapping.

"COULDN'T AGREE MORE," yelled another.

Soon, one by one, they were all standing, cheering, clapping and whistling. It was most undignified, but somehow that seemed the point and what made it all the more becoming.

Still rooted to the spot, Tank opened his mouth to cheer, but nothing seemed to come out, despite the continuing waterfall of tears. With all eyes on Richie, nobody noticed the British monarch pass the rugby playing dragon a handkerchief. Probably a good job too.

Using her hands to quieten down the crowd, and still standing by the statue, Richie hadn't quite finished what she wanted to say.

"Speaking of legends from tales of the battle that you know so well by now, this one hovering here in front of me should need no introduction... but I will give him one anyway. A weapon that knows no equal, a soul as brave and full of conviction as any I've ever met, and a wonder of a warrior, I give to you the all conquering Fu-ts'ang!"

Once again, and totally unbecoming of all the world leaders, diplomats and VIP's, the place erupted in clapping and screaming. Even the British Queen put her hands together, and that's hardly ever done.

As soon as the noise died down, Richie continued.

"I've pulled a few surprises on you, and my soon to be husband. I feel now I should get back to what I came here to do. If I don't get the chance to say it later, please, everyone, enjoy the day and embrace our bright future."

About to erupt once again, the soon to be queen used her hands to quieten them down before they'd even got started this time, before turning and walking back to her future husband and Elizabeth II. Fu-ts'ang followed briefly, before moving off into a position next to Janice, who greeted him with a hearty smile. Telepathically, they exchanged pleasantries.

And then, the official ceremony began.

As you might imagine, there was all sorts of officialdom, the signing of documents by the bride and groom and their witnesses, the sort of thing which, for the most part, was incredibly boring. Even the exchanging of vows was slightly dull, apart from the bit where Richie promised to hoard all his treasure, teach him to fly and try mightily hard not to get so carried away as to scorch him in the marital bed, something everyone there found amusing, even Elizabeth, apart from Hook, who'd already had a few close encounters.

Now you might have thought there'd be issues when it got to, "Does anyone here know of any reason why these two can't be joined?" Let's face it, there are probably quite a few, and we've only got as far as their different races. But to prevent any difficulties at this point in proceedings, any mention of this had already been removed. Better to be safe than sorry.

And that really only left the rings.

Taking the hand crafted, white gold ring emblazoned with, yes, you've guessed it... DRAGONS, Richie carefully slipped it on what she liked to think of as her husband's sausage-like fingers, before looking up into his brilliantly smiling face. Pride, adoration and love was all that radiated back. Not that she had any doubts, but in that one perfect moment, she knew she'd met her soulmate and the being she wanted to spend the rest of her life with. It was otherworldly and something she would never forget for as long as she lived.

Now Hook's turn to slip on the ring, his huge digits trembled slightly, knowing the importance of what he was about to do. Almost the dragon equivalent of a coronation, he knew that by gliding the magical ring with For'son's presence captured inside it onto Richie's finger, things would never be the same again for both of them. But it had already been agreed, and he'd accepted everything that came along with the pairing. Taking the exquisite piece of jewellery (and that was without considering its magic) from Tank's outstretched hand, giving his friend a nod of appreciation, he turned to gaze into his bride's wide and wondrous eyes, never ever imagining he'd be part of anything like this, or being caught up in a love so powerful that it made his stomach do somersaults practically every time he caught her eye. But that's how it felt, and had since their first date, only a matter of months ago. Still beaming, he mouthed the words, "I love you," for only her to see as he slipped the powerful entity onto her finger, completing not only their union but also the crowning of her as queen of the dragon realm, and the entire planet. The moment he leaned in and kissed her, not only did the whole of the Buckingham Palace grounds erupt, but the whole world rejoiced as it had never done before. A match made in heaven had been secured down here on earth, one that would hopefully stand the test of time and the trials of humans and dragons.

After that, there was only one thing to do... PARTY!

# 47 MUCH MERRIMENT

Across the world, above and below ground, the celebrations began. Magical fireworks lit up the dragon domain on every continent as false daylight turned to night everywhere, through a combination of magic and technology. Loved ones were mourned, a bright new future toasted to, as friends and family across the underground world made merry in stark contrast to all the depressing events of the last six months. In one day, nearly all the bad things were forgotten, except of course the casualties who would always be remembered, their new queen had made sure of that with monuments erected across the planet, naming those dragons who'd given their lives in a time of global tragedy. Already she'd gained a reputation for doing the right thing, no matter whose nose she put out of joint and regardless of cost. For that, ordinary dragons in the street loved her all the more.

Across the surface, nearly the entire population celebrated, again like the dragons below ground, mourning missing loved ones, but taking the chance to relish the new opportunities that were coming their way at quite a pace. Excessive amounts of food and drink were consumed, music was played, and almost everybody had a good time.

Back at the Palace, things were much the same. Politicians and world leaders danced, drank and ate themselves into a stupor. Security guards from different countries looked on in disbelief at the mess before them, upset and disconcerted at the lack of protocols being observed. They needn't have worried. The dragons, following their new queen's orders, had it all covered, having long since infiltrated every level of both the Palace and the upper echelons of security services everywhere. At least eighty percent of the catering and security staff were dragon agents in disguise, looking to make sure everything went without a hitch and that no dastardly deeds could take place anywhere within a ten mile radius of central London. Police, again dragons, were out and about, as well as covert Crimson Guards, for obvious reasons. Criminality was not an option tonight, not anywhere, and should some be discovered, it would be dealt with in the harshest manner possible, something that had been broadcast in advance across the world. Today was about peace, positivity, forging an unbreakable union, love and understanding. Nothing would spoil it. And it didn't.

"Heyyyyyy," slurred Flash, having made sure to adjust his DNA to let the alcohol have at least a little effect on his rough and tumble human guise, "if it isn't the new councillor for Australia... congratulations!"

Yoyo, all his wide eyed young charges in his wake, holding Rose's hand, squeezed his way into the circle that Flash, Amelia, Fredric, George, Tank, Hook, Steel, Jar Man and DomCon had created.

"Well, thank you," he replied, slightly embarrassed by his friend's comments.

"No... really," stated Flash. "I can't think of anyone who deserves the position more, given everything you've done. And I'm not just saying that because you've saved my life on numerous occasions."

Cue lots of drunken jeering and the raising of glasses, with barely anyone thinking that it didn't have something to do with that.

When the noise died down, Yoyo opened his mouth, only for Rose to cut in before he had a chance to speak.

"Only a short while ago I was completely oblivious to this side of my husband's character, utterly unaware of the heroic deeds he'd done in the past and of the young dragons he'd helped steer in the right direction," she said, putting her unfamiliar human arms around two of them, Trayrin and Monty, who stood by her side, much to their horror. "Having fallen in love with him many, many decades ago, with these revelations it feels as though it's happening all over again, something I'm so thankful for. And on that note, I have a little announcement for the councillor, something he's completely unaware of."

This caught Yoyo off guard and nearly made him spill his champagne.

"After a brief discussion with all YOUR young dragons whilst you were fiddling about transforming into human form and then taking an age to slip into your clothes, we all came to the conclusion that the best thing for everybody was that they should be OUR young dragons. And so with that in mind, and with the total agreement of them all, I'd like to announce that WE have adopted every single one of them, and that's official, made so by the queen herself, only a few minutes ago."

"Oh my…" was all that Yoyo could get out before all the young dragons went ballistic, jumping up and down, shouting, screaming and yelling, hugging each other vigorously, particularly Rose who barely knew what had hit her. Unsurprisingly, such a grand and selfless gesture brought instant tears to the old healer's newly formed, unfamiliar human eyes, causing a torrent of teardrops to weave their way down his cheeks, some slipping into the edge of his mouth, their salty taste tickling his tongue, others bounding off his smooth chin, heading for the luxuriously carpeted floor. Not knowing what else to do, and overcome with love for his wife, truly thankful for the life they shared, the experienced healer threw himself at her, losing himself in her arms, immersed in their own little world. Despite allowing just a little of the alcohol to take effect, Flash still had the presence of mind to whip Rose's champagne glass out of her hand before it dropped to the floor. She thanked him with a wink.

"I'd like to thank you all. You're the best friends any dragon could ever have." Turning to his wife he said with a smile, "Especially you. If anyone here ever needs anything from the new Australian councillor, please feel free to get in touch."

And with that he raised his glass for a toast. The others did likewise.

Hook, having the time of his life, glanced across the room, wondering where his newly crowned wife had got to and then smiled on noticing her white dress performing acrobatics in front of a pyramid of champagne glasses piled almost up to the ceiling, being cheered on by all her lacrosse teammates, the centre of attention of the world's most powerful men and women. For a split second he worried how it looked, but then he remembered that's what he loved about her, the no-nonsense approach to life, not giving a damn what other beings thought, yet caring deeply for her friends who she knew would have her back, human and dragon alike. So he just stood and stared, glad to be alive, lucky to be joined with the most amazing female on the planet.

"She's quite something, isn't she?" Tank declared, noting the direction in which his friend was looking.

"She certainly is."

"She's lucky to have you," observed the rugby playing dragon to his teammate.

"I think what you're supposed to say is, that I'm lucky to have her," Hook replied.

"There is that, but I'm pretty sure it works both ways. In her new role, there will no doubt be huge pressure and difficulties along the way. I don't doubt for one second that you'll help her cope. Your role will be just as vital as hers, perhaps in some way even more so."

"No pressure then," answered the rugby playing human, now one half of the world's most powerful couple.

"None whatsoever," responded Tank.

Looking down into his half empty glass, Hook reflected on what had been quite a day so far, knowing that it was far from over.

"What will they think of me?" he asked his friend.

"What will who think of you?"

"The dragons, you know, all the ones underground.

How will they react to me? Will I have to see all of them? Will they respect me or just see me as a top piece of eye candy?"

This last line was delivered just as Tank had taken a mouthful of his drink, lager in his case, straight from the bottle. Unsurprisingly, the liquid came out faster than it went in, fountaining all over the place, much to everyone's amusement.

Tank gave his friend a knowing look, sure he'd done that on purpose, having spent too much time with him in sports bars across the south of England after rugby matches.

"I don't think you have to worry too much," he mused, wiping away the excess lager from around his lips. "You'll probably be too busy at openings, cutting ribbons, collecting flowers, shaking dragon hands, kissing dragonlings on the cheeks and adult dragons on the lips to worry about any of that. It'll suit you down to the ground!"

The look on Hook's face was priceless, not knowing whether his friend was kidding or not, that is until George, Fredric, Amelia, Flash, Yoyo, Rose and all the young dragons broke into fits of hysterics. Tank had repaid his pal at least twice over.

As the music ramped up, the dancing became more erratic and frivolous, with all the VIPs, world leaders and dragons letting their hair down and getting in on the act. Phones had been prevented from working inside the Palace through some intricate dragon magic, and although the television cameras remained, they only did so outside, waiting to see if anyone of significance would come out and talk to them.

Sitting on the bottom step of a huge winding staircase, trying carefully not to spill any of the champagne from the fluted glass she held, onto the brilliant bright red carpet that seemed to cover everything she could see, Janice tried not to let the bubbles from her drink escape up her nose. Aside from the fact that she was tired from having been up before 5am, she felt exhausted from all the running around and being polite to people she didn't know. Of course there'd been questions, mainly about the battle and her part in it, as well as what it was like to have a best friend that was not only a dragon, but the queen of everything as well. While most of us would have gotten fed up after a while, not her, not with her bright and cheery outlook on life and a bubbly personality that would outshine almost anyone's, and so she answered all the questions, becoming pretty much the darling television star of the day. Right now though, it had all started taking its toll. Exhausted, emotionally drained, the happiness and excitement with which she'd started the day all used up, she sat spent, contemplating what could have been, had things played out differently at the end. Twisting the nissix ring around and around, her mind cast back to the final few seconds before HIS death, for about the millionth time wondering if there was anything she could have done to effect another outcome. Lost in a tainted dark shadow and frozen with fear as things had played out, once again even in hindsight, she couldn't find a single thing she could have done differently. It was a conundrum, a riddle and a mystery as to why her mind would constantly return to that particular moment. All she wanted to do was to move on and get her life back on track, but it seemed as though her memories had other ideas. Perhaps that would all be put to bed after the events of today... by golly she hoped so, but there was definitely no way to tell.

Abruptly, she was startled out of her thoughts by a blur of brightest white zipping around the nearest corner, bare feet skidding to a halt directly in front of her.

"Are you okay?" asked the dragon queen and her friend. "I've been looking for you everywhere."

"I'm fine," smiled the young bar worker. "Just a little tired and over emotional, you know."

Instinctively Richie nodded, understanding totally.

"Not long now. We'll wrap things up here and then be on our way. It'll be worth the wait, I guarantee it."

That brought a smile to Janice's face.

"Let's show willing and get back to the party, at least for a little while longer," suggested Richie.

Janice giggled profusely. Richie gave her a questioning look.

"Show willies?" the young bar worker exclaimed, tears rolling down her cheeks.

Richie shook her head as Janice rolled about on the stairs.

"Willing!," Richie repeated carefully. She might as well not have bothered. "If you've got a willie to show them, then you and I need to have a serious chat, young lady," exclaimed the newly crowned queen, causing a few of the staff nearby to raise an eyebrow or two and Janice to lose it completely. The glass fell out of her hand, spilling onto the carpet as she collapsed backwards onto the stairs. Richie hoped her husband would show better timing in the future and know exactly when to turn up. Since he hadn't, she dabbed the carpet with a smidgen of magic to remove the stain, picked up her hysterical friend and returned to the festivities as she should, given they were pretty much in her honour.

Across the world, beings had the time of their lives and for the most part, forgot about the tragic events that had led them to that point. Over the last few months, the dragons had used their powerful magic to rebuild not only their own civilisation underground, but to repair the human world above, specifically on their monarch's orders, doing everything they could to help their charges on the surface, and that was before the dragon world 'came out' so to speak. After that, it was all guns blazing, sharing technology, working side by side, hand in hand, doing everything they could to get things back to normal. At first, as per usual, humans were suspicious of their newly found friends' intentions, but being open, transparent and honest paid off big time, with many seeing the benefits with their own eyes as well as now feeling the effects. Homelessness had been banished in one fell swoop, something the dragon domain had always been appalled at and had secretly worked hard to correct. Now they were out in the open, it was possible to do so much more across the globe, and so they had.

Using their technology, freely given, carbon emissions were literally cut in half overnight, the results obvious within a couple of weeks with cities like Los Angeles in America now visible from some way off, whereas before it would have been shrouded in a dirty pollution filled haze. In the canals of Venice, Italy, the water was so clear it was now possible to see the fish swimming within, and even the very bottom of the famous waterways, something that hadn't happened in living memory. Also, dolphins frolicked and played throughout the watery thoroughfares and jellyfish moved in, much to the amazement of residents and the delight of tourists. These things were now commonplace across the world, immediately putting paid to most of the humans' suspicions.

And so it was that tonight's celebration was the cherry on top of the icing on the cake, as far as coming together as a planet was concerned. And it wasn't over yet.

Back at the Palace, sparkling squadrons of magical butterflies circled the room, weaving in and out of revellers, leaving a trail of shimmering dust in their wake that lit up the place. Fountains of beer, wine and spirits seemingly produced out of nothing dotted around the room, providing not only focal points for people to gather, but huge talking points, with most of the important visitors wondering how they could get their hands on such things. People danced, ate, drank and just generally had a good time, with all thoughts of politics and rivalries forgotten, at least for the time being. Huge dragon ice sculptures littered the function room, so intricately carved that they threatened to come to life. Flash made the mistake of telling his date, Amelia, that the sculptures themselves freaked him out a little... well, they would wouldn't they given everything he'd been through in Antarctica? Of course she mercilessly teased him for the rest of the evening about it, just as couples do.

Off in one corner the Salisbridge ladies' lacrosse team took on all comers in drinking games galore, with them already having put the French President and the Australian Prime Minister to shame and were currently engaging Jar Man and DomCon in an even more dangerous level of antics. From the outside, it looked as though Jar Man might well end up suffering more at their hands than he had at the talons of the ladies' sandskimming team all that time ago. Let's hope all the nail polish had been well and truly hidden.

A group including most of Garrett's assault team, with the exception of the burly Owen and all of Yoyo's young charges looked on fascinated from the sidelines, wondering whether or not to try and join in. Given the hammering DomCon was currently taking, they wisely decided not to, all having enough fun trying the vast array of different human beverages, akin to Tank, Richie and Peter on the occasion they got to watch the famous laminium ball match in which Steel took down two teeth in one go from a penalty with Silverbonce's help after slicing the ball itself in two, at Peter's house, something that seemed like a lifetime ago.

Near the doors to the outside, Steel and Tank talked everything laminium ball, much to the rugby playing dragon's delight, with Hook listening in intently, already having told them both that he was desperate to see a match when play in the leagues finally resumed. Tank told him he'd take them to the next Indigo Warriors game and that he had little choice but to support that team. Keen didn't begin to cover it, so madly was he caught up in everything dragon team sport, almost forgetting all about his wife and their big day... ALMOST!

In a tiny little alcove off to one side, three exceptionally important beings sipped champagne from delicate sparkling fluted glasses, each trying to take in the importance of what was happening around them, all wondering what the future offered.

"It's so good to see you again, Madam President, Monica," Garret remarked.

"Please Al, call me Julia when it's just us."

The 'bald eagle' glanced in Monica, the President's Chief of Staff's direction.

"Monica doesn't count. Not only is she my Chief of Staff, but she's my closest confident as well."

"Julia it is then," Garrett replied, simultaneously inclining his head and raising his glass.

"To new found friendships and possibilities," urged the President, taking a moment to enjoy what was going on all around her, knowing that there were plenty of other world leaders there who wanted to talk business. For now, they'd just have to do with waiting.

Further along, hugging the shadows, George and Fredric talked and drank, reminiscing over old times, action and missions, recounting their first meeting in Salisbridge at the time of the original capture of Troydenn all those centuries before when they were both young knights. Catching up like this hadn't happened in an age, not with everything going on in and around them and so the two friends (more like brothers actually), ended up having the time of their lives.

Another darkened table had two couples sprawled across each other, recounting tall tales of action and adventure as Yoyo and his wife got to know Flash and Amelia as a couple. And things couldn't have been going better, apart from Flash taking a few punches for his cheekiness from his other half as he occasionally tried to show off. He'd never have admitted it, but he loved every second and wouldn't change his new found life and love for anything. Two couples very much devoted to each other, one in the middle of their journey, the other just starting out.

'If everything could be like this forever, I could be quite content,' thought Flash, as Yoyo embellished yet another story.

Probably, out of all the happenings throughout the

whole room, the most surreal was the sight of Al Garrett and Owen his head of security sitting down, recounting stories with much hilarity involved, with the British monarch, Elizabeth II. Steely eyed guards looked on from the shadows, having already been waved away by the queen, as courtiers delivered a constant supply of drink to the table. Best of all was the fact that all three of them were getting on like a house on fire.

'Three more things to go,' thought Richie, one of the more self aware beings in the room, having had a little to drink, but having chosen, unlike on the odd occasion at the Salisbridge Sports club, to use her magic to quell the effects. Steadying Janice, who would no doubt have fallen to the floor without her support, still crying with laughter about willies, the newly crowned dragon queen was determined to push on with the next stage of the event, and so with that in mind, propped her friend up against the door, grabbed two silver serving platters from the nearest table, shook the remains from them onto an empty plate, and with all the significant force she could muster, banged them together. The noise was startling, instantly causing the music to stop and everyone to take note of her.

"If I could have everyone's attention please. I know some of you are keen to bestow gifts and while it's not possible for us to accept all of them in person, there are a few that I've agreed to have presented tonight. I'd very much like to get on and do that now, as I have a very special little something planned for later."

Everyone there took notice of that, wondering what on earth it could be. Extravagant, special and downright magical would best describe it. But that was for later.

"So... if you could take your seats and quieten down," she said, glaring across at the lacrosse team who looked as though butter wouldn't melt in their mouths, DomCon and Jar Man wobbling about amongst them, "my husband and I will arrive on stage in a few moments."

Having left all talk of laminium ball for another time,

Hook instantly appeared at his wife's side, ready for yet more duties.

"Sorry," she whispered, meaning every word of it.

"Don't be, I'm having the time of my life. Apparently I bleed Indigo Warriors colours... who'd have thought."

"You bet your ass you do. Who told you that anyway?"

"Tank!"

"Of course. I'm glad he did."

"He also said he'd take me to the next one of their matches when it all resumes."

"Did he? Any mention of taking me?"

Hook's face couldn't hide it, even though it tried.

"I thought not. He's for the gallows the first chance I get."

Hook laughed. Richie followed. And then it was time. Holding hands, they made their way to the purpose built gap that had been made for them on stage, both sitting on the bottom few steps, which the audience regarded as very unconventional.

With everyone in the room sitting comfortably, and even those the more worse for wear through alcohol consumption knowing to keep quiet, the first to approach the stage was the President of the United States, who looked as though she'd been enjoying herself. She was more than a little dishevelled, having totally lost both her shoes.

Acknowledging the couple with a kiss and a handshake, and getting it the right way round, she presented Richie with a huge steel tube about two feet long.

"Majesty," she started. "I'm told your people like nothing more than flying and bathing in lava. Well hopefully I can provide you with both. These are the deeds to an area of land on the Aleutian Islands around an active volcano called Shishaldin. It has massive lava flows and over two dozen pyroclastic cones on its North Western flank. The air space around the island is already restricted and we would be happy to help build you and your family a personal private getaway. This is our people's gift to you."

Taking hold of the proffered tube, the young dragon smiled at the idea of having her own volcano to play in, despite her primordial dragoness being contained by the human form she was stuck in.

"Thank you, Madam President, your gift is very much appreciated. I look forward to working with your country to make the planet a much better and rewarding place."

"As do I," replied the President, before walking back to her seat.

Next to approach was the United Kingdom's Prime Minister. Looking much more of a mess than his American counterpart, clearly having had a great time up until now, he cheekily took hold of Richie's hand and dabbed it with a huge sloppy kiss, much to her amusement.

"Majesty," he slurred. "We've searched long and hard for a gift to give you that you haven't already got and believe we've come up with something unique. Searching the entire country, we managed to find a supply of harvested charcoal dating back to the 1820's which I'm told the dragon world could quite possibly fight a war over. Of course we don't want any of that, just for you to be happy in your new life. So we'll deliver to you whenever you want and you can distribute it how you see fit. Apparently there's about fourteen tonnes of the stuff. I hope you approve."

Licking her lips, the dragon queen replied,

"I really do. Thank you so much."

Next to approach was the British Queen, strangely, flanked by Al Garrett. Richie frowned, along with most everyone else.

Not bowing or offering out a handshake, as was her wont, Elizabeth spoke up so that everyone could hear.

"Majesty, I'd like to offer you up a piece of jewellery that has been in my family for many generations. Although I'm sure you have the most fantastic collection of trinkets, necklaces, bracelets and rings, I'm quite sure you'll see the value in this."

With that, up stepped a royal courtier, carefully carrying

an immaculate black velvet box. Dropping to one knee in front of both queens, his gloved hands opened the box to reveal its contents.

Very little could surprise the lacrosse playing dragon given everything she'd been through, particularly the battle with Manson and his army of evil, but here and now she gasped. There, sparkling like a high end, brand new car just out of the showroom, was the most magnificent bracelet she'd ever seen. Most in the room would have defined it as plain, because there were no jewels, no fancy stones, just a few carvings etched into it of dragons gliding through the sky. Made from white gold, it was stunning and an item she could see herself wearing, and she couldn't say that about too many pieces of jewellery.

"This has been in my family for generations and given the inscriptions I'm guessing even back then there was a dragon connection. I hope you'll personally accept this gift from me with a promise to always be there for you and the rest of your race should you ever need anything."

"Majesty, you're too kind. Thank you very much. And let me say that I can promise that my race and I will always be at the disposal of the humans across the planet as long as they have good intentions, no matter what country they're from. I want to see us cooperate and group together for the betterment of every being on earth. That is my shared goal, and I will stop at nothing to succeed."

"Here, here," replied the Queen, before stepping aside to let Garrett approach.

"Majesty," he said with just a nod, feeling too old to drop to one knee, which she fully understood. "I'll make it brief. First I'd like to thank you for all of your exemplary work during your time at my company. Just to know you makes me incredibly proud."

Richie blushed. This was not supposed to be happening. Hook smiled.

"I have two gifts for you," Garrett announced. "First, a continuous supply of titanium for the balls used in your precious sport... if we mine it, then it's yours and currently our facilities in North America and South Africa are working overtime on extracting exactly that."

"Thank you."

"Second, I made a promise to a mutual acquaintance of ours that I would rebuild the Salisbridge sports club so that it would be better than ever. It's been completed and is ready to be opened. And take my word, it is better than ever. I'd hoped that you might consider reopening it for us... tomorrow in fact, if you're not too busy."

Using every ounce of her indomitable will, she ignored the thoughts of Peter that were trying to pierce her mental armour, assuming he was the mutual acquaintance the Cropptech CEO was talking about, knowing that a special place much later on had been reserved for all thoughts of her friend.

Throughout the room, the lacrosse team, Sam, Taibul, Tank and of course her husband held their breath in anticipation. While not the most exotic or precious of gifts that had been offered, to each of them it was no doubt the most important. They didn't have long to wait.

"Uhhhh... tomorrow. I... I... I would be delighted to, I suppose," smiled Richie, getting up to embrace Cropptech's leader, much to his surprise.

Noting her reaction to this, all the Salisbridge sport stars cheered and whooped uncontrollably, much to the horror and disgust of all the world leaders and VIP's, including Flash who, as he'd already told both his friends, Tank and Hook, had decided to give rugby a... TRY! (Get it?) Just the thought of having their club back to how it had been, let alone an improved version, gave the lacrosse girls their second wind (cue more singing and dancing) as well as getting Steel, Jar Man and DomCon to agree to come to the opening and watch some real sport as the girls put it. The laminium ball captain, never one to shy away from a challenge, agreed on one condition... that they should all come and watch his first laminium ball match back.

Immediately they all signed up, confirming with more singing and yet more dancing.

# 48 THE PRESENT

After things had quietened down, which took the sternest of looks from the new dragon queen aimed directly at her teammates, the French President approached and presented an exquisite Faberge egg, something he said the French people gladly handed over as an offer of continued friendship. Gracefully she accepted, about to call time on the whole thing, only to notice that George and Fredric had stepped up to greet her, side by side.

"What's going on?" Richie enquired of George. "Is he your plus one?"

George turned to glance at Fredric, who had absolutely no idea what she was talking about.

"What's she mean?" Fredric asked his best friend.

The former dragon monarch, shaking his head, replied.

"She wants to know if you're my date?"

"WHAT!"

Richie laughed uncontrollably, which then set George off, much to Fredric's consternation.

Rubbing the tears from her eyes, watched by the rest of the room, who for the most part hadn't heard what had happened, the queen addressed her friends.

"Neither of you should be standing here. You owe me nothing... in fact it's I that owe you both a debt."

"That's very gracious of you, Majesty," George quipped, clearly having fun with the boot on the other foot, but please let me help just a little."

With that, he proceeded to reach into his colourful shirt pocket and extract a tiny golden key.

"There's a chest about the size of a large duffel bag hidden away in a tiny cupboard under the fifth staircase from the back. This is the key that will open it. The belongings are now yours and should hopefully help you on the start of your journey."

More than a little taken aback, all that the lacrosse playing queen could think to do was say thank you. And that just left Fredric standing there all alone, with George having backed off slightly.

"Can I help you with something?" Richie asked politely.

With a concealed wave of his finger, alongside thinking three words deep within his mind, Fredric, Peter's grandfather and founder of the Crimson Guards, created a sphere of silence that encompassed him and his queen without anyone other than Richie knowing and only then because For'son, coming to terms with his new accomplice, told her so.

"What's going on, Fredric?" she asked coolly.

"I have a message from Vasuki that I wanted to relay in person," Fredric replied, all businesslike.

"Oh," was all the new queen could manage.

"He says he's taken the rest of his race into hiding, somewhere they'll never be found, and he's sorry for everything that's happened. He knows it's not directly his fault, but he does feel responsible. He said that if there's anything he can ever do to repay the debt he owes you, there's a way to get hold of him."

Fredric then proceeded to instruct her how to use the same enchantment that she'd seen him use on the cliff top at Portknockie. After that, he handed her an envelope.

"What's this?"

"Vasuki wanted me to give it to you personally. It contains the coordinates for some of the richest mineral veins in Antarctica. He hopes you'll use the wealth it creates to make up for all the dastardly deeds that were committed by his race. He really is genuinely sorry about what happened."

"So am I Fredric, so am I. It's not his fault, you know."

"I know that, and I think deep down, so does he, but there has to be a considerable time for healing, which is the reason they've all gone into hiding. Given that it wasn't their finest hour, it is understandable to some degree."

"I suppose," Richie agreed. "Is that all?"

"Yes."

"Can you remove the magic then please? People are starting to wonder what's going on."

"Oh... sure thing."

With the blink of an eye, it was done, with everything returning to normal.

And so Richie... I mean, the newly crowned dragon queen... stood. When she had everybody's attention, she spoke.

"Thank you for your patience and kind gifts, and yes I know," she said waving away all the protestations, "that more of you have offerings you'd like to present. But there's really not time now, I'm afraid. We'll sort something out. What I'd like now is for you all to join me outside on the patio... please."

Slowly, the world leaders, VIPs and friends made their way outside to the poorly lit patio where a dozen or so news anchors from around the world were broadcasting, much to their surprise.

Richie followed them all out, and in the spotlight, quite literally, addressed the waiting world.

"You have honoured me with your kindness today and ever since it was announced that I would be crowned the reigning dragon monarch. I feel truly grateful to take up this position to try to bridge the divide between our two races and form a cohesive planet that everyone can benefit from. As you can imagine, I, like many of the other dragons that walk the surface, are often asked lots of questions, and rightly so given humans' inquisitive thirst for knowledge. Whilst some will take time and much research to answer, one of the main ones, I feel I can do justice to here and now. With today being about the world coming together, and almost everything closed down in celebration, including much of the planet's air space, I thought it would be a fitting treat for those of you whose shape I take through no fault of my own, to see what glorious, wonderful and enigmatic creatures the dragons really are, with their own eyes. With that in mind, I asked a handful of dragons if they'd like to take to the air to show you just that, thinking the response I'd get would be rather... mixed. How wrong could I have been? It was emphatic and overwhelming, and so instead of what started out as a handful of them offering to take flight so that you could see through the media their grace, beauty, charm and love of flying, here in London, the idea grew beyond even my wildest imagination, with members of my kind from across the globe agreeing to participate, excepting those in the coldest of countries. And so, if you'd be kind enough to open your curtains and raise your eyes to the skies, I give you a glimpse into the future and the most magnificent of flying beasts. Behold!"

All heads turned skywards, away from the newly crowned queen, wondering what to expect. In their wildest dreams they couldn't have imagined this, and those who still had doubts, and there were quite a few, had them erased immediately as dragons of all shapes and sizes took to the air, magical mantras surrounding their prehistoric bodies, showing them off in the night skies in some parts of the world, and leaving trails of their exploits in countries where it was still daylight. Breathtaking, astounding, delightful, majestic, movie-like madness were all used to describe the scenes, and that was just in the grounds of Buckingham Palace. The crowd ohhhh'd and ahhhh'd as those who'd been chosen from the domain to participate lapped up being able to fly freely throughout the sky for the first time in living memory, not having to worry about being shot at or destroying the fabric of reality for the humans. Pairs of dragons teased each other with outstanding bursts of the brightest orange and yellow flame, playfully tickling each other's tails with it as they ducked, dived and barrel-rolled through each other's wake. High up over the Palace, two brightly coloured dragons peeled off, looking as though they were at some kind of standoff. Zipping off in opposite directions, the two giant prehistoric beasts abruptly arced around and then in a streaking turn of speed went head-to-head against each other. On the ground, everyone held their breath, wondering what the outcome of this outrageous disagreement would be, apart from their queen of course, who knew exactly where this was going. Wings flapping furiously, both approaching each other at one hell of a rate, a cone of rip-roaring flame flashing out in front of them, it looked for all the world as though there could only be one conclusion, that they would smash into each other. But at the very last instant, both rolled ninety degrees, their bellies passing within an inch of each other, the flames deflecting harmlessly away off their fireproof scales, much to the amazement of the crowd. Lazily wheeling around, the two gigantic monsters met up in the air, hugging each other for effect, friends to the last, glad to be able to show off a little of what they could do. Across the world the crowd went wild, just as they did at the Palace, whooping, cheering, clapping and whistling their approval. And so it continued, with magic being cast, fireballs thrown, aerobatics of all sorts performed, in some countries with as many as fifty dragons at a time engaging in synchronised corkscrews, rollercoasteresque drops, inverted loops, flat spins, spiral dives and ground skimming flybys at dizzying speeds. It was a treat not only for the humans to watch, but for the dragons in question to perform. People in front of their televisions, in areas too cold for dragons to fly safely, were glued to their screens, as were those in places too remote to see what was going on over the nearest cities. Below ground, dragons watching the same thing take place on home monitors, in parks and open spaces, stood agog, some weeping with happiness at the thought they might one day soon take to the open skies and feel the hot sun beating down on their flapping wings without having to pay to go to one of the famed dragon holiday spots. As surprises went, it was a pretty good one and had the effect that Richie had hoped for, by bringing both races that little bit closer together and giving them a better understanding of each other.

Sneakily, George sidled up to his successor.

"That was some move. Where on earth did that come from and how did you keep it such a secret?"

Smiling like a Cheshire cat, Richie turned to face the former monarch who she now thought of as a friend, given everything that had transpired.

"The idea had been there for some time. But as you've just said, it was all about the secrecy to pull it off. I deliberately left it as late as possible, making it look a little as though it were an afterthought so that those involved wouldn't have time to get the word out."

"Ahhh... devious. I like that," declared George, watching with envy.

Noting his expression, the queen, not quite able to read his mind, gave it a go anyway.

"I'm pretty sure no one would mind if you transformed and joined in. No one could ever begrudge you that."

For him, those words confirmed one hundred percent that she was most definitely the right being for the job of dragon sovereign. Even though up until now there'd never been a female dragon monarch, he knew without question she would be the right dragon in the right place at the right time. Although she'd suffered the devastating loss of what they'd assumed at the time was The White Dragon in the form of Tim, it had in fact turned out, as Peter had predicted, she'd been the one to fulfil the prophecy all along. He was proud to not only know her, but to have fought alongside her during the darkest time in the planet's history.

"It's okay, I think I'll save it until it's commonplace and everyone's doing it. I've had my fill of flying for a while, what with everything that went on with Manson and all that."

She understood fully.

"Anyhow... is it time?" he asked smoothly.

"I think it possibly is. Do you think all these important

people will mind if the dragon queen just slips away into obscurity?"

"None of them will really notice, not given the amount of alcohol they've consumed and the fact that the party is still going on. They might be reminded of it in the morning, but none of them will have the balls to question it, apart from Elizabeth of course, but she'll understand."

"You and her have some sort of history... don't you?"

"A good monarch should always keep a few secrets, Miss Rump, and that's one tip you can have from me for free."

"Good to know," she replied, glancing up at the sky jealously, "good to know."

"Shall we do it?"

"Let's," responded Richie. "I'll round up Janice and the humans. You grab Flash and get him to bring the rest of the dragons and we'll meet you outside the entrance."

"On it!" stated George. "See you in a while."

With the aerial antics still going on, just not at quite the same pace, some of the guests started to wander back inside, mainly in search of more food and drink. As casually as you like, Richie put one of her pale slender arms around Janice's shoulder, dragging her in the direction of the lacrosse team, much to the young girl's amusement, picking up her brand spanking new husband on the way, who, it had to be said, had absolutely no idea what was going on, but played along anyway.

"Heeyyyy... if it isn't our illustrious leader," slurred Joey, barely able to stand, much to everyone's amusement. "How's it hanging, Your Majesty?"

This made them all laugh.

"Joey... ask her the question," one of the teammates shouted.

Swaying like a weeping willow in a storm, the lacrosse playing winger had to think very carefully through the haze of alcohol as to just what that question was. But when she finally found the answer, her face lit up like a disposable barbeque.

"Oh... oh... oh... oh... you just have to answer this," she practically screamed. "Are a boy dragon's…?"

"NO!" replied Richie.

"But you don't know what I was about to say."

"NO!"

"But…"

"NO!"

The team were in absolute hysterics now.

"I was only enquiring…"

"NO!"

"But we've heard it's directly proportional to the size of their…"

"NO!" stated Richie one last time, trying to turn them all away from this particular subject without much luck. "What is it with all of you and willies tonight?" she asked.

"Ohh... that's right and you've never dreamed of asking about one ever at all. I seem to recall a certain someone at the sports club by the name of... TIM!"

And as soon as the words left her mouth, she, along with everybody else there regretted it instantly, as the good natured banter turned to stone cold silence amongst the small group.

That name, should have conjured up happy memories for her, like the evening they'd met up in Swanage and had a fabulous meal on the amazing steam railway... it should have. But whenever his name was mentioned, or she looked back on their time together, now, only one image ever appeared in her mind... that of Tim's broken body, the fabled 'White Dragon' being held aloft by Troydenn, Manson's father, as something of a trophy. Inside, the newly crowned queen fought back the bile that threatened to race up her throat, and the tears that wanted to escape, knowing all the time that if not for her, the young hockey playing treasurer would probably still be alive today. During all this, she kept a neutral look on her face, knowing that her young friend hadn't realised what she was saying.

"I... I... I... I'm sorry," uttered Joey, crestfallen, her teammates sharing much the same sentiment.

"It's okay," replied Richie softly. "I know you didn't mean to bring his name up, and I only have fond memories of him," she lied for all their sakes, using a new found diplomacy that she never realised she had. Before things got too morbid, she knew she had to recover the situation.

"Carry on partying," she announced to the team, "I just need to borrow Emma, Angela, Sam and Taibul. Come on... carry on!"

None of them minded, all only too glad to follow her orders, too drunk in most cases to even care, with those she selected following her into an adjacent room. Once there, Richie touched Janice on the shoulder first, sobering her up with just the tiniest speck of magic. As the young girl came to, wondering what on earth was going on, the newly crowned dragon queen ordered her to get Fu-ts'ang and Garrett and the rest of the Cropptech humans and meet back where they stood. Not daring to question the order from the new queen of everything, Janice shot off like an Olympic sprinter in need of the toilet. One by one, the lacrosse playing dragon queen sobered them all up with her magic, much to their surprise. In only a matter of moments Janice returned, wielding the magical blade she considered her friend.

"What's going on?" asked the young bar worker. "Are we under attack again?"

"No," replied Richie with a smile. "It's something else this time. You all have to come with me."

Of course they did, using a secret entrance in the corner of the room to gain access to an incredibly ornate staircase lit up by crystal chandeliers, the walls of which were adorned with huge oil paintings of admirals and majors, some well known, others not so much. With all of them wondering where they were going and what they were doing, to a man and a woman they all knew to keep quiet, even Janice wielding the futuristic looking Fu-ts'ang.

Everything would surely be revealed in good time.

George had rounded up all the dragons. Fredric at first, who was in on what was going on, quickly followed by everyone else... Tank, Flash and Amelia, Polkinghorne, Vimes, Yoyo and Rose as well as their newly adopted youngsters, Steel, Jar Man and DomCon.

"Is there trouble?" asked the fiery little pocket rocket of a dragon, putting a voice to what most of them were wondering.

"No," stated George firmly. "This is going to be something you'll all want to see."

With that, they made their way down into the dragon domain by quite a different entrance, all the time heading in the direction of their queen and human comrades. Before they could head out though, Nurse Conscience interrupted, having just come off her mobile phone, explaining she was needed back at the north London hospital she'd been temporarily stationed at in the domain, due to some unexpected medical emergency. The others, with just a little giggling and high jinx, allowed Steel some privacy to say goodbye to his elegant date. After that, as a group they set off, Nurse Conscience sobering up immediately, slipping out of the front door with some of the other humans, just as Polo had done about an hour earlier.

Reaching, as expected, a deserted Buckingham monorail station, all the giant LED notice boards blank because of the celebration, and the fact that none of the carriages were running. That begged the question of what the hell they were doing there, something that only Hook had the courage to ask.

The very sharp and curt reply he received from his wife was... "You'll see!"

Suddenly, out of the darkness of one of the tunnels, the lights of a single carriage appeared in total and utter silence. As if that wasn't eerie enough, instead of the usual shiny silver, this particular carriage was totally purple in colour, something that had they all known better, which they didn't, would have raised alarm bells in their heads as to just how special it was.

As it ground to a halt in front of them and the huge doors whooshed open, the queen used her hands and arms to usher them all on.

"Come on, come on, we don't have all night now."

And so they all boarded the outrageously extravagant royal carriage.

All plonked themselves down in sumptuous purple cushioned velvet that seemed to almost totally swallow up their human forms. Emma and Taibul had to try a second time, having fallen through the holes designed for dragon tails on their first attempt, much to the amusement of the others. Richie closed her eyes and instructed the dragon driver telepathically that they were ready to move off.

"Hang on a second," asked Garrett, more than a little perturbed. "I thought we couldn't go on the monorail because, and I quote, 'it has the potential to rip our faces off'."

"What?" exclaimed Angela.

"WHAT?" yelled Sam.

"Oh, well this should be fun," scoffed Owen, keen to see how fast they would go.

"It's okay, just calm down," ventured the dragon queen, slightly amused at the look currently embedded into her new husband's face. "We're not going very far or very fast, and the driver of this thing is under strict instructions to keep it slow." Turning to face Hook, she very playfully said, "we don't want your genitals spinning off into the distance now, with all the G-force we pull, do we?" which had the effect of making all the others laugh and setting them a little at ease.

They made themselves at home, most of them wondering, 'If this is slow, then what does top speed look like?' as the occasionally lit rock faces and the odd house zipped past faster than they could ever imagine. Three minutes later, they arrived at their small, shadow shrouded destination.

With their customary whoosh, the doors slid open to reveal... very little.

"Follow me," announced Richie, stomping off into the black, still in her beautiful white dress, the train of which had long since been discarded.

They all obeyed, not having to be told twice, and still having no idea what was going on. Only Janice didn't actually know, but had some kind of feeling deep inside her that it was something important, and somehow related to her.


George and Fredric led Flash and Amelia, Polkinghorne and Vimes, Tank, Steel, Jar Man and DomCon, Yoyo and Rose plus their young charges down a tight, narrow staircase to a winding passage in the basement of Buckingham Palace, with none of them knowing what on earth was going on. Stopping at an especially nondescript part of the corridor, the former monarch ran one hand vertically down the wall, whilst at the same time poking a finger from his other hand at different points in it. For all intents and purposes, the wall looked completely blank and totally indistinct. Whatever George could see to touch, was certainly not visible to the others. His actions did pay off quite spectacularly though, when abruptly a whole section dropped away, revealing stuffy, dust encrusted darkness, a foot wide shiny silver pole just visible inside.

"Follow me and don't be too tardy about it," he announced to the whole group, before taking a run and jump at the pole, and then sliding down into the darkness, screaming, "Geronimo!" at the top of his voice.

Immediately Fredric followed, yelling exactly the same thing.

Given little choice, one by one all the dragons followed, all reluctantly screaming the same word, wondering if there was some sort of secret or magical reason for doing so.

There wasn't.

Steel, being the last to exit the bottom of the pole, joined the others, wondering what on earth was so important that it could pull them all away from the reception to end all receptions. Like the others, he didn't have the answers yet, but did hope they would be forthcoming soon.

Exiting out into the dragon domain proper, they all found themselves on a large stone balcony overlooking a mighty drop. Through the darkness, they could all just make out some of the narrow alleys adjacent to the council building in the underground borough of Buckingham.

"Well," announced George, standing next to the rails of the balcony that separated him from the huge drop. "You're probably all wondering why you're here."

Lots of nodding heads ensued, apart from Fredric. George continued enthusiastically.

"It will of course become plain to see and is of the utmost importance and secrecy. But we're still not where we're supposed to be, and so you'll have to humour me a little longer and also... FOLLOW ME!" he bellowed, leaning back, allowing his human form to drop back over the side.

Fredric shook his head, sure that his friend should have gone into amateur dramatics, while the others all looked on in horror.

"Come on... move your asses. He's just fine, and playing with you," announced the founder of the Crimson Guards, bounding through them all, leaping up onto the rail, and then somersaulting off into the shadows.

'If you can't beat them,' they all thought, 'you might as well join them.' And so they did, throwing themselves over the edge one by one, igniting the transformation into their dragon personas as they did so, emerging in their prehistoric forms less than half way down, all beating their powerful wings to keep up with the impromptu leader of this makeshift group.

Some way out in front, the exhilaration of the drop

causing the scales across his back to shiver uncontrollably, George pulled up sharply from the steep dive, registering all the others following in his wake with just a touch of his magical birthright, and using his tail as the rudder it was meant to be, banked hard right, almost splitting the air as he screamed past buildings that housed businesses and upper class residences. Accelerating with just two flaps of his gigantic wings, he levelled off, glancing back over his shoulder to make sure they were all keeping up. They were! And he was delighted to see most of them making some sort of competition out of it all. Flash and Amelia fought for position, both using their cunning and guile to try and thwart the other, with the former captain seemingly coming out on top, though whether or not Flash was letting her was something only either of them would know. Whilst their newly adopted offspring careered chaotically through the air in front of them, Yoyo and Rose flew contentedly next to each other, the tips of their wings gently brushing as the air tickled their underbellies. Tank and Steel tried to outperform each other with technically tricky aerobatics, while Jar Man and DomCon both tried to bully each other out of the same air space. Like a flying ninja, Fredric appeared directly beneath George's belly, surprising the former monarch in a way he hadn't thought possible.

"Not keeping your guard up, sire?" Fredric observed sarcastically.

"I knew you were there," George came back at him.

"Yeah... right!"

About to reply with, "I did," the former monarch knew his best friend would never buy it, and so decided not to bother. What would be the point? Instead, he chose to ask,

"Are you ready for all this?"

"I think so. I'm just trying not to get my hopes up too much. I know there are no guarantees."

"It's a good attitude to have," George shouted over the whistling of the wind in his ears, "I'm not sure I could do that though."

Fredric nodded his understanding.

"It is, however, worth a try. Nothing ventured, nothing gained."

"I know. I just worry about the rest of them, including the young girl. If it doesn't work... she'll be crushed."

Barrel-rolling sharply left, around a crumbling, deserted building, George zeroed in on their destination before answering his friend.

"She's tough. We all know that, with what she's been through already, and although she'll be broken if nothing comes of this, she is at least surrounded by good beings who will help see her through it all."

Fredric nodded in agreement as they both spread out their wings and slowed their descent for landing, arriving in the secluded plaza at exactly the same time as a familiar group of humans.

"Nice of you to join us," observed the new queen, as one by one the dragons in the air dropped to the ground.

"We were just shooting the breeze, Your Majesty," replied Fredric with a wink and a look.

Around them all, humans and dragons alike looked stunned, unable to comprehend what on earth was going on. In the end it took the bold bar worker hanging on tight to her friend, the futuristic blade, to present the question.

"I have to ask," declared Janice, "what the hell is going on?"

Everyone else who had no idea, which was most of them, seconded that thought.

"We're here," announced Richie, "to follow up on some unfinished business."

It was then that Janice started to get the strangest feeling... deja vu, almost certain she'd been here before, despite her mind telling her that she most certainly never had.

About to go into more detail, out of the corner of her eye Richie noticed her friend's struggle and with a cheesy smile on her face, turned to address her.

"You okay Janice?"

"I... um... I... um... think so."

Richie laughed. That's a bit mean, nearly all of them thought. But they didn't know the truth, unlike their leader, the queen.

"It's amazing that all of you have been to this place before, and yet the only one of you with a strong enough mind to rally against the magic that keeps your memories in the dark about it is Janice."

Wow... that got their attention.

"And I say to you Janice," the dragon queen continued, "that if your love can fight and break down the bonds of the magic cast upon you, then you truly have something very, very special, and you should battle for that with all your heart."

"I... uh... ur... um…"

"It's alright, all of you, because it's time for me to explain. When I say you've all been to this place, I mean it. You all have. And yes, hang on... I know, none of you have any memory of it... yes, except you Janice, because your will is fighting back, trying to find a way around the magical barriers that were placed upon each of you... Very impressive indeed."

Bowing her head, Richie took a breath, looking for the words that would help her to explain exactly what had happened.

"Because of the secret nature of this place," she continued, using her hands and arms to signal the building behind her, "it was agreed to keep as few beings as possible in the loop as to what was going on here."

"Who agreed to that?" shouted DomCon, the pent up frustration he felt coming out in his voice.

For her part, the queen tried to hold back the laughter she felt rising to the fore.

"You actually."

"ME?!" exclaimed the explosive little dragon, sure that he never had.

"Well," continued the queen, "all of you in fact!"

Hushed whispers rang around the group as they tried to comprehend what they were being told.

"I don't remember…" started Yoyo, only to be cut off mid sentence by Richie.

"You don't remember, I know. But I assure you it's true. Better still, I can prove it."

That got their attention.

"Follow me."

Marching up to the old building, she announced her presence with a light telepathic touch to those inside who'd been expecting her. Sure enough, the huge doors opened, allowing her to venture into the high-tech foyer that lay within. This was all totally contradictory to how it seemed, much to the surprise of those who'd had their memories suppressed.

"Are you ready for us?" Richie asked the dragons behind the front desk.

"We are, Majesty," they answered.

"Good. Show them," she ordered.

"Suddenly the giant screen above the desk flickered into life, an image of everyone there, including Fu-ts'ang, gathered in exactly the same place they currently stood, only their clothes were different. Gasps of surprise echoed amongst the group watching.

On the screen, Richie, George and Fredric stood slightly off to one side. Suddenly Fredric spoke.

"And you're all completely okay with this, having your memories suppressed to help keep this place secure?"

"YES!" everyone else replied at once.

"Even though you'll remember nothing about all this until we return here together?"

"YES!

"So be it!" exclaimed the founder of the Crimson Guards, closing his eyes, whispering some unusual words under his breath, barely discernible to any of the others.

Momentarily a blue shimmering haze enveloped the

group aside from Richie, George or Fredric. In the blink of an eye it was gone.

"Now it's time to leave," Richie could be heard to say in the recording. Like zombies, everyone followed her out. And that was that, so to speak.

'Odd,' thought most of them, seeing themselves in a recording and having absolutely no memory of being there or doing that. Simultaneously, two or three of them had exactly the same thought... to pipe up and ask what the hell was going on. The queen, however, beat them to it.

"I know you're confused about what's happened, and I can assure you everything you've seen is real. You did all agree to have your memories blocked out because of the security surrounding this place and what they do inside here."

Pausing to take a breath, not for dramatic effect for once, the young queen knew that some of them were going to have their minds blown with what she was about to say, including her best friend and husband.

'Oh well,' she mused, 'here goes.'

"This place was set up in the wake of Manson's defeat with one goal, and one goal only. To help revive and repair those dragons thought too far gone, like in our laminium ball captain's case before all the hostilities began."

Steel's mind was suddenly beset with a blur of fast moving images... the laminium ball match, realising that a bomb was hidden within the shining sphere, diving deep down into the lava, the pain, oh the pain... it was outstanding and like nothing he'd ever known, even just the memory of which brought tears to his eyes, and then... nothing. A total dark blank... that is, until he awoke in the medical facility that had been overrun with deadly, dark nagas.

Closing in on their friend, DomCon and Jar Man wrapped their wings around him in some attempt at comfort as the others looked on.

"I'm sorry to bring back painful recollections, I really

am," continued Richie, "but this place was inspired by what happened to you, and will hopefully provide new advancements in technology and medical care for not just dragon kind, but humans as well."

"It's okay," snuffled Steel, "I understand."

"Thank you," replied the queen, knowing that if anybody could, it would be him.

"If Steel's okay, then what on earth are we doing here?" asked Hook, tired of playing his wife's roundabout game.

Gazing deep into her love's eyes, she knew it was time for the big reveal, to get on to the reason they were here.

"Beneath the magic, you all know why we're here, and the gamble we're about to take. I apologise for the memory loss, but you did all willingly agree to it in an effort to keep all this as secret as possible. Other than the beings here in this building right now, nobody on the planet knows what's going on. Whether we succeed or fail, I'd very much like to keep it that way. And you..." she said, pointing at Janice, should know just how special you are. It's no mean feat, a being's memories overcoming a magical obstacle like that, and can only be achieved by one thing... LOVE! For you, a human, to attain that level of recall is a testament to your relationship, strength of will and utter determination to regain the future that was stolen so harshly away from you. I think I can speak for us all when I say that there's no one I'd rather stand and fight alongside than you. GET READY!"

With a nod to Fredric, everything was undone, the memories of all those in the room, dragons and humans alike, restored.

"Oh my," squeaked Garrett.

"Wow!" observed Taibul.

"Oh my God," cried Hook.

For Tank's part, he just looked over at his best friend, tears welling up in his eyes, never believing that such a thing could be even remotely imaginable. For her part, she returned the look with interest, even though she'd known all along, that is until a flying, blonde haired ball of brown leapt right at her, enveloping all of her in one big hug.

"I can't believe it, I can't believe it," babbled Janice in Richie's ear.

Holding onto her friend for all she was worth, the lacrosse playing dragon dug deep into her emotional well of strength.

Pulling back a little, she looked Janice straight in the eye.

"There are no guarantees. You remember that, right?"

Tears streaming down her pretty blonde face, she nodded her understanding, still rightly emotionally distraught.

"I understand, I really do."

"Good," said the queen, letting go of her friend.

"I know it feels like you've all been hit by a sledgehammer, but as one of the few who has been carrying this around all this time, I'm understandably keen to get this over with one way or the other. So, if you'll follow me, we're all expected."

The reception dragons opened the way into the facility, and with Richie leading, Janice, Fredric, George, Tank and the others tagging along in her wake, they followed the same path they had previously, looking for something utterly recognisable.

Two minutes and lots of twisting and winding later, they approached the huge glass container that one of their own recognised from her dreams.

'That's exactly it,' thought Janice, stopping dead in her tracks.

"You recognise it?" enquired Richie, knowing she should, given that she'd been here before.

"I do, but not from last time," answered the young bar worker. "It's featured in my dreams, with a single scale inside."

Richie nodded, once again in awe of the young girl's ability to somehow circumvent the magic cast upon her.

Rocking up right next to the glass, the group were

unable to take their eyes off what lay inside... a mighty prehistoric beast, one that was familiar to nearly all of them... PETER! Or at least a body that looked identical to his dragon guise, a prominently brown visage with a unique green scaled pattern that made up the bent whistle markings that his name derived from, just floating there in a light yellow liquid, a mask pumping in oxygen covering the whole of his prehistoric jaw. Sharp intakes of breath could be heard from all of them, except Janice, who understandably was sobbing just slightly.

Wanting nothing more than to comfort the girl, despite their historical disagreements, Fredric, Peter's grandfather, didn't know how to go about such a thing. It wasn't so much about having a tough dragon exterior, more a fundamental rethink of everything he'd known, kind of thing. In the past he'd been wrong, only realising that on witnessing his grandson die, something he regarded as THE most painful thing he'd ever experienced and that included his stint in Antarctica and all the antics with his daughter. What had totally blown his socks off though, was the way Peter had sacrificed himself for the human girl. For the life of him, at the time, he just couldn't get his head around it. But with hindsight, he could see why and just how their love prevailed. It nibbled at his very core, chomped on his reasoning and practically tore through everything he believed in. But now he understood not only what Peter had felt for her, but what she was now going through. Still he couldn't go to her or share her apprehension and pain, not without a little nudge anyway.

"Go on," a stern voice said, accompanying the very sharp slap he'd received on the shoulder.

Fredric glared around in anger, only to find his best friend, George, staring right back at him.

"She needs you, now more than ever. And if I'm not mistaken, and believe me, I very rarely am, you need her. Get over there, you dope, and wrap your huge arms around her."

Not needing to be told twice, Fredric crossed the floor, and enveloped the young girl in his superhero-like physique. having transformed back from his prehistoric guise just like all the other dragons on meeting up with their human friends outside the facility. Both of them buried their heads against each other, the sounds of their crying filling the chamber. In other circumstances and amongst some groups of friends, the situation would have been classed as awkward... but not here and not now, not amongst this lot. They'd all fought alongside each other and nearly seen the end of the world together. After that, this was nothing. And so they all stood, giving the gentle giant Fredric and the blissfully pure Janice time to come to terms with their emotions, time to contemplate exactly what might be about to happen.

Many minutes later, and with the torrent of tears wiped away, the two of them now able to take a breath without shuddering or shaking, their broken voices having now returned to normal, they parted, each with a new respect for the other, a special bond formed, one that whatever the outcome, would outlast the deed they were both about to become part of. No words were necessary, none were spoken. Both of them just fell back to their previous positions, Fredric returning to stand next to his best friend, Janice taking her place by Richie's side, having already passed Fu-ts'ang off to Flash.

From off to one side, a dragon engineer appeared out of nowhere, ready to serve his queen.

"We need to drain the tank, Majesty," he said rather clumsily.

"Do it!" she commanded.

With two flaps of his grey and black wings, the engineer flew up to a gantry high over head, where, upon landing, he entered a series of commands into the control panel.

Metal on metal resounded from the direction of the chamber the Bentwhistle body remained encased in, before a loud gurgle emanated. Slowly, the level of the dull yellow liquid began to descend, revealing the glistening dragon body in much more detail. Visions of the battle in the king's (now of course the queen's) private residence came back to haunt them all, apart from Tank and Richie who'd grown up alongside the dragon body in question and had no doubt that it was a perfect facsimile.

Suddenly the engineer touched down next to the queen, startling her out of reverie. Realising what he'd done, for a moment he thought he was in trouble. Of course that wasn't the case. While she might have a fiery temper on occasion, she was for the most part, generous, caring, good mannered and understanding. This was most certainly one of those times.

"Can you give me an update please?" she asked softly, reassuring the dragon no end.

Watching as the remaining liquid drained away, the entire group listened to what the chief engineer had to say.

"Using a combination of gene sequencing, replication mantras, redoubling crystals and biometric gel, we've created an exact clone of the dragon in question. The body is one hundred percent perfect, functioning adequately on its own, able to breathe independently, with perfect motor function and while the brain is serviceable and the neurons firing, there is little or no activity, like a blank slate. It has no capacity for speech because it's not been taught that skill. In short, we've done everything you've asked, Majesty."

Nodding in all the right places, and considering everything she'd heard, Richie praised the dragons for their hard work and dedication to their duties.

As the last of the liquid drained away, more engineers arrived and in only a matter of moments, the glass surrounding the dragon body had disappeared completely. Two more dragons removed the mask, leaving the replica Bentwhistle freestanding, and breathing on its own.

As a group, they all stood there admiring the dripping wet form that had been created from just a single scale all those months ago. Yoyo in particular had a great deal of knowledge on the methods used and had nothing but admiration for all the scientists and engineers involved in the complicated and convoluted process. It was a moment none of them would ever forget. Tank and Richie just wanted their friend back, hearts having already been broken once on thinking him dead, Janice desperate for the future she'd once hoped for with the being she cared for the most on this much changed planet, the dreams of living with him in a huge house on a tree lined street haunting her in between the visions of the scale in the tank. Flash wanted nothing more than for his friend to return, having formed a very special bond with the hockey playing dragon, who'd accepted the dragon agent for who he was when he'd lost the ability to return to his natural form when Gee Tee had saved his life,. Not once had Peter judged him or thought any less of him, something that meant so much, both at the time and up to the present day. George and Fredric felt much the same way, invested in the young dragon whose replica body stood unwavering before them. Over the years George had come to care for the boy in much the same way as a father would for a son, because of the promise he'd made to his best friend. For Fredric, returning from Antarctica, only to be thrust into the mother of all battles, fighting alongside the grandson he loved so much, the very thought of which had kept him sane throughout his incarceration, was akin to a dream come true. That is until the adventure had led to a standoff with his daughter, Earth, Peter's mother, and the exquisitely painful death he'd witnessed. Just the chance to get him back seemed like a miracle, one he'd give his life to make work.

Garrett never ceased to be amazed by what the world had to offer. That fateful day when they'd entered what they now knew was the dragon domain had changed his outlook, opinion and frankly his take on absolutely everything, forcing him to think in almost an entirely different way. But in some ways, it had started before all that, with the young man in question who they were now trying to bring back from the dead. But it was more than that, or less, depending on how you looked at it. Surely if his mind had never died, then he'd never died, even though his body had? Having spent a lot of time thinking about all this, he still hadn't got his head around it, and then he'd had those memories wiped, or suppressed. Now they were back with a vengeance. All he could really take away from it was that he hoped his employee and friend would come back and rejoin them and him at Cropptech. Owen felt pretty much the same way as his boss, wanting nothing more than his pal and colleague to return because, simply put, he missed him so much.

Taibul, wide eyed and full of hope, didn't doubt for a second his friend and hockey mentor would chase off the spectre of death and return to his rightful place... that of the Salisbridge second XI hockey team. And when he did, he was sure they would make many more memories together, something he was hugely looking forward to.

Yoyo, despite not knowing Peter well, felt a shared connection because of everything they'd been through, from saving Flash from certain death after being poisoned by one of the deadly nagas deep in the Antarctic, to the subsequent battles with Manson and Earth. They had a bond forged in flame, one that would never be forgotten, and he hoped for all their sakes that the youngster could perform one last miracle.

It was an odd sensation for him... feeling. And he now did, after not doing so at all for a very long time. Mostly that was down to being incarcerated by the master mantra maker, but even then it had taken a shining light against the cruel blackness to bring him out of his slumber and go some way to making him whole again. Of course being totally complete wasn't possible, not being imbued inside a blade, even if it was the most magnificent weapon to grace the earth, at least, that's what he thought. But he did feel for every one of his friends in their current situation, not least the one he felt closest to... JANICE! Whilst only catching the occasional glimpse of the Bentwhistle child, he'd seen enough to know that he was a worthy mate to his closest friend and so in that respect, he wished for nothing more than a positive outcome and a repeat of the feat he'd already navigated once before.

While only having briefly shared the young hockey playing dragon's life, Amelia, Rose, all of Yoyo's youngsters, Steel, Jar Man, DomCon, Sam, Emma, Angela and all Garrett's other security squad members hoped that whatever happened next, it resulted in the boy known as Bentwhistle returning, if for no other reason than to put one over on the now deceased Manson and Earth. Whether they would get their wish, we will just have to wait and see.

And then there was JANICE! One of the heroes of the battle with Manson and Earth, an ordinary human, who in the name of love had produced heroics the likes of which had rarely been seen in the annals of both human and dragon history. Her story, already written in song, will stand the test of time and be remembered across the future to inspire others and show just what CAN be done should the need ever arise. Forthcoming generations will quote her name to their children in an effort to inspire and remind.

She'd had few, if any, true friends before Peter caught her eye at the Salisbridge sports club, and the beautiful woman's life had been turned upside down by being caught in his orbit. Disliked by both Tank and Richie at first, her love for their friend soon became obvious, leading the young bar worker into all sorts of trouble by entering the dragon domain alongside all the other humans. Daring deeds and a bond of pure innocence forged with a merciless killer made her one of the stand out heroes of all time. But it all boiled down to this. She did it for Peter, that's all. Not to save the world, that was just an added bonus to her. Just for him. And so what happens next was all about that. If he came back to her, then it would all have been worth it. If not, then she might as well have died at that very first encounter in the market place at Salisbridge in the dragon domain. Her future was quite literally on the line. With that in mind, and with part of her not wanting to go any further through fear of failure, she plucked up the courage to ask,

"What do we do now?"

'A good question,' thought Richie, and one she was supposedly uniquely qualified to answer. Only she couldn't, as she didn't know how her memories had been stored in the nissix ring… Peter hadn't told her when he'd stolen them before they'd been wiped out totally by the dragon priesthood. Both of the beings that knew how to use the damn ring were dead, well… possibly, or even probably, who actually knew? So some amount of guesswork would be required… just what they needed.

"While all your memories have been wiped, I've scoured the planet and along with Fredric and George, have tried to find out all we can about the ring and how it works."

"Great," replied Janice, buoyed by the thought of some good news.

However, the newly crowned queen wasn't finished.

"Using all the resources available to us, we haven't managed to find out one single thing… nothing! All I know is that Gee Tee told Peter it was made of something called nissix which is apparently rarer than rare. It'll automatically adjust itself to any sized finger and it's operated by depressing the matt grey triangle. That's it!"

"Oh," concluded Janice, not feeling very confident at all, mirrored almost exclusively by everyone else there.

"Polks," Richie enquired, picking out the beautiful once a year legend who stood in the middle of them all, hand in hand with the love of her life, Vimes.

"My Queen," the Santa legend replied with a mischievous glint in her eye.

The lacrosse superstar ignored it.

"Does your magic offer up any insight as to what lays inside the ring?"

"I'm afraid not. And I've never heard of, or seen anything like that strange and alien looking band. I'm sorry."

"No matter," ventured Richie, turning her head to face her relatively new best friend, "I say we give it a go."

With that, everybody's face brightened up. But she had one more piece of wisdom to impart.

"You should all, especially you, Janice, be aware there's only a small chance this will work. At best it's a gamble, one that I would have taken with any of your lives at stake. What we do know is that because it's showing a line of bright blue triangles, the ring is loaded with a consciousness of sorts. However, that consciousness might well be mine from when Peter downloaded it into the ring just before the priesthood tried to permanently delete my dragon memories. As far as I'm aware, the triangles never changed colour after that. What we do know, and I've discussed this with Janice, Fredric, Fu-ts'ang and Polkinghorne given that they were all present in the vault when Earth killed Peter, is that there was a small amount of time in which our friend possibly had the chance to download his consciousness. It wasn't long, perhaps only ten seconds at best. Whether he did or not is anyone's guess, and of course there's only one way to find out. I'm pretty sure he knew he was going to die, and you'd have to figure in one last wager he'd do exactly what we hope he's done."

Individually they knew that the young queen was trying to let them down gently, and not allow them to get their hopes up, but truth be told what she'd said didn't really change anything. They'd already seen the impossible, done the impossible, resisted and beaten the impossible. Impossible was easy for them all. Not believing was not an option. So with hope in their hearts, and a desperate willing for it to work in their minds, the moment for which they were all gathered was well and truly at hand.

Turning to face the young human who'd been her constant companion throughout her special day, the dragon queen tucked all her hope away and addressed her friend.

"Whatever happens, know that I love you dearly. I once

thought of you as trouble, not for me but for Peter. I've long since known that couldn't be further from the truth, something this very moment testifies to. We are here only because he gave you that one scale, and because of your belief that his living consciousness resides in the nissix ring you wear on your hand. Without your belief, none of this would be possible."

Exhaling sharply, looking the young girl in the eyes, both of them starting to tear up, it was finally time.

"Put it on his finger and press the button," she commanded.

Wiping her eyes with the back of her hand, Janice walked over to the newly grown Bentwhistle body. Carefully slipping the matt grey ring off her index finger, once again she marvelled at the material it was made of and the stunning blue colour of the triangles that ran around its circumference.

Cautiously taking hold of the prehistoric monster's right hand, she picked the smallest finger which was still way too big and approached its tip with the Nissix ring. Unbelievably, (even though she knew it was coming) the ring expanded in size, to something easily able to fit down onto the scaled digit, even with room to spare. Slowly, Janice lowered it as far as it would go, everybody else in the group watching in anticipation. Suddenly, the band contracted to fit the finger perfectly. Everyone exhaled, including the queen and Janice.

Afraid of what might happen next, Janice glanced over her shoulder at everyone else. Richie, Tank, Fredric and George all gave her a nod. This was enough to brush away the fear and instil in her the courage that was needed. Ready to take a step back, remembering exactly what had happened in the Indian restaurant in the centre of Salisbridge on the night that changed her life forever, the young bar worker made a wish, and depressed the button before jumping out of range.

Nothing happened. Not at first anyway, almost as if

something was taking time to register. And then, just as Janice had suspected it might, the dragon frame with the Bentwhistle markings toppled over onto its side.

## CRASH!

Startled, the whole group jumped back as one. Janice flung herself into the arms of the queen. Both women held each other tight as they watched to see what would unfold. Would anything happen at all? Would the Bentwhistle clone wake up with the queen's memories, or would they get the outcome they all wished for?

An otherworldly ROAR tore out of the dragon's mouth as its tail flailed about uncontrollably behind it. Claws scratched the rocky surface, something akin to a fierce grating echoing around the chamber, while its eyelids blinked uncontrollably.

Deep inside the blank slate of a brain, pictures, images, sounds, smells and memories assaulted all its senses at high speed. Able to take it all in, the body did, lapping it up until it was almost full. Only then did it stop shaking, stop moving, stop roaring.

Frozen to the spot, everyone there to witness what they hoped would be a great event had instinctively held their breath the moment Janice had depressed the button and were still doing so now, a minute or so later. As the dragon stumbled to its feet, its huge prehistoric head arcing round to face them all, slowly its neck arched down and around, leaving its head much lower to the ground, right in front of Richie and Janice. Breaking free of her friend the queen, the young human bar worker, eyes wide with wonder, heart full of hope, approached the huge prehistoric face that she remembered so fondly from their time fighting Manson all those months ago.

"My love?" she enquired, full of hope.

"…Janice," murmured the all too familiar voice of…

## PETER!

She was in his scaly arms, faster than a speeding bullet.

A roar with an intensity the likes of which had never been heard from so few beings resounded around the facility, shaking it to its very foundations as celebrations started that would eclipse what had already happened throughout the day.

# 49 NEW BEGINNINGS

Cue much, much merriment, both in the chamber and on the way back to the queen's private residence, tastefully redecorated after George's relocation and now made up for an out of this world celebration, one the newly crowned sovereign of the planet had kept quiet about, just in case things had gone badly.

Surrounding the plinth that had seen so much action throughout the demonic battles with Earth and Manson's wicked forces, huge, blue veined marble tables had been set up, with more seats than could possibly be filled surrounding each and every one of them, sized for both dragon and human alike. If the previous party at Buckingham Palace was grand and overflowing with excess, then it paled in comparison to this. The best chefs from across the domain had covertly been brought in, hidden in the kitchen, set up and ready for something, although what... none of the staff knew. Only that it was important and at the decree of the queen herself. The level of secrecy surrounding such a thing was off the scale. And of course, once it had been confirmed that Peter's consciousness was well and truly back where it belonged, a single telepathic command from the monarch was enough to spur all the cooks, waiters, magicians and servers into action. By the time the overjoyed group of heroes arrived, the whole place had been transformed, not only by the seating arrangements, but in every way possible. The sumptuous smell of roasted meats, cooked to perfection, wafted gently on what little breeze there was, filling the hall, making every stomach rumble with anticipation, despite the overindulgence earlier, one in particular, his newly acquainted body famished, reminiscent of the past and ready to be filled, in much the same way as it had always been.

Sixty foot high charcoal sculptures of dragons soaring high over lacrosse, rugby and hockey pitches, including players, spectators and a clubhouse, mirroring the new Salisbridge facility right down to the last blade of grass, courtesy of Garret sharing the details with his former employee, now royalty, sat dotted around the place, astounding everyone, not least the humans amongst them.

Drinks in all possible variations flowed, served by the trusted staff of the private residence, handpicked by the queen herself. From water to juices and every conceivable type of soda, to the most outrageous alcoholic drinks on the planet. You name it, it was there somewhere and available to all and sundry. The most expensive champagne bubbled and fizzed as it filled many of the humans' glasses, a treat that would not only tickle their tongues and taste buds, but would delight their minds and souls.

Yoyo's band of youngsters now bolstered by a unique amount of experience given everything they'd been through, were the first to take their seats, ordering huge amounts of whisky, gin, vodka and tequila, the servers having brought and left many bottles of each, as well as enough shot glasses for them all. In true dragon fashion, the adolescents mixed copious amounts of each, before downing them in one, each daring the next to go bigger and better, all of them sure their false human shapes could cope with whatever was thrown at them. Despite their resilience, the group were gradually becoming intoxicated with every second that passed, and increasingly loud.

Away from the noisiness, the newly crowned queen and her master mantra maker friend approached the third of their cosy trio, one who'd only just transformed back into his human guise, and one whose side Janice was never likely to leave ever again from the looks of things.

"Guys," Peter gushed, bounding right up to both, pulling them in for an almighty hug, momentarily forgetting his fully human lover.

"Look at you," Richie chuckled, "back as if nothing bad

had ever happened."

"And I have all of you to thank," Peter added, pulling back to allow Janice to join in the small huddle.

"I think most of the credit has to go to this one here," Tank reflected, playfully ruffling Janice's mane of long blonde hair.

"Without her," added the queen, "you'd have been well and truly done for."

"Ain't that the truth," chipped in Peter, before leaning in and kissing his love for all she was worth.

"Hmmm... and I thought I'd seen some sticky situations fighting against Manson and Earth, but this is almost worse," laughed Tank, shaking his head.

Peter stuck his tongue out in his friend's direction, to which the master mantra maker very bluntly replied holding up two fingers.

"So, both Manson and Earth, they were…"

"Killed, that's right," Richie replied without hesitating, knowing full well how much of a psychological hold the former dark dragon had on her friend, hoping now that for him at least, things could be well and truly over.

"We're sorry about your mum, Pete," Tank piped up.

"I'm not. Given everything she was responsible for I think the outcome can very accurately be described as deserving. I'm... over it. Let's not talk of it anymore."

And so they didn't.

"A more disorderly group of nefariousness I never did see," echoed a familiar voice from behind them.

"GRANDFATHER!" bellowed Peter, throwing himself at his blood relative, slamming at speed into the well honed physique of the former king's best friend.

"My boy!"

"I…"

"I know... there'll be plenty of time for that later on. I just wanted to come and express my thanks that you're okay and that you had the presence of mind to transfer your consciousness into the ring before setting out on your reckless course of action."

"That goes for both of us," George declared, from behind the being he thought of as a brother.

"Thank you... sire."

Everyone surrounding Peter burst into laughter, including it had to be said, the love of his life, Janice.

"What's so funny?" he asked more than a little irked.

"YOU... my young friend, have a great deal of catching up to do," Fredric announced, pulling George off towards the festivities. "I'm sure your pals will fill you in."

And with that, the two of them disappeared into the mayhem, determined to get their hands on some of the best drinks available anywhere in the world.

"WELL..."

"The king is no more," ventured Tank playfully.

"YOU'RE KIDDING!"

"Nope."

"What the hell?!"

"And if you think that's shocking, wait until you hear the rest."

"Such as?"

"The king's reign is well and truly over. Now we have a new monarch and leader, one that will unite both human and dragon kind."

"You're yanking my chain."

"I kid you not."

"If not..."

"We have a queen, Pete, and a rather able one at that."

"I thought that wasn't allowed. There's never been a queen in the history of our race."

"Correct on both counts. But due to some rather crafty planning and some fortuitous circumstances, that's where we now find ourselves."

"WOW!" exclaimed the youngster back from the dead. "Well... good luck to her. I'm sure she's going to need it, following in George's footsteps and with everything else having gone on."

"You're not kidding," whispered Richie sarcastically.

"So... who is she, this able queen who thinks she can rewrite history?"

The silence within the tiny group of four was palpable, the noise from the ongoing celebrations all encompassing.

"What is it you're not telling...?"

"It's me... ALRIGHT! I'm the queen of everything dragon and human. Now you know."

A huge grin snaked across Peter's deliciously innocent human face as he waited for the punch line, wondering where the hell all of this was going. But the silence returned and with it dawned the realisation that none of them were kidding.

"Oh..."

"Oh indeed," Richie commented. "And believe you me, it wasn't my first choice."

"You're really the queen?"

"I am, and Hook is my husband."

"NO WAY!"

"Lots to catch up on Pete, lots to catch up on."

"You look like a human youngster that's just learnt that Santa's not real," put in Tank, slapping his rather flabbergasted friend firmly on the shoulder.

"I'd rather hoped not to hear something like that coming out of your mouth," echoed a silky smooth voice off to one side, "not with everything we've been through."

"POLKS!" exclaimed Peter, throwing himself at the once a year Christmas legend, much to her surprise, before engulfing Vimes as well.

"It's so good to see both of you."

"And you, youngster," replied Vimes, "and you."

"Richie was just explaining about..."

"Yes... she's a one, that's for sure," Polkinghorne answered before he'd even had the chance to finish.

"Did you...?"

"Nothing to do with me, I'm afraid... isn't that right, my Queen?"

"It most certainly is," the lacrosse superstar reflected just as Hook sidled up to her, slipping one of his huge arms deftly around her slim waist.

"Stitched up better than a cadaver in a morgue," added the newly crowned rugby playing king, "by the former dragon monarch in conjunction with the human leaders of this world."

"Oh," sighed Peter, still not really understanding everything going on around him.

"It wasn't quite like that," Richie put in, giving her other half a brief look, one that said he might be in trouble much later on.

For his part Hook just smiled, relishing the idea of a tongue lashing from his wife.

"Perhaps," Vimes suggested, "we should all sit down and very calmly and clearly fill Peter in on exactly what he's missed."

"That sounds like a great idea."

And so they did, each ordering the drink of their choice before taking a seat in a small circle. Before anyone could open their mouths and get the conversation started, they were not quite rudely interrupted.

"A hive of scum and villainy only bettered by Mos Eisley," boomed a voice they all immediately recognised.

SMACK!

"OW!" Flash yelped, Amelia having just elbowed him very firmly in the ribs for his very unjust comments about the small tight knit group.

As one, the others all laughed.

"Amelia, Flash... please, won't you join us?" urged their new queen.

What else would you do but obey? The newcomers joined in and sat, but not before Flash had cuffed Hook playfully around the head, adding a cheeky, "Sorry Your Majesty," for good measure. Richie's other half was already planning his revenge.

As the servers departed after having fulfilled the drinks

order, it was Peter that piped up first.

"So explain once again how the hell you're queen?"

Flashing him one of her picture perfect grins that could have been straight from any of their time together ever since she'd hatched, the newly crowned monarch, light brown freckles on her pale face resembling some sort of starscape, thought carefully about where to start and how to condense down everything she had to convey.

"As you're well aware, across the course of your last day, we were dealing with multiple threats, but... there was much more to it than just that."

Peter nodded, listening intently, all the time clutching Janice's soft pale hand, something most there found extremely sweet.

"Manson died shortly after escaping the claustrophobic innards of that damn submarine, not long after the nuclear detonation in northern France had been averted, at the hands ironically, of Vasuki and a great number of his nagas."

Whilst not having a wicked bone in the entirety of his body, either dragon or human, Peter felt not only relieved that his nemesis had been killed, but glad as well. More to do with the suffering that Manson had caused Garrett, back at the Cropptech site, as well as the rest of his friends during the previous encounter right on this very spot. Hearing that was a huge weight off his shoulders.

"And just how was the nuclear warhead thwarted? I don't recall anything about all that."

"Flash, using some powerful magic applied by your grandfather, raced from Scotland across to France in the blink of an eye in the hope of containing the blast, but despite all his valiant efforts, it was not to be. With both he, Amelia, Yoyo, Rose and all their youngsters directly in the path of the detonation, as well of course as all the surrounding human population, it looked as though only a miracle could prevent the catastrophe heading their way."

Whilst all the others had heard this story a dozen times

over, Peter had no clue, hence the reason he edged ever forward towards the front of his seat.

"Perhaps," ventured Polkinghorne, "I could enlighten him about my encounter at Stonehenge?"

"Be my guest."

"You know all about our experience at Stonehenge, because Hook and I filled you in when we arrived at the Mantra Emporium shortly before our fight with Mas-crate. But what you don't know, Peter, because I didn't share it with anyone at the time, is that I had what can only really be described as an 'out of body' experience whilst trying to connect to the ley lines there."

"O... o... okay."

"It was perhaps the oddest thing that's ever happened to me, and believe you me, I've had some very unusual occurrences across the ages. Anyhow, to cut to the chase, it turns out I was interacting, through what means I don't really know, with the consciousness of the planet itself."

If Peter had looked stunned at the news of Richie being queen, well... let's just say that this was on a whole new scale once again, his mouth hanging open like a broken drawbridge on a castle.

"Long story short," continued Polks, "the planet was dying and was doing its best to convey that to me, although it was difficult to understand at the time, not least because of how delusional it appeared. Unfortunately, because of what happened during the encounter, I didn't really comprehend and... well, let's just say I didn't pick up on the hint. That took beings far more supernaturally powered than I to figure out exactly what was going on."

"WHAT! How is that even possible?"

"It's not easy to describe. Perhaps it might be best explained by the two individuals who were right at the heart of things as they kicked off. Flash?"

With Amelia having gone from playfully slapping him in the ribs, to draping her elegant human form across the whole of his lap, Flash glugged down a huge mouthful of his lager and wiping his lips with the back of his hand, sought to provide some clarity on the issue.

"Flying with little or no mass, I'd arrived just in time to witness my love here finish off a particularly despicable dragon, one that was intent, it would seem, on removing her head from her body. Anyhow, once there, we had only a handful of seconds to spare before the nuclear warhead came crashing down upon us. Fredric had shown me how to open up a naga wormhole and I set about doing just that with the help of everyone there, on a trajectory that would see the missile go straight through it. Having locked the travelling coordinates to somewhere far above the atmosphere, I cast the unfamiliar magic just as I'd been instructed to."

A hush descended across the whole of the residence, humans and dragons alike all taken in by not only the details of the tale, but Flash's brilliant storytelling.

"Sure that I'd done enough to save the day in getting there before the missile and knowing how to conjure up a portal, we did just that, only to watch agonisingly as right at the crucial moment the warhead blinked out of existence only to reappear off to the side, thwarting everything we'd so diligently planned. In that moment, the crushing weight of all the lives on the planet came raining down on me, sorrow and despair running riot throughout my mind and body at the thought of letting everyone down and losing those I'd learned to love. In all my life, I've never felt so torn and broken."

"W... w... what happened?" whispered the hockey playing dragon, totally captivated, something familiar at the back of his consciousness nibbling away at him, something to do with... hockey!

"Glancing up, we could see the fireball tail of the warhead plummeting our way. It was the scariest thing I've ever seen," chipped in Amelia, wrapping herself just that bit tighter around the courageous Crimson Guard she sat upon.

"And with time ticking down and the destruction of the

world all but unavoidable," continued Flash, "two things happened simultaneously. The first was that the nuclear missile soaring down from above exploded, something that you had to be there to believe, and then YOU of all beings turned up to save us."

"WHAT!"

"In a perfect facsimile of you, a voice claiming to be FATE herself said that there was still a way out and that the destruction of the planet could be prevented."

"But how?"

"A good question and one we both found ourselves asking at the same time. But there and then, there were no answers to be had and no time to lose, and so compelled by your exact replica that simply oozed supernatural power, we did as they directed, as fast as we possibly could."

"And what was that?"

"We dived down to where the enemy had left their stash and tossed every last piece of laminium we could find deep into the borehole with as much speed as we could put behind it."

"Wow!"

"Indeed."

"What has all that got to do with the planet?"

"It turns out... everything!"

"Whilst the ley lines act as the blood coursing throughout the body, it seems the laminium provides the heartbeat of the earth. Across millennia that particular resource has been mined to within an inch of its life because of how it can enhance dragon powers, so you can see how the planet's consciousness could very well be on its last legs."

"After my encounter with it at Stonehenge," interrupted Polkinghorne, "others were concerned for its wellbeing."

"Who would they be?"

"Fate, Luck and Time!"

"They even exist?" queried Peter, remembering a fable about the three that he'd heard during his early years at the nursery ring.

"They do, but probably not as you imagine."

"What does that mean?"

"They don't have physical bodies to start with, and can generally be found roaming an ethereal reality that coexists with ours, in and around the entirety of the planet, on the lookout for who knows what. But this time, because of what had been set in motion, even they recognised the danger and the possibility of everything ending and so decided to try and intervene as best they could."

"So it was all about self interest for them?"

"Not quite, but that probably played a big part."

"I see," mused the hockey player.

He didn't, well... not fully anyway.

"How did tossing the laminium down the borehole prevent the world splitting disaster you were all expecting?"

The planet's consciousness has, or should I say had, great supernatural power when at its best. You yourself have seen an example of exactly that, or so I've been told."

"I have?"

"Turn your mind back to the day you ended up facing your worst fear on your beloved Astroturf at the Salisbridge sports club."

Swallowing nervously, Peter took a great big gulp of his drink, his sudden nervousness evident to everyone there.

"How did that play out?" Polkinghorne asked.

"With me lying face down bleeding nearly to death, and the cowardly figure of Manson fleeing like the spineless worm that he really was."

"But why?"

"What do you mean?"

"Why did he flee and not stay and finish you off?"

"T... t... the snow. It started snowing, big time."

"Exactly! Now... do you remember, was snow forecast for that day?"

Peter wracked his brain, using his eidetic memory to return to a particularly painful time in his life.

"No... quite the opposite in fact. It was supposed to be clear and dry for days to come."

"So there you have it."

"You're saying that the planet made it snow just to save me?"

"That's how, oh hang on, I should probably have mentioned that afterwards, we found out that the consciousness we're referring to has a name... Novus, which apparently means self-made. Anyway, that's how Novus described it to me. He, or it, I don't know which and he struggles to apply any of our genders to himself, said that it recognised the threat that Manson represented and did all that it could to intervene given just how thin it had spread itself keeping an eye on the populace across the world. It knew there and then that you were special and that you needed help and did everything it could."

"Phewwww... that's a lot to take in."

"But to answer your question, throwing the laminium into the borehole allowed the planet to absorb it in the quickest way possible, boosting its ability to act, and act it did, as only Novus could.

With a little nod, Polkinghorne indicated that Flash should resume the story.

"Standing transfixed adjacent to the borehole's entrance as the fiery chariot of death exploded outward, all of us in that moment, were expecting an instantaneous death, knowing that the whole of the planet would follow shortly. Strangely though, it just... STOPPED! It was the most jaw dropping thing I've ever seen."

"I can second that," quaked Amelia, slowly shaking her head.

"But..."

Flash held up his index finger, not ready to be interrupted.

"The most bizarre thing about all of it though, was that the monster missile's thunderous engines continued to roar at full power momentarily, after which I suppose it did what it was designed to do and exploded.

"What... what... what was happening?"

"It turns out that Fate and her two cohorts, Time and Luck were spamming the world ending weapon constantly with all their supernatural, just to keep it in place. And we learnt that Fate was the one that had deliberately exploded the warhead because you see, it had avoided our wormhole by some rather wicked magic that Manson had applied to it before it had been fired from the sub, something that was dispersed after it had detonated."

"What happened next?"

"With it hanging over our heads and the three Providences losing their magical grip on things, luckily the laminium had reached the core and Novus was able to act as only he could. Poof... it abruptly winked out of existence. We couldn't believe our eyes."

"One moment," added Amelia, "it was there, right in front of us, so close that we could almost reach out and touch it, the next... it was just gone. It totally blew my mind."

"And Novus did this?"

"From his recounting of the tale, yes he did, the return of the laminium instantly bolstering his supernatural abilities, enough anyway to rid the world of the imminent threat to its destruction."

"Amazing," sighed Peter, absolutely taken aback. "Where is Novus now?"

"Probably looking on in delight," Polks laughed. "Novus does have a very unique sense of humour, especially now most of the laminium's been rightfully put back."

"What do you mean?"

"For the sake of all of us, dragons and humans alike, the laminium had to be returned... all of it!"

"How do you go about returning all of it?"

"It wasn't easy. Luckily for us, we had a somewhat expert in our midst," declared the beautiful blonde

Christmas legend.

"Expert?"

Deep within her mind, Janice reached out through the personal connection she shared with the inanimate object she'd come to know and love, their relationship mirroring that of hers with the queen.

Futuristic tip pointing firmly towards the floor, any hint of cold surrounding his blade long since gone, the renowned weapon smith from times gone by, and one of the most important Xususi the world has ever known, Fu-ts'ang hovered over to join the tight knit group.

"Peter... it's so good to see you again, and I can't tell you how relieved I am that the process to bring you back worked. And don't worry... things might feel a little odd right now, but you'll soon get used to everything."

'How does he know?' thought the hockey playing youngster, feeling as though his new bodies, both dragon and human, didn't quite fit yet, something akin to a new pair of jeans that needed just a little bit of bedding in. As if to answer his unasked question, the weapon smith continued.

"You think you have it tough my boy... imagine going from a top of the range dragon body to this fantastic blade in the blink of an eye. To say it was a difficult transformation doesn't quite do it justice."

Only then did it occur to the youngster that he'd never really thought of Fu-ts'ang as a dragon, despite knowing he most certainly had been, although not for many millennia. Janice he knew was well versed in the entirety of his back story, something she'd revealed to him on their final ride over to the Mantra Emporium, just before the beast Mas-crate had unleashed his devastating attack, but had refused to go into details. From what she'd said to him, it had sounded not only deeply personal, but harrowing as well.

"I'm sorry, I can't imagine…"

"PISH!" cried the weapon. "That was all such a long time ago, and I'm more than comfortable in my own skin... I mean look at me. Have you ever seen a more fabulous and fantastical blade?"

Of course he hadn't. No one had.

"Anyhow, back to Novus and the laminium. Ever since I hatched, many, many thousands of years ago, I've had an affinity with, and a special responsibility for the minerals of the earth. Some have even named me 'the dragon of the hidden treasures'. In my prehistoric form I was able, using all my supernatural abilities, to detect almost any mineral from a very decent height, even LAMINIUM!"

"Ahhh…" Peter sighed, sure that he knew exactly where this was going.

"So after the crisis was averted, I was tasked by George the dragon king, the human leaders of the planet, and by Novus himself, to scour the planet and round up any and all laminium. While I was doing just that, dragonkind voluntarily handed in everything they had once it was explained why, and that included every single laminium ball ever to have been created."

"Oh my."

"Indeed. It was a great deal, and coveted by many. But down to a single dragon, they all did the right thing."

"How long did it take for you to scour the world?"

"Six weeks."

"Is that all?" the youngster marvelled.

"I had help in the form of Tank and For'son. If not for them, I'd still be out there now flying around trying to locate it all."

"But you did?"

"Pretty much. Oh there might be the odd sliver here and there, but for the most part, it's all been returned."

"How?"

"We used the borehole in northern France. It seemed pretty appropriate given what had happened. Every last ounce from across the domain as well as the entirety of what Cropptech had stockpiled was thrust into the core, including your grandfather's dagger."

"Oh!"

"You disapprove?"

"No... it's not that. I just have magical memories of when the king presented it to me, telling me it was my grandfather's. To have something from him at that time, not ever having met him, was special beyond belief."

"I understand."

"Thanks."

"And that's basically that. With the laminium returned, Novus is essentially restored, or at least the majority of his supernatural is, allowing him to guide, guard and protect the world to the best of his ability, something that we think he was destined to do all along."

"Is that his job?"

"Not so much a job, Peter," Polkinghorne interrupted, "more, as Fu-ts'ang has suggested, a destiny. Novus, by his or its own admission, has no idea how he came into being. The only thing he remembers is his name, which is odd because the word 'Novus' actually means, 'self-made'."

"So he created himself?"

"No one's quite sure, and I don't think we'll ever get to the bottom of things. But what we do know is that he/it is a calm, rational being whose only compunction is to look out for all life across the planet, something he's more than capable of doing now that all his supernatural abilities have been restored. I for one am delighted to know that he's out there overseeing everything."

Everyone nodded in agreement.

"I'd very much like to meet Novus," stated the youngster back from the dead, more than a little intrigued.

"Perhaps at some point in the future that can be arranged," Polkinghorne added, "but I think for now, Novus needs space and time, something he's been assured he would get."

"I understand," Peter replied smiling, glad to have gained an insight into exactly what had happened.

And then it hit him.

"If all the laminium balls have been returned to the core,

what will the teams use to play?"

"Frankly," put in Tank, "I'm surprised it's taken you this long to ask."

Peter remained grinning like an idiot.

"So am I," seconded the queen.

"So?"

With the laminium ball season still on hold due to the ongoing rebuilding efforts, titanium has already been used to create experimental balls, all of course reinforced by magic."

"Naturally."

"Speaking of which," announced Richie to all and sundry.

"Which, what?"

"Laminium ball," the queen went on. "I've arranged for an impromptu match tomorrow to celebrate not only the return of this one," she said, cuffing Peter playfully around the head, "but to mark the opening of the new clubhouse at the Salisbridge sports club."

"Get in!" Peter yelled, buoyed at the thought of the new building, something he'd had his heart set on for quite some time.

"Where's the match?" asked Flash.

"At the sports club of course... dummy!" replied the lacrosse playing monarch.

"How are you going to...?"

"It's all been taken care of, and with magic of course. I expect you all to be there, and that's an order."

From the far end of the room, up shot George's arm, faster than a starving cheetah hunting its prey.

"I know, I know... you two are of course excused. The rest of you... be there! Tomorrow... three o'clock sharp."

"A chorus of, "Yes ma'am," echoed around the chamber amongst the merriment.

"Oh... and on the subject of the sports club," interrupted Flash, "I've got something to tell you all."

That got the friends' attention, including Amelia who

immediately sat up straighter on her lover, giving him a curious look as to what was about to come next.

"I'm... taking up a sport, a human one," Flash informed them all.

"Really?" exclaimed Peter, wide eyed.

The Crimson Guard nodded.

"The big question though," goaded the queen, "is which one? Choose carefully."

Swallowing nervously, something of a rarity for one of the most courageous heroes on the planet, sure that the monarch would want to hear the word 'lacrosse' stem from his mouth, Flash craned his neck in the direction of Tank and let rip.

"Rugby," he stated matter-of-factly, wondering what everyone's reaction would be.

"Not just the right choice," barked Tank, slapping his pal firmly on the shoulder, "but the only choice."

"And I for one look forward to training with you," added Hook. "You'd better hope you live up to your name and that you have balls of steel."

"Did I hear someone mention my genitalia," declared Steel, as he DomCon and Jar Man wandered on over with some of the humans from Cropptech.

Cue lots of laughter.

"What's so funny?" asked the laminium ball superstar, pretending to be hurt.

"Hook's enquiring about your balls," Janice ventured as straight faced as she could. It didn't last long.

"My..."

"My husband," interjected Richie, "is looking forward to getting back to playing rugby. How on earth that's going to work, I'll never know."

"Ahh... rugby," Steel mused. "An excellent pastime and one I thoroughly approve of. I'd like to come and watch you all at some point. Is that a possibility?"

"The next time we play," ushered Tank, "we'll make sure there's room for everyone to come and watch."

That got a resounding cheer.

With nearly everyone now in one huge group, through a gap in those standing, Peter spotted Garrett sitting off on his own at the far end of the chamber. Whispering to Janice that he'd be back soon, he slipped out of his seat, through a small hole in the crowd and wandered off to find the man who'd saved them all, just in the nick of time.

Lost in thoughts of everything that had happened since he'd learned about the underground domain of the dragons, the 'bald eagle' averted his eyes from the fizzy bubbles in his drink at the sound of approaching footsteps.

"My boy," he remarked jumping to his feet. "It's so good to have you back. I confess to being incredibly upset at your premature demise."

"Mr Garrett... I mean Al, it's good to see you again. I'm sorry for what you've been through."

"You have nothing to be sorry for, Peter. Without you, I'd have long since died and no doubt the world would be a very different place. I'm just thankful everything turned out okay in the end."

"Amen to that."

"You should be back celebrating with the others."

"There'll be plenty of time for that. I saw you across the room. You looked sad."

"Not so much sad, as reflecting on everything that's happened and the momentous actions of the last twenty four hours."

"Richie as queen, I know... it's pretty awesome."

"That it is, that it is. But humans and dragons sharing the world above and below ground... you just couldn't make it up."

"Pretty crazy, huh?"

"Absolutely bonkers!" the Cropptech owner stated.

"Thanks for your efforts with the sports club. I can't tell you what it means to not only me, but the others in the city. I know that Cropptech will ultimately be your legacy, but I actually think everything you've done in the rebuilding might be more so."

"You're very welcome, youngster. After all... we did have a deal."

"I know, but I still think I wasn't deserving of how much money it may have cost you."

"Oh Peter... the money, it's nothing. I have no use for it, and never really have. Life, something you'll soon learn after everything that's happened, is all about the beings you surround yourself with, not what you have or even the power you wield, but the friends you make and share memories with. You, youngster, have some of the best that history has to offer," he said, inclining his head in the direction of the group Peter had left. "As for Miss Rump, I'm so proud. If anyone can pull off this unholy alliance of different species, I know it will be her. She was practically made for the job. The planet's in safe hands, of that we can be reassured."

"I'm pretty sure you're right, but I worry about everything she's given up."

"How so?"

"The lacrosse, hanging out at the sports club with her friends, surely that's a thing of the past?"

Garrett burst into a huge belly laugh, unusual for him, as he was normally much more reticent than that.

Peter didn't know whether to be offended or not.

"My boy, the populace has known for some time that she'd be ruling the world. And do you know what? Not a thing has changed. Okay, she's become a little more serious when needed, but she's still been there for her friends, human and dragon alike. I don't doubt for one minute that she'll be flying down the pitch, lacrosse stick held up high, before drinking every one of her teammates under the table afterwards. I'm guessing that was probably a condition of the agreement somewhere."

"The agreement?"

"Negotiations between the humans and dragons hit something of a stalemate quite early on. I'd done my part by then, bringing them together, so I don't know all the details. But what I can tell you is that we're only here, where we are now, because of her. If George had wanted to cling on to power, then nothing would have been settled and the whole planet would have been back where it was before your demise. Only by George relinquishing power and having the perfect candidate, a dragon now stuck as a human as it was so callously put, did we get to this stage. Richie made all of this happen. Without her, well... I hate to think what state the world would be in. She, in my humble opinion, was the only candidate both sides could get behind, the only one who could reunify the earth."

Inside, Peter beamed with pride at what his friend had achieved, knowing just how much it would have cost her. With all his heart he hoped, despite all the security implications that she would still be found on a Saturday afternoon, displaying all her prowess at the human sport she loved almost above everything else. Only then did his thoughts return to his chosen sport, and the hope that he could now pick up his stick and once again battle alongside his teammates.

"Penny for them?" the 'bald eagle' asked.

"Just thinking about playing hockey again."

"I'm more than a mite amused at how a dragon can get addicted to a human sport."

"Not just one. Richie with her lacrosse, Tank with his rugby, and Flash has announced that he's going to join in with the big fella and the odd shaped ball."

That made Garrett smile... dragons with odd shaped balls. (First Steel and now this... I'm not obsessed you know. Really!)

"I think it does all of you credit and provides some insight into your personalities. Do you think others of your kind will want to have a go in this newfound sharing environment?"

"Maybe, but I'm guessing there'll have to be strict measures in place to ensure none of them use their inherent abilities to cheat."

"Ah yes... I hadn't thought of that."

"But it would be good to see more of them mixing and enjoying everything good the human race has to offer."

"Yes it would," the elder of the two nodded.

A thoughtful pause ensued. And just as Bentwhistle thought about returning to Janice and the others, Garrett piped up.

"And speaking of mixing, I was kind of hoping that you might want your... job back."

'Wow,' Peter thought. He hadn't even got as far as considering that, or even any part of what the future offered.

"You seem a little stunned, my boy," the 'bald eagle' laughed, deeply amused at the confused look that had come over his friend's face, as that's what they now were, not only colleagues but the best of pals.

"I... I... I hadn't really thought that far ahead, I'm afraid si... si... si... Al."

"It's alright. There's no rush. Owen's been doing a fabulous job in your absence. But I just wanted to put it out there. We'd have you back in a heartbeat if you feel that's what's right for you. Take your time, get used to being back and make the most of it with your lovely other half. She's a keeper, youngster. I'd stick with her if I were you, and never let her go."

"I intend to do just that," Peter replied, deciding to return to Janice and his friends right now. "I'm going to rejoin her. I'll see you later Al," he observed, turning to head back.

"Peter," Garrett continued, reaching deep into his right hand pocket, clutching at something shiny.

"Yes."

"Before you go, there's something I want you to have and I don't want any arguments about it."

"What is it?"

Swallowing apprehensively, with his other hand Garrett

picked up his drink and took a quick swig, the effervescing golden liquid quenching his thirst and refreshing his parched throat.

Holding out his clenched fist, Garret turned his hand over and opened out his fingers, revealing a set of sparkling silver keys in the middle of his palm.

Befuddled, the young hockey playing dragon didn't know what to do or say.

"They're for you and Janice, and as I say... I don't want any argument about it."

"What do they belong to?"

The Cropptech owner told him in no uncertain terms. The youngster's mind was well and truly blown.

Having confided in Richie some time ago about what he'd wanted to do, the future queen had allowed Garrett some recollection of the knowledge that Peter could well be resurrected. With that in mind, the Cropptech owner had gone and bought a house, and not just any one at that. On the tree lined road approaching Janice's home, a huge four bedroom monster of a thing, the perfect place for a young couple to set up with a view to having a family. It was everything Peter had ever dreamed of, something that was only now occurring to his body, as silver edged transparent tears started to stream from his face.

"My boy!"

The youngster threw himself into the arms of the man he still considered his boss, burying his head in his shoulder, the moist droplets running down his face soaking into Garrett's crisp white shirt.

"I... I... I don't know what to say," he whispered, by now having caught the attention of all the others in the huge cavern they all shared.

"Just enjoy, my young friend. And no, you're not in my debt and you coming back to work is not reliant on this. Take the keys, live a good life, have... offspring, if that's even possible. Live, love, laugh and enjoy. Now go... see your friends, hold Janice tight and make the most of the new life you most definitely deserve."

With that, the 'bald eagle' pulled away and sat back down, before raising his glass in his teary eyed friend's direction. Not knowing what else to do, Peter wandered back over towards the large group that was getting rowdier by the minute.

Looking on from amidst it all, the newly crowned queen had more than an inkling of what had just happened, her former boss having long since confided the details to her. The moment was out of this world.

Sauntering back to the huge group of friends, Peter pulled Janice to her feet and whispered in her ear exactly what Garrett had done. Blown away couldn't fully do justice to what she felt as she melted into her love's arms. Over his shoulder, her eyes met with the 'bald eagle' from across the beautifully restored cavern that had become the queen's private residence. Silently she mouthed him a thank you. Nodding, he mouthed, "You're welcome," in reply. This, she thought, was as good as things could get.

After that, and with the alcohol flowing, enough to at least lower inhibitions in most of those there, including the dragons amongst them, the party really began.

Flash, using all his inherent supernatural abilities conjured up a rugby ball straight out of thin air. Within moments, it was being tossed around by everyone, two makeshift sides having formed immediately, those experienced amongst them vying for the ball, shouting and screaming for a pass, making mazy runs around the room, hoping to see the odd shaped ball zinging in their direction. Surprisingly, it was Tank who made the first tackle, around DomCon's waist of all people, who took great offense at the effort, as he crashed unceremoniously to the floor, especially as he'd already moved the ball on. A furious scowl of epic proportions flashed in the direction of the plant loving hero from the short fused, pint sized, ball of rage. Tank, however, had long since disappeared, bounding to his feet and leaping into the crowd, the desire to get his hands on the ball all encompassing, just as it would have been above ground. His addiction to the sport he loved was proving once again all consuming.

Nearly all of them became involved, with the exception of Garrett, Janice, Amelia, Rose, Fredric and George. The humans there, despite the very real danger from all the others, opted to join in, ducking, diving in for challenges, making blocks and at one point, Judith from Garrett's squad of armed rescuers punched Flash straight in the face, stopping him dead in his tracks from leaping to intercept a pass from the opposition. Whilst the young human was mortified at what she'd accidently done, every other being there doubled up in laughter, particularly Amelia who started whooping and shouting, encouraging all and sundry to repeat the feat and give her other half an even more bloodied face. Even the Crimson Guard himself had to smile. Probably the highlight of such an extraordinary impromptu party came a massive throw from Tank that looked to find Hook from a huge distance, the ever spinning ball looping high across everyone, including those who continued to sit, its trajectory as sure a thing as you could imagine given Tank's experience and explosive power. What nobody expected was a graceful, slender, pale freckled arm to reach out midway through a treble somersault that had seen the lacrosse playing superstar leap twenty five metres into the air, and swapping sports momentarily, grab the ball one handed, then continue her tumble to land effortlessly on one of the nearby tables. Everyone, to a man, woman and dragon, stopped dead still. Well you would, wouldn't you, having seen your newly crowned queen do that in her wedding dress of all things?

In a missive to the husband she loved more than ever, she raised one of the pale fingers of her white hand in his direction, and with unerring accuracy, threw the ball in a blur towards Flash, who of course was on the opposite side. For his part, Hook shook his head and catching her eye, poked out his tongue in her direction, before once again joining the chase to get his hands on the ever moving ball. It was chaos, mayhem and most of all... FUN! For each and every one of them.

Watching from a distance as Peter got elbowed out of the way by his friend Owen, before clumsily falling to the ground and being trampled on, Janice turned to her best friend.

"Was that a wise thing to do? It certainly wasn't very regal."

"You should learn to lighten up, young lady... and that's an order from your monarch."

"YES MA'AM!" the beautiful blonde replied sarcastically.

Both women started to giggle.

"What's got into both of you?" a familiar voice whispered from in between the two of them.

"And that order applies to you as well, For'son," slurred the lacrosse playing superstar, still with one eye on the rugby.

"Is this how it's going to be from now on?" asked the enigmatic band that had done so much to preserve the planet's current way of life.

"I think it will be... yes."

"This isn't how it was with Tank."

"Are you saying that you want to be reunited with him?"

There was a long uncomfortable pause in which Richie immediately sobered up using all her dragon magic to purge the alcohol from her system.

"For'son?"

"I'm here, just contemplating your words."

"And?"

"Answering your question, I don't wish to be reunited with Tank. Well... I kind of do, because we complemented each other so well. But I want to see where this relationship with you takes me. I feel I have a great deal to offer when it comes to matters of running the planet, but not only that, I think there's a huge amount that I can benefit from being in your company. If you'll allow me to stay as your constant companion, at least for the time being, I would be most grateful."

Richie smiled.

"As far as I was concerned, you were never indebted to this position For'son, especially not given everything you contributed during the course of the battle with Manson and Earth. If at any time you want to leave, go back to Tank or even take up another position, all you have to do is ask. Your freedom should be a given, and as long as I'm in charge, it will be. Do you understand?"

"I do, Majesty," he said sarcastically.

That provoked more giggles from Janice.

"Oh... very good," declared Richie. "I think you're learning just a little too quickly for my liking."

They all laughed at that.

Off to one side, what looked like a mass brawl had become a total and utter scramble for the odd shaped ball that was on the receiving end of more wear and tear than if it had been in a dozen matches, despite the fact that they'd only been playing for half an hour or so. That, I suppose is what a group of supernatural dragons and the finest human beings on the planet have the propensity to do. Out of nowhere, up popped a huge red sack, lined with fluffy bright white fur, shovelling up the ball in one fell swoop, before disappearing into the writhing multitude.

"POLKINGHORNE!" Tank and Hook screamed simultaneously. "That's cheating of the highest order."

Taking absolutely no notice, the stunningly beautiful blonde and once a year Christmas legend, reached into her bag, took out the ball, and applying more than a little of her unique magic, tossed it in the direction of her other half, Vimes, who was waiting to receive.

Having already sussed what the fantastical Christmas legend would do, the hugely powerful Crimson Guard knew that he had to get to his friend, the dragon he'd cooperated so well with when Christmas had been in Crisis and Santa had nearly died. Just as his hands got a foothold on the ball, Vimes was struck by a freight train around the waist, smashing him to the cold, hard, marble floor. Breath knocked out of him, much to his own surprise, Santa's other half still remained holding the ball. That is, until it was unfairly snatched away.

"I'll be taking that," scoffed Flash, grabbing it before bounding up to his feet. "Thanks, old friend."

Vimes felt crestfallen. He really did think this time would be different, playing with his friends. But no... it was just like being back in the nursery ring, during all those times when he was constantly picked last.

Polkinghorne, pleased at her efforts with the sack, looked on in disbelief as Flash brutally tackled her love to the ground, before disappearing off with the ball.

'Of all the things,' she thought, being the one to encourage him to get involved in the first place. 'Right... that's it,' she mused, flooding herself with all the Santa magic, before setting her sights on the Crimson Guard and most importantly of all... the ball!

'Things,' Richie judged, 'are starting to get out of hand,' and it must have been bad if she was thinking that, given her propensity for chaos, mayhem and destruction. About to call time on all of it, especially given that some of the humans were strewn about all over the place, nursing pretty wicked cuts and bruises, and even some of Yoyo's youngsters looking pretty worse for wear, out of the corner of her eye she watched Polkinghorne intercept a pretty snazzy looking pass with her Christmas sack of all things, gaining possession of the ball and in the blink of an eye, throwing it across to her ever constant companion Vimes, who, just as he caught it, was viciously tackled by Flash of all dragons. Knowing that now was the time to knock it on the head, she just managed to catch a glimpse of the Santa legend right at that very moment. Never before had she seen something so endearing, so enraged. Knowing it was wrong on so many levels to do so, but sooooo wanting to witness the outcome, the newly crowned queen allowed play to go on, at least for the time being, desperate to see how her beautiful blonde friend, the once a year Christmas legend, would deal with the altercation between her love and the Crimson Guard. She hoped it would be something entertaining.

Flash, ball secured with his huge left hand against his chest, vaulted a series of tables and chairs with one brilliant bound, landing slightly off balance, but using his momentum and brilliant dexterity to fling himself forward, roll once on the floor before leaping leopard-like to his feet, still sprinting for all he was worth, in between moments palming some of his human opponents away, watching smugly as they flailed about in the distance behind him, sure that the only two real threats were Tank and Hook. It's a shame he didn't have more of his Crimson Guard wits about him, because if he had, he might have known that some very powerful magic was stalking him.

Glasses, broken and otherwise, as well as the remnants of all the food, lay scattered across the floor. It looked like the aftermath of a five day rock concert attended by many tens of thousands of people. The queen's residence, at least the outer chamber anyway, had turned into the mother of all messes.

Strangely though, that was all being taken care of as a gigantic electric blue ribbon of energy, five metres high and fifteen metres across, bristled across the residence, weaving this way and that, at first looking totally random on its travels, although soon it was obvious to most that it was chasing something up ahead, well... I say something, someone in fact.

Brushed off more brusquely than a bin man asking a supermodel for a date, Owen and Caren both from Garrett's squad of brave human heroes found themselves sprawled out across the shiny floor, covered in leftover food and drink, barely able to sit up after trying to retrieve the ball from the dragon in human form, most certainly living up to his name. Looking on as he skipped effortlessly over more tables and chairs, abruptly a huge surge of electric-like energy washed over them, the crackling, bright blue, rectangular ribbon of ethereal magic rolling on in Flash's wake. Oddly, to them at least, every last piece of broken glass and wasted food that the ribbon touched magically vanished, as well as all the food and drink stains on their clothes. The enchanted band was not only hot on the heels of Dendrik Ridge, but was tidying up the room as it went. Astounding!

With just a look, Tank and Hook had quickly come to an agreement, much as they would have on any normal Saturday in much muddier surroundings. Splitting up, the two decided to outflank their cocky and explosive opponent, determined to teach him a lesson about what it meant to try to show up either of them. They were so caught up in their little mission of revenge, they hadn't spotted what was going on in Flash's wake, something that might cost either of them dearly.

Standing stock still, overseeing everything with her intrinsic Santa magic humming and buzzing all around her, Polkinghorne looked like a conductor at the heart of the mother of all symphonies, willing her supernatural this way and that, keeping up with the beat, making sure the ribbon she'd launched kept time and more importantly, caught up with its so called prey. This, she knew, would be a suitable revenge.

Sensibly, everyone else in the open ended cavern had by now opted to stand off to one side and leave the three immature heroes to their sporting escapades, all now aware of what had happened with Vimes and that Santa's payback was imminent. Keen to see exactly what was coming, each of them looked on with interest, none more so than Amelia, wondering what her other half had gotten himself into this time and just what kind of outcome would prevail. Of one thing she was totally sure... this was a battle like no other, and one he couldn't possibly win.

Flash moved fast. Not as fast as he'd ever moved, because here and now, there was no using the magic of his birthright to enhance his speed, not with the humans about, and especially not given he wanted to take up this fabulous sport on the surface, as soon as his schedule would allow. No... that most certainly wouldn't have been fair, and had been an unwritten rule the moment that things had kicked off down here with the rugby ball. Speeding towards the huge rocky wall, the one below the vent through which Richie had made her way into the residence and killed Troydenn, all that time ago, the almighty Crimson Guard knew what had to be done, as he spotted both Tank and Hook on either side, looking to outflank him. Knowing he almost had enough speed, what he had planned was audacious and cunning as well as more than a mite showboaty. Still, they were all having fun and the alcohol was having at least a little effect, certainly bringing to the fore his incredible competitiveness. Watching both his friends give their all in an effort to retrieve the odd shaped ball, he was both startled and concerned when at the very last moment, both hesitated and pulled back. Unfortunately for them, it wasn't enough to take them out of the line of fire of the blazing ribbon of crackling electric blue energy that had finally caught up with the target of its ire. What Flash had planned deep within his smug, arrogant, swaggering mind, was to run up the wall with as much speed as he could in the hope that his friends would miss him completely and crash into each other, allowing him to somersault back down to the ground with the ball casually raised aloft, showing off for all to see. What happened though, was that a few of the outstretched tendrils from the ribbon of concentrated magic managed to tickle his feet and ankles just as he was about to launch himself, causing him to not only falter, but crash face first into the wall. Both Hook and Tank, unable to slow themselves completely, tripped over the Crimson Guard's prone body, all three ending up in a massive pile like the remnants of a road traffic accident. Looking a little lonely and bereft, the odd shaped rugby ball bounced off to one side. And just when things looked as though they couldn't get any worse for the trio, they did, a puff of blinding smoke encompassing them all followed by a cascading arc of bright blue electricity.

Everyone watched as the heavy, smouldering air around the three rugby obsessed combatants started to clear, waiting to see how badly each were damaged, Yoyo ready and willing to rush over and tend to their wounds. What greeted them was something nobody expected.

Scampering around on the floor, off to one side of the lonesome rugby ball, were three tiny little mice, each with long tails and bright white teeth, the grey and brown fur on their miniature bodies bristling, a sense of overwhelming panic clearly evident.

A deep hush enveloped the residence, after of course the occasional sigh, mainly from the humans dotted around the place.

And then the silence was broken by one set of serious footsteps heading directly for the three rodents at pace... POLKINGHORNE!

Much scurrying and gnawing preceded her approach, before the three mice in question backed up against the wall, their long pink tails flailing all over the place. Every other being there watched with bated breath, wondering what the outcome of such an encounter would be.

"YOU," Polkinghorne stated, bordering on being angry, "are very naughty boys. I understand your fascination with the human sport, but you've taken it a bit too far this time. If not for me, this place would look like a war zone, something that I don't think is especially appropriate, not given our cause for celebration. But that's not why you've all ended up like that. Do you know what is?"

Cue the middle mouse of the three squeaking like a rusty old door blowing in a gale.

"That's right, Flash, you did! And how do you think that made him feel?"

More squeaking, followed by another set of footsteps.

"My love…"

"NO!"

"My love," urged Vimes, putting his hand delicately on Polkinghorne's shoulder.

Slowly she turned to face him.

"They have to be told."

"I always find it adorable when you stick up for me like that, who wouldn't? But they were just boys being boys and meant no harm. Given that they probably don't even know what they've done to deserve being turned into mice, I think you should probably transform them back, don't you?"

"But…"

"Everyone was just having some fun and got a little over exuberant. There's no harm in that, and I'm sure the alcohol is mostly to blame. Please… for me, turn them back into themselves. I'm pretty sure that by now they know they've done something to upset you. And that should be enough."

She knew he was right and in typically stubborn fashion didn't want to return the trio to themselves.

'Damn him when he's so reasonable,' she thought, before turning around to face the rodents.

With a wave of her hand and yet another puff of wispy grey smoke, the three rugby amigos, one human (an important one at that) and two dragons, all reappeared standing against the wall, each looking more than a little sheepish.

"We're sorry," Tank observed, keen to apologise for all of them, despite still being unsure as to what had gone down.

"No… let me," urged Flash, stepping forward towards the still angry Polkinghorne, easily identifiable from her rosy red cheeks and the smouldering look in her eyes. "I'm sorry… I really am. It's no excuse but I got caught up in the moment, the natural urge to show off to these two trumping everything else. I meant nothing by it and would take back what I did if I could."

Santa's look said everything. Flash knew what he had to do.

Strolling up to her other half, he enveloped Vimes in the hugest hug he could and profoundly apologised, repeating his words. Being one of the most forgiving beings on the planet, and proud of his rock solid friendship with the Crimson Guard, there was absolutely no question that Vimes would not accept. He did, and finally proceedings were allowed to continue, although now more slightly subdued than before.

And so it was that they all sat down and shared stories from their adventures, but not before mocking Flash, Tank and Hook mercilessly for being turned into a trio of mice, and very frightened ones at that.

From Peter's perspective, the surprises came thick and fast. Yoyo, as it turned out, had been selected to be the new councillor for Australia, the previous one having been murdered during Manson's reign of mayhem and madness. Only then did the healer and his wife reveal that they'd adopted all the youngsters that Yoyo had taken responsibility for throughout the preceding years. And once the conclusion of that tale was reached, another revelation was revealed, this time by Flash, much to the pride of Yoyo, Rose and the entirety of their newly extended family. All the youngsters had officially been taken on by the Crimson Guards. Not in an agent capacity you understand, more in a support type of role. Think 'Q' in the James Bond movies. It was that type of position in which they would all work together in their very own department, developing magic and technology in conjunction with each other in an effort to give agents out in the field more of an edge than they'd ever had before. Peter was made up for all of them, as were their newly adoptive parents, who couldn't stop smiling.

The head of the Crimson Guards didn't stop there though. In an unusual outpouring of emotion, there and then he expressed his love for Amelia, not really a surprise for most there, but it was to the hockey playing youngster only just back from the dead. Flash then went on to reveal that once things calmed down and the world was back on track, not only was he determined to play rugby regularly at the sports club with Tank and Hook, but that they both were looking to settle in and around the Salisbridge area, not sure yet if it would be above or below ground. The friends were delighted, with hugs aplenty for the strapping male and plenty of kisses and congratulations for Amelia, who since the raging battle that had endangered the very earth itself, had become an integral part of their ever increasing friendship group.

Spurred on by the passion with which Flash had unburdened himself, surprisingly For'son spoke up, extolling the virtues of his time being bonded to Tank, throughout the course of the battle and scouring the world afterwards with Fu-ts'ang, searching out the remaining laminium so they could fully restore Novus to his full glory. Not one of the beings there would have thought it possible for an inanimate object to speak with such honesty and feeling, nearly all of them moved to tears by what the enigmatic band had to say, not just about Tank and the connection they'd shared, but about the friendship that had been formed between all of them throughout their escapades. To say it tugged at the heartstrings was an understatement, and one Richie felt especially guilty about given that as queen, she now wore the inscrutable band on her finger. Across their shared consciousness, For'son admonished her in more of a playful way than anything else, assuring the newly crowned monarch that for the time being at least, he was as comfortable with the decision as he could be, and content to be partnered with her. His words not only bolstered her spirit, but set her mind at ease.

Tank though, that was another matter. Given everything the strapping rugby player had been through, losing his dragon mentor and the being he thought of as his father, it was no surprise to find him blubbing like a toddler in a high chair, whose doughnut had just disappeared into thin air, directly in front of them. It was both poignant and heartening at the same time and a touching reminder of all those lost during the madness that had happened only a few months before.

After a comforting pause, one in which nearly everyone reflected on all that had happened and just how close the planet had come to total and utter annihilation, yet another brave soul stuck in an inorganic form decided to speak up. Yes, that's right... the master weapon smith, Fu-ts'ang!

Short and sweet, he exclaimed his love for the beautiful blonde who'd done so much to restore him to his previous self, some semblance of the courageous, loving and talented dragon he'd once been working tirelessly at his magical forge, long before he'd been chosen as an Xususi by the magic that had surrounded and inundated him. Janice had achieved it all just by being herself, something he was eternally grateful for. After which he name checked pretty much all of them... the queen, the former king, Peter of course, to whom he gave a playfully stern warning about taking care of his best friend, and even Fredric, which was something of a turnaround given the events of the standoff that had taken place right on that very spot, directly before their humdinger of an encounter with all the escaped mythical creatures. It was a moving rendition from one of the oldest beings on the planet, and one that sobered up nearly all of them.

After that, things got distinctly quieter. Okay... some were still drinking, but the revelry had pretty much died down, whispered conversations between partners being the name of the game, whilst the waiters flitted amongst them, asking if there was anything they needed between doing a standout job of tidying up. The evening, which had long since turned into morning, was well and truly coming to an end, with the guest of honour, the back from the dead Bentwhistle, having spent the last half an hour or so chatting to Owen and the Cropptech band of humans that had done so much to prevent the demise of them all at the hands of the merciless mythical maniacs under the control of the ra-hoon all that time ago.

"It would be great if you could come back to work," offered up the huge human security coordinator, the one who'd taken over temporarily from Peter in the interim.

"I'd like to, that's for sure. But currently, I don't know what the future offers. I just need some time off to clear my head and sort out everything in my mind. Coming back from the dead... it's not as easy as everyone would have you believe."

They all chuckled at that.

And then it was time to leave.

Steel, Jar Man and DomCon were the first to go, staggering back the way they'd come, all promising to attend the match that afternoon, thanking their host, each giving Peter a huge slap on the back as they passed, much to everyone's amusement. They were clearly still three sheets to the wind.

Angela, Emma, Sam and Taibul were next, all looking as though they'd been dragged through a car wash backwards, the evening and morning festivities having taken their toll, even on the young hockey playing waiter who was as expected, the only one of them still sober, despite having sampled some of the alcohol. Mostly it had been the dancing... well, that and the spur-of-the-moment rugby match. Bedraggled didn't do them justice.

As Taibul shook Peter's hand, expressing his joy at his friend returning from the grave, the youngster thanked his hockey idol for the adventure he'd been on. Unsurprisingly, Bentwhistle didn't know what to say or how to react, caught well off guard. All he could do was wish his teammate well and tell him he couldn't wait for them both to line up together on the hockey pitch. That produced quite possibly the biggest smile of the day. Emma, Angela and Sam embraced all those left, which was a thankless task as they kept forgetting who'd hugged who. In the end it was down to their lacrosse teammate, the queen, to usher them out, urging them to get some sleep, assuring them she'd see them at the sports club in only a few hours. That got them all moving.

One by one, the groups left, Yoyo, Rose and their adopted children, Garrett and his Cropptech group of heroes, all, with the exception of George and Fredric, promising to be at the Salisbridge sports club the following afternoon for the impromptu laminium ball match that had been arranged by the queen. She made sure to remind them on their way out.

With only Tank, Richie, Hook, Peter, Janice, Flash, Amelia, Polkinghorne, Vimes, Fu-ts'ang and For'son remaining, Fredric and George approached Peter, both enveloping him in a huge hug.

"It's good to see you again my boy," Fredric extolled as he broke away. "You look damn good for someone pronounced dead so long ago."

"Thank you grandfather... that means so much coming from you. Can I ask why you won't be at the laminium ball match tomorrow?"

"Ahhh…" interrupted George, "that'll be my fault I'm afraid."

"Ohhh…"

"Sorry... it's just that I promised your grandfather I'd treat him to a proper holiday when this was all over. I didn't realise there'd be more shenanigans to come, and I've already made arrangements."

"That's quite alright," Peter replied. "Goodness knows, both of you deserve such a thing after everything you've been through."

"You can say that again," Fredric chuckled.

"Just out of interest, where are you going?"

Shaking his head whilst rolling his eyes, Fredric offered up his reply.

"I don't know... he won't tell me."

"It's a surprise," put in George, mischievously.

"Hmmm... it had better be a good one, for all this fuss

and secrecy."

"It will be, old friend, it will be."

Bidding them all farewell, with each in return wishing them happy holidays, much to Fredric's consternation, the two best friends, the former king and the founder of the Crimson Guards bade their goodbyes and left, leaving the tight knit group to it.

All of a sudden and out of absolutely nowhere, Tank piped up.

"Before we all say our goodbyes, there's something that I have to tell all of you."

That got everyone's attention, especially considering he was normally the most reserved of them all.

"I wanted to let you know that the shop is all but complete."

"Oh my God," exclaimed Peter, "That's absolutely fantastic. Why didn't you say anything earlier?"

Chuckling softly to himself, the rugby playing dragon replied with a smile on his face.

"I'm pretty sure there've been more important matters going on throughout the day."

"How on earth did you get it done in such a short space of time?" asked the queen, absolutely gobsmacked. "The last time I visited it was a total mess."

"Luckily for me Zarenkesia has recovered fully from the attack and her post traumatic stress disorder. With her help we've managed to rebuild both above and below ground, making each area safer and more robust. You're all very welcome to drop by when you get the chance. I just wanted to put it out there."

"Congratulations, buddy," declared Flash, embracing his friend for all he was worth.

"Thanks," replied the plant loving shop owner.

More hugs and well wishes ensued, that is until a powerful voice rang out around the residence.

"Are you going to keep the same name, youngster?" Futs'ang asked pointedly.

Turning to face the stunning, hovering futuristic blade, Tank took a breath before replying.

"No. The shop has a new one."

Cue a round of sighing from everyone left.

"Come on then," urged Amelia, "Don't leave us hanging."

"It's called 'The Crafty Mantra Mart'."

"Catchy," put in Janice. "I like it."

And so did everyone else there.

Embracing his friend, Peter whispered in his ear as low as he could.

"He would be so proud you know... not just of the name, but of everything you've achieved. His legacy lives on in all your accomplishments."

Holding back the tears, Tank just nodded, moved by his pal's kind words, delighted at being surrounded by the best group of friends in the world.

Given the late, or should I say early hour, Janice stretched out her arms, letting out the biggest yawn she could, absolutely drop dead tired, given that the sun had long since risen across the capital of the United Kingdom some way up above them all.

"I think," she declared, "that it's my bedtime."

As the only other human left, Hook declared his support for that sentiment.

"Me too."

"Not so fast," interjected the queen, still wide awake, despite the procession of partying that had taken place across the last day and a half of all their lives.

"Come on, my love... seriously," urged the new human king and fearless rugby playing hero, who'd figured by now that he'd been through enough to deserve at least a little sleep before the impromptu opening ceremony and laminium ball match kicked off in less than seven hours.

"Hold your horses, sleepy head," Richie ventured, slapping her other half hard across his taut, six pack stomach, causing him to double over and wince more than he would have liked.

The others laughed.

"What's so important, Rich?" Tank asked, intrigue as to what was afoot just about trumping his fatigue.

"I have news," the lacrosse superstar revealed, turning to face her best friend, Janice of all people.

"What news?" the gorgeous blonde bombshell asked, wondering why the queen had turned to face HER.

"I have two announcements. One," she declared staring Janice straight in the eyes, "directly relates to you. With that in mind, you might want to decide if you want a little more privacy."

"Anything you have to say can be said in front of all these beings. I have no secrets and to a man, woman, dragon and extraordinary powerful being, they're all my friends."

"I figured you'd say that."

Janice beamed the most radiant, beautiful smile.

"So?"

"Right at the very death, or should I say... right at Earth's very death in the vault deep beneath the Emporium, you were nicked by the faintest smidgen of her unholy magic resulting from some of the despicable supernatural intent on taking your life. The wayward wisp bounced off Merlin's staff, before deflecting away and colliding with your arm. You remember?"

"How could I possibly forget?" the blonde bar worker reflected, rolling up the top part of sleeve on her dress to reveal a dark looking scar that ran diagonally across the top of her arm, something that even now, months later, looked vicious and evil to say the least.

"My love," declared Peter, rushing around the other side of his soulmate, determined to get a better look.

Janice tried to shrug him off, but he was having none of it.

"I didn't see this happen!"

"You had... other things on your mind."

"I…"

"What she means, is that you were busy uploading your consciousness into the ring. Isn't that right?"

"It is."

"So… that was caused by my mother's magic?"

Janice nodded.

"I thought… I thought…"

"Pete, it's all right. She's fine," observed Richie, partly wishing that she hadn't started all this off, but knowing that she had to move on to the bit they'd all want to hear.

"After all this time, why hasn't it fully healed and why haven't any of the dragon physicians looked at it?" Peter demanded.

"They have Pete," the queen replied calmly, sorry to see her friend all of a fluster.

"But…"

"My love," Janice urged, "please, let Rich finish. My arm's fine and barely hurts at all. Please…"

Knowing that he was well and truly beaten, the hockey playing dragon conceded defeat, turning away from the scar on his love's damaged arm to face his best friend… the queen.

"So… before I was so rudely interrupted," Richie put in, poking her tongue out in Bentwhistle's direction with a view to lightening the mood ever so slightly, despite it being about the most unroyal thing in the world to do, "we were talking about the despicable dark magic that deflected off Merlin's staff and sliced into part of your arm."

Every being there stayed silent, wondering where all this was going and whether or not their friend the former bar worker would be on the wrong end of some bad news.

"As you know, Janice, we've had some of the most proficient dragon scientists running tests for some time now."

"I feel as though I've donated more blood in the last couple of months than I have during the course of my life time, and I'm at the blood bank in Salisbridge as often as they allow."

"And that's a credit to you," Tank chipped in. "Donating is a very worthy cause. It's a shame that we're not able to contribute on that front."

"They'd get quite a shock if they stuck a needle in you and the blood came out green," ventured Flash, knowing full well that the first thing the mantras that transformed dragon bodies into humans did, was to replicate the look and feel of the blood inside the body. Not down to one specific blood type of course, that would be too complicated, but just good enough to fool most medical staff and their equipment.

"It would be amusing to see their faces at the blood bank when it happened though."

On that they could all agree.

"Anyhow, as I was saying," Richie reaffirmed, trying to get back on track. "The tests results have come back to me, and I thought you might want to know the results."

"I do," replied the beautiful young human eagerly, the damage to her arm and any potential side effects having been a weight on her mind for quite some time now.

"With magic being involved, you can never be too careful," the queen reflected out loud, with everyone there listening on. "And that's pretty much why we ran the tests in the first place. Anyhow, I can reveal that for the most part your wound is fine. Your body's natural healing process is well underway and should over the course of about a year replenish all the necrotic tissue you can see. I'm told that all the magic's done is slow down your body's natural defence system in that specific area."

"That's great to hear and a weight off my mind... thank you."

Rubbing her forehead, with a concerned look flitting its way across her face, those there could see that Richie hadn't quite finished yet.

"What is it?"

"To put it bluntly, the scientists looking at your blood

work and cells have discovered a side effect of the magic that they think stems from the contact that deflected bolt had with Merlin's staff."

Everyone held their breath, especially Peter and his gorgeous other half, both of whom were expecting the next words out of their friend's mouth to be bad news. It was anything but.

"It would appear that the staff not only nullified some of Earth's despicable magic but has caused a chain reaction throughout all the cells within your body."

"And?" asked Peter with more than a hint of urgency.

"And it's stopped them from aging at the same rate they normally would."

"What does that mean?" Janice solicited.

"From their calculations, the scientists suppose that your lifespan will now be relative to that of a dragon. You might well be able to live until you're three hundred years old."

That blew everyone's mind.

"Oh my."

"Indeed," added the queen.

Peter struggled to take it all in. First the house bought for them both by Garrett, and now this... the possibility of them each growing old together at the same rate, him not having to watch her die due to his extended lifespan. It was nearly all too much to take in.

Seeing his friend's confusion, Tank decided to step in.

"I think congratulations are in order... well done, well done," he said, strolling on over and planting a kiss on one of Janice's rosy cheeks.

Hook did likewise, flabbergasted at the news, hugging his friend for all she was worth, knowing that she could now have the life she dreamed of with Peter.

Flash and Amelia followed, both giving Janice an almighty embrace, each glad for the couple's extraordinary news, after which Polkinghorne and Vimes did exactly the same.

Fu-ts'ang hovered on over, his joy at hearing what had happened totally by accident evident from his words through their very private and personal telepathic link.

*"What a result. I was so worried... but now. Wow! That's just great news. And you can have the life you've dreamed of with your dragon other half. You must be so pleased."*

*"I am, I am,"* she answered back.

*"And do you know the best bit?"*

*"No... what's that?"*

*"I'll be there throughout the centuries, ready to defend you at a moment's notice, as well constantly keeping you in check. Can't have you getting too big for your fluffy boots, can we?"*

Deep within her psyche, Janice laughed at that, knowing her friend was only joking, looking forward to enriching their camaraderie.

Unusually, For'son stayed quiet, contemplating the news he'd just heard.

Having just about got his head around everything that had happened, Peter dived in, holding Janice tight, whispering in her ear that he loved her. Right at that very moment, she felt complete and... HAPPY, more so than she'd ever been in her entire life. I think we can probably all agree that there was no one more deserving than her, especially after what she'd been through and all that she'd given.

As Peter pulled away, up stepped the queen, taking her best friend in her arms, whispering in her ear the exact same words that her love just had. That embrace felt, for both females, as though it lasted a life time. For the beautiful blonde young human whose time on this planet had just been extended immeasurably, it was all too much. Unsurprisingly, she started to cry. And that set a few of the others off... Richie, Amelia, Peter, with even Tank shedding a few tears. It was as emotionally charged as it was possible to be and a singular moment in time that they would all remember for the rest of their lives. Interestingly though, there was more to come.

As the two heroic females parted, it was the other full human that spoke up, picking up on his wife's previous words.

"You said there were two pieces of news, my love?"

"Trust you," Richie remarked, wiping away the last of the tears, wondering if she'd just gotten herself in a whole host of trouble. Should she go on? To her at least it did seem like the perfect moment surrounded by the perfect beings. But not telling him first might cause a rift from which there was no coming back. Exploring her feelings, she came to the only conclusion that she could... that he wouldn't mind and would be grateful to be surrounded by his friends.

"I don't really know how to wrap up the other piece of news, so as you've all come to expect from me, I'm just going to blurt it out. I'm... I'm... I'm PREGNANT!"

Absolute silence reigned, well... for about a second anyway. After that, let's just say they all went absolutely MENTAL!

Janice flung herself full throttle at her bestie, both once again wrapped up in each other's arms. Peter, Tank and Flash raced forward as one, enveloping Hook, whose expression seemed to indicate that he hadn't quite grasped the significance of exactly what had been said.

"WOOOHOOO!" screamed Peter.

"MAGIC!" yelled Tank, dancing around for all he was worth, pulling the other three along with him.

More restrained and poised than any of the others, Amelia bypassed the jigging males, walking up to the two hugging females and offered her congratulations. Immediately she, and of course Santa, were pulled into the embrace with the other two, whose tears were flowing more than before.

The waiting staff off in the distance, finishing up the last of the tidying away, didn't know what to make of the events unfolding before their eyes.

After many, many minutes, the revelry calmed down as

tears were wiped away, and the instantaneous joy of what had been revealed started to sink in. As those all around took a step back, Hook stood facing his bride, the startling news now having had a few moments to sink in. By the look on his face, the lacrosse player could tell that she'd done the wrong thing for all the right reasons. DAMN!

"I'm... I'm... sorry," she trembled, carefully now trying to back track, wishing she'd told him in private before all the others. Getting it so wrong was something she just wasn't used to.

Witnessing her alarm was enough to stop all the others in their tracks, each willing to come to her rescue should the need arise.

"I... I... I should have told you in private. Please forgive me."

'Please forgive me,' Peter thought. 'Wow... it must be bad. I'm not sure I recall her ever having used THOSE words.'

With all eyes focused on him, Hook tried to gather his thoughts into some semblance of what he wanted to say.

"I..." he started.

Tears started to stream down Richie's pale, freckled face.

Hook shook his head and smiled.

"You misunderstand me, my love. I'm delighted that you've told all of us together. A greater group of friends it would be impossible to find. My... apprehension, and that's all it is, is not for the way that you've revealed this secret, but at what it means going forward. I have a million questions coursing around my tiny little brain, the main one being, is this even possible given what some time ago would have been our distinct species differences and is there any danger to the life inside you?"

Cursing herself deep within her mind for not knowing her husband better, the newly crowned queen threw herself at him. As you'd expect, he caught her expertly, pulling her in tight, revelling in the touch of their bodies, the warmth, the feel, the comfort of having his soulmate and the new life inside her so close.

"I'm delighted," he whispered, although why he was keeping his voice down was anyone's guess. It was only Janice there that wouldn't be able to hear. "I'm just worried about your and the baby's health. That's all!"

"I know," she said, the tears now flowing faster than a raging river at the height of flood season.

"Will it be alright?" he asked.

"I'm led to believe by the doctor that it will."

"That's the most fabulous news I've ever had. This day is by far and beyond the best day of my life."

"I second that," she said, nestling her face firmly into his well muscled neck, holding onto him for all she was worth.

The others looked on with a myriad of different feelings.

Flash and Amelia both wondered if they'd ever have a love as strong as their friends.

For Peter and Janice it was all about the baby, each wondering if offspring were a possibility for their now extended future.

Tank was elated for both Hook, someone he had a great deal of time for and admired greatly, and of course his best friend, who he knew would revel in her new role as not only the queen, but as a mother. Looking back, he could see now that she'd been destined for this all along.

For another of the motley crew, the moment was bittersweet. Fu-ts'ang was momentarily overcome with great joy, which was immediately replaced by overwhelming sadness. Thoughts of his life from before he was incarcerated into the blade that ironically he'd crafted into being came flooding back, particularly his time with Song Jin, the dragon he'd loved more than life itself, before she'd been brutally slain by her father, of all beings. Was this something they could have had if Fate had been kinder? He'd often pondered that question, especially in his years of solitude trapped in the vault beneath the Mantra Emporium. It was something that weighed on him heavily, that and his love's death. Over and over he'd replayed that last day in his mind, searching for the tiniest little detail that he could've changed. In all his time, he'd come up with absolutely nothing, no way out, nothing he could or should have done differently. There and then, a row of tiny tears found their way onto the shining blade from just beneath his hilt, slowly dribbling down the length of his cutting edge, little droplets one by one bounding towards the cool smooth marble surface they all stood on. Through the surrounding magic of the ley lines that pretty much now scoured the earth, Novus looked on knowing just how much the talented weapon smith had given for the planet and all those survivors to get to this point. Of all the Xususi, and there had been many, this one had sacrificed the most. He truly was the bravest of heroes.

"Blimey," commented Tank, breaking up the tear fest, "what a day! You two halfwits now ruling the world, this one's back from the dead and to top it all off, you're going to have a baby. Let's just hope when it's born it can sprout wings and breathe fire. That truly would be karma at work!"

His words did the trick, lightening up the mood no end, nearly all there laughing, save the ancient weapon smith imbued within the futuristic weapon.

After wiping away the last of the tears, Richie informed them all that she was out of surprises and that it really was time for each of them to leave, once again stating that they were all required to attend the sports club opening ceremony and laminium ball match in only a few hours' time. To a being, they all agreed as they filed out of the queen's residence and headed home for some much needed rest.

# 50 ROAD TRIP

Like most vacations it had started with an argument. This time about what clothes they would take, Fredric insisting that his friend tell him where they were going so that he could pack the appropriate wardrobe for the weather conditions. In no uncertain terms, George told him where to go (and not where they were going), stating that he was lucky he hadn't made him get vaccinations just to throw him off the scent, having met a human who'd nearly done that to his wife on their honeymoon that he'd secretly booked. That would have been a great start... knowing that you'd been through three rounds of vaccinations that you didn't need, just to keep that special holiday secret.

Once they'd got over that and had something to eat, both of them checked themselves onto the intercontinental monorail and headed west towards North America, Fredric distinctly unenthused due to not knowing their exact destination. For George's part, he remained particularly upbeat, never having been totally free to go wherever he wanted to across the planet as a whole. Okay... there was that one time, but he'd been expressly forbidden and got into a whole lot of difficulty for his trouble, not only with the bar fights, but on returning underground to the domain. This time would be different, he was sure.

On reaching New York the monorail split into two, the front half heading north through Boston before continuing on to all stations Canada. The rear coaches took a westerly direction, weaving their way through Washington D.C., Charleston, Indianapolis, St Louis, Denver, Salt Lake City, San Francisco and Los Angeles before grinding to a halt at San Diego where passengers could alight for Mexico and all things South America.

Not having a clue what was going on or where their final destination might be, Fredric allowed George to usher him off at the City of Angels, shepherding him onto a smaller carriage that unbeknown to his best friend, would travel a short hop down the line to Santa Monica, their intended secret goal and somewhere that George couldn't wait to reach. Exiting the station, the former monarch summoned details from his eidetic memory on which way to go, and soon had them both strolling along the tightest of twisting and turning shadow filled walkways, the only illumination an occasional brilliant orange glow from tiny streams of molten magma trickling beneath the pathways they were on. The more they travelled, the more impatient Fredric became, but he held his counsel, knowing how much effort his best friend had put into organising the trip and just how much he was looking forward to it. All he could hope for was that they'd nearly reached the end of all the mystery. And do you know what...? They had. Climbing a winding flight of stairs for more minutes than Fredric could count, they then slipped surreptitiously through a grubby looking pale door and onto a sidewalk, directly beside a long, straight avenue that looked to the founder of the Crimson Guards as though it headed out towards a pier. It was difficult to know exactly, because it was dark.

"Come on old pal, you're in for a real treat, because it's almost sunrise." Moving faster than his old man guise would suggest was possible, George led the way, choosing an angled path down to a car park lined by massively tall, statuesque palm trees that shimmered ever so slightly in the breeze. Crossing the tarmac, both of them strolled onto the clean golden sand, the echo of the breaking waves a short way in the distance, encouraging them ever forward. Despite it being just before sunrise, it wasn't cold, quite the opposite in fact. If not for the slight sea breeze, it might be considered a little humid. Inhaling huge lungfuls of the salty sea air, there was no stopping the former king now, having broken into a sprint and sending sand spraying up in his wake, he rocketed right down to the water's edge before striding in up to his ankles, his toes truly tickled as they kicked up tiny droplets of water. He was in his absolute element standing there next to the pier, watching the foamy white breakers lapping at the weather worn wooden supports, the renowned Ferris wheel and rollercoaster just visible in the distance on the other side, the first rays of sun bouncing every which way off the bright yellow rails that almost resembled a bowl of spaghetti.

"Is this it... a trip to the beach? We could have just gone to Swanage." (One of Fredric's favourite spots prior to his capture and incarceration in Antarctica.) "It would have saved us a whole load of time."

"Stop being so grumpy. This, I'll have you know, is just a bonus. Now... come and sit down beside me, and let's watch the sunrise. I assure you, you won't be disappointed."

And guess what... he wasn't!

Slowly, a brilliant bright ball of shimmering orange crested the horizon behind the two, lighting up the beach, the golden sand, the pier and the foamy white breaking waves, raining down an invigorating warmth that even though not in their dragon forms, both could be thankful for. With few people about at that time in the morning, it was a moment almost worth coming all this way for, and that was just Peter's grandfather's opinion. They sat looking out to sea, Fredric's shoes now off, his gigantic pale feet firmly embedded in the cool grains of sand, his mind wandering to times past, recalling not only previous adventures, but happier moments with his family. As George silently contemplated the picture perfect view, a lonely translucent sparkling tear trickled across the gnarled scenery of his friend's face, his mind and body finally at peace, despite knowing that he'd change some of the decisions if he could do it all over again. He couldn't, and so there was no sense in dwelling on actions from the past. Watching the tiny droplet plunge from his chin towards the ground, as the minute sand grains gobbled it up, he focused on all that he'd gained after surviving an ordeal most never would. Peter... his beloved grandson and the reason he'd endured that icy hellhole for so long. What a spectacular dragon he'd turned out to be. And then there was his pal George, a being he considered his brother, here with him now. It was almost as if their forced parting had never happened, all those decades of absence wiped away. They'd pretty much picked up from where they'd left off, their camaraderie as strong now as it had ever been in the past. And then there were the new found friends he'd made throughout the course of the battle, all of whom he regarded highly, any of whom he'd lay down his life for in an instant. Thoughts of them all filled him with joy as images played out across his mind, most involving magic, mayhem and life or death battles. To a being, they'd helped him and the world come through the worst of times. It was, he decided there and then, a pleasure to have them in his life.

"Oi, you soppy old tart," a nearby voice interrupted his thoughts. (An interesting term of affection I think you'll agree, and one from days long since past.)

Fredric looked up, a decisively neutral expression scrawled across his ancient features.

For a split second, George reconsidered his words. That is until his friend broke into a smile.

"Are you going to show me why we're here, or not?"

Glancing down at his watch, the former monarch could see it was time.

"Follow me," he announced, picking up his shoes and socks.

Fredric trailed in his wake, all the time stepping in the same footprints in the sand, his tradecraft kicking in without him even noticing.

Reaching the huge car park, George spotted what he was waiting for, and so after brushing the sand off their feet and putting on their shoes and socks, both of them strode across the very quiet car park towards a huge, heavy, brown coloured truck that had bright white writing emblazoned on the side. It said 'Majestic Deliveries'.

On noticing the words, Fredric screwed up his face, his mind wandering back a hundred years or so, recalling standing in a downtown part of New Orleans waiting patiently for an urgent parcel from his friend, the king. Through the heavy haze of jazz and the humid night air, around the corner had swung a dark brown Chevrolet flatbed pickup, its tiny silver door handles sparkling from the illumination of the street lights, its slim black tyres and their deep tread leaving a trail in its wake, the two bulbous headlights either side of a tall dark radiator grill making it look like a face at the front. As it had pulled up, it had the words "Majestic Deliveries" written on the side in just about the same font. Coincidence, or something else? He wondered for but a moment, before reaching the only conclusion possible.

As they approached, from out of the huge cab jumped a plain looking, dark haired human dressed entirely in dark brown overalls.

"Good morning," he said politely.

"Good morning right back atcha," replied the former king cheerfully.

"I have a delivery for... X Monarch?"

"That'd be me," scoffed George, incredibly pleased with himself at the name he'd come up with.

Fredric shook his head.

"I just need a signature, here, here and here please," said the driver, producing a clipboard and a pen from behind his back.

Signatures acquired, the driver turned to face them both.

"Give me a few moments and I'll get her out." With that, he wandered off towards the rear of the gigantic truck.

"What the...?"

"You'll see," urged the former sovereign, putting his hand firmly over his friend's mouth.

'This had better be worth it,' thought the founder of the Crimson Guards.

Waiting patiently against the backdrop of much clanging

and banging around, after three or four minutes, suddenly they were both startled by what can only be described as the mother of all ROARS, one that would put any of their dragon cohorts to shame.

Birds scattered as the thunderous sound carried on the breeze.

Just as Fredric had decided enough was enough, the rear of a stunning bright red car, reversing out of the back of the truck, dropped into view. Reaching the tarmac with the touch of a feather, the delivery driver drove on over to the pair, the wind ruffling his hair as he applied the brakes, stopping perfectly in front of them.

Climbing out, leaving the driver's door open, he gave a small bow before saying,

"She's been fully cleaned and fuelled. Enjoy your trip."

He turned and walked back to his truck, scampering back into his cab before either had the chance to say goodbye.

"Ahhh…" Fredric sighed, understanding now.

Ignoring the open driver's door, George strolled around to the front, all the time running his flat palm against the shiny, bright red bodywork, taking it all in, the sumptuous curves, the fabulous sheen, every angle, the tiniest speck of everything.

'Oh Marilyn… what a beauty you truly are!' he mused, his mind taken back to the time he'd been comforted by the real thing, one of the finest human beings he'd ever had the pleasure to meet.

With the handbrake on and the engine still thrumming away, Fredric remained stock still, only now realising the extent of his friend's attachment to the car. He'd mentioned it briefly to them all before they'd set off for Stonehenge in it, but at the time, it hadn't seemed too significant. Clearly it was.

"Marilyn… I miss you so much. The way you were treated… I'm so sorry. If I could have been there for you, I would have. I hope you know that. You, along with what happened, are some of my biggest regrets. If I could somehow go back in time and change what happened, I would in a heartbeat. Rest in peace my love," George whispered, which in itself was odd given that his best friend could hear every word.

In a puff of blue tinted grey smoke, the heavy brown truck rumbled into life, startling both pals back to the present. With a huge HONK of its horn and a wave from the driver, it barrelled around in a circle and headed up onto the main road back towards the freeway.

Glancing across at his friend, melancholy gone, the former monarch extended his arm, opened out his palm in the direction of the cherry red 1965 Ford Mustang and offered up two words.

"Shall we?"

Knowing that it was a done deal, and still eager to find out exactly what the plan was, Fredric opened up the passenger door and slid in, his huge human frame once again barely fitting, memories of the drive to the ancient monument in southern Wiltshire and everything it had entailed still fresh in his memory. Why wouldn't it be? After all, just like the rest of his race, it was eidetic.

Finally ready to go, George glided into the driver's side, the seat set perfectly for him, slammed the door shut, briefly revving the accelerator as he did so, and with his foot on the clutch, knocked it into gear. After a quick glance at his buddy, one that said, "Let's do this, shall we?" he used every ounce of strength he had to spin the steering wheel in a clockwise direction and in a hail of thick black smoke, took off like a bat out of hell, throwing in a couple of doughnuts for good measure before they left the car park, much to the annoyance of local residents.

Cruising down the freeway on the way to Los Angeles, George explained that they were going to spend a couple of weeks cruising Route 66, just as he'd done all that time ago when he'd managed to escape his shackles and be free for a short while. Fredric smiled and nodded, mainly from seeing just how much joy it gave his best friend. Given what they'd both been through, it might well have been the biggest turn around in history for two of the beings who deserved it the most. With a flick of his wrist, George turned on the radio and as the wind whistled through their long hair, they continued on their way to the sweet sound of 'Hotel California'. PERFECT!

# 51 A MAGICAL ENDING

Disappointingly, the shrill sound of the alarm instantly startled her awake. Despite her mixed physiology Richie still needed her sleep, and after the momentous events of the previous day and the early hours of the morning, she was lacking in that department. Bleary eyed and feeling wearier than she could remember, she sat bolt upright and swung her legs out of bed, the soles of her feet brushing gently against the smooth wooden floorboards. Glancing over her shoulder, she marvelled at the man she loved more than anyone or anything on this planet... HOOK, her husband and as far as she was concerned, soulmate. Momentarily a sense of jealousy nibbled at her insides, wishing that she too could sleep like that, almost baby-like, clearly far, far away in the land of nod. For her, such a thing appeared just out of reach, as she was usually lucky to get more than a couple of hours in a row. Checking the time, her mood changed immediately. Normally about now she'd become playful, but if they didn't get a move on they'd be late. So showing a complete lack of sympathy for her lover's predicament, she pulled back the luxurious, white, Egyptian cotton sheets and slapped him as hard as she could across the belly, the relaxed muscles there instantly contorting.

"Awwwww..." he yelped, shocked at being woken in such a manner.

"Morning darling," she replied with a 'butter won't melt in my mouth' expression.

Shaking his head, sliding into a sitting position, he gave her a very sarcastic,

"Thanks."

"You're welcome," was what he got back, along with, "You need to get up... we're going to be late."

And that was it, the two of them up and at it, both leaping into their separate showers to freshen up, before entering their newly designed walk in wardrobes that had taken up some of the space freed up from the previous monarch's dragon sized bed being taken away and replaced by, yes you've guessed it... a 'queen' sized human one.

Unbeknown to the newly crowned royal couple, buried only a short distance away beneath layers and layers of newly refurbished marble and complex magical mantras, a very special supernaturally charged cane belonging to the chief protagonist of all the despair and misery from months earlier, started to pulse faintly purple, out of sight and out of mind, but not totally forgotten, a misbegotten magical artefact passed down through generations. Would it, could it have repercussions at some point in the future? Only time would tell.

Under the cover of darkness, while all the others were still celebrating the return of one of their own, the queen's team of dragon specialists that had arranged and managed the details of her wedding day, arrived at the sports ground in Salisbridge, and after having gained the permission of the land owners surrounding the sports club, set about creating the perfect setting for the impromptu laminium ball match that would accompany the opening of the brand new facilities there.

With plenty to do, they first closed off roads, paths and tracks that threatened to cross the danger zone of the pitch, some of their own disguised as humans so as not to make the public feel threatened, placed strategically around the outskirts to ward off those that might intrude either by design or accidentally.

After that, it was a case of erecting the humungous stands they'd designed on the hoof, knowing that crowds would flock in from all around, once word got out... and it would. After all, who wouldn't want to see the very first laminium ball match played outside the dragon domain?

Using a combination of magic and ingenious technology, stands two hundred metres high were constructed around the outskirts of the pitch, which had been narrowed down in dimension from its usual two miles long to one and a half miles long, though it was still a quarter of a mile wide. The players from both teams would just have to make do with the reduced space in which to battle.

Once satisfied that they were reinforced enough to take the expected capacity, the last thing for the queen's specialists to do was create a goal 'mouth' with a set of 'teeth' at both ends. The use of magic completed this in less than ten minutes by a group of six of them, the imitation stalagmites and stalactites joined in the middle all but a perfect replica. Apart from the fact that everything was outside and slightly reduced in size, the setting resembled that of any of the underground laminium stadiums the best teams in the domain normally faced off in, with the exception of course that there was very definitely no molten magma surface.

With the newly constructed stands visible from across the city despite the sports club being located far out in the suburbs, intrigued humans in all their fascinating forms started turning up well before three o'clock, dozens at first, which very quickly became hundreds, turning into many, many thousands, before the opening ceremony had even thought about beginning.

The queen and her entourage, including her rugby playing husband, had been there for some time, as well as most of her inner friendship circle that had fought so valiantly together during the wicked times only months before and had partied so hard the previous night.

"Where's Tank?" Peter asked, suddenly noticing his friend was absent.

"I haven't seen him," Richie replied, using her best poker face.

"It's okay... I'll give him a call. Probably just slept in... lazy git!" Peter responded, pulling his newly acquired phone out of his pocket and hitting speed dial number three.

"Uhhhh... has anyone seen my better half?" remarked Amelia, wandering around looking more than a little lost.

"You don't know where he is?" asked Hook.

"He just left me a note this morning saying he had some things to take care of and that he'd meet me here. To tell you the truth, I didn't think anything of it, but now I'm not so sure."

"No answer... that's odd," announced Peter to all and sundry.

"He's probably on his way and in a rush," the queen implored, trying to keep everything on track.

"Are you alright DomCon?" voiced Emma, having caught the diminutive dragon wandering around in his human guise looking like a stray kitten, lost and alone.

"I was supposed to meet Jar Man and Steel here, but they don't seem to have arrived yet."

"Oh well... I'm sure they're probably just stuck in traffic and running a little late."

It was all that Richie could do to keep a straight face.

"You're probably right, you're probably right."

"Ahhh... if it isn't our Antipodean friends," teased Richie, glad to see Yoyo and Rose lead their newly adopted youngsters towards them.

"Majesty," said the healer, his usual smile caked across his face.

"Glad you could all make it."

"Uhhh..." Rose put in.

"What is it?"

"You haven't seen Monty anywhere have you? He wasn't around when we woke up and we discovered a note that said he had some stuff to do and would meet us here."

"Haven't seen him yet. I'm sure he's just stuck somewhere amongst the crowds."

"I'm sure you're right."

From out of the shadows stepped one of the queen's constant bodyguards, proceeding to whisper something into her ear.

"Right then everyone," she announced, "it's time for the opening ceremony. Please follow me."

"But what about…?"

"PETER!" Richie exclaimed, an air of feigned annoyance accompanying her every word. "They're too late. We'll just have to do it without them. Follow me... NOW!"

Shocked to the core at the brutal cut off from his best friend, and wondering if this was how ruthless she was going to be all the time as monarch, Bentwhistle gave Janice the briefest of glances that told her he loved her, before taking her beautiful, slim, pale hand into his, and guiding them both into place behind the queen, all thoughts of the missing friends scrubbed briefly from his mind.

As the entourage strolled casually out onto the section of lush, perfectly mown grass directly in front of the newly rebuilt clubhouse that looked out over the lacrosse and rugby pitches as well as the newly installed Astroturf, they were greeted by Garrett and a few dignitaries from the local council including the mayor. All this was set against the backdrop of the eye-catching cathedral some distance away, having been painstakingly rebuilt brick by brick using dragon ingenuity and magic over the course of the previous three months.

Whilst the dignitaries and Garrett all wore suits, for everyone else there, including the queen, it had been decided that the dress code would be much more informal, with jeans, smart tops, tee shirts, boots, trainers and even leggings being sported by some of the heroic crew that approached those in charge.

As those gathered in the newly built, two hundred metre high stands all turned in the direction of the clubhouse and what was happening, the city mayor grabbed the microphone and introduced Garrett, who needed very little in the way of an introduction given just how famous he'd become over the proceeding weeks due to his part in the diplomatic efforts between humanity and the dragon race.

Clearing his throat before addressing the gathered crowd, his thoughts centred on what he wanted to convey, his usual professionalism at public speaking kicking in automatically.

"Human friends, dragon folk and of course your royal highnesses, it's so wonderful that you could be here today on this momentous occasion. Not only am I proud to announce the opening of this new sporting facility for the fabulous residents of Salisbridge, to replace the one which was destroyed in all the chaos and mayhem and meant so much to so many, but as you're all well aware, the first laminium ball match to take place above ground will soon be displayed for your delight."

Cue a huge round of applause and much boisterous cheering.

"Before that happens though, I hope you will indulge me while I say a few words."

More cheering for the well liked and respected Cropptech owner.

"While it was an honour to inject the capital to see this project through, I can't take the credit for any of it really, simply because it all stemmed from someone else, someone I consider one of my best friends and one of the most brave and selfless beings I've ever had the pleasure to encounter. If not for this individual, I would have quite literally died some time ago."

This time there were many hundreds of "owws" and "aahs" echoing around the impromptu stadium, as not many people knew that particular fact.

Richie's brow creased momentarily. Of course she'd known that Garrett had been saved from the despicable Manson through Peter's bravery in uncovering the plot to steal the laminium, but what did this all have to do with the 'bald eagle' stumping up the funds to replace the destroyed sports club? Determined to put all the pieces together, the queen leaned in and continued to listen eagerly.

"The person in question," continued Garrett, "had the opportunity to accept a life changing amount of money, but instead refused, asking only that I look into rebuilding this fabulous sports club. I won't name them, because I think they'd rather stay anonymous, but still... I feel it worthy of mentioning right here and now."

Off to one side, face down, trying his best to look inconspicuous, counting every blade of grass within his eye line, Peter started to blush.

"And so here we are," added Garrett, a new cheerfulness echoing in his voice. "An alliance with a fantastic race that has always done so much to guide and protect us, about to see their most famous of sports played here, above ground, in this the most wondrous of places and now one befitting all the brilliant sport played here. I now pronounce this fantastic new clubhouse and grounds well and truly OPEN!"

A monstrous cheer echoed throughout the ground, one so loud that it could just about be heard in the city centre, three miles away.

With that, Garrett handed the microphone over to the mayor who said a few kind words, before the announcer was put back on to get the crowd riled up for the main event... The laminium ball match was of course now an ironic name for the sport given that ninety nine percent of all the laminium had been returned to the earth, or Novus as those in the know had been told. With a quiet anticipation rippling around the hastily built stands, the man on the mike got on with his job.

"Dragon kin and human friends, please give it up for the teams that are about to perform for your absolute pleasure!"

Tumultuous clapping and screaming resounded throughout the grounds.

"Gentle beings give it up for the Indigo Warriors!"

"YAAAAAAAAAAAAAAAYYYYYYYY!!!!!!!!"

"All the way from the dragon domain, I give you their superb and unprecedented captain... SILVERBONCE!"

Out from behind a thick set group of trees off to one side of the stands, up flew the outlandish and renowned mouth guard, spewing flame and performing his most acrobatic moves. The crowd couldn't get enough.

More cheering followed, combined with just a hint of curiosity as to where their normal captain was, which was echoed by the queen's longstanding friendship group. And so it continued, with giant cheers after each player's name was announced and one by one they joined their impromptu leader in the air, high up above the middle of the pitch.

"FLAMER!"

"CHEESE!"

"BARF!"

"ZIP!"

The watching humans were absolutely mesmerised at seeing some of their new found allies up close. Although most had glanced out of their windows the previous night during the marriage celebrations, this was something else altogether.

United as a team, well... almost, for the first time in an absolute age, the Indigo Warriors reverted to type and started showing off, lazy loop the loops, terrifically fast flybys, chest bumps and the most intricate bursts of flame being the name of the game. It was magical in more ways than one. After a few minutes of this, allowing the crowd a tantalising taste of what was to come, the announcer interrupted.

"Now that you've familiarised yourself with the Warriors, I think it might be time to introduce you to their opponents today."

The loudest ROAR so far rang out around the improvised stadia.

"Whilst they as a group have no formal ties to any laminium ball organisation, and this is the first time they've come together as a team, I do think you'll recognise most of them. Given all that, and the fact that they haven't even trained together, they've decided to call themselves... THE SALISBRIDGE MISFITS!!!"

# "YAAAAAYYYY!!!!!"

"Please give it up for... THE MISFITS captain... STEEL!!!!"

If the you'd thought the crowd had gone wild before, that was nothing to what was happening now, leaving the queen's elite squad that had constructed the stand worried as it very gently started to move about with all the chanting, cheering and foot stamping. The reception for that one player was extraordinary.

"So that's where he was," DomCon remarked, pleased to see his friend, but annoyed at not having been let in on the secret. 'Perhaps,' he thought, 'Jar Man has helped with the preparation in some way and that's why he's missing.' Oh how wrong could he be?

"Next... let me introduce to you the brave and heroic mouth guard for the MISFITS, I give you... JAR MAN!!!

More bouncing and cheering from the stands, each and every individual there familiar with the ginger dragon's heroics during the dark days of the previous months.

Out flew Jar Man to much celebration.

Dom Con looked as though he'd been knocked down by a titled heavyweight boxer.

'WHAT?' was all that sprang to mind.

Just as the others tried to get their heads around seeing one of their own out there with quite possibly the best laminium ball player ever, things got even more bizarre.

"Clap your hands and wings together for the one and only... FLASH!"

From out behind the trees off to one side of the sports club up flew an almighty prehistoric form, the biggest of them yet, the upper body of its gigantic frame shimmering in silver, the underside of its wings and the area around its head and sternum a delicate gun metal grey. Most captivating though was the Nordic sky blue that not only outlined the entirety of its cranium, but its wing phalanges, down the whole of its neural spine (tail) culminating in the caudal spade at the end of the appendage. Beauty, grace and more than a fair amount of menace all combined into a jaw dropping creature that every being there instantly recognised.

"You daft bugger," Amelia muttered under her breath, her love for him in his natural form more than apparent as well as her angst at his stupidity in getting involved in this.

"I never get tired of seeing him like that," observed Hook to all those around him.

"Neither do I," answered the queen, as in awe of him now as she had been when she'd dropped the shield at the king's private residence to let him and Vasuki in, right in the midst of battle, just before they'd all had their magic purloined.

"Please show all your appreciation for yet one more of the dragon heroes who not only helped save the planet, but helped unite both our species... the one, the only... MONTY!"

"YAAAAAAAAAAAY!!!!"

"If I wasn't so proud of him, I'd give him a right telling off later," suggested Rose to her Councillor husband, who... it had to be said, was beaming like a toddler who'd just rediscovered their favourite toy after a long search.

The rest of Yoyo and Rose's youngsters just looked on in utter amazement at what their brother was about to do.

"He'll have no trouble fitting in if his flying can get anywhere near matching the speed of his brain," announced Amelia, glad of the company her other half was keeping. On that, they could all agree.

And then there was a pause, a lull if you like, setting the audience on edge, all of them there watching and wondering who the fifth member of the team would be and whether or not they would recognise them. What do you think? Can you guess who it is yet?

Now while not all the details of the horrific battles involving Manson, Earth and their evil armies had been revealed to the public, a great deal had in a show of cooperation and to convey exactly what could be achieved by their two great races working together in harmony. With that in mind, prior to the wedding, details about some of the heroics performed and the heroes themselves had been released to the press both above and below ground. The friendship group surrounding the queen were all well known now, with the exception of Peter who'd been thought long since dead, the dragons particularly recognisable in both their human and dragon forms. This was important, the queen knew, and the reason that the announcer was very unsubtly trying to build the tension. Because you see, without the next dragon's cunning and bravery, none of them would be here and the world would look much more dystopian than it did now. Without him, they would all have been doomed. So she thought it fitting that he should get pride of place and expected nothing but the biggest cheer of all when his name was announced.

"Fulfilling the very last place on the MISFITS team is a dragon more cunning than one of Baldrick's plans, braver than a team of Marvel superheroes and someone we all owe a huge debt to. Without further ado, I give you one of the brightest stars of them all... TANK!"

The audience went absolutely mental at just the mention of his name, long before they could see his enormous primordial body rising out from behind the group of trees from which both sides had appeared. Easily the size of Flash and, like the Crimson Guard, able to fit Peter's squat little dragon body beneath one of his wings, the kind, caring, personable and plant loving friend to them all slowly glided into view, taking his place alongside the rest of his squad around the middle of the pitch, facing off in something of a dream, with his favourite laminium ball team of all, the Indigo Warriors.

'Things,' he thought, '*don't get any better than this.*'

With both teams hovering there mid-pitch, high up, two things happened next.

The first was that the referee appeared on the ground clutching a sparkling silver sphere, about the size of a beach ball, before jumping up into the air, flying around the two teams, before coming to a halt about fifty metres above them, both his tiny hands clutching the ball for all he was worth.

The next was that the announcer had some more information to impart.

"First things first, lovely beings... I have some details that you need to know, not only because for most of you, this will be the first laminium ball game you've ever seen, but more importantly because of where we are and the restrictions that involves. The pitch, as those of you keen underground dwellers might already have noticed, is slightly smaller than normal. There was very little choice in this, and those in charge of bringing this impromptu match about have done all that they can in this regard. On that front... there's no lava involved, something that should be obvious to all of you."

The crowd all laughed as one.

"So... there will be nothing to dive under. We did look into using water instead of molten magma, but even the most complicated magic available would not have rendered it possible. So in this regard, and this applies to both teams, so listen up, there's a magically imposed hard deck, much like fighter pilots have when they're training, of fifty metres. If any of you try to go lower than that, you'll bump into an invisible energy shield that will, to say the least, knock the stuffing completely out of you."

Once again the crowd laughed, not so much the players though, all vowing to keep an eye on that.

Glancing down at his notes, the announcer paused briefly, wondering if he should read the next line.

"Uhhh... I'm told that the usual way of making the goals at each end has had to be scrapped here today and that the 'teeth' are... false?"

Cue lots and lots of laughter from both dragons and humans alike.

"Anyhow... moving swiftly on. The ball being used today is of course not related to the name of this great sport.

There's no laminium involved in it at all, only ionised titanium. Both sides will have supernatural auras of different colours cast upon them to both distinguish the teams and limit the top speed of each individual player. That restriction will be one hundred kilometres an hour, and is in effect so that all the humans in the crowd may follow the action in real time. If not for that, everything would be a blur and there would be no point in watching. Our referee today will be Tin Tin Tumbler from the dragon domain beneath Glasgow, Scotland. With the formalities over, it gives me great pleasure to point out that the Indigo Warriors will be surrounded by a dazzling red aura, the Salisbridge Misfits will be outlined in brilliant blue, and our gracious referee will be defined in yellow. ENJOY!"

Abruptly a huge, ghostly, bright orange counter appeared directly over the clean, dull grey roof of the brand spanking new clubhouse, the number 10 hovering there in the air for all to see.

In the blink of an eye it transformed into a 9.

8.

By now the crowd had gotten the hang of what was happening.

"SEVEN" they all shouted.

"SIX!"

"FIVE!"

"FOUR!"

"THREE!"

"TWO!"

"ONE!"

And in a mishmash of prehistoric bodies piling forward and then up, the referee dropped the glinting silvery sphere into the middle of them all and in a remarkable move, doubled back over on himself in an effort to get as clear a view as possible as to what was going on.

As the chaos begin, Silverbonce and Jar Man both retreated towards their mouths just as they should, each nodding in the other's direction as they did so, totally out of respect. If nothing else this was a friendly and a chance to show the humans of this planet why the sport was so idolised and beloved below ground.

In a move that probably saw him go from zero to eighty miles an hour in the blink of an eye, Steel surged forward, using his tail to guide his trajectory and with his hands outstretched immediately got a grip on the shining sphere that was still so worshipped below ground, despite its change in makeup. Delighted at the feel of the weight in his hands, and more than a little perturbed at not having his magical senses enhanced due to the lack of laminium, thoughts of the last time he'd played in a match suddenly flooded his memory... that vile and loathsome bomb that had been placed within the ball, designed to take so many lives. Visions of swirling lava and the biting pain it had caused being beneath it for so long inundated his thoughts, making him swallow nervously, alter his heading and slow him down just slightly. And that was enough. For what I hear you ask? For Flamer and Cheese to spear tackle their unsuspecting former captain, dumping him head first into the onrushing Monty, before pinching the ball off him pretty damn quick, turning on their tails and heading for the deck. The CRUNCH of Steel's thick skull smashing into his young teammate resounded around the arena.

Quick as a flash, or in fact... FLASH, Yoyo was up out of his seat, ready to bound out into the stadia and rescue the youngster who was now officially one of his sons.

Monty's brothers and sisters gasped in horrified fascination at their brother's speedy downfall.

"Don't you dare," Rose ordered, grabbing her husband by the arm, using all her strength to keep him pinned in his chair.

"But..."

"NO! He knew what he was getting into and will have to deal with the consequences himself. Besides, I'm sure they have medics on hand if things get out of control."

'Not if,' thought Yoyo, 'but when.'

Heeding his wife's wishes, he remained in his seat, cursing the very idea of this damned match.

Watching the crunching collision from relatively close by, Flash, hero, Crimson Guard and all round good egg, had a decision to make. Every instinct in his body urged him to give chase to Flamer and Cheese but there and then he recognised the severity of what had happened between his two teammates. With that in mind, and knowing that he owed Yoyo a debt much bigger than he could ever repay, he stuck around a couple of seconds longer than he should and applied just one of the fabulous healing mantras his Crimson Guard training afforded him. It did the job on both of them, repairing bone, skin and scales in the blink of an eye, as well as making them alert and bringing them back to their best. Turning tail, he started to give chase.

"Good boy, good boy," mused the healer from the stands, delighted that his friend had stepped in where he couldn't, looking after Monty's wellbeing, just as he'd assured him he would do with all of them when they'd all agreed to go and work for him.

Having dropped back out of the melee, knowing that getting involved in the starting madness wouldn't have been playing to his strengths, Tank watched his idol Steel smash face first into the unsuspecting Monty and winced at the collision as it happened in real time, glad that the magic of the auras had reduced their top speed, determined as he would have been in any of his rugby matches to retrieve the ball and get his team back on the right side of the action. Kicking his wings into gear he dropped into a steep dive and surged forward in the direction of Flamer and Cheese, rolling over and over axially as he gave chase, his brilliant mind wondering how to part his opponents from their shining silver prize.

In a shimmer of red that all the human spectators still had trouble keeping up with, Zip hightailed off in the wake of his two teammates, looking to back them up in their attacking run, offering up yet one more option in their quest to beat the mouth guard and knock down one of the teeth, knowing that despite having their heroic captain, their opponents were still a bunch of rank amateurs and would as such likely be beaten into submission.

A way off Flamer and Cheese, but still eagerly giving chase, Tank glimpsed Zip forming up behind them, having just wheeled in from off to one side, just slightly in front of him. Familiar with every aspect of the sport, not only as a fan but from some late night, illicit experiences in the nursery ring, the competitive rugby player in him leapt to the fore, compelling him to do what any professional sports dragon in this position would. With only a thought, the raging warmth of a small sun instantly gathered inside his huge scaled belly before charging up his oesophagus, searing the back of his throat and after tickling his needle sharp incisors on the way out, rocketed free like a comet on a mission, a bright yellow flaming tail following the ever pulsating fireball. Imbued with more than enough of the supernatural, the combustible orb soared out in front of him momentarily, before smashing spectacularly into Zip's hind quarters, causing him to spiral out of control and then drop down into a sharp dive, heading for the hard deck at speed.

Delighted at getting the drop on one of the so-called professionals, the rugby playing dragon surged forward, still some way off the ball carriers, wondering just how he was going to make up so much ground in such a short space of time, especially as the two of them were now closing in on Jar Man and the mouth itself.

A ferocious beaming smile ingratiated itself across the primordial features of Flash's jaw line at what his friend had just achieved right in front of him. To take down Zip like that was nothing short of miraculous. But that was a mere distraction now. They had to get back and help out, otherwise very quickly they'd find themselves one nil down. Reaching the ball carriers was crucial, but how, that was the question.

Flapping his wings for all they were worth, muscles burning like a serial philanderer's pee, from out of nowhere that light bulb moment hit and there and then he knew what to do. Giving all he had in the briefest of pushes, the courageous Crimson Guard surged forward, topping out at the maximum eighty miles an hour, on one mission and one only, to catch up with his friend in an effort to give him the advantage that might enable them to make the difference.

An intense shiver of panic raced up his tail, encompassing the whole of him. It was something of a new experience for the ginger giant Jar Man, a dragon who was normally well in control of his circumstances, something he most certainly wasn't as the two Indigo Warriors approached at speed. Swallowing nervously, the gentle dragon prepared what he considered the most appropriate magic in his mind, got ready with the words that would set a fireball in motion, and using all his focus, set his sights on the incoming threat.

A split second, that's all that it took for Flamer and Cheese to settle on a couple of strategies as they closed in on the mouth and the terrified looking mouth guard, hovering there looking for all and sundry as though he was about to wet his pants.

Gasping frantically, having burnt up a great deal of his supernatural reserves, Flash had all but achieved what he'd set out to do. All that remained was to make contact with his pal, say the proper words and let his mana do the rest. Stretching out with his spindly little hand for all he was worth, the contact was fleeting, but it was enough.

Topping out at the apex of what was allowed, only now had it become obvious to Tank that he wasn't going to catch the ball carriers. They were simply too far ahead and moving at the same speed. And that left Jar Man at their mercy. Briefly he cursed, well... deep inside his mind anyway, that is... until he was startled back to the present as a touch of something swept across his leg. Not aware that anyone or anything was near enough to do such a thing, instinctively he glanced over his left shoulder, surprised at what he saw.

'FLASH!' he thought. "He's dropping back out of range, looking totally spent,' but only briefly because a tingling that could only have come from something magical had started to encompass the whole of his body.

*"Good luck ace. Go get 'em,"* echoed across his mind in the voice of his friend.

'WHAT?!' was all he could think, that is until he started to... SPEED UP!

'OH!' thought the rugby playing hero.

And why did he think that? Because Flash had cast the same mantra that Fredric had used on him to allow him to get to the test bore hole site in France from Scotland in record breaking time, altering his mass, effectively making him lighter. While the magic in the auras applied by those that had set up the match had limited the speed to eighty miles an hour, it could not take into account his decline in mass and thereby Tank speeded up considerably, very quickly closing in on the two Warriors ball carriers.

*"Come out and narrow the angle!"* Tank screamed at Jar Man through their team telepathic link, hoping to buy another moment or two.

Seeing his teammate's upturn in speed but not understanding how he'd achieved it, with a snarl of epic proportions etched into his antediluvian features, the ginger giant hovered forward, bringing forth sparkling white lightning onto the tips of his fingers, all the time blowing a stream of fierce fiery flame in an arc out in front of him. It had the effect of slowing the approaching attackers down for just a moment, giving them both pause for thought at the newcomer's actions.

Knowing that it would be neither pretty nor clean, Tank swept in from behind, using the entirety of his now lighter than light mass to cause the mother of all upsets.

# BOOM!

Wings, arms, legs and phalanges tumbled everywhere as the rugby playing dragon hero smashed clumsily through both Cheese and Flamer, having the audacity to pluck the ball away from them both as he did so, raising one almighty cheer from the dumbstruck crowd, each of them wondering how he'd found so much speed right at the end, when in theory it just shouldn't have been possible.

'How?' thought Peter gobsmacked.

'That can't have just happened,' mused Hook, more than a little impressed with his pal.

'Go Tank,' Janice reflected.

Richie smiled, having a pretty good idea about what had just happened, wondering if Flash would pay for using up so much of his magical energy supply in such a short space of time.

Sweeping underneath one of Jar Man's mighty wings, narrowly averting a collision, Tank darted forward towards his own mouth before kicking his tail hard left, the appendage acting like a giant rudder, allowing him to perform the tightest of turns, after which, clutching the ball in both his frail little hands, he proceeded to zoom along beside one of the stands, just out of reach of the adoring crowd. As transitions go... it was brilliant!

With the turnaround having taken everyone by surprise, including all of the players, the Misfits outfielders, Steel, Flash and Monty, each turned tail and using all their agility, headed at speed towards the Indigo Warriors goal mouth in an effort to support their friend.

'WOW!' thought Silverbonce, facing the onrushing horde of Misfit players, him being the most highly recognisable of them all there, the oldest alive still playing the game. 'Whatever it is, that's an exceptional piece of the supernatural. I'll have to get that whippersnapper to teach it to me after the match is finished.'

Abruptly, about three quarters of the way towards his destination, the Indigo Warriors mouth, Flash's speed boost, or rather Fredric's unique spell wore off without any warning, slowing the dizzy Tank down to something akin to that of his teammates.

Racing along the hard deck, having lagged behind the rest of his team and stayed in the middle, up popped Barf in front of Silverbonce in an effort to aid the cunning mouth guard, knowing that from the looks of things, he might need all the help he could get.

*"Four on two, not bad odds at all,"* Flash observed, momentarily eyeing his love, Amelia in the crowd, wondering just how much trouble he'd be in once they got home. Loads... he hoped, knowing just how playful she could get when riled.

Steel, Monty and the Crimson Guard swept perfectly into formation behind Tank, their configuration pointing directly towards the Warriors' mouth and Barf and Silverbonce who were both in the way.

*"What are we going to...?"*Tank started to ask before being very keenly interrupted.

*"He's mine,"* asserted Monty, surging out of the airborne structure they'd formed and streaking ahead.

"Oh my!" exclaimed Rose in the stand sitting next to her husband.

'My boy,' Yoyo thought to himself. 'Please don't do anything too rash!'

Determined to have his revenge for Cheese and Flamer spear tackling Steel before slamming the enigmatic captain straight into him, Monty knew what needed to be done, his mind full of everything laminium ball, having been a huge fan from a very young age. Puffing out a thunderous cone of orange, yellow and red tinged flame in front of him, hitting the maximum speed allowed by the constricting magic, eyes set on Barf, the youngster sped forwards, certain he could make the Warriors player vacate his position.

'What the...?' was all that Barf could think, fully prepared to go after the ball, but not at all expecting to see the youngest member of the opposition peel off and head directly towards him.

Caught in a split second of hesitation, having never experienced what was going on now, and thinking all their opponents (with the exception of the captain back from the dead that he'd follow into battle at a moment's notice) were absolutely mad, as the heat from the screeching arc of blistering fire started to warm the scales across his face, Barf did the only thing he could and dropped out of the way like a stone, totally forgetting about the hard deck and the magical force field that imposed it, hitting it way too hard, rolling his almighty ankle badly, causing him to be out of the game momentarily.

And that only left one player in between the onrushing Misfits and the Indigo Warriors' mouth... SILVERBONCE!

Four to one odds in this sport meant the result should be inevitable, but against the oldest, most wily and crafty of players, it was anything but, something Steel, the guest captain for the Misfits, knew better than any other being alive. With that in mind, he hatched a plan, one that he very quickly shared with Flash and Tank across the telepathic link.

A thousand calculations flitted through Silverbonce's mind for every moment that passed: angles, trajectories, how the new ball without the laminium would react in any given situation, the oncoming attackers' formation and everything in between. If any other being could have seen what was going on in his brain, even the best laminium ball players on the planet would have been super impressed. That was the measure of the dragon and showed just how much he had invested in the game he loved, despite it being a friendly and a show piece for the humans.

Having cleared the way of Barf, Monty turned tail to face his own goal, wishing his teammates good luck as they sped by, watching the rest of the Warriors try and rush back in time to stop the devastating transition from the Misfits. Proudly spitting a barrage of ferocious flame in their direction, he knew they stood absolutely no chance.

Approaching the cunning mouth guard, the three Misfit players broke rank. Tank, gripping the ball with all his might, remained on a head-to-head course with

Silverbonce, whilst Steel broke left and Flash barrel-rolled right, forming a formidable three pronged attack wing.

'Well...' thought Peter, leaning forward on the edge of his seat, 'this should be interesting.'

Richie and Hook had both unconsciously acted the same, the rugby player willing his friends on, desperate to see his first goal in this the most addictive of dragon sports.

Not by any means his first rodeo, quite the opposite in fact, Silverbonce acted instinctively as only he could. Coughing up three whopping great fireball infernos, one in the direction of each of the onrushing attackers, he darted right at first, spraying a huge line of fiery flickering flame in an almighty sweeping curve, before continuing to do so and darting back left. So thick was the fire that it formed a colossal curtain in mid-air between the sneaky mouth guard and his opponents. Now they had no idea where he was or what he was doing. The flip side of that though, was that he now had no idea where any of them were. One thing at a time.

'Oh crap!' thought Tank, his panic evident throughout the shared link with his friends.

*"Don't deviate,"* urged Steel for all of them to hear, *"that's what he's counting on."*

*"Are you sure?"* asked Flash, normally the most self assured of all of them.

*"Stick to the plan,"* pushed the normal captain of the other side, wanting nothing more than to best his comrades just this once.

And so they did, Tank rushing headlong into the gargantuan wall of flame, not knowing what to expect on the other side, wondering whether he'd run straight into the renowned mouth guard earth and be on the end of some of the wicked laminium ball wizardry he'd come to admire and love over the course of many, many decades.

Now it was Flash and Steel's turn to shine. Connected by as strong a link as it was possible to have, the captain opened up his mind and in an extraordinary feat of imagination, pictured Tank clutching the ball, soaring at speed just as he was. It was a perfect encapsulation of the rugby loving, store owning master mantra maker, one that instantly the Crimson Guard could use in a cunning ploy of his own.

Ignoring the screen of fierce, unruly flame as he shot straight through it, Flash used a little known mantra of his own, one he'd developed through experimentation in his early days as a Crimson Guard, one that fascinated him time and time again, one that had saved his life on more than one occasion. Using it here and now seemed a little wasteful but if enacted properly it should blow the minds of not only the humans, but of the opposing mouth guard as well.

Whispering the six words in the bowels of his mind, Captain Battlehard's better half applied a great deal of his remaining mana alongside all his considerable willpower. As the curtain of flame that Silverbonce had huffed into being started to dissipate, the mouth guard's sneaky ruse became evident for all to see, none more so than for Steel and especially Tank, who was just about to run straight into the aging legend of the sport, who hadn't bought everything the opposition had been selling.

But you see, that was the shrewd part of the plan, something the whole of the stadium was about to witness.

'Gotcha!' thought Silverbonce, about to surge forward, smack Tank in the stomach with his tail and gain control of the ball. Out of nowhere though, something unbelievable happened, causing the entire arena to gasp at once.

On either side of Tank, exact replicas of him carrying the ball sprang into life from out of thin air, four to his left, four to his right, leaving the defending mouth guard's jaws hanging wide open, for a moment or two anyway.

Sure that his friend and usual teammate had something to do with the highly unusual ploy, deep within his psyche Silverbonce acknowledged what had just happened.

'Well played youngster, well played.' But despite his admiration for what he'd just seen, he of all beings wasn't done, not yet anyway, and as a creature that had never given up, ever, he wasn't about to start now. Having not taken his eyes off the 'real' Tank, he leapt into action, springing forward at pace from his position hovering in the middle of the mouth, his neck arched and his talons outstretched determined to get the only thing he was focused on... THE BALL!

Something yet more extraordinary was about to unfold.

The nine mirror images of the rugby loving dragon all concertina-ed into one single being, forcing the famed mouth guard to alter his course, a slight smirk wriggling onto his face as he did so, at the fact that the magic had somehow gone awry. How wrong he was.

Abruptly one once again turned into nine, the perfect facsimiles springing out either side of the supposed individual leaving a long line of Tanks clutching eagerly onto the ball, streaming towards the mouth.

With no choice but to go with his gut, Silverbonce pounced on the one he'd continually kept his eye on, sure that he'd get not only his dragon, but the ball as well. Whipping one strong wing around to slap his opponent almost into the afterlife, his talons outstretched in an effort to nab the ball and get it quickly on the move to one of his teammates, the usually unflustered, experienced guard was flabbergasted to be scrabbling about in thin air as the flawless replica of magic and light shimmered momentarily before disappearing altogether, his efforts in vain and far too late to prevent the inevitable.

Having well and truly breached the defences of one of his absolute heroes, Tank did the only thing he could. Using both his tiny little hands, he tossed the ball up over his head, much to the crowd's consternation and surprise, allowing it to roll down his hugely muscled neck, zip the length of his powerfully arched back, before gliding seamlessly towards the end of his tail and the caudal spade, the wide bit right at the very end. Balancing it there precariously whilst still flying forward, the relative youngster used his experience from the nursery ring and THAT illicit match and slammed on the brakes, coming to an instant full stop in mid-air. In an audacious move, one that some professional players wouldn't have been able to pull off with such consummate ease, Tank ploughed all his weight forward and with that, his tail came up over his head, launching the glimmering ball on the end of his tail straight at one of the 'teeth', two in from the outside on the left. Just as he finished following through on his three hundred and sixty degree master class, the fast moving shiny sphere smashed into the 'false' teeth (called that because they'd been grown in only a couple of hours unlike those used in professional games that take much longer than that), shattering that singular one into a million tiny pieces. As the humans and dragons in the audience erupted, a holographic scoreboard popped into being from out of absolutely nowhere, mid-air high above the halfway point, showing that the Misfits now led by one goal to nil.

Peter screamed, "YEAH!" as he pumped his right fist into the air, startling Janice, almost causing her to drop her drink. He quickly apologised.

"That was epic!" screeched Hook over the noise of the crowd, turning to address his wife.

"Yes it was," she mouthed back, not sure that she would be heard. "I always knew he had it in him."

"WHAT?" asked Hook.

"Nothing my love... keep an eye on the match, it's about to restart."

And do you know what... it did!

The quick resumption led to a scrabble for the ball before a raging battle in which Cheese, Barf and Flamer very briefly blinded the entire outfield team of Misfits, allowing Zip to take off unchallenged with the sought after sphere. One on one with Jar Man, the ginger giant, stand in mouth guard and all round nice dragon, he made THE most fantastic of saves from a well struck shot that Zip was sure would level the score, just about getting the tip of one wing to the ball, deflecting it wide of the mark. Steel was able to get back in time to recover the shiny sphere and set off a quick transition towards their opponents' mouth.

Briefly the Misfits were in the ascendancy, but it didn't take long for the Warriors, led by the indomitable Silverbonce, to get back into their rhythm, passing the ball with the kind of speed and accuracy only professionals could, using all the tricks of their trade, very quickly going two one up, much to the delight of the crowd who were loving every last second of the aerobatic action.

Normally, below ground, the match would have lasted for a straight two hours, but today it had been decided it would be forty five minutes each way, with fifteen minutes in between for half time, something that had just been reached.

With the newly rebuilt clubhouse fully stocked and staffed for just this occasion and multiple vendors dotted about the impromptu stands selling an assortment of snacks and drinks, the queen and her friendship group, looking on from close to the clubhouse, decided to leave their seats, take a quick tour of the new facility and grab some drinks. Scampering down from their elevated position, they flooded through the main doors and into the open area in front of the bar. For most, those who hadn't been acquainted with the old clubhouse, there was simply a feeling of how pleasant and brand new it was. But for the likes of Richie, Janice, Hook and Peter the moment was jaw-dropping. The seating area had been increased threefold, and it hadn't been measly before, with gorgeous luxurious blue carpets stretching as far as the eye could see. Off to one side three pinball machines sat alongside a myriad of video games that all surrounded TWO brand spanking new pool tables. Sparkling new tables and chairs littered the floor, with easily enough to enable everybody to sit down on a busy Saturday.

Running the length of the huge room was a shiny polished oak bar that positively glistened, indiscriminately sprinkled with taps for all sorts of fabulous drinks as well as bar mats and towels. Inviting couldn't begin to describe it all. As well as an array of stools, a shiny full length mirror on the wall behind and the sumptuous kitchen area around the far side, that even right now was producing the most amazing aromas of sizzling food, the room itself was well lit with three monstrous televisions for everyone to watch sport on. It was a dream for all the friends and an extravagant upgrade on the clubhouse that had been here before. And that was without seeing the upstairs.

The sports playing pals, and of course Janice, were left speechless, for a short time anyhow.

"Shall I get us all some drinks, my love?" Hook asked his royal other half.

"Please," she replied, still taking it all in.

"I... just need to use the bathroom," Janice stated.

"What can I get you to drink?" Hook asked.

"A large lime and soda would be great, thanks."

Nodding, the beast of a rugby player turned and headed off towards the bar, everyone else there hanging on his coat-tails.

Following the signs, as nothing was where it had been previously, Janice quickly found the door to the ladies, marked with an elegant dark mural of a female in a long flowing dress, pushed it open and strolled inside. It was a sight to behold.

Dark grey slate tiles covered the entire floor, disappearing off into the eight spotless cubicles which were all framed by charcoal coloured doors and surrounds. Top of the range hand dryers were dotted around the light tiled walls. A massive, perfectly clear mirror running the full length of the room hung above a series of bright white countertop basins each containing a sparkling hoary plughole. Elegant silver futuristic mixer taps, that in some ways reminded her of Fu-ts'ang, hung aloft over each basin. Out of curiosity, she flicked on the tap and watched in fascination as soft bubbling water flowed effortlessly down into the sink.

'What a turnaround from the previous clubhouse,' was all she could think.

It was only then that she wondered exactly why she'd come in here. She didn't need to use the toilet, so it seemed odd. Shrugging it off and putting it down to a temporary bout of madness as you do, she opened up her handbag and pulled out her coral coloured lipstick. Flicking off the top, she leaned over the immaculate sink in front of her, pursing her lips as she did so. Momentarily she got lost, time seeming to stand still, that particular moment stretching out into eternity. Perplexed and more than a little baffled she remained stock still, staring transfixed at her reflection, her mind barely able to function. Unable to swallow and with her lips drier than an unforgiving desert landscape, out of nowhere the hair on the top of her head in the reflection started to transform, the bright blonde strands merging together into clumps, acting on their own accord, twisting and turning, zigzagging and crisscrossing, meandering this way and that. Spellbound, the young woman continued to gaze at her reflection, hypnotised. And then it happened! The perfectly pure strands of blonde hair that made up the bigger tufts suddenly transformed into a writhing nest of snakes, twisting, wriggling and squirming there, directly on the top of her head. Still rooted to the spot, unable to look away, a callous and unholy grin warped her mouth into something that was vaguely recognisable.

There and then in the deserted toilet, the merest inkling of dragon DNA had asserted itself.


# THE END
# (PROBABLY)


# THANKS FOR READING.

# ABOUT THE AUTHOR

Paul Cude is a husband, father, field hockey player and aspiring photographer. Lost without his hockey stick, he can often be found in between writing and chauffeuring children, reading anything from comics to sci-fi, fantasy to thrillers. Too often found chained to his computer, it would be little surprise to find him, in his free time, somewhere on the Dorset coastline, chasing over rocks and sand in an effort to capture his wonderful wife and lovely kids with his camera. Paul Cude is also the author of the White Dragon Saga.

Thank you for reading...

If you could take a couple of moments to write a review on either Amazon or Goodreads, it would be much appreciated.

## CONNECT WITH PAUL ONLINE

www.paulcude.com
X: @paul_cude
Facebook: Paul Cude
Instagram: paulcude

## BOOKS IN THE SERIES:

A Threat from the Past
A Chilling Revelation
A Twisted Prophecy
Earth's Custodians
A Fiery Farewell
Evil Endeavours
Earth's End
Frozen to the Core
A Selfless Sacrifice
Christmas in Crisis

www.ingramcontent.com/pod-product-compliance
Lightning Source LLC
Chambersburg PA
CBHW031727180726
48283CB00005B/1408